Mrs D. H. Jerome
Saginaw
Michigan

August 1873.

HE WAS BEGINNING SOME SPEECH OF COMPLIMENT.—p. 51.

LADY JUDITH

A TALE OF TWO CONTINENTS.

BY

JUSTIN McCARTHY,
AUTHOR OF "MY ENEMY'S DAUGHTER."

NEW YORK:
SHELDON AND COMPANY,
677 BROADWAY,
UNDER THE GRAND CENTRAL HOTEL

LADY JUDITH

A TALE OF TWO CONTINENTS.

BY

JUSTIN McCARTHY,

AUTHOR OF "MY ENEMY'S DAUGHTER."

NEW YORK:

SHELDON AND COMPANY,

677 BROADWAY,

UNDER THE GRAND CENTRAL HOTEL

LADY JUDITH:

A TALE OF TWO CONTINENTS.

By Justin McCarthy.

CHAPTER I.

NOTHING SUCCEEDS LIKE SUCCESS.

IT was the year of the first great Exhibition of all Nations in London; the year of prodigious hopes, industrial, political, and otherwise; the year of peace, freedom, and human brotherhood, which was followed by an age of war and international hatred, not even yet drawing to a close. It was the year 1851, the year of the Crystal Palace in Hyde Park; of the Koh-i-nôor, and the Greek Slave, and the competing locksmiths, and the yacht America; the year which brought into official coöperation and fellowship the three most single-minded, straightforward, disinterested men then living in the world—Richard Cobden, Arthur Duke of Wellington, and Horace Greeley; the year which seemed destined to solder close impossibilities and make them kiss; but which, so far as the people and the purposes of this story are concerned, was fraught rather with severances than unions, and brought not peace but a sword.

A very short time after the pompous opening of the Exhibition there was a great debate on some important question of foreign politics one night in the House of Commons. Every English parliamentary debate—almost, indeed, every night of such debate—has its hero; its successful speaker, who carries off the honors and the palm; and the hero of this debate was a very rising young man, already marked out, to all appearance, for great official things—Charles Grey Scarlett. Scarlett was the son of a banker, who had taken active part in the Reform agitation of 1831, and had before that time named his only son after two of his political idols—Charles Fox and Earl Grey. Charles Grey Scarlett, left a wealthy man by his father, had already made quite a mark for himself in the House of Commons. He was a handsome man, much thought of in society; his youth had been noted for its gravity and stillness; he was believed to be of pure morals, and people said he had a sweet, kind, and loving nature; he had a few, very few, close friends, to whom he was very dear; if he had enemies he did not seem to care about them. Why indeed should he care for anybody's enmity? He had wealth, station, health; a ready and eloquent tongue; the command of that capricious organ—the ear of the House of Commons; and he had a beautiful and noble wife. All that such a man could have wanted to fulfil his destiny in London society was an aristocratic alliance; and Charles Scarlett had been some two years married to Lady Judith, daughter of the Earl of Coryden. Lady Judith was a beauty and an heiress.

Charles Scarlett was, according to the standard of the House of Commons, still quite a young man, in fact a sort of precocious boy, in parliamentary life. Perhaps he was some thirty-two or thirty-three years of age. He was a man of large frame, and might perhaps have been a little like his father's hero Fox, but for the kindness of Nature, which had given him a clear and handsome face.

Charles Scarlett sat down, this night of debate, amid the ringing cheers of the House; having delivered what even his political opponents, or some of them at least, declared to be the speech of the session. With all the flush of his success full on him, he rose and left the House. Many other members left at the same moment, as the next speaker threatened to be dull, and they hurried to the dining-room, the smoking-room, the library, or the lobby. But Scarlett seemed about to leave the House altogether, for he walked slowly into Westminster Hall, avoiding all acquaintances and greetings as best he might. His speech had been delivered at an unusually early hour for a speaker of any mark; it was now only half-past seven in the evening, and men of mark do not often rise before ten to address the House. It was about dinner-time, and Westminster Hall was comparatively empty.

Scarlett walked slowly along the echoing pavement of the vast hall, amid the gathering dusk of the soft summer evening. Perhaps it was the effect of the gray deepening twilight, or the solemnity of the majestic enclosure through which he paced, that appeared to cast a shadow of gloom upon his face. Certainly you would not have thought, to see him, that you looked upon the visage of success.

Two men came out of one of the corridors almost at the same time, and walked down the hall a little way behind Scarlett.

"Well, it's a great hit, no doubt," grumbled one of the two, a stout, hard-faced, hard-voiced man, Mr. Jabez Gostick, M. P. for a north-of-England borough, and one of the Manchester school; "but I don't think there's much in it. That's the sort of thing that takes our House, Atheling, when it is talked by one of the swells. Scarlett's a sort of aristocrat; at least, he hangs on to the lot. He gets in among the peers and peeresses now behind his wife's petticoats. She's one of themselves; daughter of that Evangelical old humbug the Earl of Coryden, who takes the chair at Exeter Hall meetings. That s the way to get on in this country, Atheling. *You* are more lucky."

Mr. Gostick's companion was Judge Atheling of the State of New York, who had come to London to see the great Exhibition, and for whom his friend Mr. Gostick had found a seat that night in one of the galleries. Judge Atheling was a huge, soft-cheeked, beardless, blue-eyed man; with a complexion all white and red, like that of a schoolboy; and small, fat, white hands. He was still called judge in New York State, although he never sat in judgment now.

"Well, sir," said the Judge in a clear, quiet voice, "that is so, to some extent; and so far as it goes I am proud of it. Men don't rise among us merely because of their wives and their wives' relations; at least, they can't reckon on doing so. But I think there's something in that man. I like his forehead; it's a forehead with great brains behind it, and an immense purpose. His speech was very fine; I listened to every word of it; I had got to listen, it was so full of argument, and every sentence to the point. We don't very often hear such speeches in our House of Representatives. Who is that talking to him? is he one of your great men?"

"No, not exactly," said Gostick with a short hard laugh; "it's Tom Dysart; and I daresay he has been having more champagne than is good for him. Shouldn't wonder if there was a row."

As Mr. Scarlett was approaching the entrance of the hall there came in from Palace-yard outside two or three men together, one of whom, recognizing Scarlett, broke away from his companions, and stopped the path of the successful man. Of all men Charles Scarlett would have avoided this one. Now there was no avoiding him. Tom Dysart confronted Scarlett with flushed face and vehement gestures.

Tom Thynne Dysart was a much slighter and somewhat shorter man than

Scarlett. He had dark hair, flaming dark eyes, an aquiline nose, and white, vulpine teeth. His face was flushed; and although he was rather a handsome man, there was about him a perpetual suggestion of blended sensuousness and ferocity, which marked and marred him more than a scar would have done. Dysart belonged to a good family, had brilliant talents, and seemed at one time to have a career before him, which lately he had been spoiling as fast as he could. Just now he appeared to have received his *coup de grâce*, for his seat in Parliament, which alone had kept him of late out of the hands of the Jews and the sheriff's officers, had been disputed on petition; and a committee of the House of Commons appointed, according to the now superseded system, to try the petition, had decided that the seat was illegally obtained, and that Dysart was no longer a member of Parliament. Of this committee Charles Grey Scarlett had been a member.

Mr. Gostick, M. P., was well aware of this fact, and it was therefore that when he saw Dysart confront Scarlett he anticipated a "row."

"Look here, Scarlett," Dysart exclaimed, "don't think to escape now without hearing the truth! You are a hypocrite and a humbug, like your confounded old father-in-law! I knew that I was doomed the moment you were put on that committee—I did, by heaven! You did all you could to ruin me; and you think you have succeeded! But you haven't. I'll get over this some time, and I'll let you see that I'am not a powerless enemy—I will, by ——!" and he swore a bitter oath.

Scarlett, at first a little embarrassed, seemed to have recovered his composure.

"Mr. Dysart," he said very calmly, "I don't think any good can come of our talking over this matter, or indeed any other. If there were any possibility of convincing you, I should like to convince you that I tried to serve and not to injure you. I did indeed have some hope at one time that I might be able to serve you, but you know yourself what the evidence was."

"The evidence! You were only too ready to believe any confounded lies that perjured scoundrels were willing to swear! You are my enemy; not an open enemy but a coward!"

A little group of persons was gathering; for although even Dysart did not speak in a loud voice, yet the tones and gestures were menacing, in such a place very unusual, and therefore to idle observers specially inviting. Mr. Gostick and Judge Atheling drew near; Dysart's friends endeavored to draw him away.

Charles Scarlett grew hot and his lips quivered as he heard the word "coward." But he controlled his anger, and would have quietly gone his way.

"You need not hold me," said Dysart to his friends—he still stood between Scarlett and the entrance to the hall; "*he* knows he is safe here. If it were anywhere else, I would chastise him with this cane."

He held the cane up with a swagger.

Scarlett lost his temper utterly for the moment. He drew close to his opponent, and said in a low tone, almost a whisper:

"You evidently mistake, Dysart; you think you are speaking to your wife!"

Then, with a cry and a curse, Dysart struck him across the face.

There was for a moment, only a moment, a scene of wild confusion, strange indeed in that solemn, sad, majestic hall. The vastness of the place, the growing darkness, the comparative insignificance in extent of this one little excited group, which made but a moving speck on the broad dim spaces of the pavement—all combined to prevent the quarrel from becoming a public "row" and scandal calling for the rush of the police from all the doorways. It was over in a moment, and the police were none the wiser.

When the group reduced itself to form again, Dysart was securely held by his friends, and indeed seemed to have somewhat regained his self-restraint. Judge Atheling had picked up Scarlett's hat and handed it to him. Scarlett thanked him with a word and a bow. Scarlett was now perfectly composed.

"I take you to witness, gentlemen," he said, in a calm steady voice—"Mr. Gostick, and you other gentlemen who have seen all this—that I did not return Mr. Dysart's blow, nor attempt any retaliation. I am sorry that I so far lost my temper as to say some words which provoked him. No quarrel between him and me can come out of this."

He raised his hat to the group, and, no longer molested, walked slowly out of the hall and into Palace-yard. Dysart and his friends went the other way toward St. Stephen's Hall.

"Your swells, as you call them, don't always seem to have much courage," said Judge Atheling to his companion. "I never saw a man take a touch of a cowhide so philosophically."

"Humph!" replied Mr. Gostick, M. P., reflectively, "I don't much like the man; but you may depend on it Scarlett does not want courage."

"He's big enough to be brave, anyhow," said the Judge.

"No want of pluck there," pursued Gostick. "There's something in all this that we don't understand yet."

CHAPTER II.

"ALL HIS HOUSEHOLD GODS LAY SHIVERED ROUND HIM."

MR. SCARLETT crossed St. James's Park on his way homeward. He lived in one of the fashionable streets off Piccadilly. He walked very slowly, and sometimes came to a stand altogether for a moment or two, and looked back. Once he caught a glimpse, through the trees, of the Houses of Parliament, and he sighed audibly and shrugged his shoulders.

"No one," he murmured, "ever valued success there more than I did, more than I do now at this very moment, when I give it all up forever. Well, it is something to know that there *is* a sacrifice on my side."

Then he turned and walked more quickly homeward. Arrived at his house, he opened the door with a latch-key, and went quietly into his library. He unlocked a desk and took out two documents—his will, which he had lately altered, and a paper containing a statement of certain instructions addressed to his solicitors. These he read over carefully, and enclosed in an envelope which he sealed and directed to the solicitors. Then he wrote two short letters, one to an intimate friend and old college companion; the other to his wife, Lady Judith Scarlett.

When he first entered the library his servant, hearing the master's step, came into the room with lights. Mr. Scarlett did not speak.

His letters finished, Scarlett walked listlessly up and down the room. Once or twice he stopped before some favorite volume on the shelves, took it down, looked at it with a sort of affectionate regard, and put it back in its place again. There was one book, however, over which he lingered. It was a volume of illustrations of Goethe's poems; and Scarlett opened it by chance just at a page which showed the third scene of the fourth act of Faust—a wood and a cavern, and Faust alone; and underneath the opening words of the famous soliloquy of despair:

> "Erhabner Geist, du gabst mir, gabst mir alles
> Warum ich bat!"

Terrible confession! Spirit supreme, thou gavest me all, everything I prayed for—and now, behold, this is the end!

"Was it not so with me?" murmured the successful man, as he stood alone this night. "Did not the Unknown Spirit of Life and Creation grant me all, all I ever asked for or dreamed? Health, fortune, success in every field I cared to enter? Is there a name in England which speaks already of higher promise than mine? Lead us not into temptation? I never was led into temptation, in the common sense. I never knew the ignoble impulses that have drawn other men astray. I had love, and hope, and everything that could gladden life; and one mistake, one misconception of my own nature and soul, has marred it all. Supreme Spirit, you gave me all indeed; and what have I made of the gift? I was to have been an instrument of happiness, and good, and honor to others and myself—and I steep two lives at least with my own in misery and shame. And my name will be remembered as that of a coward and a criminal!"

He looked into the face of the Faust in the engraving, as if he sought some likeness there. "That expression ought to be like mine," he said bitterly; and he closed the volume and replaced it on its shelf. Then he sat down in his arm-chair, leaned his chin upon his hands, and seemed absorbed in thought.

The little timepiece over the fireplace gave a sudden silvery chime, and Scarlett started up. His eyes fell on the letter addressed by his own hand to his wife. He took it up with an air of determination or desperation, and left the room. He crossed the hall, and ascended the stairs until he reached his wife's room, which he knew he should find empty just then; for Lady Judith had gone to one of her father's solemn, almost sacrificial, dinner-parties. A dim light was burning, and the room looked more like an oratory than a lady's boudoir. It had a large open Bible on a reading-stand, and over the reading-stand was a crucifix, and on the table were divers prayer-books and hymn-books.

Scarlett laid on the table the letter he had written, and was turning away, when he took up, half unconsciously, a volume that was near. It was a small and handsome copy of the New Testament. Scarlett held it a moment irresolutely in his hand, as if uncertain whether to open it and look into it or not. He decided at last: he put the book down without opening it, and he left the room.

A few moments afterward Mr. Scarlett quitted the house. His servant took it for granted that he was returning to his place in Parliament; but the hero of the night's debate—the most rising orator of the session—the coming minister—the successful man, who people said might even be looked upon as a predestined premier—did not return to the House of Commons; his place in Parliament knew him no more.

It was a streaming wet night when, some hours after Mr. Scarlett had crossed his threshold, his wife's carriage rattled up to the door, its lamps gleaming through the wet and darkness almost like the dragon of the great Pendragon ship, "making all the night a steam of fire." So, at least, it might have seemed if he had only read the "Idyls of the King," or if the poems had then been published, to the ragged little boy who lay coiled up on Lady Judith's steps, and who was startled from his sleep by the crash of the wheels and the horses, and opened his dazed eyes to the glare of the two great lights that suddenly flashed upon him.

The footman who sprang up the steps to knock at the door, the servant who opened the door, were alike horrified and disgusted to find a ragged brat crouching there.

"Be hoff hout of this, this instant minnit!" said one, pushing the boy forward.

"Git hout of the way!" said the other, giving him a push sideways, in order to open a free passage for the lady of the house.

Lady Judith's eye fell upon the little social sinner who had come uninvited to her door.

"Stay, Francis," she said to one of the servants, as she gathered up her draperies and mounted the steps; "don't send him away. Come here, boy; come in here under this light."

She was standing in the hall, and she motioned the child to come in. The little fellow pulled off his cap, and squeezed it to get the rain out; then he scrubbed his feet, bare as they were, on the scraper; and thus made ready for polite society, he entered the hall and stood beneath the lamp. If any new illustration could possibly be found of the contrast between rich and poor, it might perhaps have been extracted somehow from this lady and this child, who now gazed at each other. Lady Judith Scarlett was a magnificent woman—tall, stately, somewhat pale, no doubt, with a forehead white as that of a statue, and luxurious masses of dark hair. Hers was a face and form to impress, rather than to fascinate; almost, one might say, to repel, rather than to allure. Infinite power and fixity of purpose spoke in the eyes and lips and chin; while even the full white shoulders and noble bust, which her shawl now hardly concealed as she stood in the sheltering hall, did not quite suffice, with all their feminine beauty, to invest their owner with that softening halo and allurement of womanhood which is woman's highest charm. The rich lady's arms and bosom were as naked as the poor boy's feet; but there were diamonds on the former, and only mud on the latter.

The boy was some five or six years old. He was very wet, ragged, and dirty; but he had really a pretty face, and under his uncombed curls there gleamed a pair of eyes as bright as Lady Judith's diamonds.

"Have you no home, my boy?" Lady Judith asked, in the clear imperative tone which ladies accustomed to Sunday-schools and ragged-schools naturally adopt when catechising a doubtful claimant, and which seems intended to intimate at once that it is no use trying on any nonsense.

"No, ma'am—I mean to say, my lady; at least, I haven't any home to-night."

"Where's your father?"

"Dead, ma'am, ever so long."

"And your mother?"

"In the hospital, over there." He jerked his head, as if to indicate in the precisest manner possible the locality of the institution.

"Don't I know your face, my boy? Is not your mother the Italian woman who used to play on a guitar, and whom I visited when she was sick in Stalley's buildings, in the court yonder?"

"Yes, my lady." The boy's lip began to quiver, and his eyes to fill with tears.

"What was your father's name?"

"Volney, my lady."

"Yes, I thought so. Well, that will do; you must not sleep on the doorstep in the rain. Your mother is a decent poor woman, much to be pitied; as, indeed, most women are. Francis, let this boy sleep somewhere in the house to-night, on a hearth-rug or anywhere, and give him something to eat. Remind me of him in the morning before he goes away."

Lady Judith turned and went up stairs; her maid, who followed her, pausing an instant to exchange a glance of wonder and sympathy with the servants whom the inexplicable caprice of a lady had burdened with the odious charge, even for a night, of a ragged and dirty little boy.

To reach her bedroom, Lady Judith had to pass through the room already described—the boudoir converted into an oratory. In passing through, the lady turned her eyes reverentially toward the figure of the crucified Christ; and then, looking meekly downward, she saw the letter addressed to her in the handwriting of her husband. She knew the hand. Does it seem idle and ridiculous to say that a woman knew her husband's writing? Perhaps it seems so; but Lady Judith had had few love-letters from Charles Scarlett—they say a woman never forgets the writing which even once told her of a love—and their brief prime of wedded tolerance over, she had had few letters or scraps of writing of any kind from him. For three months before this night they had been almost as strangers to each other. Her charities and her piety had never won him back; his rising fame had not warmed or softened her. She knew his writing, however; and she knew that when he wrote to her, and left a letter on her table, there must be grave and solid reason for it. No possibility of little scribbled messages for her about delays in the House or business in the city, accompanied with the tender phrases of playful excuse and affection, which loving husbands write and happy wives receive. No; when Charles Scarlett writes to his wife Judith, look you, there must be matter in it.

So Lady Judith thought; for she sent her maid away, and opened the letter alone.

She opened it with a firm hand; and though her eyebrows contracted, and her lips had to be firmly compressed while she read it, yet she did read it steadily to the end. Then she read it again. It was very short; it gave her to know that her busband had left her forever—that he had given up every hope which could delight ambition—every splendid possibility which political genius and parliamentary influence might realize—in order to be free from her. One can understand the feeling of blended pride and remorse with which a woman, even a guilty woman, learns that a gifted and successful man has renounced all that earth can offer for the sake of being with her. It is less easy to comprehend how a woman, not consciously guilty, but indeed, on the contrary, believing herself all virtue and religion, feels when she learns that such a man has renounced pride, power, and success, for the sake of being free from her.

Lady Judith went into her bedroom, and presently got rid of her maid. She did not sleep that night, but she allowed her woman to undress her, and she went into bed. Her future part in life was too uncertain to be settled at present without long grave thought; and she would do nothing by which an excuse could be afforded for precipitate talk and scandal. No one would observe her husband's absence for one night, and the morning might have counsel to bring. So she acted just as she ordinarily did until her maid was gone.

Then she felt as if she could not remain lying down—as if the weight of her bitterness would stifle her. She left her bed and walked the room, and sat and thought and prayed. Prayed for patience and heavenly support in affliction, and the strength to pardon those who had done her wrong? Oh no; but for courage and fortitude to wait and compass and witness the punishment of those who had sinned against her. Probably she did not say this in actual outspoken words; but this was the soul and spirit of her prayer; and like some other devout people, she was liable at moments to forget that the Power she supplicated can detect any wrong interpretation which the lips may happen to put upon the message of the heart.

Brooding over the past through that weary night, did Lady Judith never think, never once think, that perhaps things might have gone better but for some fault of hers? Did she reproach herself with nothing? Did she not suspect that there must have been something besides man's inherent wickedness to explain the sudden fall into shame and sin of one generally so pure of heart and character, so full of ambitious and steadfast purpose, as her husband? Was she not conscious of any error in always coldly standing aloof from him and his ways, and making him aware that she shrank from him as an unbeliever, and thwarting him whenever she could, and avowedly hating all persons and things he loved? Nay, did she not think with regret and compunction that when, soon after their last quarrel and their subsequent tacit separation, she had come to know something which might have gladdened and softened his heart, and brought them back to each other, if anything on earth could, she had proudly and purposely kept from him the knowledge that a hope long deferred was at last likely to be gratified? No; she felt no regret, no compunction; she saw in herself only a victim, a wronged being, a sufferer throughout—one other pure and religious woman made a sacrifice to the cold cruelty and selfishness of man. She even felt a thrill of something almost like pride and joy to think that she had kept from her husband all knowledge of the hope which had lately begun to throb beneath her bosom. For Lady Judith's religion was only her own strong will converted into a divinity and a code, and prayed to, worshipped, and obeyed. That it led her so often into works of charity and goodness is not surprising after all. No oracle always gives forth wrong counsel. False gods flourish on the good deeds which, despite of them, their votaries sometimes do.

Lady Judith sat, or walked, or knelt in her white night-dress, looking like a beautiful stately ghost come back to earth for some stern business of revenge. The night wore away, and when day was bright she returned to bed; and her maid, coming to call her at the usual hour, found her apparently fast asleep.

The news gradually spread itself over London that Charles Scarlett had flung away his career, and had committed a political, social, and moral suicide. There was no sudden shock; the story only suffused itself by imperceptible degrees and shades, like a dawn, over the sky of London society. Those who were privileged to come near the real facts of the case learned that Scarlett had been for two days at least making very deliberate preparations for his self-outlawry. He had penned a brief, quiet address to the constituency of the borough which he represented in Parliament, merely announcing that he had determined, for private and personal reasons, on withdrawing from political life, and thanking his constituents for the confidence they had always given him while he was their representative. This letter he had enclosed to his solicitors, with instructions that the necessary steps should be taken on his behalf to obtain the stewardship of the Chiltern Hundreds—in other words, the permission of Parliament to resign his seat as a member. He had taken with him a sum of money which, although considerable in itself, was quite insignificant when compared with the wealth which he possessed and left untouched. Concerning this property he made certain conditional dispositions which it is not necessary just now to explain. Lady Judith Scarlett was in any case a wealthy woman; and her money and lands were absolutely her own.

In fact, Charles Scarlett seemed to have done just what any man of his position might naturally have done who was about to travel—say to explore Africa, or seek sport in South America—for a year or so. Nothing contained in any of his written and formal instructions could have given any one to understand whether he did or did not contemplate an early return to England. But public scandal started a good many theories of explanation; and soon a general consensus seemed to have settled upon one.

"Now, Atheling, you have a pretty fair specimen of the ways of our aristocracy, or of the fellows who try to be like them. Egad! I think the imitators in these, as in most other cases, are the worst. Look at this Scarlett. His father was a respectable man, and made his money honestly; but this fellow must be an aristocrat. To gain his social place he must marry an earl's daughter; and then, to show that he was worthy of his station, he must carry away another man's wife."

"Then that is the true story?" Judge Atheling asked.

He had called this morning to say farewell to his friend Mr. Gostick at Mr. Gostick's lodgings in Manchester buildings, Westminster. Mr. Gostick was a very rich man, and kept up a heavy imposing sort of style in his Lancashire home; but when in London for the session he lived in a couple of shabby rooms, for which he paid two guineas a week.

"That is the true story?" Atheling asked. "Always the woman in the mischief." And a smile twinkled over his broad benignant face, on his full soft lips, and his blue kindly eyes. It is an odd thing that even pure-hearted and good people should be so ready to smile when they hear of somebody carrying off another man's wife; but they do smile at such things—at least, they did twenty years ago.

"Of course, that is the true story. Tom Dysart's wife, you know; the fellow who struck Scarlett in Westminster Hall the other night. That was the reason Scarlett did not hit him again. I told you at the time there was something or other up which kept Scarlett so quiet. Well, sir, Scarlett paid him off. When Dysart got home that night, or next morning very likely, his wife was gone."

"With Scarlett?"

"Well, I suppose it is not uncharitable to infer that much; at all events, Dysart is yelling it all over the town—that I know for certain. Poor thing!"

"Poor Dysart?"

"No, no; Dysart's a ruffian. The poor wife, I mean. She must have had a hard life of it with him. She was a beautiful girl; and a good, sweet girl, too. My wife knew her very well. Why she married him I don't know; but he was a handsome fellow, and was cousin to a lord—that's the curse of our social system in this country, Atheling."

"Well, it's a bad affair altogether," said the Judge, who had now wholly ceased to see the comic aspect of the situation, and who indeed could never read the story of the woman bidden to "go and sin no more" without tears rushing into his eyes. "A bad affair; all the worse that some of these people don't seem to be bad people. I never saw a face and head I liked better than that man Scarlett's. If you were a phrenologist, my friend, you would know what I mean."

"Phrenology!—fudge!" interjected downright Mr. Gostick.

"Ah, well, you don't understand; and would not be convinced, like a genuine Briton. But I liked the man's head. The moral qualities seemed particularly well developed. Then you know, after all, there really is a sort of misguided heroism and devotion about a man who throws away such a career as he had, and regularly ruins himself for a woman."

"And ruins the woman, too. And the other woman, his wife? That's heroic too?"

"No, you have me there," said Atheling. "You will look at all sides of a question, and will not allow me to keep to my sentimental side. Still he has given up everything; that must be allowed. He's as good as Marc Antony, anyhow."

"Stuff!" grumbled Mr. Gostick. "My esteemed friend, you know nothing of our ways here. This man Scarlett will come back to London somewhere about the middle of next session; and his friends and admirers will like him all the better for what he has done. Given up! He has given up about half a session of the House of Commons, and he has gone on a holiday trip. That's about the size of the thing. He has only won his spurs as an aristocratic chevalier."

"Well," said Atheling, "you know your people best; and I must not lose my train or keep my wife waiting. I am obliged to you, Gostick, for all your kindness; and if ever you do cross the Atlantic——"

"I'll come and see you. But you and your wife will pay us another visit here in the Old World before long?"

"Not very soon, I think. We have set our hearts on making a great journey to the West—quite a big thing; to the Rocky Mountains, and further perhaps."

"Is not that a heavy undertaking for a woman?"

"Not for my wife. She and I are still only like a big schoolboy and schoolgirl. Nothing tires us or puts us out; and we are good company to each other. Then we have a restless fit always on us of late. In fact, since we lost our sweet little girl, our one only infant, my wife can't rest long anywhere; and no more can I. The moment we begin to feel as if we were settled and at home anywhere, we hear the patter of her little feet again; and we know she is dead."

The Judge's large blue eyes were watery. Gostick too was touched. The one soft place in his heart was that which belonged to the domestic virtues. He had no sympathy with irregular emotions of any kind, heroic or otherwise; but the griefs of honest proper married people concerned him.

"Say, Gostick," said the Judge suddenly, "there weren't any little children mixed up anyhow in this Scarlett affair, were there? *He* had no child, I hear."

"No, *he* had no child; but I think there was a little Dysart—a girl, I believe. Mrs. Dysart certainly had a little girl; but I don't know—perhaps she's dead."

"Ah, let's hope so. It would be better so, surely. I don't like to think of a girl whose mother dare not look frankly into her child's eyes. Let's hope the child is dead. Yes, yes; no doubt she is dead."

Judge Atheling seemed to take quite an anxious personal interest in the fate of the child, of whose existence, problematical as it was, he had never heard before that moment. He was an eccentric sort of man, with a kind of religion of his own, which sometimes, when provoked, presumed to be sturdily antagonistic to other people's dogmas, but was indeed at bottom only a mere unorthodox mush of charity and love and pity.

Atheling talked with his wife over the story of Scarlett's disappearance and the possibility of the fugitive Mrs. Dysart having a little girl, whom perhaps she had to leave behind to the heedless hands of a profligate and brutal husband. Mrs. Atheling, however, would not hear of this conjecture. If the child were alive, she insisted that the mother would have taken her away; and this, she admitted, would be dreadful under the circumstances. No; if the girl were alive, Mrs. Atheling ruled that the mother would never have run away, but would have borne with anything rather than bring shame upon her daughter. So they agreed that the child was dead and buried. But if they had not had to leave England at once, they would never have rested until they had found out all about the matter; and on many a night, as they steamed across the Atlantic, there seemed to rise over the waves, out of the moonlight, the sweet sad face of a deserted little child; looking like their own lost daughter somewhat, but looking as she never did—pale and unhappy.

Meanwhile London soon began to forget Charles Grey Scarlett. He did not fulfil Mr. Gostick's prediction; he did not return about the middle of the next session. His enemy Dysart obtained a sort of consolation for his loss by receiving a high official appointment, which gave him a large salary and the control of a department of revenue. Some people said the ministry owed this to Dysart, because he had worked long in their interest, and had lost his seat in the House mainly through his over-anxiety to keep his vote at their service. Others declared that some of his aristocratic relatives insisted that a good place must be found for him, to keep him out of debt and harm. And others again positively affirmed that the place was obtained for him through the pertinacious and urgent exertions of the Earl of Coryden, at the command of his daughter. For Lady Judith, they said, was so high-minded and good a woman, that she felt it a point of conscience to do some substantial service for a man whom her husband's sin had so cruelly wronged.

Anyhow, Tom Dysart got a good place, and spent his salary splendidly. It must have been a great comfort to his friends to know that his domestic calamities had not broken his manly heart.

Other rising men came up in the House of Commons, and Charles Scarlett was forgotten there. He had not had celebrity long enough to become even a tradition. Scandal soon ceased to talk of him; friends, acquaintances, rivals ceased to think of him. There was no one left in England who had ever loved him; only hatred kept his memory green.

CHAPTER III.

BORN IN BITTERNESS.

THE great Exhibition of 1851 is over, and the Crystal Palace no longer cumbereth the earth of Hyde Park; the house of glass is transplanted to Sydenham, and the Exhibition has become a memory; the Duke of Wellington is dead, and well-nigh forgotten; the Prince President Louis Napoleon has become Emperor of the French; the Crimean war is over; Garibaldi has freed Sicily, and the kingdom of Italy has been made; Darwin has written his book, and Buckle lies in a grave at Damascus; Abraham Lincoln has been elected President of the United States, and there has been a Southern Confederacy and a great smoke of battle, and the Confederacy is gone and Lincoln is murdered; Prince Albert is dead; Richard Cobden is dead; people who can remember the Exhibition of 1851 begin to feel almost like old fogies as they stand with their juniors on the Champ de Mars, Paris, and criticise the Exposition of 1867. So many years have passed since the last chapter.

It is a bright day, not too hot, in the late summer or early autumn of 1867 in Paris. It is about the time of year when Parisians who belong to society have ventured on their grand annual expedition to the sea-shore, or Baden-Baden, or their provincial *châteaux*, and Paris is, for the most part, abandoned to the stranger. An English party, weary of the crowd and the courts, and the Tunisian palace and the Russian cottage—weary of Spanish minstrel-girls who could speak no language but Clerkenwell English, turbaned Turks who answered any question in the most fluent French, and such other wonders of nature and art—had sought refuge and repose in a gallery devoted to sculpture. He who knows anything of such scenes knows that around a really great pure work of the sculptor's art is solitude. Let conspiracy, if it would discuss its plans in safest secrecy, seek out a great popular exhibition and shelter itself near a noble marble group. No idle crowd gathers there.

No conspiracy, however, was in process of concoction by this English party. They only sought a little rest; one of them at least looked utterly wearied and out of humor, and this was the youngest of the group. The party consisted of an elder lady and a younger, and two young men. The younger lady was apparently not more than sixteen years of age; she was very small and of delicate, almost frail *physique*, with thin, white, nervous-looking hands, one of which could be seen just now, for she had plucked off her glove with an impatient fretful eagerness. Her features were small and regularly formed; her complexion was perfectly colorless. Her dark hair was smooth, and arranged without a chignon; her eyes were dark, glittering, and restless. The elder lady was by no means elderly—perhaps forty, certainly not more. She too had dark hair and a pale face, but she was of splendid physical proportions and a noble, queenly bearing. Yet no one could look at these two women without feeling satisfied that he saw a mother and daughter.

One of the young men had the regulation whiskers, moustache, light complexion, and white teeth of the fashionable and well-bred Englishman. He was unmistakably a gentleman, or what his countrymen would have called a "swell." The other had something of an olive tinge in his face, and short, thick, curling hair of deep brown, which looked almost black when contrasted with the bright locks of his male friend, and positively light when one compared it with the "raven down of darkness" on the foreheads of both the ladies. This young man wore a short moustache, and had otherwise a beardless face—not shaven, but beardless. The group, taken altogether, had somewhat of a distinguished appearance.

"How I hate all this sort of thing!" broke out the younger lady, with a grimace and a shrug of the shoulders.

"What sort of thing, Alexia?" asked the elder.

"This exhibition, and this detestable looking at sights and odious people; nd Paris, and all the rest of it; and everything. Where are you going next, mamma?"

"I am going to the service in the Protestant church.'

"Why don't you call it 'temple,' mamma? The Protestant temple—that is the proper slang phrase for it among your religious set of people, I think."

"I don't talk slang, Alexia."

"I call it all slang, that sort of thing; and I hate religious slang worse than any other. Charles Escombe's slang, which he picks up among billiard-markers and vulgar actresses, I believe, is much less odious to me than the slang of your people, dear mamma."

Charles Escombe laughed a good-humored British laugh, showing his bright white teeth.

"Pray don't attack me, Miss Scarlett. I am not equal to the encounter, I assure you. Besides, I hardly know a billiard-marker by sight; and, I declare, don't know any actress, vulgar or otherwise, except so far as seeing her from the stalls may be considered an acquaintanceship."

The young lady disdained any reply to, or even recognition of, his remark; and, looking at her mother, said:

"Then, mamma, if you are going to the Protestant temple, or whatever you call it, I am going home. I hate being in the hotel, but it is better than this."

"Very well, Alexia. You can take the carriage."

"Thank you; I don't want the carriage. I mean to walk."

"Alone, Miss Scarlett?" asked Escombe, smiling.

"Alone, of course. You don't suppose I want anybody's company?

She laid a peculiar emphasis on the word "anybody," and fixed her eyes on him with a glance of gleaming scorn, which he bore with perfect good-humor.

"But it isn't quite the thing, you know, for a young lady to walk alone in Paris."

"Is it not? Then it is just the thing I mean to do."

And the young lady arose with a very resolute air.

Her mother glanced at the darker young man, and they exchanged looks.

"I, too, am going home," he said. "I have had enough of this, and I am not in a humor for the service at the church. I'll walk with you, Alexia, and Charles Escombe will stay with Lady Judith."

The young lady looked up at him, fixed her eyes on his, and then said, still holding him, and him only, in her gaze:

"Perhaps mamma would prefer that you remained with her."

"I should certainly prefer Angelo to remain with me," said her mother calmly, "if you did not wish to go away. But if you will go, some one must go with you."

"Then if it is left to my selection, I prefer Angelo, certainly. Let Charles Escombe stay with mamma, and help her to pray for the conversion of the Faubourg St. Germain to the principles of Dr. Pusey or Lord Shaftesbury, according as she feels disposed. I hardly know one from the other, and I don't care if the French never were converted."

The agreeable conversation was here interrupted for a few moments by a party of visitors who came into the gallery as if they had been there before, and wished, for a special reason, to study one of the groups of sculpture again. For they walked directly up to one of the masterpieces of modern Italian art, and stood gazing at it. The new-comers were three—a tall, stout, heavy-looking man of sixty, a tall, thin lady about the same age, and a young woman of nineteen or twenty.

"What a beautiful girl!" said Alexia, in quite an audible tone, apparently as if she did not care in the least whether the object of her admiration heard the praise or not.

"I think she has heard you, Miss Alexia," Charles Escombe whispered.

"If she did, she probably did not understand; Frenchwomen hardly ever know English."

"But I don't think she is a Frenchwoman."

"What then? English, perhaps? Do you suppose that sort of graceful figure and that walk are common among our countrywomen?"

"Miss Scarlett is cynical," said Escombe, smiling; "and we know that she is always unpatriotic."

Meanwhile the subject of the discussion, with her companions, turned from the group at which they had been gazing, and passing close by our English party, left the gallery. Alexia calmly surveyed the lady from her bonnet to her boots, as if she were studying a statue. The young lady looked at her in return, and their eyes met. Apparently the stranger was almost as much struck with Alexia as Alexia had been with her; for, as the three new-comers passed out of the doorway, our party distinctly heard the young woman say to her companions in English, but with a somewhat peculiar accent:

"What a pretty pale girl that is! Can she be English?"

"A case of mutual admiration," said Escombe. "She is a very fine girl indeed. Splendid eyes! Did you see her, Lady Judith?"

"Yes; she is handsome, I think. But I did not much observe her. What sort of people were those with her? They look wonderfully uncouth."

"I thought the ancient pair must have come from the French provinces somewhere," said Escombe. "The man looked like a personage who might be a *maire*, or something of that kind. But they are some sort of English people by their talk."

The dark-complexioned young man, who had for the last few minutes been sitting in silence, here rose, and said:

"If you will go, Alexia, I shall be glad to go too."

Alexia looked inquiringly into his face.

"Not with you!" she answered, in a low undertone.

He only smiled a grave, sweet smile, and took her arm and drew it under his.

"You are not angry with *me*, Alexia?"

"O no," she replied, after a moment's pause, and in a softer accent; "I am not angry with you."

They presently passed through the door and into one of the open gardens; and the young man talked cheerfully to the girl, who began at last to answer in a genial voice and with gentler gleams in her glittering eyes. Suddenly she broke off in the midst of something she was telling him, and said in vehement accents:

"I sometimes think that I hate every one in the world except you!"

Just at that moment they heard footsteps approaching; and from one of the side-paths which opened on the broad walk—where they were treading amid enormous stone vases of gorgeous flowers, amid ferns, and trees, and gleaming statues, and jets of water sparkling in the sun—there came forth, so close to them that one or other group must give way to allow the other to pass, the girl and her companions whom Alexia had lately criticised.

This group was certainly remarkable. It was made up of a very tall, very stout, ungainly, fair-cheekd, blue-eyed man, with bald forehead and yellowish hair hardly yet touched with gray; an equally tall, remarkably thin and shrivelled lady, with complexion yellow almost as the gentleman's hair, and twinkling brown eyes that peered everywhere and took in everything; and a young woman, with fair hair just long enough to reach her shoulders, and allowed to fall there in its natural curls, seeming almost like the *chevelure* of some brilliant young cavalier of the days of the Stuarts. This girl was rather tall, although she appeared of moderate proportions indeed between her two high-reaching companions; and she walked and moved with a certain grace and strength and springiness as unlike to the measured and stately movements of a fine Englishwoman as to the mincing prettiness and coquetry of a fashionable Frenchwoman's gait. She had certainly, as Escombe remarked, splendid eyes; eyes of a deep, changing blue, which in some lights looked gray; eyes that had a thoughtful depth in them, that filled the gazer with emotion as they turned even by chance on him; eyes that were tender and sympathetic, and yet telling of a high aspiring soul. Egeria might have had such eyes perhaps, or Corinna.

For the rest of the face, one forgot it almost at first, because of the eyes and the hair; but it was a face full everywhere of beauty; more girlish than a stranger would have thought, while the gravity and melancholy which always shine out of really beautiful, lustrous, untwinkling eyes had still their full, fresh command over him. Indeed, this was simply a handsome girl; only there was something in her look which seemed to say that she was a girl with a past and a future—with a history and a destiny.

Alexia Scarlett and her companion looked at the girl alike with a feeling of admiration. She, of course, knew them again; and there was something almost approaching to a glance of open recognition exchanged. The eyes of the strange young lady and those of Alexia's companion met for an instant. Then she passed on; and Alexia turned and looked after her. She wore a dress of some light summer fabric and of violet tints; and the dress was at that time somewhat remarkable because of its short skirts, adapted for easy walking. A small, black, cavalier-fashion hat, with a drooping black feather, contrasted picturesquely with her fair hair.

It must be owned that it was not Alexia alone who looked after this graceful disappearing form. Alexia's companion, too, stood and gazed with undisguised interest along the path she was so lightly and firmly treading.

"I wish she had looked back," Alexia said at last. "I should like to have seen her face again. Not because she is pretty—in fact, she is not pretty; I don't care for pretty faces—but there is something peculiar about her—something of character and expression. I think I should like to have a sister with such a look in her eyes."

"I wish you had a sister, Alexia," said the young man, looking down upon her with an expression partly of tenderness, partly of pity.

"Do you? Then I don't. She would be very good, of course, and delightful, and angelic; and you would all praise her and love her, and hold her up in perpetual contrast with me; and I should grow to detest her very soon. I feel quite sure Eve was perpetually torturing her wretched son Cain by holding up to him the example of his sweet little brother Abel."

"I am glad I have nothing angelic in me but the name, Alexia, lest you should hate me."

"Would that vex you much?"

"Indeed, it would—very deeply."

She stopped, and looked up at him. Unluckily, perhaps, he was just then glancing back once again along the path where the fair-haired girl had been. Alexia's eyes sparkled with a quick, fierce light; and she caught his arm, and said in a tone of sudden sharpness:

"Did you ever see that girl—that person—before? Come, tell me—did you?

"Never, Alexia. Why do you ask?"

"Because of the way in which you looked after her."

He smiled.

"Come, tell me why you smile. You did see her before?"

"Only when we all saw her—in the room where the sculptures were."

"But did you not meet her, you yourself, somewhere before, or hear or know something about her?"

"Never saw her, or heard or knew anything about her, until to-day."

"I don't believe it!" she exclaimed passionately; and her hand clasped his arm more fiercely. "She looked at you as if she knew you; and I detest her already."

"Don't you believe my word, Alexia?"

"No—I don't. Well—yes; I suppose I do. But I thought you looked at each other as if you had some sort of acquaintance."

"If we had, Alexia, what would it have mattered, and why should I not have told you?"

"I don't know. Perhaps because you think I am bad-tempered and malignant, and all the rest of it, as mamma is always telling me; and perhaps you thought I might have taken some freakish dislike to that girl; but I only hate her far worse now."

"Because I don't know her?"

"No; because I have made myself ridiculous about her. Do you know another reason why I don't like her?"

"Indeed, Alexia, I do not."

"Because she seemed so familiar and so happy with those old people, whoever they were—her father and mother, I suppose. Did you ever see such a frightful old yellow creature as that tall thin woman? And yet that beautiful girl seemed quite fond of her; and they were affectionate to each other. Very well; did you ever see mamma and me affectionate?"

"My dear Alexia, you know you are very peculiar in your ways sometimes, and you don't try to accommodate yourself to your mother's likings and habits."

"You think me very malicious and wicked?"

"No; I think you want self-control, Alexia. But I think you might govern yourself if you would. You are very young; you have time to improve."

"How much older, pray, are you than I am?"

"I don't well know, several years certainly; six or seven at least."

"That is not much. How do you manage to control yourself? How are you always so kind and sweet to mamma?"

"My dear Alexia, because I love her so dearly.'

"Love her dearly! Stuff!"

Angelo laughed.

"Come, Alexia, you are not half so bad as you give yourself out to be. You *are* fond of your mother; and you and she would be tender and loving friends if *you* would only give way a little. I know your mother better than you do."

The girl shook her head.

"Yes, indeed, I do. I ought to know her well, and to love her. No one in all the world, I do believe, ever was so good to another as she has been to me. I would give my life to please her—or to please you, Alexia, for that matter; although, if it were a question between one and the other, my dear little sister, I must cling to *her*."

Alexia paused for a moment, and then said:

"Listen to me, Angelo. You don't know my mother fully; *I* know her by instinct. She is fond of you, in her way, because you devote yourself and your life to her. It has often made me more perverse and malignant than ever when I saw how devoted you were—looking up to her as if she were a saint or a goddess. Let me tell you, good example is sometimes worse in its effects on wicked people like me than bad example would be. It offends and aggravates us. No matter. What I want to say is, that you don't know my mother. Some day you will cross her in something—you will refuse to sacrifice your will or your pleasure to hers: and then she will crush you, and throw you away, and trample on you as I do this wretched faded old flower."

She plucked a flower from her belt, crushed and crumpled it in her fierce little white hand, flung it on the gravel walk, and stamped and trampled on it.

"It was Charles Escombe gave you that flower," said Angelo calmly. "You ought not to treat it thus."

"I care nothing for Charles Escombe or his stupid flower; and you know that perfectly well. You say such things only to offend me."

"Indeed, Alexia, I never say anything to offend you; and Charles Escombe is one of the best fellows and the truest friends living."

"Yes; very well; let him be so. But, my meek Angelo, I see already that a time will come when you will quarrel with my mother."

"Never, Alexia; the thing is impossible."

"Why? Are you above all human passion?"

"Not I, dear; but I hope and believe I am above outrageous ingratitude; and it would be nothing short of such a crime if I were to quarrel with Lady Judith. Don't think of it. There is nothing I would not do rather than displease her."

Alexia laughed a short, bitter little laugh.

"My dear, good, devoted, sweetly-filial Messer Angelo, there are things you would not do to please even her. Do you think I don't see that you can have a will of your own, just as strong as hers or mine? Some time you will have to choose between offending her and giving up something you have set your heart upon; and you will offend her without a pang of hesitation. The time will come when I shall hear her denouncing you as a monster of ingratitude—as she does most people. Look out for yourself when that time comes! She will not spare you! I shall look on and laugh and be glad. I delight in the thought already."

"Don't, Alexia—don't talk so foolishly and bitterly. It pains me to hear it; and I know you do not wish to do that."

"Sometimes I do; and to-day especially. I think that when I was born, I must have been consecrated by mistake to some demon. My mother is so very devout, that she would naturally have sought for a patron saint for me; and as she never was quite a Roman Catholic, or fully acquainted with the names and histories of canonized personages, she probably vowed me away to some fiend in mistake. If so, this must be his fête-day and mine. I feel delightfully insane and wicked to-day."

Any one who could have seen and heard this young man and young woman —the latter hardly more than a child—as they thus talked during their walk through the Champs Elysées, which they had now reached, would assuredly have been struck by the patience, good-temper, and moderating, protecting pity, with which Angelo bore himself towards her whom he called his sister. No expression of impatience, no word of anger, broke from him. She was now doing her best to torment him; saying wild and fantastic things just because she knew he did not like to hear her say them. And he knew this; and was only grave and tender with her, waiting until the evil fit should pass away, and the better mood of this freakish and bitter Undine of the night should have command once more. It did, indeed, seem sometimes as if the cradle of this slender, pale, and beautiful girl had been rocked by Sycorax herself. Tetchy and wayward was her infancy as that of Gloster ; a legendary changeling could hardly have shown less sympathy and instinctive affection for the woman on whose breast she was imposed than Alexia Scarlett did for the mother who bore her. The strange thing was, that hardly any one hated her—her who was so full of capricious hate. The servants whom she insulted, and sometimes almost maltreated, had compassion and a charitable word for her; and even at this moment, as she walked homeward in her ill-humor, and tried to annoy her patient escort, there were words whispered of her into her mother's ear which a very Griselda of meekness and virtue might have gladdened to hear.

These words were spoken by Charles Escombe, who had taken advantage of Alexia's sudden departure to speak to her mother of certain hopes and schemes he had already been forming. Charles Escombe was a younger son of an aristocratic house. He would never, in all human probability, come to enjoy a title, except his present prefix of Honorable; but, more fortunate than most younger sons, he had received by bequest a tolerable property. He was one of a class of young aristocrats growing numerous in England of late years—young aristocrats whose creed is philosophical Radicalism, and whose practice is systematized philanthropy. If there were a Young England party of the present day, Charles Escombe might be taken—not, indeed, as one of its leaders; for he had not genius enough to lead anything—but as one of its average representatives. The Young England of Disraeli's better days believed in a paternal nobility, wearing white waistcoats, doling out alms to bedesmen at sound of bell, and playing cricket with a grateful tenantry. The school of which Charles Escombe was a member believed in Stuart Mill, workhouse reform, and the overthrow of the Established Church. This school was equally strong on sentiment and on statistics. If one could combine Gradgrind and Rousseau, he would thus have constructed an idealized symbol—a *beau idéal*—of Charles Escombe's Young England. Escombe believed in the regeneration of the world by the universal suffusion of the democratic idea; but if you misquoted by a single word any clause in the Reform Bill, or exaggerated by half-a-dozen souls the population of any country or county whatever; he would have come down upon you hard and fast with his incontrovertible facts and figures, and demolished you.

A certain similarity of pursuits, or at least a common earnestness in pursuing anything which seemed desirable, had brought the Hon. Charles Escombe into close relationship with Lady Judith Scarlett. The fact that her Protestantism was illumined considerably by Pusey, while his was tempered by Auguste Comte, did not much divide them. Escombe had a profound respect for Lady Judith's intellect and energy, and he kept his Comte all to himself when she was present. He had no mother; his only sister was married to a Scotch lord, and was of a hard Presbyterian turn; and he drew towards Lady Judith and her family with a frank liking for each of its members. Towards one, indeed, he began already to entertain feelings which now were finding expression.

Lady Judith and Charles Escombe were still in the sculpture gallery. Escombe had said his say; Lady Judith looked uncomfortable.

"I wish you had not told me this so soon," she said at last. "Do you know how old Alexia is? She wants nearly a month of sixteen."

"Of course, Lady Judith, I know all that; she will be sixteen on the 27th of October. Yes, I know all about that; but I thought it right to tell you; not that I want to bring matters to a crisis now, you know, but that you should understand my motives and objects, and so forth, and that you should not disapprove when you see me doing my best to win Alexia, and to make her love me."

"Are you sure, quite sure, that you love her?"

"O yes, indeed I am. I have thought it over very calmly, Lady Judith; I have put it to myself in a variety of ways. You can't think what trouble I have taken to make myself understand it thoroughly. What with that and the workhouse-reform business, and the compound householder, I have had quite a hard time of it. But I see my way; I do indeed. I know Alexia is only a mere child, one might say; but I know that I love her, and I could not take any step in the matter until I had first spoken to you."

Lady Judith looked at him with a gaze that spoke at once of curiosity and of pity.

"Granted, then," said she, "that you understand yourself; are you quite sure that you understand *her?*"

"Well, yes, I think so. I know what you would say, Lady Judith; and very frank and generous of you, I am sure. I know that Alexia seems a little odd at times, and hasn't a very mild temper, and does not care always about pleasing everybody. But you know, Lady Judith, the very best people sometimes don't get on together. My sister and I never could hit it off together, somehow—not that I am one of the best, or even of the second best, Heaven knows—and I think sometimes—I think, you know—" Here he hesitated, colored a little, and then plucked up courage and went on: "I think, Lady Judith, you and Alexia don't seem very well adapted to each other. I don't say that either is to blame; but I think she requires, perhaps, a different sort of treatment. Now a man and a woman may get on very well indeed, where two women, whatever their relationship, can't manage to agree; and, in short, I am not afraid of trusting my happiness to Alexia, if I had her all to myself to manage; and if you'll only give me the chance, I'll set about trying to win her."

Lady Judith rose from the crimson-velvet seat on which she had been resting, and crossed the floor, and studied with much appearance of keen critical interest the knee and ankle of a marble dryad which formed one of a group. Then she returned to Escombe, and said:

"I think I hear people coming. Suppose we go into the open air."

He gave her his arm, and they walked in silence into the garden which Alexia had lately traversed. Near a little fountain, scattering its waters into a basin, and trickling sadly in its fall from the noses and bosoms of a cluster of bronze nymphs, there was a seat; and there Lady Judith and Escombe sat down. He waited for her to speak. She spoke at last.

"Charles Escombe, if my daughter were of my mind, she would not marry mortal man—the best that ever lived. If my advice were likely to have the slightest influence for good with her—if, indeed, it were not likely rather to impel her into doing the very thing I advised her not to do—I would urge her to drown herself sooner than trust her heart and her happiness into the keeping of any man. Let me say something more. If you were my son, and my counsel could guide you, I would urge you not to trust your happiness into the keeping of any woman. My bitter experience of life is, that either the one or the other must prove treacherous and false. But I know that neither you nor she will take my advice, and I don't thrust it on you. I would rather, for my daughter's sake, that she did not marry you; I would rather, for your sake, that you did not marry her. But I put all that aside, and I only say that I cannot refuse to do anything in my power to make you happy, even in your own way—which I think a wrong way, leading to late repentance. Now, then, let me ask you, have you any special reason to believe that Alexia cares for you?"

The young man looked embarrassed and uneasy; but he was a thoroughly manly fellow, and he came out with his answer frankly.

"No, Lady Judith, none whatever; but I would try to win her, and do my best."

"Don't you think that if her extreme youth, and her temper, and her odd ways, allow her any feelings of the kind at all, Alexia's inclinations turn in a different direction?"

"You mean," he said with some hesitation and difficulty, "Angelo Volney?"

"I do."

"I don't think there is much in that. I should hardly have said a word if I thought *he* would be injured by it; but I don't believe he has any feeling towards her more than what is natural and brotherly, and that kind of thing; and I think any feeling she has is merely girlish, childish. Do let me try, Lady Judith!"

He spoke in quite a pleading tone, and looked, indeed, a handsome, winning fellow as he spoke.

"Let me still deal frankly with you, Charles Escombe. My own first wish would be, that my daughter should not marry. I think, apart from all personal or individual considerations, that there is much great work to be done in the world especially in England, which can only be done by women who are free; that is, by women who are not married. But I suppose I cannot have that wish. And my next desire would be, that Alexia should marry (if she will marry) Angelo Volney. There are many reasons why that seems to me so natural and desirable an arrangement, that I sometimes have thought it might even be providential. But I know my own unworthiness too well" (and as she spoke, Lady Judith raised her head, and looked supremely proud and beautiful) "to presume on my capacity to interpret the decrees of Providence. If, then, Alexia will marry, and if she and Angelo do not choose to join hands, you are the only man left on earth to whom I would willingly give my daughter."

Charles Escombe took her hand and pressed it to his lips, having previously, in accordance with his character—blended of the practical and the sentimental—glanced around the garden to be certain that nobody was looking.

"But remember," Lady Judith went on when this unwonted demonstration was over, "there must be nothing precipitate. Remember that she is still a child; and I will have no marrying of children. You will start presently on your tour through the United States?"

"Yes, certainly."

"Quite right. I would have nothing to prevent, or even to postpone that. That ought to be the grand tour now; Europe is grown old, used-up. No young man of rank can do anything useful, or take any high place, who has not seen and studied the republican States of America. Canada, of course, you will visit; but I don't care so much about that; there is no new problem of political and social life working out there. You will go, then, to America at the time you have already fixed upon."

"I meant to sail in the early part of September; but I began to think lately of waiting for—well, for Alexia's birthday."

"Not at all; don't think of waiting; go at the time you originally marked out. Let us avoid all sentimentalism and nonsense. Now listen: I have made up my mind that Angelo Volney shall go with you."

The young man flushed and looked very glad.

"Indeed, Lady Judith! I am delighted; and so, I am sure, will he be. I would have suggested it long ago, and so would he; but I hardly thought—we hardly thought, I mean—that you could have spared him."

"I am not accustomed to think of myself in anything; and I *can* spare him. I dare say he can bear leaving me."

"Well, now, really I don't know. Of course, he would like to go; every fellow would like such a trip, I suppose. But I don't think he would enjoy it, or would go at all, in fact, if he supposed that you wanted him here."

"I don't want him here; and I have special reasons—two at least—for wishing him to go. Then this is our understanding: you go upon your American tour, and you take him with you. Until you come back, you are to make no approach whatever to Alexia—I mean no approach of the kind you have indicated. When you return to England, if you are still of the same mind, you are free to try your fortune; and I shall pray for you both, and shall accept with resignation the result, whatever it be."

"Lady Judith, I ask for nothing more. This contents my uttermost expectations. How shall I thank you? how shall I prove that I am grateful, and that I appreciate you?"

"By not alluding to the subject any more until after you have returned from the United States. You can keep a word and a purpose; and so can I. We understand each other—at least as well as a man and a woman ever could understand each other. We need not speak of the matter any more. Let us go and see something."

"Certainly. What do you wish to see?"

"The Prussian village-school model first, and then some of the machinery. We are late for the service in the church with all this talk, and I regret that."

So they went and inspected the Prussian village-school, and Charles Escombe could explain everything and give the exact figures of everything; and then they saw some machinery, and he could explain all that too. And not a word of sentiment or love escaped the lips of that good young man during the whole of their instructive ramble. But when they were leaving the Palace for the late dinner which Escombe had been invited to share, the autumn moon was already rising over the trees, and fountains, and colonnades, and statues which had sprung up so suddenly out of Bellona's barren bosom, the Field of Mars, and its light was falling tenderly, poetically over the Champs Elysées, and over the quiet Seine; and surely no lover, though inflated like a very windbag with political ideas, and crammed full as a cornsack with facts and figures, ever yet looked at the moon without feeling a throb of sentiment pulsate within him. So Charles Escombe thought of the pale pretty child he loved, and he looked on the pale beautiful face of her mother; and as he assisted Lady Judith into her carriage, he pressed her hand and softly whispered to the stately lady:

"You have done a good deed, Lady Judith! You have made a man happy!"

Lady Judith looked at him with an expression of pity and sadness. She almost sighed. Perhaps for a moment, thinking of her own drear and barren life, she envied the emotion which could thus gladden so earnest a heart, and make the wise happily unwise, and the desert of practical philanthropy blossom with the roses of sentiment. But if she felt any such softening sensation, it was soon gone, and she returned to her wonted condition of mind, in which pity and scorn of mankind and conviction of mankind's inherent foolishness and baseness were predominant. She gazed at the handsome, true-hearted, manly creature before her, and thought with wonder, curiosity, and compassion that the whole world was now changed for him because he had some hope of winning the worthless love of a freakish, fantastic, ill-humored, malignant little girl in whom she, Lady Judith, the mother who had borne the child, could see nothing that was not pitiable, despicable, or hateful.

"*I* never was like that," Lady Judith thought to herself proudly; "I never could have been thus infatuated about any human creature. Man is man, and woman is woman. I never could for a moment, even when I was a girl, have been deceived and humbled into fancying that either was an angel. I never could thus abase my intelligence and my nature before any poor human creature!

So she pitied Charles Escombe for the folly of his love, and prided herself on the wisdom and strength which could not stoop to such emotions. She was indeed, and ever had been, wiser in her generation than the children of light.

CHAPTER IV.

"MOTHER, YOU HAVE MY FATHER MUCH OFFENDED."

"I WONDER any one would take the pains to rear a daughter!" Such is the heartfelt utterance of the perplexed and half-distracted mother in the "Beggar's Opera"; and having in it that touch of nature which makes the whole world kin, it might have commended itself to the sympathy of Lady Judith Scarlett. This lady had indeed never seen or read the "Beggar's Opera," and would have been simply disgusted with it if she had; but she was almost every day brought into unknown and unconscious kinship with honest Mother Peachum by the sensations which the capricious and unmanageable character of her daughter aroused within her. Lady Judith's world in London pitied her because of her daughter, and sympathized with her, and marvelled why it was that so good, devoted, and religious a mother should have been afflicted by the existence of such a child. Only those who came very near the mother and daughter —the servants, for example, of whom mention has already been made—ever had a word to say for the poor child of misfortune, "born in bitterness and nurtured in convulsions."

When Lady Judith Scarlett was left in a condition worse than widowhood by the events described in the first and second chapters, she did her very best not to yield mentally, morally, or physically to the stroke. She looked Calamity and Humiliation boldly, sternly in the face, and strove to stare them out of countenance. She had youth, beauty, wealth, rank, and an almost universal public sympathy to uphold her. But even these gifts and good fortunes cannot wholly unsex a woman or give her nerves of steel and a framework of gutta-percha; and Lady Judith's physical nature yielded somewhat, at last and after a struggle, to the pressure, and strain, and excitement which she had ordered her soul to bear. The result was, that Alexia Scarlett came prematurely into the world; was first a sickly baby, then a cross-grained, elfish, malignant child; and is now a young woman, precocious in passion and in self-will, humorous as winter, full of fierce and often meaningless angers and suspicions; antagonistic almost to everybody in everything; hoping little, believing little; seldom laughing, but at the vexation of others; never allowing others to see her tears, but weeping freely and bitterly when she could enjoy the luxury of solitude and tears together.

Always had Alexia Scarlett, since she came to distinguish persons, been haunted and tortured by a distrust and dislike of her mother. The girl could not help it; it was apparently instinctive, and belonged to her blood and the laws of her being. Perhaps when physiology and morality and the principles of social life shall have come to a full understanding and reconciliation among each other, we may see more clearly than we now do the inexorable justice, physical and religious, which would brand with a practical and visible condemnation such unions as that of Charles Scarlett and that Judith whom man's law made his wife; and we shall have no more difficulty about recognizing the consequence of such as shown in the temperament of an Alexia, than we now have in acknowledging that consumptive mothers are likely to bring forth consumptive children. However that may be, it is certain that Alexia Scarlett never loved, or believed in, or confided in her mother; and that the older she grew, the deeper the gulf seemed to be which sundered the souls of these two women. Her mother's religious devotion Alexia scorned, believing it to be nothing but hypocrisy—which it certainly was not. Her practical beneficence and systematized philanthropy Alexia openly gibed and scoffed at.

"The absent are always in the wrong," was not a maxim which governed Alexia Scarlett. On the contrary, the present almost always were in the wrong with her. Distrusting and disliking therefore the mother who was present, it was but natural that her thoughts should turn habitually to the father who was absent. For many years Alexia was allowed to believe that her father was dead. Whenever anything displeased her or went wrong with her—which happened rather often—she was accustomed to attribute all her wrongs and sufferings to the absence of a father's care, and she was wont to hide in her own room, and shed passionate tears over an imaginary grave. Once when Lady Judith strove to teach her to say her prayers correctly, and told her she must address her petition to "Our Father who art in heaven," the little girl looked up with a scornful anger as keen and proud as that of Hamlet himself when he makes his bitter retort upon his mother, and she only said, "*My* Father who art in heaven!"

But Alexia was precocious almost in every way; and she soon began to conjecture shrewdly enough either that her earthly father was not yet in heaven, or that there was something uncommon and mysterious about the death which had left her fatherless. She had no direct means of learning the truth, for Lady Judith's first act when she began to compose herself to her widowhood had been to make a clean sweep of the servants in the house; and not a creature now in her employment knew anything whatever of Charles Grey Scarlett. Tom Thynne Dysart had long disappeared out of London society. The official position he got was given too late to save or even serve him. He only spent money ten times as fast as ever on the strength of his appointment; and after two years' occupation of the place, its accounts became hopelessly muddled, much of its revenue had vanished, and Dysart suddenly disappeared. When he was gone, it was found that he had spent and wasted the official receipts with a wild hand; that he had borrowed and swindled; that he had even forged great names, and rendered himself in various ways liable to the operation of the criminal law. The thing stirred a great scandal: a virtuous Opposition publicly and often denounced the Government for having made such an appointment; the independent newspapers insisted that Dysart might have been arrested if the heads of the Home Office really desired his capture. But Dysart was gone. Afterwards it was reported that he had died miserably in a wretched exile; and he too be came forgotten, and one other witness was removed out of Alexia Scarlett's world who would only too gladly have told her something of her father's story.

Chance had intervened during this visit of the Scarletts to Paris to bring the mystery of her father's disappearance back with fresh curiosity and bitterness to Alexia's mind. In the hotel where they were living she came on some old volumes of the "Illustrated London News," dating from the year of the first great Exhibition; and turning over the leaves, she discovered a portrait of her father, who was described as one of the rising celebrities of the day. Then, going carefully and pertinaciously along over page after page, she came at length to certain mysterious paragraphs of gossip about the extraordinary disappearance of a distinguished political man; authentic contradictions of this rumor, delicate and doubting allusions to that other, and so forth; and she was easily able to establish, to her own satisfaction, the date of the event, whatever it was, which had left her fatherless. Her conclusion was prompt and characteristic. She at once assumed that, driven to despair by her mother's unloving coldness and harsh fanaticism, her father had killed himself.

Alexia was a lonely creature at best, much given to the secret perusal of the dreariest tragedies and the grimmest romances. It fed her morbid soul with a kind of cruel delight to dwell upon this hideous solution of the mystery that had curtained her childhood. She spoke to no one of what she believed herself to have discovered, but brooded over it, and allowed it to take utter possession of her.

This evening, after her return from the Champ de Mars, she hurried into her own room, sharply announced that she did not intend to come to dinner, and that she would not see or speak with anybody. The windows of her room looked across the gay and glittering Rue de Rivoli and through the gilded gates of the Tuileries into the gardens, where a well-trained band was making joyous music among the chestnut trees. The gladness and life of the outer world found no way into the lonely heart of the sad and self-tormenting girl. She first pulled down the blinds, that she might not see the gayety and happiness of people outside; then she locked her door; and then she flung herself down on the floor and hid her face.

Many things had conspired to distract her on this unlucky day. To begin with, she awoke out of some strange dream about her father—some ghastly dream about her having come upon his dead body, half hidden with leaves, in the brown depths of an autumnal forest, as such things happen in the weird romances she loved to read; and that her mother was standing by, and that the corpse bled anew when Lady Judith came near; and Alexia screamed, and thus scattered her hideous phantasy. But its memory brooded over her; and now, as she turned her face to the floor, it glared upon her closed eyes again. Then she had not liked Charles Escombe's manner all day. She could only tolerate Escombe in her best moods, and she hated him in her worst; he was such a favorite with her mother, and always so sure to be right in everything he said and did. Again, she had been vexed somehow by Angelo's admiration for the strange girl in the Exhibition gardens—Angelo, the only person she yet knew for whom she had any gleam of affection, or in whom she felt any confidence. Then she had been trying to be very good; and there are some people with whom, as in the case of the lover resolving to forget his faithless love, the hard struggle to forget is itself a new temptation to remember. Poor Alexia never analyzed her emotions or their causes; but she knew that things had gone ill with her that day; and she felt the coming on of a raging mood, as one feels the coming of a headache. As she lay there, it seemed to her as if ghosts came around and moaned over her; as if demons came and tempted her, or mocked her. Perhaps these latter visitants were indeed of just the same brood as the fiends that of old came to lonely struggling men in ascetic caves and tempted and maddened them.

The outer world would be better than this. She sprang to her feet, pulled up the blinds, and opened the windows. It did not seem, however, as if either solitude or society was destined on this unlucky day to bring soothing to the fretful mood of this poor, self-torturing child. For, as she looked out of the window and strove not to rage at those who seemed happy underneath, she saw an open carriage drive past, in which were seated the elderly pair and the young woman whom she had seen in the sculpture gallery that day. The broad soft face of the man positively beamed and rippled all over with delight; the thin wrinkled countenance of his companion broke into countless little grimacing dimples of pleasure; and the beautiful girl looked like a living symbol of health, womanhood, intellect, and gladness.

"I wish I knew her," sighed our self-imprisoned child. "I think I could trust her and love her. No, I don't. I hate her, because she is so happy and so beautiful, and because Angelo looked at her, and because she has her father."

She turned away from the window and flung herself on her bed.

Two or three times there was a tapping at her door; but Alexia would not open or make any answer. This indeed was commonly her way. As the evening wore into night her maid came, and through the keyhole offered her services, but was sharply bidden to begone. Then Alexia thought she could best escape all the further persecution of a wicked and tantalizing world by undressing and going into bed unassisted. She had nearly undressed, with no other light than that of the moon, which was shining in, when a somewhat imperious tapping was heard at the door, and Alexia knew that her mother was there. The young girl's heart beat fast. Not often did Lady Judith trouble herself personally about her daughter's fits of ill-humor or sudden disappearances into solitude. Lady Judith had no sympathy with whims. She believed that she had thoroughly disciplined her own nature; and she made as little allowance for women who could not discipline theirs as a man who has never felt a pang of fear is likely to make for one who is constitutionally a trembler.

"Open the door, Alexia," said Lady Judith calmly.

"Pray, mamma, do you very much want to see me? I am nearly undressed."

"I want to speak to you, Alexia. Open your door."

There was something in Lady Judith's voice which always carried with it, when the owner so desired, a sense of inexorable resolution. Alexia felt that she could not fight the quarrel, if there was to be one, upon that ground; and she sought strength in an utter abandonment to the rising power of her own evil temper. She opened the door, and Lady Judith entered.

The mother and daughter confronted each other, and were indeed a contrast all the more striking because of the points of resemblance. Assuredly all the physical advantage was on the side of the former. The moonlight showed her firm and stately figure, the white forehead, the dark hair, the floating robes of silk, the gleaming bracelets and sparkling rings, the queenly opulence of form and of apparel, the supreme self-composure. It showed too the small, fragile, pallid girl shrinking back in her little frilled night-dress, contracting her forehead over the fierce and fitful light of her dark eyes, and eagerly clutching at something on the table as her mother entered.

"Alexia, have you prayed to-night?"

"No, mamma. I am not quite in the sort of mood, I suppose, which makes a prayer acceptable. *I* cannot have the prayerful mood always ready."

"You ought to pray for a better spirit. You ought to pray for guidance and for light from above——"

"Light from above? Yes. I want light from above! Do you know for what? To show me how my father died, and who it was that caused his death! Mother, where is my father? If he lives, I will go to him, if he were at the other end of the earth! If he is dead, tell me where his grave is, and who killed him! Keep your preachings and your prayers from me, and tell me of my father, or I will kill myself here before your eyes!"

And indeed the young woman held in her hand a glittering weapon, and looked like a being well capable of making her threat a deed.

CHAPTER V.

LADY JUDITH'S PUPILS.

THE Lady Judith Scarlett would probably have made an excellent tamer, or at least conqueror, of wild animals. She had always that indomitable conviction of her own rectitude of purpose and justice of vision which is the soul of all conquest. She had, of course, great personal courage. Most women have. Nothing can be more baseless than the conventional notion that women excel in patience and fail in courage. As a rule, only men are patient; as a rule, women are fearless. They seldom pause at a crisis to count cost or consequences; and therefore have no fear. Add, in this case, to the uttermost courage of woman, woman's strongest will and faith in self, and it will be seen that Lady Judith Scarlett was not likely to flinch or even to hesitate.

Moreover, if she wanted any other advantage over her daughter, it was given her by Alexia's own demand. The one thing on earth about which Lady Judith was most certain—and she was certain about nearly everything—was that in regard to her vanished husband hers was the story of a victim and a martyr. The very existence of the pale girl who stood before her was, under such circumstances, a new wrong to her. It seemed to Lady Judith that Alexia's whole life ought to be one of penitence and meek apology, for the injury she had done to her mother in being born of such a father.

Lady Judith had some tact, too, which women of iron will do not always have. There are people who threaten to kill themselves, and do not mean it, and for whom open contempt and ridicule will be found the best treatment. Lady Judith, however, was by no means certain that a word or even a look of incredulous scorn, a phrase or glance tending to show that she considered her daughter's threat a piece of mock-heroic display, might not prove the very thing to send the weapon into the child's passionate heart. So she spoke as one who is dealing with a grave reality.

Calmly and sadly, full of faith in her own martyrdom, Lady Judith spoke.

"Alexia, you have no need to use such threats, offensive and alarming to me, still more lamentably offensive to heaven, in order to extort from me some painful truths. You ought to know that I could only have kept these things from you because I wished to spare you much useless pain. Now you have grown to be a woman, and you have a right to ask and to know all that you will. Give me that knife."

It was a pretty little Eastern dagger, to which Alexia had taken a fancy at one of the stalls in the Exposition, and which she would buy whether her mother wished it or not.

She laughed her bitter little laugh.

"No, indeed, I mean to keep this, mamma. It makes me mistress of the situation. Tell me about my father."

"Had you not better at least go into bed, Alexia? You will take cold,"

Again a little laugh. Alexia believed herself to be winning the game.

"Take cold! That is like the story of the wretch on his way to execution; the rain began, and some one offered him a cloak lest he should get wet—as if it mattered then! No, dear mother, I don't care about a possible cold just now; I may use this pretty plaything yet. Tell me of my father. I don't care for life, I am sick of life, unless *he* is living. If he is dead, I will go to him. Tell me the truth in one word. Is he dead? Yes or no?"

"No."

"He is living?"

"He is. At least I believe him to be living."

"This is no deceit—no pious, motherly fraud to stay my hand and save my life?"

Lady Judith smiled a cold smile that was almost like a sneer.

"Child, I would not tell a falsehood to save the lives of all my race. I believe your father to be still living."

"Then, thank God! I will live and find him out."

She flung the little dagger contemptuously from her, and it rattled on the floor. Lady Judith did not take it up, or even glance towards where it lay; that would have looked like weakness.

"Alexia, your father was a bad man."

"I don't believe it!" the girl fiercely interposed.

"I wish you had not forced me to convince you of it. Before you were born he deserted me and you. He disgraced and abandoned us; he turned away from his God. My miserable story was the scandal of the day. The pity and sympathy of the good, the coarse curiosity of the vulgar, the ridicule of the wicked, were poured on me, and on you while you were yet a baby. Ask no more about your father. You had better not have heard this much; do not try to know any more. Pray for him, that he may be converted and brought back to good; and pray for yourself, Alexia, that you may have a better spirit."

"Where is my father? I must know that."

"That you cannot know; that no one knows."

"You are trying to deceive me, mamma. If you know that he is living, you must know—at least you must guess—where he is."

"All that I know of his present existence," said Lady Judith, rising from the chair where she had seated herself—while her daughter now stood upright, with one hand resting on the arm of a little sofa—"all that I know, Alexia, you know. I have told you so much, not because of any petulant and wicked threat of yours (here, however, Lady Judith stooped and picked up the dagger), but because I did not believe myself justified in withholding from you at your present age the knowledge you asked for. Now listen to me. I *may* come to know something of his present existence; I only say that I *may*. But should I do so, I will not allow *you*, while yet you are under my care and guardianship, to write to him or hear from him. When you are eighteen years old, I shall consider you responsible for your own acts; and if you then know anything of him and will go to him, you are free from me for ever. I hold no parley with wickedness. 'Come out from amongst them, and be separated from them,' is a law to me. Providence has seen fit to afflict me as a mother and as a wife. I hope I can bow my head to affliction, and bear it; but I cannot hold terms with sin. Now we have talked enough of this, and you know my resolution. Go to bed, Alexia, and good-night."

She turned away and left the room, closing the door behind her; but she remained a moment on the outer threshold, and noiselessly listened. She heard her daughter sobbing bitterly within. Lady Judith's face brightened.

"She is safe now," the mother thought to herself; "and the worst is over. It is right that she should sob and suffer for her wickedness. May her heart be touched and softened!"

So firmly steeling her own heart against pity, Lady Judith Scarlett left her daughter.

Yes; Alexia Scarlett had flung herself on the bed the moment her mother's eye was removed, and burst into passionate tears. Was her little world of fancy and hope and wild longing really, then, shattered all around her? Had she no father—or a father who was worse than none? Of late her sick and morbid soul had only fed itself on dreams about a noble, true, and loving father, driven into exile, or perhaps even to death, by the very influences which so often seemed destined to crush the life from her own young heart; a father still living for her, here or in the skies, and longing for her, and ever ready, when fate should allow, to stretch forth his loving arms and shelter his daughter on his breast. And was this story she had heard the truth? Was this lost father only a selfish criminal, a degraded outcast? In spite of herself, the cold cutting firmness and apparent sincerity of Lady Judith's words had wrought upon her, and the light of her hopes seemed for the moment to have been rudely blown out for ever.

Suddenly the girl heard a quiet footfall stealing away from her door; and springing towards the threshold with the silent alertness of some swift animal, she could distinctly hear the rustle of her departing mother's dress.

"She has been listening; listening to hear whether I was crying," said the girl to herself, with a fierce quick light of mingled anger and triumph flashing up in her dark eyes. "She has been watching me, she has been deceiving me. I know it now; I know it by that one sign alone. It was not true all that she said about my father. It was false; and I believe in him and not in her. My father—he is still my father; and he lives and does not know he has a daughter who loves him and longs for him, and who will find him yet and hold him to her heart."

Ah, Lady Judith, why play false, even that one moment, to the grand and conquering power of sincerity? That one little scrap of harmless insincerity, of innocent double-dealing, that short moment of listening at your daughter's door, has simply spoiled all. She is a sceptic and a rebel now more than ever.

But Lady Judith believed in her own triumph and was content, although the affair had not been without alarm for her. Her daughter was a trouble to her, just as it would be a trouble to have to watch over a panther or a maniac, or some other creature on which the eye of supreme power must always rest, and which a single glance of hesitation or timidity may set free to do any nameless work of wild destruction.

She returned to her own rooms—a dressing-room and bedroom—looking into the great courtyard of the hotel, with its roof of glass, its palm-trees and its lamps. As she glanced into the courtyard, she saw Angelo Volney enter it, and she watched him, in the blended light of sky and lamps, as he crossed the broad space that even still echoed with footsteps and murmured with voices. She watched his graceful form and handsome head as he sprang up the great staircase; she even leaned out of her window to see him yet another moment, and then Lady Judith drew back and sighed.

She rang her bell, bade her maid have the lamps lighted and the windows closed; "and tell Mr. Volney I wish to speak to him here."

Lady Judith settled herself gracefully and picturesquely in an arm-chair; adjusted the bracelets on her wrists, the pearls on her neck, the silken skirts around her feet. Her chair stood near a small table; she took from the table a little volume, opened it, and began to read. It was "De Imitatione Christi" in French.

A knock at the door, and she called "Come in;" and Angelo Volney entered. Lady Judith's face looked glad. The one only creature in life who seemed heart and soul devoted to her, and for whose devotion she had a deep regard, was this young man, Angelo Volney. He was a handsome youth, with a face of bright intelligence, and ways that were at once sweet, grave, and caressing, such as some women like to whom high animal spirits seem to savor of vulgarity, and habitual mirth-making to denote frivolity and want of soul.

"I want to talk to you, Angelo," said Lady Judith, pointing to a chair near hers.

He sat there, and leaned towards her with a manner full of confidence and affection, as if he were her son.

"I have something serious to say to you. You have been walking with Charles Escombe!"

"Yes, Lady Judith; I walked a little way with him towards his hotel."

"Did he tell you what he and I had been speaking of to-day?"

"He did; he told me that you wish me to go with him on his tour through the States."

"Of course you are willing to go?"

Lady Judith's eyes, dark and majestic, rested with something of curious inquiry on him as she spoke.

"Dear Lady Judith, it is just the one thing in the world I have been most anxious for."

She dropped her eyes.

"Yes, Angelo, I wish you to see the United States. I wish you to continue to study, as you have done, in the life of realities, and not in schools; in the living present, and not the dead past. So I wish you to see America. Did Charles Escombe speak to you of nothing else?"

"No, nothing in particular."

"Nothing about Alexia?"

"Nothing at all."

"Well, he is a sensible, discreet young man, and probably thought he had no right to speak of it; but he might have talked of it to you. No matter; it is better, indeed, that it should come from me. Angelo, Charles Escombe has been talking to me about his wish to have Alexia for his wife one day, when she is a little older than now."

Angelo looked up and smiled.

"Is that the news—the secret? Why, Lady Judith, I could have told you *that* was coming any day for the past three months. I am sure I am delighted if you are."

She looked at him once more keenly and curiously, and then said:

"I am not delighted, Angelo; such things don't delight me. But I see no reason to object, and little use in objecting so far as I am concerned. What do you think Alexia will say?"

"Oh, I don't know; I think she likes Charles well enough, although she rails at him now and then. Where could she find a finer creature?"

"True. I don't care myself about what people call love. I suppose she has no such feeling towards anybody?"

"Alexia? Oh no! At least, I suppose not; I never thought of such a thing I can hardly imagine her having such a feeling; she is very young and whimsical. I should think she likes Charles Escombe as well as she could like any one."

"Except you, Angelo."

"Yes, Lady Judith, except me, of course. We have been so much together, and she is so familiar with me, that we are, in fact, brother and sister; and naturally she is more attached to me than to any one else, as I am to her. But that would have nothing to do with Charles, or with any one she might consent to marry. That, of course, would be quite another feeling; and I don't see why it should not grow up for him as well as for any one else."

Lady Judith looked at him fixedly, and slightly raised her eyebrows. After a moment's silence, she went on:

"Well, we need not say any more about this just now; there is something else I wish to speak to you about. Angelo, do you know how much I have done for you?"

She spoke in a low, grave tone, and she leaned her chin upon one hand, the arm of which rested on her knee, and the deep, steady light of her eyes was full on his face. He looked up surprised, and something of a color suffused the faint olive tints of his cheek.

"Surely, Lady Judith, I do know it. I know that you have been to me what few mothers have been even to a favorite son."

"You do not know all or half. Do you know that you were a beggar-child, sleeping on my doorstep—the orphan, at that moment, of a mother who lay dead in a workhouse hospital? Do you know that you are no relative or connection of mine, however humble or remote? that I never saw your father, and know nothing of him, but that he died a wretched, worthless idler and vagabond? and that I knew your mother only as a suffering poor creature to whom I gave alms?"

Angelo started to his feet with a cry of surprise, and then flung himself into his chair again, and covered his face with his hands. Lady Judith looked down upon his emotion with a gaze that had something of kindness, almost of tenderness in it, and then she laid her hand upon his heaving shoulder.

"All that is true, Angelo. Your mother was an Italian guitar-player, who died in the hospital; you crawled to my doorstep, and my servants found you there in the rain. And since then you have been as my son. Did you know all this?"

"No, no. O my God! Some painful, horrible memories I have of a miser able home, and of hunger, and of my mother being carried away somewhere, and of my wandering into the streets. I knew that my first years were passed in wretched poverty; but I always believed that I belonged to your family—that I was your nephew, perhaps, the son of some brother or sister who had been unfortunate, and that you took me into your house because of my birth when I was left an orphan. I always thought this; I took it for granted. Oh, Lâdy Judith, how blindly ignorant I must have been!"

He sprang from his chair, and walked up and down the room.

"Sit down, Angelo; sit near me."

He obeyed her, but he kept his eyes averted.

"Listen to me, Angelo. The night you came to my doorstep, a great calamity, a profound disgrace, had fallen upon me and mine. My life was made desolate and blasted. The hour that brought you brought this revelation. When I first saw you, after I had known all, there was something in your face which pleaded powerfully with me; and it seemed to me more and more as if Heaven had sent you to my threshold, in order that by doing some good for a human being, I might atone for the sin of one who—who once was linked with me. I felt as if Heaven, which had sent me a cross to bear, had also sent me a crown to win. I resolved to save you from the life and the vices of the streets, and I did so. But I never thought then of making you, as you have made yourself, a son, and more than a son, to me; that came later, and step by step. My daughter is hardly as a daughter to me; the blood that runs in her veins has poison in it, Angelo—poison and sin. Do you know why I tell you all this?"

A proud flush came into the face of the young man, and he looked firmly into her eyes as he answered:

"No, Lady Judith, I do not know; but I feel sure your motive is kind and just. Whatever it be, I have learned at last what a worthless and dependent idler I have been; and I will, with Heaven's help, be so no longer. I may have begun life as a beggar, but I will not so continue it. You have done for me already more than ever Christian lady did for an unknown outcast. You have reared me, taught me, saved me! I must make the rest of my way in life myself. You shall not have cause to be ashamed of me, or to think your good deeds thrown away."

Angelo's voice began to tremble, and there were tears glittering in his eyes. He was half an Italian, let us remember, and brave men among Southern races are not ashamed to shed tears.

"In other words," said Lady Judith, with a return to the cold smile which her lips often wore, but which had vanished in the earnestness and heat of her recent utterances, "you would show your gratitude and your spirit by leaving me when your presence had become most needful and valuable. I might ask, with the dying Emperor, 'Is this fidelity?' But, indeed, it would be very like man's gratitude always. Such thanks have I usually had."

Angelo threw himself on his knees, and seized the hand of his benefactress, and kissed it again and again. Lady Judith colored—almost started—but did not draw away her hand.

"You know," Angelo exclaimed, "that you command my life—that your word is my will—that I would die for you!"

"I don't ask you to die for me," calmly replied Lady Judith, with something of a softer light now in her eyes; "I only ask you to live for me. Is not that easier to do?"

"Not always. Just now I feel so crushed by this disclosure—by the weight of your goodness—by the hopeless, impotent impulses of my gratitude—that, indeed, Lady Judith, I wish I had a chance of doing something for you which would cost me my life."

"Now, however, Angelo, I especially want you to live. You can serve me. I may say that you alone can do so. Stay—don't break into any protestations, but listen to me; I have something more to tell you."

He rose and resumed his seat beside her. She drew a deep breath, set her teeth firmly, as if with the fixedness of some painful resolution, and spoke in a low tone at first, with her eyes upon the floor, until she grew into heat and bitterness as she went on:

"There is a man still living—a bad and wicked man—who did me the cruellest wrong. He is still living, as I believe; perhaps prosperous and successful. He is my husband, Angelo—the husband who deserted and disgraced me—the father of that unhappy girl, whom sometimes I almost detest because she is his child. There is much in her that reminds me of him, although he was not wayward and fitful in manner as she is; and I dread more than anything on earth his meeting her one day, and claiming her, and gaining influence over her, as he could do over most people, and leading her into his own profane and irreligious and godless principles. My greatest purpose in life is to save her soul, and to keep her and him asunder. You can help me in this; and now you know why I told you of your birth and your poverty, and of all I had done for you.'

He looked at her inquiringly.

"Don't you still understand?"

He shook his head.

"To bind you to me, Angelo—to pledge you to my purpose."

"Lady Judith, I am pledged to any purpose of yours, for I know that it is just and right. Even if I did not know this, I fear it would hardly make much difference: I am bound to you in heart and soul."

"I want you to help me in keeping my daughter from this man. You have more influence over her than any one else has. She does not care for young Escombe; she never will care for him. Angelo, I want *you* to marry my daughter."

Volney colored and started.

"Why do you start? Is this a difficult thing I ask you to do?" Lady Judith asked sternly.

"Oh, no, no; but it surprises me. Alexia and I have always been like brother and sister, and I am sure it has never occurred to her to think of me otherwise. And then, Lady Judith, I cannot now forget that your daughter will be a woman of rank and wealth, and that I am a pauper dependant; that I was a nameless outcast, that I was a beggar who sat at your threshold and cried for bread. Does she know that? Do you think if she did it would not alter her feelings towards me? Lady Judith, I have the warmest affection for Alexia, and I know there is far more in her that is good and noble than you—than some people, I mean—may think; but I do not believe she has a soul great enough for *that*."

"But if she comes to love you, Angelo? Do you think that with her impetuous soul she would care for any such consideration then?"

"Perhaps not; but even then, would it be right or manly in me to trade upon her generosity and her affection?"

"Angelo, this is idle talk! Either you speak the truth when you say that you have pledged yourself to my purpose, or you have talked the mere babble of unmeaning politeness. I tell you I have set my heart on this, and I will have it so, unless *you* refuse! If it depended wholly on my will, no daughter of mine should ever marry even you, Angelo, whom I believe to be an exception among men. But as I know that she will marry, I wish her to marry you. You can already influence her as no one else can, and I can trust you to stand between her and *him*. Do you refuse me?"

He smiled faintly.

"Lady Judith, you crown a course of unheard-of beneficence by making me an offer of almost incredible generosity—and you ask me if I refuse! What could I hope for better than this? If I hesitate, it is because I am ashamed to take advantage of such splendid goodness. But, after all, it is not I who have to refuse or to accept. What of *her*—of Alexia?"

"There is time enough for that. This thing, of course, is not to be approached at once. She is too young. But I think she already looks towards you with something that will be love; and I therefore wish you to know that her mother desires you to foster and strengthen and accept that sentiment. I wish you to feel that your interest in her is likely to be enduring. I have told Charles Escombe that he is to make no advances to her for the present—nor need you. But I know that she will refuse him, and I think she will accept *you*. That is all for the moment. Don't we understand each other now, Angelo?"

"I think so, Lady Judith."

He spoke in a low meditative tone.

"Well, then, let me tell you of *this man*. I have heard a vague rumor that he is somewhere in the United States. He has, of course, disguised his name; but he has great gifts and great strength of mind, and he is likely to have made a success—for he was consumed with worldly ambition—and to have become conspicuous and influential. I should like to know, if it were possible, whether he is living in America, and whether he is prosperous and successful, and what manner of repute he bears. Find out this, Angelo, if you can; but avoid the man yourself; for he is my worst enemy. Guard against the influence of his plausible manners, the gravity and purity he used to assume; and remember always what he has been to me. I have no clue to his discovery or his whereabouts—none whatever—and yours may be the idlest wild-goose chase; but I will give you such dates and descriptions as may help you. Find out something of him, if you can; but avoid him. We have talked too long, Angelo; it will soon be dawn. When in London we can talk of this again. Now, good-night!"

She rose with her usual decisiveness of manner and gesture. Angelo Volney again touched his lips to her white cold hand, on the fingers of which glittered jewels bright and cold as her eyes or her intellect; and he left her without a word.

"I know," she said between her teeth, "that he is a successful and an honored man somewhere. And if I find him out, I will strip him of his false reputation, and pull him down! I owe it to myself, to society, to religion, to see that he shall not masquerade in the robes of honesty and virtue, and feed his profane ambition, and deceive and betray others as he deceived and betrayed me."

Then she rang the bell for her maid; and she again opened the "Imitation of Christ," and sighed fervently more than once, and shook her head, as she bent over the pure pages.

Angelo went to his room with throbbing pulses and a swimming head. If one could be born full-grown, full-brained into the world, to him all new and strange, inexplicable, thrilling, bewildering, he might have felt somewhat as Angelo Volney, son of the Italian guitar-player, felt when he quitted the presence of his benefactress. The past and the future were alike confusion and chaos to him; a jangle of wild discordant bells; a rushing of mad winds; a deafening roar of waters in the ears. He sat up a long time; lay long awake on his bed; and when he did sleep at last, he dreamed first that he was a ragged boy wandering through cold black streets; then, that he was pursuing fiercely, at the angry bidding of Lady Judith, a flying enemy, who hid his face until they two were remote from all gazers, and then turned round and smiled upon him sweetly and sadly with the deep planet-like eyes of the girl he had seen in the garden that day. This face, those eyes, followed him from that hour through all his phantom-haunted dreams; and ever the face seemed to be a part somehow of his coming mission and his coming history; and ever it seemed to be blended with, to alternate with, the dim and shadowy features, hardly seen through a veil of mist, which belonged to the being he was sent to pursue. His sleep—if such fever-dreamings may be called sleep—was unrefreshing; and Angelo was glad when he opened his eyes at last upon the bright sunlight, even although the very first moment of wakefulness brought with it the painful consciousness that there was opening on him a new life under wholly unexpected conditions; that the old familiar past had fallen utterly away from him; that he was a dependent, a waif, and an alien in a sphere to which he had no right, but from which the very nature of his dependency did not allow him manfully to withdraw. Yesterday he was in honorable and loving service; to-day he was a purchased slave. This was the first thought which morning brought to him.

Angelo Volney is the hero of this story. There was nothing very heroic about him, either in the meaning of the military gazette or of the modern novelist. He had never fought in duel or battle, although, perhaps, "he was likely, had he been put on, to have proved" as brave as most others. He was not of tremendous strength; not given to vast feats of drinking; not pitiless in the maltreating of less sinewy men; not addicted to the corruption of women. Indeed, some of your swashbuckler heroes of the modern novel would have probably thought that there was a good deal of the milksop about this young fellow. Perhaps, not being a hero, he was a little of a hero-worshipper, or heroine-worshipper at least. His earliest idolatry was for his poor mother. When a worthless and idle father died of heart-disease and rum, and left the poor Italian woman in misery, little Angelo used to beg for her, and tinkle the guitar for her, and go to the pawnshop, and thence to the bakery, for her. He would rise at daylight—in the bitter winter months often before daylight—and go out in the streets twangling a guitar as big as himself, poor little miserable mite! And if he brought home a few halfpennies, he was proud and glad. And if she had a few cold potatoes saved up for him, he would take them quietly into his peculiar corner of the garret, and sit there and eat the potatoes contentedly out of his little red fists—red with the wind and the work. Life begins so soon with creatures like this, that Angelo felt rather advanced in the world when he was six years old, and his mother grew so sick that she had to be taken to the hospital, and he, weary of her absence and his loneliness, although the people from whom the miserable garret was rented were not unkindly, wandered out into the streets, and fell asleep at last on Lady Judith Scarlett's doorstep.

After that Angelo seemed to have been changed into another sort of creature. It has been already told how Lady Judith took pity on him. She had, indeed, always some pity for the poor; and her stern religion—the monasticism of Roman Catholic Middle Ages under a new name—bade her to accept the suffering inflicted on herself as a command to arise and do some good deed. It was her pride to show that no calamity falling on herself could make her forget a duty to others; and the very day that she found herself deserted she went to visit poor Mrs. Volney at the hospital.

"Heaven has been kind, very kind to your mother, my poor boy," said Lady Judith to Angelo that evening.

"Oh, ma'm, is she better?"

"Better? Yes; much better. Better than *I* am. She is dead."

The little man gave a great scream, and fell on his face.

All that passed like a dream. Angelo began to awake to a new life; a life to him as bewilderingly luxurious as that into which Christopher Sly or the "sleeper awakened" of the "Arabian Nights" was summoned. He always had enough to eat and drink; he had a beautiful white bed to sleep in; he never had to go into the streets when it rained; when the cold weather came, there were always coals enough in the house to make every room quite warm; and when the fire burned down, no one groaned or shivered or seemed uneasy, but at once more coals were brought, and the flames were made to leap up cheerily again. For a short time Angelo was allowed to go about the house like a little dog, running from room to room. Then Lady Judith took him in hand for a certain time each day, and taught him something; and then the boy transferred his idolatry to her: he simply worshipped her; thought her an angel of beauty, genius, and goodness, sent to save and make laws for creatures like him. Gradually there arose upon the horizon of his life an odd, eccentric, fitful little human comet in the shape of a pretty, sickly, elfin girl, whom the nurses pitied and girded at, whom Lady Judith, her mother, shunned as much as possible, but of whom Angelo grew unaccountably fond, and whom he soon could manage when nobody else could. Thus the boy became a sort of necessity to Lady Judith; and perhaps his open idolatry of her mollified and touched her—she had never before been anybody's idol—and at length it came to be recognized that she had adopted the lad, and was bringing him up as her son.

Of course her relatives grumbled and sneered a good deal, but no one remonstrated. Lady Judith was not the sort of person on whom any one would have tried a remonstrance. She never allowed Angelo to go to school or college, or to associate with other boys; she had tutors to instruct him after plans and principles of her own, which included little Latin and less Greek, but plenty of French, German, history, political economy, and chemistry. She never went into society, but she had frequent philanthropic and charitable meetings in her own house, and Angelo always acted as her secretary and amanuensis. Charles Escombe was one of the very few human creatures who had the general right of entrance to her house on the footing of a friend.

Lady Judith burned always with an implacable sense of wrong. She never for one moment, even when at her prayers, forgot that she had been wronged by her husband. She fed her soul on the memory of her injuries. When she did good deeds, she did them with a certain proud sense of greatness in thus trying to save a world wherein she had suffered. If she relieved the destitution of a man, she said to her own soul that she was thus heaping coals of fire upon the head of the sex which had made her to suffer. Nay, when she performed some beneficent action, she seemed to look up into the face of Heaven itself, and say, "Behold what I am doing in your service, although you have allowed me to be wronged and humbled!" Her grievance was her idol, and she offered up all her thoughts, words, and actions upon its shrine. Of course Angelo Volney saw nothing of this. He never suspected for a moment that there was anything stern, or hard, or implacable, or egotistic in her nature. She was to him his Madonna, his guiding and governing angel, his star of the sea. He never analyzed or criticised her at all; only bowed to her and worshipped her.

Thus he grew up, living in London and in the midst of a certain luxury, but almost as entirely apart from the ways of what is called society as if he had been still following the footsteps of his poor guitar-playing mother. A certain grave sweetness was his most prominent and obvious characteristic. He had much of the gentle, gracious, natural courtesy of the land from which his mother sprang; and perhaps the shadow of his childhood, with its poverty, hunger, and orphanage, had fallen on his youth and his early manhood, and darkened what might have been its sunny brightness.

Up to this time he had lived wholly for others; not deliberately, or from any purpose or principle, but because it was part of his gentle, patient, unselfish nature to do so. He was the very opposite of Lady Judith in this: her best deeds were but a glorified egotism; the ego hardly existed at all in any consciousness of his. Perhaps the first question of self-examination that ever hinted itself to him was when his patroness told him that she desired him to become hereafter her daughter's husband. Even then the question rose less out of any personal doubt than out of the utter novelty of the suggestion. He had been so long accustomed in his quiet, devoted way to accept Alexia as a sister, that the idea of his marrying her seemed almost as strange as if he had been bidden to marry Lady Judith herself. But as yet no question of whether he loved Alexia or did not love her, whether the affection he felt towards her was the thing called love or not, or what love really was, had shaped or realized itself in his mind. He was some twenty-four years old, wonderfully efficient and acute in many ways, the right hand and often the guide of his benefactress, but as yet the real being within him had hardly been awakened. That handsome, olive-tinted, shapely youth, with the sweet, grave smile and the thoughtful air, is as yet only a soulless boy. Motion and strength, muscle and brain, are alive; but the soul, the reality of being and manhood, is yet to come into its inheritance. The first summons to it to arise and take possession was given when Lady Judith Scarlett told Angelo Volney the story of his childhood, and pledged him anew to her service.

CHAPTER VI.

"OUR ISOLIND."

"QUEEN of the western waves!" A city girt by three rivers and gazing on the ocean; a sea Cybele; a city lying on the edge of a bay not less beautiful than that of Naples, and gladdened by a sky of more than Italian purity and azure brightness; a city whose suburbs already stretch along banks and at the feet of mountains which well may rival those of the Rhine; a city from the roar and bustle of whose busiest wharves and thoroughfares, outroaring the loudest din of London bridge or the docks of Liverpool, you cross a stream and escape in a few moments into green woods fit for the revels of Titania; a city of stupendous contrasts—the most hideous streets, the most beautiful streets—masses of squalid huts, avenues of palaces—something worse than the Ghetto or Bluegate-fields here, something fairer than the Bois de Boulogne or Kew Gardens there—in summer the fierce heat, the blazing, blinding sunlight, the tremendous thunder storms, the drenching torrential rains of the tropics—in winter the snows and the furs and the sleighs of St. Petersburg; a city in which everywhere, physically and morally, in buildings and in breasts, the prosaic and the poetic, the uttermost energy of the practical, the dreamiest visions of the ideal, are always contending—where men who have faith in nothing save railways and money do daily business with other men who see visions passing those of Swedenborg, and people the common air with forms dearer and brighter than those of any Rosicrucian dream; a city where nothing is held to be settled or certain—where John Law, or Fourier, or Johanna Southcote, or the Witch of Endor might be expected to appear any day and have a following—and where yet the highest teaching of European science is welcomed and studied as it is not in Europe's old schools themselves; a city of paradoxes; a city of magnificent possibilities contemptuously disregarded, and of seeming impossibilities conquered and reduced to the servitude of the practical and the real; a city which first repels and ends by fascinating:—such is, in short, the city of New York.

At this moment, however, the reader who follows the story can see New York but faintly. It lies there on the low lands across the waters of the bay: you can see two or three spires rising into the evening sky, and beneath them a darkling mass like a fog bank on the water, which darkling mass is one of the river-fronts of the city with its shipping. Islands are scattered everywhere over the water—some almost as large as an Ionian isle on which battles have been fought and of which poets have sung; some only large enough to hold a few buildings and two or three trees. Steamers of all sorts and sizes are coming in and going out: the long, lithe, narrow ocean steamer familiar to every port; the vast white floating castles or palaces which carry New Yorkers to Boston or to Albany, and the sight of one of which on the Thames or the Mersey would create almost as much surprise as if a Roman war-galley or Noah's Ark itself were to appear there; little yellow fierce-snorting, vicious-looking tugs; the tiny tidy boat of the Associated Press running to meet one of the great screws from Liverpool or Southampton; the ferry-boats, whose name is legion, panting across to the islands and the railway stations; the flag-ship of a famous and popular admiral who has just come into port; perhaps a Monitor, irreverently compared, for its odd structure, to a couple of Dutch cheeses on a raft; here and there a genuine raft laden with timber, telling of the Hudson and reminding of the Rhine. Over all is a pure lustrous blue sky, glowing towards the west into a sunset so gorgeous that Turner himself could harldly have pictured it or even fancied it, and deepening on the opposite horizon into magnificent and wondrous effects of reflected purple and gold. Truly the whole is a beautiful sight. Let the Rhine (not of Emmerich, but of the Drachenfels or St. Goar) flow directly into a vaster bay of Dublin; scatter the flags of all nations and the commerce of every port broadcast over the waves; let the atmosphere of Salamis shine upon the scene; and you will have constructed in your imagination something like the picture which the New Yorker may gaze upon any fine evening.

Not every feature of this, however, can be discerned by the group of persons now seated on the "stoop" or portico of a handsome villa that stands on a lawn looking down upon one section of the bay of New York. It is a beautiful evening of October, a little too early perhaps for that most exquisite, dreamy, poetic of all seasons—the incomparable Indian summer of the Eastern States; that Indian summer of which Hawthorne sadly remarks, that it has "a mist in its balmiest sunshine, and decay and death in its gaudiest delight;" the last and most captivating gleam of the dying year's beauty, the lighting up before death, before the grave of snow in which all verdure and purple are soon to be buried The house in front of which the living group is seated is an elegant unpretentious building of stone, with creepers and flowers and shrubs everywhere around its verandahs and its "stoop," and in the grounds to the rear are masses of trees—the huge willow, to which that of England looks so small; the sumach, the tulip-tree, the hickory, and—seeming oddly out of place here to the stranger's eye—the poplar, which speaks of the Arno and the Po. It is too late in the year for the myriad fire-flies of summer to flash and glitter on the grass and among the trees; but the shrill, peculiar, double-action throb of the katydid's manifesto is beginning to make itself heard from the groves and bushes.

The group consisted of an elderly gentleman, an elderly lady, and a young lady. The first was huge, heavy, fair, and benignant-looking; the second tall, withered, and yellow; the third bright, shapely, and beautiful. They were, in fact, the persons whom Alexia Scarlett saw at the Paris Exposition. The gentleman was Judge Atheling, the elderly lady was his wife. The Judge and his wife were seated on cane chairs; the young lady was standing a little behind, and was looking out across the scene with eyes that spoke most eloquently of content and admiration.

"Glad to see the old place again, Issy?" said the Judge, looking up at the girl.

"Please don't call her Issy, Atheling," remonstrated his wife.

"Why not, love?"

"Well, because it isn't fit for her, anyhow."

"Is not genteel, I suppose?" said the Judge with a kindly laugh.

"No, Atheling; but it don't sound nice, I think; it reminds one of a little girl in pantalettes."

"And not of our stately Isolind? Very well, love; I'll try to call her by her full name."

"Dear," said Isolind herself, coming behind his chair, and putting one of her hands on his shoulder, "I don't mind what you call me, if you like it. Indeed, I think 'Issy' pleases me, because it makes me fancy myself still a little girl under your care. But let mamma have it as she will; she knows best what is good for all of us."

"Anyhow, you are glad to be here again, Isolind?" said the Judge.

"Glad! Yes, indeed. I wonder what place on earth is like this. I feel a positive delight every moment in thinking that we are here at home again."

"And you don't want to go abroad any more?"

"Oh yes; I want to see every place—every place that I have not seen."

"Even England?" asked the Judge, with a twinkle in his blue eye.

"Well, yes; even England. But not just yet."

"When your patriotic fever cools down—when you can forgive her."

"Now please don't laugh at me. I cannot forgive her just yet; and I don't understand how *you* can."

"Nor I, Isolind," interjected the Judge's wife. "But that's Atheling's way always."

"Too forgiving, eh? Well, I suppose that's the way with men. Women are not much given to such weakness, eh, Isolind?"

"Indeed, I think women are generally far too forgiving; and so you have often said yourself."

"When you or the old lady wheedled it out of me, dear. Ah, well, I suppose it is quite true; only I think perhaps women forgive in the wrong place, and are unforgiving at the wrong time."

"Everybody—I mean every man—laughs at women," said Isolind, with darkening brow. "We are not even thought worth the dignity of an argument."

"*Chérie*," said the Judge, "what chance should I have of holding my own in an argument with you? My dull, prosaic ways would prove as ineffective as if I were to undertake to debate in rhyme with your 'Atlantis.'"

Isolind colored a little, and then smiled and asked, "Why *my* 'Atlantis'?"

"Because the poems are just the thing to delight you; they have the same sublime dreams about woman's place in life, and the same magnificent anger against poor old Mother England."

"Stepmother England, dear," said Isolind.

"Well, stepmother, if you will. But, my dear girl, we all belong to England, don't we? Were not my grandfathers and grandmothers the Athelings of Devonshire? Didn't the old lady and I see their tombs and their monumental brasses, and all the rest of it, in England in 1851? And I can tell you *she* nearly shed tears."

"That is just why I feel angry, because our common parent cast us off, and was false to us. We do not care for injuries from the hands of strangers; it is the wrong done by dearly-loved hands that touches us."

The Judge looked up with a satirical gleam in his pleasant blue eyes.

"Why, Isolind, I fear you are plagiarizing, or you have been studying 'Atlantis' rather too closely. *She* says all that kind of thing."

"Does she? Does she say it well?"

"Yes, she does. Perhaps I am not much of a judge of poetry; but I do think there is some good stuff, some of the genuine ring, about her verses. Don't you think so, mother?" he asked, rolling his great frame round on his chair, to get a look at "mother," and to put his question to her with expression.

"Why, certainly, Atheling; of course I do. But then——" and the old lady looked at Isolind, and applied a dainty kerchief to her face, and peeped out from behind it, and laughed.

"But what, my love? and what are you laughing at?" asked the Judge in wonder.

"Pray don't tell him. Keep him in ignorance; don't let him know yet; it would punish him justly for his obtuseness," Isolind interposed, all blushing now.

"Here's mysteries!" exclaimed the Judge in genuine surprise and affected anger. "Have we, then, plotters here in this peaceful nook?—spies, *mouchards*, Copperheads? What is all this confusion and ostentatious secrecy about? My wife, I command you! Break the seal of silence!"

"Why, you great goose——"

"Come, that begins well; that is conjugal devotion!"

"You great goose," continued the thin and tall old lady, rising to her feet, and patting her husband compassionately on the head, "didn't you say you had read 'Atlantis's' poems?"

"Why, certainly I did."

"And admired them?"

"Admired them—yes. I could not help admiring them; they are so fresh and genuine, and beautiful too, for that matter. I did not always agree with their notions; but I hope I didn't like them any the less for that."

"And you didn't think them like any one you knew? The thoughts didn't remind you of any one?"

"Well, I don't know about that. Yes, they did, though; that is to say, I reckoned they were just the sort of thing that would suit our Isolind. I seemed to hear her talk sometimes as I read them. That is why I bought the volume and brought it home. Poetry in general don't take hold of me somehow."

"Then you did like the little book, dearest?" said Isolind, seating herself at his feet, and throwing her arm over his knee; "you did like it, and thought it worth writing and printing?"

"Of course I did, child. But it does not much matter what I thought, does it? Others, whose judgment, as Hamlet says, cried on the top of mine, have gone wild over it; indeed, it is the talk of New York—so far as New York can ever be said to talk over anything literary."

Nothing could adequately describe the pantomimic expressiveness of the delight which Mrs. Atheling exhibited while her husband thus spoke out his opinion. She smiled, she pursed up her lips, she drew her lips far apart, she threw her head back on her shoulders, she craned her head forward, she kept up a sort of running accompaniment or beating of time to her partner's words with the fingers of one hand on the palm of another; and she directed the whole performance at the blushing Isolind.

Mrs. Atheling was a woman who could sometimes, on due provocation, make use of a pretty sharp tongue, even to her husband; and she had been known to call him "a great booby" when he declined to do something which she thought necessary for his personal health and comfort. But she fully believed her husband to be the wisest and best man on earth; and she would have abandoned or adopted any opinion, any relationship, any friendship, at his bidding. She had already changed one form of worship to please him; she would almost have become a Mormon to please him, if he had taken it into his head to accept Mormonism as the true faith. He was original, eccentric, even crotchety in his very benevolence, as he was generally in his views of religion and social duty. She had no views or identity of her own, but passed for being original and eccentric, just because she did as her husband bade her. The good Judge was always starting something new: he had a fresh sort of creed, religious or political, about every other week. Only he always remained faithful and orthodox as regarded his beneficent spirit and his broad love of humanity.

While Judge Atheling thus laid down the law, and his wife expressed her approval and delight, Isolind sat with her eyes fixed upon the ground. Then she said, looking up at him:

"Dear, we are only too proud of your approval. It was a little scheme, a piece of harmless fraud, of mamma and me. We published the poems without your knowledge; we gave them to the publisher before we sailed for Europe, in order that they might appear in print during our absence, and we might be spared the agony of any cruel criticism."

"But who in creation are *we?*"

"Why, we two, of course—mamma and I."

"You don't mean to say mamma writes poems!"

"No, dear, not exactly that. She gave her advice, and was a party to the conspiracy."

"And *you* made the poems?"

"At least, dear, I put my true and honest thoughts into the best rhymes and verses I could make."

"Then our Issy is a poetess!"

The Judge actually rose from his chair, in order to allow free scope to his wonder.

"Our Issy is 'Atlantis'! our Issy is a poetess!"

Now the Judge's rising created some little disturbance. His great Newfoundland dog had been coiled up close to his master's feet; a large yellow cat was seated and purring on the Judge's left shoulder; a gray parrot had walked out of his cage on the "stoop," the wire door being left open for his convenience, and had taken up a position in the Judge's lap, where he was amusing himself by stretching up to bite the Judge's finger. The Judge loved all manner of animals, and was instinctively, and on the very shortest notice, accepted as the friend and confidant of all of them. No four-footed creature, no feathered creature, but took kindly to this good and loving man, and trusted in him. Had it been a different hour or season, flights of birds would probably have been observed descending and settling round this portly figure, waiting for crumbs of bread, and chirping notes of friendly welcome. Sometimes the Judge was to be seen meditatively walking up and down on his greensward with his cat on his shoulder, his parrot on his wrist, the Newfoundland dog plodding gravely at one side, and a saucy little gray pony trotting at the other side, and endeavoring to thrust his nose into his master's unoccupied hand. The Judge might be said to speak the language of animals. He could have tamed spiders if he wished it; and his friends used sometimes to insist that he was the hero of the old story about the man who had taught an oyster to follow him about the house like a dog.

Just now, as he stood up amazed, the Newfoundland dog, feeling himself routed from his pleasant place, rose and shook himself lazily, and cast a look of remonstrance, and almost of reproach, at his restless master. The cat rocked to and fro for an instant on the moving shoulder, but easily contrived to hold her place, steadying herself by fixing one claw among the Judge's thick and yellow hair; and being thus reassured as to her security of tenure, resumed her interrupted purr, as if to announce that all was right with her, and that her bearer might go on if he thought fit. The parrot made an immense flapping of wings and clattering of feet, but succeeded in attaining somehow the Judge's wrist; and having accomplished so much, proclaimed in tones of shrill exultation that "Polly wants a cracker!" after the fashion of parrots educated in New York. And while the Judge thus stood, with his happy family, human and otherwise, so grouped around and upon him, a "colored" boy, dressed, not in livery (to which the Judge objected on principle), but just as the Judge's son would have been if he had had one, came out of the house and handed him the cards of some visitors. The grounds, it should be said, sloped in front down to the water's edge, and were inaccessible on that side except by boat. On the other side the road passed through the property; and visitors coming that way entered the house by a door opposite to that at which the Judge now stood.

Atheling looked at the cards.

"It's Vansiedler, mother," he said. "Glad he has come. I have not seen him since our return. And there are two strangers with him apparently. Let us see. 'Mr. Angelo Volney. Wonder who he is; anything to the Ruins of Empires? 'The Honorable Charles Escombe, London, England.' Now then, Isolind, here's a dreadful ordeal for you, poor dear patriot and poetess! This is one of the bloated aristocrats of England, my dear. 'Honorable' there doesn't mean that the honorable personage was once a member of a country school-board. It means that the person is a son of a lord. Shall we admit him, Isolind, or bar the doors and fire on him, or take him prisoner and hold him as a hostage?"

"You may laugh at me, dear," said Isolind calmly; "but I am prepared to dislike him all the same."

"I must go and dress," said Mrs. Atheling in alarm. "Isolind, you will not receive him that way?"

"O yes, of course she will," interposed the Judge; "and you too, mother stay here; you are all right enough."

But "mother," who had a little weakness for dress, and perhaps for looking younger than Nature, or even art, would encourage, disappeared precipitately. The Judge went off with his cat on his shoulder and his parrot on his wrist to welcome his visitors. Isolind remained just where she was. She leaned against the porch, and was apparently absorbed altogether in contemplating the purpling sky of evening, and the waters which trembled and changed under its glow.

Isolind Atheling has been already described. She was in every sense of the word a beautiful and noble creature to look upon: a face full of thought and force as well as beauty; a figure rich with the evidences of a feminine strength and health not perhaps very common among the fragile, exquisite flowers of American womanhood. As she stood now, bareheaded and very simply dressed, with a certain expression upon her face which faintly spoke of pride, or sullenness, or defiance, and thus cast a kind of poetic shadow over features whose habitual look was bright and free, no one could have seen her without interest and admiration. Perhaps a poet looking upon her might have said that her face was that of a Corinna, and ought to have shone beneath a myrtle crown; but a painter or sculptor would probably have seen in the figure a form to bear a corslet, and be symbolized on canvas or in marble as some beautiful Amazon, some Penthesilea, some Camilla, or, grander and truer far, some Maid of Orleans.

Such thoughts, perhaps, passed through the mind of Angelo Volney, child of a mother from the land of art, as he advanced with the other men, and saw the girl who stood at the porch. She looked up as he came; and in an instant she recognized him, as he had done her, and for an inconceivably short space of time their eyes met. Then the Judge came forward and presented "our Isolind"—it was thus he spoke of her—to the Honorable Charles Escombe and Mr. Angelo Volney, both of London.

A certain quick inexplicable sense of relief went through our Isolind's breast. The dark-complexioned young man whom she remembered so well having seen in Paris was not the English aristocrat. That was something.

Judge Atheling's friend, Mr. Vansiedler, was one of the Knickerbocker tribe. What is a Knickerbocker? One of the grand old legendary families who live in what may be called the Faubourg St. Germain of New York; one of those who had grandfathers and ancestors, and are proud of them; who date back to Peter Stuyvesant and his peers and paladins; who are republicans with a picturesque old-world dash of legitimacy over them; who shrink back from Shoddy as a Larochejaquelein might from a Mirès; who would rather be poor, if needs were, than be mixed up with any of the vulgarity of modern wealth; and who would be offended if they were mistaken for residents of Fifth Avenue. Leave the luxurious vassals of Fifth Avenue, Murray Hill, and Madison Avenue, you inquiring European stranger of intelligent and pensive mind; wander towards the East River, until you emerge from shops and noise and traffic and modern activity into the solemn, stately monotony and majestic silence of Second Avenue. There dwell the Knickerbockers in dignified isolation, fading grandly away, *cito perituri*, but touching and sublime in their fall. Modern degeneracy has not reached them. Go there, contemplative stranger, in the twilight, and not in the garish day, and say whether even New York has not its ruins and its romance; whether even modern commerce may not have its old *noblesse*, democracy its traditions of gentility, republicanism its legitimacy and its stately futile protests against a too clamorous and vulgar progress. The Coliseum has been done to rags; the Alhambra is "played;" the Faubourg St. Germain is worn out. Will no poet of melancholy spirit feed his sad soul with meditations among the Knickerbocker mansions of Second Avenue, New York?

Mr. Vansiedler had a town house in Second Avenue; but he had a country seat near the home of the Athelings.

"Our friends from London, Judge," he said, "have been kind enough to consent to spend an idle day or two with me before plunging into sight-seeing and travelling all over our country. Mr. Escombe you know already very well by name; and I knew you would all be glad to make each other's acquaintance."

Atheling had, in fact, no previous knowledge of Escombe's name. A name must have a great sound indeed to send its echo across the Atlantic.

"I am delighted to meet both gentlemen," said Atheling; "and I pledge myself to wait several weeks at least before I ask them how they like our country."

Everybody laughed; and Escombe acknowledged that he had had the question put to him many times already. Then Mrs. Atheling came up, now very much dressed indeed, displaying robes of youthful fashion, and looking very old and withered, but full of genuine simplicity, sweetness, and cordiality of manner. After regular presentations and formal words, Angelo Volney talked with the elderly lady; and Charles Escombe, bursting with desire for information from anybody and from everybody's point of view, dashed into a conversation with Isolind: asked her what she thought of the Woman's Rights movement; what was the proportion of women to men in the Eastern States; whether she had ever studied the public-school system of Massachusetts; and whether there were any new poets coming up in America.

Isolind found the British aristocrat a very agreeable person, despite his thirst for facts. She thought his manners friendly and pleasant, although he seemed to her utterly wanting in depth and in soul. He had hardly color enough to be set down as a butterfly; so she classed him rather as a quick, industrious ant, or perhaps a grasshopper. But he was interesting in his way, very animated, and thoroughly good-natured, besides having great intelligence and a vast amount of knowledge. And Isolind felt disposed to respect him as well as to like him.

These two parted on the friendliest terms, frankly expressing to each other their hope to meet often; and Escombe protesting that he would not leave the country until he had converted Miss Atheling from her hostility to England. Angelo did not during the interview exchange one word with Isolind. He bowed to her at coming, he bent to her at going; and that was all. This was their introduction.

The English travellers were to dine that evening with Mr. Vansiedler, and sleep at his house. The Athelings, who led quite a simple country sort of life, had dined hours before, and were, indeed, about to have their evening meal very soon. But the Judge promised that they would all go round and spend an hour or two with their neighbor that night.

"How do you like them, Isolind?" asked the Judge.

"Mr. Escombe very much indeed. He must be quite an exception to his order."

"Why, my girl?"

"Because he appears to know something, and yet not to be self-conceited."

The Judge laughed.

"I don't believe they are all such dreadful creatures, these British lords,

Isolind. Take care that when you go to England some time you don't fall in love with one of them. How did you like the other young man, the handsome one?"

"Not at all. At least he did not seem a sort of person to like. He seemed cold and proud. *He* ought to have been the aristocrat. Or perhaps he is one of the class of Englishmen who think it beneath them to speak to a woman, she being the inferior animal."

"O poetess! O sibyl!" and the Judge put his arm round the girl's waist. "She divines England as Talleyrand said our Alexander Hamilton divined Europe. She never saw the dear little island, and hardly ever spoke to an Englishman; and yet she can describe and define this class of Englishmen and that class, as if she were a Dickens or Thackeray in petticoats!"

"Besides, Isolind," said Mrs. Atheling, "the dark young man talked to *me* a great deal, and very nicely. He seemed a modest, agreeable person."

"And to crown all, Isolind," the Judge added, "I don't believe he is English. But let him be what he will, I want to hear something more now about your mysterious poems. My love, I am proud of you; and I wish to read the volume over again, and more carefully, that I may be all the more proud."

Isolind's handsome and expressive face flushed with pleasure. Any praise from him was joy to her.

What were the poems of which so much has been said already? But, first, what of the poetess?

"Our Isolind" must have had a singularly clear, simple, and noble nature not to have been spoiled by the life she had led under the roof of the Athelings. In that sweet and happy home she had long been the absolute mistress. She was always known to the world as "Miss Atheling"; and she was always heard to address the Athelings as if they were her parents. Yet those who were intimate with the Judge and his wife were well aware that they had had but one child, who died an infant. Many years ago the Athelings returned from one of their long journeys, bringing home a pretty little girl, two or three years old, whom they called Isolind; and this was she. The adoption of children is too common in the United States for such a fact as this to set any one wondering or inquiring; and Isolind was soon accepted as a component part of the household.

At first the good Athelings were merely fond of the little child, as of a child. But she gradually came to impress them with a feeling of something more than mere affection. Her grace, her beauty, her sweet ways, were not her only or her chief attractions; as she grew into womanhood she proved to have intellect, talents even, of a rare order. She could learn anything and do anything. She was a musician, a botanist, an eager reader of all manner of literature that was worth the reading; and she practically contradicted the old-fashioned theories about literary women by displaying a perfect genius for the management of a household. She could darn stockings, if need were, or cook "scrambled eggs" or "succotash," much better than the hired lady from "the gem of the ocean"; and she had occasionally to prove her skill when such lady took it into her head to leave the family in the hour of uttermost culinary need. Isolind knew the details of the household much more intimately than Mrs. Atheling did, and was ever and anon referred to by Mr. Atheling when he wanted information about the value and condition of some of his sources of income. At the same time there was not the slightest appearance of command or determination in her. Whatever she did, or regulated, or ordered, seemed to be done—was actually done—only that she might save her benefactors the trouble of doing or ordering it. Then the Athelings were plain people; in the English sense, homely. Despite the Judge's descent from some grand old Devonshire family, his ancestors had begun in poverty their American career, and worked up gradually into successful commerce and profitable land-buying; and Atheling was conscious that he and his wife wanted the graces which commend people to society. He was proud, therefore, of the gifted, graceful girl, who grew up to be the ornament of his household, who attracted so much attention and admiration wherever they went, and yet whose sweet, unspoiled ways never changed to those around her. Isolind was the eye, the brain, and the beauty of the Atheling home; and the master and mistress of the household cared little what they did, if it only pleased her and won her approval. Lately they had been travelling widely over Europe, and into Egypt and the Holy Land; and they deliberately avoided England to gratify Isolind's one whim: a keen spirit of hostility to poor Britain, born of Britain's puzzle and blundering during the American Civil War.

Yes, Isolind had perhaps one other whim, and it may as well be brought out at once. With her it was a principle, a creed; probably most people would call it a crotchet; it was a faith in some high and special destiny for woman ("Destiny" perhaps ought to be spelt in this case with a capital letter); some grand redeeming, elevating business in the scheme of human society, not limited to the mere producing of children on the one hand, or the registering of votes on the other. Pray don't turn away from her as unwomanly, ye on one side of the question; she had no ambition for the wearing of pantaloons, and would not have supported a woman as a candidate for Congress. Prithee do not scorn her as feeble, and lacking in proper regard for her sex, ye on the other side; for she disapproved of all legal limitations to woman's pursuits in life, and she did sometimes chafe against the tyrant man. Poor tyrant man! There was little indeed that Isolind claimed for her sex which the tyrant would not gladly have yielded to her; and there never was a man so prejudiced and stupid as to have denied to her, with all her aspirations and her demands, the charm of a true and perfect womanhood.

Isolind, then, had Views; and was a believer in woman's Destiny. Her belief, such as it was, became a passion with her. She would have died for it. Could she define it?

Perhaps not very clearly. Perhaps she could not easily have reduced it to a satisfactory formula. Truly, if no one ever were to die for a belief which he or she could not logically define, the bead-roll of martyrdom would not be long. But we may say that Isolind did not care much about woman's rights; believing that, after all, what woman really needs is the means of knowing and accomplishing her duties. She saw, or thought she saw, terrible danger for woman and her best influence between George Sand on the one side, and Susan B. Anthony on the other; between the freedom which threatens to be impure, and the freedom which tries to be masculine. Vaguely, perhaps, but very firmly, Isolind maintained, as the indispensable conditions of woman's destiny, Knowledge and Purity. To reconcile Knowledge and Innocence—to show that man's science can be combined with childhood's simple, stainless purity—such was the work of woman, according to Isolind's creed. To be the priestess of such a faith would have been her highest ambition.

Perhaps there were moments when she even dreamed of such a possibility. Perhaps in the nights when her poems welled up vaguely within her, or in the bright early mornings when they shaped themselves into sprays and streams and jets of song, she may have had some dazzling hopes. But she had too little of the egotistic in her to indulge in the intellectual sensuousness of any such dreamings; and she only did her household duties and went her quiet way, and made life happy, so far as she could, for others, and enjoyed it herself. She had a nature rich in capacity for enjoyment; no thought of beauty, no gleam of light, no strain of music, no breath of fragrance was lost on her. When her volume of poems (by "Atlantis") appeared, they showed themselves the outpourings of an affluent and fruitful nature; of an earnest, almost passionate soul filled with noble hopes and pure ambition; they were, above all qualities else, sincere; they struck the rock of many hearts, and "bade the living fountain gush and sparkle." They were the outcome of a young, fresh, generous, fearless nature—the nature of a woman without egotism and without affectation. Thus, and not otherwise, they were a success; and, at any rate, they created a sensation.

The night of the evening just described, a pleasant group was gathered in the drawing-room of Mr. Vansiedler's house. Vansiedler was a man of taste and travel, and he had means enough to gratify his tastes sufficiently, although he was far indeed from being a wealthy man in the New York sense. His house had a good library, and every new book worth reading was sure to be found upon his table. He had a few genuine paintings, some bronzes, and one or two beautiful statues by American artists. In his pleasant rooms there were open fireplaces, not too common in New York; and this October evening logs, not coals, were glowing on the hearth.

Mr. Vansiedler, his wife (like himself, a genuine Knickerbocker), and their pale and pretty daughter, the Athelings and Isolind, Charles Escombe and Angelo Volney, and two or three other people, were present. They had been discussing, among other things, the poems by Atlantis, the authorship being still a secret; and Charles Escombe had been showing, to the great amusement of Judge Atheling, that the volume was clearly written by a man, not a woman; because woman never really had any of the sort of ambitions and aspirations attributed to her by the poet.

"I don't deny that it's cleverly done; in fact, it's deucedly clever; but then, you know, women of that kind don't write in that sort of way. They go in for woman's rights, and that kind of thing, or they go in for nothing."

Angelo was sitting alone, looking at engravings and photographs and suchlike. He had dropped out of the conversation somehow, and it seemed to Isolind that he looked melancholy. She had not yet spoken a word to him, and he had not approached her. But in America that which French diplomatic phraseology calls "the privilege of the initiative" seems to be vested in woman, unmarried as well as married.

"He is thinking of home, perhaps," Isolind said to herself. And she left her place, and went across and took a seat by his side.

"I hope you are not lonely," she said, entering at once into conversation. "I fear you are sorry to be away from home."

Angelo looked up with a bright smile, and the ice was broken.

"Not lonely in that sense," he said. "Indeed, I feel very much at home in this pleasant house, where there is such a welcome. But I have never been far away from my own home before—I mean from the place where I live," he corrected himself somewhat hastily, remembering, poor youth, how he had lately come to know that it was no rightful home of his; "and perhaps I do sometimes feel a little strange, although everything I see is full of vivid interest for me."

"I never was away from home—I mean, we always carry our home with us, we three; we never break up our little camp. So, I may say that I have never been away from home. In our tents in Syria, it was still home. After all, home means people, not places."

"With some, yes; but with others home means places, not people."

"Not with you, I am sure," said Isolind, looking quite earnestly at him.

"No, indeed; I care little for the place, and all for the people."

"I knew that must be so."

"Indeed! Tell me how you knew it."

"Oh, I can't tell. One divines things sometimes—by the expression of the face, or in some such way."

"And one is wrong sometimes?"

"Yes, indeed. I think I had an impression about you first which was wrong."

Angelo nearly blushed. It is so delightful to a young man to learn that a beautiful woman thought him worth so much consideration as would go to form an impression.

"What was your first idea of me then?" he asked.

"I thought you were a typical Englishman, cold and egotistic, and——"

"To begin with, I am hardly half an Englishman. But go on."

"Well, I thought you were one of the class of men—are they not very common in England?—who look down on women with disdain as inferior creatures, and will hardly condescend to speak to them."

Angelo laughed and felt delighted. But in his breast there was a certain wonder. "This beautiful being," he thought to himself, "with the noble head and the eyes through which there looks such a glorious soul, can she really suppose that any man could think her an inferior creature?" The thing was to him almost inconceivable. To an ingenuous, pure-hearted young man, with poetical susceptibilities, a handsome girl is still simply an angel; and he can hardly understand that there are people to whom she is only flesh, bones, talk, and clothes.

He said, "I don't think such men are common in England. I don't know any such. For myself, I have been brought up almost exclusively among women; and I can hardly realize your meaning when you speak of looking on them with disdain. There is a woman in England who is a very divinity to me."

"Ah, I think I know who she is," said Isolind softly. "The beautiful pale girl I saw with you in Paris?"

Angelo smiled.

"No, indeed. I love Alexia very dearly, but she is not a divinity. I spoke of her mother, who has been my mother too."

The conversation was growing more and more interesting to these two. Angelo, naturally rather a shy and silent young man, was charmed wlth the frank and fearless ease of Isolind's manner, which had to him—only accustomed to English reserve—the piquant charm of novelty. But just then Mr. Vansiedler struck in, and broke the *tête-à-tête* by addressing Angelo directly.

"I have been telling our friends here, Mr. Volney, that I suppose you want to see all the remarkable personages you can during your run through our country, and that therefore I had invited quite a remarkable sort of person to meet you at dinner to-day. He wrote to say that he could not come to dinner, but that he will be sure to present himself at a later hour; and he will spend the night here. He's a representative man in his way—a representative of one peculiarity of this age and this country; although, by the way, I don't believe he's an American by birth. Judge Atheling knows him well—Chesterfield Jocelyn, Judge!"

"Why, you don't mean to say Chesterfield Jocelyn's here!" exclaimed Atheling.

"Yes, he has just come to town; and I have some little affairs on hand in which he is condescending enough to profess an interest; and I thought our friends ought to see him."

"Why, certainly," Atheling said. "He is an institution—not one perhaps to be very proud of; but, all things considered, he is a wonderful creature in his way. Do you know, Vansiedler, this is an opportunity for me too. I never saw him."

"You, Judge, never saw Chesterfield Jocelyn? Is it possible?"

"Never set eyes on him."

"Well, that is wonderful! Never saw Chesterfield Jocelyn!"

"Who is Chesterfield Jocelyn?" asked Angelo.

"I have read something about him," interposed Escombe, who could not admit the idea that there was anybody or anything he had not read something about. "Great railway speculation man, mixed up somehow with Mexican miners, isn't he?"

"Well, yes, as he is mixed up with everything. At present his chief enterprise is a scheme for the importation of Chinese into the Southern States from the West; but he is also concerned in a plan for the purchase of Cuba from Spain; and he is raising a loan here for Lopez in Paraguay. He made a heap of money years ago in San Francisco and Mexico; and he had a leading part in a plot for the secession of California in 1861. That fell through; and then he worked hard for the South. There are sensible people who say he ought to have been hanged or shot; and he has been in everything almost

"Rich, of course?" Atheling asked.

"Well, I don't know about that. No end of money must go through his hands somehow; and he ought to be rich. He is always bursting up, and then making a fresh start. He is a wonderfully able fellow—a man of inexhaustible resources. He is here to-day; heaven knows where he may be to-morrow or the day after. Quite a person to see, Mr. Escombe."

"Is his name Chesterfield?" asked Escombe. "It sounds oddly—Chesterfield Jocelyn."

"Oh, no; his name is Edwin Dare Jocelyn, or something of the kind. People give him the nickname of Chesterfield because he is so tremendously polite—the florid, old-fashioned politeness, Mr. Escombe, which is not very common out among us rough, new people." Mr. Vansiedler himself was a courteous and polished gentleman.

"It gets late," Atheling remarked. "I am doomed to be disappointed, Vansiedler. Your Chesterfield Jocelyn is not coming."

"I hope he will not come," Isolind quietly said.

"Why not, Miss Atheling?" asked the host with a smile.

Isolind was allowed the privilege of saying anything.

"Because I think it a sin of our society that such a man, a traitor you say, and a reckless devotee of gain, should be welcomed among us. To my mind, Jocelyn is a traitor as deep-dyed as Benedict Arnold."

"With a heavy dash of our Railway King Hudson," suggested Escombe.

Further discussion was cut short by an immense crashing of wheels and trampling of horses outside, and much bustle and hurrying about of grooms and helps; and then a colored attendant entered the drawing-room and announced, "The Honorable Edwin Dare Jocelyn."

The flush was still on Isolind's cheek, the sparkle was in her eyes, when the new-comer entered the room. He was a man of some fifty years of age, perhaps, rather above the middle size, and so stout that his figure might almost be said to approach corpulency. He was nearly bald—the forehead and temples were quite bare; but he wore a full dark beard and moustache, covering up the whole of his face from the aquiline nose downwards. Magnificent diamond studs flashed from his vast expanse of white shirt-front. On one white finger was a ring with an emerald, on another a ring with a ruby. He held in one hand a double eye-glass mounted in gold and suspended round his neck by a thick gold chain, while a gold chain of different make was attached to his watch. He made a bow of quite surprising depth and graceful flexibility, considering the portly bulk of his figure.

"Delighted to have the honor of meeting you once again, Mrs. Vansiedler, and especially charmed to see that you enjoy such radiant health. Vansiedler, my very dear friend, it is indeed a pleasure to stand upon your genial hearth. Honored, I am sure, to be presented to Mr. and Mrs. Atheling." (In Vansiedler's house the old-fashioned and very convenient ceremony of introduction was carefully retained.) "The distinguished name of Judge Atheling is well known even in the wild West. I rejoice to have the privilege of being presented to the Honorable Charles Escombe. I had the honor of being acquainted with Mr. Escombe's noble father—it surely was his noble father?—some years ago in Paris and in Madrid, when my noble friend—if his son will now permit me so to call him—was attached to the embassy of my other noble friend, the Earl of Clarendon."

Thus did Mr. Jocelyn get through his introduction with a compliment to every one in turn. Hitherto Isolind had kept in the background; but the host, partly out of good-humored sportiveness, insisted on bringing the new guest toward her. Isolind, it must be owned, looked somewhat sullen, and acknowledged Mr. Jocelyn's low bow with the coldest recognition.

He was beginning some speech of compliment, when he suddenly paused and gazed into the girl's face with a look of actual wonder. His words, whatever they were, seemed to die upon his lips. He glanced quickly round, as if he were about to ask some sudden question, then recovered himself, and repeated his bow, and that introduction was over.

In a moment or two he drew his host quietly aside and said,

"Your pardon, Vansiedler, I did not quite catch the name of that young lady yonder, to whom you did me the honor to present me."

"That young lady? Oh, Miss Atheling."

"Daughter of our friend the Judge?"

Mr. Vansiedler assented.

"Indeed! Of course I might have known it. Such a wonderful likeness to her father—I mean, of course, to her mother."

Vansiedler quietly smiled, much amused by this latter compliment.

Mr. Jocelyn seemed oddly discomposed.

"I dislike that man," said Isolind in a low tone to Mr. Atheling. "His presence fills me with a strange sense of fear and pain. The room seems to me to have grown cold, as if a harsh wind breathed through it, since *he* came in. Why does he fix his eyes on me?"

The Judge smiled.

"Admiration, no doubt, Issy; but I don't like him any more than you do, so far; and it seems to me somehow as if I had seen him before. Yet that can't be. I'll go and have a talk with him."

Isolind only repeated in her low tone, "I don't like him. I wish he had not come."

All this was lost upon the company generally; and Mr. Jocelyn now was in full and fluent talk again. But nothing that had happened was lost upon Angelo Volney. He had noted, with his quiet gaze, Jocelyn's start of surprise and the kind of shudder that had passed over Isolind.

CHAPTER VII.

THE CHAMPION OF A DISTRESSED DAMSEL.

LADY JUDITH had a hard time of it with her daughter after Angelo Volney had left England for the United States. Alexia became almost unmanageable. She had discovered that her mother detested scenes and passionate public demonstrations of any kind; and she did her very best to *exploiter* this weakness on the part of the elder lady. Indeed, there was something admirable in the marble, or at least stony, endurance with which Lady Judith bore up against displays *coram publico*, which were to her detestable and degrading. She raised her proud head firmly to meet them, and did not so much as wink an eyelid during the worst raging of the ignoble storm. Think what it is to be haughty and sensitive, to abhor all scandal and whispering comment, and to know that your family quarrels are the incessant theme of your servants and your neighbors; and yet never to make your mental suffering manifest! Talk of Talleyrand, who could be kicked *à posteriori*, and yet never show in his face one hint of any mental or physical discomfort! Talk of the Duchess of Burgundy, of whom Saint Simon tells that she underwent so very trying an operation in the same room with her awful sovereign and marriage-relation, Louis the Great, and never by one grimace allowed His Majesty to suspect that something uncomfortable was going on under his own august eyes! The patience and self-restraint which enabled a woman so proud and so sensitive as Lady Judith Scarlett to bear without writhing the more and more frequent displays of her daughter's fierce temper, may surely deserve as much higher respect and admiration as the triumph over mental anguish transcends in dignity the conquest of purely physical pain.

Lady Judith at last began to think that her daughter was really going mad. She invited the attendance of a great physician, who called on Alexia, opened a friendly conversation with her, tried on her the force of a glance which had awed full many a patient—penetrating, indeed, and powerful as that with which George III.'s medical custodian is said to have made Edmund Burke to shrink —but which was wholly thrown away upon the audacious Alexia. The girl quite understood the meaning of the visit, and, with her elf-like skill, was at once prepared to frustrate it. Raging in her heart, she preserved a demeanor of the most perfect composure; she answered every question with a prompt and cheerful serenity; and finally, the eminent doctor was compelled to take his leave, and to tell Lady Judith that he could find in her daughter no symptoms of madness whatever.

Then, when he had gone, Alexia locked her door, tore half her clothes off and scattered them about the room, flung herself on her bed, and almost cried her heart out. While the doctor was trying to get at the reality of her condition, Alexia had done her very best to keep herself sane; now she was doing all she could to drive herself into madness. Like Shakespeare's Constance, she wished to heaven that she were mad. Oh, how it would have relieved her passion-charged soul if she could all at once have felt that the frail barriers between receding reason and advancing frenzy were broken down, and that she could have floated heedlessly, joyously, along the fierce rush of the tide of insanity!

To certain natures there is no luxury like the luxury of utter, reckless desperation. Alexia resolved, with fierce delight, upon doing something which should shame and grieve her mother. The girl would have killed herself somehow, dashed her head against the wall, flung herself from the window, or stifled herself by holding her face down in her washing-basin, but for the new purpose and hope which had possessed her, and which bade her seek for her father. But she bitterly resented the visit of the doctor, and resolved that her mother must suffer for having thus insulted her. She could think of nothing better to do than to run away at night and get lost somewhere—as had happened to many heroines of the romances she loved to read. So when came the night of the day on which the physician had accidentally dropped in to pay her his prearranged officious visit, she made up her mind that she would run away and get lost somewhere. It was not difficult to try this experiment, for the doctor had expressly recommended that no semblance of watching her should be kept up, and that no opposition should be made to the indulgence of any whim which was not actually unreasonable. She had therefore, on this particular day, greater personal liberty than for a considerable time before, and she availed herself of it. When evening darkened London she dressed herself, put on a hat and shawl, stole down to the front door, opened it, and glided quietly into the street.

Lady Judith had never left the home of her early married life. The human weakness which would shun the scene of a great sorrow or a great shame she despised. Her religion, she said, did not teach her to avoid or evade suffering, but the rather to court and seek it, and compel it to give a blessing, as Jacob did the angel. With Lady Judith, religion and the law and the prophets meant the saving of one's own soul—the extracting from the sins and sufferings of the whole world, if need were, the means or medicaments whereby one's own individual salvation was to be assured. The blood of a vassal generation was to be freely spilt, if necessary, that the feet of one superior creature might be warmed in the sanguinary bath. So she made it one other way toward celestial happiness to confront unflinchingly the cruel memories and ghastly shadows of the house in which her lost husband had left her to a premature and peculiar widowhood. This house was in a street running at right angles out of Piccadilly, very near Cambridge House, which Lord Palmerston had so lately tenanted; and of course, when Alexia stole from her threshold, she had only to run a short distance along the great thoroughfare to reach the railings of Hyde Park.

Two gentlemen happened to be walking along Piccadilly toward Apsley

House and Hyde Park, and to be crossing the street in which Alexia's house stood, at the moment when the girl was rushing away from her home. She passed them quite closely—they had to draw back, indeed, to make way for her impetuous movement—and the light of a lamp at the corner of the street fell directly on her pale face and dark hair.

The younger and taller of the two gentlemen peered downwards into her face, and then, as she flashed onward, he said in a tone of wonder:

"Why, I know that girl's face! It's Lady Judith Scarlett's daughter! How strange! They say she is a little touched in the head."

"Shouldn't wonder," the other gruffly observed. "Her father must have had a touch of madness about him, to go off in the way he did."

"Did you know him? Stop!—there she goes toward the Park. Let us follow her."

"Follow her? For what? Are we detectives or penny-a-liners, or the guardians of every half-crazed young woman in the West End of London?"

"No; but I am a little curious to see where she can be going, or what she can be doing alone, at this hour, in the streets."

"Follow her yourself, then, and make a heroine of her, or a poem about her if you like. I shall be at the Reform Club by and by. If you want me, you can find me there any time up to twelve to-night, or at breakfast to-morrow; but I don't see that any more talk with me will do you much good. Anyhow, I sha'n't be in town more than a few days; and I think you are making an ass of yourself."

The younger man paid no attention to this piece of genial confidence, but followed with his eyes the figure of the girl. She had not yet entered the Park, but was close to the gate.

"Just a word, my uncle," he said, "before I set out on my chase, which perhaps is not quite so unmeaning as your practical mind supposes. You once knew this girl's father?"

"Knew him? yes, in a sort of way. Never were much of friends; not likely."

"There was, then, some mystery or other about his disappearance?"

"Of course there was—a nine days' wonder. It was not his going away that surprised me, but his staying away. What would Belgravia have cared if he had carried off half-a-dozen women?"

"You must tell me all about it to-night or to-morrow; that, dear uncle, won't cost you anything, and it may be useful to me."

"Glad to find that anything inexpensive can be useful to you," said the uncle, with a grim smile.

The young man laughed, and darted on in pursuit of his quarry; the elder trudged his way alone.

This elder was a stout, thick-set, square-shouldered man, with a large gray head, heavy jaws, thin lips, and whiskers of the approved British mutton-chop pattern—in color, gray like his hair. He was very plainly dressed, wore cotton gloves, and an old-fashioned cravat which always had a tendency to work itself round, so that the tie came under one of the wearer's ears. Yet there was something about the man which would at once have satisfied any experienced observer that there was plenty of money to line the pockets of the shabby and wrinkled old trousers which hardly reached to the thick unshapely shoes. No Englishman without plenty of money ever shouldered his way along Piccadilly as did now our old acquaintance Mr. Gostick, M. P.—grown a little more gray and stout and square and "bumptious" than he was when last we saw him, some sixteen years ago.

The young man who claimed him as uncle was a very different-looking sort of personage. The peacock might, with as much apparent reason, have proclaimed himself of kin with the owl, or the panther have boasted near relationship with the steady domestic ox, as this young man have declared himself a nephew of Mr. Gostick. He was very tall and slender; he had black hair arranged in curls which were almost like the ringlets of Disraeli's bright youth; he was dressed with extreme elegance, bordering indeed on richness; an artist blessed with a large private property, and mixing in fashionable society, or a young aristocrat affecting authorship, might have dressed and looked as he did. For he was not the ordinary young "swell" of Rotten Row and the opera stalls; there was nothing of the Guardsman about him; there was in his curls, and his costume, and his very walk, something which indicated a real or affected affinity to the brotherhood of letters and art. He was a handsome young fellow too, although he had a restless sort of eye, which always seemed to be seeking for something not obvious and apparent in the group, or the personage, or the conversation which might have appeared to engross him. While he talked with Mr. Gostick this might have been specially noted by any observer. The quick eyes kept glancing now to where Alexia Scarlett moved along; now suddenly and surreptitiously into Gostick's face, as if endeavoring to find out some hidden meaning there; and again at this side or that, as though they looked for the admiration of stray passengers.

Gostick looked after his nephew for a moment, and laughed a short dry laugh.

"What on earth is his game now?" he grumbled to himself. "Thinking of capturing an heiress perhaps in some romantic sort of way? I shouldn't wonder. Egad, he's vain enough, and empty-headed enough, and, for that matter, unprincipled enough too, to suit the best of them. I never could make out whether the lad is more of fool or knave; but he is quite enough of both to make a good way among the lords and ladies."

So the practical philosopher dug his hands more deeply into his pockets, and went on.

The nephew, even in the earnestness of his pursuit, glanced after the square form of his disappearing uncle, then stroked his dainty moustache and his little peaked artistic beard, and sighed.

"And that miserly old miscreant," he said to himself, "is my uncle—my mother's brother! And he has all the money—with that accent and those shoes! Good heavens! it is enough to make a sensitive man proclaim himself an atheist!"

Alexia Scarlett had now entered the yet open gate of the Park, and wandered purposeless along one of the walks, glancing around her like some startled wild animal, some creature which has escaped from its cage and is scared by its unwonted loneliness and liberty. It was in October, and somewhere between seven and eight o'clock, and there were but few figures to be seen along the broad walk which she had entered. The night was fine, but a little chilly; and the October air, the darkness, the dreariness of the place, fell coldly on the nerves and spirit of the poor girl. One or two idlers addressed a word to her as she passed, and this caused her to stand and confront them with fierce and flashing eyes; whereat they only laughed and went their way, and she felt inclined to burst into tears. She did not know what to do; she had no notion of going anywhere in particular, only of "running away" and being found somewhere under a hedge, and thus afflicting and punishing her mother. Perhaps the poor bewildered child had had some vague dream—who knows?—of finding her father somewhere in the great outer world, where never, until this hour, had she been for one moment alone. But now in the cold, and the dark, and the vulgar harshness of reality, all such dreams seemed to vanish, and it appeared to her as if in such a world she could not have a father. She was utterly wretched, and yet she would not turn back. Perhaps if she had come to the water just then she would have sought shelter there, and left a corpse as a bequest and reproach to her mother. But there was no piece of water near her path, and her movements, moreover, were closely watched and followed.

"Where *can* she be going?" thought her adventurous pursuer. "Is she mad? This looks like it. How am I to manage an effective introduction? Why are there no highwaymen, from whom I might heroically rescue her? By Jove, a grand idea!"

At that moment the object of his interest threw herself upon a seat at the side of the walk, and covered her face with her hands. The young man stopped and looked anxiously about him in every direction. A short distance off he saw two ragged rough-looking youths tossing for coppers under a lamp-post. They were rather more than boys, hardly yet men. He went up to them, and entered into a short conversation, which had evident reference to the young lady on the seat, for he pointed her out to them, and gave them some explanations and instructions, whereat they grinned, and a couple of shillings each, whereat they grinned still more. Then they darted on, and he followed them at some distance.

Alexia was just rising wearily from her seat, when two creatures, who seemed to her like demons of some particularly vile pit of the lower regions, pounced upon her with fierce gestures.

"Your money or your life, Miss!" said one, who had apparently been a student of the "thieves' literature" of London, and knew the parlance of the gallant Turpin and the sweet Duval.

"Fork over all you've got, young woman," exclaimed the other, "and look sharp about it, will yer?"

Alexia sprang to her feet.

"You cowardly wretches!" she screamed, clenching her thin little fists and darting a fierce futile defiance out of her glittering eyes, "how dare you address a lady?"

A burst of laughter only followed this demonstration; and one of the fellows said, "Your money, or we'll kill you!" while the other laid his dirty paw upon her arm. In the vehemence of her emotion Alexia struck at him, and he seized her, and his comrade seized her, and she was powerless in their clutches, and she thought her last hour had come, when suddenly there was a cry of wrath and scorn, and strong hands flung her assailants one to this side, one to that—and they fled in dismay, no doubt—and she was rescued; and there stood before her her deliverer in the person of a noble-looking young man, the *beau-idéal* of a hero and a cavalier, who took his hat off and held it in his hand while he bowed to her, and hoped she had sustained no injury at the hands of the flying miscreants.

Nor did the rescuer of the distressed damsel wait for any answer. With a delicate consideration for her natural embarrassment, he spared her the trouble of saying anything for the moment by keeping the talk all to himself. He told

THERE STOOD BEFORE HER HER DELIVERER.—p. 56.

her that the villains who had assailed her were evidently members of a gang of robbers who notoriously infested the parks, and with whose outrageous exploits all the press of London was ringing; and Alexia did remember, although she never could be said to read newspapers, having seen many letters in the "Times," as it lay on her mother's table, about robberies and assaults, and other such frightful doings, occurring at nightfall, and almost under the very windows of Buckingham Palace. These things had made little impression indeed upon her mind hitherto. She had paid about as much attention to them as one pays to the paragraphs which tell of a brigandage in Mexico or a revolution in Central America; and now behold she had become, on her very first visit alone to the outer world, the heroine of such an adventure! Her thoughts were, however, diverted even from that subject when her deliverer, in a tone of blandest courtesy, asked to be allowed to have the honor of escorting her home, and dropping his voice, said:

"I presume I have the honor of addressing Miss Scarlett, Lady Judith Scarlett's daughter?"

"I am Lady Judith Scarlett's daughter," the girl replied, with a dash of bitterness in her tone which did not escape the notice of her escort. "May I ask how you came to know me? I don't remember having ever seen you before."

"Perhaps not, Miss Scarlett; but I have seen you often, and your face is not easily forgotten. I am happy to have the opportunity of seeing you to your home."

In truth Alexia had no choice but to go home. The running-away project had ended very ignobly, and she was by no means wild enough not to be sensible of the ridiculous vulgarity of the adventures which apparently awaited fugitive maidens in the wilds of West End, London. Besides, there actually had been something done; her mother would have the humiliation of knowing that Alexia Scarlett had been attacked by robbers in the Park at night, and rescued by a gentleman who apparently was familiar with her face and her family history. So she took the arm of her champion, and set about walking home. The wild adventure and escapade was ending, seemingly, in mere prose.

"I have met Lady Judith Scarlett once or twice," said the champion—"that is, I have been at places where she was—but I never had the honor of being presented to her. You, Miss Scarlett, do not much resemble her in face." (He had noted, as has been said, the girl's bitterness of tone when she mentioned the name of her mother.) "You seem to me to bear a stronger resemblance to your distinguished father."

He uttered the words slowly and emphatically, in a low, sweet, sympathetic voice, which appeared to Alexia to lend an infinity of meaning to the sentence. She started and clutched his arm, and a thrill of triumph and delight went through him.

"Did you then," she asked, in eager stammering accents—"did you know anything of my father?"

He paused, and looked down at her.

"Does Miss Scarlett—Lady Judith Scarlett's daughter—really desire to know something of her father?"

"Oh, can you doubt it? Sir, sir, I do not know, I cannot guess, who you are; but you are welcome to me beyond all power of words to express, if you can tell me anything of my father. You *do* seem to know something—your tones as well as your words imply it—and this strange, mysterious meeting! Oh, pray tell me!"

"Miss Scarlett, I may have little to tell, and I may not be the fittest envoy.

"Envoy! From whom? From *him*—from my lost, dear father?"

"Let me not say too much; let me not claim too much, or arouse hopes I may not be permitted to realize. Only one question I will ask. Miss Scarlett, do you still love your father?"

"Love him! Oh yes, beyond all power of language to say!"

"You have not, then, been tutored to forget him?"

"Mamma never willingly speaks of him; but I cherish his memory. As you now, I never saw him."

"Never saw him! Oh no, of course not."

"He had disappeared from the living world," said Alexia simply, "before I was born."

"Yes, yes; of course—I was aware, well aware of all that. But you still are true to his memory, and you love him?"

"His memory is all I have to live for. I hate my mother!"

This startling confession was made in a tone of such sudden energy and earnestness, that no one could have failed to recognize its sincerity. The listener seemed both amazed and amused.

"Lady Judith is perhaps not all that a mother might be," he said, with a gentle sigh. "But I am glad to hear that your father is still dear to you, and that you have not forgotten him. More I do not dare to say now."

"Yet, sir, one word more, since you have said so much. He is still living?"

"Your father?"

"My father. Speak, sir!"

"He is still living."

"Oh, thank God!"

"Thank God if he be living," thought her guide to himself—"especially if he do not happen to turn up too soon. He would be dreadfully *de trop* for some time to come. I suppose he *is* living—I think my uncle said so. No doubt he is living."

Then he said aloud and gravely:

"You have reason to thank God, Miss Scarlett. For the moment, I can tell you no more. This is your house. But we shall meet again."

"Oh, surely, I hope so."

"May I call to-morrow, to satisfy myself that you have suffered nothing from your alarm?"

"I at least shall be glad to see you—I cannot promise for mamma. But if you succeed in seeing her, and will talk with her about religion—the conversion of the Jews and the Catholics, and all the rest of such people—I dare say she will like you very well. *I* owe you a deep obligation, and as yet I have hardly even had the grace to thank you."

"Do not speak of thanking me, Miss Scarlett! There are reasons which ought to render thanks from you to me superfluous. Forgive me if I can say no more now—and good-night."

"But stay—your name? You will surely let me know the name of one to whom I owe so much, and who appears to know so much concerning me of which I myself am ignorant."

"My name, Miss Scarlett, is as yet an obscure one. The time may come when it will be better known. Such as it is, there is at least no stain upon it."

He had rung and knocked; and the door was now opened. The footman stood wondering on the threshold. The stranger handed a card to Alexia, raised his hat, made a graceful bow, and turned away. The girl sprang up the steps, and hurried to read under a lamp the name on the card. It was that of "Mr Eric G. Walraven, Albany Chambers."

The "G.," it may be said, represented the plebeian name of Gostick, which Eric did not care to make too prominent. His mother, once a Miss Gostick, had married a very poor and proud clergyman, and had insisted on having the name of her wealthy brother added somehow to her son's appellations. Gostick, M. P., had consented to become the godfather of his nephew, but had expressly made it clear that he thereby accepted no obligations, whether spiritual or pecuniary, which were not of a strictly ceremonial and merely nominal character; and so far as he could resist the pressure occasionally brought to bear upon him, he had kept his word.

Mr. Eric G. Walraven left the door of Miss Scarlett's house, and walked again into Piccadilly, and along it toward the Regent Circus, meditating as he went—unless when he happened to pass any shop still open in which there were looking-glasses, and of such a delightful chance he never failed to avail himself, but always paused and contemplated with fond and loving eye his own manly symmetry and beauty. Eric Walraven was to the full as deeply in love with himself as ever Narcissus was, but he served his idol a good deal more wisely and satisfactorily than Narcissus was able to do.

"I venture to think," thus ran the current of his hopeful meditation, "that I have already made an impression on that girl. It is nonsense to speak of her as mad. She is a little wild, but she is no more mad, in the legal sense, than I am. No court of law, for instance, could attempt to dissolve a marriage—stay! I am going rather too fast. It is clear that her weak point is her father. I must find out something about *him*. Old Gostick must put me on the track. On the whole, I rather hope he is dead—his suddenly turning up might be awkward. He might not like *me*. Yes, I hope he is dead. But for the present he shall live, so far as she is concerned, and be a benignant and distant influence, and all that kind of thing. I really see a great chance ahead, and I do so want to cut that hideous old beast Gostick—and how can a man like me, with genius and without money, afford to cut the only relative who has a guinea to give away? She is a pretty girl too—beautiful hair and eyes. I think I could quite fall in love with her if that were necessary. At all events, I am pretty sure I could make her fall in love with me—which is a good deal more to my purpose."

Mr. Walraven had spoken or thought of himself as a man of genius. This, in the ordinary sense, he certainly was not. He was the author of one or two volumes of poems, which had made a sort of sensation, because of the cleverness with which he had contrived to blend meaningless pietism with meaningless impiety, so as to make people doubt whether they were studying hymnology or flat blasphemy as they puzzled over the ingenious pages. Simple religious persons claimed Mr. Walraven as their laureate, while he was the momentary idol of a certain clique of the noisier and shallower infidels. Mr. Walraven understood his public, although he overrated himself. He knew that in England it matters very little what you do, but a great deal what you say—above all, what you say in print. As the Queen of Spain, when there was such a sovereign, was not really supposed by etiquette to be guilty of any sin or shame in having legs, but only to be aggrieved by any public recognition of the fact in the form of an unlucky and officious gift of stockings, so the censors of morals in British literature are often very much shocked at printed recognition of certain passions and sins, about the actual existence of which the same people are in dulgent and charitable enough. Mr. Walraven understood this by artistic instinct, and he took good care that no anatomical allusion of any kind, no hint of the existence of illicit emotion anywhere, should sully the mild purity of his feeble blasphemies. There are a good many people who never would know soft-voiced and demure impiety from true religion; and with such therefore Mr. Walraven passed off for a Keble, while with another section of his admirers he enjoyed something like the fame of a Shelley.

Human character is said by certain philosophers to require the presence, in proper proportion, of three elements, in order to make it as near perfection as anything human may hope to be. It must have the element of the moral, the lovable, and the æsthetic. Now in the composition of Mr. Walraven's character the first and second of these elements seemed to have been left out altogether. There was nothing whatever of the moral or the amiable about him; he had the instincts and tastes of the artist without his soul. Milton's Satan has been described as genius without God. Eric Walraven was a considerably lower sort of thing: he was æstheticism without soul or conscience. He loved and revelled in the sight or sense of all things beautiful and bright and rich; and he never in his life knew what a gleam of human affection or a pang of human remorse or pity might be. There was nothing actively wicked about him; he was not even a very immoral man in the common meaning of the word; he was rather unmoral—he had no sense whatever of right or wrong. Nothing in human life perhaps is more utterly remorseless—not love, not hate, not ambition, not vanity; nay, not even stupidity—than the artistic or æsthetic instinct morbidly developed to the suppression of conscience and feeling. Eric Walraven fed upon the sight and memory of beautiful objects and the indulgence of emotion. He could not live without emotional stimulant and satisfaction. He might have belonged in a humble rank to the school of the artist who tortured a slave to death that he might study the changing expressions of human agony. Once he picked a quarrel with a foolish girl who loved him—as many girls did; who had sacrificed much for him—as many girls would have done; and of whom he was tired. He was leaving her; and in the grief and rage of the separation the girl flung herself on a sofa, and covered as well as she could her face with her hands, and sobbed and shivered there. Her attitude chanced to be one of the finest accidental illustrations of picturesque agony; and Walraven was literally delighted with it. The dishevelled hair, the tears escaping from under the hands, the position of the body, the folds and fall of the dress, the manner in which one foot, ankle, and part of the symmetrical leg were exposed—all combined to make up a picture so pretty, so fascinating, that Walraven gazed at it in intense artistic rapture, only marred by the dread lest the sufferer in her emotion should change it for some position less graceful. This she did in fact, very soon—showed a tear-blurred face, and huddled up her limbs quite awkwardly; and Walraven left her. But the beauty of that first attitude lingered always in his mind; it was a joy forever to him. Time after time did he recall that lovely picture, and dwell in memory on all its details, and feed his senses on it, and be glad because of it. In many little vexations and discordant conditions he brought it back to his recollection, and was cheered and brightened by it. What became of the girl herself he never knew or cared to ask. The one substantial, important, and abiding reality to him in the whole affair was the picturesque and beautiful illustration of feminine suffering. The girl was an accident—a nothing.

Now if Walraven had been a man of genius (and if one could suppose, which it is difficult to do, that there could be genius without feeling), he might perhaps have made a great name for himself in the world. If he had been a man of fortune, he might well have done without the great name. But having neither genius nor fortune, he was driven to make a way for himself; and he hoped to make his way through Society. He was one of the first to see that Bohemianism in literature was "played out"; that a reaction was setting in; that Belgravianism was to be the next phase through which the literary man was to reach *ad astra;* and he was one of the very first to assume boldly the new part of Writer in Society. We all know that some years ago many worthy honest fellows, personally averse to all irregularity and excess, model husbands and fathers, who paid their bills steadily, did nevertheless affect to be wild Bohemians and reckless men of genius just because that was the whim of the hour, and it seemed difficult to obtain a recognition in the guild of literature without conforming to its laws. So in later days many a modest and quiet youth, who hardly knows Clicquot from old gooseberry, or ever handed his card to a Belgravian lacquey, nevertheless tries to be thought an authority on little dinners, and professes to scorn anybody who is not in Society, because such is now the humor of the thing; and literature, weary of putting on the ways of the ruffian, has taken to imitating the manner and jargon of the footman. Eric Walraven had many advantages and opportunities for this sort of thing; he played his game earnestly and spiritedly; he had full faith in himself; and he did actually, as Belgravian literary man, contrive to edge his way a little into Society. He knew the names and faces of most persons of rank; he was invited occasionally to a few houses during the season; and he soon made up his mind that his noblest ambition and most practical object must be to marry a girl of good family and fortune. He now thought he saw this ambition made a possibility by his adventure as the champion of Alexia Scarlett.

Meanwhile the young woman for whom this honor was thus designed, hastening up to her room after her little escapade, was met on the stairs by her mother.

"Where have you been, Alexia? I have been much alarmed about you."

"I have been out in the Park somewhere; I don't exactly know where."

"What new folly is this? Why did you go into the Park alone, and at such an hour?"

"Because the whim took me. I think I meant to run away."

Lady Judith turned paler than usual with vexation and anger, and with some alarm too.

"Alexia, I sometimes believe you would like to break your mother's heart!"

"Oh no, mamma; I am not quite so ambitious or self-conceited as that. I know the strength of my mother's—did you say heart, mamma? Well then, 'heart,' if you will have it so—to suppose that I have power to fracture it. But I am mad, Lady Judith, am I not? You had your mad doctor, you know, to examine me and report. Why do you wonder, then? Mad people do all sorts of queer things, don't they? Perhaps I ran away to escape the strait-waistcoat. Did you intend me for Bedlam, or one of the asylums Charles Reade describes? But I forgot that you don't read novels."

"No; I have seen what comes of such reading where there is no strength of moral principle or religious grace to sustain. What did you do in the Park? and why did you——"

Lady Judith was about to say, "why did you come back, if you were so anxious to run away?" But she checked herself suddenly, because she had serious dread of the effect of anything like a sneer upon a girl of Alexia's temper.

"I had quite an adventure: was attacked by robbers—murderers, in fact—and rescued by a gentleman."

"Is this serious, Alexia, or only extravagance?"

"Nothing could be more serious, dear mamma; and I thought you would like to hear of your daughter being the heroine of such adventures, and having her name perhaps get into the papers. 'Extraordinary Adventure in the Park: Lady Judith Scarlett's daughter attacked by murderers.' Will it not be nice? I shall become quite celebrated. Would you make any objections, Lady Judith Scarlett, to having your daughter's portrait taken for the 'Illustrated London News'?"

There was method in all this sort of madness, as Lady Judith well knew. The method was to alarm and annoy her by threats of reckless exposure. If the good old customs of the elder Mirabeau's time were prevalent in England, perhaps Lady Judith might have found some means of persuading her conscience that religion and duty exacted the use of a *lettre de cachet*, and the consignment of her daughter to some sort of effectual *duresse*. But she had no such resource, and so she asked, with aspect of entire composure:

"Who was the gentleman, Alexia, who rescued you from this terrible band of murderers? Did he give you his name?"

"He did; and he will call to-morrow to see you, mamma, and to receive your thanks for the rescue and protection of your daughter. Perhaps, on the whole, you had better be civil to him; that is, if you really don't want to allow me the pleasure of being a heroine in the newspapers. *I* shall be civil to him; he has a claim on *me;* for he knows something of my father!"

With this parting shot the girl swept past her mother and hastened to her own room.

Lady Judith was perplexed. She did not know whether to attach any substantial meaning to the words her daughter had just uttered, or to set them down as the sheer ravings of growing insanity. Oh, how miserable this wretched little girl made her! How perpetually her personal pride and dignity were threatened by the temper and the escapades of such a daughter! How lonely, uncounselled, almost helpless she felt! Even prayer sometimes seemed to lack its soothing efficacy, and Lady Judith, on her knees, felt her mind wandering away from the business of her soul's salvation to the flighty, peevish, perverse daughter whom Heaven had been pleased to give her, not as a comfort and a stay, but a vexation and distraction. Now that Angelo was gone, there seemed no woman in all London more lonely than Lady Judith. She had no one whom she could consult; she whom so many—the poor, the lame, the halt, and the blind—were always free to consult. She had for her daughter only a wild and fantastic enemy, who might be trusted with no purpose, except indeed the purpose to torment one whom she ought to reverence. She had no husband now—and the thought but added a fresh bitterness, a new sense of injury to the catalogue of grievances registered in her stern heart against the man who had given her such a daughter and then deserted her.

Next day brought some relief to Lady Judith, in the shape of a visit from Mr. Eric G. Walraven. Mr. Walraven's appearance was prepossessing; his manner was quiet, gentlemanlike, and pervaded by a certain tone of sympathetic sweetness and sadness, as if there were already something like an inevitable confidence between himself and Lady Judith. He told the lady with an easy brevity, which had obvious purpose in it—the purpose of a gentleman who, knowing more than he desires to imply, hurries lightly over a communication which may pain the listener's ears—that he had seen her daughter in Hyde Park the previous evening, that he recognized her face, that he happened to be going in the same direction, that she was assailed by two or three rough-looking fellows, who meant probably to frighten merely, and not to rob or injure her; and that on his coming up they of course ran away. He made very little of his own share in that part of the adventure; but insinuated rather than stated that there had been some little difficulty about inducing Miss Scarlett to return home, and that he had shown some skill and delicacy in persuading her. In short, Mr. Walraven's manner and words gave Lady Judith to understand that he quite appreciated the difficulties of her situation, and was acquainted with the peculiarities of her daughter's temperament; but that he was far too refined and honorable a personage to lend any distinct or direct utterance to anything he might happen to know. Lady Judith was impressed and pleased by him.

She was very anxious to know if there was any meaning in what Alexia had said about Mr. Walraven's knowledge of her father. Having thanked him earnestly for his services, in a tone which implied that she thanked him for his delicacy also, she added:

"My daughter said something, Mr. Walraven, of your having had some previous acquaintance with some members of our family I did not quite understand her meaning; and I do not remember having met you before."

"I have had the honor of seeing you at Lady Martha Sidon's, but of course you would hardly remember me. Miss Scarlett did, however, dwell upon a word or two which I let fall inadvertently. I spoke of having seen Mr. Charles Grey Scarlett many years ago. Although I was quite a boy at the time when I heard him speak in the House, his eloquence delighted me, and I have not forgotten it yet."

Lady Judith felt relieved to hear that this was all, and she sent for her daughter to thank Mr. Walraven in person. Alexia came. Mr. Walraven was quite formal and distant; Alexia was sullen and silent. But, before Walraven took his leave, his eyes and hers quietly met; and Walraven was satisfied with his visit.

He broke in upon his uncle's lodgings that day, and accosting Mr. Gostick with an imitation of Fechter's Claude Melnotte, which the worthy Lancashire man utterly failed to comprehend the meaning of, he exclaimed:

"Geef me choy, dear uncle! I have won ze bra-ize!"

"What play-acting is this?" inquired the grim elder.

"I am going in for a prize, uncle mine; and I mean to win it. Now, first of all, tell me everything you know—give me every scrap of possible information about Lady Judith Scarlett's escaped husband; and then I'll tell you something in return, if you care to hear it. How can you live in this hole, smothered among these hideous blue-books?"

"I pay for my lodgings," was the uncle's significant reply.

"Very likely. I mean some day to have lodgings a little more picturesque without paying for them."

"I thought imprisonment for debt was abolished, and I didn't know that they ever went in much for the picturesque in Whitecross street," was Mr. Gostick's genial commentary on his nephew's exultant declaration.

"Not bad, uncle; not bad at all for Lancashire. But now to business; unbosom yourself of all you know, and help me to win my prize."

"Tell me first, without rhodomontade and in plain English, what you propose to do."

Mr. Walraven frankly confided his purposes.

"Your mother," said Gostick composedly, "is a worthy and respectable woman. I never heard anything said against your father, except that he was a preacher of a State-paid church. They are honest and poor: I am honest and rich. How does it happen that our family is favored with the addition of so shabby a rogue as yourself? Go your own ways, sir; I'll give you no helping hand or word to bamboozle a half-crazy girl, and to creep into society and fortune by alternately flattering and cheating a proud aristocratic woman, who does not think you or yours fit to untie her shoe-strings. Go, break stones, or enlist, or do penny-a-lining, or sell cheap photographs; but live like a man anyhow."

And Gostick was inflexible; and Walraven, shrugging his shoulders and moaning over the abominable vulgarity of his uncle, left the place sincerely disgusted. But he soon became a regular attendant at all the philanthropic meetings held in Lady Judith's house, and other meetings elsewhere which she was likely to attend; he was allowed to give her advice on many matters, and even occasionally to write letters for her; and though Alexia and he did not talk much together in public, they had their momentary glances of mutual sympathy and confidence. And Alexia grew less ostentatiously fantastic and fretful; and might indeed have seemed, to a close observer, to have acquired at last something like a purpose and a seriousness in her life.

CHAPTER VIII.

CHESTERFIELD JOCELYN.

DURING the remainder of the evening spent at Mr. Vansiedler's on the edge of New York Bay, Mr. Edwin Dare Jocelyn, or Chesterfield Jocelyn, was by far the most prominent and talkative of the company. He knew everything, and had been everywhere. So, at least, one was led to believe from his anecdotes and his assertions. Nobody's opinion was of any value when compared with his. He spoke of great schemes involving millions on millions of dollars, in which he was concerned here, there, and everywhere, with as cool a carelessness and ease as an ordinary man might allude to a projected change of lodgings, or a seaside visit in the autumn. He professed to know every eminent public man of every country under the sun. When he last had the honor of talking with Gladstone, Gladstone consulted him on the Alabama question; and he, Jocelyn, pointed out the easiest and fairest way of settling the matter; and he had reason to believe—of course he spoke now in confidence—that when next Gladstone came into power, *that* would be the plan. Louis Napoleon certainly did make an awful mess of that Mexican business; but Jocelyn begged the gentlemen present to believe that *he* had advised the Emperor against the scheme from the very beginning. In fact, it was he, Jocelyn, who persuaded General Prim to break off at the eleventh hour. Bismarck had just been writing to him, Jocelyn; he had the letter here in his pocket, and there really was nothing private about it. No; unluckily he had left it at the St. Nicholas Hotel; but there was no mystery about the business at all; everybody knew that Bismarck and he were old allies. As to political opinions, he, Jocelyn, professed to have none: he was just as much attached to his friend Horatio Seymour as to his friend Charles Sumner or Wendell Phillips; and really, of the two, he thought John Bright was a pleasanter companion than Disraeli. No; a man like him should be as impartial in politics as in science; and he never could say, for the life of him, whether he preferred his friend Richard Owen or his friend Tom Huxley.

So Mr. Jocelyn went on—not dogmatically or noisily, but blandly, and without seeming purposely to engross the conversation. All through the flow of his talk he kept casting thoughtful and anxious glances at Isolind.

Angelo Volney was, for the most part, a quiet watcher. Nature had endowed him with a wonderfully quick perception or instinct for the reading of character, between the lines of mere conventionality and talk. While Charles Escombe was half disgusted and half amused by Jocelyn's extravagance and egotism, and was every now and then tempted to break into futile controversy, Angelo took quite a different view of the character of their new acquaintance. "All this is play-acting," Angelo said to himself; "this is a cool strong man playing the part of a gasconader and a fribble; there is an iron hand under this glove of velvet—a powerful daring brain beneath this cap and bells."

Mr. Jocelyn contrived to approach Isolind.

"I have seen Miss Atheling before," he said; "hers is not a face to be forgotten. We have met—in Rome, I think, Miss Atheling?"

"Perhaps so, sir. I have been in Rome, but I do not remember seeing you."

"Naturally you forget. The sun, Miss Atheling, can scarcely be expected to remember the face of every sunflower: but the sunflowers still turn to the sun."

"I believe they don't, as a matter of fact," broke in Charles Escombe. "I am told it altogether depends upon the manner in which the sunflowers are——"

"Pray don't spoil my poor effort at a tribute to Miss Atheling by your practical prose, Mr. Escombe. Clytie is a reality, I insist upon it. But forgive my awkward attempt at a compliment, Miss Atheling. I have no skill in such things."

"I forgive you," replied Isolind coldly, "on condition that you attempt no further offence."

"Offence! Is, then, a poor phrase of sincere admiration an offence?"

"To me it seems so. Not a purposed and deliberate offence, Mr. Jocelyn; but still an offence. That kind of talk implies that a man thinks he is speaking to an inferior being, whose weak mind he can delight by flattery. Men don't pay compliments to men, unless for some mean purpose, and where they suppose the objects of the flattery are feeble enough to be pleased by it. In every such sense, therefore, a compliment is really an offence."

"Then I shall restrain all expression of my genuine feeling, at whatever cost, rather than displease Miss Atheling, or lead her to doubt my sincerity."

"Thus, Miss Atheling," interposed Angelo quietly, "you compel Mr. Jocelyn to become insincere, in order that he may not be suspected of insincerity."

Isolind sent a glance of bright humor across to Angelo. These two, who had hardly exchanged a dozen sentences, were already beginning to understand each other.

"Pardon me," replied Jocelyn, in nowise disconcerted; "Truth has continually to stifle her voice, lest she be mistaken for exaggeration. Nothing is so wonderful as the real. No opinion, for example, that I could form of *you* would be so strange but that you could, from your knowledge of your own history, make it seem poor and incomplete."

"True enough," thought Angelo—"a very palpable hit. No one here, indeed, could guess my true story. I wonder what is *his*."

"Forgive me," said Jocelyn blandly, "for selecting you as an illustration,

Mr. Volney. Of course I did not mean you in particular, but anybody, everybody. For instance, I am confident that I have met Miss Atheling before now, although she does not remember me. I am convinced of this, and yet I do not venture to contradict her impression on the mere strength of its being utterly impossible I could ever have forgotten so remarkable, so beautiful a face. I am compelled to be silent lest I should seem to be a flatterer; yet I *do* feel convinced that I have seen Miss Atheling before now. I said it was in Rome; but I was clearly mistaken in that conjecture. No, I now remember it was in England that I saw that face."

"Then your memory cruelly refuses to justify your compliments, Mr. Jocelyn," said Isolind. "Be warned against further flattery of women by this very instance. I never was in England."

"Never in England?"

"Never."

"You quite surprise me!—Judge Atheling" (the Judge had just joined the group), "is it possible that your dear daughter was never in England?"

"She was never in England, sir. Let me tell you that it is her own fault; for we wished her to go there the other day, when we were in France; but she has got her head crammed with patriotic extravagances, and she would not consent even to tread the soil of perfidious Albion."

"Ah, then I am altogether mistaken as to the scene, at least; though I still cannot admit the possibility of my having been mistaken as to the face and figure. I think you spoke of going south, Mr. Escombe. The season's favorable now. Come with me, you and your friend Mr. Volney. I can obtain special cars, or at least free passes, anywhere and everywhere; and I have many schemes on hand south of Richmond just now, and shall be proud to show you the country. Meantime, suppose you dine with me at Delmonico's to-morrow or Thursday? Just a little pleasant party. Our dear host Mr. Vansiedler, and our distinguished friend Judge Atheling, will come, I hope?"

"I am sorry to say that I cannot go any day this week," said Mr. Vansiedler.

"I'll go with pleasure," said the beaming Judge, "if my wife will only allow me."

"Pray permit me to persuade Mrs. Atheling. Then you will come, Mr. Escombe?"

"Delighted, I am sure! Thursday, did you say?"

"Thursday, yes; let it be Thursday, at seven. Mr. Volney will come?"

Angelo bowed and murmured a formal willingness. Perhaps he of all the invited guests was really most anxious to go. He wished to study Mr. Jocelyn, and, if possible, to understand him.

Escombe engaged Mr. Jocelyn in conversation about the condition and prospects of the South, regarding which he had a theory, as he had about most things, and several rows of figures, making up tabulated comparisons, to support the theory. Mr. Jocelyn never admitted that there was anything in anybody's theory except his own; and he met Escombe's carefully-arranged figures—all taken from blue-books and the reports of British consuls—by other figures utterly contrasting and incompatible with Escombe's. Hence a lively discussion, during which Angelo drew under the light of Isolind's eyes, which somehow seemed to invite him.

As he came to her side, she glanced over towards the group amid which Jocelyn stood, and said suddenly in a lowered voice:

"Mr. Volney, I wish you would avoid that man.

"Mr. Jocelyn?

"Yes. There is something about him I dislike and don't understand."

"There is something about him I too don't understand, and don't much like; but I want to know more of him for that very reason."

"I wish you would avoid him."

She looked at Angelo with a quiet earnestness, which had no gleam of coquetry or affectation about it, but which made Angelo's heart beat.

"Why do you wish *me* to avoid him, Miss Atheling? Your father seems rather attracted by him."

"My father is only amused by him and curious about him. He studies him merely as something odd and interesting."

"So do I, Miss Atheling; and I am not likely to be drawn into any vast speculations by his influence, I can assure you. I am indeed the empty traveller who may sing before the—speculator, let us say, not to be too rude and harsh to our new friend."

"I cannot tell why it is, but the man's eyes fill me with a kind of dread. They seem full of evil omen towards me every time they turn on me. If it were not foolish to say such a thing, I should say that his presence is surcharged with evil towards me—and towards one other person here."

"And that other person is——?"

"Yourself, Mr. Volney."

"But why do you think his presence is ominous to us—to you and me—and not to the others here?" asked Angelo with a smile, and with a strange sensation at his heart, caused by the coupling of her and him together, and the interest thus suddenly manifested in him.

"I cannot tell. Perhaps women can divine things by instinct. Perhaps there is something in certain antagonistic natures which may subtly warn one against the other, and which may some day be discovered and recognized as a reality by science itself. You smile at me, but I don't know why such things should not be possible. However that be, it seems to me that that man's eyes beam danger and pain on me and on *you;* and I almost fear him, although I am not given in general to feminine fears. Will you promise me to avoid him?"

"I cannot, Miss Atheling. I cannot tell you how much I feel delighted by your kindly interest in me. Indeed, it gives me the highest pleasure; and I only wish there were some danger of any sort to justify it, that I might feel for the once a little heroic. But there can be nothing in this person to alarm any one who has no money to lose in speculations; and I have some special reasons for wishing to study him."

"We are going, Isolind," the Judge called out at this moment; and Isolind rose to leave, and the confidential conversation was over.

The Athelings had only a very short distance to go, and most of the company came out on the lawn, some departing, some saying good-night to the parting. Angelo walked a little way by Isolind's side, and they talked of indifferent things—of the beauty of the night, the charm of the scene. The autumn moon was shining brightly upon the water and the islands, and the moon shone to Angelo as it had never beamed on him before; and when he bade Isolind good-night, and felt the touch of her hand in his, and saw the white rays rest upon her beautiful face, it seemed as if she were the soul and spirit of the place and the delicious hour, awakening him to a new, a glorified, and a sanctified existence.

When he had left her he walked back in silence; and knew not why it was that while he thought of her he found the sufferings of his childhood once more brought in array before his memory, but brightened now, and made sweet and sacred. All the past looked beautiful and tender, all the future silvery and sad; like the light that fell now upon the water—like the light that had lately rested upon her cheek. He had only spoken a few words to a beautiful girl, had touched her hand, and looked into her eyes; and the old world of his life was all laid in ashes for him, that a nobler and more sacred existence might be raised upon its ruins. To-night was not as yesterday. From life to death, from nothingness into life, could hardly be a greater change than that through which, as yet all unconscious of its meaning, Angelo Volney had passed.

As he came near the porch of Vansiedler's house, Mr. Jocelyn, smoking a cigar, emerged from a little group of smokers enjoying after their fashion the sweet night air, and approached our hero with a demeanor of friendly confidence.

"A very charming and highly-gifted girl, apparently, is the daughter of our good friend Atheling, Mr. Volney."

"Very," assented Volney.

"Quite a woman of genius, I am told. Perhaps you have a prejudice against women of genius? No? I am glad to hear it. You will meet many remarkable women in your travels through the States. She does not, I think, greatly resemble our friend Atheling. Did any resemblance strike you?"

"No, indeed," replied Volney, very conscientiously.

"Nor is she remarkably like her mother. By the way, Mr. Volney, I have been watching for an opportunity to ask whether you are not a son of my old friend Colonel Sir Richard Volney, of your East India Company's army, whom I had the great honor to know in Bengal?"

"No, Mr. Jocelyn; no relation whatever."

"Indeed! You certainly do not resemble my gallant friend, but the name is a little peculiar; and I thought that—but perhaps, indeed, you are related to my eminent friend Dean Volney, of Stortford-cum-Kingscote, in England?"

"You may spare yourself useless conjectures, Mr. Jocelyn. I have no relatives living, so far as I know. I don't know anything of my father, except that his name was Volney, and that he died miserably poor. I was brought up as an adopted son by one of the best women who ever lived—Lady Judith Scarlett."

Angelo looked steadily at Mr. Jocelyn as he spoke, and he felt sure he saw the lines of that dark face quiver for a moment.

"Lady Judith Scarlett!" exclaimed Jocelyn. "Why, she surely had a child of her own?"

"A daughter—yes; but no son. Did you know Lady Judith?"

"Yes—oh yes; a long time ago; that is, I used to meet her in places. She does not go out much of late, I am told."

"Hardly at all. You seem to keep up your acquaintance with England very well, Mr. Jocelyn."

"Keep up my acquaintance? Yes, sir, I do. In fact, I regard myself as an Englishman. My father was born in England; and I have been there a great deal, but not very lately. My father spent his fortune in England, Mr. Volney, before he was twenty-three years of age, and he came out here to make a new fortune, which *I* spent. But I re-made myself in San Francisco. I am a Forty-niner. Do you know what we call a Forty-niner? No? One of those who settled there at the beginning—at the outburst of the gold-digging mania, when San Francisco was only a few canvas tents. You should see it now—you *shall* see it, and thoroughly too, if you will only stay long enough to make the journey. They know Edwin Jocelyn in San Francisco, sir; everybody going along Montgomery street—from the Governor of the State to the dirtiest John Chinaman—knows Edwin Jocelyn. I have made fortune after fortune there. This is the land for fortunes, sir. I'll put you up to a good thing if you feel like it."

"I am afraid I have nothing to tempt Fortune with, Mr. Jocelyn. She is like a Gipsy, and requires to have her palm crossed with silver before she will say or do anything. Does she not?"

"Well, sir, that surely could be managed too. Our friend Atheling, I suppose, is a rich man?"

"Really I don't know; I only made his acquaintance this very evening.

"Indeed! I thought you were old acquaintances—the young lady and you especially. His only daughter, I believe?"

"I suppose so."

"And will have all his money, no doubt. You spoke of Lady Judith Scarlett, Mr. Volney, and her retirement from the world—a sad condition of things surely for a woman so splendid as she was. Of course you are acquainted with all the circumstances of that affair?"

"Not all the circumstances. I only know that she had a bad husband, who deserted her and disappeared. I have never sought to know more."

"Has she ever heard anything about him?"

"Nothing direct, I fancy; but she believes that he is living, and somewhere in America."

"I don't believe it!" broke out Jocelyn almost fiercely; "and as you are a friend of Lady Judith's, don't you believe it either. Does she want to find him out? has she sent you to look for him? Does she want to be reconciled to him, and to take him back, an interesting penitent? It can't be. If she is anything like the woman she was, that is about the last thing she would think of doing. She is not such a fool; and even if she was, it can't be and it sha'n't be!"

"I know nothing of Lady Judith's purposes, Mr. Jocelyn, and I neither understand your meaning nor your warmth."

"Pray, my dear Mr. Volney, excuse me! A thousand times excuse me! I am really quite ashamed of a warmth which must have seemed to you as rude as it was inexplicable. The fact is, that the story of Lady Judith's wrongs impressed me at the time very deeply. I had known her, as I told you; and she became quite a—well, a sort of heroine in my eyes; and of course I hated her husband—for that reason, you know—and my soul revolted at the idea of his being restored to society and to favor. But I have no doubt the fellow has been dead these many years."

"Lady Judith thinks she has reason to believe that he is still living."

"Has she any better reasons than guess and fancy, and all the other nonsense that women call reasons? Anything that a man of sense, with two ideas in his head, would call reasons?"

"I know nothing in this case of Lady Judith Scarlett's reasons, Mr. Jocelyn; but I know few men who are better able to form a sound opinion on any subject."

"Indeed! No doubt; of course you are quite right. In any case, my dear Mr. Volney, it hardly concerns me. But I wish you English people would not look upon this country as if it were the camping-ground and refuge of all the scoundrels your capital chooses to cast out. Shall we join our friends on the 'stoop,' as we call it here in New York? A delicious night, certainly, for a quiet smoke in the open air."

The Vansiedlers were early people, and had already remained out of bed to an unusual hour for them. Jocelyn would apparently have sat up all the night, and so would Charles Escombe; these two opposing irreconcilable theories and comparing incompatible facts. Escombe had a slow steady fluency of talk; Jocely streamed away like a rushing river. Before Escombe had grasped some paradox clearly enough to begin refuting it, Jocelyn had pelted him about the ears with half a dozen others. Jocelyn, moreover, assumed in every dispute the manner of a practical man who is calmly putting down erroneous theories and correcting ignorant assumptions. He disposed in every instance of Charles Escombe's blue-books and other authorities, by coolly observing that he had himself actually lived in each of the places referred to; that he knew every foot of the soil and every individual worth knowing; that nobody else knew anything at all about the matter. How many lives would it have taken, as a mere question of time and the hour, for Jocelyn to have lived in all the places and known all the people described by him? Old Parr, Methuselah, the Wandering Jew, could hardly have accomplished so much. Yet the difficulty in judging of the man's true character was great. It might have been easy enough to dispose of the matter by setting him down as a mere braggart and liar. But if you are entitled to test a man's professed acquaintance with subjects and places unfamiliar to you by the genuineness of his professed knowledge of subjects and places with which you are familiar, it must be owned—and Angelo Volney had several times during this night to own it to himself—that Jocelyn had a wonderfully wide and exact amount of information. For example, it was clear to Angelo that Jocelyn knew England, especially London—its politics and its actual society—much better than Charles Escombe did. Indeed, although Angelo could not well suspect his new acquaintance of modesty, it seemed to him almost certain that Jocelyn rather underrated and suppressed the varied and intimate extent of his familiarity with English affairs and English people. Then, again, Mr. Vansiedler was no fool, and Judge Atheling was well acquainted with most parts of the American States and most subjects of American controversy. And yet they were both apparently much impressed by Jocelyn's acquaintance, at once broad and exact, with regions, topics, and people whereof they had themselves special knowledge.

In fact, it was evident to Volney that Jocelyn had completely talked over and conquered Judge Atheling, and much impressed even Mr. Vansiedler, a graver man of less emotional kind, slow to sympathies and new ideas. Judge Atheling was always on the lookout for novelties in opinion, and had almost invariably some new theory, notion, or crotchet on hand. Vansiedler, as became a genuine Knickerbocker, respected the majesty of the old and the past. Yet he, too, was clearly a good deal taken with some of Jocelyn's views; while Atheling seemed perfectly ardent about certain enterprises recommended to him. After the Athelings had gone, Jocelyn turned his attention principally to Charles Escombe, with whom he debated in the manner just described.

Escombe entered Angelo's room for a few minutes when the *séance* had concluded.

"An amusing fellow, that Jocelyn," he said. "There's a good deal of a certain sort of cleverness about him, but he doesn't know anything well; and he is awfully shallow. I suppose he is what the Yankees call a smart man, but he wants strength and depth altogether, I think."

"On some things," Angelo replied, "I think he knows more than he pretends to."

"Do you really? Now that didn't strike me at all—quite the reverse, in fact Anyhow, he is well worth studying. He seems a perfect type of the Yankee."

"I am convinced," said Angelo smiling, "that he is just as much of a Yankee as I am."

Escombe laughed.

"What a contradictory fellow you are, Volney! Come, here's something you can't contradict. Atheling's daughter is a handsome girl, and an uncommonly intelligent and agreeable girl too."

"I like her very much indeed—very much."

Escombe looked at him for a moment thoughtfully, bearing in his mind certain fears which had been urged upon him regarding Alexia Scarlett, and wondering whether the attractions of Isolind Atheling might not prove of happy omen for his own love-suit. And Angelo, as he answered his friend's remark, was thinking too about Alexia, and felt, he knew not why, a sudden strange pang of pain when he remembered his pledge to Alexia's mother. So the two young men stood looking at each other for a moment, both wrapped in the same subject, one with his silent growing hope, the other with his silent pain, each alike ashamed to acknowledge in words, or even in distinct thoughts, the growth of the hope and of the pain.

When Angelo was left alone, he sat down and gave himself up to puzzling thought on one chief question. Who was Edwin Jocelyn? Was he indeed merely that which he gave himself out to be—a dashing, daring, scheming American adventurer? Or was he somebody playing a part, and having behind him a history and a mystery which he had some motive for concealing? The very suddenness and apparent unreasonableness of the conjectures or suspicions which, from the very outset, Angelo had formed regarding him, only lent to a thoughtful half-poetical mind like his stronger reasons for believing that there must be some foundation for such an instinctive assumption. True, there seemed something extravagant in thus fancying he had detected a mystery in almost the first man brought directly under his observation on American soil. Yet would it not be still more extravagant and irrational to admit that such an idea could have entered into his mind, utterly without plausible foundation or excuse, in the instance of the first casual stranger he had taken the trouble to observe? It counted for something, too, that a girl with the brow and the eyes of Isolind Atheling should have at once and instinctively assumed that round this fluent and audacious adventurer there hung some veil of ominous mystery. The more he thought of the manner and the words of Jocelyn, the more Angelo became convinced that the extravagant compliments, the fluent, almost frivolous audacity, the hyperbolical pretensions, were but the playing of a part.

Jocelyn's sudden surprise and subsequent heat of expression, when Lady Judith Scarlett's name and history were brought up, seemed absolutely irreconcilable with the vague interest of a mere stranger. But who, then, could the man be? Lady Judith's denounced husband and enemy—the man about whom Angelo had been bidden to inquire? If this were he—if, almost immediately on his touching American soil, Angelo Volney had been brought face to face with the very man for whom he had expected to have a long and toilsome search—what more extraordinary incident could be introduced into the pages of the most fantastic romance? Yet this was the idea which had thus far taken possession of Volney's mind. Lady Judith had told him of one who was profoundly selfish, worldly-minded, ambitious, plausible, and clever, who was sure to rise to the surface anywhere, and to become influential and conspicuous. Did not all this correspond with the appearance, character, and career of the adventurer calling himself Jocelyn? It did indeed seem hard to Angelo to understand how such a man as he had seen before him that evening could ever, at any time, have won the affections of a woman so pure, serene, and elevated in soul as Lady Judith. But youth is a great enchanter; youth is easily enchanted. Lady Judith twenty years ago, this man twenty years ago, may have seemed very different beings; she had spoken of him as impressing people with a belief in his austerity of virtue. Why might he not then have chosen to play the part of a saint, as now he found it convenient to assume the character of a mere adventurer?

Angelo brooded over the idea. It fascinated him. When he fell asleep he dreamed of it and of Isolind's face; and when he awoke he remembered how, before leaving England, he had dreamed of following out the track of Lady Judith's enemy, and how in that dream, too, the pure and beautiful face of Isolind had arisen and shone upon him.

When the company were finally breaking up that night, Mr. Vansiedler accompanied Jocelyn to the door of his room, and there for a few moments the host and guest stood in light and pleasant talk.

"Then you will leave us to-morrow?" the former said.

"My very dear friend, I must indeed. Think of my engagements! You don't know how many thousand men stand waiting for my word of command to begin operations! I am pledged, positively pledged, to the Barings and to Lafitte; and for that matter to dear old Vanderbilt too. But I don't leave New York for a few days yet, and we may meet again. The fact is, my esteemed Vansiedler, you must break, postpone, forfeit, or otherwise get rid of your inconvenient engagements, and dine with us on Thursday at Delmonico's. I have my equals, Vansiedler, in most things, and even, I don't hesitate to say, my superiors; no, it is no affectation of modesty! I am quite aware that there are men in certain fields superior to me, but in the art of arranging and ordering a dinner, none whatever. No, sir, none whatever! There I stand alone!"

Vansiedier smiled, again excused himself, and they parted for the night.

Jocelyn held his door open for a moment, and looked after his host with his habitual expression of jaunty braggart *insouciance* on his face, and then he drew back into the bedroom and closed and bolted the door. Then the expression of his face underwent so sudden and complete a change that an observer, could such have been present, might have been startled by a doubt whether the man before him was really the same man who had that moment entered the room. The removal of a mask could hardly have created a greater and more instantaneous change. Bold, bright, genial self-conceit and self-satisfaction beamed on the face of the man who stood at the yet unclosed door; a sort of almost boyish audacity and complacency; an expression which amused, and indeed rather attracted, the spectator; a heedless, harmless, egotistical *bonhomie*. But the man who closed and bolted the door showed a countenance which was stern, harsh, almost ferocious; which had a fierce and haggard expression in its eyes, and a compression of selfish unscrupulous energy, daring, and hate about the lips. "He may have his faults, but he is a regular good fellow at bottom," anybody might have said about the wearer of the first expression. "That is a man to shrink from, to dread, and to detest," anybody might have said of him who now stood in the room alone.

Thus had Chesterfield Jocelyn's face changed its character in a moment.

He did not speak aloud. There are men who do, when alone, pour out to themselves their thoughts in audible words. There can hardly be a greater mistake than to suppose that the trick of talking aloud thoughts that ought to be secret is unknown to any save the personages of the dramatist and the romancist. But Jocelyn was not a man to run such a risk. He never talked to himself where there was any possibility of a listener being near. Long, long experience and practice had trained him to caution and to a self-restraint which was only at rare intervals broken in upon by the vehemence of a naturally impetuous temper. But he stood now at the window overlooking the lawn, and he thought; and we may follow the current of his thought and give it expression in words.

"So then *he* is alive," thought Jocelyn; "he is alive, and *she* knows it, and is seeking for him! I thought if he had been anywhere above ground my hatred must have found him. Can it be that she is really seeking to bring him back—that she is now weary of her long years of widowhood, and is ready to receive him after all? I thought better of her—much better; but this would be like a woman's cursed sentimental weakness and folly! This would indeed be a fitting and goodly end, that he should be restored to his place, another prodigal son, while I remain here in this hateful exile! Curse it, I am sick of this place, sick of every place here, and of the miserable excitement in which I seek for relief, and of the part I have to keep up, and of the trumpery triumphs and failures. Good heaven! one-tenth, one-twentieth of the patience, the self-control, the craft I have been employing here these years back would have made and kept a splendid place for me in London; and I care for no spot in the world but London. Ten thousand curses on him, my enemy, rival, and plague from our very school-days; my victor only because of his cold and bloodless phariseeism! To him I owe my ruin—to him and to *her*. Where is *she* now? If he is living, why not she?

"*If* he is living, I now shall find it out. This demure boy, whom Lady Judith sent over, evidently knows much more than he pretends. I will work upon him and find out through him; and if I can but once come face to face with Charles Scarlett, I shall be ready to give up all in this world or the next, if I fail to have one sweet half-hour of revenge.

"But who is that girl of to-day? Good God! what thoughts came back upon me when first I saw her face! I could almost have struck her, so strong and hateful was the resemblance to that accursed woman who was my bane and shame. I never saw such a likeness! Can it be possible that she is really—? The thing seems too wild and absurd even for a dream, and yet what a likeness!

"That riddle I must endeavor to solve at once. These Athelings are rich and foolish; she will, perhaps, have all their money; another chance!

"I wonder if I could venture back to London? Could people recognize me there? Heavens, I have surely undergone enough to change any one's face, and to defy discovery! Atheling talked of going over to England next year; perhaps I might go with him, and in that way help to evade scrutiny.

"This evening has been a terrible trial. All the devilish agencies seem to have combined to torture me. The thought of *his* being alive, the possibility of his finding his place again—the cold hypocrite who always tried to injure me, the coward whom I chastised, the cause of my ruin and banishment! And if he is alive, why not she? And then, who is that girl whose face haunts me—whose resemblance to *her* is so strange, that I wonder I can look on and not betray myself?

"Things are darkening round me, and I am growing weary and desperate. If he be living, I don't care what happens to me, provided I can only have revenge! It would atone for all the past. I begin to be sick of life and of excitements that lead to nothing, and I would welcome ruin gladly for myself, if first I could only stop him as he was about to return once more to society and his place, and strike him down and trample him to death!

"Too much for one day—too much—the thought that he still lives, and the face of that girl!"

Thus Chesterfield Jocelyn, the debonair, the bright, the audacious, communed with himself; and he bit his lips and his nails, and clenched his hands as he thought. Of course his moods did not express themselves coherently and in order as the words have here been written down; on these pages have only been given the sum and meaning of his ravings as they passed through his disturbed brain, and mirrored themselves in frowns and lines and contortions upon his passion-seamed face. He sat up long and late, and all the past streamed back upon him, and brought him only a renewal of savage hatreds and bitter regrets, but brought no remorse or repentance. He slept heavily at last, and woke early to new bewilderment and conjecture, new emotions of hatred, and new resolves of revenge. But then he dressed himself most carefully, and perfumed his hair and his beard and his whiskers, and made elaborate use of his tooth-powder and his dyes, and put on all his rings, and pins, and chains, and trinkets; and having likewise put on, with yet greater care, his habitual smile of genial self-conceit, he sallied forth on Mr. Vansiedler's lawn, the same gay, audacious, complacent, egotistic, reckless, pleasant creature as he had shown himself the night before.

CHAPTER IX.

A MORNING WALK.

ISOLIND ATHELING had a good many household duties to look after. When a woman shows a gift of managing and ordering domestic affairs, she is certain to be allowed abundant opportunities of displaying it, and whatever her position in the family—whether she be wife and therefore legitimate sovereign, or sister or daughter, or even only governess—she is equally sure to become the practical ruler. Good Mrs. Atheling had long since withdrawn from all active and laborious interference in the arrangement of the family affairs. Isolind was mayor of the palace; she kept the keys, gave the instructions, composed the quarrels among the "helps" and attendants, reconciled—oh, hardest of tasks! —the Irish ladies in the kitchen to the existence and propinquity of the dark-skinned men and brothers who drove the carriage and kept the stables in order; and she did all this without noise and without bustle. Of course it broke in a great deal upon her time for reading and study, for music and the composing of poems, for keeping up with the doings of the political world, as most American-bred girls of any intelligence are anxious to do, and indeed for nearly all other things in which mere intellect and taste can take delight. But Isolind's creed of Woman's Mission was rigid as to the necessity of doing the nearest scrap of duty first. Just now, at this present moment, see that the family shall have some dinner to eat, and that the clothes go to wash—that done, then set about the regeneration of humanity! An English girl whose family had wealth, or something approaching to wealth, could hardly understand how much of constant domestic duty fell to the share of Isolind Atheling. The Athelings came into the city in the winter, and then they lived in one of the quietest of the best class hotels, and Isolind was nearly free of all trouble. But in the months when they occupied their place on the edge of the bay, her duties of arrangement and supervision, and sometimes of direct personal coöperation, were multifarious and continual.

With all this she lived a very happy life, a life indeed of almost ideal and

Arcadian happiness. While the Athelings were in their country home one day was for Isolind very much like another, so far as events and external conditions were concerned. But the girl's thoughts were always fresh, vivid, and changing; and while there was a new tint on a leaf, a new breath to ripple the water of the bay, a new cloud to float across the sky, life could have no monotony for her.

She always rose early. Her bed-room opened on a flower garden at the rear of the house; at least if we call that the rear which looked towards the road and away from the water. When she raised her window, she could step out on a broad path among flowers; and rarely indeed did she make her appearance at the window but that the head gardener, a gray-haired Irishman, came over to greet her with a bouquet of flowers, or, at the proper season, a bunch of grapes, or some of the delicious peaches which gladden in such prodigality of numbers and juciness the palates of New York. Isolind's was a pretty room, fitted up simply but very tastefully with rose-colored curtains, which sent a rich glow over her fair complexion and sunny hair; a few well-chosen prints, and one or two statuettes—among them an excellent miniature Parian copy of the incomparable Venus of the Louvre—several medallions brought from Italy, and various little mementoes from the East. The furniture of Isolind's room was plain—unpretending maple, or some such wood—but the taste which chose its ornaments lent it an appearance of luxury. There were a sofa and a table, and on the latter were writing materials and a few books.

Let us see what were Isolind's books. A Shakespeare, a Schiller, a "Don Quixote," a little sewed copy of Molière's "Misanthrope," Robert Browning's poems, Lowell's "Biglow Papers," Hawthorne's "Mosses from an Old Manse," John Stuart Mill's "Essay on Liberty"—with daily draughts of which latter Isolind refreshed her convictions as to the supreme human need of individuality, and the bane of mere conventionality—Lessing's "Laocoon," and an odd volume or two of Victor Hugo. This young woman's reading was in the highest degree desultory and unsystematic. If you wanted to speak in the language of compliment, you would call it eclectic or catholic; if otherwise, irregular and scrambling.

She dressed herself and arranged her hair without ever dreaming of the intervention of a lady's maid. The grand difficulty of modern womanhood, the arranging of the hair, troubled her in no wise. Her hair fell about her neck, but not quite to her shoulders; and it would not grow any longer, and it could not be made smooth and flat by any arts known to *friseur*. Therefore Isolind merely combed and brushed it through, then threw it back from her forehead and ears—and there it was. No pomades, no oils stood upon her modest dressing-table. This particular morning she put on a pretty white cashmere dress trimmed with blue—a dress cut so short as to be quite off the ground, and to show a good deal of a very neat, picturesque little boot of buff-colored leather coming high above the ankle, and fastened with a row of buttons. Short dresses were at that time not very common in Europe, and an English girl might perhaps have been a little astonished at the free display of Isolind's boots and ankles. But Isolind's dress never needed to be raised as she walked through her garden, and therefore she never showed more than boot and ankle; whereas the most modest wearer of a long skirt would sometimes when suddenly endeavoring to save her silken sheen from damp or dust make unexpected display of calf and stocking to a height perfectly alarming. Sir Walter Scott, in his "Anne of Geierstein," makes special mention, when we are first introduced to his heroine, of the firmness and symmetry of the legs which her short Swiss kirtle reveals. Emboldened by his example, let us say that Isolind's feet were a pretty sight in her buff boots, and that her limbs were straight, firm, and shapely.

One of the ornaments of Isolind's room was a fine engraving of a Düsseldorf picture from Fouqué's "Undine." This picture was before Miss Atheling's eyes every day; yet this particular morning she seemed to look on it with peculiar attentivenss and interest. She wondered perhaps whether Undine felt any the happier when love had given her a soul; and whether the whole legend was not sadly discouraging to Isolind's own Equality of Womanhood theory, seeing that poor Undine only obtained her gift of soul when Tyrant Man was good enough to love her. This view of the situation had not struck our heroine before, and she smiled at it; and yet was, for some reason or other, anything but quite gladsome.

The business of life, however, broke in upon her meditation, and she went to give orders and make arrangements for breakfast. Scotland, Switzerland, and the United States are the regions where breakfast really is a meal to think about, plan, order, and arrange—where it actually has a *menu*. The Athelings were simple in their tastes, but yet their breakfast-table had hominy and succotash, which the Judge liked; "milk-toast," in which his wife delighted; buckwheat cakes; stewed apples; preserved peaches—the fresh peaches were gone with the summer; "scrambled" eggs; potatoes done in various ways—the sweet potato and our old familiar mealy friend; apple sauce; and several varieties of bread, besides tea (which only Isolind drank); chocolate, which pleased Mrs. Atheling; and a great bowl of milk, to be swallowed by the Judge, who never touched tea, coffee, or any such beverages. It is almost needless to say to any one who knows New York, that great glasses of ice water stood beside each plate.

When Isolind had seen to all this, she went into the garden, and gathered such flowers as the season allowed, made two pretty little nosegays, and laid one beside the plate of each of the elders of the family.

"Our flowers are nearly gone, Martin," said the girl to the gray-haired gardener.

"There's one of your own favorite still for *you*, miss," said the gallant veteran; and as she thanked him with her sunny smile, and was returning to the house, he looked after her, and murmured or rather growled to himself, "Divil resave me if ye aren't the purtiest flower yerself that ever was seen in a garden! God bless you! you're good and beautiful enough to be an Irish colleen, my heart!"

In this kind of way Isolind's days began and went on for the most part. There was a daily beauty in her life. Her most prosaic duties gave her pleasure—partly because she had a truly poetic soul. As to the pure all things are pure, so to the poetic all things have poetry in them. Isolind was surrounded by natural beauty, and by the moral beauty of a peaceful, happy, loving home. She was utterly unconventional. None of the fears, anxieties, and longings on the subject of fashion and gentility which torture so many pretty New York girls ever vexed her. She never bestowed one single thought upon her social position or that of her neighbors. She never cared whether Fashion approved or disapproved of her. Then she was equally free from the dread which harasses some good Englishwomen so much, the fear of doing or seeming to do something improper. The thought of impropriety never entered into the girl's pure, free, and womanly soul. She talked as frankly to men who were her friends as to women; she never stopped to think whether she was speaking too long to this man if she liked his conversation, or smiling too kindly on that man if her heart felt genially towards him. It need hardly be said, that girls in America are allowed a personal freedom which even elderly married women are not permitted in England, and which would be utterly impossible in France. In America, therefore, the question of impropriety—factitious or constructive impropriety—can hardly be said to arise in the intercourse of educated young women with their friends and society. Girls are not vexed and harassed with invented and imaginary sins. Nothing is improper which is not really and in itself wrong. A clear bright line is drawn. When once society sets about devising constructive improprieties, there is no bound to the ingenious refinement of ultra-delicate imagination; but as yet the social opinion which endeavors to rule the lives of American women in cities seems to concern itself more in laying down laws for the preservation of the gentilities than for that of the proprieties. Now, for the former rules Isolind cared nothing; and of the latter she took no heed. She was as free and fearless on the score of gentility as any really well-bred and intelligent English girl could be; and never doing or thinking anything improper, she was troubled by no doubts or dreads on the side of propriety.

Therefore she enjoyed a true freedom, and had all the pure and noble virtues which only grow up in the atmosphere of freedom. What women in civilized countries mostly want is magnanimity. Men of high minds are constantly disappointed when they find this lack of the magnanimous revealing itself in the character of some woman who otherwise seems so admirable. But men themselves have hitherto, in Europe especially, so shaped and limited the moral training of women as to render magnanimity a virtue of almost impossible attainment. The errors of women are in their degree almost always the common errors of servitude. But there is something more than that. The whole training of womanhood is directed to the culture merely of one virtue. It is not indispensable or even necessary to a woman's honor and repute that she should be truthful, or generous, or beneficent, or brave. She has no need or inducement to cultivate the magnanimous qualities. Society only asks her to be chaste. If you will cultivate but one flower, you cannot have a *parterre.* In days not far removed from our own, a man was only called on to be brave and truthful—he might be as ferocious and voluptuous as he chose; therefore his common vices were ferocity and profligacy. Women are commonly trained even now to believe that so long as they are "virtuous," it is not requisite that they shall be sincere and magnanimous; therefore their common defects are insincerity and meanness.

Isolind Atheling was free by nature and training from these defects. She had all the purity of a woman, all the magnanimity of a noble-souled man. So she went through life bright, clear, and free; infusing an ideal purpose and beauty into the most ordinary domestic duties; full of faith in the present and hope for the future; always with a soul for every great cause, and a heart for the slightest enjoyments. She thus extracted unconsciously from life nearly all the good and the joy it can well be made to give.

This morning, after the night described in the last chapter, she rose early as usual, and set about her various domestic duties of order and arrangement. But somehow her heart was hardly as much in her work as it ought to be. Everything looked a little dull, almost uninteresting. A vague, restless, strange sensation was in the girl's heart; a sensation of craving, of mingled pain and pleasure, of dread and longing, which had kept with her through all the night, through all her dreams; which awoke with her now in the morning, which she shrank from openly confronting and examining, and would not have dared even to attempt translating into verse. Eyes noble and gentle seemed to look into hers in vain; a sweet deep voice was in her ears; the thrill of a hand, touched but for a moment, was still on hers.

She was restless; and when breakfast was over and the time allowed her, she strayed out into the grove behind the house; the grove in which the orange and purple and crimson tints of the fall were already beginning to gladden, or perhaps, as Isolind now thought, to sadden the scene. She had still the flower in her hand which she had received from the old gardener, and she inhaled its perfume with delight.

"What a world of thought, of rapture, of hope, and passion, and joy is in fragrance!" the young poetess said within herself. "The scent of this flower opens up a whole new world to the senses and the soul, as the microscope and the telescope do to the eye and the intellect! I have only to smell this leaf and I pass into a land of magic, where everything is rich, aromatic, and delightful; where every yearning finds an answer, and every dreamy hope becomes a beautiful reality. It is like the mysterious ointment in the Arabian story, which rubbed upon the eyes made one to see all the riches of the earth stored together. Nay, this flower is better; for it makes me mistress for the moment of all the riches and the rare delights which the earth has not, and can never have. Now I withdraw it; and I come back to the real world out of my perfumed palace of imagination. Poor little flower! poor little talisman, that opens the wonder-world! it seems a pity to throw it away, even though it already wilts and droops. Can it not give so much joy then, and live too?—I am growing sentimental," she said suddenly to herself; and she smiled not over brightly, and threw the flower away.

At that moment she heard the step of some one coming through a little opening among the trees to the path on which she was walking; and she started, and did not dare to look round, but she felt that despite of herself her pulses were beating fast, and her cheek was growing crimson.

Some one picked up her rejected flower and stood before her, hat in hand. Her face underwent a sudden change, from agitating hope and fear to blank disappointment, and then to displeasure; for it was the portly figure of Chesterfield Jocelyn which approached her—it was his aquiline nose, his thick full beard, his dark eyes, his white, fat, ring-bedizened fingers on which she looked.

"Good-morning, dear young lady! How strangely, doubly fortunate I have been! I took the liberty of entering my distinguished friend Atheling's grounds in the hope that I might meet the honored Judge or his dear wife; and I have now the yet greater pleasure of meeting you, and the rare happiness to secure this little fragrant memorial which you had thrown away. 'Dearer is the withered flower which has been worn and thrown aside'; is there not a ballad in that strain? I am indeed somewhat of a musician myself, but I take perhaps a more ambitious range than that of the ballad; and I ought almost to apologize for mentioning a trivial ballad to so accomplished an artist as yourself, who doubtless delight in the lofty and classical music."

Hospitality's sacred laws compelled Isolind to be civil; and perhaps she was a little penitent for her demeanor of the previous night towards Mr. Jocelyn. So when he approached she held out her hand, which he took with a bow such as a courtier might have made to an empress, and she constrained herself to endure his compliments with a smile.

"Indeed, Mr. Jocelyn," she answered, "I cannot pretend to call myself a musician; I have had hardly any scientific training, and have picked up much of what I do know in rather a scrambling sort of way. I am very fond of ballad-music, and rather prefer, generally, to sing without any instrumental accompaniment."

"Surely there is no music more delightful than the simple melody which seems to speak out the soul! May I hope to have at some happy moment the extreme delight of hearing you sing in your own favorite strain?"

"You would hardly care for it, Mr. Jocelyn; I may assure you without affectation. I often sing of evenings to please my people; they are no musicians, and it gives them pleasure; but you would care nothing for it. No, no; indeed I don't want a compliment."

She checked him good-humoredly, for she feared that he was about to say something meant to be delightful.

"I know, since last night, your hatred of compliments. You think they are only fit to flatter weak and foolish men?"

He spoke now in an altered tone; quite grave and calm.

"I do, Mr. Jocelyn."

"And you are right, Miss Atheling. When I spoke to you at first, I addressed you in the common jargon that men use to women. I soon saw that it was not fitted for a woman like you; and I ask your pardon, and will address such language to you no more."

"Why address it to any woman? Why thus help to foster in them the weakness and folly you condemn? Why not help them to prove that they have souls, by addressing them as creatures with souls, like men?"

"Miss Atheling, it is the common curse of our social system, that men and women seldom look at each other except through masks. Once in a life or so we meet with some being whose very glance bids us to stand up, be truthful, and put our masks away. *You* wear no mask; let me, in your presence, remove mine."

Assuredly nothing could be more complete than the change his whole manner, almost his very appearance, had undergone. Instead of the fat voluptuary with the fribble manner and the sinister expression whom she had seen the previous night, there now stood by her a strong and earnest man with a look almost of sadness on his calm dark face.

They were slowly walking along the broad path under the trees.

Jocelyn looked gravely into her face and said:

"When you saw me first, Miss Atheling, you disliked and distrusted me?"

Quite taken by surprise, Isolind frankly answered:

"I did indeed, Mr. Jocelyn. I beg your pardon for allowing any such hasty impression to show itself."

"Ask for no pardon, make no apology; the impression, sudden as it was, does you only credit. You thought I was playing a part?"

"I did."

"You were right; I *was* playing a part."

Isolind drew back, quite amazed at this unexpected revelation. She looked into his face; it was earnest, composed, apparently quite sincere. She was almost utterly puzzled, and hardly knew how to take so odd and embarrassing a confidence.

"Why tell this to me? why speak to me at all of this?" she asked at last.

"There are reasons, Miss Atheling, as strong as they are strange. Your face is one which speaks to me as none other on earth could do. Now don't start, and draw back, and look displeased! Nothing is farther from me now than the thought of paying you any idle compliment. Your face is the very face of one I shall never see more, but which is made sacred by memories and associations that are laws and gospel to me. You think I am talking wildly? Then look at that picture."

He drew from his pocket a case containing a photograph—or rather, indeed, a daguerreotype, of the fashion of twenty years since—and handed it to Isolind. She took it mechanically, almost unconsciously; but the moment she looked at it her eyes lighted up with wonder.

"Why do you look surprised?" he asked.

"Because at the first glance I thought it was a photograph of myself! And even still—although as I look at it closely I do not now see that there are differences—it seems quite wonderful. At first I might almost have thought I was looking into a little mirror! Mr. Jocelyn this is quite astonishing! Whose portrait is this?"

"Don't ask me that," he answered sadly; at least, just yet. The memories, and still more the doubts, it brings back are too painful. I show it to you, that you may be the better able to understand and appreciate the nature of the impulse which commands me to be sincere to *you*, and to try to serve you. This much you will own, that the impression produced on me by your likeness to that photograph was no mere phantasy."

"Indeed, I have never seen anything more surprising—it is quite a wonderful likeness. Yet it is a sad face, I think; and I, Mr. Jocelyn, have never had any cause to be sad. So far it is not like me."

"Hers was a sad life; and it stamped itself on her face. Is it not a beautiful face?"

Isolind blushed and smiled.

"I hardly know how to answer the question, Mr. Jocelyn. I hope it is very beautiful, as it is like me; although of course one knows perfectly well that there can be a decided likeness between a face which is really beautiful and one which is not so. Frankly, then, that does seem to me a beautiful face, although it is like mine. Her life was a sad one?"

"Very sad. Her whole history was sad; and it bequeathed to some others, Miss Atheling, the memories of repentance and remorse which cannot die! Can you wonder, that when I look into your face it becomes consecrated to me."

Isolind was a poetess; and in any case she had, like most girls who are worth anything, a deep suffusion of the romantic in her character. She was touched by the apparent depth and sincerity of Jocelyn's emotion, as well as by the halo of melancholy mystery that now seemed to surround him; and she silently held out her hand, which he pressed in his.

"The resemblance is all the more strange to me," said Jocelyn meditatively, after a moment of silence, "because there can hardly be any relationship, unless the most distant possible, between your family and hers. She was an Englishwoman who had never been out of her own country; your family have been for a long time settled in America?"

"For several generations."

"And came originally from Devonshire?"

"I believe so."

"Yes; Judge Atheling has told me so. She was of Irish rather than English extraction. Yet I cannot believe that this wonderful resemblance is wholly the work of chance. At least, Miss Atheling, I claim that it gives me a sacred right to be your friend and to serve you."

He laid so much emphasis on the word "serve," now introduced into the conversation by him for the second time, that Isolind could not but notice it.

"To serve me, Mr. Jocelyn? You are very kind; but I need no service."

"Don't be too certain, Miss Atheling. I speak to you as I speak to no mortal. I am a man much abused by the world; partly because I have been very successful, partly—I don't deny it—because I have been somewhat unscrupulous. I have sought excitement; I have sought to drive away the memories of a deeply-repented wrong in success. My waters of oblivion have been the wild waves of speculative struggle; and woe to the weaker swimmer—I own it—who has ventured to be my rival! You are shocked at me?"

"O Mr. Jocelyn, if you have suffered and are full of regrets—and I do most earnestly believe it!—why not seek peace and atonement where alone such blessings can be found—in striving to be good to others? Forgive me if I talk to you thus; I am no preacher, only an ignorant girl. But you have great gifts; you have made great successes. Why not consecrate those gifts to some noble end, and thus find happiness most surely?"

Poor earnest Isolind! There were tears in her deep lustrous eyes, and she gently laid one hand on his—her slender white hand, bare of all adornment, on his fat white hand glittering with rings. Jocelyn looked down, and perhaps was a little struck by the contrast. Possibly it occurred to him that romantic repentance and remorse did not look quite in keeping with such an overload of brilliants. At all events, he gently withdrew his own hand and thrust it into his breast.

"Miss Atheling, no word of yours, believe me, is lost on me. But there is a destiny in things sometimes against which the strongest of us struggles in vain. Perhaps such a destiny has brought me here—no matter! Let me now come to the point. I spoke of serving you, and my words had meaning. Miss Atheling, your father has become suddenly fascinated with one of my schemes, and means to risk nearly all his fortune in it. You know what a risk that is; and you must prevent him from attempting such a step."

"But, Mr. Jocelyn, I am powerless in such a case; I know nothing of the matter, and could not understand it probably; and he is no wild speculator, but a man of ability and clear intelligence, singularly unavaricious and unselfish. Anything he does must have good reason to support it. What could I say to dissuade him, I who know nothing?"

"You know (I saw it in half an hour) that he is enthusiastic, impulsive, credulous, always athirst for new ideas. Now, Miss Atheling, this great new enterprise of mine counts for comparatively little with me. Should it utterly fail, it is but one ship gone down; the very *éclat* of failure would be a sort of new splendor for me. In this country, to have one's name loudly trumpeted in any way is a guarantee of success to one who makes enterprise his occupation, as I do. But Atheling would be swallowed up in the wreck, never to emerge again. To him, a childlike sensitive man, the very failure would be a crushing calamity and disgrace, from which he could never recover; to me it will be an exciting incident, a piquant episode, a sensation."

Isolind shuddered.

"Is this, then, man's pastime?" she asked.

"This is to some men what the "noble game of war"—so Napoleon called it, regretfully, in his exile—is to others. To me it is the noble game of war

I do not spare myself, nor others usually; but, Miss Atheling, I would spare your father."

"Then why do you not yourself dissuade him? why did you lead him on?"

"I did not purposely lead him on; I explained my project to him and to Vansiedler; and as I went on I warmed naturally to its advantages and its temptations; and he became fascinated. Dissuade him now I cannot, he would not believe me; he would think I was but endeavoring to get rid of him in favor of some one else: and besides, Miss Atheling, I cannot, I dare not—at least, I *will* not—publicly disclaim and discredit my own enterprise. No; there are others and other interests involved to which I must be true. The general may allow one raw recruit to be privately warned against the forlorn hope, but he must not openly repudiate the movement he himself has ordered."

"Then, Mr. Jocelyn, what can *I* do?"

"Simply ask of him, beg of him, that he will undertake no speculation—with *me* if you wish to put it so. Give him no reason; let him think it womanly weakness, or girlish fear, if he will; only prevail upon him. You can do anything with him; do this, and save him."

"Is the enterprise then hopeless? May it not prove a success?"

"It may; but I begin to doubt it. This very morning, before you were awake probably, I have had telegrams in cipher which are ominous. Don't ask me for any more explanations—I have already done for you what I have never done for a mortal; but be you prompt and save *him*. Think of me, if you will, as a brigand who had some good qualities in him—as a filibuster not wholly without honor, pity, or hope. Think of me, in any case, Miss Atheling, as your devoted friend, who claims a right he cannot *yet* explain—cannot *yet*, I say, explain—to be your friend and to serve you. Hush! somebody is coming. You see, Miss Atheling, what it is to be an early riser, and what an advantage it gives even to a grim and grizzled old cavalier like myself over a brilliant youth like our friend Mr. Volney here! For shame, Mr. Volney, to be anticipated on this beautiful morning by one of my age, and, alas that I must add it! of my weight."

It was Angelo Volney who now approached. He had (doubtless with love's light wings) o'erperched the wall which divided Mr. Vansiedler's land from Atheling's, and he had been wandering through the trees, disturbing the squirrels, in the hope, unexpressed even to himself, of meeting Isolind Atheling.

None of the party but Mr. Jocelyn retained even the semblance of self-composure. Angelo was vexed and disappointed to find Isolind in company with Jocelyn, and his vexation and disappointment had surprise added when he observed, as he could not fail to do, her evident agitation. Her cheeks were flushed, her hand which she held out to Volney was trembling, she kept her eyes down, her whole demeanor was that of one disturbed and distressed.

Jocelyn looked perfectly serene and smiling. He was once more quite the Jocelyn of the previous night, and he flourished a dainty cambric handkerchief with pompous action, and he ostentatiously flashed his diamonds and rubies in the sunlight of the autumnal morning.

"It would be quite unpardonable in me," said the bland Jocelyn, "to monopolize any longer so charming a companion. Mr. Volney, I yield my place, gracefully, I hope, if not quite without reluctance! May I pursue my way to the house, Miss Atheling, and seek for my esteemed friend, your distinguished father?"

Isolind bowed assent. She was too confused to speak.

"Should I fail to find him there, you will not perhaps forget, Miss Atheling, the message you were kind enough to undertake?"

She raised her eyes till they met his, and she said, still looking earnestly at him, "I shall not forget it, Mr. Jocelyn. But we shall meet again to-day, I hope?"

"Need I say that the hope is echoed by me? In fact by a whole tumult of echoes, like that of the Lurleiberg! Meanwhile allow me to offer my thanks for your exceeding courtesy, and to wish you a good-morning."

He bowed profoundly to Isolind, less profoundly to Volney; then turned and sauntered away.

"I have hardly had time to speak to you, Mr. Volney," said Isolind, making a brave effort to recover her composure, and greeting Angelo with a smile of unmistakable sincerity and welcome. "It is very kind of you to come to see us. Will you walk to the house?—this way."

"Thank you, I shall be very happy. But is not Mr. Jocelyn going that way just now?"

"He is going to make a call. But let us walk more slowly, if you like. Or will you allow me to show you our garden, if you don't care to meet Mr. Jocelyn again just now? I know you are not one of Mr. Jocelyn's admirers."

"Nor are you, Miss Atheling, I fancy. Only last night at least you warned *me* against him."

"And I do still, Mr. Volney—I do still indeed, and most earnestly; although I believe now that there is more of good in him than I then thought. Then indeed I knew nothing of him."

She stopped somewhat confused, afraid she had said too much.

"And now, Miss Atheling?"

"Now, I know little more. But I have been talking with him. I met him here this morning by chance, just as I have met you" (Angelo, it may be noted, looked a little confused at this); "and he has convinced me that although he is a dangerous man, he has some truth and generosity in him."

"He seems to have alarmed you a little," said Angelo boldly

"Perhaps he did, without meaning it—at least he surprised me. There is a mystery about him which I don't pretend to understand; but I believe there is good in him."

"Miss Atheling, I have no right to ask you any questions; but I do wish you could give me any hint as to the identity of this man. I have a purpose in asking—a serious, earnest purpose."

She opened her eyes in wonder.

"More mysteries, Mr. Volney! You too! Have you then any knowledge of this Mr. Jocelyn?"

"None—that is, no certain knowledge. But I have some suspicions."

"Have you?" she asked quite eagerly. "Can you tell me what they are? I have a deep interest in knowing."

He shook his head.

"I cannot indeed. They are as yet too vague; but I had some hope that——'

"That I might help you out with my revelations, and have no satisfaction for my own curiosity, Mr. Volney! Come now, was that fair—and to a woman, too? O no; honorable exchange of ideas, or nothing."

And Isolind smiled, and endeavored to treat the whole question as a laughing matter.

"But then," Angelo pleaded, "you began by warning me against him—and you must have known something. So you have tempted me to ask for your reason."

"Ask a woman for a reason! Do the women, then, give reasons in England? Women are free here, Mr. Volney, I warn you; and we give no reasons. Why may I not have had an instinct warning me against Mr. Jocelyn?"

"And why, then, may not mine too be an instinct?"

"Nonsense! men don't have instinctive beliefs. Anything they believe they have some sort of reason for. The gift of divination is denied to them. The oracles were women, were they not?"

"Yes; and therefore they were not dumb."

"But very doubtful sometimes! Seriously, Mr. Volney, it is a very strange thing that you and I, who never met hardly until yesterday, should be both vexed by a vague sense of mystery about a man whom neither of us ever saw until last night. I would freely tell you what he said to me if it were mine to tell, and if it would avail you to know. But it could not: it only affects others."

"And it has changed your opinion of him?"

"In a certain sense it has. I still fear him, Mr. Volney, and I don't understand him—and I still warn *you* against him, as I would warn any friend. Keep away from his schemes, and even from himself! He is a dangerous man. But he has done me a service; he has some good in him; and he professes to be my friend—for a strange reason, and yet not a reason difficult to understand. There! I have already said too much. Don't tempt me to say any more."

"Miss Atheling, distrust that man, and don't believe in his pretence of friendship, or of services! My life on it, he is playing a part for some evil purpose. Don't think me rash or wild in saying this—your own instincts already said the same to you. If he is the person I begin to suspect, he has been guilty of the base betrayal of one who is as dear to me as my own mother could be—one who is as noble a woman as ever lived!"

Isolind started and flushed. Why, these words spoken by the excited young man at her side did indeed confirm and tally with the vague hints and half-confessions let fall by Jocelyn!

"Mr. Volney," she said, interrupting him, "I fear you are already prepared to find an enemy in this man. I don't pretend even to guess how far your conjectures may be justified; but I would beg of you more than ever to avoid him. Men may have done great evil and repented. He may be one such."

"Then you *do* know something of him?"

"Oh, pray don't press me—indeed I know nothing more than the vaguest hints and words could tell me. He gave me some advice—with a good motive, I fully believe."

"Don't trust him, Miss Atheling; look in his eyes and disbelieve him. I pledge my existence that there is in him nothing true—nothing that is not sinister and false!"

Angelo was as sincere and disinterested a young man as could easily be found in New York State or elsewhere, and he really believed that in speaking as he now did he was impelled only by a just distrust of Jocelyn. But it may be taken for granted that the sort of confidence which he perceived Jocelyn to have pressed upon Isolind, and still more the sort of qualified praise Isolind now bestowed upon the man, had a large share in embittering Angelo's distrust and dislike. He felt inclined to resent Jocelyn's attention to the girl; it angered him to see such a man endured in anything like companionship by her.

Perhaps it vaguely occurred to Isolind that there was a little of a personal and special warmth in Angelo's manner; for she endeavored, not without a dash of heightened color in her cheek, to put the whole discussion aside.

"Well, Mr. Volney, we are both forewarned—let us both be forearmed; but meanwhile we must not make too wonderful a mystery out of this Mr. Jocelyn. He will probably turn out a very commonplace sort of person after all. Bold and heedless speculators with rather odd antecedents are as common among us as fireflies in the summer evenings. How do you like our foliage? The tints will soon come out in glorious variety and richness. I believe you can boast of nothing like them in England."

"No, indeed; but forgive me, Miss Atheling, if I return to this man."

"Again this terrible Mr. Jocelyn! He is your *croquemitaine* apparently."

"You laugh, Miss Atheling, but you do not look as if you thought lightly of the matter. Let me beg of you to be careful how you admit that man to any confidence."

"Pray, Mr. Volney, don't speak to me as if I were a child and this personage a strolling gipsy with an eye to kidnapping. There is no danger to me; and I can take care of myself."

"You are offended with me because I have been presumptuous enough to offer you my advice?"

"No, not offended; but a little surprised perhaps at your urgency and earnestness."

"Because I feel convinced that this man is not what he represents himself to be, and that he has some sinister plan at present in his mind. Wait a few days—I only ask you to wait a few days—before you put any confidence in him."

"Mr. Volney," said Isolind gravely, "whatever may be the ground of your conjectures, I thank you sincerely for your interest in me. I am not offended by your advice; indeed I invited it by venturing first to offer you advice on the same subject. It is strange that we should be brought into this confidential relationship in such a way and on so short an acquaintance; but I tell you frankly that there is something in your face, your manner, your expression, which draws me into friendship with you, and makes me glad of your sympathy and believe in your goodness. Come, what would be said of one of your English girls who should make so unreserved an acknowledgment of sudden friendship? But as I have said so mnch, I need not be afraid to offend you if I say that we have warned each other enough against this mysterious personage, and made quite enough of mystery about him, and had better let him go his way for the rest."

Volney felt much flattered, and a little hurt. The frank acknowledgment of friendly regard was the salve to the little wound inflicted by Isolind's positive rejection of his further services as Mentor in the matter of Jocelyn. He could not help wondering within himself why the gentle words of Isolind hurt him, whom the wildest freak and the sharpest language of Alexia Scarlett never discomposed.

"I see that I *have* offended you," he said, in a low sad tone.

"Indeed no, you have not. I understand your kind purpose; I appreciate it; but—but, in short, Mr. Volney, let us talk of something else, something bright and pleasant."

Then they did talk of something, of many things bright and pleasant; and they seemed to forget that they were to go into the house. They walked up and down among the trees, and spoke of books and places and scenery, and American woods and lakes; and when Isolind earnestly urged him to hasten to Niagara, he felt pained as Longfellow's Paul Flemming did when Mary Ashburton advised him to leave Interlaken and speed on to Mont Blanc. For there seemed something unsympathetic, unkind, and almost cruel in thus pressing him to go away; to go and see any place, however glorious, where she was not to be. But they talked of other subjects, and Angelo forgot his pain, and thought he had never known so fresh a mind, so delightful a fancy, so pure and womanly a nature as that of the fair-haired girl into whose deep eyes he gazed. The sun came out brightly, and shone almost as warmly as the sun of early June in England. There was a fallen tree, and Isolind being a little fatigued sat upon it, and invited Angelo to rest there too. He sat there at her side, near to her, and the delicious moments went by. On her face there was now no shadow of embarrassment. She talked as freely as if they had been friends for years; her eyes met his as frankly and fearlessly as though they were utter strangers brought together that moment by chance for the first time. Because she, at least, had as yet no perception of whither they two were certainly drifting. She only enjoyed the hour, the sunlight, the scene, the conversation; was happy and not afraid. But in Angelo's heart was already some tremor, some conflict of delight and pain. For he could not deceive himself any longer, or doubt the reality and the meaning of the emotions which were rising within him. Their very strangeness compelled a recognition of them. What was this wild, ecstatic, terrible emotion, which he had never felt before? What should it be—what could it be but love? Yes, he knew it—he was in love with Isolind Atheling! And he remembered the pledge he had given to Alexia Scarlett's mother—to her who had been his benefactress, who had lifted him from hunger and misery, who had held him in her heart, and had asked him—as the sole return he could make for such boundless beneficence—to become the husband of her daughter.

CHAPTER X.

YOUR DUCATS, AND MY DAUGHTER.

CHESTERFIELD JOCELYN, or the person thus called, had begun life with brilliant talents, a fierce, energetic, animal nature, and an unscrupulous will. He employed many of his early years in gratifying every desire just as it rose; and his principal desires were three: women, the spending of money, and incessant occupation. He had a nature so restless in its fierce vitality that he must always be doing something or striving for something. At a critical period he played for high stakes, and lost. There lay before him the choice of three courses: utter disgrace and social annihilation, suicide, or escape into an entirely new career.

He chose the last. He flung himself into the seething, fierce current of speculation in America, and he gave full vent to all his physical and mental energies there. It pleased him to obtain the stamp of a distinct individuality; and whereas in his younger days, living amid the most polished society of the Old World, he had been noted for a certain *farouche* roughness of manner, he took on him in New York and California the antiquated and florid politeness which soon procured for him the nickname of "Chesterfield." Perhaps he thought such a style might help him to win many a game of speculation, by disguising his real force of character among a class and in places where energy and intellectual strength are almost always rugged in their expression. Of course he had strong reasons for wishing to conceal his identity and to sever himself from his

HE SAT THERE AT HER SIDE, NEAR TO HER, AND THE DELICIOUS MOMENTS FLEW BY.—p. 86.

former career. Possibly, as he must always be doing something, he enjoyed this continuous playing of a part. Perhaps all three reasons combined. Anyhow, he did play the part, and "Chesterfield Jocelyn" became, in his way, a famous sort of personage. He was a man to know, a man to dine with, to boast of having dined with. People were fond of saying "Chesterfield Jocelyn has been telling me," or "I dined with Chesterfield Jocelyn yesterday," or "I have just been introducing our friend somebody or other to Chesterfield Jocelyn." Jocelyn was an authority on dinners, on wine, on the points of horses, the limbs of the ballet, as well as the many and more serious branches of practical knowledge we have already indicated. In his peculiar way he was a marvellous success. His hands were always full, his mind was always on the stretch; his name was always on people's lips and in the newspaper paragraphs of a country where journalists think nothing beneath their notice which concerns the private interests of humanity. A very moderate celebrity in America is enough to secure to one the pleasure or pain of seeing a reference to himself and his affairs at least once a day in the newspapers. The name of Chesterfield Jocelyn might have been "kept standing," as the printers say, so constantly did it make its appearance in the columns of the American journals.

Yet Chesterfield Jocelyn was not happy. Men who have suffered poverty in their early days are sometimes kept miserable even in boundless wealth by the dread of a possible return to penury; the man who gratifies himself by playing the spendthrift in youth not uncommonly gratifies himself by playing the miser in old age. So, or in some such fashion, Jocelyn had begun of late to be tortured by a perpetual dread of failure and want of money. Like Will Watch, the bold smuggler, and other familiar heroes of the nautical ballad, he was always of recent years making up his mind that he would accomplish some grand success, and then leave the stormy sea of speculation forever, coil up his hopes, and cast anchor on shore. More than that, he began to weary of, to sicken of, to hate the life he had been leading. Cavour used to say that the Austrians never settled in Venetia, but only encamped there. Jocelyn certainly never settled in America, he only encamped there; that anatomical structure which he called his heart was far away. It spoke highly for the force of the man's intellect, the power of his self-control, that for so many years he had lived thus bold, bustling, careless, apparently joyous, revelling in the most audacious freedom of speculation—ordering and helping to eat good dinners; a familiar figure in Wall street, New York, and California street, San Francisco; and likewise in the theatres, green-rooms, and first-class restaurants of both cities—while all the time he was gnawing his heart away with bitter, vain longing for the scenes and the society of his earlier life. Never did Parisian *flâneur* more dearly love the Boulevards of his lifelong affection, never did Boston *bel esprit* cherish in fonder veneration the sacred city of Massachusetts, than Chesterfield Jocelyn adored the home and the haunts of his early manhood, where he had been so happy and so wretched, so gay and sinful and brutal, and from which he now saw himself exiled. It is only bare justice to Jocelyn to say that he never in his life gave way to any pang of feeling for any human creature but himself; and yet there was something almost sentimental, touching, tender, poetic, in his yearning for the paradise of brick and stucco, clubs and lobbies, dinners and divisions, from which he had so long been banished. Alas, we can none of us be perfect; and in the magnificent Napoleonic splendor of Jocelyn's selfishness there was one dim spot—the weakness of his longing for his native place. The robber or murderer who escapes from prison is seized sometimes with this unconquerable longing; he creeps of nights back to the pot-house of his early affections, to the *chère amie* whose eyes he blackened just before his incarceration; and the police, knowing his fatal weakness, seek him there and find him.

There were times when Jocelyn felt tempted to run this risk.

At this moment, however, his attention was distracted by two or three heterogeneous schemes. He had brought nearly to the verge of success a project of marriage with a widow of enormous wealth, when he chanced to fall in with the Athelings. For reasons which readers will probably guess, and which in any case will appear clearly hereafter, he had been thrown into wild surprise by the face of Isolind Atheling; and when, the first shock of this surprise over he got time to think more calmly, he resolved that it would be essential for him to obtain if possible a strong control over the mind of the girl. The Athelings were rich, and she would doubtless be their heiress; and supposing that a certain wild conjecture he had formed should prove to be correct, their wealth might one day come into his hands. Supposing this conjecture to be merely wildness, it would still be possible to get hold of Atheling's money in the regular and legitimate way of speculation; and for this purpose too it would be necessary to have this girl, this favorite and spoiled child, on his side, or at least not against him.

Studying the girl's face and manner, taking into account her manifest dislike towards him, he came to the conclusion that her sympathies must be conquered by a *coup de main;* by some sudden and audacious appeal to the romantic side of her nature. Mr. Jocelyn was proud—among many other sources of pride rather especially proud—of his knowledge of woman. He had studied the subject closely, long, and in every possible light, and he flattered himself that there was, to use his own phrase, not a turn in a woman that he did not understand. He had not the faintest possible prejudice for or against virtue, and therefore he was quite ready to do justice even to good women; and he was utterly above the weakness of many men somewhat akin to him in nature, which leads them to assume that all women are bad. Mr. Jocelyn was entirely selfish, but he was not by any means an egotist. He was quite aware that there were natures unlike his, and he was willing to make allowance for and able to understand them. As he liked dry champagne and detested sweet, but yet was prepared to understand that other persons might honestly choose the latter, so he was fully aware that there were human beings, women more especially, to whom vice was really distasteful. Now he assumed that Isolind Atheling was a girl with a pure heart, and an unselfish and somewhat romantic nature; and it is but justice to him to say that he did not on that account cherish any prejudice against her. Of course in a companion such qualities as purity and virtue would be insufferable nuisances; but Chesterfield Jocelyn was growing more and more tolerant as regards the outer world, and he was prepared to live and let live. Even pure-minded girls might have their uses.

Therefore he determined to assail the generous and romantic side of Isolind's character, and we have seen how far he succeeded.

As regards Angelo Volney, Jocelyn had quite other purposes, less needing immediate concealment. He proposed to discover through him whether Charles Grey Scarlett still lived, and if so where; and whether one other being in whom likewise he had a deep interest, and whose reappearance just now would have been highly inconvenient, was also above the ground. If, however, Scarlett lived, and he, Jocelyn, could find him out, then revenge, revenge, above all considerations and at any risk. This man's nature had so much of the antique herc in it, that he would now at any moment surrender all dearest personal delights and burning ambitions for the sake of destroying his enemy. High above covetousness, and above lust, there ruled supreme in his nature the majesty of hate.

Jocelyn sauntered pleasantly and briskly away towards Atheling's house when he had left Isolind and Angelo together.

"That girl knows nothing about the matter," was his mental comment as he walked along, humming while he went an opera tune. While Jocelyn was thinking over any perplexing question he always kept humming an air—from the teeth outward. That is to say, his teeth were firmly closed, and gleamed through his dark beard and moustache, which were divided by his parted lips.

"*She* knows nothing about it. If any scheme has been going on, it would be useless to try to get at it through her. The thing looks preposterous, almost impossible—and yet such a likeness as that cannot mean nothing. I never saw a face and figure so like. She is a fine girl and a good girl; and yet by the Lord I could have hated her as she stood there, because she was so like that cursed woman! How do you do, my dear Judge? Delighted to see you. I trust your excellent wife is well, and that she enjoys this delicious morning."

The Judge advanced from the portico of the house, and held out to Jocelyn one big hand, while the wrist of the other formed a perch for his parrot. The dog was at his feet as usual; and the dog somehow did not appear to like Mr. Jocelyn, but showed his teeth and looked out of temper.

The Judge gave Jocelyn a warm and friendly greeting. The two men formed a curious contrast. Both were large and heavy, but there was gentle good-nature in every line of Atheling's soft, round, beardless face, in his twinkling blue eyes, in his infantile chin, in his ungainly form, in his sweet bright smile. Jocelyn's aquiline nose, dark-bearded face, and keen glowing eyes spoke of fierce energy kept steadily in check, and selfish passion hardly suppressed.

Atheling was an utterly unsuspicious man, and had already been effectively talked over by Jocelyn. It was easy enough for the latter to touch a soft place by descanting on the beauty and evident goodness of Miss Atheling. The Judge soon became eloquent, and Jocelyn now listened with an eager interest which he could hardly keep down.

"No man, Mr. Jocelyn, ever had so good a daughter, I verily believe; and let me whisper in your ear, sir—I don't want it talked about, because the dear girl herself does not know it—she is *not* our daughter."

Jocelyn and Atheling were sitting on the "stoop" of the house, overlooking the lawn, when these words were spoken. Not Hamlet himself, when the Ghost first confirms the awful suspicions of his prophetic soul, could have started with a more genuine pang of blended wrath and triumph than did Chesterfield Jocelyn when Atheling announced that Isolind was not his daughter. A flush deep as the color of old port-wine suffused his face; one great vein in his forehead swelled and became a rope of livid blue; his eyes were bloodshot. He sprang to his feet, and clutched Atheling's shoulder fiercely and feverishly.

"I knew it!" he exclaimed with a savage oath, all the long-stifled ferocity of his passion breaking out in one hideous imprecation; "I knew it from the first moment!"

"What in all the nation did you know, from the first or from the last?" asked Atheling, quite bewildered by Jocelyn's demeanor.

But Jocelyn broke away, and strode up and down the portico like one utterly driven beyond self-control. The dog—who disapproved of this proceeding, and evidently was disposed to construe Jocelyn's whole manner into a hostile demonstration against his master—growled so fiercely, and showed such an inclination for a sudden spring, that Atheling, as a measure of precaution, promptly stooped and seized him by the collar. There, then, sat the portly and fair-haired Judge, holding his angry dog with one hand and supporting his screaming parrot on the other; and gazing meanwhile with round blue eyes of utter wonder at Jocelyn's sudden and passionate outburst.

Jocelyn stopped at last, and confronting Atheling, said in a hoarse harsh tone:

"Judge Atheling, I want to have some talk with you in strict privacy."

"Why, we are private here. There is no one round."

"No, this won't do; somewhere in a room where we can lock the doors, and be alone and safe."

"Certainly. Come this way then, into my study."

Atheling led the way without further speech. Something now told him that he had to do with serious business. The fierce emotion of his companion was no longer visible, but there was no trace of the debonair and jaunty Chesterfield Jocelyn on that dark face. And as it darkened and gloomed, it seemed somehow to Atheling more and more as if old, vague, long-forgotten associations were coming back into life and settling round it. The heart of the good Judge beat violently, and his trembling hands betrayed his emotion. Where had he seen that fierce and scowling face before, and what had its owner to do with our Isolind?

"Now, sir," said the Judge as he entered the pleasant study, well lined with good old books and some good new ones, "we are quite private here."

As they passed through the hall Atheling had taken the precaution, necessary in the interests of peace and quietness, to put the loquacious parrot back into his cage. The dog, however, insisted on forcing his way into the study, and the Judge thought it hardly worth while to dispute the point. So the shaggy familiar entered the room and stretched himself on the hearth, carefully watching Jocelyn out of his blinking eyes, and apparently waiting confidently for the moment when it should become necessary for him to spring upon the ill-omened stranger.

The Judge pointed to a chair, and took one himself. Then he waited in silence for Jocelyn to speak.

"Mr. Atheling, I am not in a condition of mind for ceremony; I want to know where you found that girl."

"Meaning by 'that girl' our Isolind?"

"Where did you find her?"

The old shrewd professional instincts were still strong with the Judge, and before answering so direct a question he felt disposed to know the reason why. Examination of that sort brought him back to something like composure, as the old soldier becomes cool and self-possessed in the presence of the enemy.

"Mayn't I ask, Mr. Jocelyn, why you put the question, or what interest you can possibly have in the matter?"

"You shall be told, Judge, rely upon it," answered Jocelyn, with a savage smile. "An interest which you will hardly refuse to acknowledge. That girl is my daughter!"

And he dashed his hand so fiercely on the table that the dog thought the war-tocsin had sounded, the hour had come, and rose to his feet growling, to settle down again discomposed and disappointed after a moment.

To Atheling it seemed almost as if he had received a bullet in the head. It was a shock like that of being accused of murder or suddenly told of the death of some dearest creature—a shock bewildering and stupefying, unsettling all the regular conditions of things, not to be comprehended in its full force at the first. The fierce earnestness of Jocelyn's manner served so far to carry conviction with it that the Judge had to collect his senses before he quite remembered that such an assertion would have to be proved before it could be accepted.

"That girl, Mr. Atheling, is my daughter! I knew it the moment I saw her! She is the daughter of my runaway wife! I swear it. I can prove it. Tell me, sir, one word first, quickly and right out—is that infernal woman alive or dead?"

"What woman are you speaking of?"

The Judge was glad to seize upon the chance of asking a collateral question while preparing his mind to grapple with the main issue.

"Her mother—that girl's mother—the woman that once called herself my wife."

"Mr. Jocelyn, I hardly understand what you are talking about. Our Isolind has been always known to me only as an orphan. She never knew anything of her mother, nor do we. You say now she is your daughter. Are you serious in this? And have you any evidence whatever to offer in support of such an extraordinary assertion?"

"Where did you find this girl? Answer that."

"No, Mr. Jocelyn," and there was a slight evanescent revival of its pleasant habitual twinkling in the Judge's eye; "that is rather too much. I am now somewhat in the position of defendant in this action. I *have* our Isolind, and I want to keep her; and I mean to if I can. You claim her, and I tell you candidly that from what I have just seen of you you are by no means the sort of father to whose guardianship I could be glad to hand over my sweet girl. You may have some motive in all this that I cannot fathom, and I am not bound to supply you in advance with a stock of evidence. You must give me some reason to believe that there is anything serious or solid in your claim before I proceed even to reply to it."

"Too clever by half, Judge Atheling! Why fall back upon your pitiful country-lawyer tricks and dodges if you were not already afraid of your case? But you shall be convinced. First look at *that!*"

He took from his pocket and laid before Atheling the little portrait he had so lately shown to Isolind herself. The Judge adjusted his double eyeglass and attentively studied the face. There could be no doubt that the likeness to Isolind was something wonderful. It was indeed a paler and sadder Isolind—Isolind robbed of the glow of health and the free and noble outlines. It was Isolind's face painted by care and disappointment. It was the pallid ghost of Isolind. A sweet sad face, altogether unspeakably beautiful and pathetic. The Judge looked up from that face to the fierce, dark, selfish, scowling visage of the man before him; and he thought he could read *there* the explanation of the melancholy tale suggested by the picture.

"Do you see the likeness?" Jocelyn slowly asked.

"To Isolind? Oh, yes; it is beyond all denial or question. Whose face is this?"

"The face of her mother—of my fugitive wife."

All this time something of a painful recollection had been crystallizing itself into definite form in Judge Atheling's mind while he studied the expression on Jocelyn's face. Half unconsciously he said aloud:

"This, then, you tell me, is a likeness of Mrs. Jocelyn; but how am I to be satisfied?"

"I never said it was a likeness of Mrs. Jocelyn," the other replied, with a hard and scornful laugh. "I said it was a likeness of my wife. Give me the portrait"—he almost snatched it from Atheling's hands—"and I can show you name, and date, and place on the back, inside the case. My name is not Jocelyn, most learned Judge, any more than that girl's is Atheling."

"Stop!" exclaimed Atheling, rising abruptly from his seat, as a light of clear recollection broke in upon him. "Don't tell me who you are—you need not. I remember you now perfectly well, and I shall presently recollect your name. You are the man I saw in Westminster Hall, London, sixteen years ago—the man who struck Mr. Grey Scarlett! Your name is Dysart; and every one said even then that you were an infernal scoundrel."

"I don't care for your coarse language, Judge Atheling—your age saves you from the chastisement which you say you saw me give to Scarlett. I am Thomas Thynne Dysart, and I am, if you like to have it so, a refugee here from the criminal law of England. I am not the only one in New York, Judge, whose antecedents are not pleasant or inviting to look into. Only for one cursed mistake, I might have held up my head still among gentlemen of my own set in my own country, and not be driven to associate with cads in this. But I am also—and this is what concerns you, Judge Atheling, my venerable friend—the husband of the woman whose likeness is there, and the father of the girl you have adopted as a daughter."

The perspiration stood in great beads upon Atheling's forehead, and his hands trembled and shook with agitation. Perhaps Virginius felt hardly a deeper shock of agony when his daughter was claimed as the child of a slave than Atheling now felt when our Isolind, the darling and pride of the house, was claimed as the offspring of this acknowledged swindler and forger, this outcast of European society, this scandal of England, who stood and scowled before him.

Innocence and truth, we are told in most good books, invariably stand up firm and fearless in the presence of guilt. You may know the one from the other, if such evidence be needed, by the proud and upright port of the innocent, the drooping head and trembling nerves of the guilty. Just so! Mr. Atheling—who never wronged mortal in all his life—was now crimson, perspiring, quivering; while Jocelyn or Dysart was composed, cool, ferocious, absolutely, to all appearance, master of the situation.

"Mr.—a—a—Dysart," Atheling began.

"Call me Jocelyn, Judge! I still prefer to be Edwin Dare Jocelyn, if you please. Under that name I retrieved myself—so far as I could retrieve myself in this cursed country—and I choose to keep it. Tom Thynne Dysart is dead and buried. I myself prepared his obituary, and I don't care to have him revived. If I am to claim my daughter, I suppose she would hardly desire to have her father adorned with Tom Dysart's antecedents."

"Well, then, Mr. Jocelyn, you know of course that there must be some proof of this."

"You shall have proof enough, man, crammed down your throat. But you must yourself lend a helping hand. You must tell me everything about your finding this girl. I presume the excellent and virtuous Judge Atheling does not mean to juggle a father out of his child by withholding information that might help to establish her identity? No, Judge; you and I will lay our heads together, and compare dates and facts, and we shall find proof enough. We don't want the strawberry mark on the right arm in this case. You admit that this girl is not your daughter. I say she is mine, stolen from me by a false woman and a hypocritical scoundrel. My daughter was two years old when I lost her; this girl must have been just about that age at that time. I produce that likeness of my wife, and I say there is no man or woman living who would not admit the wonderful resemblance to your adopted daughter. Come, Judge, there is what I may literally call a *prima-facie* case. Out with the whole story, and let me embrace my daughter."

"Poor mother!" murmured Atheling. "This will be a heavy blow for her."

Jocelyn caught the word "mother," and his face again became purple with excitement.

"Did you speak of her mother?" he cried. "You do then know something about that woman, although you pretended a moment ago that you knew nothing! Come, then, tell me all about her; let us have the truth at last!"

"I know nothing, sir, about your unhappy wife; and if I did know anything, you could not bully me into betraying her to you. I hope and believe the poor woman is in heaven. I was thinking of my own wife, who loves our dear Isolind as if she were her own daughter, and to whom this story of yours will be a bitter blow if it prove true. I say if it prove true, Mr. Jocelyn, or whatever you choose to call yourself; because your antecedents hardly entitle you to expect that anything whatever could be credited on your word alone."

"You are talking foolishly, Judge. Don't you perceive that the worse you make me out to be, the greater shame you bring on my daughter?"

Jocelyn said this with a contemptuous sneer.

"I do indeed perceive it! My poor dear Isolind!—the purest, sweetest, most sensitive creature in all the world—what a cruel fate for her! May God pity her and avert this blow! My sweet Isolind! *You* will think me very weak, Mr. Jocelyn; and you are free to laugh, if you like; but that girl has been to my wife and to me the best daughter a home ever had; she has been the brightness and the happiness of our lives: often and often have we said that Heaven had sent her specially to be the stay and comfort of our old age, in the place of the child—the one only child—of our own love, whom Heaven saw fit to take from us when we were young. We have sometimes wondered how we could endure it when the time should come to part with her to some loving husband worthy of her; and now—and now!"

The Judge was tramping heavily up and down the room, his lips and hands quivering with excitement. He had to take off his spectacles and to wipe the moistened glasses, for a mist was rising before his eyes.

Jocelyn bore all this very patiently. Assuredly he thought Atheling a very silly old man; but he knew that there were many silly and affectionate people in the world, and it was convenient for him, rather than otherwise, that the Judge should prove to be one of them.

Atheling suddenly stopped in his walk, as if some new thought had occurred to him; and, pausing in the rubbing of his spectacles, addressed Jocelyn in a tone which, for Atheling, was almost fierce.

"Suppose your conjecture, or whatever it is, should prove true—suppose this sweet child should turn out, unhappily, to be your daughter—what then?"

"Then of course, Judge, I should claim my child."

"Is it 'of course'? Do you really mean to claim her? Are you a man to care for playing the genuine part of a father?"

Jocelyn laughed and stroked his beard.

"You are pretty shrewd, Mr. Atheling, for all your simplicity. You don't think I am a sort of man to be troubled with much paternal feeling, or to relish being hampered with parental responsibilities. Well, Judge, you are about right in that. I don't mind being quite frank with you. I have not one gleam of that sort of feeling. I am perfectly certain that that girl is my daughter, and I have in fact better reason for believing her so than many fathers, whose conjugal relations seem absolutely perfect, have perhaps for the same sort of belief. Yet I really don't love the girl particularly—I don't in fact care one cent about her—and it would never disturb my sleep if I were not to see her again. You shudder, Judge; but you are such an exemplary person."

"Then if this is so—and I can almost believe it of you now—why do you raise the question at all?"

"First, because the girl is my child—mine, a part of my property, out of which no one shall cheat me. Tell me, Judge, do you think I cared for her mother—my wife? Not I. I married her for her money, which I spent; for some family influence which I supposed her to have, and which she had not; and of late I hated the very sight of her. Yet I pursued the man who carried her off, and I would have hunted him to the very death. I will do so yet if he be living! So, if this girl is mine, no one shall keep her from me without my consent. Next, I hope to obtain some advantage by means of her."

"Then I am to understand, Mr. Jocelyn, that you are open to negotiations in this business?"

"Certainly! I am quite open to negotiation. You say, you and your wife are fond of this girl, that she has twined herself round your heart-strings, and all that sort of thing. Your object, I suppose, is to keep her as a daughter still. I have none of those tender feelings; perhaps a daughter just now would be in the way, rather than otherwise. I have other objects, Judge; and in these you must give your full coöperation. That is my price."

"Suppose I denounce you as an escaped swindler and forger—as Thomas Dysart, once of London, who escaped transportation by flight?"

"Who would listen, Judge, or care, except my daughter?—who is sensitive, as you say, and would feel disgraced. Your treaty of extradition does not touch me. And who in Wall street, New York, or California street, San Francisco, would care one curse for anything I may have done, or have been charged with doing, more than fifteen years ago? Judge, you are a baby! Don't you see that if anything is to be told, all must be told? If I am a swindler, then our Isolind, as you call her—where the devil did you get that absurd name?—is a swindler's daughter."

Atheling again strode up and down the room.

"Let us come to an ultimatum, Judge. I will claim that girl, and make her miserable, unless *you* can tempt me to leave her unclaimed and happy. Don't make any mistake about *me*. I am in every way what people like you would call a bad man. I could not, even if I tried, care for anybody but myself. I never had any kind of feeling but one towards women—except, indeed, for my wife, whom I hated. Think, then, whether I am likely to make my daughter happy."

"What do you want me to do, supposing I should consent to debase myself for my darling Isolind's sake and her happiness—to debase myself by entering into a shameful compromise with you? What would you have?"

"First, your aid, comfort, and coöperation in certain schemes I shall more fully unfold to you. I think I can realize something splendid, if I only have enough of the sinews of war to begin the battle. I want your moral coöperation, as well as your material aid, venerated Judge. You must lend me the weight of your good character. I did at first think of drawing you in by the ordinary baits; and I may as well confess to you that I tried a little device on 'our Isolind' of rather an ingenious and brilliant kind for the same purpose, or, perhaps, I should rather say, for the purpose of having two strings to my bow. But I did not then know that I was so near to getting a firm hold of your heart-strings, my dear and venerable friend. I had then only had my mind perplexed by a vague and almost impossible conjecture. I had not then learned from your own lips that this girl was not your daughter, or your wife's. Now I think finesse a waste of time; and I merely propose to dictate terms. Judge, you must risk your money and your name with me as I shall direct."

"And in return for all this? If I do, in my old age and my weakness, consent to hold terms with villany, if I do sell my soul, what am I to have in return?"

"Your Isolind, Judge, to be still your daughter—at least until she gets married, which must not be, let me tell you quietly, without my full approval; because it is of the utmost importance to me—or it may be so—that my son-in-law should be a man of credit and substance. In plain words, although you and I will still consult and concert with each other privately regarding my daughter's future, I will make no claim to her filial affection, nor ever obtrude myself upon her notice. Atheling" (and here Jocelyn's half-sneering manner suddenly changed again into sternness and ferocity), "If you do love that girl really, then save her at all cost from being associated with me. For it may be that the blood of her mother's paramour—the blood even of the false mother herself—may yet be on these hands."

"Mr. Jocelyn," said the Judge, "I do you the credit of saying that I did not think earth contained so utter a villain, so remorseless and base a scoundrel. I would even gladly think, for the credit of human nature, that your words are extravagant, and that bad as you may be in heart, you are not so utterly depraved."

"Think nothing of the kind, Atheling. I have played the hypocrite so long, that it is a positive relief, a kind of joy, to speak out the full truth to you—as a fellow who has been long compelled to keep sober against his will finds a delight in getting madly drunk on the first opportunity. I tell you, man, I have neither pity, nor scruple, nor fear! My father was the worst profligate of his day, and I have seen him horsewhip his second wife, my stepmother—and I was devilish glad to see it, too! They say his father was rather worse; and I profoundly believe I am the worst of all. Everything they did I have done, with a little swindling thrown in which they would have shrunk from. Think if I am likely to be much moved by the tears of a girl. I want to make a grand *coup*, Atheling, and be done with it; and I want even more than that to have a full and magnificent draught of revenge! Come, then, what will you give, most loving husband and father, to save 'our Isolind' from *me?*"

Atheling's mild blue eyes were lighted with a flame of horror, and, for once, of hatred. There was a something of dignity even in his ungainly form and awkward deportment, as standing firmly before Jocelyn, he said:

"I have already told you how I love that girl, how dear a child she has been to me. Let me convince you of my sincerity. Prove to me that the being I call Isolind Atheling is your daughter, and to save her from you I will risk any sacrifice—all I have of money, of credit, of reputation on the earth."

. . . .

Ten minutes afterwards Jocelyn left the house, not however without having paid a visit to Mrs. Atheling, and tendered to her some of his most florid compliments.

"Was there ever such a guess as that?" Jocelyn said to himself, as he sauntered along by the broad walk which led to the little grove behind the house, and thus to the gate on the landward side. "The moment I saw the girl first the thought came on me like a flash! Proofs does he ask for? *I* need no proofs but her face and the thrill that went through me, the cold shiver of old hatred coming back like a ghost, when first I saw her. Nor has *he* any doubt of it—I could see that all through. He might as well have told me all about the thing, without standing out for his day's delay. But it really matters very little now; the thing is certain; and if I play my cards only decently, this is the opening of a little mine of money and of opportunities to me. Why, that girl, if taken to England, might marry a marquis—and then there *must* be an amnesty arranged somehow for the new peeress's loving father. All that looks well, and may come to pass; but passion has dashed the cup of opportunity from my lips before, and may well do so this time too. I would fling all away here deliberately this moment for a fair chance of revenge. The Power that made me put a dash too much of hate into my composition. Let it be so. I did not make myself, though I have unmade myself pretty often."

Jocelyn suddenly came to a stand, and surveyed with an apparently profound interest some objects in the scene before him. Indeed, it was a bright and gracious scene. The walk along which he had been treading was crossed by another and a narrower path; and it was down this latter path, to the left, that Jocelyn now gazed. The trees, in all the glowing splendor of their autumn tints, had yet begun to shed a carpet of leaves along the path, and the colors on the branches were thus reflected, one might say, on the ground. Birds chirped and chattered, tiny insects whirred and rustled among the boughs and through the mosses. A sky of luminous and stainless blue arched over the grove; and on a fallen tree at one side of the path two figures were seated. They were the figures of a young woman and a young man, both graceful and picturesque. The group adorned the landscape, added new beauty and vital interest to the scene—and Jocelyn studied it with a peculiar smile on his lips. The girl was speaking, and the young man was listening in an attitude which told of intense devotion. The girl was our Isolind; the youth was Angelo Volney.

Jocelyn smiled—a fat, bearded, bejewelled Mephistopheles—thinking, perhaps, as did his more slender prototype, of the God that made boy and girl, and blandly tolerating the pair to whom such vague and mild enjoyment could bring pleasure.

"I wonder who the devil that Volney fellow is?" thought Jocelyn. "He seems already in a fair way to constitute himself my son-in-law. No, you don't, Mr. Volney, until I am quite satisfied! Shouldn't wonder in the least if Judith Scarlett really had adopted that lad, and would leave him her money just to spite everybody else. She had always a magnificent capacity of hate, had that woman—like myself. What a pity she and I could not have married, and engendered a race of human tigers! Well, if my demure Volney is Lady Judith's heir, he may have my danghter and my paternal blessing; but if not, Mr. Volney, your love-making is all thrown away. I shall be able to turn that girl round my finger.'

He trod as silently as might be over the fallen leaves, until he was fairly out of sight and hearing of the youth and maiden. Suddenly he drew back once more, and looked this time down at the path before him. A snake lay coiled up there. With all his knowledge of America, Jocelyn was still but a stranger, and did not yet always know how to govern his English dread and dislike of reptiles. The little creature now on his path was the common garter-snake, as it is called, of the American woods, as harmless as a British cricket. Jocelyn carried in his hand a pretty silver-headed cane, which looked light and slight, but had a thin, flexible, strong blade of good Damascus steel within. With a motion quick as light he unsheathed the weapon, and pierced the wriggling snake.

"Pooh!" he said; "only a poor little garter-snake. I'm glad I've killed him. Of all living creatures, I think a snake without poison is about the most worthy of contempt!"

CHAPTER XI.

THE POET'S FRENZY.

THERE are certain days in winter when London looks well. These are days when there is no fog, but just a sort of silver-gray haze, through which the golden sunlight slants with a gentle ray, and the shapes of the bare trees in the Parks are softened into something like a vernal tenderness and delicacy, instead of standing out steely and sharp. It is an atmosphere that accords well with London, and looks kindly on it.

On such a day a girl stood at a window of a house in a street running out of Piccadilly, and gazed, as well as she might, obliquely into such fringe and section of the Park as could be seen from that spot. The sunlight fell winsomely on the girl, and gave a look of brightness to a face almost perfectly colorless, and of habitually sad or bitter expression. Perhaps it was not only the rays of the sunlight either; for there surely was a glance of expectancy, or even of longing, in those dark, restless, glittering eyes, which had nothing to do with atmosphere or ray. The girl's whole manner was eager and impatient. Suddenly a light passed over her face, and a faint color sprang into her cheeks. She started from the window and drew back into the room, and then seated herself at a piano, and played hurriedly some careless chords. But her ear was eager to listen for all sounds below.

A servant entered the room with a card on a salver, and looked round.

"Some one for mamma?" asked the girl carelessly. "She will be here presently. Let me see the card. Oh yes; let him come in here. Mamma will be here in a moment."

Then a tall, dark, slender, handsome gentleman was introduced, who bowed and spoke a word or two of formal courtesy to the young lady, and heard from her the assurance that her mamma would presently be visible; and then the servant had left the room, and the visitor and the girl were alone. Thereupon the visitor quickly crossed the room, seized the girl's small white hand, and pressed it passionately to his lips.

She trembled all over with excitement and delight as he touched her, and she sent her glances of apprehension everywhere around the room. At last she said:

"Eric, my Eric!"

"My beloved Alexia! my soul's idol!"

"O Eric, I have so longed to see you!"

"And I, sweetest, to see *you!*"

"Have you indeed longed to see me, Eric, and thought of me always?"

"Love, don't you know that I have?"

"Yes, I do; I think I do; but still one likes to hear it said again and again."

"Then let me say it again and again in all the softest and tenderest words that I can think of. No words could be too fond and tender for my beloved Alexia."

"Eric, tell me first one thing; and oh, tell me truly, as you believe in me—I was going to say, as you believe in heaven; but I don't think you do believe in heaven."

"Sweet, how can you accuse me of such want of faith?—me, to whom heaven has sent *you?*"

The girl, who had been leaning fondly with both her clasped hands on the arm of the young man as he sat beside her, and was gazing upward into his face, as one might gaze upward to some planet, now shrank together as he spoke these last words, and withdrew her hands, while a sudden contraction of pain came over her pale and delicate face. Her companion saw the change at once, and hastened to seize her hand, which she suffered him to retain, although the look of pain remained upon her face.

"Alexia, my own love!" he pleaded, "why do you look on me so coldly, so doubtingly? Can I have offended you?"

"Because I do doubt you," the girl fiercely replied; "because I would doubt any one who talks to me in that way. I hate that sort of cant. It has poisoned the air around me since my cradle time, I think, and I detest it. Don't talk to me of heaven! Keep that for my mother, if you will; she lives on that stuff, and has made me hate it. I was fond of my brother, my more than brother, Angelo, because, although he was good, he had no pious slang on his lips. Eric, I loved you first because you made me believe that you were a rebel like myself against false gods, and that you hated sham religion and cant."

"And so I do!" the young man exclaimed in a fervent tone, turning his dark eyes fully and almost fiercely on hers. "I hate the false gods whom the world adores, and the vile jargon of pietistic cant, which blasphemes religion and outrages the human heart! Am I not a rebel against the whole code and sacraments of their conventions and creeds? Did not my heart first leap forth to meet yours because I saw in you a spirit as daring and scornful as my own? What would be to me the heaven they preach of, compared with the fellowship of a soul like yours, were it but as outcast spirits in the darkness of Gehenna? And now she doubts me!—Alexia doubts me!"

His passionate energy conquered the girl. Won upon word by word, she showed that she was yielding by the softening emotion on her face; and at length she clasped her hands around his arm, and gazed devotedly into his eyes again.

"Oh no, my Eric; I do not doubt you—not now, in my better mood. Only, for the moment, while you spoke, there was something in the words which sounded hollow, and—I don't know—no matter. You forgive your poor wild Alexia, who always speaks out what thought she has, and never could deceive anybody—I mean anybody except mamma. I don't count deceiving her anything, because I know she is always deceiving me and herself too; and, besides, she does not much care what I do, and we are old antagonists. But I should not doubt you, Eric. When I doubt you, I had better be dead. You will forgive me, won't you?"

"Sweetest, you have but to ask me; I am but too glad to forgive;" and Mr. Eric Walraven assumed the air of an injured angel. "But where is the question you were going to put to me, and which I was to answer so faithfully?"

"It was this, Eric. Oh, do tell me! Am I doing anything base and shameful in—in meeting you in this way? Think for me—I cannot think for myself—and protect me, Eric, as I am one day to be your wife. Don't let me do what is degrading. If it is so, tell me, my Eric, you who are wise and brave."

"My own Alexia, fearlessly trust to me. Who could be as tender and careful of you as I would be? Let me be your guide and your conscience. When you are Eric Walraven's wife, let us see who will dare to reproach you. But, sweetest, the precious priceless moments run away, and I have some words to say to you which must be said."

"About my father?"

She started with almost convulsive eagerness.

"Yes, dearest; about a deeply injured man."

"You have found him? You know where he is?"

"Sweet Alexia, I have not yet exactly found him; but nothing can be more certain than that I shall be able before long to bring you and him together, and to obtain his consent to bless our marriage. Dearest, what a day of triumph and pride that will be for me, when I shall place my Alexia in the arms of the father from whom she has so long been separated!"

"He will love you, Eric. I know it; I feel it. He will love you better, ah, far better, than he can love me; for I am so morbid and savage, and you are so good and firm and patient. But may I not know anything more than this? May I not know what you are doing, and how you hope to reach him? It seems to me wonderful how you have been able to discover anything; but you have such a genius! Hush! here comes my dear mother."

All this conversation took place in Lady Judith Scarlett's drawing-room. It will serve to show how far things had progressed between Eric Walraven and Alexia. This conversation was one of many which the pair contrived to have when Mr. Walraven came to make a call on Lady Judith. They found an easy way of adjusting matters so that Eric should call at an hour when Lady Judith was sure to be somewhat engaged; and Alexia would take care to be at hand in the drawing-room. Thus a few sentences and promises and vows and phrases of love could be exchanged. But they interchanged letters too, and contrived even to have sweet stolen interviews not under Lady Judith's roof; sometimes not under any roof. The poor girl had fallen madly in love with Walraven's dark eyes, and his poetry, and his mysterious promises and semi-revelations about her father. He studied her moods, and played upon them with audacious skill; for he rather enjoyed the game itself, apart from the advantages he proposed to find in t. He liked playing with the wild ways of this eccentric, passionate girl, who n some of her moods was very beautiful. As to Alexia, she began to know, for the first time in her life, some glimpses of happiness. It was true love, so far as she was concerned; it was first love; it gave to her in her better moods such heavenly glimpses now and then, that it might almost have made her believe in heaven.

Lady Judith came in serene and stately, and looked a little displeased to see Alexia there, but said nothing on the subject while Walraven was present. Lady Judith, indeed, was only too happy to escape without a disagreeable scene whenever there chanced to be any one in the room with herself and her daughter. Nothing could be further from her mind than any idea of assuming the offensive. She received Eric Walraven with a courtesy that was almost friendly; for of late she had come to like him, and he had made himself useful to her.

Alexia remained in the room, only now and then uttering an interjected word, and during most of the time turning over a parcel of books newly come from some library, and which her mother regarded with special dislike and distrust. When Alexia had exhausted other means of displeasing her mother, she sometimes privately sent for terribly unorthodox or full-flavored books from the library, and left them lying where her mother must see them. She wanted Lady Judith to suppose that she had got the books secretly for the pleasure of reading what her mother would have wished her not to read. In truth, unless in the case of some very alluring romance, Alexia never read the books thus obtained; she only wanted her mother to suppose that she read them. She cared nothing about the forbidden fruit as a food or a dainty; she only desired the reputation of having greedily eaten it.

Walraven did not remain long. He had only come to speak about some one of Lady Judith's philanthropic schemes; and he soon took his leave. Departing, he exchanged a glance full of meaning with Alexia; and as she held her hand out to him, he contrived to press into its little palm a tiny scrap of paper.

Alexia enjoyed all this sort thing with a fierce delight. It gave her an almost irrepressible pleasure to see how completely Walraven could hoodwink and deceive her mother. She looked on from her corner, looked up from her books, and was proud of her admirer's skill in deceit—as a Spanish girl might have felt pride in the cruel art of the matador her lover. Walraven was her champion, she thought; he was deceiving Lady Judith on her account and in her cause. Was he not clever and brave? How much better than Angelo!—who, although he was fond of Alexia, was yet always advising her and remonstrating with her, and holding up her mother as a model. Alexia positively hugged herself in her champion's adroitness and courage.

If there is any one who holds it to be inconsistent with human nature that the girl should thus take pride in her lover's power of deception, and yet have no fear that that power might now or at some other time be practised on herself, then that person ought to learn a little of human nature out of real life. If he opens his eyes and looks at people around him and their ways, or perhaps looks boldly into his own heart and his own life, he will see that Alexia Scarlett might have been his twin sister, so far as that goes.

Walraven went away, and with him went some of Alexia's courage and all of Lady Judith's fears.

"What books are those you have had from the library, Alexia? I did not know that you were sending there to-day."

"I didn't intend to send at first, mamma; but then the whim took me."

"What books are they?"

"This is Renan's 'Vie de Jésus'; a delightful book which you must read, dear mamma; but perhaps you have read it already?"

"I have heard of it; and I believe it to be a detestable book. Give me that book; you shall not read such things, Alexia."

"Dear mamma, I have read all I want of it. Is it very dreadful? Will it sap the foundation of my faith? What a pity if it does!"

"What is that other book?"

"A novel—a charming one—'M. de Camors.'"

"A French novel?"

"Oh yes, dear mamma; about such a delightful lady; a little elderly, who was in love with a young man—much younger than herself; and, as she could not well marry him, she gave him as a husband to her daughter. Was not that a good idea?"

Lady Judith flushed slightly, and looked keenly at Alexia. But the girl met her scrutiny with an air of the most utter innocence.

"Give me that book, Alexia."

Alexia handed it over, and Lady Judith opened its pages at random and began to read. Presently her face crimsoned and her lips quivered.

"You have not read this book, Alexia; you cannot have read it."

"Why not, Lady Judith?"

One of Alexia's pleasant ways was thus sometimes to address her mother as Lady Judith."

"You would not have dared to read such a book and then tell me of it!"

"Charles Scarlett's daughter might dare many things," Alexia answered spitefully.

"She might, if she would resemble her father, dare many things indeed, which other people would shrink from—people who value purity and religion. Still, Alexia, I don't believe that you have read *this* book. You are not given to saying what is not true. Did you read it?"

"Oh no, not I, mamma. I opened it just where Madame somebody or other is asking M. de Camors to marry her daughter, because she thinks it would be hardly convenient for him to marry herself. That is all I know about it, or care to know. I dare say I should read it every word if I felt inclined that way, but then I don't."

"Then why did you say it was a charming book?"

"I think I said it to spite you, dear mamma."

"Does it give you pleasure to spite me, Alexia?"

"It does, Lady Judith."

This dialogue, so far, was carried on with the utmost apparent composure on both sides, and in low, calm voices. Lady Judith sighed and rose from her chair, and walked toward the window, where she stood for a moment buried in thought. Her heart was bitterly wounded by the conduct of her daughter; and the bitterness was perhaps all the greater, because Lady Judith conceived that her own conduct, and her wisdom as a mother, had been beyond reproach or cavil. She was in perplexity, and almost in agony of doubt as to what course she ought to adopt; and she hit instinctively upon the one course out of several which awed Alexia the most, and served her the least. An ordinary soft-hearted mother might have burst into tears; which would have amused and pleased Alexia mightily. A true, loving, wise, and tender woman would have taken her daughter to her heart, full of compassion and excuse and pity for her, and tried to win her into love and confidence and a better spirit; and Alexia would simply have melted into softness on the breast of such a mother, and would have been as a little child at her feet. Another, again, would have raged and stormed; and this—even if it shook Alexia's thrilling morbid nerve-system—would have gratified her sense of power, and soothed her vanity with a consciousness that her proud mother's temper was at her mercy. Lady Judith resolved coldly and firmly to ignore the matter altogether—to show no indication whatever of having felt or heeded Alexia's sting. This was the course which always awed and bewildered the girl most; this evidence of a proud, cold self-reliance, which could not recognize a wound, which treated the uttermost efforts of another's spite as a subject of calm indifference. Alexia could bear anything better than this marble patience and indifference. It only aroused new fires and new bitterness in her fierce little heart.

Calmly, then, Lady Judith turned to her daughter and said:

"I have had letters from America to-day, Alexia."

"From Angelo?" and a gleam of genuine interest and emotion lighted up Alexia's face.

"Only a short letter from Angelo, and for myself altogether; he says he will write to you very soon. But I have a long letter from Charles Escombe, which I should like you to hear. It is full of instruction."

"Thank you, mamma; I dare say it is; but I really don't care to hear Charles Escombe's dreadful prosings. If Angelo won't write to me, and you won't read to me what he writes to you, I altogether decline Charles Escombe."

"Charles Escombe is a young man of great ability and great goodness."

"Yes, I suppose he is; he is delightfully good, and wonderfully clever, and a dreadful bore. Why doesn't he go into the House of Commons, or write for one of the reviews, and get rid of all his superfluous cleverness and energy there? I pity poor Angelo with him; although Angelo deserves nothing from me since he has not written to me."

"Angelo is not with Charles Escombe now."

"Indeed! How luckily for Angelo! Where, then, is Charles Escombe?

"Mr. Escombe has gone south—to Richmond."

"And Angelo, mamma?"

"Angelo remains for the present in New York."

"In New York—all this time? What can have kept him there?"

"Some reasons which he explains to me."

"Has any pretty girl anything to do with them, may I ask, dear mamma? They say the American girls are charming."

Lady Judith looked angry.

"You talk idly, Alexia. Angelo Volney is not a frivolous boy, to——"

"My dear mamma, what do you know about boys, frivolous or otherwise, you who don't read novels or poems? I think Angelo is just the very person to fall desperately in love with some *belle Américaine*. That would be delightful! How I should laugh when she came here with him and presented herself to you! Of course she would say, 'Wall, stranger,' and 'I guess,' and 'old hoss,' and that sort of thing. And I presume all the American ladies smoke and chew. Depend upon it, mamma, he has fallen in love with some Pocahontas out in the backwoods, Philadelphia, or California, or some such place. Didn't he say anything of the kind in his letter?"

Lady Judith disdained reply.

"Not a word? Then that makes it all the more likely, mamma. Such depth, you see, already! *Comme l'esprit vient aux garçons!* Take my word for it, Lady Judith—as I heard Francis the footman say the other day of somebody—my demure Angelo is gammoning you. Isn't that a pretty word?"

"I don't understand slang, Alexia, and I don't listen to the talk of servants or care to hear it repeated. You are not in a mood for serious conversation now, my poor child, and so I shall not read Charles Escombe's letter to you. I am going to take a drive. Get ready and come with me."

"But are we going to any dreadful schools, or garrets, or societies, or that sort of thing?"

"You are coming with me, Alexia, and you will see."

"Ah, *mon Dieu*, I suppose so. Then don't we leave town any more this year, mamma?"

"Yesterday, Alexia, you complained and murmured when I talked of returning to Brighton; and I gave up the idea."

"To please me? Mamma, this is wonderful! and to think that I should be so ungrateful for such a sacrifice as even to forget that I ever invited it, and to be now rather anxious to get away from town! No matter. Is the carriage ordered, mamma? I shall be ready in a very few minutes. But take my word for it, Messer Angelo is engaged to some *belle sauvage*. He is like the egotistic person in 'Locksley Hall': 'I will take some savage woman; she shall rear my dusky brood!'"

And Alexia disappeared, exulting within herself that she had sent a shaft of annoyance into her mother's heart. But when she reached her own room, she thought how Angelo had not written to her, and how he did not care for her any more; and she burst into tears. Then she put her hand into her bosom and plucked out the tiny crumpled note which Walraven had given her; and she kissed it and wept over it, and passionately declared that he, her Eric, alone of all the world cared for her, and—and loved her; and she wished that she could have the luxury of killing some enemy of his, to please him, or of lying down and dying at his feet.

Lady Judith sighed again when her daughter had left her, and leaned upon the chimney-piece, and laid her head upon her hand, and sadly wondered why Heaven had been pleased to visit her with so heavy a dispensation. She had always, she thought, done her duty; and yet Heaven had decreed her so much ingratitude and so much suffering. Thus thinking, she raised her head, and chanced to see her face and form reflected in a mirror; and she could not help seeing that that face and form were noble and queenly. Where could anything more like a queen, in an artistic sense, be seen than that face, with its broad white forehead, its coronal of luxuriant dark hair, its clear marble outlines, and the feminine majesty of that splendid bust, that stately figure? For the moment, while the glance endured, Lady Judith was a very woman, and wondered how, with that face and figure, no man had ever loved her. She was even now hardly more than forty years old. She would have challenged admiration at a drawing-room in St. James's Palace, or a ball at the Tuileries; and yet she was given over to mental solitude and philanthropy, and the care of a daughter who scorned and defied her. Lady Judith prepared for her drive with a sad, stern heart. She assumed that Heaven was ordaining all this for her spiritual good; but how hard a trial to have to climb even to Heaven by the weary rounds of such a ladder!

Scenes such as have been just described were of common occurrence between this mother and daughter. Perhaps, if at any time some resolute, daring, loving Christian creature could have understood the situation, and torn away the mask of egotism and pride from these two women, and showed their souls and natures naked one to the other, that mediator might have brought Lady Judith and her daughter Alexia together, never to separate. But such friend there was none; and the mother and daughter only drifted away from each other—further and further away.

Meanwhile Mr. Eric Walraven was going home to his rooms in the Albany. He was quite jubilant in soul, and his joy almost expressed itself in manner. His mental orchestra accompanied him with "See, the conquering hero comes," all the way down Piccadilly. He glanced admiringly at his own reflection in several mirrors as he passed by the shops of upholsterers and pastry-cooks; and he was so absorbed in his own triumph, that he only paused to admire two pretty faces, one head of bright hair, and three pairs of neat ankles, as he went his way. His triumph consisted in the fact that he now had Alexia quite at his mercy—to marry her when he pleased. In every way this suited him. First of all, the poet adored the aristocracy, and would rather have married the cast-off mistress or the illegitimate daughter of a nobleman than have wedded another Corinna. Think, then, what his exultation was, when he found that it was quite within his power to run away with the daughter of the cold and proud Lady Judith Scarlett—with the granddaughter of the Earl of Coryden! Secondly, the poet sadly lacked money; and he felt convinced that if once he became, by any means, the husband of Lady Judith Scarlett's only daughter, he would never again be allowed to feel the pressure of financial difficulty, even if there should prove to be no foundation for the story that Lady Judith's husband had left a vast fortune to be given to his daughter on her marriage. Thirdly, the poet dearly loved *éclat* and sensation; and he thought with delight and exultation over the fame it would bring him, and the *prestige* it would secure for his coming volume, if, while its announcement was yet conspicuous among imminent things in the columns of the "Saturday Review" and the "Athenæum," it should become whispered about in society, and hinted at in newspaper columns, that the poet had run away with the daughter of the proud aristocrat Lady Judith Scarlett.

Walraven was a little—just a very little—troubled by the fact that he had obtained much of his influence over the distracted mind of poor Alexia by professing a mysterious knowledge of her lost father, whereas in good truth he knew nothing whatever about the matter. He had had at first a kind of dim idea of finding a track, following it up, and obtaining some genuine information, and thus presenting himself to Alexia in the guise of a real benefactor and champion. But it was very hard to find out anything, or even to get on the path of discovery; and Walraven was luxurious and lazy, and he found it so easy to invent lies suited to the circumstances of each day. He therefore kept on inventing lies, feeding the sick heart of poor Alexia on lies; and sometimes he feared, not that he might be detected, but that he might be detected prematurely. If he could but once make Alexia his wife, he would care little for the rest. He felt no doubt he could easily deceive and satisfy her; and even if he could not, what would it matter then?

For all reasons he felt satisfied that he could not too soon bring the campaign to a close; and to-day it seemed to him that he had good reason for believing the time and the means of successful conclusion to be quite within his own hands.

Therefore Eric Walraven walked down Piccadilly a hopeful and proud man. He could not help smiling at the thought of the poor little girl and her credulous nonsense about her father; and he was rather amused by the reflection that he himself knew absolutely nothing about the personage in question.

"He must be dead," thought Eric to himself as he sauntered along; "I should say he certainly *must* be dead. What could keep a man like him, if he were alive, from returning to his home and his wealth and his position? Lady

Judith is a magnificent woman too—not a finer woman in London, I think. *I* should rather enjoy her coldness and stateliness if I were her husband; a new piquancy and pleasure would be added to the conjugal relation. It would be like compelling a goddess to come down and be one's wife—by Jove, a new idea for a little classical scrap of poetry! I think I could do something very taking about Anchises, and his feelings when Venus consented to come down to him. I'll think of Lady Judith and some ordinary fellow marrying her; and I fancy I can work out the idea."

When he reached his own threshold, he was still turning over this idea, and trying to realize, in an artistic sense, the feelings of some one who had conquered for his wife a woman like Lady Judith Scarlett.

"Alexia's very pretty," he thought incidentally, "and really at times looks quite attractive. But she wants form and the richness of womanhood, somehow. She certainly is not quite my style; but then she is so very young. Perhaps when she is thirty years old she may be almost as fine a woman as her mother. How she would rage, if she knew that all my acquaintanceship with her father's mystery was only a daring flight of poetic imagination! Well, am I to blame, O Athenians, for having given you one happy day? Am I to blame, Miss Scarlett, because I have fed for a few days the cravings of your odd romantic little heart?"

Walraven's chambers in the Albany were a sitting-room, bedroom, and dressing-room. They were small, but they were fitted up quite luxuriously. His bedroom and dressing-room were little marvels of elegance and ornament; they would almost have suited Edmond About's Madelon, or some other luxurious nymph who comes easily into the possession of money. Walraven was always more or less in want of money; but his rooms spoke of cultured opulence. In his sitting-room were some costly editions of illustrated books, and some fine engravings; among the rest, Gérôme's Phryne, and one or two others of the same class by the same daring pencil. For the broad manly humors of Hogarth, or the robust nudities of Rubens, Mr. Walraven had as little relish as he had for Rabelais or Chaucer. He liked his sensualism tinted and enamelled and scented. He enjoyed Alfred de Musset, but not Shakespeare; the "Dame aux Camélias," but not "Humphrey Clinker." He once tried to admire Fielding; but when he came to that passage in "Tom Jones" where sweet Sophy Western, peerless among English heroines, is thrown awkwardly from her horse, and thus makes a display of her limbs, whereat the rustics in the stable-yard grin and chuckle, Walraven put the book away, simply disgusted. Talk of a novelist having any claim to art who made his own heroine seem ridiculous! If Walraven were to write a romance, his heroine would be something different indeed from pure and fresh Sophy Western; but let her make what sweet romantic havoc of the Decalogue she would, she should never be seen in an awkward attitude, or allowed to raise a smile of mirth on the face of any one.

Walraven's furniture, pictures, and books were in full keeping with his æsthetic canons of taste. The place looked tempting and bright, and Eric cast an eye of pride and affection over everything.

"Marry or not marry," he mentally resolved, "I'll never give up this crib. I dare say I shall be only too glad to get a snatch at bachelor life here every now and then. No man ought to be always with his wife; it spoils her and him. No; I'll keep this place for an occasional retreat."

His table was covered with letters, papers, and bills, at which he gave a weary glance, like the look of one on whom food is forced while he is already well nigh to nausea. He drew a chair, however, and set to work with a sigh at the task of reading, or at least inspecting the correspondence.

"Poole's bill; well, I needn't look at that, nor Fortnum and Mason's, nor Gunter's. I can't pay these people. That bill from the Star and Garter I am perfectly sick of seeing. I thought I had paid that liveryman's account for little Julia's brougham. Confound her! lucky for me that I am out of *that* affair. Oh, hang it all, there's poor Kitty's scrawl again! Well, I can't do anything for her; I have no money for myself, and she must get along as well as she can. She has really no claim on me; it was her fault as much as mine. I wish she would let me alone; and I won't read a line of her letter. Dear old mother, how sweetly domestic and virtuous her fine square hand looks, there among all this ruck! Well, I'll not read her letter to-night either; I am not quite in the mood—it would be a sort of desecration to the good old lady to read her in such company. Besides, I dare say, I know all she has to say pretty well beforehand; and so we'll just put you by, *ma mère*, for a better hour, along with your last dear letter, and read both some calm evening."

He rose and opened one of the little drawers of his desk, which he reserved specially as what he called "the family altar." There he was wont to put letters from home—from the quiet old home away by the Trent—until he found a suitable opportunity or pressing inclination to read them. He knew that one letter from his mother—her "last dear letter"—was lying there unopened already; but he had quite forgotten a previous arrival, and he was now a little vexed to see that two maternal missives already lay unopened there. It made him wince a little, not from any feeling of remorse or affection, but because he thought of the mountain of good reading that must accumulate for him, if he did not make a bold effort somehow, and get through the arrears of the correspondence. He sighed, shrugged his shoulders, and grimaced; but the thing had to be done.

"It wouldn't do," he sadly thought, "to put them all in the fire at once. There may be something in them, although I don't suppose there is. No; it's no use trying to escape one's responsibilities. This comes of having a mother. I must read them; poor father may be sick, or dead, perhaps, for that matter; and how the deuce am I to get a decent suit of mourning just now?"

Eric looked at his watch. He had time enough for plenty of work; for it was not yet five o'clock, and he had no engagement until eight, when he was to dine at the house of a literary peer. He was, indeed, at present, rather hard at work upon his new volume of poems, to be called the "Mystery of the Universe"; but still, the reading of the letters from home could not well exact more than half an hour. So he put on a dressing-gown, seated himself pleasantly in his arm-chair with the "velvet violet lining," drew the soft-shining lamp to his elbow, and resolutely set to work to get through his mother's letters. Like a wise man, he began at the latest first, not without a hope that it might save him the trouble of reading the others. It was lucky for his credit that he had done so; for the letter did tell him of an alarming illness that had attacked his father; and Eric was just thinking what a hideous bore it would be if he should have to go down to the country now, when he heard a heavy step on his threshold, and a loud knock at his door; and the step and the knock were alike familiar to him.

"Gad, it's Gostick!" said the poet to himself. "How lucky I read that letter! What on earth should I have said if I had put it aside without reading? I think I can turn this to account with old Gostick."

He hastily arranged his mother's letters, all of them that he could find, on his table, keeping the latest one half-crumpled in his hand. Then he flung himself into his chair in an attitude of utter abandonment, spread his arms out upon the table, and laid his head on them, so that his luxuriant hair fell over the arms and hands; but allowed the one hand to be seen—that which, now all veinous and knotted and quivering, grasped as if spasmodically the crumpled letter. Eric's arrangement of himself was remarkably picturesque and effective. It might have suited the student in Poe's poem, just before the tapping comes to summon him to admit the raven with his three syllables of despair.

Again the knock was heard at the door, and this time Eric languidly called "Come in." And the door was opened, and Mr. Gostick, M. P., made his appearance.

The Lancashire manufacturer stood in the room a moment or two unnoticed, and wondering much at the attitude of his nephew. At last, as he was about to utter some gruff interjection, Eric raised his head, and showed his fine dark eyes literally floating in tears. One of Eric's most wonderful and useful endowments was a gift of tears. He could cry, when he liked, as readily as Mrs. Thrale's lovely friend Sophy Streatfield; and, like Sophy, he could weep without marring his good looks. Indeed, Eric himself, who had often and carefully consulted the looking-glass on the subject, thought he looked handsomest when his bright eyes were gemmed by a manly tear. Many a secret sovereign had those tears extracted from his poor loving mother; many a time had the hoard of the honest proud-souled curate and teacher, his father, been unduly and unjustly pinched to dry those sparkling drops of ready sorrow. More than once had those tears made sad havoc with other feminine feelings than those of his mother. It may be supposed that if Eric set the fountains flowing now, it was not because he imagined the mere sight of manly beauty in tears would have any effect on stout Mr. Gostick; but he was well aware of Gostick's weakness for the domestic virtues, and he thought he might now be able to water that weakness to some purpose for himself.

"What's the matter, Eric? what's the matter, boy? Don't mean to say you are crying like a school-girl that has had a whipping?"

"Oh, uncle, have you come from home? How is my father? Have you any message from my dear mother?"

"Well, yes. I was passing through that neighborhood, and I saw your father and mother; and he's rather bad; but I don't know that you need be much alarmed. It's overwork—all overwork, you know—and not half enough to eat. I promised your poor fool of a mother that I would call and tell you all about it; not that I fancied you were likely to trouble yourself greatly on the subject."

"Oh, uncle, how can you speak so! I am no longer ashamed that you should have found me in this condition. Think it unmanly, if you like; but let it at least prove the sincerity of my feelings."

"I thought perhaps it was something especially poetic," grumbled Gostick. "I was very fond of my good old father—much fonder, let me tell you, than ever you appeared to be of yours; and when I heard that he was on his death-bed, I didn't sit down and blubber. But I suppose poets take things differently."

"Uncle, the things *are* different. You had no feeling of self-reproach, of remorse, blending with and adding to your grief; you had always been a good and faithful son."

"Well, I had always tried to do my duty."

"And I have not done my duty—I have not been a good son—I have sadly neglected the noblest of fathers, the most loving and tender of mothers. This is the thought, uncle, which lends such bitterness now to my grief—which has plunged me into the condition you see, but of which I am not ashamed. My dear kind mother, your own only sister, uncle! See, there is a heap of her letters, some of them faded and yellow. I have treasured them, uncle—I have treasured them; for I have been neglectful, but not wholly worthless, not utterly without a son's affection. Strange, I had them all out just now—all but this last—and was reading them over, little thinking of what was to come, when the postman brought to-day's letter; and then, uncle, the shock was too much for me—the shock of mingled sorrow and remorse; and I confess I did break down, as you see."

A new rush of tears filled his eyes, and choked his utterance; and Eric sprang from his chair, and turned away his head, to hide of course the evidences of a grief which would not be suppressed or conquered.

Gostick was quite taken aback. He did not remember ever to have seen an Englishman in tears before. He had seen Italians, and Germans, and people of that sort crying; and he had looked on with curious contempt and pity, just such as he felt when he saw bearded men kissing each other at Teuton railway-stations; but an Englishman shedding tears was a sight he never thought to see. To be sure, the Englishman was a poet. Mr. Gostick mentally classed poets somehow with foreigners, and women, and other eccentric impulsive creatures, on whose ways no man of common sense could pretend to calculate. However, there was the man crying plenteous tears; and the man, with all his faults, was the son of Gostick's sister, and was crying because of her grief; and Mr. Gostick was touched. It was in this one case lucky for Eric that he was a poet. Had he been a manufacturer, or a banker's clerk, or a porter, or anything else, high or low, that was manly, Gostick would never have believed in the genuineness of the tears, and would have walked out in disgust, convinced that his nephew must be either drunk or shamming. But Gostick did not profess to understand poets; and he was not prepared to deny off-hand that poesy, as well as the petticoat, might honestly claim the privilege of tears. So he looked at his weeping nephew with something like a real compassion.

"Well, blood's thicker than water, certainly," was Mr. Gostick's observation. "It was an old saying of my good father's, Eric, and I see there's a great deal in it. I never thought you had so much nature in you, boy."

"Uncle, I don't wonder that you misunderstood me—indeed, I deserved the worst interpretation my conduct could receive. But there is hope, uncle; you say there is hope?"

"Hope of what?"

"Of my father."

"Oh, pooh! Yes, of course there's hope. It's only overwork, I tell you—a ew days' rest will bring him round."

"And my mother never told me anything in any of her former letters."

"Why, how could the woman tell you before it occurred? Doesn't she say then, in her last letter, that it began suddenly with a fainting fit the day before yesterday?"

"Yes, yes, to be sure; in my excitement and remorse I forget everything. (Thank Heaven," thought Eric, "it only began the day before yesterday, so that there couldn't be anything about it in the letters which I didn't read.) Then, uncle, had I not better hasten to my father?"

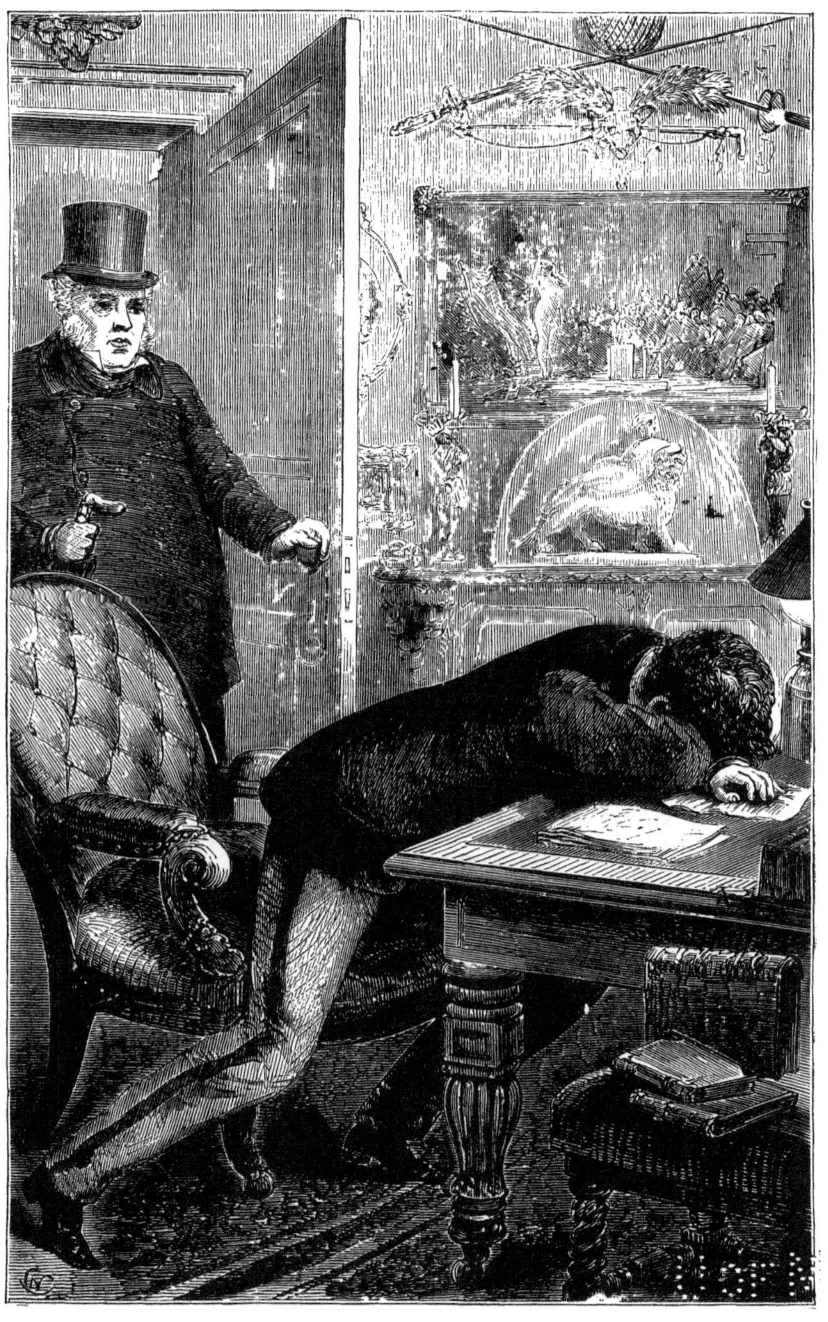

THE DOOR WAS OPENED, AND MR. GOSTICK, M. P., MADE HIS APPFARANCE.—p. 107.

"Your mother thinks so. I should if I were you; for although I think it will be nothing, still——"

"Still my father is overworked and weak (I really shouldn't wonder in the least," Eric said in his own mind, "if the poor old boy were to drop off this time; he must be dreadfully worn out), and I ought to be by his side and by the side of my dear mother. My time is very precious here, uncle; I am working hard, endeavoring to make up for weeks of indolence; but I will sacrifice all, rather than remain away from home at such a time."

"Well, hadn't you better go this evening by the mail train at nine?"

"If I can—if I only can contrive it."

"How contrive it? Isn't there plenty of time between this and nine o'clock to get to Euston square?"

"Yes, uncle, but I must see some persons—my publishers, in fact. They will perhaps advance me something for the work I have in hand. In honest truth, I am ashamed to present myself penniless at my mother's door. I cannot and will not do it. I will have money somehow; I will draw half the price of my work beforehand, if I have to live on macaroni and cheese when I return to town."

"It's a bad thing, that discounting one's profit and drawing one's pay in advance. I don't like it."

"Neither do I, uncle, and I never do such things" (in truth, Eric's work, such as it was, had invariably a publisher's mortgage on it long before its issue); "but I will stop at no slight scruple of etiquette where my mother needs help. No, uncle, I'll hunt up the publishers to-night, and start by the first train in the morning."

"Why do you keep these expensive rooms? Why don't you sell off all that costly trumpery? That would be my idea of independence—to live cheaply, within my means, and not waste my money on such trash. What do you want of these statues and brass candlesticks and old cups and saucers?" (This to some wonderful gems of *virtu*.) And how do you think your decent mother, if she could come here, would like to see these pictures of naked women all about the walls?"

Eric smiled a sad smile between his tears, like Andromache.

"My dear good uncle, I am more economic than you think; these things are not mine. By the way, these pictures which offend you are considered works of art of a very high class, although I don't say that they are just such as I would have of my own choice in a room of mine."

"Room of yours? Whose rooms are these?"

"Well, uncle, you see I have been forced of late to have recourse to the severest economy. You smile at the idea of these being economic chambers; but the truth is, they are put at my disposal by a kind and intimate friend, young Oscar McAlpine, the Hon. Oscar McAlpine, son of Lord Glenbinkie, uncle; he is away travelling in the East, and will not return for some months, and he would insist on my having these rooms in his absence. So you see, uncle, I am more economical than you could have guessed."

"I don't think I should like to be under a compliment to people of that kind, who only look down upon you and your class," grumbled Mr. Gostick; in his heart, however, somewhat pleased to hear of his nephew's intimacy with the son of a lord, and still more pleased to hear that the chambers cost him nothing.

"Dear uncle, you do my young friend and men of his rank a great wrong; they are far from having the foolish notions you ascribe to them. My friend Oscar McAlpine has no more idea of looking down upon me than a brother could have. Indeed, we are like brothers; he knows that I am poor, and that makes not the slightest difference. There are no people who are less likely to turn their backs upon a man because he is poor than the aristocracy of these countries. I do wish, uncle, you would cease to hold off from them as resolutely as you do."

Mr. Gostick smiled a grim smile. This was a very happy hit of Eric's, and it was all the more effective because of the earnest tone of almost aggrieved remonstrance in which it was made. Mr. Gostick was pleased to be enabled to regard himself as a stern plebeian whom the patrician crowd in vain endeavored to draw to their side. He had hitherto hated the aristocracy because he assumed that none of them would condescend to associate with him.

"Yes," continued Eric, who noted that his daintily-feathered shaft had sped home, "Oscar himself often said to me that your rejection of every advance was a matter of talk and of complaint among his set. They can't understand it. Lord Glenbinkie went into the peers' gallery of the Commons purposely to hear your speech on the church-rates bill, and he thought it capital; and he wanted some people to meet you at dinner, but he said, It is no use thinking about asking Gostick—he won't come. So Oscar told me himself. But I know I can't convert you, uncle" (Eric became a little afraid of carrying the thing too far), "and indeed I am not in spirits enough to convert anybody to anything now. Thank you for coming to see me, thank you for not laughing at my weakness. I'll make all right to-night, uncle, and go down to-morrow."

"No, no, you must go to-night. See, look here—lend me your pen. Will a poet's pen sign a check? All right—here, take this. Anybody will cash it for you at once, and it will pull you through. I don't like the notion of eating up one's pay before it becomes due. Come and dine with me at the Reform, and you can go off at nine."

"But this is too much; I really didn't think—how shall I thank——"

"That'll do; let's have no more talk about it. Come and have some dinner."

"Thousand thanks, dear uncle; but I have so much work to do, and I have already dined."

"Dined already? Half-past five o'clock?"

"Dinner enough for one who has work to do, and means to do it. A chop and some pale ale—call it luncheon, if you like—it shall serve for this day. I'll have a cup of tea and a sandwich at the railway station before I start. My dear, dear father!"

The tears were springing again, and Eric turned away his head. In fact, he was now very anxious to be rid of Mr. Gostick, and he thought a fresh shower would probably frighten the veteran away. So it did. Gostick could not stand any more tears. He wrung his nephew's hand with a genuine warmth, and bade him farewell. As he was going he paused for a moment, jerked the point of his thick stick in the direction of the Phryne, and said:

"I think I would take these things down if I were you, or turn their faces to the wall at least. Let your friend the owner of the rooms have them if he likes, but they don't suit your mother's son."

"Perhaps you are right, uncle; I hardly observed them until now; but you are right."

Dashing away a tear with his white handkerchief, and then throwing the handkerchief on the table, Eric gravely rose and deliberately turned Phryne and her judges, and one or two other works of art of the same class, with their naughty faces to the wall. His uncle nodded approvingly, again said "Good-by," and disappeared.

"I never thought that fellow had so much feeling in him," muttered Gostick, as he emerged presently into the gaslight and the noise of Piccadilly. "And so much shrewdness and economy too! I shouldn't wonder if he were to become a respectable man after all."

As for Eric, when he was certain that his uncle was fairly gone, he flung himself on his sofa, and gave way to a ringing peal of the most genuine laughter he had enjoyed for a long time. He did not even stop to look at the amount of the check, until he had had full revel in the artistic enjoyment of the droll scene which had just taken place, and which gave him the same kind of delight that some brilliant piece of comedy by Ravel or Charles Mathews or Jefferson might have done. Indeed, as to money there was nothing meanly mercenary about him in detail; and, feeling confident that there would prove to be a pretty decent sum at his disposal, he did not care much about the precise tale of the pounds sterling. He laughed, and laughed again.

"What a jolly old snob Gostick is, for all his Radicalism!" laughed the poet. "Nothing hit him so cleverly as that touch about his holding off from the aristocracy. Come, my fair Phryne, now you may turn your face to the light once more. What a dull old beast he is! I would not have a soul like that, so dead to all beauty and art, for all his money. Let us see what he has given me."

Eric took up the check, and almost started when he looked at it.

"Why, this is an uncle! Two hundred pounds—I expected fifty! How my genius must have warmed and softened that tough and withered old heart! Two hundred pounds for a touch of flattery and a few tears, idle tears—no, by Jove! not idle tears this time. This positively sets me up. I can actually marry Alexia with this; and I don't think I can possibly do better than bring the affair to a close at once. Heaven knows when I may have so much money again in a lump. Two hundred pounds well managed would cover all expenses, and carry us on for a couple of months perhaps; and of course Lady Judith would have given in long before that time. Poor uncle has little notion of his check being devoted to such a purpose as the carrying away of an earl's granddaughter. Confound it, though; I hope nothing will happen to poor father just now. The thing would have to be postponed somehow if he were to go off. I'll go down to-morrow morning and return next day, if all's well—the trip altogether can't cost more than a five-pound note; and dear old mother will never tell Gostick that I didn't give her any of the money, even if the old screw should ask her. Yes, I'll go down to-morrow; and if nothing happens there, I'll come back to town and complete my heroic enterprise."

It need hardly be said that Eric's story about the ownership of the rooms, and the kindness of the Hon. Oscar McAlpine, was among the bold poetic imaginings of the young minstrel. The chambers and the *bric-à-brac* and the nudities were as absolutely his own property as anything for which a man has made himself legally responsible can be said to be his property. He alone owed the money for them.

He would not of course forego his invitation to dine at a peer's house; and he smiled at the notion of dining at the Reform Club with Gostick, whose barbarous notion of a dinner consisted of a cut off a joint, with potatoes, and two glasses of sherry. So he dined joyously at the house of his noble friend and patron—an obese nobleman, who had written one or two poems, and concocted a biography of a distinguished ancestor—and he went down to the country next day. He found his father looking miserable, and with the shadow of death evidently on him, but apparently not doomed to die that very week. So Eric declared himself delighted to find that father was so well; rejoiced to think it was only a false alarm; affirmed that he himself was constantly in the habit of having precisely similar seizures, which after all came to nothing; was intensely affectionate to his mother; alarmed her almost beyond measure by describing the life of severe study and hard work he was leading in London; and hurried quickly back to town, having kept his word for once, and not spent upon the whole expedition more than a five-pound note.

CHAPTER XII.

ISOLIND AND ANGELO.

NOTHING could well have been more remarkable than the change that came over the atmosphere which had hitherto surrounded the household of the Athelings from the time when Chesterfield Jocelyn paid his first ill-omened visit. Judge Atheling seemed to have lost nearly all the clear serenity of his manner; he went about like one burdened with a gloomy secret; he took little joy in his books and his animal pets; his wife could not understand him; Isolind could not understand him. He had frequent letters from the city, which Mrs. Atheling was not allowed to see—a strange and novel restriction for her—and he had evidently business affairs in hand, about which he would not consult Isolind. Of course Isolind had spoken to him earnestly about keeping out of speculations with Jocelyn; but he put her admonitions and entreaties away with a quiet, melancholy firmness which she could not conquer. She told him of the portrait Jocelyn had shown her; but the Judge made no remark, and hardly appeared to hear what she was saying. The Judge was indeed wonderfully altered. From seeming like a happy child he had grown moody and silent, taking pleasure in little; walking alone very often about the grounds with his hands in his pockets, and with knitted brows and puckered lips. He never was peevish; indeed, he showed rather an increased tenderness now and then for his wife and Isolind. Once or twice, when Isolind asked him some question, he made no reply, but put his arm round her waist and drew her toward him, and gazed into her eyes until his own big blue eyes seemed wet with tears; and then he turned away and left her.

Sometimes Mrs. Atheling feared that his health must be wholly failing. She happened to read in an English magazine an article called "Sentenced to Death," or some such name, describing the mental condition of a man whose physician had warned him, while yet he is apparently in the enjoyment of full health, that he has but a very few months to live; and she became possessed with the idea that Atheling had had some such warning. But the Judge assured her that his health was perfectly good; and the family physician, whom she privately consulted, said the same thing.

Mr. Jocelyn came occasionally to dine, in the intervals of his journeyings and enterprises, and was always so gently complaisant and demonstrative in his attentions to Isolind, that Mrs. Atheling, who cordially detested him, became possessed with the hideous idea that he meant to propose for the girl; at which idea, when she spoke of it to Atheling, he laughed, a grim hard little laugh, very unlike his genial boyish laugh of other days.

These were troubles for Isolind; but she had other troubles, too, of a more directly personal nature.

One was but a small vexation. Her volume of poems had created only too great a sensation. Respectability and piety had chosen to see in her pure aspirings and truly womanly protests against conventionality and cant and falsehood and baseness an assault upon society and the churches; and the press in general shrieked out against the book. Now, as it had appeared anonymously, and Isolind would not have sought to gain celebrity by the poems had they won to the utmost the public fancy, she might well have been excused for sheltering herself behind her anonymous position, and might have heeded little the misconception and the clamor. But it hurt the girl bitterly to find that she was thus misunderstood; and the unjust reproaches stung her like personal calumnies. She had, moreover, gone in rather strongly against the tendency to level all distinctions of habitual occupation and pursuit between men and women; and she had thus brought the voices of the strong-minded in shrill chorus against her. Thus the young poetess was attacked by a cross-fire; and her own sex assailed her rather more sharply even than the other.

Still Isolind, being a girl of spirit and of pure and lofty principle, could have borne all this well enough; but there were other trials upon her, for which philosophy can do as little as it can for the toothache.

Angelo Volney came frequently to the house. He had lingered in New York for some reason, while Escombe went south; but now he too must soon go; and Isolind dreaded to think of his going, and blushed and was ashamed to think how much she dreaded it. From the first moment when they spoke together, there had been something strangely sympathetic between these two fresh, unselfish, and generous natures. For some time their intercourse was free, unconstrained, and delightful; but of late it had become to each only as a kind of fearful joy—something too dangerous to be indulged, too exquisite to be resigned. Angelo remembered his pledge to his benefactress, and did not dare to give one word's expression to the new fierce passion that consumed him. Isolind, only too deeply conscious of her own love, was perpetually haunted by the dread lest she should by some look or tone betray her secret to one who had perhaps no love to give her in return.

At last poor Angelo, torn between his love and his pledge, resolved that this must end, that he would go away and see Isolind no more. He was too young and inexperienced to know that the girl loved him. She was far too beautiful and gifted, he thought, to care for one like him. To him still a fair and sweet girl was a being of a different order from man; and he thought that his heart alone and not hers would be wrung by the agony of separation.

So having, as he thought, made up his mind to the very worst, being resolved to keep his secret and go, he left the city one bright morning, crossed one of the ferries, and then took the train for the place where the Athelings lived. It was one of the most exquisite November days that even America could show. The waters of the bay slept in the soft sunlight of the Indian summer; and the woods had still their gorgeous garb of crimson and purple and orange. When the train landed him at the quiet little railway station—a plain wooden shed reached by a huge ascent of rough wooden steps, which rose directly from the edge of the line of rails—Angelo mounted the steps, and gazed for a moment on the broad quiet beauty of the scene. Only a few minutes ago he was among the muddy roaring streets of one of the noisiest cities in the world, and now he stood and gazed upon a scene which looked as lonely as it was lovely. The train had rushed onward towards its goal, and even its cloud of smoke and steam soon faded. There was no one at the station. The station-master, an awkward hobbledehoy, and the station-master's sister, a pleasant young woman with bright eyes and plenty of talk for every one, alternately attended on trains coming and going, but always disappeared the moment a train departed; and Angelo now had the platform all to himself. Its elevated position enabled it to command the whole landscape: the water that seemed to flow just beneath the gazer's feet; the wooded island in the bay, on Angelo's right; the clumps of firs and hickory and willow amid which he knew the home of Isolind to be; behind him a broad and smiling plain, dotted with wooden houses, gleaming in the white-and-green of walls, shutters, and porticos, and with here and there a church-spire rising; and in the far distance the belt of woods again, behind which at evening the sun would go down in a very blaze of gold and purple and fire.

Angelo could not choose but gaze upon the loveliness of the scene. But he was yet far too young to love Nature purely for her own calm beauty; and while he gazed and admired he still thought of Isolind, and of his deep vain love. How long was it since first he looked upon this place? It seemed half a lifetime—it was perhaps a month. How much he had grown in heart and feeling during that time! and what a new and bitter sense of shame, strange and new even as his love, had been rising within him! What was he after all—this was the thought that now hardly ever left him—but a pauper and a dependant? He was living on the bounty of Lady Judith; the very money he was spending here in New York was her money, the few cents he had paid as his fare to-day, that he might come and look on Isolind, were from Lady Judith's purse; and she held him bound to marry her daughter, whom now he could not love. He had never had a shilling of his own; he did not know how to set about earning a shilling. Were he to be free to-morrow, and were Isolind to love him—nay, to offer herself to him—he must ask her to marry a very beggar, or he must pass from abject dependence upon one woman to abject dependence upon another. Sometimes he could not help thinking that Lady Judith, with all her unspeakable beneficence, had been cruel to him in this kindness which disregarded the noblest qualities of manhood, and made of him but a pet and a pampered bond-slave. One thing seemed to him clear: that this must end; he must make a career for himself, and no longer depend on any bounty, however queen-like in its generosity. While he was yet unconscious of servitude it brought him no disgrace; now that he knew his own condition and felt its meaning, every day that he wilfully bore it was but another day of degradation.

Sometimes he had thought of speaking to Charles Escombe on the subject, and asking Escombe to help him to a career, that he might henceforward help himself. Again, he felt tempted often to unfold his own heart to kind and manly Atheling, for whom he had begun to feel quite a warm affection; and now he seemed to think that it was perhaps due to Lady Judith that she first should hear of the resolution he had made.

Thus meditating sadly enough over his past and his future, he turned away from the little station, and walked slowly to the landward gate of Atheling's modest grounds. He entered, and went on and on until he had reached the broad path where he sat next to Isolind that bright sweet day. And as he came within sight of the fallen tree, there seated on the tree, her face turned from him towards the sun and leaning on one of her hands, was Isolind herself.

Involuntarily he sprang towards her. The sound made her start and turn round, and her face flushed and her eyes sparkled when she saw him. She rose and went to meet him.

I am so glad you have come!" she said, and her lips quivered in spite of every effort at self-control. "Do you know that I thought you would come to-day? Everything looked so bright and lovely, that I thought, when you saw the sun shining on Broadway, you would reflect that it must shine far more brightly still on our beautiful bay, and that you would come to see."

"And you are glad I have come?"

"Oh, yes; very glad!" Then she stopped, afraid that she had spoken too warmly.

"I have come," said Angelo, trying to look bright, "on an errand, Miss Atheling, which rather spoils the sunlight for me. I have come to say good-by."

"To say good-by! So soon? Are you then really going to leave us already?"

"Will you sit for a moment again on this friendly old tree, Miss Atheling; and may I sit beside you?"

"Yes, surely."

She resumed her place on the fallen tree, and Angelo sat near her.

"It was here, Miss Atheling, I first sat beside you; and it seems only fitting that here I should say farewell—forever."

"Forever, Mr. Volney! Oh, surely not! Why should you speak of leaving us forever? You will pass through New York again, when you have joined Mr. Escombe, and travelled through our States; and, besides, may we not hope that you will be tempted to pay us another visit? Englishmen don't often come here a second time; but you do not feel so coldly to us—you will come?"

"Perhaps I may return here some day," said Angelo in a low firm tone; "but none the less do I now say farewell to you, Miss Atheling, and to this delightful scene, and to many a dear and sweet association. May I tell you a short story—and ask an advice?"

She started and blushed.

"The story I will gladly hear; the advice how can I promise?"

"Yet I beg for your advice; and, believe me, I am paying no idle compliment when I say there are few creatures on earth whose advice I would beg so earnestly. May I go on with my story?"

"You may."

She now kept her eyes fixed on the ground.

Then he began and told her his strange tale; how the Lady Judith had found him a beggar-boy on her steps, and took him in and brought him up as though he were her son. Isolind listened with wonder and ever-deepening interest. He said nothing of the offer of her daughter's hand which his benefactress had made to him. But he told how, when he came to know the whole truth of his past life, there grew on him scruple and shame that he should have lived a life of mere dependence, and now at manhood have no other career before him but that of a dependant; and how he had felt driven to break away and make a man's independent path in the world for himself; and how he was distracted between his gratitude to Lady Judith, his fear of giving her pain, and his sense of shame, and of the duty he owed to himself and to common manhood. All this he told with glowing fervor and animation, carried away even into something like eloquence by the strange delight of having such a *confidante* to whom to pour out some at least of the passionate demands of his soul.

Isolind listened with kindling eyes—soon with moistened eyes. When he had finished, she pressed his hand in obedience to an irresistible impulse of sympathy and regard, and she broke out at once with her counsel:

"Mr. Volney, your duty is clear, and your heart and mind have already seen it. Do not—oh, do not consent on any account, for any bond of gratitude, to lead an idle and dependent life. No sense of thankfulness can extort from you such a sacrifice of the finest part of your nature. Your benefactress herself, if she truly loves you, cannot but be glad to see you make a career for yourself, and be a man among men. Mr. Volney, I chafe to think even of a woman leading the life of a dependant and an idler. I lament the conditions which excuse and justify so many women who do this; but I cannot believe that any man is born for such a life. You have gifts and energy; you can easily make a bright path for youself. Stay in this great country, where all paths are open, and where the poorest youth may rise to the highest fortune. Stay here, or return here, and cast in your destinies among us. You are sure to succeed. I predict it for you; every friend who knows you must predict it."

Isolind was carried away by her sympathies and her interest, and she spoke with rapid, eager utterance, and with profound emotion. Angelo listened and held his breath and fixed his eyes on her—felt raised, for the first time in his life, to a sense of pride in himself by her manifest sympathy and friendly confidence.

"Miss Atheling," he said, "I thank you from my very heart. If I had needed decision, this would have decided me. I hardly know why or how I ventured to speak to you of my own affairs. I fear you will think it a strange piece of presumption; but I felt impelled to it, and only hope you will forgive me."

"On condition," she answered, with a friendly radiance in her eyes, "that you speak no more of saying farewell to us."

Angelo's expression grew dark and sad.

"I must say farewell all the same. I cannot stay here. I must say farewell to many things, to most things that so far made life dear; but above all——"

He stopped.

"Above all?" she asked, gently echoing his words.

"I am almost afraid to go on—afraid to say something which might offend you."

"How can that be, Mr. Volney? How is it possible you could wish to say anything that could offend me? I trust you as you have trusted me. Why must you leave us forever?"

The poor youth looked into her eyes for one bright short moment, and felt his heart glow and thrill in their kindly, frank, sympathetic light. Her face, so sweet and earnest in its expression, so pure and noble in its outlines, seemed glorified in the sunlight; and the bright hair which fell upon her neck borrowed some of the gleam of the sun itself. Strange that in the moment while he gazed upon her, as once before when he thought of her, his childhood and its sufferings came back upon him; but this time with a pang of grief and wild dismay, because he seemed as one who has been lifted from lowest darkness into light and heaven, only that he might be plunged back again into lonely hell.

"I must leave you," he exclaimed in a passionate outburst of emotion, all of the heat of southern nature, which he inherited from his mother, glowing up within him—"I must leave you, because I dare not see you any more—because I love you only too much already. Miss Atheling—Isolind—Isolind, forgive me that I cannot keep back my words. I never meant to speak out my soul in this mad way, but I cannot now keep my feelings from betraying me. I love you! I never, until I saw you, had any faint thought even of what love was, except such as I felt for Lady Judith and—and for Alexia" (he stammered a little as he pronounced the name, and felt a pang of regret and shame)—"for Alexia, whom I used to think of as my sister."

Isolind gently interposed. She had not expected this; and her bosom heaved with emotion, the true strength and source of which the impassioned Angelo had not divined, but she endeavored still to preserve her self-composure.

"Why not allow me to think of myself as your sister too? Believe me, n sister could feel a truer interest in your future and your success."

Angelo smiled, a wild smile, and tossed back his hair from his throbbing forehead.

"You are only too good and kind to me, Miss Atheling; but the love of a sister, even if you could really offer it to me, would be thrown away on me—from you. You cannot know how dark all things look to me in the future, or how much I leave forever when I leave you. But I love you, and I do not ask you—I dare not ask you—to offer me one encouraging word. I could not accept such a word, and I even thank Heaven that your heart does not suffer in the parting which tortures mine; but I must not see you any more."

Isolind sat with her eyes averted from his and her face crimsoned with emotion. She could hardly speak. If he would but have asked her to love him If he would but have offered her his love without reserve! But the young man, in the wildest vehemence of his emotion, seemed still to set a barrier between himself and any possible return of his love, and to forbid even kindness and pity to pass that bound.

"Here then, Isolind," exclaimed Angelo, and he sprang to his feet, "I look for the last time on this scene and on you. Always and wherever I go, the memory of that water and of those lonely woods shall remain inseparable in my soul from the thought of you, and I shall love them as I love no scenes of boyhood and youth. I never knew what life was until I saw you: I never knew my own heart, or its impulses, or its possibilities, until you taught it how to feel. I thought my utmost emotion was only in such affection and gratitude as I had for Lady Judith, whom I called my mother, and for Alexia; but at last I have learned what love is, and that I love you. Do not repel me—it is needless. I ask nothing of you—not even a refusal—for I have nothing to offer. The moment which brought me near you severed me forever from my past life and from past affections, and drives me away to be an outcast once again. Good-by, Isolind, my love—for once, this once, I will call you so. Forgive me if you can—even forget me if you will—and farewell."

He seized her hand impetuously, pressed it to his passionate lips once, only once, and then sprang from the place. Isolind heard the crash of his swift feet among the brushwood and amid the trees as he sped upon his way and left her.

She remained for a while seated on the fallen tree, and did not raise her head, but kept her eyes fixed upon the ground. The sun seemed to have suddenly faded from the sky, and the soft balmy air of the delicate Indian summer to have changed into the drearest and coldest winter wind. Thus, rigid and silent, she remained for a while; and then suddenly looked up with glowing cheek and flashing eye, and cried out, "Angelo! Angelo!" so that the little wood gave back the vain call; and then the girl fell upon the fallen tree again and hid her face in her hands, and broke into a quick tempest of tears.

That night Angelo Volney wrote a short letter of kindly farewell, warm thanks, and good wishes to the Athelings. He did not even mention Isolind's name. Perhaps he thought there would be a sort of deceitfulness and meanness in alluding in any commonplace and formal words to one who had heard from his own lips that day's wild avowal. However that might be, he did not mention her; and he wrote no line to her. He told the Athelings that he was compelled to leave New York; that he regretted he could not see them once more before his sudden departure; that he should always keep in bright recollection their kindness and their friendship; and bade them farewell. That very night he followed Charles Escombe down south. Angelo was inclined at once to tell his friend of his new resolve, and receive what counsel he might. But he was determined that nothing should alter his purpose. The inherent manliness of the youth's nature, the steady and single-minded devotion which had been his childhood's virtue while he gave up his earliest years to hunger and drudgery in the service of his poor mother, remained true to him now. It was now impossible that he could love Lady Judith's daughter; impossible, therefore, that he could remain a dependant on the woman whose one sole wish he could not gratify; equally impossible that he whose life lay all dark and difficult before him, and whose only hope was to enter resolutely and doggedly into any way of existence, however humble, in which he could make a subsistence honestly, could dare to seek the love of such a girl as Isolind Atheling. His lot seemed a hard one: to have to renounce love because he resigned worldly ease; to renounce that ease because he had known love. But that lot he was firm to encounter. Just now indeed he had but one thought ruling in his heart—the thought that he loved Isolind Atheling; that he must love her always, and that he had lost her forever. This dominated even over the bitterness of the reflection that he must repay the kindness of his benefactress with a seeming ingratitude; and the occasional throbbings of a fierce, almost savage pride, in the conviction that the poor beggar-boy could show himself more proud than the proudest who would befriend him.

And Isolind—how was it with her when she was left by him, when she knew he had gone? Love came to her, as life comes, with throbs and agony; and for the first time in her life the young poetess knew what it was to be unhappy. For some part at least of that day, when Angelo proclaimed his passion and his renunciation, she did almost wholly give herself up to grief. She did what in all probability the weakest-minded and the strongest of her sex would alike have done. She hid herself in her room, locked her door, threw herself upon her bed, and wept bitterly. It would have seemed less sad and trying to her if she could even have told him of her love; could have answered his passionate avowal by an equally passionate avowal of her own, and sent him forth on his strange new struggle with the world cheered and strengthened by the assurance that her love followed him like a blessing. She reproached herself sometimes that she had not had the courage to speak out; she called that a false pride, a cruel and mistaken sentiment of delicacy, which allowed her to send her lover on his bleak and weary way without one word or sign of her love. Had he been prosperous and rich in worldly blessings, as he once seemed to be, then, indeed, she might well have forborne to speak. But to hear from the same lips which proclaimed his love the story of his misfortune and his self-accepted poverty, to know, as she could not but know, that he had refrained from asking for her love only because of the darkness which hung over his path, and yet to have withheld from him the only words which could have given gladness to his heart—this smote upon Isolind's warm and generous bosom as a cruel and unwomanly piece of coldness and rigid restraint. For it need hardly be said that, like a true woman, she found Angelo more dear than ever because of the strangeness of his history and the poverty and hard struggle which he was resolved to accept. So she mourned with all the bitter self-reproaching sorrow which one feels who knows that the friend is gone forever whom kind words would have gladdened, and that the kind words have been withheld in a mood of wilful, irreparable silence.

But the realities of life left Isolind little time for the luxury of lonely tears. She knew that there is a sensualism of grief which the heart with a high purpose can no more indulge than the sensualism of joy. She arose and went about her daily tasks, taking no pleasure in them, but still striving to give pleasure to others. The household was, indeed, sadly changed. A cloud seemed to hang always over it. The fall and the Indian summer passed away, and the Athelings left their home on the shores of the bay, and migrated to New York, where presently the snow came down thick and heavy, covering every street many inches deep from the Castle Garden to the Central Park, and from the North river to the Brooklyn ferries. The sleigh-bells rang merrily in the streets all day, and the snow-plough was often called into use to clear away some of the depths of snow and allow the traffic to get somehow up and down Broadway. Isolind, who usually watched with ever fresh delight each change of the seasons, seemed to care little whether it was winter or summer. The beauty of the snow was lost on her, as the glory of the sunlight would have been. The heart that nature never betrays must, in truth, love nature only, and nothing else; and as Isolind's was not such a heart, nature refused to console it.

Mr. Jocelyn came as usual at random frequent intervals during these months. He was more bland than ever to Mrs. Atheling, but had frequent talks with the Judge, from which he sometimes emerged with a fierce moodiness of face. His keen black eye soon noted a change in Isolind.

One evening when the two happened to be left a few moments alone, Jocelyn turned to Atheling and said:

"Do you resemble justice in being blind, Atheling? Have you no eyes? Don't you see the condition into which that girl is sinking?"

"Good heavens! our Isolind?"

"Our Isolind, indeed. Can't you see? can't your wife see? The girl is pining away; she will be in a consumption presently if you don't take care. As soon as winter is over, with the first fine weather, you must take her to Europe."

Atheling listened like one on whom the shock of a paralyzing surprise had fallen. He had never thought of Isolind but as the living symbol of health, the strength as well as the brightness of the house.

"Take her to Europe," continued Jocelyn. "You yourself had better, on the whole, be out of the way about then. And that girl must have an entire change of air and scene. Look here, Atheling, you must take her to England—to London."

"My God, I would travel round the earth with her," exclaimed the Judge, "rather than my sweet child should lose one tinge of the color in her cheek!"

"Color in her cheek! Judge, if you will only be good enough to open your eyes and look at her, you will see that there is little color left there now; and what there is will soon fade if something be not done. For England, Atheling, before it be too late."

"But Isolind does not like England; she will not go there."

"Stuff, man; that was her nonsense of six months back—ten thousand years ago. She will go to England gladly now, and she will recover her roses there."

"Why do you say so? How do you know?"

"Do you make no allowance," asked Jocelyn, suddenly assuming, or resuming, his habitual air of jaunty *fanfaronnade* which he had for a moment laid aside, "for the instincts and inspirations of the paternal heart?"

"In your case," replied Atheling sternly, "none whatever."

"So, then, most wise Judge, your love would let the girl die, and never know that there was anything wrong with her until it was time to order her coffin. I don't profess any particular depth of affection for her, and shouldn't feel much were she my child twenty times over; and yet I can see that that girl suffers, and that you—or shall I say *we*, Atheling?—are likely enough to lose her if something be not done."

"I'll call in Dr. Sharp to-morrow," stammered the alarmed Atheling.

"Spare yourself the trouble and her the alarm, Judge; there is nothing in Dr. Sharp's pharmacopœia to meet such a case as hers. Once more, take Isolind to England."

"Why England?" Atheling asked, still puzzled.

"Perhaps because England is her native air," Jocelyn coolly answered. "You forget, Judge, that our Isolind is an English girl, although you have trained her up to be so sadly unpatriotic. But her heart is in England now, and the sooner she follows it the better. My heart is there too, Atheling; and I only wish I could follow it, and her and you, and never return here again."

"Hush, here she comes," whispered the Judge; and Isolind entered, looking pale and sad indeed.

CHAPTER XIII.

ALEXIA'S DEFIANCE.

THE spring of the year is opening. The little children are again beginning to make their voices heard of evenings in the smaller and shabbier streets of London—in the streets where the parents are not so poor as to leave their children to play on the pavement in all seasons and at all hours, yet poor enough to welcome the first breath of milder weather which frees their little parlors from the noisy sportiveness of the young ones. The snow is beginning to disappear from the great thoroughfares of New York, and the hills of the Hudson will soon look brown again. The fresh breath of the spring fans the pale cheek of Isolind, who is eating her heart away with love, which she fears it is unwomanly to confess. The same air plays unheeded around the forehead of Chesterfield Jocelyn, who has been hatching a winter of daring and desperate enterprises, and is already looking with bold and bright eyes to the crisis which is to make him or undo him quite. It seems to bring some hope of healing on its wings to Judge Atheling, who grows a little like his old self with the growing year; and it inspires to new courage Angelo Volney, who is resolute to begin at once a fresh, untried, momentous chapter of his existence. It breathes or lulls unnoticed by Lady Judith Scarlett. Lady Judith could name every star visible to the naked eye, and she knew botany well; but she cared nothing in particular about the perfume of a flower; and the midnight sky was to her only a map of the constellations outspread over her head.

Meanwhile she labored hard and patiently at her life's occupation of doing good—or at least of trying to do good—to people upon her own interpretation of their moral and spiritual needs. But a certain change was slowly, almost imperceptibly, making itself felt in her character. Perhaps she was of late beginning half audibly to ask herself the hitherto unknown question—Why is this? With all her singleness of purpose and patient earnestness of effort, she did not seem to have the power of making the good grow around her. She sowed good seed apparently, and thistles and tares came up. Sometimes, therefore, she could hardly help asking herself whether perhaps there was not something in the way of sowing the seed, or in its selection, which earned such failures. In other words, she was at least on the threshold of that condition of mind which would cease to believe in its own infallibility. This is indeed a change in the character of egotism. Lady Judith was only an egotist. She was absolutely unselfish. This story must fail of its purpose sadly if its readers will not bear in mind that selfishness and egotism are totally different qualities, and that the egotist and the selfish person may be contrasts and counter-agencies not only in fiction, but in the real business of life.

Lady Judith sat at her desk one morning writing letters. She was very busy, having a great many schemes on hand, and had given orders that she was not to be disturbed. Lady Judith was a good letter-writer—concise, direct, and pertinent in style—and she sat at a desk like that of a professional secretary rather than the sort of toy which women love to have who play at letter-writing and business. Her beautiful white hand—not too small, but of perfect shape, and glittering with rings—went firmly and rapidly across every page. As each page was written, it was finished and done with. No word required alteration or expunging. There were no blots; there were no letters left blind for lack of a dot over them, or powerless for want of a cross-stroke.

The entrance of a servant, bringing a card, disturbed her, and she said in a cold decisive tone: "I gave orders that I was not to be interrupted. I am engaged."

Lady Judith never tolerated any such social figments as "Not at home." To say, in any form of conventional politeness, the thing which was not, meant a lie to her. She was incapable even of the most pious fraud.

The servant explained that the gentleman who brought the card said he had business so pressing, that he must ask Lady Judith to see him.

Lady Judith looked at the card. It bore the name of Mr. Gostick, M. P.

Now the name of Mr. Gostick was quite familiar to Lady Judith. Most cultivated Englishwomen of her class pay attention to the proceedings in Parliament, where they probably have husbands, brothers, or sons; and Lady Judith studied politics closely. She knew quite well that Mr. Gostick was a Lancashire member, a strong nonconformist, and quite a notable person in church-rate debates and reform-bill discussions, Lady Judith was herself a Liberal of the Whig aristocratic kind; and she considered Mr. Gostick and men of his class simply as coarse purse-proud Radical clowns, whom Liberals of position and culture were compelled to tolerate. But she took it for granted that Mr. Gostick knew his place and hers. She assumed, as a matter of course, that Mr. Gostick considered Lady Judith Scarlett a personage utterly out of the range of possible acquaintanceship or familiarity; and therefore she came instantly to the conclusion that he must have some serious motive for his visit. Further, she remembered—and the recollection made her cheek color and her lips close even now—how she had heard from many sources that Mr. Gostick was one of the last persons who had seen her husband in London.

So she ordered Mr. Gostick to be admitted; and she bent to him with stately courtesy as he entered.

Mr. Gostick came in, bearing his hat and cane in his hands, on which hands were cotton gloves of the kind called after the capital of Prussia. Lady Judith took him in from head to foot at a glance, and she did not shudder. It was just what she had expected. As for Mr. Gostick, he was quite undismayed. The richness of the furniture and general surroundings did not impress him. His own house in Lancashire was furnished still more expensively; and he liked his shabby old rooms in Manchester Buildings rather better. Neither did the beauty of the lady's face, nor the grandeur of her figure, make any effect on him. Women did not interest him particularly; he had hundreds of them in his employment in Lancashire, and he found that they were good and bad, just like men; but he never observed whether any one of them was handsomer than another.

Lady Judith motioned to a chair. After all, Mr. Gostick was a member of Parliament, and thus entitled to a sort of official courtesy from every person of recognized position responsible for the maintenance of social order.

"I beg pardon for disturbing you, Lady Judith," Mr. Gostick began, "but my business is rather pressing; and I think it concerns you more than it does me. In fact, I shouldn't have thought of disturbing you on business of mine."

Lady Judith drew herself back, and looked at the intrepid Lancashire man with cold proud wonder.

"You have a daughter, Alexia, ma'am?"

The lady inclined her head and contracted her eyebrows.

"Yes; I've seen her—and I have a nephew. You know him—at least he says you do—Eric Walraven?"

"I have the pleasure of knowing Mr. Eric Walraven—not very intimately. I never knew that he was a near relative of yours."

"No, I dare say not. He's not very proud of the relationship when he gets among what he calls the aristocracy; but you should hear him boast of it down in Lancashire, or when he wants to borrow money."

"May I ask you, Mr. Gostick, to favor me with the object of your visit? I have not yet heard anything of that."

"Certainly, ma'am; and don't blame me if I come to the point directly. My nephew, Eric Walraven, is a scamp, and he proposes to run away with your daughter and marry her."

The blood rushed into Lady Judith's face as if she had received a blow That any man should dare to hint at such a thing! That she should be exposed to the insult of listening to such a statement! She would not, however, stoop to the degradation of exhibiting any anger. She rose from her chair with stately calmness, as if to bring the interview to an end, and said with complete self-composure:

"All that I have seen of Mr. Eric Walraven has shown him to be a well-conducted and honorable young man. Even were it otherwise, your words, Mr. Gostick, are quite absurd—unworthy a man of your years and respectability. My daughter Alexia is a foolish child sometimes, but she has never deceived me; and she knows her position—and the thing is impossible."

"I tell you, ma'am, the thing is settled. If you don't look out, it will be an accomplished fact. My nephew is perfectly unscrupulous and a consummate deceiver. Why, it's only the other day that he took me in completely—me who ought to have known better! What chance has your little girl in dealing with such a fellow? Why, he has succeeded in imposing on you. Come, Lady Judith, I'm an old man, and I have girls of my own; and I suppose girls are made of flesh and blood in every class; and you may be sure it's no pleasure to me to come and expose the shabby conduct of my sister's son. I do it, ma'am, because I think it my duty to warn you."

"I thank you, sir. I am sure you mean it well; but you have perhaps hardly considered——"

"I have, Lady Judith—I have considered everything. I very seldom act upon impulse, ma'am, and I never say a word without being able to prove it. Come, Lady Judith, forget for a moment that you are an earl's daughter and that I am only a plain man of business. I am a father, and I talk to you, a mother, for the sake of your daughter, and to save her from a runaway marriage with a bad young man."

"Well, then, Mr. Gostick," said Lady Judith, resuming her seat calmly, "let us, if you will, forget everything for the moment but the fact that you have a nephew and that I have a daughter. What ground have you for asserting that my daughter has deceived me?"

"Did you ever, ma'am, give your daughter permission to receive love-letters from my nephew?"

"Assuredly not."

"Well, I thought not. I need hardly ask if you ever allowed your daughter to write love-letters to my nephew."

This was perhaps as great a trial as Lady Judith's temper had ever borne. But she surmounted it triumphantly, and replied composedly:

"As you say, Mr. Gostick, you need hardly ask me such a question. But since you have asked me, I had better give you an answer. I never authorized my daughter to write letters of any kind to Mr. Walraven. I never supposed it possible that she could think of writing to him. I do not still think it possible."

"Then, ma'am, you are entirely mistaken. I saw some of her letters myself with my own eyes. The fellow had the impudence to show them to me because I wouldn't believe what I supposed to be his brag and lies. But I saw the letters, ma'am—downright love-letters; silly stuff—no harm in it, if the girl were writing to a decent man with the consent of her mother."

"You saw them—read them—letters of my daughter to this low deceitful wretch?"

"I saw them—love-letters signed 'Alexia.' If they are forgeries, you can easily find out by asking your daughter. God knows, I almost wish they were; for the fellow couldn't be any worse than he is, and the poor girl would be safe. As you say, Lady Judith, he is 'low' indeed. My father—his grandfather—was a working weaver, ma'am. But it's odd that *he* is the only one of the family who ever kept company with aristocratic acquaintances, and he is likewise the only one of the family that ever proved himself dishonest. Now I have warned you, Lady Judith Scarlett, and done my duty. It was not an agreeable duty, but it's done; and the rest is your business, not mine. I wish your ladyship a good morning."

Lady Judith hardly heard what he was saying. The proud forlorn woman's heart was swelling as though it were indeed about to burst. The bitter sense was growing on her that she was destined to meet with nothing but treachery, and that she was incapable of coping with the falsehood around her. While Gostick was speaking she sat supporting her chin with one hand, the arm resting on her knee, and looking with sad, cold, rayless eyes into vacancy. That which the Lancashire man took for the haughty impassive bearing of the scornful aristocrat was but the growing, conquering agony of the woman. Gostick might have pitied her if he could but have known how she was suffering.

His somewhat brusque good-morning recalled her to herself.

"This seems an honest man," she thought; "he is a man who tries to do his duty and to do me a service. God help me!"

"Mr. Gostick," she said, rallying together all her powers of self-control, "I will not deny that this is a sharp blow to me, unless it prove that you are mistaken, or that this man has forged the letters. In any case, I am obliged to you, deeply obliged. You have acted like a man of conscience and of high principle, like a father, and like—and like—a gentleman." (This last word she brought out with a great effort, for even in that moment she thought Mr. Gostick looked very unlike a gentleman.) "Now, tell me one thing. If this is true, what does this man want?"

"My nephew?"

"Yes; this Walraven."

"Money, Lady Judith, and the honor of marrying anyhow into the aristocracy."

Lady Judith winced and shuddered.

"But the girl has no money, unless what I may choose to give her."

Gostick laughed his hard dry laugh.

"He thinks when once he has married her you will have to do something for him, for your own credit's sake. And more, ma'am, he has got into his head the notion—well, perhaps I ought not to go on. I am treading on dangerous ground, and I don't want to offend you. I want only to do what's right."

"Please, Mr. Gostick, go on. I can hear anything that has to be said."

"Yes; I don't want to say anything that hasn't to be said, you may depend upon it. He has got it into his head that Mr. Charles Grey Scarlett may have left some of his property to his daughter."

Lady Judith felt her cheeks flush with passion.

"This base intrigue shall be foiled," she exclaimed. "I thank you, Mr. Gostick, for what you have told me. In return, will you let me tell you that this man Walraven shall never gain one penny of money from me even were he to satisfy his wildest hopes, and carry out his abominable plot by marrying my daughter in some secret way? I will take steps, depend upon it, to foil any such plot. But even were it to be successful, *he* shall gain nothing. My daughter shall perish of want before he shall be the richer for one coin. Of her father's will *I* know nothing; I have never asked a question of any one on the subject. But I am still convinced that he is not dead; and either he does not even know that he has a daughter, or he has shown himself utterly and wickedly regardless of his daughter's existence. Your nephew is mistaken if he founds any hopes on that quarter. Tell him that too from me."

"I sha'n't tell him anything," said blunt Mr. Gostick. "I hope I shall never have any need to speak to him again. I gave him warning plump and plain that I would tell you—your ladyship—all he had told me, and that I would warn you against him."

"You told him that? What did he say?" asked Lady Judith eagerly, catching at a ray of possible hope.

"He only said it was too late now; that the girl was madly in love with him, and that she would run away or drown herself to-morrow if he only asked her. And, my lady, you had better be very cautious, for, from what I have seen, I believe it's true enough. Sorry I've had to disturb your ladyship, and worry you with this disagreeable business; but I couldn't help it, and I ask your pardon. I have daughters myself, and I'm sorry for you."

So Mr. Gostick made a hurried, rough sort of compromise with a bow and took his leave, putting on his hat before he had got half-way down the stairs, and thinking, on the whole, rather better of Lady Judith than he was disposed to do before entering the house.

"Sorry for me!" murmured Lady Judith, echoing his last words. "Sorry for me! I wonder who is there who knows me and does not pity me? What creature so poor and mean who would not think me an object of pity if he did but know? Great God! that I should be brought so low that any clown may tell me he is sorry for me, and I can only meekly own that I am indeed a woman who merits pity! This base deceitful wretch—and this most miserable girl! It is true—it is all true! I feel it—I know it! These weeks back I have seen an insolent light of happy defiance in her eyes—a look for which I could not account—a look that seemed to boast of being quite independent of me, of having found a source of happiness all her own! I could not then understand it; I never should have guessed the meaning of it; but now, now it comes on me as if Heaven had revealed it! The wretched, wretched girl!"

A light step was heard on the threshold, and the wretched, wretched girl herself entered the room. Truth to say, she did not look very miserable; on the contrary, there was a certain radiancy about her whole demeanor such as Alexia did not often wear in other days.

"Mamma, who was that dreadful person who has just been visiting you? Only that I don't suppose you have personal interviews with the tax-collectors, I should have set him down as one of the fraternity. Was I right? Income, mamma, or water-rates? He looked angry, I thought. Is our water to be cut off?"

"That person, Alexia, was one in whom *you* ought to have a peculiar interest."

"Oh, indeed! A mad doctor, or a keeper, mamma?"

"Alexia, that gentleman was Mr. Gostick, uncle of your friend Mr. Eric Walraven."

Lady Judith turned round in her chair, and came face to face with her daughter, watching the expression on the girl's countenance as Alexander the Great might have studied the visage of the suspected physician before swallowing the famous draught of medicine. Alexia's face betrayed her. A faint color rose upon those pale cheeks, the lips quivered, and the girl's slender figure seemed to shrink together. Only for a moment, however. Alexia at once saw that the game was up, that her secret was discovered. She was fairly driven to bay, and now she heeded nothing.

"Indeed!" she said coldly, as she threw herself on a sofa and took up a book; "I should never have thought it. Where did so handsome and noble a creature as Eric get such an uncle?"

"Then it is all true, Alexia, what he told me?"

"I don't know, Lady Judith. What did he tell you? He looks the sturdy plodding sort of person who would be terribly truthful and literal."

"Is it true that you, my daughter, have been carrying on a silly shameful love-affair with this Mr. Eric Walraven, nephew of that man?"

"No, mamma; it is quite false."

"False?"

"That I have been carrying on a silly and shameful love-affair. But that I love Eric Walraven, and that I have told him so, and that I mean to be his wife, is as true as gospel, Lady Judith."

"You have been writing love-letters to him?"

"Indeed I have. Why not? I love him."

"And you have deceived me—cruelly and basely deceived me—all this time! Alexia, I could have believed you capable of anything but deceit."

"Thank you, mamma. I never knew there was anything bad of which you did not believe me capable. Tyranny, Lady Judith, engenders deceit. I think I remember reading that somewhere. Women and slaves are generally liars; deceit is their weapon of defence. You were always my tyrant, dear mamma; you had all the weapons of oppression. I should have some shield, you know."

"You can look me in the face, can boast of your unwomanly love for this man, and you do not blush—you are not ashamed!"

Lady Judith was now sitting once more in the attitude already described, leaning one arm on her knee, and with the hand supporting her chin, while with sternly gleaming eyes she strove to carry humiliation and terror into the heart of her daughter. Alexia sprang from her sofa, went over to her mother, kneeled down on the carpet, put back her hair from her face, and then looked straight up into Lady Judith's eyes.

"Ashamed, mamma? Look at me. Do I seem ashamed? Do I not look you in the face? I tell you I was never in my life proud of anything before; and I am proud of my love for Eric Walraven. I love him—love, love, love him! Unwomanly? Since when has it been unwomanly to love? Don't provoke me, Lady Judith, or I may speak of what *is* unwomanly—not to love at all, not to understand a noble love when it is offered."

"Unhappy girl! what is to become of you? May God forgive you!"

"Forgive me for what? For loving one of the noblest of His creatures? Of course He will forgive me. He is God, and not a petty, passionate, implacable mortal. Did you call me unhappy, mamma? How little you know of my feelings! I never before knew what happiness could be. I know it now for the first time. Eric has taught me what it is. Shall I tell you, Lady Judith? It is love."

Alexia sprang to her feet again, and stood up in an attitude of cool defiance.

"Do you know, Alexia, that you are still under my guardianship and control?"

"Oh yes, mamma, I know all that. How could I ever forget it? But I can wait; I shall be my own mistress some time. I don't mind waiting, if it must be so, nor does Eric."

"Perhaps you are not aware that Eric, as you call him, shows your silly letters to everybody, and boasts that he is going to marry you because he thinks you have money."

Alexia laughed in utter scorn.

"So Mr. Gostick has been trying to deceive you, my poor mamma! So he has been telling you *that* story! I knew how much he hated Eric because Eric despises his low, miserly, vulgar ways; and this is his effort at revenge! Clumsy, like the man himself, as I have just seen him. Lady Judith, Eric Walraven has the purest and noblest soul ever given to man. Tell these false calumnious stories to some one who might believe them, some creature incapable of appreciating a soul like *his*. I only laugh at Mr. Gostick's tales."

"Listen to me, Alexia. You know whether I do not always keep my word. Marry Eric Walraven, and I cast you off forever. You shall never have one coin from me—never, never! Tell your lover *that*, and see whether his ardor does not cool."

Alexia laughed again.

"Poor mamma! So you really cannot believe in love? I don't wonder at the fate of my father! Why, Eric has told me over and over again that he knew you would cut me off utterly; and he cares as little abont the money you please to withhold from me as I do. We don't want your money, Lady Judith. Eric has genius and a name; and we sha'n't want for food, mamma, depend upon it. You talk really as if you were a reader of the old-fashioned romances, in which the disconsolate heroines, turned out of doors by their flinty-hearted parents, could only sit on door-steps in their night-dresses, in the drenching rain, and weep."

"I had hoped for a better fate for you, Alexia."

"To be the happy bride of Charles Escombe, mamma? To have blue-books read to me of afternoons, and to be pressed into expeditions to the Lambeth vagrant sheds? No, thank you. Let that good young man find somewhere a good young woman with a healthy taste for political economy. I never was good, Lady Judith, as *you* can testify."

"It was not Charles Escombe to whom I had hoped to see you some day married; it was Angelo Volney."

A faint color came on Alexia's cheek, and she dropped her eyes.

"Angelo Volney is far too good for me, mamma. I am not jesting now, or speaking of him as I would of a dry prig like Charles Escombe. But Angelo is too grave and sweet and good. His life would be worn away with trying to keep me in order; and besides, Angelo never cared for me, except in the beloved-brother sort of way. Nor could I now love him to marry him, whatever I might have done once."

There was something unusually calm in Alexia's tone, and her mother could not fail to observe it.

"You talk, Alexia, as composedly of marriage and love as if you were a mature and experienced woman, not a girl who had hardly yet passed beyond the years of childhood."

"I have left the years of childhood long behind, Lady Judith. I sometimes doubt whether I ever was a child. I can only remember being always moody and uncomfortable—always vexed about something or other. But I have grown very old within the last few months; and I am so happy now, that I don't care to think of the past. Mamma, *you* never gave me one hour's happiness. Look in my face, and dare to tell me that you will now endeavor to stand between me and the only happiness I have ever known!"

"Child, child, you are bringing misery, not happiness, on yourself! Could I have allowed you, when you were an infant, to swallow poison because its color seemed tempting to you? Just as little will I allow you now, if I can help it, to take a step which would be as fatal."

"You cannot help it, Lady Judith! Nothing on earth shall prevent me from becoming Eric Walraven's wife whenever he thinks the right time has come to ask me."

"But if I can convince you—convince even you, foolish and headstrong child—that this man is only deceiving you; that he is a false and selfish adventurer——"

"Hush, hush, Lady Judith! Not a word more of that kind; not a word against my Eric! Nothing you could say could have any effect on me. You, who never loved, do not know what it means to have faith in a man. I do. I would cling to him and believe in him though one rose from the dead to preach against him!"

"What if his own words were to convict him?"

Lady Judith laid her firm white hand upon the shoulder of the girl, who tried to shrink away from the touch. Alexia's eyes flashed fire.

"You talk impossibilities, mamma. But if you will talk them, let me give you an answer. My whole soul and heart are bound up in the love of Eric Walraven. Prove to me that he does not love me—only, thanks to the good God who made him what he is, and made him for me, you cannot do it—and I will kill myself. You remember, Lady Judith, the little dagger I bought in Paris, and that you took from me? I got it into my hands again, and I have kept it since. I have kept it always inside my stays, and I have had it under my pillow of nights. Do you know why? Because I did not know when my dear mother might not think it wise and right and religious to send her daughter to a lunatic asylum; and I was glad to have always ready to my hand the means of saving myself from *that.* Now things are changed with me, and I have no more inclination for killing myself than the most resigned and pious of you all; I love life now—oh, so fondly! But I love it only for Eric. If he were dead, or if you could prove to me what you say, then this little toy would become very useful Now, Lady Judith, you have my answer!"

Lady Judith's hand fell from the shoulder of her child. It was not the threat of the girl which appalled her mother, although she believed Alexia well capable of carrying it into desperate execution. It was the recklessness which dared to do wrong, which could resolutely promise and purpose to commit a crime, could defy Heaven to Heaven's face—this it was which paralyzed and bewildered Lady Judith. She shuddered as one who hears some dreadful blasphemy issuing from lips which ought to have breathed only a prayer. Nothing could shake Lady Judith's courage or nerves but the thought of a deliberate crime. For the moment she quailed before the fierce little girl, and repented of the words spoken by herself which had provoked this outburst, as one might repent of some hasty ignorant utterance which called up a demom.

Before she could recover herself, Alexia had left the room; and Lady Judith had lost the battle, and knew it.

She laid her hand heavily upon her broad breast, as if she could thus keep down the pain that was swelling there. "I am not able to cope with this girl any more," she bitterly said; and she flung herself upon her knees, and asked of Heaven, in almost fierce expostulation, why a task had been imposed upon her which was beyond her strength to accomplish.

Let us do Lady Judith justice. She had little or none of that which is called a mother's feeling. Even when she gave her bosom to the infant Alexia, she had not loved the babe as happier mothers love their children. For years back she and her daughter never had known one bright hour together. Lately their life had become but as a trial of strength, and the weaker nature always came off in the end victorious, because of its very weakness. Lady Judith was, in the contests with her daughter, placed at almost such a disadvantage as a man is when he quarrels with a woman. Alexia was but weak, fretful, and freakish, while Lady Judith was calm and strong; but Alexia had no restraining moral sense, no heed of exposure, no thought of dignity or propriety; and thus she often carried her point. But now Lady Judith felt that a graver crisis was at hand, and that her daughter was about to break away from her forever. The justice, then, we ask for her is, that she shall have full credit for the unselfish sense of duty which made her now as anxious to save Alexia from what she deemed a calamitous and degrading marriage as though the love of a mother's full heart were vainly poured out on her daughter. Probably, to save the splenetic little girl who defied and insulted her, Lady Judith would at this moment have sacrificed the dearest legacy and treasure her bosom still cherished—the treasure of a bitter memory, the precious legacy of a sense of wrong.

Lady Judith rose from her knees, softened and strengthened so far as to be willing to take a step from which she had always hitherto shrunk as from an intolerable personal degradation. It was not a great thing in itself; but to her it was so much that it involved a positive self-conquest. There was a great deal of the heroine about this proud and beautiful woman. She had many of the splendid magnanimous qualities which mark the greatest natures and the greatest deeds. Hers might have been a noble scheme of life had she not disdained to admit into it the element of human love. "Soon or late," in another sense from that contemplated by the poet, "Love is his own avenger." And this is the truth which Lady Judith was destined by sharp experience to learn.

CHAPTER XIV.

"DOES MY OLD FRIEND REMEMBER ME?"

IN many parts of London, long before one has reached the suburbs, may be found quaint old-fashioned houses standing in a sort of isolation, and with large gardens around or behind them. Perhaps the gardens are surrounded by a wall, tall and blind as that of a Syrian mansion, and the passer-by never knows that he is not looking at a brewery or a soap-boiling concern, or a House of Correction; whereas inside that dull barrier banks of roses are blooming in the summer, and clusters of grapes are ripening on the southern wall. Perhaps, however, the brick-and-mortar fences are low, and then the pedestrian, fagging through miles of weary dusty streets, gets tantalizing glimpses of fruit and flowers, and sees the green boughs of trees waving over his head. These little sacred spots are usually places which the lucky occupier holds under a very long lease, and which therefore so far have defied the progress of building works and terrace rows. As each lease falls in, the enterprising proprietor is pretty sure to pull down the old house, cut up the garden into lots for building purposes, and soon a genteel terrace of houses, small enough to suit the tenancy of dolls, is run up, or perhaps the beginning of a new street is made there; and the very spot on which the late resident watched his grapes growing purple in the autumn sun is occupied by a corner ginshop.

On the south side of London, near the inner fringe of the suburbs, but yet well built around by busy streets, stood lately, and perhaps still stands, one of these old houses. Looked at from the front, it was an old shabby structure, with a sort of monastic appearance about it—a small house with a little Gothic porch and a tiny window on either side; a building that seemed as if it might once have been the lodge of a convent. A wooden paling with a very rickety door divided it from the road, and within the paling were two or three trees large and leafy enough almost to mask the whole front of the house. Behind the house, however, was quite a spacious garden—a garden that would have counted for something even in an inland county town. Once in this garden, the visitor seemed to have no more to do with London than if he were in the heart of the New Forest. The garden had trees so tall and apparently so old and venerable, that wandering rooks frequently took them *au sérieux*, and perched and cawed in the branches. Smaller trees and shrubs were dotted everywhere. The sumach's shaggy branches, looking like the paws of a cinnamon bear, clawed you as you paced the walks. A noble copper beech had a commanding place on a patch of greensward. Strawberry-beds lined the base of one wall. Vines mantled the side of another. Ivy crept all over the back of the old house, which looked upon the garden

Apple-trees made the place bright with their blossoms at one season and rich with their fruit at another. There were a few rose-trees and pinks; but the occupier did not appear to give much attention to the culture of flowers. The walls were so high that no glimpse of the roads could anywhere be seen, and only a portion of one neighboring building obtruded itself on the gaze of the lounger in the garden. By an odd chance, too, this one only evidence of an outer world was a quaint gable of some old almshouse which stood near; a gable covered with red tiles much overgrown with ivy, and having one little lattice-window in it. This therefore added to instead of detracting from the appearance of venerable loneliness which gave so strange a charm to the place.

One of the early days of the budding spring the occupant of this little oasis in the London desert was pacing up and down his garden, with a book in his hand. Sometimes he glanced at the volume, and sometimes he inspected the condition of the trees and the promise of the buds. He was a thin man, rather below the middle size, very shabbily and carelessly dressed. He might have been called seedy, but for the scrupulous cleanliness shown in his shirt and collar and wrists. He did not look old, although his hair was white as snow, and he wore a white moustache and long full white beard. His face was perfectly bloodless, yet it looked fresh and healthy, and his quiet gray eyes seemed to express a sort of languid resignation rather than melancholy. One could hardly glance at him without having the idea of Defeat called up to the mind. A general who had failed and given up his sword and retired from the world, or a prisoner restricted on parole to a life within certain bounds, might, if manfully resolved to make the best of things, have come in time to wear such an expression.

Indeed, Robert May was in some sense a defeated man. That is to say, he was like thousands of men who start in English university life with apparently great talents and much aptitude for culture, and whose co-mates look on them as certain of great success; but who prove in after years to lack the fibre out of which success is welded, and in the strain of life grow limper and limper, and at length relax altogether. May did not get on; in fact, he got off. He was cursed with a little income, just enough to live on decently without struggle, and not nearly enough to help him to any career. Even this little property faded out of his possession somehow after a while, and then some of the friends who had not wholly forgotten him obtained for him a permanent appointment as principal teacher in one of the foundation schools with which England abounds. Robert May therefore was principal of an institution endowed a century or two back for the purpose of teaching Greek and Latin to boys belonging to that parish and the Protestant Church, whose fathers had been killed in fighting against the French. The most liberal construction of the purposes of the founder did not in Robert May's time entitle a very large class of scholars to enjoy the benefits of the institution, but it still did have the grandchildren or great-grandchildren of a few heroes who had fallen at Waterloo or Corunna. Therefore to direct the classic studies of these gave Robert occupation enough to prevent him from regarding himself as an idler, or perceiving too keenly that his life had been a failure. The school was near his house, and the walk thither and back formed almost his only expedition outside his own walls. His sister Tessy, or Teresa, managed his home for him, and they kept one old woman as a servant. Hardly anybody ever came to see them, except some of May's pupils, who were invited to tea and to eat fruit in the garden at the proper season.

The reader may perhaps not have forgotten that on the night memorable in this story, when Charles Grey Scarlett was about to leave his home, he wrote two letters. One of course was to his wife, the other was to "an intimate friend and old college companion." Robert May was this old friend and companion. To this placid obscurity had life come down with him.

This was a holiday, and May was enjoying it. To him the daily visit to the school had become quite an active and arduous occupation, and he much appreciated the relief and quiet of the present hour.

"Robert, Robert!" called his sister—a pleasant, almost pretty little woman, prematurely sealed and devoted to old-maidenhood. Tessy was perhaps thirty-five years of age, and might have looked quite young as a married woman, but was almost antique as a spinster. She was a marvel of neatness as to her hair, her apron, her cuffs, her collar, and her slippers and stockings.

Robert slowly sauntered up to meet her.

"Robert, my dear, a lady wants to see you."

Tessy was quite excited apparently at the sudden visitation.

"Does she, Tessy? I don't want to see her, my child. You must tell her the school is the place to make all inquiries about pupils and presentations. They ought not to have sent her here."

"I don't think it is anything about the school, Robert. She has come in a splendid open carriage, and she says she wishes particularly to speak to you."

"Tessy, my good girl, you know I don't see people—women especially—fine ladies more especially still. She can't have any business with me personally; it must be something about the school. Can't she tell it all to you, whatever it is? Go now, like a dear, and explain that you understand everything just as well as I do, and get rid of her somehow."

Tessy tripped away, not unwilling to do all the talking herself; and May went on with his perusal of Hobbes and his occasional inspection of the blossoms.

Presently Tessy came back, looking a little put out and disconcerted.

"Robert, my dear, she says she wants to see you and no one else, and that she is sure you will see her. Here is her card, dear."

May took the card with a weary air, as of one who fears that further struggle is useless. But the moment he read the name his expression changed—first a look of surprise, then one of sadness or sternness.

"Yes, Tessy, I will see her," he said; "though I cannot understand what object she can have *now*. Seventeen years ago I asked her to see me, and she refused point-blank. No matter; I will go to her, Tessy. Is she still in the carriage?"

"Oh no, dear; I brought her into your study."

The study was a very small room in a sort of wing of the old house. Little as the room was, it took in the whole width of that part of the building, and had a small window looking on the patch of ground in the front, and another commanding the large garden at the back, but almost blinded by the foliage of the copper beech already mentioned. Robert May's desk and arm-chair stood in the corner near this window. The room was nearly full of books; but they were not heaped about pell-mell in common scholarly disarray. May was orderly in his habits, and his books were properly arranged on shelves and tables. One or two really valuable prints ornamented, so far as they could be seen, the darksome little study.

An unwonted sight now disturbed the monotonous gloom of Robert May's study. A tall and stately lady, rich in the glow and rustle of silk and velvet, was standing there.

May entered the room, and having motioned to his sister to fall back, said:

"I need hardly ask if I have the honor to address Lady Judith Scarlett?"

"That is my name, Mr. May. I have ventured to disturb you, and to ask for the favor of a few moments' private conversation."

May placed a chair for the lady. He was about to hand her his own little arm-chair; but a momentary mental estimate of the amplitude of her skirts and draperies made him abandon that effort of politeness, and he placed another seat for her. Then he closed the door and seated himself.

"Mr. May," Lady Judith began, in her cold, clear, vibrating tones, "you did me the favor, some seventeen years ago, to offer to call on me, for the purpose of giving some counsel or explanatlon which you thought would be of service tc me."

"Pray, Lady Judith, excuse me," Robert May said, with more of a quiet ease and dignity than might perhaps have been expected; "it was hardly that. I thought I might perhaps be able to say something which should help to clear the memory of at least one very dear friend."

"In any case, Mr. May, your motive was a good one, and I was wrong in refusing to see you. At the time I thought of you only as an old and intimate friend of a man who had cruelly wronged me; and I took it for granted that you wished to make some defence of him, to which I would not listen."

"Charles Scarlett and I were old and dear friends, Lady Judith. At Eton and at Oxford we were friends and rivals, to some extent; but he had gifts which I had not, and he had ambition; and while I have naturally remained here, he would have become a great man but for——"

"But for what, Mr. May? Speak plainly out, and don't spare *me*."

"But for his too sensitive heart, Lady Judith."

"His sensitive heart!" she said in scornful tone. "*His* heart! But I don't mean to dispute with you on the virtues of your friend, Mr. May. I don't care to go back to the past in any way. I am now only concerned with the present. If any one is in the secrets of Charles Scarlett, *you* are. Can you and will you tell me anything of him? Is he living? Does he know that he has a daughter? Oh, if he has the heart of a human creature, and could know what cruel danger that wretched girl is in, and how, poor weak fool, she looks to *him*, and dreams and raves of him, it might touch him, and revive in him some sense of duty!"

May shook his head sadly.

"Of Charles Scarlett now, Lady Judith, I know no more than you do."

"Is he living?"

"I fully believe him to be living, because he pledged himself to make it certain that, in case of his death, the news should reach England, and especially should reach me. His solicitors, as you know, still act as if he were living."

"I do not know; I have never gone near them, or had any inquiry made of them. It is not about his property I am concerned; it is about his unfortunate child. Heaven knows I have tried to do my duty by her; but she baffles me; and I now fear that a most fatal, insane marriage awaits her, and I cannot holo her back. She often talks and raves of her father in her mad romantic way. Perhaps he could save her. If he will, let him have all the merit, such as it may be; and let it atone for the past. I can do nothing with her any more. I speak to you, Mr. May, as his friend. There is not another being in the world tc whom I would thus lower myself."

May acknowledged the confidence by a bow. There was a moment's silence, and then he said:

"Lady Judith, I am sorry to say that for years and years I have known nothing of Charles Scarlett. When he was leaving home he wrote me a few lines—I need not go over their contents; they told me he was about to take a step against which I had often argued——"

Lady Judith started and colored. Her husband, then, had discussed with another man the propriety of abandoning her! Could it be wondered that she hated his very memory? This was her bitter thought.

"But he begged of me," May continued, "by all the sacredness of our old and dear friendship, not to endeavor to trace him out; and he pledged himself, as I told you, to take measures which would make it certain that his death, should it occur, would be notified to us here. I have never heard from him since. I assume that he is living. Where, how, in what part of the world, I do not know."

"Is there no way of finding out?"

"None, I think. At the time *you* took no steps; his own solicitors, of course, took none; I took none, to follow or trace him. Any attempt now would be idle."

Lady Judith had for some time been bracing herself up to a great effort. At last she asked:

"Do you know anything of *her*—of that creature? Is *she* alive?"

"What creature, madam?"

"That wretched woman for whom he abandoned me, his home, and his God!"

"If you mean, Lady Judith, as I presume you do, the ill-fated wife of the profligate swindler Dysart, you are speaking of one of the purest as well as the most unhappy women who ever lived."

"Mr. May, do you speak thus to me—to *me*—and of that woman?"

"As sure as God is in heaven, Lady Judith, you wrong that woman!"

"Wrong her?" exclaimed Lady Judith, springing to her feet and flashing on the gentle Robert May a look of superb scorn—"wrong *her!*—the wretch who fled from her husband to become the mistress of a married man!"

"I don't believe it," May replied, with a sudden energy almost equal to her own; "on my soul, I maintain that it is not true! I knew her, Lady Judith—ay, madam, and I loved her!"

"Indeed! You were not the only one——"

"No, she was a woman to be loved. She did not love me, Lady Judith; although there was a time when I was foolish enough to hope that she might have been content with a poor, nerveless, unambitious, unsuccessful creature like myself. But she did not care for me in that way; and my love for her was my ruin, if so helpless and good-for-nothing a being as I am could be ruined."

"She seems to have had the gift of ruining men," Lady Judith interposed, with icy contempt.

"She would have been the happiness and salvation of any man who had any good in him, and who could have called her his wife. That Thomas Dysart was an utter and irretrievable scoundrel was best proved by the fact that even she could not redeem him."

"Mr. May," said Lady Judith coldly, "I did not come to hear the praises of a person whom no self-respecting woman could name without a blush. It may perhaps be cruel to undeceive so devoted a worshipper; but in common justice to myself and to you, I must tell you of the true nature of your lost idol. Learn, then, that Charles Scarlett left a letter for me, in which he told me that he was about to leave me, and to take that woman as his companion."

"Even that does not shake my faith, Lady Judith—no, not one jot. I have no doubt that Charles Scarlett, in his desperation driven wild by pity for the unspeakable sufferings of that ill-fated woman, did make up his mind to try to save her at the ruin of his own hopes and reputation—at the ruin of his own soul, if you will. But I am satisfied that she never consented or could be persuaded to any such sin. For his sake, as well as for her own, she would have refused it."

"Perhaps, Mr. May, you will endeavor to persuade me that she did not leave her husband at all?"

"Oh no, Lady Judith. She did indeed at last leave that abandoned villain. I think she fled at once from the man she hated and the man she loved."

"These words, Mr. May, it hardly suits *me* to hear."

"Yet listen, Lady Judith—only for a moment or two. Listen, as you are a Christian woman—do not refuse to hear what can be said to vindicate a woman whose sufferings were surely far greater than even your own."

"Mr. May, your enthusiasm does you much credit, and your simplicity of character is evident. I can well understand how easily a bold, unscrupulous, and, I suppose, beautiful woman—I never saw the person we are speaking of—would impose upon *you*. But I am not a man; and therefore I am not quite sc susceptible to the magic of a woman's smiles and tears. Have you any evidence whatever, beyond your own boundless faith, of this creature's innocence?"

May rose and paced the little room irresolutely, with one hand pressed to his forehead, as if he were trying to force into coherent argument wild thoughts that would scatter. At last he answered:

"Lady Judith, I have only the evidence of my own profound conviction. I knew her well and long; you did not know her, and therefore I should vainly endeavor to inspire you with my belief. I knew her, and I can only declare once more my solemn faith that there never lived on this earth a purer, more devoted, and more high-principled woman. I do not know where she fled to, or where her grave is made—for I am convinced that she is dead; but if ever Charles Scarlett should reappear on earth, I know that he will vindicate her memory and establish her innocence."

May threw himself back into his chair, trembling all over with excitement and emotion, and covered his face with his hands. Lady Judith stood in her cold proud attitude, and gazed down at him first in scorn, then in wonder, then at length with a growing pity and something not unlike respect.

"Poor creature," she murmured; "poor weak creature, deluded slave of a pretty face and a sympathetic voice! Like all men! I can hardly hate their crimes when I am forced to pity their miserable weakness."

May now looked up, and seemed much embarrassed.

"Pray excuse me, Lady Judith," he said in a tremulous voice. "At least if I seem worthy of your contempt, let the emotion which I am not strong enough to conceal bear witness to my sincerity."

"That, Mr. May, I cannot doubt. I respect your sincerity; and I am sorry to have given you pain. Let us say no more on such a subject. I don't even apologize for having troubled you by this visit; much rather should I apologize for not having sought you out long before. Can I—can I—in any way—serve you?"

"In no way, Lady Judith. My life is clear and quiet, and just what I would have it. I have no need of any service. But I am sorry, very deeply sorry, I cannot help you in your search. If I can think of any way, or light on any way of finding out anything, I will take the liberty of at once communicating with your ladyship. But I fear—I fear greatly—that Charles Scarlett has buried himself somewhere out of the reach of any tidings from the living world. Never, never would he have allowed her name to be condemned to seventeen years of merciless defamation if he knew anything of what was passing in England."

"You are not a parent, Mr. May," said Lady Judith bitterly, "and it is perhaps not wonderful you should think the reputation of such a woman ought to appear of greater importance to a man than the fate of his child. I thank you for your good-will, however, and I again ask pardon for not having acknowledged it long ago. That you cannot aid me is not your fault. Aid me? No one can. I have to walk my way alone!"

She spoke not one other word as May conducted her to her carriage, and she did not see that both Tessy and the old servant had posted themselves one of the windows to study her appearance and criticise her clothes. She bowed to May as he handed her into the carriage; and as she drove off was seen sitting erect and stately, with no sign of emotion visible on her white proud face.

"Not now, Tessy, my good dear," said May gently, as he reëntered the house and put aside his sister, who came bustling up to ask all manner of questions. "In a few moments, my lass, I may tell you something. Just now I want to be alone, and to smoke a pipe."

So Robert went back to his study, and lighted a great old winding hookah—his solace in all moods and moments of restlessness and perturbation—and smoked in silence, now and then fanning away with his hand the white circling clouds. But the hookah had hardly now its wonted power to soothe; and May's face looked very sad, and deep lines showed themselves under his languid eyes

He put away the pipe with a sigh. He rose and went to his desk, and opened a secret drawer there. Thence he brought out a tiny parcel wrapped carefully in paper of silver tissue, and tied with an old piece of ribbon. With a trembling hand he untied the string and unfolded the parcel. It contained an old glove and three faded scraps of paper. The first piece of paper was a little note in a woman's hand, dated twenty-three years back, and merely thanking "dear Mr. May," for his present of books, and signed "Agnes Revington." The next bore date some years later, and contained these words:

"MY DEAR FRIEND: I thank you from my very heart for your kindness. If any one could serve me, *you* would, I know, and there is no one whose services I would more willingly accept or ask for. But indeed you cannot aid me, even with advice; and I can only thank you. AGNES DYSART."

The last leaf of paper was written hurriedly, and bore date in the year 1851. It said:

"Farewell, dear old friend! Think of me always as you have known me. Believe no evil of me—hold me always in your sympathy and pity! We shall never meet again. AGNES DYSART."

These letters were creased and old and yellow. As Robert May looked at them his memory went back to the bright and happy girl whom he loved so well and so vainly; then to the young wife whose happiness so soon was clouded, whose gentle face grew to wear the sad look of hopeless disappointment he had watched so often with a tortured heart; and then he thought of the stormy night of early summer when the last of the letters was put into his hand, and he learned that he was to see her no more. He looked at the letters; and he looked at the little glove, which she had dropped somewhere long ago—long before her marriage—and he had found and kept, to be the only treasure and trophy of his true and futile love. And then if any of the boys of the foundation for the descendants of British heroes could have peeped into the little study, they might have seen an odd and curious sight—the gray-bearded principal crying regular tears over some old papers and a glove which he held in his hand.

CHAPTER XV.

"DO AS THOU WILT, FOR I HAVE DONE WITH THEE."

LADY JUDITH did not fail to take energetic measures for the preservation of her daughter. She wrote a stern letter to Eric Walraven, telling him that she had discovered his base attempt to ensnare the affections of Alexia, declaring that she would never give her consent to such a marriage, and warning him that, in the event of her daughter marrying against her will, the daughter would be simply a penniless gril. She also wrote a letter to Angelo Volney, urging, and almost commanding, him to come back at once, without losing a day, to Europe; for she had a hope that his influence, should he arrive in time, might have some good effect. Finally, she resolved at once to quit England for the present, and live for some time at least in Rome.

"Alexia," she said a day or two after her return from poor Robert May's house, "we are leaving London to-morrow night."

"Indeed, mamma! For Brighton?"

"No, Alexia."

"Might I ask, mamma—might a poor worm ask, as the man says in Dickens's novel—where we are going?"

"I don't mean to tell you just now. You shall know after we have actually left."

"What a dear delightful little mystery! Shall we be long away, Lady Judith?"

"I am not certain. Perhaps we shall not come back until you have returned to obedience and good sense."

"A lifelong exile then awaits me! Farewell, England, much as I have loved thee! Of course, we are leaving England? You don't propose that we should spend our lives in Birmingham, dear mamma, or Walton-on-the Naze?"

Lady Judith gave no answer. She had resolved that Alexia should know nothing of their destination until they had actually quitted England; and that she would journey to Rome by such short stages and roundabout ways, that it would be impossible for Alexia's lover to find them on the road. At Rome Lady Judith's own parents were now staying; and though she had long been estranged from them, and laid on them all the bitter blame of her marriage, yet in her present miserable condition they might perhaps be of some service to her. In Rome, too, the secret marriage of a young Protestant lady of rank against the will of her mother and guardian would be almost impossible.

So Lady Judith kept her counsel from every one but her own maid, a woman whom she believed to be wholly devoted to her. The woman, in truth, sympathized altogether with Alexia, regarded her as an injured creature, and was quite enraptured with admiration for Eric Walraven. Walraven, indeed, had won her favor first with flatteries, and then, when he had got hold of Gostick's check, with money. Poor Lady Judith's little plot was at once made known to both the lovers; and Walraven resolved that the time for action had come. Lady Judith's warning letter to him only amused him. He flattered himself he knew what that sort of thing meant. Unrelenting mothers he put down as creatures to be classed with mermaids and fairies and real patriots, and other inventions of poetry and romance. He, too, was of Arcadia; he was a poet, and he understood all about that kind of business. He would confidently give Lady Judith three weeks to hold out—not a day more. So if Lady Judith made her arrangements in confidence, he made his in still greater confidence.

The night of the journey arrived. Lady Judith, her maid, Alexia and her maid, were to leave London by the night-train for Dover, and to cross the Channel at once. Lady Judith was not a woman to require much assistance in the arranging of her plans; and although she had but a short time for preparation, she had done everything necessary. They were to go from Dover to Calais; and there a courier was to await them. From Calais they would go into Belgium; and after staying here and there on the way, get on thence to Cologne, and thence to Switzerland, and so to Italy. Alexia's maid had not been told by Lady Judith where they were going, not being considered worthy of confidence.

The evening was cold and raw; and as Lady Judith stood in her own room, waiting for the time of departure, she felt peculiarly unhappy and lonely. Even her resolve and her sense of duty could hardly bear her up. Few beings in the shape of woman are there who do not feel weak and depressed in any hour of doubt for lack of the decisive counsel and the strong arm of a man. Lady Judith now felt her widowhood terribly. The responsibility of her daughter's welfare was a bitter burden to her. So heavily had it weighed on her, so much change had it already wrought in her, that it was a profound disappointment when she learned that Robert May knew nothing of her lost husband. Ah, what a sickening trial it had been to that proud heart to humble itself so far as to confess that it needed help! to acknowledge that it would welcome even the help of him who had so misprized and wronged it! Yes; it had come to this. Judith Scarlett would almost have welcomed, in her cold stern way, the return of the erring husband, if only she might have said to him, "There is your daughter. Relieve me from the hopeless task of trying to control and guide her. She claims you; she loves your name, while she hates me. Though you and I should hate each other, yet save her if you can; and Heaven pardon you the rest!'

So she had humbled her proud heart—in vain.

As she stood now in her room the memory returned—when, indeed, was it long absent from her mind?—of the night, that fatal night, when she found Charles Scarlett's letter telling her that they were to be divided for ever. The remembrance now brought a sick and shuddering sensation to her. The growing darkness of the room oppressed her in a manner which at another time she would have thought utterly impossible. The very flame leaping on the hearth had something ghostly in it. The crucifix she kept on her table seemed to send a sad wan warning to her. The ticking of the little clock deepened the sense of loneliness. Everything seemed to tell the widowed woman of her desolation.

While she stood there, and thought of her loveless youth and her dreary widowhood, and of the struggle and torment that awaited her with her stubborn and malignant child, a sound on the stairs suddenly startled her. It was a man's tread—a tread she might well have known; but for the moment her mind was bewildered. Her impending departure and the weary time it promised, the sense of her loneliness, the gloom and darkness of the room, the sad retrospect of that cruel night which in this very place pronounced her doom of widowhood—all this confused and distracted her mind so that the past became mingled with the present, and imaginings seemed as realities. The approaching tread, familiar to her, and yet not heard of late days, sent a wild thrill to her heart. Who was coming to her? Great heavens! if it now should be he—if it should indeed be that husband of her youth, coming back, perhaps heaven-sent, to ask for pardon, to help and guide her, could she truly welcome him? Could she bring her heart to forgive him? Her face flushed, her fingers trembled, almost her heart stood still. If at that moment the lost Charles Scarlett had reappeared on her threshold, and had caught her in his arms, and confessed his own errors, whatever they were, and claimed her as his wife, perhaps the living waters of affection might have streamed at last from that breast which seemed of marble. Even now was it not something that the proud egotism of that perverted splendid nature had so far yielded as to admit a momentary question of itself? In the thrill and wonder, the fear and hope of that solitary darksome hour, Lady Judith for the first time distinctly acknowledged to her own soul that she too, like the rest, might have erred.

The step was now on the threshold. A hasty and yet hesitating step it seemed, as of one who comes hurriedly with sudden news, but is doubtful of the nature of his reception, and halts at the last moment. Then was heard a knock at the door.

Lady Judith said, "Come in!" with a calm and steady voice, and leaning one arm on the chimney-piece, turned half round. Whatever her emotions, she now gave no outward sign of them.

A man entered and came eagerly toward her, holding out his hand. The room had grown so dim that Lady Judith at first could only see a vague figure. He, however, could clearly see her tall form outlined against the firelight.

"Lady Judith!" he said in a sweet low voice, with an undertone of appeal and pathos in it.

"Angelo!" she exclaimed, and rushed toward him, all her proud coldness melted and gone in a moment. "Oh, thank God you have come!"

And Lady Judith threw her arms round Angelo Volney's neck, and he heard her softly address him as her son, and he actually felt her lips touch his forehead. Could this be Lady Judith, whose very noblest qualities had always seemed to him to have the lofty distance of cold divinity in them?

"Thank God you have come, Angelo!" she again exclaimed, as she raised her head from his shoulder and looked into his pale and agitated face. "I have so wanted you. I have been so lonely and so distressed. You have come in time, I hope—I hope. I knew you would come the moment you got my letter.'

In her excitement and sudden sense of relief Lady Judith had actually forgotten for the moment that her letter to Angelo had only been written the day before. Then she saw doubt and wonder in his face, and she recollected herself, and said in a tone of surprise:

"But I wrote only yesterday! You could know nothing about it. Why have you come back?"

There was a sad blank expression in the face of the young man which even in the dim light she could see, and it bewildered her.

"My dear, dear Lady Judith, you seem quite alarmed and distressed. What is the matter—what has happened? I came back only because——But I will tell you all presently. Never mind me now. Tell me about yourself, and about—about Alexia. Where are you going? They tell me you are leaving town. I know nothing. I only reached Liverpool this morning, and came here at once."

"Angelo, I am in misery about Alexia. She has fallen in love with a wretched hypocritical adventurer; he has taught her to deceive me systemati cally and shamefully. She defies me, and tells me to my face she loves him and will marry him!'

Angelo Volney was surely not a selfish man, and he would at any time have given his own life to save his benefactress from pain. Yet it must be owned that amid the sensations which this sudden announcement called up there was a wild thrill of relief.

"Who is the man, Lady Judith?"

"A man named Eric Walraven—a poet, a wretch! He has bewitched the unhappy child. I, too, am to blame. He imposed himself on me as a man of honor and a Christian. I received him here—and now, this is the result!"

"Walraven—Eric Walraven? I have met the man, and have seen his name in newspapers and reviews. I have read some of his poems, but I didn't care about them. They seemed showy and hollow. He is well spoken of, though, in literature; quite a rising man, I think. Charles Escombe knows him and likes him. He did not impress me; I thought there was something artificial and insincere about him; but I know nothing bad of him."

"Can there be anything good in a man who teaches a child to deceive her mother, and boasts to his friends that he means to marry her because she has money and rank? Angelo, *you* must prevent this marriage, and save this wretched girl. You are the only one who has any influence over her; *I* have none!"

Lady Judith rang her bell and called for lights. When these were brought, she noted again a peculiarly anxious and melancholy expression on Volney's face. He saw with deep emotion, and with a certain conscience-stricken feeling, the wasted, haggard look that veiled the splendor of her beauty. She seemed to have grown older, her complexion looked more transparent, there were deeper lines beneath her eyes, the eyes themselves looked more eager, lustrous, and wan than when he parted from her scarce six months before.

"If this is serious, Lady Judith," he said sadly—"if Alexia really loves this man—not as a child, but as a woman—what can I do, what can we do, what ought we to do, to prevent it?"

"Anything!" exclaimed Lady Judith, turning on him with a sudden change to fierceness of manner. "Anything! If I could lock her in a convent or a bastile, I would do so! If I could bind her in chains, I would do so! You ask me what we can do or ought to do? Do you think I will consent to surrender a child of mine, body and soul, to a villain like that? Are you too turning against me?"

"Poor Charles Escombe!" murmured Angelo. "The last words he said to me when I parted from him were about *her!*"

"You speak of Charles Escombe," said Lady Judith bitterly, "as if he alone were concerned in the welfare of my daughter. I might have thought that you too had some interest in her happiness, and in mine. Is this the comfort and counsel you bring me? I might as well have been alone."

"Where is Alexia herself? Perhaps this thing is not so serious."

"Alexia is leaving London with me to-night. I am taking her away—to Italy. Will you come with us at once? Or will you stay behind and see this man, and compel him to cease from pursuing her with his false deceitful persuasions?"

"Yes, I will stay; I will see him; I will know, at least, what manner of man he is. If he be the deceiver and traitor you speak of, he shall never marry Alexia, Lady Judith, depend upon *that*. But where is Alexia herself?"

Lady Judith rang the bell again.

"It is time that we were leaving," she said. Then to her maid who entered: "Ask Miss Scarlett to come here, and then bring me my cloaks and shawls. Is everything ready?"

"Everything is ready, my lady."

The woman disappeared, and returned in a moment with face of well-painted wonder and alarm.

"Please, my lady, Miss Scarlett ain't in her own room, nor yet her maid Frances, nor yet her cloaks and things."

Lady Judith started, and became white as a ghost; but she recovered herself, and said:

"They have probably gone down to the carriage. Go and see."

"This is one of Alexia's ways of vexing me, and showing sullenness and disrespect, Angelo," said Lady Judith when they were alone again. But she looked very anxious and alarmed.

Her maid returned.

"Oh, please, my lady, Miss Scarlett's not anywhere about—not in the carriage, nor in the house. And James and Thomas both say they saw two females go out of the house 'alf an hour ago, with cloaks on, which they thought was me and the maid Frances. And coachman thinks he saw a gentleman put them into a cab down the street, and they went away. He says it was none of his business; for he thought it was Frances and me sent on some message."

"She's gone!" exclaimed Lady Judith. "The graceless girl is gone—is lost!"

"It is not too late to save her," cried Angelo. "Even if she be really gone, it is not too late to overtake them. A telegram will go before them wherever they go; and they can only leave London by certain stations and lines. Lady Judith, if this is really true, this man is a villain, as you say; and we must save her from him. Leave it to me. Is she not as my sister? I will save her!"

"Stay!" said Lady Judith sternly. "I must first find out for myself, Angelo, if she be really gone. She will probably have left some letter for me in her room. That is the regular course of proceeding, I think, in the poems and romances on which she loved to feed her mind and heart. I shall find some such relic, I have no doubt."

The quest was vain: Alexia had left nothing behind her in the shape of a missive. She was gone, and her maid was gone; and that was all that could be known for certain. Even that might have been doubtful; at least, it would have been possible to suppose that Alexia had gone out on some freakish but harmless mission, were it not for the positive assertion of the coachman that he saw two women, one of whom he knew to be Frances, Alexia's maid, and the other of whom he supposed, from her dress, to be Lady Judith's own maid, come out of the house, and walk to the Piccadilly corner of the street, where they got into a cab. He thought he saw a gentleman get out of the cab in the first instance, and then hand them in; but he was not quite certain of this—he didn't take particular notice, he said.

Angelo urged that all further inquiry now was loss of time; that the only thing to do was to telegraph along all the lines of railway out of London.

But Lady Judith listened with little heart to this recommendation. Nothing now could avert another scandal from her darkened life. Nothing could undo the reality of the fact that her daughter had fled from her house—had eloped with a lover. Indeed, the poor lady began to suspect that the one great end of Walraven's plot had been already accomplished when Alexia left her home in his company; that the irreparable scandal had been achieved, and the adventurer now justly assumed himself to be master of the situation. Moreover, there was a look somehow in the eyes of her maid and one or two others of the servants which seemed to tell her of treachery. Once again she had been betrayed: her faith in herself was breaking down.

Angelo was still urging her to authorize him, to allow him, to take some step, when the maid again entered.

"Please, my lady, a letter, just left by a messenger, who said there was nc answer."

Lady Judith quietly glanced at Angelo, and bade the woman leave the room.

"This is from *her?*" Angelo asked eagerly.

"Oh yes! This will doubtless explain the mystery of the melodrama."

Lady Judith opened the envelope with a hand which trembled no more tnan if it had been unfolding the subscription-list of a Mayfair charity. Angelo was quivering with anxiety.

Lady Judith took out two letters.

"One is from *him*," she said. "Man is the nobler being—the lord and master of woman. Let us do homage, therefore, and read the man's letter first."

So she read in a firm clear tone:

"MADAM: Only the devoted and unconquerable love I bear to your daughter can excuse—if even that can excuse—the step I have taken. I could not live without Alexia. I am proud to believe that I am needful to her existence. I dare not hope to obtain your consent, and I have therefore braved everything in obedience to the highest law of all. When I have made it certain that my darling Alexia is all my own, secured by marriage-bonds against the possibility of severance from me, I shall fling myself—we shall fling ourselves—at the sacred feet of her mother, and implore forgiveness. Only forgiveness—we will ask nothing but that. With Alexia for my wife, I ask no more of earth or heaven. My love may be wild—may even be unscrupulous—but I would ask Alexia's mother to believe that it is unselfish and disinterested.

"As I have braved your anger and the condemnation of the world, I have felt bound to make it certain that the reputation of my Alexia was not perilled in vain. Any pursuit will be hopeless. Nothing can now prevent me from making her my bride.

"With the deepest penitence and homage, yet with a heart full of hope and joy, I am devotedly yours,

"ERIC G. WALRAVEN."

"Angelo," said Lady Judith, turning to Volney with a cold light as of steel gleaming in her eyes, "I was kind to that man! I trusted him, and welcomed him to my house!"

That was her only comment on Walraven's appeal.

"Now," she continued in her cold quiet voice, "let us read my daughter's etter."

"DEAR LADY JUDITH: I told you I would marry Eric Walraven, and I am going to keep my word. He is the only being who ever loved me. Please don't make any scenes, or send any detectives or spies after us, or otherwise make yourself and us needlessly ridiculous. We have so arranged matters that all the detectives in Wilkie Collins's novels could do nothing to stop us.

"You never loved me, mamma; you were always cold and hard. I could have loved you, if you would only have allowed me; but you never cared for that sort of thing. Please, then, don't try to prevent me from being happy in my own way.

"But I should like to come to see you. May I—soon? I could say a great deal more, but to what end? You would only think me sentimental. But I am happy and sorry, and I should like, if it might be, that you would try to make some excuse for me. After all, mamma, I am your daughter. If we had only been a little better to each other! ALEXIA."

Lady Judith read this letter to the end without the slightest tremor in her tone. Angelo was deeply moved.

"Is it too late?" he asked; "too late to save her?"

"Quite too late now; she has made her own bed, and must lie on it."

"Something may be done. Let me telegraph, if this man really be as bad as you think. Let me go."

"Nothing can be done now. With my consent nothing shall be done. The girl has doomed herself to misery; any efforts of ours to save her would now only add public scandal and disgrace. She's lost!"

"Poor Alexia! Lady Judith, she has a great heart."

"I suppose so," said Lady Judith calmly. "I have suffered much from people with great hearts. What day of the month is this, Angelo?"

"The twenty-fourth."

"Of March?"

"Yes, Lady Judith; but why do you ask?'

"I thought it was the twenty-fourth. They should have waited two months—just two months—and this letter would then have come on the anniversary of the night when, standing in this very room, I read the letter from her father which doomed me to a worse than widowhood. Will you tell them, Angelo, please, that the carriage need not wait? I shall not leave London now."

"Lady Judith, you will forgive her? She is, as she says, your own daughter, and she is only a child."

"She has made other and dearer ties, Angelo, and she owes me no duty any more. Forgive her? Of course I shall forgive her—shall try and pray to forgive her; but she has chosen her road in life, and she must walk it alone for me."

"If this man should prove a deceiver, if he should not treat her well!" Angelo began, with dark flashing eyes, clenched hands, and an expression which carried a *vendetta* in it.

"If he should not treat her well, Angelo," said Lady Judith, quietly interposing, "he will be her husband and master, entitled to treat her as he pleases."

"She is my sister!" exclaimed Angelo fiercely. "I will have his heart's blood if he dares to treat her ill."

"She is my daughter," said Lady Judith, "and she has deceived and deserted me. I surrender her wholly to the man she has chosen for her husband. Listen, Angelo; I have been deceived by her, and by him whom she has now preferred to me. I was deceived and abandoned by her father. It only remains that you desert and betray me, and I shall then have nothing but treachery and desertion for which to thank this earth. Your turn ought to come; you ought to be the next and the worst, for I have done most for you and loved you the best."

Angelo turned away from her piercing eyes. He could not at that moment meet her gaze. His heart was torn with grief and pity for her, and yet he knew that he too must leave her

CHAPTER XVI.

JOCELYN'S MORNING CALLS.

BROADWAY lies all white and glittering in snow. The snow had come down, at first, with a rush and in a tempest, paralyzing and reducing to nothing for the time all the efforts of traffic and locomotion to compete against it For several hours no trains could leave the stations, no carriages of any kind could move along the streets of New York. The pedestrian, fighting his way home through the thick fog of snow-flakes, plunged, if he had to step off the foot-path or "sidewalk," through snow up to his knees. All the time the snow was thus falling on the silent though not solitary Broadway, the sky was veiled in one vast cloud. Nothing more cheerless and drear could well be imagined than the aspect of the almost interminable thoroughfare which is the backbone of New York. Broadway is usually one of the brightest and most animated streets in the world. No two houses in all its vast length (and it is as if the Strand intersected London from end to end) are like each other; this side of the street is never like that. A huge building of white marble stands next to one of brown stone, both of the newest and most glaring hues; and then comes a quaint old Dutch looking house of the days of Stuyvesant, and then again something little better than a shanty. On this side you are reminded now of the Rue de Rivoli; cast your eyes across the street, and you see a scrap of the New Cut or a bit of Wapping. Here a side street runs across which seems borrowed from Liverpool; a few yards on is another which, with its quiet uniform red brick houses, its double row of trees, its cleanliness and its quaintness, appears to have been transplanted from Delft or Utrecht. Nearly everywhere along the line of Broadway, the shop fronts bristle and glitter with signs, and thrust out huge symbolical devices, and flutter with flags. There are more banners and insignia hung out on Broadway every day, than might be seen in the Strand on the occasion of a royal pageant. A Chinese city is not more party-colored, bright, eccentric, fantastic, in its devices to attract the attention of the passenger. To the European stranger this most practical and money-grasping of all streets seems as if it were perpetually playing at a sort of Venetian carnival; a huge frolic, mask, and mummery. Only when the snow begins to come down with its sudden overwhelming power, and hides the heavens in gray and swallows up the street in whiteness, does Broadway cease to be brilliant, glittering, and *bizarre*.

Now, however, the snow has ceased to fall, and it is frozen over and forms a hard, white, gleaming pavement. Snow in London is soon merely a gray and dingy sort of mud; in New York it sparkles for weeks, bright as the sugary crust on a wedding cake. The air is intensely clear. The sky is as blue as that of the Egean Sea; the sun is brilliant. There is summer in the heavens and winter on the earth. It is cold to be sure; it ought to be piercingly cold; but somehow the atmosphere is so exhilarating, the sunlight is so radiant, the sky is so glorious in its azure, that one forgets to be chilled, and is delighted with the whole condition of things. The street rattles and rings with the tinkling sleigh-bells; for nothing on wheels, except the staggering little city omnibuses, can now be seen along Broadway. Tiny basket sleighs with one horse, bigger and more pretentious sleighs with two, with three, with four horses, glide along with jingling bells and gay caparisons, with silver-embossed housings and gorgeous buffalo robes. The English traveller, looking on with unaccustomed eye, can hardly believe that this sort of thing means business. It seems like some fantastic piece of Christmas revelry or a scene from a play. Nay, it hardly looks like a living reality of any kind. The radiant sun, the laughing blue sky above, the hard and gleaming snow beneath, the almost interminable stretch of incongruous street, and the never-ceasing rush of odd, brilliant, picturesque vehicles, become bewildering to him. He is disposed to think that if he shuts his eyes for a moment and opens them again, the whole scene will have vanished in the momentary interval.

Such, however, is the common—to New Yorkers the commonplace—appearance of Broadway in the winter. Such was the look it wore one particular day in the winter we are now describing—a day to which we will turn back from the regular course of our story, to have a glimpse of certain of the recent occupations and enterprises of Mr. Edwin Dare Jocelyn. He had just dismounted from a sleigh at the entrance of one of the principal hotels.

Jocelyn's was a magnificent equipage. His "team" consisted of two splendid black horses, whose harness sparkled with silver knobs, and bells, and ornaments. The sleigh was filled with superb and costly buffalo robes, from amid which Jocelyn might properly be said to emerge as he threw the reins to his colored groom and leaped—lightly for a man of such bulk—on the pavement. Across his broad chest was buttoned a magnificent garment of fur; gloves of delicate lavender kid outside and thick fur lining within protected his hands; a powerfully flavored Havana blazed between his lips. A hot-house flower was glowing in his buttonhole; a ruby flamed in his cravat; perfume exhaled from his hair and his beard; a gold-rimmed double eyeglass dangled on his breast from a chain of gold.

At the entrance and in the hall of the hotel stood a straggling crowd of loungers. There were men who represented business and fashion, Wall Street and Fifth Avenue, at once; men with kid gloves of wonderful fit, and coats which Poole himself might have admired; but who had an ostentatious air and an apparent consciousness of being dressed which would have been fatal to them in Rotten Row. There were lank and sallow Southerners, stiffly upright in bearing and having a curious chronic aspect of offended dignity about them. There were huge Western men, loosely-clad giants, with quick restless eyes and astounding neck-ties all awry. Mr. Jocelyn swaggered in among the crowd, and apparently found personal acquaintances in five out of every six of them, and had the sixth portion immediately presented to him; for during his passage into the hall he seemed to have shaken hands with every individual there. For some he had a friendly familiar word; for others a patronizing and gracious touch; for others a florid bow and an overwhelming compliment.

The great hall of the hotel was so crowded with loungers that Jocelyn was slow in working his way up to the office, or what would be called in the more old-fashioned parlance of London the bar. Behind the counter of the office were two or three magnificent clerks with hyacinthine locks shining in pomade, and resplendent diamond pins adorning vast breastplates of hard and snowy shirt-front

"Delighted to see you looking so well, Captain," said Chesterfield Jocelyn, extending his hand to one of these gentlemen.

"Mr. Jocelyn, sir! Up from the South already!" exclaimed the martial clerk. "How's your health, sir?"

Mr. Jocelyn explained how his health was, and gravely sought some particulars relating to the health of the friendly questioner. Then he shook hands with the other two clerks, one of whom introduced to him a casual acquaintance who just then chanced to come in; and finally he turned once more to the Captain and remarked that he wished to see the Hon. Ezekiel Verpool, if that gentleman happened to be in his room.

The Captain touched a shrilly little gong which stood near him, and a black functionary started up from a seat in the hall and approached.

"Take Colonel Jocelyn's card to the Hon. Ezekiel Verpool—No. 214," said the Captain.

Jocelyn never pretended to any military rank, and the clerk, if he had stopped to think about the matter, would have known perfectly well that he did not. The title "Colonel" was given off-hand, just as a courteous and ornamental way of introducing a name. So a stranger in Germany receives a card of invitation which addresses him as high and well-born; or in England, if we wish to be civil to the green-grocer or the chimney-sweep, we confer on him when we have occcasion to drop him a line the title of Esquire.

Presently the messenger returned with the intimation that Mr. Verpool was in his room; and thither Chesterfield Jocelyn was conducted.

The apartment was simply a bedroom; and the Hon. Ezekiel Verpool was seated at a table up to his ears in papers. Up to his ears too was the collar of his coat; and he had his hat on.

The Hon. Ezekiel Verpool was a long, lean, skinny man, with a bent neck and stooped head, and a skin from which every light and shade of complexion appeared to have been eliminated. He had no whiskers or beard, except a few starved iron-gray hairs on his chin. He had an eagle beak, a cold, gray, lustreless eye, and thin straight lips. He was shabbily dressed in clothes which did not even affect or pretend to fit him. He had his back to the door as Mr. Jocelyn entered, and he did not rise or move, but sent a rearward glance out of the corners of his gray eyes; and then when his visitor had come within range held out to him a curved and corrugated claw, almost smothered in a superfluity of coat-cuff.

"How d'ye do, Jocelyn?" was the cordial and eloquent welcome.

Jocelyn stood now in front of his friend. Broad, beaming, gorgeous in costume, grandiose in manner, the corpulent adventurer shone in radiant contrast to the shabby skeleton at the table. He looked down at his friend with a glance of irrepressible contempt and pity; his friend looked up with a caustic glance which for a moment spoke of contempt and pity.

"How does Vermont's most illustrious son, the prince of philanthropists and sovereign of speculators?" Jocelyn asked, at the same time drawing from hi breast pocket a silver cigar-case and helping himself to a fresh Havana.

The prince of philanthropists and sovereign of speculators made a motion with his lean fingers as if he were reaching for a pinch of snuff. Jocelyn understood the gesture and held out, not perhaps very readily, the cigar-case. His friend surveyed its contents slowly and keenly, and picked out what seemed to him the best cigar of the lot. He made another clawing motion, which Jocelyn replied to by handing his own blazing cigar. Mr. Verpool lighted his fire at the flame of his friend, and took a puff or two in silence.

"I don't very often smoke, Jocelyn," he then observed, "but you do have such good cigars. Cost fifty cents each these now, I should say? You can afford it—you can."

"Yet you see I am not proud, Verpool—I am not ashamed to associate with honest poverty like yours." Mr. Verpool gave a short, dry chuckle. "Patriotism and poverty naturally go together, my dear Verpool. A devoted citizen who executes so many government contracts is naturally led to sacrifice his own interests to those of his country."

"Well, I did make a good thing out of that last little affair, I tell you," said Verpool. "You were wrong there, Jocelyn; you ought to have gone in with me—I told you so."

"Yes, I dare say. I am always too impatient for that sort of thing. I can't stand all that lobbying and hanging about Washington. I know there is money to be made, plenty and safe, by fellows of your cool and cautious kind; but it is not in my line. I always kick the pail over just when it is nearly full."

"That's so," his friend complacently observed. "You can project a thing Jocelyn, as nobody else can; but you want some one to work the thing out for you."

"Therefore, I have secured at present the coöperation of the Hon. Ezekiel Verpool. So we come to business, dear friend. When did you leave Washington?"

"Last night."

"And you return—when?"

"To-night."

"So soon?"

"So soon."

Mr. Verpool, it may be said, was a man who passed at least half his life in "the cars"—the railway train, that is to say. He was always going off somewhere or other. It was as ordinary a part of his life's work to get into a sleeping-car and pass his night in travelling, as it is to a London city man to mount the omnibus every morning.

"Then things must be looking very well, or confoundedly ill," said Jocelyn.

"Well, they ain't looking bad. On the whole, I guess they're looking about as well as can be expected. It will be a big thing! Atheling's name has done wonders."

"I knew it would," Jocelyn exclaimed with kindling eyes.

"Yes, sir, Atheling stands well; he has a good name! Folks will believe anything when they hear that Atheling vouches for it. Say, Jocelyn, that was a great stroke of yours; but do tell, how did you ever get hold of Atheling and bring him into this?"

"That, my venerable Verpool, is one of my secrets. Genius must work in its own way, and it wouldn't profit you to know."

"Guess he wants to make money, anyhow."

"Wrong, Verpool, for once! You are lacking, Verpool, I fear, in the finer dramatic instincts. Inconceivable as it may seem at first to you or me, it is yet the humiliating fact that Atheling does not want to make any more money."

"What in the nation does he want then?"

"I should despair of making his motives clear to you, my dear Verpool; and I had rather shield our friend's weaknesses from your too severe criticism. It is enough that he has his little defects of moral constitution, and that we are able to make use of them for his profit and ours."

"Something soft here?" said Verpool, touching his forehead.

"No," replied Jocelyn carelessly, as he knocked the ashes off the tip of his cigar; "I should rather say something soft *here*," and he lightly touched that part of his frame beneath which the heart is supposed to pulsate. "But you wouldn't understand, my dear Verpool; and it doesn't matter. If we make Atheling a millionaire against his will, he will owe us all the deeper debt of gratitude."

"Does he understand the business?"

"Not he; there is no need that he should. Whom did you see in Washington, and what did you do there?"

Jocelyn drew a chair close to that of his friend, and the pair talked for a few moments in a low tone. Mr. Verpool seldom mentioned proper names in the course of his explanation, but helped out his meaning a good deal by nods and gestures and sideward jerks of his head, as if he were pointing out visible personages.

After a while Jocelyn stood up again, and drew a deep breath.

"Well," he said, "I think things are looking promising enough. I like your courage, Verpool. I was a little in doubt as to whether you had pluck enough for the business; but I think you'll do."

"I want to know! Why, I didn't quite fancy you had courage enough, Jocelyn, for all your tall talk."

Jocelyn laughed.

"I have not much to lose," he said, "even of character. I am the Bohemian of speculation, my excellent Verpool, while you are a respectable citizen—a proper Philistine—an elder of your church congregation doubtless. You go into the race handicapped with respectability. Will you dine with us to-day? Delmonico's—at half-past six."

"Who are us?"

"Only four or five besides myself. An Englishman (son of a lord—you respectable Pharisee ought to go anywhere to meet the son of a lord), Charles Escombe; Chauncey Pyne, General Derners—one or two others perhaps. Come."

"No, thank ye. I don't much care about dinners—and then you see I have to pay for my board here all the same; so it seems like throwing away one's money not to eat what one pays for. Then I should be running away to the cars. I know Mr. Escombe—met him in Washington."

"Indeed. What do you think of him, Verpool?"

Verpool shut his eyes, cogitated, made a sound and movement as if he were expectorating, but did not expectorate, and said:

"There's nothing in him. He don't amount to anything."

"Just my own opinion," said Jocelyn with a smile.

"But there was a smart young fellow with him, Volney by name—half an Italian, or Cuban, or something of the kind, I guess."

"Yes; did you see much of him?"

"Met him twice, and came with him in the cars from Richmond. We talked all the way, and he seemed sharp and smart. Couldn't get anything out of him."

"Verpool," said Jocelyn gravely—and he resumed his seat—"I never knew any one who could see into people and judge of them as well as you can. Nay, do not think I flatter—why should the poor be flattered?"

"Come, Jocelyn, don't go on like that; I never said I was poor."

"I was only quoting from 'Hamlet,' my Vermont Crœsus."

"Oh, that's it. I don't read many plays."

"But I was saying that I have always admired and believed in your judgment of men. Not of women, my good Verpool—you have not much taste, I think, for the study of that branch of humanity—but of men. Now, I want you to tell me about this lad Volney. I could not quite make him out; but I confess I was rather disposed to set him down as a soft and spooney sort of fellow."

Verpool shook his head.

"I was wrong?"

"Teetotally wrong. I take him to be a sharp, quick, deep fellow. I think he is a fellow to make his way here if he tried. I told him so. I offered to give him a hand-up if he would settle here."

"What did he say?"

"Well, he seemed kind of struck with the idea."

"But he has gone back to Europe."

"Has he? Yes, I believe he has. But I shouldn't wonder if he came back here again. He told me right out that he wanted to get on, and that he hadn't any dollars of his own."

"What could you do with him?"

"Well, I don't just know. Make a goodish sort of secretary, wouldn't he? He talks French, and Italian, and Dutch" (Mr. Verpool always described German as Dutch), "and he takes notice of all that's going on and don't let out much; and he has a sort of face that induces people to give him their confidence. Yes, sir, I liked him. I guess I could make that chap useful."

"Does he know anything of my relations with you?"

"I guess not."

"Don't let him know anything. Get hold of him by all means, my dear Verpool, and let me know all about him. I have a kind of interest in him, now that you assure me he is not the harmless sort of person I was disposed to think. Then you won't come to Delmonico's and dine with us?"

"No, thank ye; I am not all right to-day anyhow, and eating much would not agree with me."

Nothing could well have been further from Chesterfield Jocelyn's mind than the idea of really having Verpool as a companion at the dinner-table. He had given the invitation knowing that it would not be accepted. Verpool was a man who never dined for pleasure, or connected any notion of social enjoyment with dinner or tea. He had lived all his life in hotels and boarding-houses, and always dined in the solitude of a busy, hurrying, indiscriminate company. He ate to live, and he lived to travel in "the cars," and buy "lots" of land, and speculate in new railways and joint stock companies, and other such enterprises. He ate his dinner just as he had himself shaved, because it was a thing proper to be done once a day, and each operation cost him about an equal length of time and gave him an equal amount of enjoyment.

So Chesterfield Jocelyn took leave of his friend and swaggered down stairs.

"I wonder what the devil that fellow's motive in living can be." Such was the nature of Jocelyn's cogitation. "He can have no possible enjoyment in life; and it would be a clear saving of expense to him if he were dead! What a beastly old cad he is. It is a cursed misfortune for a gentleman to have to associate with such an uncouth old savage. But the brute has a wonderfully long head—I feel like a child in his hands. He must be right about that semi-Italian brat, this sentimental lover of little Isolind. I never knew Verpool to be wrong about any man yet. I believe that old gray eye of his can see round a corner or into a millstone. Well, if we can do this trick, I'll cut the whole concern and go and live in Paris. I think I could venture on Paris.—My dear Governor Strange! This is indeed a pleasure. When did you come to town? and how are they all in Iowa?"

For Jocelyn's reflections had been cut short by his nearly running over a stout, white-haired man, with a florid face and a pompous manner, who, having been lieutenant or deputy governor of a State some seven years before, still retained the full title (or indeed enjoyed a rather higher title than was his by right even when in office) and the aspect of conscious importance.

Meanwhile Mr. Verpool was paying his mental tribute to the character and endowments of his departing friend.

"He's a smart man, Chesterfield Jocelyn—a remarkably smart man—but he wants ballast. Kind of frivolous somehow. He'll soon be played out if he don't take care. Ideas splendid, but not practical. This is a grand idea of his, this new one; but he could never work it out himself. Too much champagne and clicquot" (Mr. Verpool was not much of a connoisseur of wines, and did not know whether clicquot might not have been red burgundy), "and dinners at thirty dollars a head, and late hours. A man should never see the wrong side of ten o'clock at night. I shouldn't wonder if Jocelyn were to die without a red cent—or come to a violent end perhaps. There's something in his eye that looks like that somehow."

With this cheering prophecy Mr. Verpool mentally dismissed his associate and went on with his financial calculations and his plans and papers.

Mr. Verpool was a man of some sixty-five years. He was reputed to be immensely rich, and though always speculating, and thus of course liable to have his losses, he was believed to have bought up real property enough to provide substance for a dozen Fifth Avenue families. He had neither chick nor child, and if he had any poor relations, they remained poor for all that concerned him. He came originally from the Green Mountain State, but he had not visited the home of his boyhood for years. He had no house or local habitation of his own anywhere. The papers announced his arrival now at the hotel in New York where he is at present a guest (a man is called in the States the guest of a hotel where he pays five dollars a day for the hospitality), and again at the Parker House, Boston, the Continental, Philadelphia, the Tremont House, Chicago, or Willard's at Washington. All the nights, and they were many, that he did not sleep in one of these hotels, he slept in "the cars." He never thought of any sort of amusement or social enjoyment. If he ever had an hour absolutely to spare, he would have utilized it by going to sleep. He took not the slightest personal interest in politics, although when occasion required he did not refuse to vote with his party, even though the doing so exacted a patriotic sacrifice of half an hour of precious time. He had never been guilty of an immoral action (in the common meaning of the word), and had probably never felt an immoral impulse in his life. He never drank, or swore, or gambled—at least with cards or dice. He subscribed liberally to the building of churches; he had built one church all at his own cost and of his own design—the most hideous specimen of ecclesiastical architecture to be seen east of the Mississippi. He had built a college which bore his name, in a town which he himself had founded. He was pitiless to unsuccessful men, but took something like a connoisseur's interest in the progress of smart and promising men, whom he looked upon with the sort of professional, almost personal interest which a recruiting sergeant might feel in a strapping young bumpkin. Such persons were interesting, were worth looking after, might perhaps be made useful and turned to account somehow. A new and likely man might even indirectly and unconsciously suggest a new and likely scheme, which his own capacity might be utilized in working out. Mr. Verpool was much respected everywhere. When a poor farmer's son, he used to have mush and baked apples for breakfast; now that he was a rich man, he had nothing better than mush and baked apples still.

Jocelyn, meantime, had mounted to his seat in the sleigh once more. He drove up Broadway, past the fashionable Grace Church, the porch whereof glitters and sparkles on Sundays with the most gorgeously dressed congregation of fair penitents to be found anywhere in the civilized world. Then he turned into Fifth Avenue and rattled through the monotonous grandeur of its huge brownstone palaces, very stately and costly structures indeed, but looking about as cheerful and homelike as a double row of State penitentiaries. At one of the largest of these he checked his horses and got out of the sleigh. He rang the bell, asked for Mrs. Braxton, and seemed to receive the answer confidently expected when he was told that the lady was at home. Jocelyn appeared to be on familiar terms in the house.

He was shown into a large and handsome reception-room, furnished with extravagant splendor, and crammed or choked with paintings, statues, statuettes, and ornaments. There were pictures there of genuine value and beauty by rising American artists; but these were rather in the background; they were hidden away in corners or leaning up against chairs and the arms of sofas. The most conspicuous places were given to poor and tawdry copies of great Italian masterpieces, or trumpery pretentious daubs done by artistic humbugs who had the good luck to bear Roman or Florentine names. The chimney-pieces—there were two in the room—were loaded with ornaments and curiosities; the tables were almost hidden with gorgeously-bound albums and specimens of *bric-à-brac*. In this recess you nearly stumbled over the Greek slave; Ariadne and her lions stopped your progress yonder; marble busts were sprinkled about like footstools. The whole room would have reminded an English visitor of a gorgeous and glorified curiosity shop from the regions of Holborn or Soho.

Mrs. Braxton was the rich widow who has been mentioned in an earlier chapter of this story as the prize, or one of the prizes, Chesterfield Jocelyn was striving to win. She was the relict of a man who had worked his way upwards from hawking buttons and stay-laces to be the owner of a "store," and then a speculator, and then a millionaire. He had fallen in love with the bright eyes and plump figure of the woman whom he made his wife, and whom he loved to infatuation and indulged to extravagance. Lucinda Braxton had had very little education to start with, but she had a certain odd, misleading kind of talent, and a vast amount of egotism and self-conceit. She had made many efforts to get into society during her husband's lifetime, but failed. Shoddy itself demurred to her, and laughed at her. After his death she became a passionate devotee of spiritualism, and her passion was nourished by some who found a profit in her weakness and extravagance. Jocelyn heard of her immense wealth, vanity, and nonsense, and thought he saw a splendid chance of making a grand *coup*. In him she met for the first time anybody who even pretended to social position. He humored all her whims, and the woman became gradually more and more fascinated by him.

Here, amid the embarrassment of riches, Jocelyn knew his way about, and therefore did not stumble over any marbles or become entangled in a forest of bronzes. He had some time to wait and look around him if he cared to see the art-treasures of the room, for the lady of the house was engaged in making herself as ornamental as her apartments.

At last, however, there was a rustling and rushing of silken and velvet draperies, and Mrs. Braxton stood before Chesterfield Jocelyn, who first bowed almost to the ground, and then advancing took the hand extended to him and pressed it to his lips.

Mrs. Braxton was a lady of rather short stature, but otherwise ample proportions. She was not young. A census-collector anxious to do a flattering and graceful thing might have put her down at fifty. She had a large head, with a broad face and forehead and rather fine dark eyes. Her hair was almost quite white, and was arranged in a profusion of long thick ringlets falling about her neck and shoulders, but gathered carefully away from her face so as to display the broad forehead, of which its owner was especially proud. Her mouth was large, with full lips and good white teeth. She might have been called a fine-looking woman. She certainly was very remarkable. Anybody would have turned and looked after her as she passed in the street. Nobody could have seen her in a crowded room without asking who she was. She might have looked noble and queenly if her head, with its prodigality of white ringlets, had only surmounted a frame less plump and less short, and if, too, there had not been an uncomfortable expression of oddity about the twinkling restless eyes.

Mrs. Braxton was dressed in glowing ruby velvet, and her broad bosom was like a jeweller's window for its profusion of chains and brooches. Her fingers were incrusted rather than ornamented with diamond and emerald rings.

Mrs. Braxton appeared to take the courtly salutation of Chesterfield Jocelyn very much as a matter of course. Jocelyn then handed her to a seat and took a chair near hers.

"I had almost given you up for to-day," said the lady, turning her twinkling eyes upon him and indulging in a faint sigh.

"Did I not promise, dearest lady? And was the promise needed? Could Edwin Jocelyn come within a hundred miles of New York and not find a way to see one who is all in all to him?"

He was venturing to take her hand, but she gently withdrew it, and sighed once more.

"All in all?" she repeated reflectively, and gazing on him again.

"Dearest Mrs. Braxton, dearest Lucinda, can you doubt it? Do you not know only too well——"

"*They* do not say so," she murmured in a sad monotone.

"They? Who? The miserable babblers of New York, the wretched coteries who can understand me as little as they could appreciate you?"

"Not so, Edwin Jocelyn," replied the lady solemnly, and laying now her jewelled hand on his. "Not the coteries of New York. These I scorn as much as you can do. But there are higher intelligences which do not refuse to watch with ours and guide us! Edwin Jocelyn, I have been warned. The spirits!"

The impulse of Edwin Jocelyn undoubtedly was to exclaim "Damn the spirits!" But he knew that to indulge in such a profanity might prove just now a luxury purchased at a vast sacrifice, and he repressed his emotion. He was well aware of Mrs. Braxton's profound faith in the guidance she believed herself to have received from other spheres. Only indeed a moment of surprise, and the general knowledge that New York suspicion might have had a good deal to whisper against him, had led him to mistake the source of Mrs. Braxton's doubts.

"Dearest Lucinda, you know me well enough to believe that I value as highly as man can do the guidance of those souls on a higher plane of being than ours. *I* have been thus led, and have walked under the guidance of angels. Such guidance has led me to *you*."

"I did indeed believe, Edwin, that in you I had at last found my affinity. Never, never could the souls and beings of the late Mr. Braxton and myself have commingled in a celestial union, to endure through all the spheres and ages! You appeared, and you proclaimed yourself my other being, my affined nature, my affinity. Hush, do not speak—I have been warned to beware!"

"But, dearest Lucinda, I must speak. You know better than I do—you whose starry nature can rise to loftier spheres than mine can yet pretend to soar to—you know that there as well as here are malign and wicked spirits, who delight in thwarting the happiness they cannot share, and vexing the pure souls they envy and hate! Some such creatures, hating and envying you, may have tried to pain you by traducing *me*. You know there are such spirits."

Mrs. Braxton shuddered. "I do indeed," she said. "But, Mr. Jocelyn—Edwin—it was not one of these! I have lately been so happy as to find myself wholly *en rapport* with and under the guidance of one whose ministrations I can accept with the utmost trust! John Bunyan," she exclaimed, rising to her feet and looking upwards with a gaze of excited devotion—"John Bunyan is my companion, friend, and guide! He calls me Faithful! He comes always when I summon him, and has promised to devote himself to me! Edwin"—and she lowered her voice once more to a sad undertone—"Edwin, I have spoken to him of *you*."

Jocelyn was not, in the common meaning of the word, a mirthful personage. Stern, ferocious, and sensuous was his nature; and when he smiled, it was at some human weakness, or else for the sake of seeming genial and good-hearted. Now, however, it cost him no small trouble not to laugh outright. The utter oddity of the notion of John Bunyan's being applied to on the subject of Chesterfield Jocelyn's character was so delightfully comic, that he felt for a moment tempted to fling up all chance of Mrs. Braxton's money and enjoy a wild laugh at her folly. Prudence, however, triumphed. Jocelyn had been for years disciplining his nature in a school of self-restraint.

"You honor John Bunyan, Edwin?"

"Surely, surely," Jocelyn replied, having at the time a dim recollection of an illustrated copy of the "Pilgrim's Progress" which he used to delight in when a child. "But even Bunyan may be misled. There are impulses of our own natures, my Lucinda, which come from higher sources than even the wisdom of

Bunyan." Jocelyn was, meantime, vainly racking his memory for any quotation from Bunyan which might come in appositely on his side of the question. He could think of nothing, and therefore suddenly asked:

"Why has Bunyan warned you against me, dearest Lucinda?"

He put the question with a merely affected warmth and earnestness. Against information supplied by John Bunyan he thought he could easily contend. A hint from the police detective department of London would have been much more formidable.

"He warns me, Edwin, that your soul is not the true counterpart of mine."

"Oh, that's all," thought Edwin. "I guessed as much." Aloud he said: "Of that, Lucinda, Bunyan cannot judge. Your soul and mine have recognized each other, and alone can decide their mutual destiny! Your soul is now mine—I claim it and will hold it!"

Jocelyn did not feel quite at home in the spiritualistic controversy, and hoped to cut it short. Claiming Mrs. Braxton's soul as his, he sprang up and with chivalric ardor flung his arm around her waist. She did not wholly disengage herself, but drew back a little and murmured pensively:

"I wish I could believe it wholly. I know there is within you, Edwin, a sacred germ growing up which will one day become an illumining power and a beacon to the world! Edwin, I see in your eyes a penetrating light, which ought to be capable of piercing into the furthest worlds, and holding communion with the brightest spirits. But is this germ developing and growing? Have you been lately cultivating it with fidelity?"

Jocelyn hastened to vow that he had never relaxed in the task of cultivating this sacred germ. He confined himself, however, to a vague earnestness of vow. He vowed as the Scotchman in the story swore—"at large." He did not choose to venture into details, for he could not even guess at what the sacred germ might be.

"Bunyan does not think so," Mrs. Braxton went on, laying her hand upon her ample bosom. "Bunyan thinks you are unfaithful to your mission, and so does Swedenborg!"

"Oh, is *he* in the business too?" thought Jocelyn. "These illustrious persons are evidently all in a story. They appear to take more interest in me than I do in them." He drew Lucinda more closely to him, and said in a deep, grave tone:

"My Lucinda! perhaps I have not been all I m ght have been. We men have natures at once grosser and less sublimely tenacious than yours. Always with us the tendency of hard and busy life is to darken the spiritual world, to withdraw our duller eyes from the higher visions and our souls from the grander intercourse around. Let me own to you—and I am not ashamed to make the confession—that mine is a nature which needs perpetual companionship and guidance. A pure spirit must minister to me and lead me! *If* I have any spiritual gifts——"

"Oh, Edwin! *If* you have—with your brow and your eyes!"

"If I have any such gifts," Jocelyn went meekly on, "they can reach their fullest development only in a lofty and serene companionship such as yours. Lucinda, in you I see my guide! I too have known what it was to wither in an uncongenial companionship. Save me and guide me! Divine Lucinda, sweet sublime soul, be mine at last—now, now and forever!"

Lucinda's breast heaved and fell until the chains and trinkets that lay upon it rattled and clanked. She was yielding, her upturned eyes looked tenderly into Jocelyn's, and for a moment the adventurer felt himself in virtual possession of a great fortune. Nay, for a moment, his thoughts overleaped even his success, and he began to say to himself what a pity it was that triumph could not be had without alloy, and that the absurd woman must be taken along with the coveted wealth. He looked down at the handsome, ecstatic, foolish face, thrilling with vain delusions and preposterous sentiment, and he had to say to himself "At last I shall be really a rich man," in order to keep up the courage of his wooing.

"Then you do indeed love me?" the yielding lady murmured.

"Love you, Lucinda!"

"And you do not hesitate to make the sacrifice?"

Jocelyn supposed she was alluding to her years.

"Any sacrifice—all sacrifices—would be welcome for your sake. But, my Lucinda, do not give me a merit I cannot claim. What sacrifice can there be in a love which gives to me beauty and genius like yours—a soul like yours?"

"I knew they wronged you," Lucinda exclaimed, and in her ardor she withdrew herself wholly from the embrace of her lover and gazed at him with eyes of pride and gladness. "Even the higher souls are not without their errors. I knew you loved me for myself alone."

"Did the spirits then so wrong me as to tell you otherwise? Lucinda, at this moment I wish that you were poor of every earthly possession, and stood there with no gifts but your intellect and your charms."

"I knew it; I knew it!" the poor woman again exclaimed. "Then you care as little for the sacrifice as I do? Did I not say so?"

"What sacrifice, love?" Jocelyn was growing puzzled.

"The sacrifice of this vulgar and worthless wealth—this tinsel and trash!"

"But why sacrifice it? Why despise the power of diffusing enlightenment which it confers? My Lucinda, your wealth is your own—I care nothing for it, except in so far as it contributes to make you happy. A face and form like yours are in their proper setting when framed in magnificence."

"Then when it is no longer mine, shall I look less beautiful in your eyes, Edwin?"

"No longer yours? I don't quite follow you, Lucinda. Do you think I am the man to rob you of your wealth and misapply it? Surely, it will be my care to preserve and to increase your store, whatever it may be."

Meanwhile Jocelyn's brows were contracting and his lips trembled with anxiety and surprise; and a quick, ominous fierce light was darting from under his dark eyelashes. If the vain, dreaming woman, who again drew near to him, had been a little less subjective in her mental constitution, she might have read a warning in those flaming eyes more distinct and direct than anything her spirit-voices had disclosed.

"But, Edwin, when I marry you all this ceases to be mine! Don't you really know? Can it be?"

"Dear Lucinda, you are playing with me—or trying some foolish and useless test of my love! Do speak plainly!"

"I always thought you understood! Oh, you *do* understand! My late husband was a jealous man; his being and mine had no affinity. I told him so many and many a time; I told him that in the higher spheres he and I could never be linked together. I then believed that it might be my fate to wander on through long æons of eternity, looking for some kindred soul to mate with mine! Now, Edwin, I am happier!"

She turned a languishing gaze towards the face of her suitor. He made heroic and even desperate efforts to look love in return, but his anxiety was intense, and hot drops of perspiration already began to moisten his forehead.

"Yes, dearest, yes; but go on!"

"My husband, jealous and low-minded, told me that on this earth at least I should have no mate but him. He judged all men by himself. He knew nothing of the destiny of hearts or of disinterested love. In his will he left me all his wealth, provided I remain a widow to the end; but all is to pass away from me the moment I accept another husband! This is the sacrifice, Edwin, your love must bear. To you I know it is little; yet it was but right I should tell you of it. I thought you knew it always!"

This was indeed a thunder-clap. Jocelyn had never thought of anything like this! For years he had seen this woman revelling in the possession of wealth which she seemed only eager to lavish. It had never occurred to him to think that there could be any limit to her absolute ownership.

Yet even now Jocelyn was by no means satisfied that his original assumption was wrong. The late Mr. Braxton had been notoriously so adoring a husband, so devoted a slave, to a wife whose audacious although not actually sinful coquetries might have driven another man into wild rebellion, that Jocelyn could hardly believe him capable of repudiating even in death his unqualified allegiance to the government of the petticoat.

"This is a trick!" Jocelyn thought—"a device; a woman's little plot to find out whether I am quite sincere, and that sort of thing. Some of her train of humbugging *protégées*, alarmed at my advances, have been putting her up to this."

Mrs. Braxton was always surrounded by a swarm of pretended devotees—women who were mediums, women who were apostles and disciples of spiritualism, and who made a good thing of her weakness, her vanity, and her generosity. In New York, and indeed in London for that matter, the Tartuffe and Lady Tartuffe of our days ought to be represented as Spiritualists and Mediums. Our Organ is usually a rich elderly lady, with a fancy for receiving direct personal messages from the higher spheres, and vanity enough to believe herself a fitting companion for John Milton or Dr. Channing.

Naturally, Mrs. Braxton's followers would take alarm at the possible prospect of Mr. Edwin Dare Jocelyn's becoming the husband of the lady, and virtual master of her wealth. That indeed would be *à corsaire corsaire et demi* with a vengeance.

Therefore Mr. Jocelyn ordered his soul to be reassured. But the whole situation was still terribly trying. The promptest decision must be taken, and a mistake either way might be fatal.

Jocelyn decided. There was but one way by which to secure a safe retreat in case of the worst, and yet to save the lady's self-love and keep her on his hands in case of the best.

Lucinda was about to throw herself upon his bosom. He raised one hand as if to stay her approach, and the other hand he pressed for a moment to his forehead and eyes. Lucinda stood amazed.

"You *have* then doubted me, Lucinda," Jocelyn said at last, removing his hand from his eyes, and speaking in a deep sad monotone. "You have not believed in my love! You have suspected me of some design upon the miserable wealth which now surrounds you! Your trust has not been wholly given to me—as mine has been to you!"

"Oh, Edwin, do not say so! Oh no—indeed, indeed, I have not doubted you!"

"Then why speak to me of this unhappy old man's jealous precautions? Why speak of your money at all? Why name such conditions" (Jocelyn's voice grew louder as his manly anger carried him away), "as if we were paltry traffickers adjusting some commercial bargain! What to me is your wealth—what would be your poverty? To me, Lucinda Braxton poor is as Lucinda Braxton rich! I—thank Heaven!—have brains and energy enough to maintain for my wife her fitting place in society, were she endowed with no coin of marriage fortune. I have been misunderstood—Lucinda has doubted me! No, Lucinda, it is not *your* work. At least it is not the prompting of your own mind. Some mean and jealous enemy has suggested the doubt; and you have fallen into the snare! You have listened to the whisperings of envious and malignant tongues! Lucinda, adored and ever trusted, farewell!"

And he turned away as if about to rush from the room overpowered by his emotions. In any case, he began to think, his horses had been kept standing rather too long. From the spot where he stood he could see through the window that his groom had kept the sleigh still before the door.

"Oh, Edwin, Edwin, forgive me—I never doubted you!"

"Forgive you, dearest! I have nothing to forgive. But I cannot bear to speak of this just now; I feel too deeply and sensitively! Think again, Lucinda—commune with your own heart in the silence of this night! Ask yourself whether you can wholly trust me—whether you indeed believe me to be the vile adventurer your friends—yes, your friends—would paint me! Then, if your heart answers as I would have it answer, send for me. Send me a line, a word, a flower—and Edwin Dare Jocelyn will be at your feet, to prove whether his love is that of pure devotion or of vile self-seeking! Lucinda, till then farewell!"

He seized her hand, pressed it to his lips, and hastened from the room, leaving her in an agony of bewilderment and remorse. The poor, fat, foolish woman flung herself on the sofa, covered her face with her hands, while tears came trickling through her rings.

Oh, how she had wronged that noble, disinterested nature! How meanly she had listened to unworthy doubts! "Bunyan!" she exclaimed in her grief. "John Bunyan, you have misled me! Was this well of you? Was it right to whisper suspicions of a man so great and pure, a spirit so sublime? He loves me for myself alone—do you not hear? He knows all, and he cares nothing for the miserable money-sacrifice! I have but to send him a word, a line, a flower, and he will hasten back and be mine! Why, oh why did I ever offend him! But he will forgive me, for he is all goodness! Edwin, my Edwin, come back!"

But Edwin had taken good care to be well out of hearing. He only wanted to gain a day's time, and to leave her bewildered in the interval. The poor woman, when she had a little recovered her wonted composure, resolved to have instant conference with Bunyan and Swedenborg, remonstrate with them, and reassure them on the subject of her lover's devotion. Unfortunately she was not herself a medium, and had to commune with the other spheres through the agency of some of the personages whose influence Jocelyn justly suspected that he could discover in the spiritual doubts of his moral integrity. Mrs. Braxton's waiting-maid, an astute French girl, was, strange to say, a wonderful medium, and was a frequent gainer at the hands of her mistress by her spiritual acquire ments. John Bunyan, however, chiefly conversed through the intervention of a Scotch lady, the wife of a tailor, and once poor and shabby, but now living comfortably on Mrs. Braxton's bounty, and receiving substantial rewards for celestial ministrations.

Mrs. Braxton summoned this seeress, and was soon deep in conference with the author of the "Pilgrim's Progress."

If any one supposes there is exaggeration or even unintentional extravagance in this picture of a weak and credulous nature feeding upon the garbage of imposture, the writer can only say that the painting is subdued and colorless indeed when compared with what he has himself known and seen. Lucinda Braxton is a poor and commonplace illustration. Reality, anywhere you may chance to look for it, will show you types of credulity far more remarkable. In fiction one has to soften and weaken these things in order to be believed; the real, strong truth would be too much for the readers of romance.

Meanwhile, Mr. Jocelyn began to breathe a little more freely as he drove along the gleaming snow. He had at least gained time. In a few hours he could easily find out whether Mrs. Braxton's story had been really a pious fraud, a loving woman's device—as he was still inclined to believe—or whether she was really doomed by the Parthian shaft of a dying husband's jealousy to a choice between poverty and perpetual widowhood. In either case he felt sure that she would send for him; and he would go to her or not just according to his knowledge of the real state of affairs. It would be a heavy blow for him if his long siege of the widow's heart should prove to be thrown away; and Jocelyn ground his teeth as he thought of the hours of weary homage he had possibly wasted, the sickening absurdities he had had to endure and to take part in. There were times when the best fruits he could gather in life tasted bitter in the mouth of Chesterfield Jocelyn.

But he dined joyously that evening at Delmonico's, talked in his grandiose way, and boasted prodigiously, and left Charles Escombe at last in doubt whether he, Escombe, really knew anything—even of the condition of English work-houses.

"When you begin to see a little of America," said Jocelyn to Escombe, as the pair stood in Delmonico's hall lighting their cigars before parting for the night, "you will take a different view of things."

"But, my dear fellow, I think I have already seen ever so much of America. I have been to Boston and Philadelphia—and Chicago—and Cincinnati—and St. Louis—and down South—Richmond and Atlanta—and New Orleans—and no end of places."

"Ah, that's nothing! Nothing at all, my dear Escombe, I give you my word! You don't begin to know the country yet! When you have gone a few times across the plains, and carefully studied all the mining regions of Nevada and Montana—and so on—and completely investigated the resources of California on the spot—and the Oregon river and country—and lived among the Indian tribes a little—I know Black Kettle myself intimately—and gone all through Texas—and of course over all the Northern States—and had another visit or two of more extended range to the South—then, my dear Escombe, you will begin a little to understand the surface of things in this country."

Escombe was aghast. He thought he had done everything that the most enterprising and conscientious British traveller in quest of and athirst for knowledge could be expected to do. He began to think that he should never be able to know even the surface of things in the country, and that he might as well go home at once and confess himself a defeated man.

CHAPTER XVII.

OUR HEROINES.

In a great London square, which once was fashionable and even aristocratic, but from which lately fashion and aristocracy have been travelling westward, there was a brilliant gathering of a certain kind one evening. It was the home of a veteran author, who had acquired considerable distinction with the public and still greater esteem and affection among his fellows, and who, with the help of a genial and charming wife, contrived to draw around him now and then all that was celebrated or promising in the art and letters of the capital. Members of the House of Commons, and even peers, who had literary tastes, were common visitors there; and eminent strangers from other countries were almost certain to be taken there, and quite certain to be welcomed. Of late years there have been so many descriptions of literary and artistic gatherings crowded into novels, that the outer public must have begun to weary of the subject. Therefore there shall be no general account of this particular evening's entertainment or of its guests. But there are some of the company who need a special notice.

There are two ladies present, for instance, who have been dividing between them the attention of the assembly. They are unconsciously the rivals of the night. One is a tall girl, with brightly fair hair falling upon her shapely shoulders, and a noble look of health and womanly strength about her. She is plainly dressed, and there is something in the cut of her clothes (if that be the proper word to apply to a lady's dress and general get-up) which shows readily enough that she is not at home in London. Nor is she; for this is Isolind Atheling, who is now on her first tour in England, and making her first acquaintance with the society of London. She looks in better health and spirits than when we saw her last. The change of air and scene perhaps has done her good. Or there may be other reasons, too, still more effective. Whatever the cause, she looks animated, healthy, and very beautiful. Indeed, Isolind has surprised and disappointed many of the company, who expected to see in an American girl something far more fragile and delicate. The tall and firm figure, rich in every womanly development, the bright hair, and the fresh, fair complexion, were not what they would have looked for. Indeed, some who came into the room and saw for the first time both the ladies now spoken of, fell into a very natural mistake, and assumed that not our Isolind but the other girl was the living representative of that slender, delicate, fragile, sparkling kind of beauty which may be seen in an American city.

Very strange and striking is the figure and appearance of this other girl. As she leans forward now from the low chair in which she is seated, she seems well to merit the interest and curiosity which surround her. She is small and slight; her face perfectly colorless, her hair deep black and falling behind almost to her waist. She is dressed in a white robe, high to the throat, and in fashion more like the drapery of a classic Greek or Roman girl than the attire of a modern London lady. Nothing breaks the flow and fall of the white dress but a belt—one is tempted to call it a zone—round the waist. She wears gold bracelets on her slender wrists, and her belt is of golden material. The contrast between the dark hair and eyes and the white drapery is almost startling. The girl's face is decidedly handsome, and to-night the eyes are sometimes sparkling with excitement of an unwonted kind—the excitement of delight. Most of the ladies present criticise her sharply, and say that her style of costume is mere caprice and insolent affectation. One fair critic, whose display of arms, neck, and bosom, rising out of billows of lace and gauze, suggests a Venus Anadyomene, asks of a matron near her whether the dark-haired young lady has not made a mistake and come in her night-dress. But the wearer of the white robe is happy and heedless of censure. She has dressed thus to please her husband, whose æsthetic taste delights in seeing his young wife draped like a Pompeiian lady, and takes all the pride of ownership in observing the attention she attracts. There he is yonder—that very tall and handsome man with the dark poetic curls. Even while he talks with the fair-haired girl from America, he glances across every now and then under his eyes to see whether people are admiring his wife.

He is Mr. Eric Walraven, and his young wife was very lately Alexia Scarlett. They have been married but a short time, and London society is still ringing with the fame of their audacious escapade. It was quite romantic in every way, for the fugitives made their escape from London in a yacht, the property of one of Walraven's friends, which lay at Greenwich to receive them on the evening of their flight, and wafted them to Scotland, where they became man and wife. This was entirely out of the common way of doing things, and created quite a brilliant sensation. Now they were settled in a tiny Richmond cottage—at least, if not settled, they were for the time lodged there—and Walraven was going about London proud of himself and of his wife, delighted to exhibit his charming prize everywhere, delighted to figure in the new and striking character of the Lochinvar of a Mayfair damsel, delighted to think that he could show off an earl's granddaughter as his bride, and delighted to make her dress in any way that gave special artistic effect to the peculiar style of her beauty. Alexia, for her part, has hitherto been equally delighted, because of her newly-acquired freedom and her gratified love. She loved her husband with a passion that was ecstatic and feverish. Even now, happy though she is, she grows a little impatient because he is not by her side. She would have liked to sit at his feet for hours with her head resting on his knee. She begins to grow somewhat *distrait* and even petulant, as she sees that her husband is still hanging round the chair of the fair-haired girl, whom Alexia remembers and recognizes with an odd sort of pang, thinking of the day in Paris, and how angry she was because Angelo Volney stopped to look after that shapely figure and those fair curls.

As for Walraven, he liked every one to see and know not merely that he had carried away and married the beautiful daughter of the aristocratic Lady Judith Scarlett, but likewise that he was the girl's absolute master; that he could dress her according to his own whims, and talk to her only when he liked. The conqueror would lose nearly all the joy of glory if he might not parade his captives for the public gaze, and show that they were his captives, not his equals.

Therefore Alexia was, after a while, left positively alone. The quickness and the somewhat sharp and scornful tone of her replies and remarks puzzled and disconcerted people. Though all the men admired her, most of them rather feared her. It was her aristocratic pride, some thought and said. She was Lady Judith Scarlett's daughter all over. Whereas in truth the granddaughter of a hundred earls (the Corydens go back to William Rufus at least) was only vexed because her plebeian husband whom she worshipped would not come near and allow her to bask and nestle in the light of his beautiful eyes.

Walraven looked over and saw that Alexia was gradually becoming isolated. That would never do, so he asked Isolind if he might not be allowed to make her and his wife acquainted.

Isolind was growing weary of the poet, whose fine phrases were sadly empty and whose air and manner were not pleasing to her. Her eyes indeed had long been darting anxious and frequent glances round the room—thus far apparently in vain. She was glad to have an opportunity of speaking to Alexia, whom she remembered having seen in Paris, and whose face had a peculiar attraction for her.

So, without waiting for Walraven, and in her quick impulsive way, which seemed a little out of tone with the steady, formal movements of English society, she crossed the room and placed herself at Alexia's side. She was glad in any case to have a chance of escaping from Walraven.

"May I not introduce myself?" said Isolind in her frank, free way. "I have been talking to your husband this long time; and for many reasons I feel as if we ought to know each other. I remember so well seeing you in Paris at the Exhibition, and admiring you so much."

The demon of petulance had at that moment an unlucky hold of Alexia. She looked up coldly and said:

"Thank you. May I ask to be favored with your name?"

"I am Miss Atheling. I thought you knew my name—pray forgive me if I have intruded."

"Oh yes. Your name is known to me," Alexia replied. "I have heard of you a good deal. You are, I think, Lady Judith Scarlett's latest favorite. That isn't much of a recommendation to me perhaps; and on your own account, Miss Atheling, I advise you not to be seen speaking to me. You would lose all favor instantly in the eyes of my dear mother."

Isolind colored; the audacity of this reception surprised and hurt her a little, but she did not mean to be offended.

"Lady Judith Scarlett has been very kind and friendly to me," Isolind replied as calmly as she could. "So have many other English ladies. So have all indeed whom I have met—except you."

Isolind always went frankly to the heart of a question when she had to deal with it at all.

Alexia smiled scornfully. "I have not been quite famed for my kindness, Miss Atheling. My dearest friends will bear witness to that. As you know some of them, you ought to know so much."

"I do know some of them," said Isolind softly, as certain tender memories rushed upon her and gently disarmed any anger she might feel.

"So I have heard. Then they will readily give me even a worse character than I could give myself."

"Indeed, I never heard you spoken of by those I mean but with affection."

"Lady Judith Scarlett, for example?"

"I have not spoken to Lady Judith Scarlett of you; she did not speak of you to me, and of course I knew there had been a temporary quarrel between you.

"Temporary quarrel! When I am old enough it will have become a thirty years' war! It was not Lady Judith then who displayed all the affection? How odd! Mothers generally are very affectionate and all that, aren't they? I only ask for information, Miss Atheling. I don't know anything of the kind from personal experience. Your mother, I dare say, is very kind to you. I think I observed as much at Paris, and I believe I detested you for it; I mean I didn't quite regard you with that feeling of sisterly affection which good girls ought to feel to other good girls. You are now of course a model good girl, and people are all very kind to you."

Isolind had now ceased to feel offended or angry, and was in fact a good deal amused by the unnecessary petulance of the young bride. Besides, she had heard something of Alexia's eccentricity and temper before; and then there were the tender memories! She laid her hand lightly, gently on Alexia's thin, white little hand, and said:

"You can't offend me, Mrs. Walraven. It is of no use trying. We are not to quarrel. I like you, and I know you have a brave and generous heart."

"I have no heart of any sort now—I have given it all away. But why do you like me? I assume now, you perceive, that you speak the truth—I think your face looks like truth. A wonder! Nine out of every ten of our wretched and detestable sex are liars! I have myself told I don't know how many delightful little fictions to my mother, and she believed them; for to do her justice, she has not the faintest idea of ever telling anything but the truth. You look truthful too. Come, then, why do you like me?"

Isolind's kind, frank eyes smiled as she replied: "Perhaps I should have said I am inclined to like you."

"Ah, yes—that makes such a difference! So many things we are inclined to do, and can't do. But I take the compliment such as it is, and make the best of it. Why are you inclined to like me?"

"Because you have individuality and a character of your own, and because I know you have courage and a heart, and because I admire your hair and your eyes and your pretty figure—and because some whom I like are attached to you! Now, have I not been frank enough? Only one little word of frankness more—I think if you knew me you would not dislike me."

"Are you not afraid to offer a friendship in that way? Afraid of coldness or rudeness, I mean? We English are so very cold and rude."

"No, not in the least afraid. I am never afraid when I am doing what I think right. If you had persisted in being rude and cold, I should not have been pained for myself; I should feel that I had not deserved it."

"As a rule," said Alexia meditatively, "I hate women. I hate their little mean ways and prides and spites, and I seldom see a woman without thinking that a whipping would do her a great deal of good. But I don't think so of you. I think there is something in *you*."

"There is good purpose at least in me; and I think there is that much in most women for all their faults, and men too. I don't hate women as a rule. I endeavor to love them."

"And men too?" asked Alexia smiling.

"Yes, and men too. Why not?"

"No 'why not' that I know of—only I hope that in some one case at least no severe endeavor will be needed. Miss Atheling, there is something about *you* that *I* am inclined to like. I think we had better not swear an eternal friendship; that kind of thing ends badly generally—among women at least. But I ask pardon for having been rude to you. More than that, I will do penance by compelling myself to tell you the very reason why I was rude."

"I am not curious to hear."

"You shall hear. Not because you are handsomer than I—oh, yes, nonsense—you know you are, just as you know you are taller. No, I don't dislike women for anything of that kind. First, then, Miss Atheling, I was rude because I had heard that you were the latest pet and favorite of Lady Judith Scarlett. Second, because I thought my husband talked too much to you—and he is a poet and you are a poetess, and I am not. Third, because you seemed so happy at the Paris Exhibition and so much loved and caressed by your parents: and because Angelo Volney admired you."

It must be owned that a deepening color came into Isolind's face as this last in the catalogue of reasons was set forth. Alexia did not fail to observe the flush of that emotional dawn.

"You know Angelo Volney—my brother, my more than brother—do you not?"

"Oh yes!" Isolind's eyes lighted for a moment and then dropped.

"Then you know one of the truest gentlemen alive—the finest specimen I could show you of our grand British aristocracy. Don't you think so?"

Isolind looked up amazed and hardly knowing what to answer. The saucy Alexia understood all her emotions.

"I see, Miss Atheling, you *do* know him, and he has told you more than he ever condescended to tell me. But he is none the less one of the finest gentlemen alive. I wish you saw some of the born aristocrats I know! Yes. I have heard all about Angelo's antecedents, as you have evidently, and I think him all the nobler gentleman. He is a plebeian, and so is my dear Eric, my handsome, gifted husband; and so, in one sense, was my lost father, whom every one describes as the finest of true gentlemen. The plebeians have the best of it. If you marry in England, Miss Atheling, be sure to marry a plebeian. But they tell me that in America you all adore peers and peeresses, and are in fact what we call—may I break into slang?—downright snobs. Is that true?"

"Not of the Americans I know, certainly. But we live very quietly and among quiet and rather old-fashioned people, and I can't pretend to judge of Americans in general; only I should not like to believe such a charge, and indeed I can't believe it."

"Well, let us pass for that, Miss Atheling, and come back to our possible bond of friendship. What is your name?"

"Isolind."

"What an odd, pretty name! May I call you Isolind?"

"It will give me real pleasure to hear my name from your lips."

"I like you, Isolind, very much. I do indeed. I have not talked so much and so familiarly to any woman before in all my life, I think. We must see each other often, even though you are a favorite of Lady Judith Scarlett. Tell me something about your country, Isolind. Do you all hate us and want to make war upon us and overthrow our institutions? I am sure I don't care how soon you overthrow half of them. And is it true that the men all carry revolvers, even at dinner, and that the American ladies would scream if they heard of the naked truth, and would faint if they were accused of having legs?"

Isolind smiled.

"You English people know as little of us as you do of the Chinese, I really believe," she said. "I don't think you would be surprised in the least if I were to tell you that the shores of New York bay are swarming with crocodiles, or that Bunker Hill is one of the Rocky Mountains."

"I am sure I should not be surprised," Alexia replied. "Why should any one be surprised? Are there no crocodiles in New York—and what does it matter where the Rocky Mountains are? I dare say mamma knows, and I am sure Eric does not."

Eric himself approached at this moment, and magnificently displayed his most imposing attitude before taking possession of a vacant chair near the two ladies.

"I have been gazing with admiration on the exquisite artistic combination and contrast with which you two perfect specimens of bright and dark are unconsciously gladdening our eyes. If I were only a painter now, what a charming illustration of Morning and Night, or perhaps of Light and Darkness. Miss Atheling, does your country produce many living embodiments of fair-haired beauty at all approaching to that which I now am happily privileged to see?"

"There are fair-haired girls in America, Mr. Walraven, if that is what you mean," replied Isolind, who was repelled by the man and his compliments, and anxious to ignore the latter at least; "and many of them are very pretty."

"But you do not look like an American—at least what we have been taught here to regard as typically American. So noble and stately a presence; such a rich artistic womanhood."

"Thank you, Mr. Walraven, for the pretty compliment which I suppose is implied, but please don't compliment me at the expense of my country. Tell me I am the true type of American women, and then you may see a delighted and grateful smile."

"Beauty is of all types and tints. We consider—certainly I consider—Alexia my wife as the very perfection of the dark-haired and slender form of womanhood. A poet naturally thinks—and I do not forget that you, Miss Atheling, have been crowned with the poet's wreath—a poet naturally thinks——"

But what the poet naturally thinks did not seem destined to find expression from this authoritative mouth. For Mr. Walraven suddenly stopped in his speech, seeing a light of sudden and glad emotion flash at once over the faces of both the women he was haranguing; and Alexia actually rose from her seat and made an eager step forward to meet a new-comer.

"My dear, dear Alexia," the new-comer said, while Eric turned surprised and sharply round in his chair and confronted the speaker.

"My best brother Angelo!" And the impulsive little creature threw her arms round his neck, drew him down to her, and kissed him.

"Eric, my love, this is my earliest, for a long time my only friend—my brother, Angelo Volney! You know him well already. But you must know him better! You two must love each other. O Angelo, I am so happy!"

"How do you do, Mr. Volney?" the poet coolly said, and he shook Angelo's hand in a very calm and business-like fashion. "Often heard of you from Alexia. Hope we shall see you at our house."

"My sweetest Eric, what nonsense you talk! Of course we shall see Angelo often and often."

"That is the hope I have expressed, my love," the poet composedly observed. He was prepared to dislike Angelo. He could not forgive the interruption of his eloquent speech; he was angry that Angelo's coming should have called up such a light of joy in the eyes—of Alexia? Was the poet already jealous? Oh dear, no, not in the least. He understood Alexia's affection for Angelo perfectly well, and thought it quite right and silly and proper when he thought about it at all. He was angry that the light of joy which kindled at Angelo's approach should have gleamed from the eyes of Isolind Atheling.

Meanwhile, Isolind had drawn back a little. But Angelo's glance sought her out, and in a moment their eyes met. Now, however, she was almost encircled by a little group, and Angelo's approach was cut off for the moment. But her eyes and his, even in the short instant of time before hers drooped again, had exchanged a new pledge, and Isolind and Angelo knew that in that crowd their souls were together and alone. Once and again, during the few moments which elapsed before Angelo could approach her, those quiet signals were interchanged. What to Isolind was the babble of those around her? What to

Angelo were the chilling ways of Walraven—or even, alas that it must be said! the feverish welcome of Alexia? Love is terribly selfish—terribly self-forgetting.

"Where have you been, Angelo, that you did not come to see me before?" Alexia asked impatiently. "Did my dearest mamma forbid—did she threaten banishment or the rod, if you dared to come near her graceless daughter?"

"My dear, I have been out of town—I have been travelling for days and nights. I only got into London this evening." And here his eyes again glanced towards Isolind. He had indeed been travelling with wild and constant speed to make his appearance that night in those rooms, where he knew Isolind would be.

"You must come at once and have a long, long talk with me, Angelo. But not now—oh, don't be alarmed! Don't think I haven't eyes, sir. Go and talk to her; her cheeks have already lighted up their bonfires for your arrival! I like her, Angelo, now—although at first I thought I should hate and detest her."

"Hate and detest whom, dear Alexia?"

"Stuff, sir, you know perfectly well—Lady Judith's new pet from the backwoods—your charming Pocahontas—your Yankee Corinna, Miss Isolind Atheling. Don't look so sad and angry, Angelo! I don't mean to vex you, my dear brother. I am so happy myself—a new thing for me to say, Angelo!—that I want everybody else to be happy too."

"And you are happy, Alexia?" the young man asked in a tone of deep affection and some anxiety as he took the poor child's hands in his—her fragile thin white hands, on the finger of one of which it seemed so strange to see a wedding-ring shining. "You are happy at last, my dear little sister?"

"Oh, Angelo, I am as happy as any woman ever was! I never thought to be so happy! But how could I be anything else? If you only knew my Eric! Look at him! Is he not handsome and noble?"

"Yes; he is indeed very handsome."

"I think he is like a god! Sometimes I think he is a god. You will love him, Angelo, when you know him! Will you not?"

"Any one you love, Alexia—any one who loves you—must be dear to me."

He pressed her hand tenderly, and as he glanced around the crowded room caught a glimpse of the god-like poet bending over Isolind's chair. The expression that came over Angelo's face certainly did not denote unmingled approval of the husband of Alexia. But he soon forgot the poet in the light of the welcoming smile and the yet more tenderly welcoming blush and tremor which invited him to the side of Isolind.

While they talk, this pair of happy lovers, in low delighted tones—the poet having found himself plainly *de trop* and reluctantly receded—something may be said to explain the meaning of our Isolind's appearance in London in the novel character of Lady Judith Scarlett's friend and favorite.

When Chesterfield Jocelyn urged the removal of Isolind to Europe, the Athelings were only too glad to follow his advice. They left New York in the spring and crossed the Atlantic. Isolind now raised no patriotic objection to a landing on English soil. The voyage was happy and hopeful. Atheling's own spirits seemed to lighten with every hour on the sea. He grew like his old gladsome boyish self by the time they landed in Liverpool. His wife was joyous in his joy. He had a youthful zest of pleasure in showing Isolind all the famous places of the old country; and the girl herself felt a thrilling delight in every scene she looked upon. "This dear old beautiful England!" she exclaimed many times; "how could I ever reproach it or turn my eyes and heart away from it!" Once, as she was wandering with her people somewhere through a sunny lane in the northern suburbs of London, she stopped and was silent for a while, and then looking up at Judge Atheling said: "I understand now why our people call England home! All this day I have been haunted by the feeling that here I am at home—that some place like this must have been my home." Atheling's face wore so strange and embarrassed an expression that she suddenly added: "But oh, don't think I could ever compare any place with our own dear New York home! Only there is something in the very air here which affects me with a strange, sweet, and tender sensation, as if I were looking on some long-forgotten scene of early childhood! I feel almost like the poor girl in Cooper's novel who was stolen by the Indians when a little child—I feel almost as she might have felt when she was brought back to look upon the valley of her childhood, and asked if she had never beheld such a valley in her dreams! I seem to have seen places like these—to have been breathed upon by an air like this, in my dreams."

Atheling was silent. His gloomy mood seemed to have seized him again for the moment, and Isolind forgot all about her peculiar sensations in the effort to brighten him once more.

In London Atheling made many acquaintances and friends who understood and esteemed him. After all, no city on the earth gives a kindlier welcome to the stranger, and opens its great arms more willingly to him, than does dear, darksome, unlovely old London. The Athelings had no end of genial invitations. And Isolind found herself in London a social success and a social sensation. The beautiful young American girl was sought after everywhere. Her face, her form, her fresh, frank, independent manners, the occasional piquancy of her somewhat aggressive patriotism, were found charming everywhere. A publisher brought out an English edition of her poems, and they were quite a success. Their freshness, courage, and simplicity pleased many a wearied critical palate. There was something about them which was essentially womanly, but not womanish. Such as they were, they were real. They were evidently written out of the fulness of the heart. They were "sung as the song-bird sings." The singer might not be a great poetess, but she was in her place a genuine poetess. So Isolind became, to her own great surprise, a celebrity of the season in London, and West End drawing-rooms were delighted to welcome her.

The Athelings were very proud of all this. The Judge used to stand for a whole evening in the heat and crowd of a fashionable party, his broad face beaming over, his very spectacles glistening with delight. He, too, was liked by every one. Educated people in London are probably more tolerant of mere peculiarities of manner and appearance than any other class of people anywhere; and Atheling's noble heart, gentle ways, sound knowledge, and bright good sense, combined with a certain flavor of originality in his way of looking at things and expressing himself, made him respected and appreciated. Cabinet ministers would feel and show an interest in talking with him, and obtaining information about his own country. Peers of ancient title would press him with the kindliest invitation to visit their country-houses. A bishop escorted the Atheling party to hear a great debate in the House of Lords.

Isolind's head was in nowise turned by the flattery of this quite unexpected success. Her heart indeed was so deeply occupied by feelings which Society's favor could not touch, that it would have kept her head right if such steadying power were needed. She knew well enough the value of her own poems. She had weighed them in the balance with other poems, and she knew that they were wanting, and why. She thought they deserved some sympathy and a little praise, but she knew they could not live beyond their hour. For her, too, she knew that their hour had already passed away. She could make no verses *now.* Her love had taken the place of her poetry. She gave up her heart to the thought of Angelo; and her brain would not work alone. "Genius," said Isolind to herself, "is independent of all this, and works despite of heart and fate. Mine is no genius; no inspiration—and I don't care! I would rather have a touch of Angelo's hand than hold the sceptre of song. I would not give up my love for him to be another Sappho."

Meanwhile, Angelo did not appear as yet; and Isolind's eyes and heart yearned in vain. But being deeply interested in all that belonged to the education and the elevation of womanhood, especially among the poor, she was brought within the sphere of Lady Judith Scarlett's ministrations; and Lady Judith whose mind was already disposed to welcome anything from practical and progressive America felt strangely drawn towards the girl. Isolind's poems and her conversation were not without some little dash of complaint against the despotism of the Tyrant Man—poor fellow!—and they were full of very sincere if rather vague and unpractical aspirations after the elevation of woman. All this appealed to the seared and lonely heart of the proud bereaved woman who had lost and suffered so much, and who believed her sex to be the slave and victim of man's inherent selfishness and cruelty. Her pride and courage had driven her into society since her daughter's *escapade* much more than had been her wont. Lady Judith would not allow the world to suppose that the disgrace of a malign and disobedient child, could break or bend her spirit. So she went out a good deal; she met Isolind often; she would more and more have Isolind with her.

Isolind, for her part, sincerely admired the proud, sad, beautiful woman. She saw what good deeds Lady Judith could do; she had little opportunity of observing her sterner and harsher qualities. She saw that every great cause, every noble purpose, had the help and the approval of this haughty lady. We have already spoken of Lady Judith's as a "perverted, splendid nature." Isolind saw as yet nothing perverted in it. To her it was only splendid. Need it be said, that she saw in Lady Judith above all things, the benefactress who had done so much for Angelo, and to whom Angelo was so deeply devoted? Isolind could not criticize Angelo's benefactress, had she been so disposed. She could only admire and revere Lady Judith.

Meeting Lady Judith, Isolind of course met Angelo. But they met, at first, only as friends. At least no word passed between them to bespeak a dearer possibility. Their eyes and tremulous hands might tell tales to each other; but for a while there was nothing save friendship in their words.

Yet Angelo knew she loved him. It was not even from her eyes that he first learned this secret. One evening he was near her when many others were around. Isolind was seated on a sofa on which other ladies too were sitting; Angelo stood alone behind the chair of Lady Judith, which was placed near Isolind's sofa. Isolind by chance laid her bare arm and gloved hand on the arm of the sofa. Angelo was so near, so temptingly near, and there were no eyes on him! He could not help himself—he could not resist the inexplicable impulse. He laid his hand, oh ever so lightly, so gently, on Isolind's arm. He felt the sudden little tremor that passed through it—the tremor of recognition and of confession! For though his hand rested there for but some poor fractional part of a second of time, that instant of contact was enough, and Angelo Volney knew as if by a certain revelation that his love was not poured out in vain.

His course of life then became clear. He resolved to return to the United States, make a way there for himself, and win Isolind. He would not come to her as a dependant and a pauper; he would work and win her. He told her soon that he had resolved to go to America and make a living there—make a fortune if he could. Her eyes kindled with gratification and hope. He did not say that he would strive to make the fortune in order that he might win her, but she knew it, and he knew that she knew it. They made no pledge of love and constancy. But their hearts were irrevocably pledged, and each was sure of the other, and both were happy. Isolind had sense and spirit enough to honor the manhood of the lover who would not ask as a beggar for her love; and he knew that he was understood by her. What true-hearted woman of older days would not have loved her lover all the more because he would win his spurs before he sought her hand? Angelo was entering into a battle more trying to youth and love than any adventure with the Saracens or the giants, and his heart was as chivalrous as any that ever beat under the breastplate of a Lancelot or the Cid.

As yet he had not announced his resolve to his patroness. While the wound inflicted by Alexia was still open and bleeding—for he knew that it bled although the sufferer might make no sign—he could not desert her. He had, too, some hope of bringing the mother and the daughter together again. Therefore for the present he remained in Europe—not lingered, but purposely and resolutely remained. He still acted as Lady Judith's counseller and secretary, and had just returned from Italy, where she had sent him on a business mission to her father, the solemn old Earl of Coryden. To the last Angelo would serve his benefactress. Nothing, however, could change his resolve to go away and be independent, and do battle with the giant Paynim world for his true love.

Happy for that night were Isolind and Angelo. They sit and talk together low-toned as long as may be, and all the world and the future seem sunny and musical and radiant with the rainbow of hope. Love's roseate colors and youth's purple steep their hours in glowing, glorious hues. When they parted for the night, the pressure of the hand was to each a new delight, making parting itself sweet and ecstatic.

Angelo walked home. It was a soft and beautiful night, still in the spring or in the faint flush of summer's first dawn. There are such nights when London is delightful, and a walk through the quiet streets, in the soft, bland air, already redolent in anticipation of the breath of summer, is as pleasant as any ramble through rustling woods or over breezy downs. To Angelo just now the air was all balmy with hope and happiness, and the streets were more musical than Paphian groves or the valley of Tempe.

When he reached home—he still called Lady Judith's house his home—and passed by his benefactress's room, he saw that light was still burning there. Glancing in, he saw Lady Ludith seated at her desk reading a letter by the soft light of her shaded lamp. The light fell upon her sad and beautiful face, which, now that she was alone, wore less perhaps than it was wont of a cold or stern expression. The lines of the face looked deeper and darker, the cheeks more wan, the eyes more hollow than Angelo was used to see them. Unspeakable pity and tenderness filled the heart of the young man as he saw that time and sorrow were, for all her courage and stern self-control, working their will at last upon the noble face of the proud woman who, to him at least, had been so good. He longed to throw himself on his knees before her and ask her forgiveness, since he too must desert her.

Lady Judith heard his step, and without looking up called him in her clear, firm voice: "Angelo!"

He came in and stood by her chair.

"I am glad you have come; I have been waiting for you. I want to speak to you. I have had a letter, Angelo, from Charles Escombe."

"Poor fellow!" Angelo said involuntarily.

Lady Judith looked up quickly. "He is fortunate, Angelo—fortunate, though he does not think so now. He ought to thank the kind Heaven that has saved him from a partnership of misery. He is a good young man, and I am sorry for his pain."

"How does the poor fellow—I mean how does Escombe bear it?"

"He writes bravely enough," Lady Judith answered with a sigh. "He does his best. But he is not coming home just yet. He is going to California, and thence will sail for China and Japan. He will go round the world, in fact. He will come home cured, I hope, and able to take his place and do his duty in life. I think it is rather a weak thing to go wandering round the world merely to shake off the burden of a disappointment. Better to shake it off by some work of active good. But Charles is not very strong, though he means well always. There is his letter, Angelo—you can read it. Whom did you meet to-night?"

"For one, Lady Judith, I met Alexia.'

"Indeed. And her husband?"

"Yes—him of course."

"Any one else?"

"She was looking pale, poor child!"

"Who was?"

"Alexia, Lady Judith."

"Mrs. Walraven, you mean?"

"Your daughter, Lady Judith—your daughter Alexia! It pierced my heart to see her."

"Why so, Angelo? Has she not made her choice? Is she not happy? Is she already disappointed?"

"Oh, no. She does not say so at least, and she never was able to disguise her real feelings."

"You do injustice to her talents, Angelo. She had greatly improved of late in the art of deception."

"She declares that she is very happy, and she appears to love that fellow—I mean her husband—passionately."

"I am glad. It is the duty of a wife always to love her husband, I believe, without the slightest regard to his merits or personal character. So good a daughter ought to make a model wife. But why, then, do you feel so miserable on her account?"

"Because I know she will yet be unhappy, very unhappy! I watched that man, and his demeanor towards her; and towards others. I looked in his eyes, and noted his expression; and I wish he had been dead before Alexia ever saw him. If he is not destined to make her unhappy, then I shall never again try to find a man's character written in his face."

"My good boy, I dare say he will make her unhappy. Nothing is more likely. We are all made unhappy by some one, unless when we are making others unhappy. Why is Mrs. Walraven to be exempt? Is it because of any special grace about her, or that she has done her duty so much better than anybody else?"

"Lady Judith, she has been very foolish and wilful, but she has not been wholly to blame; nor is she the only one to blame."

Lady Judith's eyes flashed, but she retained her composure.

"I am to blame, Angelo, you would say? I did not understand or appreciate her—did not fondle her pretty wilfulness, and try to humor her into love and obedience? Is that what you mean?"

"Yes, dear Lady Judith, something like that."

"Angelo Volney, I don't think the less of you because you defend my daughter and accuse myself. You were always a brave lad, not afraid to side with a losing cause. But between my daughter and me no man could possibly judge, nor woman either, indeed. Heaven alone must decide between us, and condemn me if I have not at least faithfully striven to do my duty. I am not afraid to stand the test! Now then, tell me who else was there to-night?"

"But you will forgive this poor girl. You will see her; you will help her in life? Oh, Lady Judith, listen to the pleadings of your own good and generous heart—how good and generous Heaven and I alone can know! Don't be unforgiving. The more you are in the right, the better you can afford to forgive. She is destined to misery if you cast her off."

Lady Judith rose from her seat and stood with one arm resting on the marble chimney-piece. She was not wholly composed. Her lips trembled slightly; her bosom heaved and fell. A moment passed before she could speak. Then she said, in cold distinct tones:

"Angelo, we must finish this subject once for all. It is idle to talk of my casting my daughter off. She cast me off. Let us strip this whole affair, if you please, of all romance and melodrama, and look at it as it is. I never cast off my daughter. She deliberately deceived me; made her choice and left me. She gave herself over to an adventurer—a swindler—who only takes her because he believes he and she can prey upon my supposed weakness, and that he will become rich with my money. Is not that the plain truth?"

Angelo was silent. He feared only too much that it was the plain truth.

"Very well. Do you think I will allow this man to win his base game? Never, Angelo! He has played and lost! No power on earth shall ever induce me to grant him the reward of his villany! Let him support his wife as he has taken her; let her share his fortunes as she has chosen him. Is there anything unjust in that? Let us talk no more of my casting her off. I will not enrich a swindler merely because he has cheated me out of my daughter—that is all."

"But you will see her—you will not refuse to receive her?"

"Surely I will not refuse to receive her. I hope and trust I have forgiven her. Whenever Mrs. Walraven pleases to visit me, I shall of course receive her. Not him, Angelo—not him! If you are good-naturedly acting as their emissary, please to remember that I will not see him! But you do not really suppose that Mrs. Walraven looks forward with any particular longing to a meeting with me? You are a child, Angelo. Let them know as my certain determination what I have already told you, and you will hear no more of any loving desire for the joy of an interview with me. No, Angelo, I can't hear any more. You must spare me now. I too have my feelings, and weaknesses, and sufferings, although I don't poser myself as a heroine of romance. I have something else to say to you. Whom did you see to-night besides Mrs. Walraven—I mean what woman?"

Angelo colored. He knew the meaning of the question and he did not th[illegible] of evading it.

"Miss Atheling was there, Lady Judith

Lady Judith smiled a faint, sad smile.

"I am glad to hear of her, Angelo. I like her much. She seems a good, dutiful, faithful girl, and she has spirit and brains. Women without heads are to me the most contemptible creatures. I like her in many ways. But there is one thing, Angelo, which gives her a peculiar value in my eyes."

"What is that, Lady Judith?"

She laid her hand gently, almost fondly, upon the young man's shoulder, and looked into his face with great pitying eyes.

"Because you love her, my poor boy, and because she loves you. Oh, Angelo, many, too many, have been false and ungrateful to me! You have been true—although I have loved and served you. Since you two have set your hearts upon each other, and fancy you can only be happy by being man and wife"—Lady Judith paused, and slowly repeated the words "man and wife—O my God!—I should like to help in making you happy, even in your own way!"

CHAPTER XVIII.

"LET NOT THE SIN OF HER MOTHER BE BLOTTED OUT."

ANGELO left Lady Judith that night with a heart which seemed scarcely able to bear the burden of his wonder and his gladness. He had long believed that his love for Isolind and their unspoken pledge and betrothal would be bitterly resented by his benefactress. He was prepared to bear Lady Judith's anger—nay, that he heeded little in comparison. He was prepared to bear even the knowledge that he must forever rank in her mind as one of the most ungrateful of human creatures. All this, however, he would have borne. There was something in the nature of the young man which made love—true, reciprocal, and passionate love—sacred to him. He would have renounced all the world, borne all the world's wrath and censure for Isolind, because he loved her; more than that, he would have felt that he was not obeying a passion, but following a sacred and divine principle.

But the one being on earth to whom after Isolind he felt himself devoted was Lady Judith. When, therefore, she spontaneously approved and ratified his love and offered to assist him in securing its object, the world seemed to have hardly anything more to promise. The manner in which Lady Judith anticipated his inmost wishes was as surprising as anything else. She had divined his determination to be independent. She was practical and clear-headed in everything she undertook, and she now proposed that her patronage, or guardianship, or whatever it might be called, should end with one present benefaction—that she should find him a career or the means of opening one for himself. That done, let them be friends hereafter and nothing more. She would have liked Angelo to attempt a diplomatic career, and had quite influence enough to secure him a start. But her clear good sense saw decided objections. The English diplomatic service is essentially aristocratic. Angelo's birth would be terribly against him. Worse still, the service in its junior grades is very badly paid. The young men who enter that career are not supposed to want money. It is part of aristocratic policy not to pay the junior ranks, because thus a new barrier is raised against the entrance of clever and humble young men. Angelo as an *attaché* of a diplomatist could not support a wife unless by means of her fortune or of Lady Judith's generosity. Lady Judith would gladly, oh, how gladly, have been generous! She was rich, and she cared nothing for money. She would have been delighted to remain his benefactress always, but she had lately begun to learn the difficult art of understanding the pride and principles of others, and she appreciated the young man's impatience of further dependence. Therefore she proposed that a consulship should be obtained for him in some French or Italian port, his knowledge of modern languages being his special recommendation for such a post, and that he should endeavor to rise in that less pretentious and aristocratic branch of England's foreign service. She would like him and his wife to remain near her; and anywhere in France, or Germany, or Italy she called near. But she made no conditions. Her desire was to make Angelo independent and happy. She was willing even to part from him wholly. She had travelled far in self-development lately, and had learned to acknowledge the right of individuality and to distrust the infallibility of her own will.

"I have spoiled your life, Angelo," she said—"spoiled it at least in one way. I did not see that to be a lady's page is hardly the best business for a man. Even the pages of great ladies, I think, were expected some time or other to become my lord's squires and go to battle and win their spurs. Let me repair my error, Angelo, and send you to battle decently armed for the fight. You will win, I know—and I shall see you sometimes."

Angelo could not speak. He could not say what he wished. He wanted to pour out his gratitude and devotion, to tell her how magnanimous and noble he thought her—in his heart he wondered at that moment why her husband had not adored her—but he could say nothing articulate. He kissed her hand, she kissed his forehead, and then he left her.

Judith Scarlett fell upon her knees and prayed. She prayed for patience, and strength, and light. Ah, this woman's life was all prayer! She had never taken any step in existence without asking for guidance. She had never consciously done an unjust or a wrong deed. Yet she had done many things that were wrong. She had made many sad mistakes, and now at last she began to know it. Hers had been a hard task in life—to struggle against the influence of a proud, egotistic, imperial nature—a nature which saw things only by its own light, and whose first instinctive impulse was to compel all other natures to bend to its command. Lately she had begun to learn a better wisdom. It was bitter to her to part with Angelo. In a strange, inexplicable way she loved and honored the young man. No one else had ever been frankly devoted to her; and yet no one else had ever ventured so bravely and calmly to oppose her wishes. She had learned not merely to love but even to respect the *protégé* whom she had raised from beggary, and who yet loved Love, and Duty, and Right more than he loved or feared her.

So she had resolved on a new and final sacrifice. She would give up this loved and heaven-sent boy, this son of her affection, this brother of her intellect, this companion of her occupations and her mature years. She would give him up to another woman. Only God could know what that sacrifice, so cheerfully made, meant for Judith Scarlett.

It somewhat, but not much, lessened the burden of the sacrifice that Lady Judith had grown into such regard and affection for Isolind Atheling. The pervading earnestness of the girl's nature had in the beginning a charm for her. She was attracted toward a woman whose whole conversation and conduct proclaimed that the *humani nihil alienum* was the essential principle of the one sex as well as of the other. She was attracted by a girl who did not acknowledge that girlhood gives any exemption from interest in the great purposes and duties of life, any more than from its sufferings. In Isolind Atheling she saw the first woman—at least the first unmarried woman—whose principles avowed and conduct proclaimed the faith that common human duty begins and ends only with consciousness. There was, too, a freshness in Isolind's manner, a fearless originality in her conclusions and expressions, which had a special zest and flavor for Lady Judith. Therefore Lady Judith made her a favorite.

Observe that Lady Judith was given to making favorites. All women are whose capacity of love has not been developed, or if developed has not been filled to its utmost measure. Catherine of Russia might have been one of the purest, as she was one of the greatest of her sex, if she had only had a Cœur de Lion, a William the Silent, a Frederick, or a Napoleon for her husband. Doubtless the same causes which dispose women to make favorites dispose them to quick variations of mood and sudden, strange, strong dislikes.

Now, however, Isolind Atheling is Lady Judith's favorite *en titre*, and for her sake the aristocratic and high-bred English woman accommodates herself to Judge Atheling, and—a yet more difficult task—finds attractions in Mrs. Atheling. The Judge himself was an individuality; he had a strong, clearly-defined character. He was all goodness and charity, and he had much knowledge, shrewdness, and observation. But his wife was only his loving, faithful little planet. She was nothing in herself. Lady Judith nevertheless constrained herself to find merits in Mrs. Atheling. She wondered to herself many times how such a woman could have such a daughter as Isolind, and how Isolind could prove herself so dutiful and devoted to such a mother. What was the mysterious reason, she often and bitterly asked of herself, why the most commonplace women, with nothing of surpassing goodness about them, so often have affectionate and dutiful daughters—and she, Judith Scarlett, who was not commonplace and had always striven heart and soul to do her duty, must have only an Alexia for her child?

"If *I* had such a daughter as Isolind Atheling!" the bereaved woman would many and many a time whisper to herself. How often had not poor Alexia in the bitterness of her heart murmured to herself, "If I had only had such a mother as this girl from America has, perhaps—who knows?—I might have been as loving and obedient a daughter."

Perhaps Alexia was thinking of this that very night as she lay perturbed, feverish, and sleepless, beside her peacefully slumbering husband. The meeting with Angelo, the talk with Isolind, had unsettled the poor girl, and she could not sleep. Eric had lain awake for a little, thinking of several things. First, whether Lady Judith would soon come round. Next, what on earth he should do if she did not soon come round. Third, what a confounded nuisance it was that his new poem, "The Mystery of the Universe," was not receiving prompter notice from the reviews. Fourth, what a charming creature that young American woman was. Fifth, what a puppy and cod that fellow they called Angelo was.

In his thoughts, then, was there really no memory whatever of the dark-eyed passionate child who had given herself to him, and who lay by his side? Oh, yes! He had thought several times what an awful sell it would be if Lady Judith should actually not come round, and should positively leave him with Alexia clung on to him; and he had thought more than once that, despite all his artistic taste in dressing her, Alexia looked nothing when compared with that splendid girl from New York. Therefore Eric could not be accused of having forgotten his wife—his wife, who when at last he fell asleep hung over him and gazed in rapture at his face and his curls as the faint moonlight showed them, and fancied herself like one of the women in story with whom a god had fallen in love, and whom he had admitted to his bed.

Next day, as early as might well be done, Angelo hastened to the lodgings of the Athelings. They lived in pleasant quarters near Eaton Square, and the distance from Lady Judith's was not great. But, early as he was, the Athelings had already gone out. They were seeing London in all its nooks and corners, as Londoners never do. They would endure an hour's jostling in Eastcheap, just because once upon a time, and when Eastcheap was not, as it is now, all insurance offices, cheap houses, and jewellers' shops, Prince Hal and Falstaff had drunk sack and rattled the window-shutters there. They had gone in quest of the Soho house, where De Quincey sought a refuge from the cold lap of the stony-hearted stepmother, Oxford street. They had wasted ever so much time exploring Shore-ditch until they found out Bevis Marks, where Mr. Swiveller acted as clerk to Mr. and Miss Brass. They had looked up admiringly to many a window in the dull squares and courts of the Temple, believing that in chambers like those brave George Warrington must have smoked his pipe and listened to the aspirations of his friend Arthur Pendennis—that in yonder porter's lodge poor Fanny Bolton must have smiled and sorrowed and been comforted.

This sort of thing was half the delight of their visit, as it is of most true-hearted Americans who come to London, and who set, alas! far higher value on most of London's literary associations than the Londoners do. Show me the born Londoner who ever walked one street out of his way to see any spot which the genius of Shakespeare, or Fielding, or Addison, or Dickens, or Thackeray had made sacred!

Isolind and her people had gone out, then, this morning, on some exploring expedition. They had of course little notion of an early visit from Angelo. Isolind certainly had no such hope, or the dearest associations of London streets would have been powerless to draw her out of doors. Indeed, if the truth must be told, she had gone out with the hope of seeing Angelo; for she was resolved some time that day to pay a visit to Lady Judith, and there was at least a chance of finding *him* there. Of course, too, no girl in love ever goes out in a city where her lover happens to live without the hope of seeing him at every street corner. Observe the palpitating hopes and desires of Miss Austen's heroines in London and Bath; and Miss Austen's heroines are surely the most charming, sweet, and womanly cluster of women known to the world since Shakespeare drew Imogen and Beatrice—since Cervantes painted Dorothea and the Duchess.

Isolind's eyes sought for Angelo at every turning; but they found him not. He had gone to look for her, had heard that she and her people were gone out driving—knew what one of Judge Atheling's exploring expeditions meant—and went disappointed and restless into Kensington Gardens, where he wandered through the glades and sat near the Round Pond, and was quite unreasonably discontented and aggrieved with fate. When a man has believed himself hastening to the very threshold of felicity, the interruption and delay of even a pebble in the way will distract him. Angelo was as anxious and impatient because he had missed seeing Isolind just this once as if the hour's delay had opened a new gulf between them. There seemed to be something of evil omen in the delay and disappointment, and it began quite to vex and darken his usually serene mind. Nothing ever wholly banishes the tinge of superstition from the nature which has any of the Latin or Celtic constitution. A young Briton or American in love, and failing to find his mistress at home when he very much wanted to see her, would have been terribly disappointed doubtless, but he would hardly have had occasion even to defy augury; for the idea of any evil augury in the matter would never have occurred to him. But it was not so with Angelo.

Being, however, a youth with an earnest and practical turn, even in his love-making, he felt at once that the only way to shake off the cloud that hung over him was to go and do something. He made up his mind that he would go to see Alexia and endeavor to like her husband. He called once more at the Athelings' lodgings, found that they were not expected home until six o'clock, and then took the train and went to seek Alexia.

Meanwhile Isolind, having explored a good deal, was taken with a not unnatural desire to call on Lady Judith. Isolind did indeed greatly admire and look up to Angelo's benefactress, and not merely for Angelo's sake. Lady Judith's sad story had impressed her deeply; and she had many times heard Mr. Atheling describe the strange and memorable scene which he witnessed in Westminster Hall when Lady Judith's husband, so soon to disappear from the eyes of men, was assaulted by Dysart. Of late Atheling had dropped talking of this, and when he and Isolind entered Westminster Hall for the first time together, and she wished him to point out the very spot where the meeting took place, he seemed unwilling to say much about it, and gave a hasty, vague sort of description, and hurried on. But the story had sunk into Isolind's heart, and the strange, romantic, inexplicable events connected with it threw all the powerful charms of mystery and wonder over it. Lady Judith was in her eyes the heroine of a marvellous story—the typical victim of woman's wrongs and sufferings. Isolind's heart yearned toward her, and the two women drew gradually close to each other.

So Isolind gladly gave up part of her time this day to visiting Lady Judith She would have done so even had she no had hope, as she had, of meeting Angelo. Mr. and Mrs. Atheling did not accompany her, but they promised to call for her after a while. In truth, they did not care much for the society of the proud and stately London lady. Do what she might, her presence chilled them.

Isolind found Lady Judith seated at her desk, reading letters. Lady Judith was cordially glad to see the girl, and came to greet her with quite a warm smile upon a face that just before had been very sad. Nay, she even kissed Isolind, who blushed somehow at this mark of favor and affection. Our Isolind, who usually passed for a rather stately and queen-like specimen of womanhood, seemed quite girlish and slight beside the superb Lady Judith, who petted her and even caressed her as if she were something *mignonne* and fragile.

Lady Judith asked some questions about the previous night. Isolind, not without some tremulousness, endeavored to put in a word for Alexia; but Lady Judith would not give her a chance.

"Have you seen Angelo Volney to-day?" suddenly asked the great lady, looking keenly but very kindly at the young woman.

"No," replied Isolind, crimsoning; "not to-day. I thought perhaps he might be here. But indeed that was not the reason why I called."

And then she became a little embarrassed as she felt that the very protest was itself a confession.

Lady Judith smiled.

"I thought he intended to call on you to-day."

Isolind looked up disappointed—almost startled. The thought of Angelo having gone to see her and failed to find her was dreadful.

"Oh, I shall be so sorry," she began, "if he came this day, of all days, when we were not at home since ever so early in the morning."

Lady Judith kindly laid her hand on Isolind's and said:

"My dear, you know what I think of Angelo Volney; I have told you again and again. But I want to know what you think of him. Come, tell me. We are women, and alone; and I sometimes feel as if I ought to have been your mother. What do you think of Angelo Volney? Or, rather, how do you feel toward him?"

The blood rushed again into Isolind's forehead, and a tremor passed through her. But then she looked up quietly and met Lady Judith's large bright eyes, and said in a low, clear voice:

"Lady Judith, I love him."

"I knew it, dear. Do you know that he loves you?"

"I suppose—I hope he does. Oh, indeed, I should not speak as if I affected to doubt him! I know he does."

"You know each other's feelings, in fact?"

"Dear Lady Judith, I am afraid he knows mine. I am afraid I took little trouble to conceal them. Was that unwomanly? Would an English girl not have done so? I am not a prudent and pale-blooded person, and I fear there are times when I think as little of propriety as of punctuation. From the moment when I thought Angelo cared for me, I am afraid I was only too eager to let him know how I felt toward him. Indeed, Lady Judith," added Isolind, with a bright, irrepressible smile, which glittered through an equally irrepressible tear, "I only hope I did not show him my heart a little before he told me anything about his."

Lady Judith sighed faintly. She was thinking of her own unloved and loveless youth; and Isolind knew it and softly pressed her hand.

"Well, my dear, I am not much of a matchmaker, and, indeed, have no great impulse to join people in marriage; and when I did try to do such a thing, I failed. But I should like to assist you and Angelo. I think you are worthy of him. Don't be offended at my putting it in that way."

"Offended, Lady Judith? What higher compliment could you pay me? I don't believe I am worthy of him; but Heaven knows I will try to be."

"You are at all events the only woman I know who is or could be worthy of him; and he is the only male creature I know or ever did know whom I should like to see any pure, good woman intrust with her heart and her destiny. You know that he is poor—you know, of course, his history?"

"Oh yes; he told me all, long ago."

Lady Judith smiled.

"I knew he would tell you all; but was it so very long ago? You met him for the first time—when?"

"Only last fall. But I seem to have known him always. And it does seem very, very long ago since he told me all about himself, for he went away immediately after, and we were separated for several——"

"Weeks, I believe, my dear?"

"Indeed, for some months, Lady Judith, and you don't know how long it seemed."

"No, dear, I don't know much about it," and Lady Judith's brows contracted, for she was once more thinking of her own youth; "but I can take on your word anything you tell me. Well, then, what do you propose to do?"

"Alas! I don't know; I don't propose anything. I wish I might!"

"What would you propose?"

"I would just find out what *he* wished to do, and I would propose that right away," said Isolind, bursting in her excitement into a flash of American slang. Even poetesses in our day will now and then help out the effects of the vernacular by a touch of slang.

"Well, my dear, I think you had better wait and hear what he says. I don't think he will keep you long waiting. For one, Isolind, I will do all a woman may do to help you and smooth your way. I will not encumber him—or you—with a sense of obligation. He is proud, as you know, and he will not care to be weighted with too many favors, either from your good father and mother or from me. What I would do for Angelo is not the question; the question is what he would allow me to do for him."

"He has talents, Lady Judith, and can make a way, and we can wait. I would wait for him until he thought the right time had come. I would wait for him until my hair grew white. I do feel that my soul claims him. I do need him. I do love him!"

And the tears, proud and glad tears, tears of love, and hope, and devotion, shone in Isolind's eyes.

Lady Judith looked at the impassioned girl with a quiet, kindly, pitying gaze, such as perhaps the worn and disappointed veteran may give to the enthusiasm of the young conscript, or the sobered and gray-haired penman to the exulting confidence of the ardent literary novice. She was about to make some very kindly and encouraging answer, suited to Isolind's condition of mind rather than to her own, when a servant entered and handed her a card on a silver salver.

Lady Judith read the name, and an expression partly of surprise, partly of downright pain, showed itself on her face.

"Mr. Robert May," she murmured. "What can he want? Can he have heard anything? Too late now if he has, and I care nothing!"

All the old bitterness rushed for a moment back into her heart. Perhaps the contrast between Isolind's young, glowing, and confiding love and her own premature widowhood and desolation helped to produce the sudden emotion. She thought of her own blighted life and of the child who had deserted her, and the name of Robert May recalled all the fading sense of wrong and revived the expiring flame of resentment against her husband.

"Show Mr. May in," Lady Judith said in her coldest, clearest tone, all the gentleness and warmth quite gone.

"You have a visitor; I will leave you." And Isolind rose.

"No, Miss Atheling; stay, please." Even to Isolind her voice had not for the moment its wonted kindness. "I had rather you were present. Be as a daughter to me, Isolind, if you can."

Isolind resumed her seat, not without some wonder at the sudden change in Lady Judith's manner, and perhaps for the first time beginning to have, in spite of herself, a faint awakening perception of a possible explanation as to the reason why Charles Scarlett had not loved his wife. She was, however, far too generous and too sincerely devoted to Lady Judith to allow such a thought more than a momentary occupation of her mind.

Robert May entered, Isolind awaiting with some curiosity the appearance of the visitor whose mere announcement had caused so much agitation. She was filled with a certain blending of pity and admiration at the sight of the sweet, melancholy expression on the gentle, worn face, and the snow-white hair. Robert May walked in, Isolind thought, as if some ancient picture had stepped out of its frame. He wore an old black velvet coat, rather loose for him, but, with its quite unfashionable and ancient shape and its color so strikingly contrasting with his white hair, giving him a marvellously pictorial appearance. Isolind could not help thinking of some prisoner who had been confined in the Bastile or Chillon and suddenly sent back to the living world when his eyes could hardly bear the light of day, and he had almost forgotten the ways and the speech of men.

But Robert May found his tongue. Indeed, he hardly waited for Lady Judith's formal salutation, but he began at once:

"I am sorry to interrupt you or intrude upon you, Lady Judith, but I have heard something which I thought it right that you should know. I have heard ——Here he became aware that there was another visitor in the room, and he stopped, rather embarrassed, and then for the first time saw Isolind's face.

Had he seen a ghost come from the grave, the sight could not have wrought on him a more startling effect. A light of wild surprise and joy came into his eyes, and he trembled in every limb. The two women gazed at him in utter amazement. There was an instant of silence, and then May cried aloud:

"Agnes! Agnes Revington!" and he sprang forward and clasped both the hands of the astonished and now pitying Isolind.

"It *is* Agnes Revington!" Robert May went on in broken accents. "I will not call you by that villain's name, Agnes! And you have come back, and were not dead after all, and you have come back to clear your name." And he darted a quick glance at Lady Judith. "Tell me—tell me all."

"Indeed, sir, you mistake," said Isolind, gently withdrawing her hands. "I do not know you. I don't know what you speak of." She looked at Lady Judith with inquiry and wonder.

"You are not quite well, Mr. May, I fear," said Lady Judith calmly, and with a quiet force she drew him away toward a chair. "You have heard some news, perhaps, which has startled you, or you have been reading too hard. Pray sit down and rest." Lady Judith was all kindness and consideration when any one within her reach was stricken down by physical illness of any sort. She had set down May on a former occasion as a man of feeble character and excitable, nervous temperament, and therefore was at once assured that too much study or something of the kind had momentarily shaken his intellect. "Take a seat, Mr. May. This young lady is from America, and you do not know her."

May sat down and passed his hand across his forehead, as if thus hoping to bring his thoughts into coherent order. He murmured:

"I believe the boys sometimes think my brain is muddled. Heaven knows. Perhaps they are right. What could have made me forget the long years that have passed since poor Agnes vanished, or suppose she could reappear in all the bloom of youth?" But here, rising from his chair apparently to fulfil his mission, whatever it was, his eyes again turned upon Isolind, and again he scrutinized her face with eagerness and wonder. Then he turned to Lady Judith and said with trembling lips:

"In God's name, Lady Judith, tell me who is that young lady?"

"That, Mr. May, is Miss Isolind Atheling, of New York, who has but lately come to this country for the first time."

"Can it be possible? Can I be really deceiving myself? Young lady, may I look at you a little closer?"

There was so much of respectful earnestness in his manner that Isolind was touched by it, and could not feel alarmed or offended.

"Certainly, sir," she said; and she approached him with fearless cordiality. "Perhaps I resemble some one you have known. But I have never seen you before; and this is my first visit to England."

Robert May gazed into her face steadily for a moment. The gaze was so intense and eager that Isolind, for all her courage, could hardly help wincing and coloring a little.

Lady Judith looked on with scornful impatience.

"I am not mistaken!" came at last a cry, a positive cry, from May's lips. "Nothing on earth shall convince me that I am mistaken! Young lady, where is your mother? Alive or dead? Speak quickly!"

"Alive an hour ago, certainly," Isolind replied, smiling.

"O God! Alive, and here in London?"

"Yes, indeed; here in London."

"Mr. May," said Lady Judith, firmly interposing, "I think I can hardly allow you to cross-examine this young lady any more. She has been very patient and good-natured so far, I think. Even if she is like some one you know, or if you do know some member of her family, there is hardly any occasion for so much excitement. Pray compose yourself. Have pity on our feeble feminine nerves, Mr. May, and don't alarm us too much."

Lady Judith spoke in good-humored scorn. She despised mental weakness and eccentricity.

"But, Lady Judith, pardon me; you don't know—you don't yet understand. It can't be that you know the truth and yet take it so calmly."

"Then will you kindly tell me the truth, sir, and let us have an end of all this wonder?"

"Lady Judith, the presence of that young lady and her mother in London are the signal for the refutation of a fearful scandal. I always said it would be exposed and refuted, but little did I think that my dearest friend was herself alive to refute it. I presume you, Lady Judith, have not yet seen this lady's mother?"

"I have seen her, Mr. May, many times."

"Seen her! Did you not recognize—did you not guess who she was? Why did she not proclaim herself? Why did she not come to me?"

Isolind meanwhile could not but remember the portrait Chesterfield Jocelyn had shown her and the emotion he had expressed. She was evidently very like in face to some unhappy English lady, and this chance resemblance was the whole cause of so much confusion.

"I think, Lady Judith," she said gently, "I can throw some light on this little mystery. This is the second time my face has proved to be very like that of some lady who, I believe, lived in England, and was very unhappy. In my own country I was shown a portrait of her, and it certainly did bear a striking resemblance to me. But, Mr. May, I am not that lady nor any relation of hers, and I don't think you could make anything romantic or mysterious out of mamma. Besides, I don't resemble her in the least."

For the first time during the discussion Lady Judith began to listen with a close attention and a quickening pulse. What strange and ominous sensation was it that seemed to send the blood rushing back to her heart, and made the air grow misty and dim, and caused a painful tingling in her ears and a thrill in her limbs?

Robert May caught at Isolind's last words, and with a heavy sigh he exclaimed:

"Ah, she is dead, then, as I feared, and the lady from America is not your mother! But you are *her* daughter as sure as God is in the heaven over us all!"

Isolind turned pale. She was about to speak, but Lady Judith interposed, and with an immense effort at composure brought out the words:

"Whose daughter, Mr. May? A plain, prompt answer, please, without any sentimental outburst!"

"Agnes Revington's daughter! The unhappy Agnes Dysart's daughter! The daughter of the purest woman that ever lived and suffered!"

"Miss Atheling," said Lady Judith, turning upon Isolind with a livid smile and eyes that burned with wan, unearthly light, "do you understand the compliment this gentleman would pay you? Forgive me if I speak a little plainly. He is anxious to believe that you are the daughter of a vile and wanton woman—the daughter of an adulteress—of a woman who left her husband to become my husband's mistress!"

"No, no!" May almost screamed, "the daughter of a suffering victim——"

"For whom, and in whose company my husband left his wife, his country, and his God!"

The scene was terrible to Isolind, although she could not understand it. The stern, vindictive earnestness of Lady Judith, the wild, emotional demonstrations of Robert May, gave it an appalling reality. The amazed girl looked on with some such feeling as one might have who had come suddenly on an awful incantation scene, the dread purpose of which might be gathered from the faces and features of the actors, even though they sang their wild chant and shrieked their weird words in tone and language unintelligible to common mortals.

"Disavow the compliment, Miss Atheling," said Lady Judith, again fixing her gleaming eyes on the bewildered girl, "and prove to this excited gentleman that you are not the child of sin, the daughter of a strumpet."

A wild ejaculation broke from May's lips. The word had stung more than the lash of a whip could have done.

A servant entered the room bringing some cards.

"Show them in here," said Lady Judith. "Miss Atheling, here are your father and mother."

"Thank God!" murmured Isolind.

"They will, perhaps, satisfy Mr. May that you cannot accept the vile pedigree he proposes for you! Mr. and Mrs. Atheling, you are welcome!"

The big Judge entered blinking benevolently through his spectacles, and with him his wife, all peering kindly eyes and shrivelled cordial smiles. Isolind started from her place, ran to the Judge, and drew her arm through his. The manner of Lady Judith for the last few moments had been terrible to her.

At once Atheling saw that something strange and ominous was going on. Not so his wife. She began some gentle compliments to Lady Judith, her face still puckering over with smiles.

"You have come opportunely," Lady Judith said, addressing the Judge. "That gentleman, Mr. Robert May, has set up a claim to your daughter, whom he declares to be not your daughter, but the child of a dear friend of his—an adulterous and outcast woman! I don't suppose, Mr. Atheling, that you usually carry your daughter's certificates of birth and baptism about with you; but you can probably satisfy this gentleman that she is your child. He will hardly, I presume, doubt your word and your wife's."

A cold perspiration broke out on Atheling's face and a mist dimmed the crystals of his spectacles. His heavy frame quivered with emotion of pain and pity. He pressed Isolind's arm closer to his side, and looked down at the girl with affection and pathos all unutterable. Mrs. Atheling quivered and shivered; she hardly knew why Lady Judith's excitement grew greater every instant. May was now the least disturbed of the party. He felt confident that he was right.

"Who is this gentleman?" Atheling sternly asked at last. His impression was that the white-haired, earnest man might be some emissary or accomplice of Chesterfield Jocelyn.

"The oldest and most devoted friend of that young lady's mother," May said, in sweet and gentle tones. "One who would believe in Agnes Revington's purity though all Belgravia had ten times over tried her and found her guilty!"

Atheling regarded him fixedly for a moment, and then said with a sigh:

"Your motive, sir, I am sure is good; I guess I can read that pretty plainly in your face; but I wish you had been less impulsive. You have done no good, sir; you may have done a dear and innocent girl much harm!"

"Then he is right," said Lady Judith, drawing back from the whole group with a kind of horror. "The man is right. Once for all, Mr. Atheling, whose daughter is that girl there?"

"Lady Judith, I am every way grieved to say she is not my daughter nor my wife's. Nay, Issy, don't faint or fall, my girl; you are always the daughter of our hearts and of our love—dearer to us, my child, than many real daughters are to their true parents. Here, mamma, come and support our child and comfort her."

"She has need of comfort," Lady Judith broke in fiercely. All the bitterness of her heart was now stirred up, and she thought no more of Isolind's feelings than the soldier in the heat of battle cares for the sufferings of his enemy. "She has need of comfort if she is the daughter of that adulteress! Of *her*, my God—and perhaps of him! Give me an answer, sir. Is that girl the daughter of my—of Charles Scarlett?"

"No!" cried May; "it is impossible—I say it isn't true! If ever there was a virtuous woman on earth, it was Agnes Revington!"

"I say, sir, speak,' said Lady Judith sternly, appealing to Atheling. "We have surely had mystery enough already; it is time there should be some truth and plain speaking."

"I am thinking of this sweet child's feelings; Lady Judith they are more to me than the feelings of any other in this sad business. Isolind, my love, this is hardly a discussion for you to hear! Will you not go home, child, with mamma; and I will presently come to you."

"Yes, my dear, let *us* go," whispered Mrs. Atheling to Isolind.

But Isolind had now recovered from her first bewildering shock, and felt the simple strength of her pure womanhood. She stood erect and stately, still leaning on the Judge's arm, and said:

"I will stay, dear, thank you. I have the best right to hear all that has to be said. Whatever the truth may be, it is only fitting that I should hear it. I am not a child, but a grown woman."

"Once more, then," said Lady Judith, "I have to ask, whose daughter is this young lady who has been presented to me and welcomed in my house as the legitimate child of virtuous and respectable parents?"

"If I desired to do so, Lady Judith, I might perhaps evade the truth by giving you the most direct answer in my power. You ask me whose daughter is this girl. I could say with perfect truth, I don't know. But there are strong evidences which lead me to believe that she is the daughter of the unhappy woman whom this gentleman calls Agnes Revington. I suppose he means the wife of Edwin—I mean of Thomas Dysart."

"And her father?"

"Her father I believe to be the scoundrel—I mean the person who was once Thomas Dysart. The other part of your conjecture, Lady Judith, I am happy to think is wholly unfounded. I think so, I believe so; I might almost say I am sure of it. God knows the thing is sad and shameful enough without that. Thomas Dysart, my lady, was more merciful than you. He never suggested that this girl was not his own daughter."

"Then you know him—he is still living?"

"He is."

"Did you know that this girl was his daughter, or his wife's?"

"He told me so himself; he laid claim to her. He gave me no proof that would amount to anything in a court of law. But I confess he did, much against my will, bring home to my moral judgment the conviction, or the strong impression at least, that my darling Isolind was his daughter."

A new pang of grief and shame passed through Isolind's heart. She did not need to ask who was the man claiming her as his child. She knew now only too well that it was he whom from the first time she saw him she had dreaded and disliked—the adventurer and profligate Chesterfield Jocelyn.

"But I had heard of this man Dysart's death."

"Possibly, Lady Judith. He is quite equal to any such contrivance. He lives, however."

"And his wife?" Robert May sadly asked.

"She is dead."

"Ah, I knew it! I knew that if she were anywhere in life, she would find means to vindicate her fame and that of her child!"

"I saw her laid in the grave," said Atheling solemnly; "I saw the sand and the sage-grass of the prairie opened to receive her remains, and closed and trodden down on them. At least if it was she in whose arms and on whose breast my little Isolind lay an infant, I saw her buried in the desert. But I know nothing more. The woman my wife and I helped to a decent burial was too worn and discolored and disfigured by sickness and toil and fear and suffering of every kind, to be recognizable in her last moments even, I should think, by her own relations."

"And you knew who this girl was—you knew who her mother was; and yet you kept the knowledge to yourself, and you allowed me—*me*—to receive her as a friend—me whose very blood might be expected to curdle at the mere approach of the child of such a mother!"

"Lady Judith, I'm not saying I did right; I don't suppose any manner of deceit ever is right or can end well anyhow. But I thought of this dear girl, who is innocent of everything, and I did do my best to conceal from her any knowledge of the truth. She never dreamed of it. I didn't tell my own wife what I had found out lately. She must forgive me; this is the only secret I ever kept from her since our marriage; I wanted to spare her feelings too! I did it all for Isolind; to save her from undeserved shame and from contact with a bad father, who only wanted to make money out of his claim to the child! Heaven knows the amount of the price I paid to him, for *I* don't know it yet; but I don't care much about that. Yes, I did all that; and for her sake I would do it all again. And please to remember, Lady Judith, it was not *me* who sought you, but you who sought us—her at least; and she hadn't sinned against you anyway, and she is fit for the society of the greatest lady in your land, from your Queen Victoria down."

The Judge's voice was a little tremulous, but his heart was very firm.

Isolind withdrew her arm from his and advanced with unfaltering step, though with drooping eyes, toward where Lady Judith was standing. Instinctively the latter shrank back.

"I don't mean to approach too near," said Isolind, in a sad, firm tone—"I don't mean to touch you; I don't blame you, Lady Judith, for drawing back. I can understand your feelings and make allowance for them. I know how bitterly you were wronged, and I did so admire and love you! Oh, forgive me that I have, though not meaningly, caused you a new pang. Think that if your burden is great, it is but light to mine! You have only suffered; you are not shamed! Oh, think what this blow is to me! Think of all we spoke of to-day—just before this"—and Isolind's voice nearly broke down and her eyes filled with tears—"think that all that is over for me; that I must renounce it forever—friendship, and the pride of womanhood, and hope—and—and—love—and all! Think of this, and as you are a woman pity me, and do not hate me! I shall always think of you with gratefulness and kindness."

But Lady Judith stood pale, cold, and unmoved as a marble statue. Even as the beautiful, proud, humbled girl pleaded to her, she only thought, "This, then, is the face which blighted my life, which made me an object of scorn and pity to the world. Perhaps such pleading, tearful tones won my husband to betray and desert me."

So she said aloud:

"We had better bring this unpleasant scene to an end. Mr. Atheling, I ask for no further explanations, and I care to hear none. Your story is romantic, and may probably have interest for Mr. May. It has none further for me. The one fact is enough. Miss Atheling—I prefer for decency's sake to call you by that name, in speaking to you, I hope, for the last time—you are only to be pitied, not condemned in all this, and you have indeed, as you say, a heavy burden to bear. You must bear it, as others have done. But I tell you openly that an angel of light with that face would now appeal to my sympathy in vain."

Lady Judith touched her bell.

Robert May crossed the room, seized Isolind's hand, and pressed it to his lips.

"Young lady," he said—and his manner was now firm and dignified—"have no fear. No shame will come on you. The pure fame of your dead mother will yet be made clear, even in this house! I was sorry at first that I should have spoken out so rashly; but I am not sorry now; it is better as it is. The truth will be made to shine all the sooner."

Atheling drew Isolind to his side again, and they left the room.

Robert May paused a moment. "Does your ladyship desire to hear the news—if it be news—I came here to tell?"

"Not now, thank you, Mr. May. Quite enough of revelations for one day, I think. In any case I presume it comes too late, and it can matter little now even if I should never hear it."

May bowed formally; she bent her head, and in a moment she was alone.

May overtook the Athelings on the threshold and laid his hand gently on the Judge's arm.

"You must not blame me and think hard of me," he said. "It was a sudden impulse which I could not control. You can't know what my feelings are."

"I don't blame you, sir," Atheling replied. "You couldn't help yourself, and the thing must have come out somehow. But I want to learn several things of you."

"And I have many questions to ask of you. Perhaps we may come together on some track. May I have the honor of calling on you?"

"I shall be happy—but I beg your pardon, Mr. May, I would rather for many reasons"—and he glanced at Isolind and his wife, who stood waiting in the street—"I would rather go to see you where we could talk the whole thing out alone, in the first instance."

"Surely; surely, you are quite right. Here is my address. Any hour of day or night to-day, to-morrow, the day after—when you will. Good-by, sir; good-by, madam. I wonder," he added in a low tone, "would *she* speak to me—can she forgive me?"

"Isolind, my love," Atheling said, "you will speak to this gentleman—to Mr. May? He fears that you blame him, and he was your mother's friend."

Isolind came back and put her tremulous hand into that of May. Her veil was down, and he could hardly see her eyes.

"I thank you, sir," she said in simple earnest tones. "You spoke some words for which I thank you from my very heart."

Then the Athelings entered their hired brougham. And it was thus that Isolind left Lady Judith's house. So high and bright a hope in the noon, so sudden and utter a prostration in the afternoon, had surely seldom been ordained to one creature even in the story of the sufferings of woman. As the carriage drove through the crowded streets Isolind seemed to herself to be passing through a cold and silent graveyard, lying wan in a livid dusk and peopled by dim and melancholy ghosts.

CHAPTER XIX.

"LIKE ROCKS THAT HAVE BEEN RENT ASUNDER."

POOR Isolind! All the objects and idols of her life seemed falling into ruins around her. Her love and her pride were assailed at once. Since she had come to know anything of the great mysteries and trials of life she had been a devotee of the purity of woman. As poetess, as dreamer, as thinker, after her own fashion as woman, she had profoundly, passionately, proudly believed that pure womanhood was to be the grand redeeming force and agency in modern society. She had faithfully believed and bravely asserted—not without some peril and even penalty, as we have seen—that those of her own sex who endeavored to find woman's redeeming power in any other influence than this were leading womanhood astray. She believed, with all the force of faith, that society was to be regenerated by the union of knowledge and purity in woman. Not that innocence which is only ignorance refined, but the noble, sublime thought of purity combined with intellect and understanding. This was her creed, her dream, her passion. And now behold! She learned that the mother whose breast her lips had drained was a hissing and a by-word to the virtuous of the earth. Her father a profligate adventurer—a man whom she herself had once classed with Benedict Arnold and such like; her mother an outcast!

It would have been a bitter and grievous thing merely to know that she was not really the daughter of the Athelings, whom she so loved—of Mr. Atheling especially, whom she looked up to with all a daughter's reverence and admiration as well as all da aughter's best affection. But to find that instead of Mr. Atheling she had for a father Chesterfield Jocelyn ; instead of sweet, simple, stainless Mrs. Atheling, a woman who had abandoned her husband to fly with the husband of Lady Judith. Lately she had looked up to Lady Judith with reverential pity. She had often thought over her hard and cruel fate, and wondered what manner of woman that could be who had made herself the accomplice in such a deed of heartless wickedness. She had wondered how such a woman could exist, and whether any pleading angel could find aught to say in defence or palliation of her deed. And now the truth had come to light, and the guilty woman was her own mother !

No wonder Isolind covered her face with her veil and with her hands, and wished that she could be hidden from the light of day. She bore up tolerably well until she reached the lodgings. Then she said :

"Mamma—I may call you mamma still ?"

"Oh, my sweet child !"

"Well, I think I should like to be alone—quite alone—just for a little. I should like to think all this out. It is too much for me just yet."

So she hastened to her own room. Oh, how different, she thought as she entered it, from her dear little room on the shores of New York bay ; and then, womanlike, she flung herself on her bed and prepared for the work of "thinking all this out" by a wild, passionate, hysterical flood of tears. Good heavens, what a fountain of tears that was which sent forth, like a geyser, its scalding waters ! The girl thought she should never be able to rise from that bed again, so often and so completely was her effort to get up and be calm mastered anew and swept away by a fresh and more vehement torrent of grief.

At last she arose, and the dusk was already gathering. She could not help glancing at her looking-glass—for this is no true heroine, look you, but only a woman and a sister—and what was the first thought that flashed across her tempest-tossed soul ? Alas ! she will probably forfeit for evermore the respect of many readers when they learn what frivolity could even at such a moment assert its presence in her and its momentary control over her. For as she saw her face in the glass, and saw that her eyes were red and swollen, her cheeks blotted and blurred, there arose in her mind the thought, "If Angelo should see me now, would he still ?——" and then the foolish thought was swept away in a tempest of fresh sorrow, for she remembered that for her there was no Angelo any more.

Yes, in the first shock of the revelation, and now that she had grown comparatively familiar with its terrible meaning, the same conviction rose solemn and clear in her breast. If this story was true, she could never marry Angelo. If this story was true—and how could she doubt it, when Judge Atheling was satisfied of its truth ?—she could not think of marrying the adopted son of Lady Judith. She could not allow Angelo to put this cruel insult on the benefactress of his life. More than that, were Lady Judith now dead, or had she never lived, Isolind was resolute in her own mind and soul that she must not be the wife of any man. She would bring a stained name and memories of dishonor and infamy to pollute no man's hearth. That was not her idea of the sacred sanctity of marriage ; and she loved Angelo far too well to endow him with a bride of sucn tainted, nay, infamous parentage. Every feeling of the girl's heart, every fibre of her frame revolted against the thought of marriage with such a plague for a dowry. It was nothing to know that she herself was innocent. She would likewise have been innocent had she sprung from insane or leprous parents: would she then have brought hereditary insanity or leprosy as her marriage portion to make glad some good man's house?

While she was touched by and grateful for Robert May's passionate protestations of her mother's innocence, she was compelled sadly to regard them as of little importance. The man was an outward dreamer, a prematurely aged enthusiast to all eyes; and what Isolind had seen of him had not impressed her with any respect for his judgment. No, she thought it idle to fight against the cruel, inexorable truth. She had heard Lady Judith's sad story twenty times over—from the Athelings, from Angelo, from Lady Judith herself lately. Lady Judith's husband and that woman—O God, Isolind's own mother!—had disappeared from London the same night, and Scarlett had left for his unhappy wife a written confession of his purpose, which mentioned the partner of his flight. The woman's husband believed it—"My father!" Isolind thought with a shudder; all the world of London believed it; even charitable and gentle Judge Atheling thought it beyond a doubt; no one had ever arisen to dispute it; no one ever disbelieved it except poor May, who had only baseless and chivalric faith to justify him. Isolind would fain have hoped even against hope, and believed even against belief. But to what avail? The thing was clear.

Perhaps a heroine of romance—especially of French romance—would have believed in the spotless innocence of the mother whose very existence she could not remember, in the teeth of all evidence, merely because she was her mother. In French sentiment, to name *ma mère* is to name an angel. But Isolind was not a heroine of romance—especially of French romance. She was not ignorant. She could read, and she had eyes to observe. She knew that the earth was "bursting with sin and sorrow." She knew that men led women astray, and likewise that women just as often led men astray. When the Athelings took her of nights to the opera or the theatre, and she saw in the glittering Haymarket bevies of noisy young women, gorgeous in paint and silks, she did not suppose that these were innocent young English maidens out for a harmless evening's walk. She knew that in every land and every class of life women have sometimes fallen—that the story of the woman taken in adultery has never yet lost its meaning. So, though she would gladly have given her life—alas! not now a very precious possession—to prove her mother innocent, she was compelled to bend for the hour to the too cruel evidences that seemed to declare such proof impossible.

She had, then, lost all by one cruel blow—parents, lover, and the sweetness of an untainted name. She purposed to raise her head against this fearful storm some day like a brave, true-hearted woman; but for the moment she acknowledged its strength irresistible, and she could only fling herself down on the corpse of her ruined happiness and weep insatiable, useless tears.

When at last she sought the company of her protectors, her true parents, the Athelings, it was in a timid, shame-faced way. She felt reluctant to look up at them—she, the daughter of the profligate father and the outcast mother. The Athelings were waiting for her, and when she came the big Judge rose from his chair and ran to her and folded her in his arms, and without a word deposited her in his own seat, his own peculiar and favorite possession, the rocking-chair, which had been bought for him in London, and which his wife even never offered to sit in. Poor Isolind had never sat in this royal seat before. Indeed, it was a very uncomfortable seat, and Heaven only knew why the Judge supposed that it would in some way soothe the girl's sorrows if she were placed there. Just then, however, it was the only way he could devise of conveying to Isolind the assurance that her grief had but given her a higher place in the heart's love of himself and his wife, and Isolind understood his meaning and felt her eyes overflow anew with tears at his simple kindness and affection.

Then gradually they all came to talk somewhat calmly over the situation, and Isolind learned as much of her story as the Athelings could tell her. About her mother they hardly spoke at all. Atheling merely said once, in a hasty sort of way, that he supposed Mr. Grey Scarlett must have died, or abandoned her. From what he had heard of Scarlett, he thought the former the more likely explanation.

Isolind endeavored to learn the nature of the agreement Atheling had made with Jocelyn or Dysart; but the Judge refused to give any information on this subject, and seemed painfully reluctant even to allude to it.

Isolind unfolded to her tender companions two deliberate resolves: one she spoke firmly and frankly out, the other she conveyed in broken sentences with starting tears and blushes. The first was her resolve that, come what might, she never would accept her position as the daughter of Edwin Jocelyn. A proper heroine of romance would of course have yearned for her father and rushed to his bosom, whatever his crimes. But no voice of nature called on Isolind to turn toward the man who had never sought her, and who, when the knowledge of her existence was at last forced unexpectedly upon him, had used it only as a means of ignoble and base extortion. To the end of her life she would regard as her father the man who had found her when an infant and taken her to his heart and his home, and brought her up from childhood to womanhood as a dearly loved daughter.

Atheling of course approved of her resolve, and, in fact, took it as a matter of course. He did not tell Isolind how unlikely he thought it that Chesterfield Jocelyn would care to claim his paternal rights, save as a possible means of raising money.

"My darling Issy," Atheling said cheerily, "you are our daughter by right of love and habitual and prescriptive possession, and everything else that holds good. We mean to keep you, despite all the Jocelyns in the world. We will give you up, my love, to a husband whenever you like; but not to a father."

Then Isolind came to her second purpose: she would never marry. At which declaration they were only soothing and kind, and did not seem to attach much importance to it. So with a great burst she announced that she would like very much to leave London and not to see Angelo Volney any more. Then they both became earnest and serious, and tried hard to reason with her. But she was firm; she would not bring him a tainted wife; and, thinking that Lady Judith had been to him what the Athelings had been to her, she resolved only the more earnestly that she would not be the means of tempting him to add the crowning shame and sorrow to the sufferings of his benefactress.

"He is very young," said poor Isolind, "and he has not known me long. He will soon—I mean he will some time—forget me, or learn to be happy without me, and he will love some one else." And thereupon her heart, though not her purpose, failed her, and she broke down again in tears.

At that very moment Angelo himself was standing within a dozen yards of her. He was in the street, outside the window. He was returning from Alexia's, and he had found, of course, that his shortest and only way home was through the street where Isolind lived. He stood and gazed at the windows, and saw no light. The Athelings had been sitting purposely in the twilight; they seemed to talk more freely without the glare of lamps. So the poor youth assumed that they had not yet returned, and did not like to knock at the door for the third time that day. He took a few turns up and down the street, vainly hoping to meet them, and yet half ashamed to be found there; and then at last he made up his mind and walked resolutely home.

His mind was somewhat disturbed on another subject. He had spent the whole day with Alexia, and had come away greatly uneasy on her account. He found her alone, and much perplexed and worried even by such light household cares as fell upon her in her toy cottage at Richmond. Her own maid Frances was with her, and was still faithful to her, and there was something in that companionship which softened the strangeness of her new life. But although Angelo remained the whole day, and dined with her and had tea with her, he saw nothing of her husband. When first Angelo came, Alexia, delighted to see him, insisted that he must stay to dinner. Dear, darling Eric had gone to town; he had to see his publisher, or reviewer, or somebody; but he would be home to dinner, and he would be so glad to meet Angelo. Angelo, who knew that Lady Judith dined out that day, willingly remained. Alexia and he walked in Richmond Park, and she told him a great deal about the virtues and charms of Eric, and how some stupid, envious journals, especially the "Saturday Review," were purposely ignoring his last volume of poems out of mere jealousy and spite. She "chaffed" Angelo a good deal about Isolind, and was a little tormenting in her old way, which, however, he did not much mind. But they returned to the cottage, and the god-like poet did not make his appearance. Dinner hour came, but no Eric. Then Alexia said he always told her not to wait for him—that he was sure to be punctual if something connected with his publishers and his poems did not compel him to remain in town and dine there. In fact, she never did wait for him; oh, yes, he sometimes was kept in town, poor boy, and could not come. So they dined together, *tête-à-tête*, Angelo and she, and were rather dismal.

After dinner Angelo tried to talk to her about the necessity of conciliating her mother, but Alexia was growing wild and unmanageable, and only answered with saucy sarcasms. The absence of Eric affected her terribly—she was so much in love with her husband. She only blamed fate, not him; for she never supposed that he would not have come to her if it were humanly possible. But his absence made her fretful and restless, and, in her childish way, savage; and her guest, who was really very dear to her, had to bear many a sudden and sharp reply.

Meanwhile Eric, however, was dining gayly at Greenwich with a joyous bachelor party. It was very delicious to play the bachelor now and then. He did not much care for dining alone with his little wife. When they were invited out to dinner, that was very pleasant. He made grand display of her beauty and her rank, and her devotion to him, and he was quite happy. Eric Walraven would almost have been ready to follow the example of King Candaules rather than allow the treasures he had won to remain unknown to the world, to the detriment of his own personal glory. But to live alone with Alexia flattered his vanity now in no wise, and he thought it very slow work. So he had business in town this day, he said; and he called upon the Athelings in the hope of meeting Isolind, wherein he was disappointed, and then he went to Greenwich with his pleasant bachelor friends.

Angelo and Alexia had tea together, and the god-like poet did not come. At last Angelo must return to town without seeing Mr. Walraven.

Alexia grew softer as the hour for parting arrived.

"You will tell mamma you have been to see me?" she said in a doubtful tone.

"Certainly," he replied. "Why not, Alexia?"

"Well, I don't know. Oh, there is no reason; only I don't think I should like her to know that Eric was away. She wouldn't understand a bit. She knows nothing about publishers and all that, and she might fancy—I hardly know what; but she always thinks badly now of my darling Eric, and I don't want our affairs talked about, Angelo. Tell mamma, if you like, that I should much wish to go and see her, but that I will never go near any one, were she twenty times our mother, as Hamlet says, who will not receive my Eric! Tell her that, Angelo, if you tell her anything, and if you are not afraid of her! There, don't look angry or heroic; greater men than you, my best of brothers, have trembled at the wrath of woman. But I don't believe Eric is one particle afraid of me, and I hope you never will be afraid of my fair-haired New Englander. Is she a New Englandeı? Well, it doesn't matter. Good-night, Angelo. I am sorry you have to go."

"I am sorry to leave you here alone, dear." And then he wished he had not said just that.

"Are you really sorry? I do believe you are! That is kind of you, and like you, for I tease and worry you, too, Angelo, as I do most people. But you and I were always brother and sister, and loved each other—as such! Did you know, sir, that my lady mother wanted to make us rather more to each other? We may talk of it now."

"I knew it, my dear," said Angelo, smiling.

"She told you so, I dare say?"

"Well, she said something——"

"She proposed for you, in fact, on my account, and you refused me, no doubt?"

"Indeed I didn't; and she only talked of possibilities."

"Well, sir, abate your self-conceit, and learn that whenever she made hints that way to me I always rejected you point-blank. Come, now, Angelo, make honest confession. Are you not very glad you did not have me for a wife?"

"Tell me first, Alexia, are you not very glad you did not have me for a husband?"

She smiled and colored. "Indeed, I would rather have my darling Eric than all the world; and so, Messer Angelo, you must never have the face to hint to Miss Américaine that you might—or—if you would—and so forth. This is all silly nonsense! Good-night, my brother! No sister could ever love you more than I do."

She raised her pretty lips toward him and kissed him affectionately. She stood at her cottage door to see him go. He looked back more than once and still saw her child-like figure, her pale face, her dark hair framed in the cottage porch, as she gazed after him and once or twice waved her hand in farewell. The soft air of early summer was dawned, the light of fading day was shining gently and tenderly on her. The ripple of the silver Thames was faintly heard. Over the whole scene there was a sweet, sacred, melancholy atmosphere. The little figure in the porch seemed to look sad and almost unearthly as Angelo glanced back and saw it still there, pale, beautiful, infantile, and lonely. He thought of that evening, that parting, that solitary little figure, the young wife waiting for her husband, many a time afterward. He will never forget that picture framed in the cottage porch. There was a time when he hardly dared to recall it to his mind—when he could not bear to think of it.

Lady Judith went to her dinner-party. She never broke engagements, and would never allow society to suppose that anything had disturbed her self-command. It was a very heavy and dull dinner-party; but that was nothing to Lady Judith. She disliked dinner-parties of any kind, even the best and brightest. Perhaps she disliked the best and brightest rather more than the others. She only went out to dine when she thought for some reason or other it was a sort of duty to go; and in the discharge of her duty she had just as soon be bored as not. But having performed her task, she came away early, and was at home before Angelo returned.

She went into the library, where she knew he would come, and waited for him. She dreaded the interview in a strange kind of way, and yet was resolved to go through with it at once. She dreaded to find that Angelo would cross her purpose and refuse to see things as she did and prove ungrateful to her, as she would have called it, and leave her. The patrician lady was positively afraid that she could not command the allegiance of the beggar-boy she had taken from her doorstep and reared up as her son. In truth, while the young man had wonderfully twined himself round her lonely heart, he was the one being in the world of whom she felt any fear, before whom she doubted the power of her own will to prevail. There always seemed a principle in whatever Angelo advised or did which she could not bear down by the mere weight of her moral dignity. She had heaped on him services enough to have made him her slave, and yet she shrank from a discussion in which he would be likely to oppose her. Like most women, even when the tyrant was strongest in her, she despised slaves.

Before long Angelo's step was heard, and he appeared in the library.

Lady Judith began at once.

"Angelo, have you seen the Athelings to-day?"

Angelo replied in the negative, and was conscious of feeling a little awkward as he made the acknowledgment. It was not his fault if he had not seen them.

"Then you don't know that a most painful and shocking discovery has been made?"

How the blood rushed into Angelo's face, and a thrill of wild, nameless, unspeakable alarm quivered through him. Something painful and shocking—and the Athelings! All the keenness of his sudden superstitious auguries of the morning revived. Isolind! Had anything evil befallen her?

He could only ask in anxious, stammering accents:

"What is it? I have heard nothing. Is it anything to affect——"

"Isolind—the girl they called Miss Atheling? It is, Angelo! Stay, don't speak till I have told you all!"

She told him the story in quick, brief words, every word falling like a spark of fire. He held his breath till all was told, and then he found himself relieved and almost happy in the reaction. Why, he had been driven nearly wild by the dread that Isolind was dead, or had suffered some cruel misfortune; and she was alive, and the same to him whether her mother were saint or Magdalen! He was grieved because the discovery must so grieve and wound Isolind, and because it seemed to have reawakened all Lady Judith's old sense of wrong. But for the rest, he had Isolind still.

"And this is all true—all certain?"

"Mr. Atheling himself confessed it."

"Confessed, Lady Judith?"

"Confessed, yes—acknowledged—anything you like to call it—that he found this girl somewhere, I don't know where—I don't care to know—and brought her up as his own child."

"He has a noble soul," said Angelo enthusiastically; "he has a soul like your own, Lady Judith! Then Isolind owes as much to him as I do to you! But it is a sad and cruel thing for her. Why should they have told it to her? Such a secret might surely have been allowed to rest in its grave."

"Is that all you have to say on the subject, Angelo? Does it not affect your own course and your future?"

"Mine, Lady Judith? Not in the least! You surely don't believe I could think the less of her, or love her the less, because of her mother? I must only endeavor to show that I value her all the more because of this calamity; for it is one. Now she is dearer to me than ever. My dear Lady Judith, I told her all the truth about my father, and it didn't affect her in the least. But why did they publish the secret now which had been so well kept all these years?"

Angelo indulged in no protestations or heroics. He hardly thought it necessary to go even so far as he had gone in reaffirming his unalterable love and purpose. He was thinking almost entirely of the pain this disclosure must cause to Isolind, and the strange unwisdom of making the revelation now. Thus engrossed, he did not perceive Lady Judith's drift. But he soon was made to see it.

"You seem not to understand, Angelo. Your love for this girl dulls you, I think. Are you thoughtless enough to suppose that I could encourage or countenance your marrying such a girl—that I could bear the insult and agony of her presence?"

"Lady Judith!"

"Think of it, Angelo, and you will see that it is impossible! Think that she is the daughter of the base woman who shamed and ruined my life! Think that all the suffering I have ever known came from the poisoned breath of that girl's mother; and then, remembering what I have been to you, speak, if you can, of loving and cherishing her! Angelo, I will not believe it of you!"

"Good God, Lady Judith, do you really think I could desert her—tear her from my heart—live without her! I love her, dear Lady Judith—I love her with all my soul, with every fibre of my strength. And, thanks to kind Heaven, she loves me!"

Lady Judith rose to her feet. "What is this girl to you when compared with what I have been to you? How long since you saw her first—how many months or weeks? Can a pretty face and bright hair turn a man, then, into an ingrate and a traitor? Are all men, then, indeed alike? Angelo, I should never have believed this of you!"

"Lady Judith, I don't even understand you. Is it to be an ingrate and a traitor not to desert Isolind Atheling because she had a weak and bad woman for her mother?"

"It is being an ingrate and a traitor," Lady Judith turned on him impetuously, "for you to refuse to give up that wretched girl or any other girl when I ask you to do so. Have you forgotten what you owe to me?"

"I have not forgotten it, Lady Judith," the young man replied in a low, sad tone; "I have not forgotten it, although until to-day you seem to have always striven to avoid even a word which could remind me how much I owed to you. No one on earth ever could have owed deeper obligations to another than I owe to you. What, then, would you have me to do?"

"Give up that girl. She cannot think of holding you to an engagement made in ignorance of this horrible secret. If she has any spirit, or principle, or even true regard for you, she will not think of allowing such an engagement to go on."

"She may perhaps think herself bound to renounce it," Angelo admitted with an agonizing pang; "but I will not allow her to refuse me. She shall not sacrifice herself and me to a mistaken sense of duty and self-denial. We love each other!" That seemed to him enough, and decisive.

"Angelo, one thing is certain—you must give up this girl or give up——"

"Stay, Lady Judith—and out-say the word——"

"Or give up me, Angelo! If you will cling to her, you have lost me! Think of it—think of it until to-morrow—and then tell me."

"No, Lady Judith—no, my dearest and most honored benefactress, I have nothing to think over. My way is clear. Isolind has given me her love; nothing in life has so strong a claim on me as that. Oh, Lady Judith, why did you not leave me to poverty or death? It would have been a thousand times more merciful and charitable than to bind me to you by such bonds of duty and gratitude, and then summon me to surrender my heart's love, to sell my soul—ay, to sell my very soul—in return! Lady Judith, this is cruelty——"

"Angelo, I have loved you as if you were my son——"

"And if I were, I still could not do what you now ask me. No son would have a right thus to destroy two lives because his mother ordered him. Lady Judith, *you* will think of this! You will allow your generous soul to prevail——"

"Never! You must give up her or me! My last word, Angelo! Choose!"

"I do not choose," Angelo answered, sadly but quite firmly. "You expel me from your presence and from your affections, Lady Judith, that is all! You cannot, even by this, undo all that you have done, or make me forget it. But there is no choice for me. I have long thought that I had no right to lead this dependent, helpless, womanly life. Was it kindness, after all," he demanded, growing more bitter in feeling despite his loving and patient nature—"was it kindness to bring up a human being to mere dependence? But no matter—too late to think of that now. I must leave you, Lady Judith."

"Angelo," said she, suddenly pouring all the cold light of her eyes on him, "the night when my daughter left me I reminded you that had she waited just two months she would have chosen for her flight the very anniversary of the night when my husband deserted me. Do you remember that? Do you know that this night is the very anniversary? A fitting night to make your choice, and to leave me for the daughter of the woman who ensnared my husband!"

Angelo almost started. It was indeed the anniversary of the fatal night, the twenty-fourth of May. In all his own grief he was touched and thrilled with pity for the woman who stood before him.

"Oh, Lady Judith," he pleaded passionately, "do not lay this heavy curse of seeming ingratitude on me! Have some pity and spare yourself and me. I will do anything you ask me—but that. I will wait—*she* will wait—as long as you like—until time has quite softened the bitterness of all this. But do not try to make me seem to myself a monster of ingratitude because I cannot do what it would be a moral murder and moral suicide to do. You would not ask me to give her up even for you if she were my wife. In my heart and hers we are as much pledged to each other as if we were married."

Lady Judith made a scornful gesture of her white hand, as if to wave away all such pleas as that.

"You cannot reason thus with me, Angelo. I cannot reason on this subject at all; it touches me too deeply. If you marry that girl, you renounce me. I will never form a link in a chain which would bring me in any way nearer to the daughter of such a mother. I say nothing against the unfortunate young woman. I pray that she may have escaped the contagion of such a mother's nurturing. But her friends can never be my friends; her lover, her husband can never be my son!"

"Then, Lady Judith, good-by. Seventeen years ago this night you brought me into your home. I shall never forget all that you have done for me; nothing can ever cancel that bond—nothing can ever repay your goodness. Perhaps you are only following a just and natural impulse even now; perhaps any further intercourse between us would be a pain and an insult to you. I don't pretend to blame you; but my course is clear; I have no choice to make I go where my heart and soul lead me. I would walk that way, I hope, to death. Good-by once more!"

He took her cold hand and raised it to his lips. She looked at him with a somewhat surprised glance, and asked in a tone that had lost a little of its wonted composure:

"You will wait until you are ready. You are not going now—to-night?"

Her womanly instinct—womanly weakness, perhaps—revolted at the idea of his going out upon the world at night. There was a hard, chilling, miserable realism about that little fact which shocked her. She had no thought of giving way. She knew that they must part, and she would have held to her conditions though her heart-strings snapped. But there was something in the bare fact of the young man turning from her door to go out into the cold world at night which for the moment pierced her more keenly than anything else. She made a gesture almost as if she would lay her hand upon his arm to detain him.

"Every moment that I remain," he said, "after you have decreed our separation, is an intrusion on you and a humiliation to me."

"Then go!" she answered bitterly. "I might have looked for this ingratitude, to crown all the rest! I said, the night when Alexia left, that *you* ought to be the next; and so it has come to pass!"

She stood nearer to the door of the library than he, and as she spoke those words she suddenly turned from him and left the room That was their farewell. So closed her seventeen years of beneficence.

Angelo hastened to make his preparations. They were not many or complicated. He would have wished that he could depart taking with him nothing that had belonged to his patroness. But this was simply an impossibility. The very clothes he wore were bought with her money. Of course he had for several years back acted most efficiently as her secretary and almost her *factotum*, and had rendered good and valuable service. That was some consolation. He had a sovereign and a few shillings in his purse. At first he took them out and laid them on his table, meaning to leave them there. Then a better thought prevailed, and he reflected that such an act could only seem like a wanton and unmanly insult to the woman who had been so kind to him, and toward whom even now he felt no anger, but only pity and affection. He put the few coins into his purse again, ashamed of his petulance. Then he packed a few clothes and books into a portmanteau.

Then he surveyed certain articles of property that were his own. Let us see what these were.

He had rendered much willing service for years to a benevolent society, and on its dissolution, when its special work was done, it had presented him with a gold watch and chain. That was his own.

Charles Escombe had given him a diamond ring and diamond pin. These were his own.

He had won at shooting matches on Wimbledon Common a splendid silver-mounted rifle and a revolver. These were his own.

That was his property. He proposed to sell the watch and chain and rifle at once, to keep the diamonds and sell them hereafter if necessary, and to keep the revolver as his travelling companion. It might prove useful, for he proposed to wander to the far, far West—the West of the Western World. His idea was to sail for New York at once, find out old Verpool, and try to obtain a start from him somewhere in the West. He did not stop to think of the particular career he was to have. Once in the West, he thought the rest would follow. He could talk French, Italian, and German; he was a good chemist and generally well up in science; he could write a capital hand; he could hold his own with a rifle at a target or at a deer; he never heeded either heat or cold; he had patience, energy, and capacity. He was a capital amateur actor, and could sing and play on two or three instruments. How could he fail to make a way somehow in a new community where these gifts and acquirements were surely not possessed by every one, common as they might be in London? The idea of failure never occurred to Angelo. He would simply go to the West, conquer a fortune or at least make a career, and then return to New York and claim Isolind. Had she not bade him to seek fortune in America?

He wrote a few lines of warm-hearted, grateful, affectionate farewell to Lady Judith, and then he went quietly down stairs and left the house. He paused a moment and looked back. There was the threshold on which he had crouched, a little miserable outcast, just seventeen years ago. He could remember it perfectly now; could recall all his sensations; could feel the chill, sick shudder of cold and hopeless misery which came over him as he coiled himself up on the doorstep; could feel again the wet of his childish tears as thinking of his poor mother he gradually fell asleep. He recalled with a wonderful distinctness his sensations of bewilderment and alarm, when somebody roughly roused him and his eyes were dazzled by the flash of the carriage lamps; and he was again awed by the stately presence, the clear commanding voice of Lady Judith. His heart softened with gratefulness to her, but he was not sorry to leave her and be free.

Always since his coming near to manhood he had found it hard to repress his longings for freedom. Now, freedom meant Isolind, love, and life. Angelo felt the blood rushing warmly and passionately through his veins. He was almost happy.

He slept at a small hotel that night, or rather he lay in a bed there, for he could hardly be said to sleep. Next morning at nine o'clock—he thought he could not venture to present himself earlier—he hurried to the lodgings of the Athelings. They were not at home! They had left at seven o'clock—gone to the country somewhere, the servants thought. Mr. Atheling was to return some time that day, but not the ladies, she believed. Angelo tried to get some clearer information, and the mistress of the house was summoned; but nothing came of it. She understood that the ladies had gone to the country for a few days; but that Mr. Atheling was to be in town some time to-day, perhaps every day, but not to dine at home.

Angelo went away bewildered and disheartened. That Isolind would send him some message of explanation he did not doubt, but still he felt cruelly anxious and depressed. He wanted to see Isolind once—only once—have one long interchange of sympathies and pledges, and then leave England.

He wandered about the streets for a while thinking. Then he sold his rifle and his watch, and got nearly fifty pounds. Plenty of money, he thought, for the present; quite enough to take him to the New World and start him there.

He returned to Atheling's, but the Judge had not been there. Resolved not to miss seeing him if he should come, he accepted the landlady's invitation to go in and wait. He sat in the drawing-room where he had so often been welcomed by Isolind; he sat in the chair he had often seen her occupy; he touched and opened the books he knew her to have loved. In one book—it was a copy of Lowell's poems—he found a little pencil-case, left there perhaps by accident, perhaps to mark a place. But it was Isolind's, and Angelo began his new career by a theft, for he stole the pencil-case. He put it in his pocket and kept it. Glancing over the pages it had marked, his eye fell on some words in one line which thrilled him like an omen:

All strength shall crumble except love!

"And is it not so, to the letter?" thought Angelo. "Have I not myself even in my own experience seen the strength of human character, human purpose, pride, and principle crumble—all except love?"

A cab drove up, a latch-key was heard in the hall-door, there was a heavy tread on the stairs, and in a moment Judge Atheling entered the room. He came alone. His face looked anxious and distressed. He held out his hand cordially to Angelo, but he kept his eyes uneasily averted.

"I am glad to see you, real glad, Volney, my dear boy," he said. "We have taken flight to the country just for a little, but of course I meant to write to you. I was going to write this very—— day"

"How is Isolind?" Angelo exclaimed.

"Oh, she's very well—that is, she is only pretty well. She has suffered, you know, poor child! You have heard all about it, Volney, have you not? Well, well; girls will feel these things, you know."

The Judge was making tremendous efforts apparently to take the matter coolly, and seemed all the time embarrassed as a man would be who had some unpleasant announcement to make.

"Yes, yes; surely, it is a cruel thing for her. But I want to see her, Mr. Atheling. I want to see her this very day. May I not return with you? You know all about it, Mr. Atheling. You know that I love Isolind with all my soul and that she loves me. Well, then, I want to see her."

"I am afraid you can't see her to-day, my dear boy," the Judge replied sadly.

"Good God! Is she then so ill?"

"Well, she's pretty bad; but no, it's not that. She's not sick, Angelo, in any way to be alarmed about—for her physical health, I mean. But her mind is distressed. Sit down, Angelo, and let us have this thing over. I have a letter for you from Isolind."

A wild thrill of delight passed through Angelo. The horizon of strong emotion is always a narrow boundary. Just now to Angelo a mere letter from his love seemed ultimate bliss, all the joy his heart could hope for or hold. He stretched his hand out eagerly.

Atheling gave him the letter, and muttering something about "a few things to look after, return presently," left the room.

Angelo opened the letter and read:

"MY DEAREST LOVE, ANGELO: I must do a thing which will seem cruel to you, and is utter cruelty to myself; but I must do it none the less. I must leave you, dearest, forever, and I never loved you so devotedly as now. I loved you always, from the very first. The very moment my eyes first rested on you my heart leaped up, and I thought I would give all the world to win *his* love. I think for the moment, too, I half disliked you, for I thought you were a proud, self-conceited English aristocrat, who could never care for me; but if I did for the moment dislike you, it was only because I loved you and was angry with myself for it. Then we came to know each other and our hearts rushed together, and the uttermost dreamings of my girlhood were made real and living in you. Oh, my lost love, let me for this once, this first and last time, be wholly myself to you, and pour out all the passionate emotion that fills me! I will not now starve or stint my language; I will give my whole heart out in expression, if only that, knowing how measureless is to me the agony of the sacrifice, you should know that I must feel it to be inevitable and will pity me, not blame me. You did not know, Angelo, you could not have known, how passionately, how utterly I love you. Every pulse and fibre of my frame seem instinct with this love. Oh, dearest, when we are separated remember this, and pardon and pity me. You will never, never again be loved in life as I love you, as I always shall love you.

"But I cannot marry you, Angelo. The curse which has rested upon my people shall at least sink into the earth with me. I will not bring that heritage of shame and sin to any man's hearth. I *could* not marry you; the deeper my love the more my soul revolts against the thought. Ah, do not think me weak, or too sensitive or sentimental. You, even you, with all your tenderness, cannot understand how a woman feels such a shame as this. No, Angelo, I can never marry. Even were you not Lady Judith Scarlett's adopted son, even if that fearful obstacle did not exist, I could not marry you. I have thought of *this* all the night through. I have thought and prayed, and this is what every principle, every instinct, every prompting of conscience order me to do. Oh, my dearest love, my adored Angelo, this is what I *must* do.

"I have thought that we had better not meet again. It would be only agony in vain, and I shrink with a cowardly fear from the struggle in me between duty and passion, should we meet now. My love, why should you endeavor to prevail on me to do wrong? Spare me, as I would try to spare you, useless suffering or the temptation to forsake a high and sacred principle of duty.

"I will not ask you to forget me. Love like ours is not forgotten. Oh, remember me; remember me always! You will be loved again—though not as you are loved by me; you will love—though not perhaps as you have loved me. But in whatever happiness and sweet fulfilment of wishes, keep a place for me in your memory—a little sacred place.

"I take your hand in mine, I press it to my lips. Farewell!

"ISOLIND."

"Mr. Atheling," Angelo exclaimed—for he heard the tread of the Judge on the stairs—"Mr. Atheling, come here, for God's sake"—and he leaped to his feet. "I must see Isolind! Where is she? I must see her this very day! You shall not take her away—you shall not let her stir—until she has seen me!"

"Sit down, Volney, my dear boy," said the Judge, laying his heavy, kindly hand on the shoulder of the excited young man. "Sit down and let us talk this matter over calmly."

"I can't, sir; I can't talk of it or anything! I must see Isolind! Do you know what she writes to me? Great God, does she think I could give her up? Mr. Atheling, do you know what she asks me to do? I'll never give her up—never, never—and I must see her this very day."

The Judge's eyes were watery. "I feel for you deeply—I feel for you like a father," he said; "but what is to be done? We can't quite understand the nature of such a girl as Issy. Even you can't, though you love her so much. You see we are men after all, and these things don't touch our hearts so. She says her conscience commands her; and I'm afraid it would be hard work to make her go against her conscience; and I don't know that a man ought to try, anyhow."

"I will try!" cried Angelo. "Conscience! madness! She and I love each other. That's conscience; that is above everything else! Nothing shall come between me and her; no, nothing. I will save her from her own scruples and doubts as I would rescue her from a fire! Only let me see her. Where is she, Judge? You would not keep me from her—no, no, you would not!"

"I would not, indeed, boy, if I could—that's so. But what am I to do? I talked to her and mother talked to her, but it didn't amount to anything. She thinks it's her duty, and she does it, though she suffers more than even you, I do believe—ah, more than any man could suffer."

"My God! am I not to save her from that suffering? Why may I not see her—just for once? I am going away—to America. Am I not to see her for once to tell her how I love her and will live only for her? Judge, I *will* see her."

"Well, yes; that's natural enough. But don't you see the poor thing is only a girl—flesh and blood like ourselves—not made of adamant, not even a Joan of Arc, only a warm-hearted girl, wild almost with love of *you*. Can't you see that she's afraid her resolution will fail her if she lets you come and talk to her?"

"Of course, of course," cried Angelo in wild excitement. "She would never be so cruel as to refuse me if once I could see her and speak to her. I know I can prevail upon her. What is this sudden scruple of conscience, this sentiment, that it should be stronger than our love and make our lives wretched? Are the living to be sacrificed to the dead? Judge, where is Isolind?"

The Judge tramped heavily up and down the room, much perplexed and excited. All his instincts and his sympathies pleaded for Angelo's view of the question. The injunctions and entreaties of Isolind lost the day.

"Look here, boy," he said, "I believe you're about right. My feelings go with you, and I'll break my promise for once and help you to see her."

Angelo clasped his hand and pressed it fiercely.

"Gently now, a bit. You haven't much time to lose. We are to leave this country to-morrow. Well, you shall see Issy, and persuade her if you can. I'm with you. I don't see that a dead mother's sin—if it was sin, poor thing—would be made any the better by a living daughter's misery. Now listen. We are staying at Forest Hill—here's the direction." He gave Angelo an address and a description, the young man listening with hungry ears and throbbing pulses. "Go there this evening after I have left town. Don't go knocking at the door and all that, giving people time to think. I dare say you can climb a wall—the house is only the third from the road. Get over the walls and through the gardens as quietly as you can, and come on Isolind unexpectedly. I'll take care that she walks in the garden between eight and nine, alone if I can, but if not it don't matter. Then plead your own cause, and God prosper you! This is your best way, Angelo; if you ask to see her, Heaven knows she may have strength of purpose enough to refuse."

"My dear, dear friend! Oh, you have saved me!"

"Gently again. Now, Volney, listen to what I've got to say before you do anything. God knows if I am doing right in this. My feelings all go with you, but may be I have no right to help you in conquering the conscience of this dear child. Now, then, don't break out; you must hear me. I tell you I have a perfect reverence for the pure soul and the high principle of that girl, and it seems sometimes like a sort of spiritual seduction to lead her away from any resolve. Now, now, don't go on so. I am on your side, but I must have a condition. When I leave you, Angelo Volney, ask your God for advice. I'm no theologian, and I don't care how you address Him or where you find your evidences that He is. But I tell you to ask Him to guide you. He will answer. If He bids you go to Isolind, go in His name. But if when you appeal to Him some doubt of the rightness of conquering her conscience is sent into your heart, then in God's name accept the warning, and be a man and conquer yourself, and leave my little girl to her suffering and her sense of duty. Don't dare to tempt my little girl unless you know from Heaven that you are leading her right."

Mr. Atheling was detained in town rather later than he had anticipated. He met one or two Americans and heard some news which disturbed him a little, and required the writing of a letter or two. Then he hastened to Forest Hill. He reached the house at nine o'clock. He had promised Angelo that Isolind should walk in the garden between eight and nine; the time had hardly lapsed as yet, and lovers are patient. He felt quite sure that Angelo was already in the garden waiting and watching.

Isolind was in her room, trying to read, and trying not to cry. She had not been out. She seemed to dread the very sky. The Judge with kindly pressure forced her into the garden. He was not good at deceit, and he was anxious and much agitated.

Angelo was not there. Atheling kept Isolind out until Mrs. Atheling sreamed that she must not remain longer in the night air. Then Isolind went in; but the Judge paced the garden until eleven o'clock.

Angelo did not come.

The Judge put off their departure from London for two days. Angelo never came or wrote.

"He must have thought better of it," Atheling said to himself. "He must have felt some scruple of conscience, and he has given her up! But I should never have thought it! I wouldn't have done so when I was young; that's so! And he has not even written to her! My poor Isolind!"

No, Angelo had not come and had not written. Isolind made no complaint. She assumed that Angelo had felt compelled to bow to her decree and accept their separation; and, judging of what the struggle would cost him by what it had cost her, she came to the conclusion that he did not yet feel calm enough to trust himself to write to her. Perhaps she was glad to be spared another struggle between love and principle. Perhaps—Heaven knows—she was disappointed. She was utterly unhappy, even although the bitterness of death seemed now to have passed.

But the Judge wondered, and shook his head sadly, and felt almost inclined to grow cynical. The third day after the appointment of the rendezvous which never took place, the Athelings left London for the Continent—and nothing had been seen or heard of Angelo.

CHAPTER XX.

EXPLANATIONS AND FORESHADOWINGS.

THE very evening of the revelation and the scene at Lady Judith's, Atheling hastened to visit Robert May. He was impatient to compare notes with the one friend of Isolind's mother who appeared to be still above the ground, or at least was accessible to ordinary eyes. The place was easily found—although even Judge Atheling, mentally oppressed as he was, could not help wondering at the sudden strange aspect of isolation and solitude which seemed to belong to the quaint old house and garden.

"This is the kind of place," said the Judge to himself with a half-melancholy, half-humorous shake of the head, "where a sad secret seems the right thing to talk about.'

May soon presented himself, still in the old velvet coat, and the Judge was made acquainted with "Tessy," to whom he was very polite in his old-fashioned way, addressing her as "Ma'am."

In a few moments Robert May and Atheling were walking up and down the neat, sad old garden, and had plunged into the subject which brought them together. Atheling walked with his great shoulders stooping, his hands behind his back, his face puckering and working, but no word escaping his lips, while May talked, unless when he felt himself compelled to ask a question in order to keep the track of the story. May told him in rapid words—eloquent by virtue of their clearness, their sincerity, and their emotion—the facts of Agnes Revington's unhappy life. He spoke of her husband, of her life before marriage, of her early love for Charles Scarlett, of Charles Scarlett's father having set himself utterly against the match, and of Agnes herself renouncing it because she feared to bring her lover into a bitter quarrel with the father who adored him. Then he told how Thomas Thynne Dysart became, in his wild, selfish way, a lover of Agnes, and how her father urged the match—being dazzled by Dysart's talents and position—and how all went wrong from that time forth. May assumed that Charles Scarlett, since he could not marry for love, thought he could be contented with marrying for ambition, and so married the beautiful, aristocratic Lady Judith. It was well known that they did not live together on very affectionate terms; but people in Belgravia don't much heed that sort of thing. Dysart began soon to treat his wife ill. Himself the most profligate of men, he was wild with jealousy of her. Undoubtedly he knew of her love for Scarlett before he married her; but after marriage the thought became hateful to him. Shocking stories of his conduct to his wife began to float about the world. At last came the night of scandal. The most rising man in the House of Commons disappeared from the world, "and at the same moment," added May, "the purest woman in England."

"You don't believe the two went together?" Atheling asked.

"I am convinced Agnes Revington never defiled her soul!"

"Evidences look terribly against them both," said the Judge, shaking his head. "And, my good sir, what about Scarlett's own letter—the letter to his wife?"

"Mr. Atheling, suppose anybody came and told you that the girl you brought up as your daughter had committed some crime or some base action? Would it matter to you what evidence he brought? Would you not feel convinced that two words from her lips would clear up the whole thing?"

"Why, certainly—of course I should."

"But why?"

"Why? Because I know her. I know it isn't in her to do anything wrong."

"Just so! Mr. Atheling, I knew Agnes Revington, and I know she couldn't do wrong. Don't let us waste our time on impossible conjectures. Take it from me that Agnes Revington fled not more to save herself from her husband than to save the man she loved from temptation and danger."

"And to save herself perhaps, poor thing," said the Judge in a low tone. "A woman may be the best in the world, Mr. May, and yet know that she isn't made of stone or hammered iron. I begin to go with you. But why would she never have taken any steps to clear the fame and the birth of her baby—her innocent baby?'

"Your tale tells me that, Mr. Atheling. She died on her way to some place of safety. Since I heard you tell your chapter of the history, the whole grows clear as light to me. Now before I give you my conjecture—my conviction rather—tell me again all you know."

Atheling had not much to tell. In the milder opening weeks of the early summer of 1853, his wife and he were making an expedition to the Rocky Mountains. The plains west of the Missouri, or indeed even of the Mississippi, were then a region rarely explored save by the passing of the emigrant trains. At one of the forts and mail stations the Athelings found that a small party which had passed had been compelled to leave behind them a dying woman and a child. The woman, it appeared, had had money enough, and had paid liberally for being allowed to accompany the party and have their protection. She said she was going to seek her brother, who had settled somewhere among the Wahsatch Mountain valleys, far to the west of the Rocky range. But she became weak and sick; she could not go on, and nothing could be done better than to leave her in charge of the wife and daughter of one of the men at the station. Just as the Athelings arrived she died. Their hearts yearned to the child, and they took her and adopted her. They saw the mother buried, and that was all. None knew her name. She had no papers or letters. The Athelings left their name with the people at the station and the fort, where indeed Atheling was already well known. They advertised in New York and Western papers in vain.

No one ever inquired after mother or child. The sage grass of the prairie covered the mother—the child was now Isolind Atheling.

"So it was thus then you died, Agnes?" murmured poor May to himself. "Thus was your grave made—far away from any heart that knew or loved you—in the desert, where now no eye can ever trace out your last resting place! So much beauty, and grace, and goodness, so much love and truth; and this is the end! Mr. Atheling, I don't ask you to excuse my weakness. Sir, that was the only woman I ever loved."

Atheling put his arm round May's shoulders in his ungainly, tender—unspeakably tender—way, and then withdrew it gently, and made no other answer.

"Now, Mr. Atheling," May resumed, apparently gathering strength, "this is the way in which I read this sad story. Agnes Revington once had a brother—her only brother—some years older than herself. He was somewhat eccentric in character, and he had led a wild life in his youth; and he had brought some trouble on his father and misery on at least one other person. This was long before Agnes's marriage. He became suddenly stricken with a deep and stern penitence after he had stood by a certain deathbed—never mind his story—and he left this country to bury himself, as he told his father, in solitude and gloom forever. Advice and appeal were thrown away on him—for good or ill they always were useless with him—and he disappeared. He never wrote to any one but his sister, who dearly loved him and whom he loved, and to her only at the longest intervals. I don't know whether he ever even told her where he had buried himself, but I always heard vague reports that he was living a kind of hermit life far away beyond the borders of civilization in your American desert. For twenty years and more I have never heard even his name mentioned. I was not in the way of meeting poor Agnes much. But I am now as certain as of my own existence that the distracted, despairing woman went out to seek him, to place herself and her child under his protection, and there to vindicate her own character and clear the future of her daughter from stain or cloud. Mr. Atheling, I see it all: Agnes Revington fell dead on the road to her brother's protection!"

"Had she then no friends here?"

"None, sir, except this one" (and May pointed to himself), "whose interference would have been worse than useless, and that one other whom she died to avoid. What friends could she have? Her father died, her mother was long dead, and her scoundrel husband allowed no one to come near her. I dare say she was only too glad to keep back in the darkness. She was too proud to display her sufferings. No, sir, she had no friends. If you knew England better, Mr. Atheling, you would know that one of the privileges of a bad husband is to decree that his wife shall have no friends. In this country, Mr. Atheling, a man's wife is his own; let him treat her as he will, no one shall dare to befriend her."

May was growing wildly excited as he spoke.

"Well, well," said Mr. Atheling, "things are growing better now, I believe, but I dare say they were bad enough at that time. You don't know whether this poor creature had found out where her brother was living?"

"I know nothing about it, but I think it likely enough that even if she did not she would have made a wild plunge in the hope or faith of finding him."

"True enough, true enough; it's just the thing a woman would do. You don't know whether the brother is living yet?"

"As I said, I have not even heard his name breathed for more than twenty years."

"How about Scarlett? Do you suppose that he went to America?"

"Certainly not. *She* must have gone to America knowing that he was not going there. That to me is clear and obvious. She went to America to find her brother and to be lost to Scarlett."

"But Scarlett, certainly believed that she was going with *him?*"

"Perhaps it may be; I can't quite account. Who can tell what Scarlett's letter really said, or how far his wife in her frenzy may have misunderstood it?"

"Frenzy or no frenzy," said the Judge, again shaking his head, "Lady Judith Scarlett seems to me the coolest and most self-contained woman I ever saw; I doubt if she would make a mistake of a comma. But no matter, that's not much to the purpose; and I want not to argue, Mr. May, but to be convinced, if I can."

"Suppose that, seeing no other way of escape—suppose, O God! that she, doubting even her own strength, allowed Scarlett to think that she would yield to his appeal—merely to gain time for escape, and to save herself and him. Is that impossible—is that unlikely?"

"Not impossible, certainly; not even perhaps quite unlikely; but yet——"

"Mr. Atheling, in this case anything is possible, anything is likely, but that Agnes Revington became the mistress of any man. Don't look down on me as a weak old dreamer and romantic fool; but believe me that I know the nature I am talking of, and take that from me as a fact to begin with. Your Isolind is the daughter of a woman as pure as herself."

"Mr. May," said Atheling, suddenly stopping in his walk, and laying one hand on each shoulder of his companion, "when I cease to believe in the possibilities of human nature and of woman's virtue, I shall cease to believe in everything—heaven and God and everything. I am with you in this affair, and I am ready to believe that your theory is the true one and will come to be proved so. But it isn't enough that you and I believe it, Mr. May. That would go for not much with the world; it wouldn't enable my darling Isolind to hold up her head and be no more ashamed. The memory of her mother must be cleared somehow by more distinct proof. There may be one man still living in the world who can do it; and that man is Scarlett."

"And at last," exclaimed May, "I have come on some proof of his existence!"

"You have! Good heavens, can it be? Why, this is the rarest of good fortune!"

"I have! That is why I hastened to-day to see Lady Judith Scarlett; I thought she ought to know, if she had not heard already. Look here, look here!"

With trembling hands May pulled from his pocket the "Times" newspaper, a copy several weeks old.

"Look at *that*," May exclaimed, folding the paper so that a certain marked advertisement came under Atheling's eye. "Read *that!* If I had only seen it before! But I hardly ever read the papers; I shouldn't have seen that but that I promised to draw up an advertisement for tuition for a poor girl, and I looked in the 'Times' to see how such things were done; and think how I started when I saw *that*."

This was what Atheling read:

"To My Daughter, A. S.: Fear not; I live and will appear at the fitting time. Trust meanwhile to the one devoted friend you have found. Through him we shall meet. C. G. S."

Atheling studied this mystic scrap over and over again, with anything but an appearance of satisfaction. Then he looked at May, who was gazing upwards with brightening eyes.

"That don't amount to much, Mr. May," said the old lawyer, sadly.

"Good heavens, Mr. Atheling! Is it not as clear as light? Are not those Charles Scarlett's initials—are not those his daughter's initials? Is it not plainly a message from him to her?"

Atheling read the lines again. "Did your friend," he asked quietly, "your friend Mr. Scarlett ever write for the New York 'Ledger'?"

"How, sir?—I don't understand——"

"Well, what's your great penny romancist here? The London 'Journal' or the 'Family Herald'? Was Mr. Scarlett in the habit of contributing much to either of these periodicals?"

"Mr. Atheling, I don't understand you—I don't like levity. It—it surprises me at such a time and on such a subject!"

"Forgive me, Mr. May. I am as much in earnest about all this as you can be. But, my dear sir, I don't know much about the ways of your English aristocracy, it is true; but I saw Mr. Scarlett and heard him speak, and I am an old lawyer, and it surprises *me* that you can think a man like Scarlett ever penned that advertisement!"

"Why not?"

"Why not? Don't you see it's all in the regular dime-romance—I mean penny-romance—sort of style? Take my word for it, Mr. May, Scarlett never wrote a word of *that*."

May looked quite dashed and disconcerted.

"Then, Mr. Atheling, in Heaven's name, who did write it?"

"Ay, just so. That becomes a very important question. Somebody is in the game evidently—somebody is looking over the cards—that you and I don't know of."

"Somebody directed by Scarlett?"

"Oh no, I think not. Why should he act in that roundabout sort of way? Why shouldn't he write to his daughter right away—or to you, his old friend—or to his lawyers?"

"True, true; I never thought of all that. I am a muddle-headed old fool sometimes, Mr. Atheling. Nothing could be less like Scarlett than such a way of notifying his existence. But yet there is the advertisement; it must have been put in the paper by somebody who knows all about Scarlett?"

"Why, no, Mr. May. I don't read it so, at all."

"You don't read it—how?"

"I take it that whatever the thing means, and if it isn't merely a chance coincidence of initials, it was put there by somebody who knows nothing about Scarlett. I think what strikes me as an unlikely thing for Scarlett to do, me who only saw him once, would never be done by anybody who knew him. If we were betting men, Mr. May, I would even bet you a trifle the person who wrote that thing believes Scarlett to be dead, or at least out of any possible chance of ever hearing anything about this advertisement. It is worth looking into, and I'll try to hunt it up. Do you know, I think the point of the thing is all in that clause about trusting to the devoted friend, and so on. Don't you see, Codlin's the friend, and not Short? Take my word for it, it was Codlin who wrote that!"

"Codlin? I don't follow you, Mr. Atheling. Who is Codlin?"

Robert May never read modern novels, and knew no more about little Nell and Short and Codlin, than Goethe's Hermann did about Pamina and Tamino. Moreover, the Judge's ways puzzled him; the tone of humorous levity jarred on his nerves. On the other hand, Atheling was now somewhat disposed to undervalue May's judgment, and to attach little importance to his convictions of Agnes Dysart's innocence. The advertisement in the "Times" was, to Atheling, so obviously either a reference to some quite different business and people or a trick of some kind, that he could not believe the man whom it deceived could have much insight into any character. Therein, however, he was wrong. May was peculiarly qualified by nature to understand to the depths a soul like that of Agnes Dysart; but the least little morsel of deceit or concealment was too much for him. Even the simple humor of Atheling left him behind. He failed to see that Atheling was as profoundly in earnest as himself, because Atheling now and then put things in an odd sort of phraseology which savored of levity.

Atheling did not wait to explain who was Codlin and who was Short, and how they came to be mixed up in Scarlett's affairs. He took a note of the advertisement and its date; he left with May the address which would find him on the Continent, and they parted with mutual promises to write in case of anything coming to the knowledge of either which seemed worth communicating. Next day, when Atheling had bestowed his family at Forest Hill, he went to a London lawyer whom he knew, and instructed him to endeavor to find out the author of the advertisement. It might, of course, have no relation whatever to Mr. Scarlett and his daughter. Still, Atheling thought it had; and he had even formed in his own mind a shrewd suspicion as to the identity of the Codlin, not Short, who was to be trusted as the devoted friend of poor Alexia.

When Atheling saw Angelo that evening other thoughts occupied him, and, carried away by Angelo's passionate entreaties and his own sympathies, he forgot to say anything about the advertisement, although he had fully intended to call the young man's attention to it, and take his opinion.

"I will speak to him to-night about it," said Atheling to himself, "when he comes."

But, as we know, Angelo did not come, and the Athelings left England and heard nothing of him.

The whole course of this story would have been changed if Angelo had seen Isolind that night. Not a single being, perhaps, now holding a prominent place in these pages, whose destiny will not prove to have been profoundly affected by the chance or ill-hap which prevented Angelo from entering the garden where the woman he loved was to be found.

Angelo was early at the rendezvous. The garden belonging to the house where the Athelings lodged was the third inward from a little road or lane that ran off the highway. The wall of the outer garden was not very high, and Angelo saw little difficulty in quietly climbing over it and getting through the gardens intervening between him and Isolind. There was only a faint young moon, he heard no voices in any of the gardens, and he hoped to make his transit unobserved.

But he did not know that the outer garden belonged to a furious naturalist, who cultivated ferns, and dahlias, and tulips with all the passionate devotion of idleness. He did not know that this naturalist had lately had some of his choicest roots and flowers stolen, and had vainly applied to the police (on principle without giving them any stimulating half crown), and had therefore resolved at last to mount guard himself over his property, armed with an air-gun of his own improved construction. Our sage had watched some nights in vain; but this unhappy night he had only mounted his place of observation when he saw in the dim light the head and shoulders of a man rising over his wall. Another moment, and the figure was seated on the wall; another, and it would have dropped into the garden, but the naturalist took aim and fired, and Angelo Volney uttered a short, sharp groan, and swayed for an instant on the wall, tried to keep his place and look round for his assailant, and then fell heavily back into the lane, with two swan-shot in his shoulder.

In a moment Angelo scrambled to his feet and found that his head seemed spinning round, and that his shoulder, at first benumbed, was now in an agony of pain. The whole meaning of the situation flashed upon him at once; he knew he had been taken for a robber and fired upon accordingly; he thought the hurt was not very grave, and his one uppermost desire was to get away, so that Isolind might know nothing of the unhappy accident and might be spared all alarm. He had, for the time, no thought but this—to get away—that she might not know, that she might not have added to her other troubles some fear and grief for him. Therefore he rose to his feet and staggered and ran like a wounded felon who strives to drag his life away at any pain from the pursuit of avenging justice.

He dragged himself along through several suburban streets, not knowing or heeding whither he went, and feeling his strength give way more and more every moment. At last a sickening sensation came over him, his forehead and brow were wet with a cold perspiration, strange sounds rang in his ears, the stars seemed reeling in the sky, and he fell senseless.

Meanwhile the naturalist had rushed out to capture, not the robber, but the local policeman on duty, to drag him to the spot, and convince him by the sight of the plunderer's fallen body that the complaints about the stolen roots were not unfounded. But when the officer of justice was captured the robber had escaped, and thus only renewed and strengthened official skepticism rewarded the naturalist for his heroic pains.

Another policeman, however, found poor Angelo lying, and at first assumed that he was drunk—the London policeman's natural explanation of everything. Then observing that, drunk or sober, the prostrate man was certainly wounded, he had him conveyed to the nearest hospital, and there poor Angelo lay for several days, and would not tell his name lest the story should reach the ears of the Athelings or of Lady Judith. The wound he had received did not, however, amount to anything serious. While he lay still almost insensible the naturalist came to see him, brought by the captured policeman, the one who had not found Angelo. The naturalist, of course, could not pretend to identify the alleged robber, whom he had only seen as a dark form against the faint moonlight; but the policeman, who sometimes did duty at the Crystal Palace, at once recognized Angelo from having seen him frequently there with Lady Judith and Alexia.

"I say," he whispered to the philosopher, "are you sure that's the man you hit?"

"To the best of my belief."

"Never mind your belief, sir," said the stern policeman, imitating the style of a criminal lawyer whom he much admired. "Is that the man, yes or no?"

"Well, I only saw him in the dark, and I couldn't undertake to swear; but it must be he; it can't be anybody else."

"Can't it? Very good! Wait till he comes to hisself and won't there be a row in the building! I say, my man, you've been and done it this time. Do you know who you've been a-shooting of?"

"I've been defending my property against a robber."

"No you haven't. This here gentleman ain't no robber. It is Lady Judith Scarlett's stepson. I know him as well as I know my own inspector, and she's daughter of the Earl of Coryden, and they're among the proudest lot in all London. She's a bitter pill, I fancy; and if they don't make you jump about, call me a Dutchman. I wouldn't be in your shoes for a trifle."

"But what the devil then brought him over my wall?"

"Don't know, I'm sure; but it wasn't to steal cabbages and dandelions, you may take your affidavit. Perhaps there was some pretty girl in one of the gardens—these young swells are always after something in that line. Anyhow, I think if I was you I'd say nothing about the business. You'll be only too lucky if you get off scot-free."

The poor naturalist took the semi-official advice and held his tongue. He began to think the policeman's conjecture as to the motive of the visit paid by "Lady Judith Scarlett's stepson" must be correct; and as he had himself no wife or daughter, or even pretty housemaid, to attract daring gallants, he owed the intruder no ill-will, and was only too happy to be out of the whole affair.

The policeman was for some time in doubt whether it would be more profitable to him to go at once and tell the great Belgravian lady of her "stepson's" mishap, or to keep the matter secret and go for a bribe for his discretion from the young man. Finally he decided on the latter course; to go to Lady Judith with an unpleasant story might beget ill-will, not reward. So when Angelo was recovering, the policeman told him how he had made the discovery and kept it secret, and Angelo was glad to pay him a reward out of his small stock of sovereigns.

Angelo explained his wound as accidental—which in one sense it was—and the medical officers of the hospital pressed no inquiries. In a very few days he was well and free; but Isolind and the Athelings were gone.

He wrote a letter to Atheling explaining all, and enclosed one for Isolind, in which he utterly and passionately refused to accept her farewell; declared that he would never give her up in life or in death; and announced that he was going at once to the United States to make a free career for himself, as she first advised him to do, in order that he might be able honestly to claim her. He wrote full of love and passion, and pathos and hope. The letters he addressed to the care of Bowles Brothers of Paris, the famous bankers and agents who keep the gates of the paradise for good Americans. In their recording leaves he assumed the name of Atheling would be some time found.

Also he wrote a letter of loving and brotherly farewell to Alexia and a few lines of grateful devotion and good-by to Lady Judith, and then he seemed to have closed that volume of his life forever. Quietly and unnoticed he left London. He had never had many friends, and those whom he knew he now carefully avoided. As he got into a third-class carriage at Euston Square to reach Liverpool, whence he was to sail, it seemed to him as if an earthquake had swallowed up all his old life and the people whom it enclosed, and that he was alone in the world. He could hardly have started to seek his fortune more slenderly provided and in more humble case even if Lady Judith's door had never opened to him that night when he crouched upon its threshold.

"Oh, Eric, my love," exclaimed Alexia Walraven that same evening when the poet's curls and graceful form returned to her little drawing-room at Richmond,

"I have such shocking news! Mamma and Angelo have quarrelled, and he has left her, and now he's gone to America to seek his fortune!"

"Glad of it, I am sure," was the poet's sympathetic answer.

"Glad of it—oh my Eric! Why glad that poor Angelo should be driven out into the world? And now I suppose that American girl will never marry him.'

"If he is gone, all the better for us, dear. Besides, *I* never liked him. I think he was a presuming cad. Why should he think of that splendid American girı? Wasn't he a beggar-boy or something of the kind?"

Alexia looked curiously and wonderingly at her husband. Was it really he who talked in this kind of way, and talked of Angelo, who was so dear to her? She felt a chill steal over her, and involuntarily she crept up to the poet and put her arm round his neck to satisfy herself that she still had her own Eric. Her arm, however, disarranged the locks of her own Eric, and the poet therefore quickly set free his neck and his curls from the soft seizure which he had not solicited.

"Yes," he went on, "I call it quite a good thing for us that the fellow is gone. I say, Alexia, is there any chance of Lady Judith becoming reconciled to him again?"

Alexia shook her head.

"Not unless he made some fearful submission, which he will never do, for he is sure to be in the right and mamma altogether in the wrong. I knew it would come to this—I told Angelo so long ago—and I used to say I would laugh and be glad when it came; but now I don't feel at all inclined to laugh, and I am very sorry for Angelo. I must have been a very dreadful creature in those days, Eric! Because I was unhappy, and no one loved me. Now I am better, because you love me, Eric."

"Then she won't take this fellow back?"

"Angelo?" in a tone of remonstrance.

"Yes; she won't open her arms, and that sort of thing?"

"Dear Eric, you don't yet know mamma. She never forgives!"

Eric got up and moved uneasily about the room.

"Good God, Alexia," he said fretfully at last, "you don't really mean that you think your mother will not be reconciled with *us?*"

"Indeed I do. She never will; never, though our summers to such length of years should come as the many-wintered crow, and so on: don't you remember Tennyson?"

"Talk sense, please, Alexia."

"If I can, love. She never will, then, unless we go on our bended knees and humble ourselves, and perhaps not even then."

"Hadn't we better do it?"

"Do what, my Eric?"

"Humble ourselves, as you like to call it. We had better humor her, Alexia."

"Not I, dear. I'd rather starve. I have done nothing to be ashamed of. Why should I humble myself? I am very proud and happy. We can live without our gracious mother's pardon. I don't believe in parental blessings."

"I wish to Heaven, Alexia, you would talk sense. How do you propose that we shall live?"

"Is Providence, then, so very busy feeding the young ravens that no time can be spared for our young ravening appetites?"

"I have some work to do, Alexia, and I expect one or two fellows out here to-night. I had better go and write. I should have liked to talk with you a little first, but you are in no mood for reasonable conversation, and I am in no mood for nonsense."

Alexia looked up quite bewildered and alarmed.

"My darling Eric, don't go away and leave me alone—I have been alone all day; or let me go with you into your study, and I will promise not to disturb you, or even to ask you a question. Stay with me and I'll talk sensibly—I will indeed. I can—I know I can; it was only the excitement of your coming home which made me go on in such a way."

She clung fondly to the poet's arm. She was torn by a quite new sensation of positive terror, the dread of Eric's being angry and punishing her by leaving her without his companionship. The idea of Eric's being tired of her had not yet arisen ever so dimly in her agitated mind.

But Eric was vexed and out of humor, and weary of her ways, and terribly afraid that he had made a complete mistake; and it relieved him to punish her and make her unhappy. He coldly put her away, and when the poor child began to cry he was greatly gratified. It gave him much pleasure to see her cry and to note how genuine were the tears. Walraven always liked to see women weeping on his account, it was so gratifying a tribute to his power. But in this case it was specially soothing and flattering. Here was the granddaughter of an Earl, the girl whom her mother had found utterly unmanageable, now humbled to the dust and dissolved in tears because he was angry with her. And he *was* angry with her, and she *ought* to be punished. So he let the little thing cry her fill, and he looked on and enjoyed the sight until he thought it was time to show his power and supremacy in another way, by pardoning and restoring her. Then he was kind to her, and took her in his arms and dried her tears. But it was long before Alexia's convulsive and choking sobs were wholly stifled, and at the end she bore his pardon and his petting, rather than snatched at it or was gladdened by it. In fact, Alexia had had quite a new sensation and could not yet wholly understand it; could by no means guess whither it might be tending with her.

All that night the girl had her sleep haunted and made hideous by wild, frightful dreams—the kind of dreams that used to visit her pillow when she slept alone, but which had vanished in her early weeks of marriage and of happiness. She dreamed of ghosts and dead bodies and frightful fiends; of demons that urged on people to do murder. She dreamed that she was clinging with her hands to the edge of an awful precipice, and that she cried to Eric for help, and that he came and busied himself in smilingly endeavoring to unloose the clutch of her fingers, that she might fall and be crushed. She dreamed that Eric was trying to kill her with her own dagger; and that her mother looked on and smiled a cold contemptuous smile. She dreamed at last, that Eric himself lay bleeding and dead at her feet, and then she gave a wild scream and awoke. She was alone; Eric had not yet come to bed. He loved to sit up late and read. He was an independent creature in all his movements, and hated to be constrained by regular hours and habits; and Alexia commonly now passed half the night alone.

CHAPTER XXI.

CERTAIN PEOPLE FALL OUT.

TREMENDOUS excitement in Wall street, New York. Excitement too, hardly less great, in Chestnut street, Philadelphia, and in Montgomery street, San Francisco. An audacious speculation, nay, rather an outrageous gambling-plot, having its focus of conspiracy at New York, had suddenly burst into shivers, carrying unheard-of commercial and financial destruction along with it. The plot had been of the boldest and subtlest nature. It had worn on the face of it an astonishingly deceptive appearance of innocence, and of legitimate operation; and men had been drawn into it who beyond all doubt had never comprehended its full scope. Had the plot succeeded, it would have placed at one *coup* the whole of the railway share market and the whole of the gold market literally in the hands and the power of a small cabal and clique of utterly unprincipled and reckless operators, who might then have enriched themselves simply as they pleased and beggared whom they would. New York is not easily shocked or alarmed in the matter of financial speculations; but it did almost literally and universally shudder over the discovery of this. It was so audacious, so tremendous, so incredible, so impossible; and yet it went so very near to success! Discovered and frustrated as it was, the very frustration yet involved wide and ghastly ruin; and even those who were not ruined trembled and groaned over the dangers they had passed, and the fearful approach to success which the scheme had made. Why, people declared to each other in wonder and affright, if the thing had had only half an hour, just half an hour more of secrecy, it must have succeeded! Wall street simmered, fumed, foamed, roared, and swore for six-and-thirty tumultuous hours. There was more banging of doors, crashing of glass, flinging down of hats, and tearing open of neck-cloths, than ever had been known before in the neighborhood of Trinity Church, Broadway. The newspapers brought out fresh editions and fuller particulars every ten minutes. The little riotous imps of journalism, the stormy petrels of civil and political commotion and disaster, the New York newsboys (the New York newsboy is a good deal more amusing, original, and grotesque than the Paris *gamin*), were never done yelling, "Here's yer extra edition, more news from Wall street!" The excitement in the city of London on the famous Black Friday some four or five years ago was not nearly so stormy or so eccentric in its turbulence as that which raged and raved along and around Wall street. The sweltering policemen made no effort to check the boisterous overflow of the commotion, but resigned the corners and sidewalks of Wall street completely into the occupancy of the shouting crowd. Excited groups ran from office to office, from door to door, up steps and down steps, almost every one open-throated and perspiring, and everybody talking wildly to everybody he met. The drivers of the Broadway "stages" or omnibuses, rumbling from far "up town" to the Battery, as they sheltered themselves from the glaring sunlight under gigantic yellow umbrellas fixed upright in their box-seats, craned their necks while they jolted past Wall street in the hope of catching some sort of knowledge of how things were going. Dainty little ladies, as, shimmering in all colors, they danced in and out of the stages in their high-heeled boots and with bundles of silk trussed up on their backs, or rather on the dorsal region below their waists, to facilitate the requisite "Grecian bend"—even they had eyes and ears for what was going on, and caught the wonder, alarm, and excitement of the hour. The stranger from England, who, ignorant of the state of affairs, happened as he descended the lower part of Broadway to glance into Wall street, would probably have conjectured at first that an extemporaneous prize-fight was delighting the population of that quarter, and that the police of course were conveniently out of the way.

Wall street is as to its functions the Lombard street or Threadneedle street of New York. In appearance it looks like Old Broad street, with a dash of Grace Church street and a distant suggestion of the region of Wapping Old Stairs. There is a sort of turbulent and boisterous horse-play about its gravest and most practical operations which distinguishes it cheerfully from Lombard street or the Place de la Bourse. The younger financiers in especial are apt to blend with the spirit of business an occasional gleam of a frolicsome temperament, like that which among the old lawyers of Edinburgh used to find its relief in the pastime of High Jinks. Therefore, when Wall street writhed with passion or contorted itself in despair, there was a certain element of the grotesque and even of the comic made manifest in the passion or the despair, which did not relieve the monotony of emotional vehemence in the neighborhood of Lombard street, London, on the famous Black Friday already mentioned. Likewise, there was some personal and dangerous ferocity now and then apparent in Wall street, which found no vent in its London compeer; and at one period of the crisis there was ominous talk, not to be despised as mere empty threats, of executing summary justice on the principal ringleaders of the plot which had so nearly succeeded, and which even in its failure had brought down so widespread a ruin.

But who were the ringleaders? Foremost and most ostentatious was, or rather had been, Mr. Chesterfield Jocelyn. In all the early stages of the work Jocelyn had made himself so very conspicuous as the prime mover, that people began to doubt the reality of the position he so boldly assumed, and to suspect that there must be yet more powerful movers in the background who did not choose to be publicly known. Jocelyn's grandeur and ostentation were as tremendous as his cool composure or his magnificent get-up. His shirt front, his diamond studs, his white waistcoat, his gossamer summer clothes were perfection. He smoked unnumbered cigars; he made no end of jokes. For a long time the real drift of the financial game was not fully apparent. Wall street thought it a bold piece of adventure, and wondered who were really in with Jocelyn, but was not aghast. At last, however, the reality of the enterprise became apparent; and horrified Wall street was not able then and there to grapple with the difficulty. When this point became reached, the complete success of the conspiracy would depend only on two things: the timely bringing up to Jocelyn's aid of certain financial reserves on which he counted for a final grand charge along the whole line; and the inactivity of the Government. The latter power, if made acquainted prematurely with the real drift of the scheme, might interfere by throwing its financial resources and potentialities into the scale on behalf of distracted Wall street. But Jocelyn believed care had been amply taken on his side in both matters; and he awaited the crisis with composure and confidence. "Half an hour more," he thought, "and I am a millionaire, and I will go to live in Paris!"

But soon he began to grow anxious; his lips were compressed; his eye wandered. He kept up his jaunty, defiant, *insouciant* manner well enough; but his mind was misgiving him. The financial reserves were not coming up, and the crisis was awful. Where, where were old Blücher-Verpool and his Prussians? Worse than that, ominous rumors began to float about that the Government at Washington had had its eyes suddenly opened, and had telegraphed to its agents in New York to intervene. Big drops of perspiration stood on, Jocelyn's forehead; he clenched his cigar fiercely between his teeth, and thrust his hands into his pockets that the quivering of the fat, ring-laden fingers might not be seen.

Yet a little, and it became evident to every one that the Government had taken the field; while to Jocelyn, who kept close account of time and chances, it was equally clear that the scheme must have been prematurely disclosed to the Government by one of the parties to the enterprise. And Verpool's reserves did not come up.

None knew so well as Jocelyn did that the crisis was now over, and the whole plot a failure. Wall street was still in feverish and frantic excitement and alarm, when Jocelyn knew to a dead certainty that the last of his hopes was gone; that his enterprise, so long in preparation, so daringly projected, so skilfully planned, was a mere heap of ruins. The one contingency on which alone he had never counted, came to pass; the scheme had evidently been abandoned, betrayed, denounced to the Government by one of its leading promoters. Jocelyn well appreciated the difference between success and failure in the financial operations of Wall street. He knew that he had by no means taken much trouble to steer clear of the criminal law; for he had counted on success, and he knew well that were he only successful the very men whom he had ruined would have a kind of admiration for him, and that no legal machinery would prevail, or even try to prevail against him. But if he should fail, and bring ruin, as he must do, to so many in his failure, then indeed he would be a mark for every hand, and public opinion, in Wall street at least, would equally applaud the judge who sentenced him to a dozen years of imprisonment, or the angry enemy who blew his brains out, or the mob who lynched him at the nearest lamp-post. An Ottoman pasha sent to lead the imperial forces against an enemy has hardly so much personal stake in the issue of success or failure as a daring gambler in the financial market of New York.

Jocelyn drank iced draughts and smoked cigars in vain. He could not keep his composure. His lips were dry, and he was constantly striving to moisten them with a tongue hardly less parched. The game was over. Hundreds of men were ruined by him, and he, too, was ruined. Eyes began to look desperately at him; fierce tongues swore at him. The crowd and the confusion were yet so great that he, the leader of the mischief, was hardly isolated enough to be in much apparent danger. What he feared was that when the mere excitement of the battle was over passion and despair would have time to turn on him. As he endeavored to make his way out of the press he jostled against a man whom he had deceived and beguiled into the enterprise and ruined, and this man, recognizing him with a yell and an oath, seized Jocelyn by the throat, tearing off his gorgeous cravat and sending his diamond pin glittering and clinking under the heels of the crowd. The man seemed endeavoring to strangle Jocelyn, who struggled and gasped; and the impulse once given to violence seemed likely to have terrible results, for several other men clung round Jocelyn and dragged him hither and thither, and cursed him and struck at him, and raised wild cries of lynching him then and there. But some of the police charged manfully and dragged him out; and indeed the density of the crowd and the still unrelaxed tension of the crisis were in his favor, and he was carried away with purple, bruised face and torn clothes, out of the tumult, and put into a carriage and driven up town. By the time he had reached the Fifth Avenue Hotel he was as safe from turbulence and in as serene an atmosphere as though he were pacing the cloisters of a sanctuary.

The Fifth Avenue Hotel happened just then to be his temporary home, and he hastened to his bedroom, and as quickly as he could removed or concealed the evidences of the late struggle. Then he rang the bell and ordered up some champagne and ice and sat down to think things over.

He was ruined, to begin with. He had many times undergone something like ruin before, but never aught so comprehensive and complete as this. Atheling's money, Mrs. Braxton's money, every dollar the poor *protégée* of John Bunyan could lay her fat hands upon, the money of scores of other persons less innocent, had gone in the general crash. Everywhere around him now he must look to find unrelenting enemies. Things did not show half so dark and dangerous when first he came a fugitive to the United States, and then the new career was all before him, and he was fifteen years younger than now. Ruin, utter ruin, was now his doom.

Yet it was not this which was uppermost in his thoughts. His whole mind and soul were filled with fury by the conviction that he had been juggled with, thrown over, betrayed. Only Verpool could have done the trick. Verpool had seen the way to a more safe and profitable stroke by throwing up the game and betraying his partner, and Verpool had sold him accordingly.

Evening came on, and Jocelyn left the hotel. In New York, and in one or two other cities where he had many occupations and acquaintances, Jocelyn kept a quiet little room or two in some house in a leading street, where he could at once work, and think, and observe undisturbed. Such a little retreat he had in Broadway—two small rooms in a huge house, which was on the ground floor a furrier's store, and which had bonnet-sellers, linen-collar-sellers, medical practitioners of dubious character, and various other inmates located through the upper ranges of chambers. Jocelyn's rooms were not occupied in his own name, but in that of a clerk who hardly ever went there unless when he was bidden expressly to do so. Jocelyn always had a key and went there and let himself in when he so pleased. He made appointments and received visitors there whom it would not always be convenient to receive at one of the hotels. Like a man who knew what he was about, he had established this retreat in the most crowded part of Broadway. Nobody's attention would be much aroused by the sight of Chesterfield Jocelyn entering or issuing from a door in Broadway a dozen times a day, if such a thing were to occur; but his appearance even once in some particularly secluded place would be almost sure to set somebody's suspicion or curiosity on the watch. Of course many of Jocelyn's personal acquaintances were in the secret of the little rooms. The acquaintances who visited him there were generally well dressed, but even of the very best dressed among them it would have been safe to say without fear of offence that they were "no gentlemen." They did not pretend to be. They professed to be ladies, but in their pleasant, confidential hours with their friends, they laid aside even that profession as wearisome and superfluous to sustain.

To this retreat, then, went Chesterfield Jocelyn on the evening of his defeat. It was a beautiful evening of early summer, and the spring had been somewhat late, and people had hardly yet begun to think of fleeing from New York, and so Broadway was still crowded with mere promenaders. In the bright, pure light it looked quite a picturesque street, and Jocelyn could see from the door of the house he was now entering clear up to Grace Church at the one end, or down to Trinity Church, close by the scene of his defeat, at the other. Jocelyn had had to make his way through a dense double stream of promenaders—ladies for the most part, dressed in radiant silks and tissues, such as in sobeıer Europe no woman ever exhibits except in a drawing-room or a ball-room. He had chosen to walk in the hope that the walk might compose him, but he only found his heat of fierce passion inflamed and aggravated anew by every group of pretty, daintv obstacles which barred his progress.

But he reached his den at last, and opened the window and sat there and smoked. He allowed as little of his face and form to appear as well might be; but he kept a keen eye to the pavement in front of the entrance of a great hotel just underneath. For this was the hotel which Verpool frequented when in town; and Jocelyn had ascertained that Verpool was expected there that evening. Assuming the treason of his accomplice, it looked a likely part of Verpool's plan—the very thing indeed he would probably do—to select that very day for quietly travelling to New York in order that the world might see his ignorance of or his indifference to the whole affair. A conspirator would surely take care to arrive in time to help or watch the plot; or else he would keep away altogether. Jocelyn was convinced that Verpool's quietly arriving on the evening of the fatal day was only another evidence of the sinister and deliberate purpose which had prevented him from arriving on the morning of that day or of the day before.

He had not very long to wait in expectation. Presently a "stage" or omnibus came slowly jolting and staggering up Broadway; a New York stage always staggers as if it were toiling through a freshly-ploughed field; it halted before the door of the hotel, and Mr. Verpool came out of it. Mr. Verpool had never in his life taken a carriage where a stage or street-car would enable him to perform the journey. He descended from the stage holding a shabby old carpet-bag in one hand, and he shambled into the hotel.

Jocelyn gave a snarl of ferocious anger and exultation, and descended into the street.

He sauntered with as much appearance of jaunty ease as he could assume into the office of the hotel, where his presence created just then a little sensation among the resplendent clerks who had evening editions of the papers in their hands, and he ascertained the number of Verpool's room, declining to give any one the trouble of showing it to him.

Verpool had hardly had time to settle himself in his room. He had just opened his carpet-bag, which contained a greater quantity of papers and documents than of wearing apparel. He was busily sorting the papers when Jocelyn entered without knocking. Verpool started, very slightly but yet perceptibly.

"How d'ye do, Jocelyn; how's your health, sir?" was his greeting, and he held out slowly and dubiously one skinny claw.

Jocelyn swaggered towards him with fierce and frowning eyebrows. On entering the room Jocelyn had glanced eagerly at the lock of the door, but the key was not in it, and the door had no bolt.

Verpool saw the movement, partly understood it, and chuckled to himself.

"Who betrayed us?" exclaimed Jocelyn; "was it *you?*"

"What d'ye mean, Jocelyn? Is it true that the thing's busted? I heard something of it now in the stage. Have you got any of the evening papers?"

"Dry up with all that damned nonsense. Don't think you are dealing with a fool——"

"Wall, you don't seem to have been extry smart in fixing this business, Jocelyn. That I will say."

"You old swindler, you have sold me and the whole thing at Washington. Don't attempt to deny it; I see it now in your very eyes! Fool and ass that I was to trust to a scoundrel like you!"

"Wall, I don't know about all that. You see, Jocelyn, you should have trusted out and out or not at all. Half measure don't run no chance with me. You are just too smart by half, Jocelyn, and I saw right through you, that's all. I had my suspicions roused, you see, and then I found out quick as a flash that you were trying to grind your own axe and going back on me; and then I thought it was every one for himself, you know. Hope you haven't lost much anyhow."

"Lost? Damn you—lost? Everything! I'm ruined; and you—I swear you are well rewarded for your treachery."

"Rewarded? Oh, nary red cent; but I guess I've saved myself, that's about it. But I say, Jocelyn," and Verpool looked at his accomplice with an expression of genuine curiosity, "you don't really mean to say you have lost everything? Why, how cussed badly you must have managed!"

"So badly, Verpool, that I don't much care how things go for the rest of my time, and that I will have one scrap of revenge at least, whatever comes next."

"What d'ye mean—what—d'ye mean? Keep off, keep off, or I'll call for help! You wouldn't murder an old man! Oh, oh!"

A choking, gurgling sound only was heard as his further utterance of complaint, for Jocelyn had flung himself with all his weight on Verpool, forced him to the ground, and griping his throat with one hand struck him savagely about the head with the other. With a cunning which all his ferocity and passion did not banish, Jocelyn had refrained from flinging his victim roughly to the ground so as to make a noise. He rather laid than flung him down, keeping from the first a tight hold upon his throat so that the unfortunate captive could not scream. A savage light flamed in Jocelyn's eyes, and all the ferocious, wolf-like passion of the man's nature—the furious passion which had throughout his life been his conquering foe, triumphing at last over every resolve and plan formed by craft and selfishness—seemed to find delight in the work which engaged him. That work appeared as if deliberately intended to be nothing short of the murder of Verpool. Jocelyn, while he struck him again and again with remorseless force on the head and face, still kept tight hold of his throat and shook his victim to and fro as a wolf worries his prey.

In the fierce joy of his revenge he did not hear a light tap at the door. Then the door was suddenly opened and a man looked in—rushed in—and flung himself on Jocelyn.

The new-comer was young and strong, and Jocelyn was fat, scant of breath, and pretty nearly spent by his unwonted exercise. The intruder dragged Jocelyn from his prey, and forced him to the other end of the room; then he lifted poor old Verpool on to the bed, opened his necktie, and dashed water in his face. All this time not a word was spoken.

Then the young man said in a low tone: "For shame, to attack one so old as he is! Would you murder the poor old man?"

And he moved toward the bell-handle as if to summon help.

Jocelyn interposed. He now perfectly recognized the intruder (who in his surprise and in the growing dusk had not recognized him), and he at once assumed his customary manner of florid assurance.

"Don't trouble yourself to ring the bell, Mr. Volney! You'll find that our venerable friend Verpool would prefer for himself that our little dispute should not be made public. He is not destined to go to the devil this time; tell him with my compliments that he owes his wretched and detestable existence to you, for I should most certainly have consecrated him to the infernal gods. He is not so old as you think, my dear Volney—he is very little older than I am—and I was merely inflicting the punishment he well deserves. It is a principle of law, you know, that malice supplies age in the case of the young—supplies youth's deficiency in responsibility. I think it should also be held to perform the corresponding service for age. No, don't trouble yourself to ring the bell! If your friend Verpool desires to prosecute me at law, he can do so, but he won't. He'll think himself well off as it is."

Volney, uncertain how to act, still kept near the bell-handle, and between Jocelyn and the door, when Verpool himself slowly opened his eyes, groaned, shuddered, and said in a low, half-choking tone:

"Let him go, let him go! As Dannel Webster said, I still live—and I don't want this here thing talked about anyhow—and let him go!"

"You hear, my dear Volney? The wisdom of age, you observe, even in its somewhat confused moments, rebukes the precipitateness of youth. Verpool, you owe your life to this young fellow, and perhaps on the whole I am not sorry that he came in time. A pitiful wretch like you is not worth a gentleman's risking his neck for. Good evening, Mr. Volney. You have just come from Europe, I presume? How are Lady Judith Scarlett and my excellent friends the Athelings?—I was wreaking the honest Judge's wrongs as well as my own when you interfered—and, above all, how is our sweet young friend Isolind?"

"Oh, oh!" groaned Verpool, "ain't he gone yet?"

"You must leave the room at once, Mr. Jocelyn," said Angelo, leaving the groaning man and sternly approaching his punisher.

"Thanks. I shall linger only one moment." Stepping quickly aside, he approached the bed and took a moment's glance at Verpool—a glance hideously expressive of satisfaction at the bruised and wounded face.

"Poor consolation there, after all," he said, "for the ruin he has brought on me. I ought to have killed the scoundrel, though the devil came between us. But even that is better than nothing, and the rest may come some day."

Then Chesterfield Jocelyn swaggered out, closed the door carefully behind him, and disappeared from the sight of Angelo, of Verpool, and of New York. Verpool and New York never saw him more, but Angelo and he met again.

"I feel very bad," groaned the wretch on the bed. "I guess I'd have been dead, Mr. Volney, only for you. That's a desperate fellow, Jocelyn, but he's a fool and he's a dead-beat now; and I guess I've about fixed him. How lucky you came in time. I'm much obliged to you, and I'll prove it. Now send one of the niggers for a doctor, won't you? I must be able to get down town to-morrow anyhow.'

This was Angelo's first adventure on his return to New York, and it proved somewhat important to him. He had been in town a few days, had already seen Verpool, who gave him some encouragement, and told him to come and see him this very evening. When Verpool arrived in the hotel he paused a moment at the office to say he expected a young man whom he was likely to employ, and that if he came he was to go up to Verpool's room "right away." This was a piece of Verpool's cunning; an appointment that evening with an insignificant young foreigner looking for employment would seem the kind of thing most unlikely to be made by anybody deeply interested in the events of the day. So Verpool took special pains to be loud and clear, and even garrulous, in his directions at the office; and probably his caution saved his life. Otherwise the clerks would surely never have allowed an unimportant stranger to disturb a conference between two such persons as Mr. Verpool and Chesterfield Jocelyn, and the latter would have had his will.

Next day and for days after New York still simmered and seethed with Wall street's commotion. Ruin was abroad. Of the many victims, public curiosity was specially active about Judge Atheling, for his name had been used everywhere, and without contradiction, by Chesterfield Jocelyn as one of the decoying agencies in the enterprise; and yet people refused to believe him a party to the plot. Mrs. Braxton went about everywhere dissolved in tears and denouncing Jocelyn as having plundered and beggared her, which was but the truth. Other victims were more guilty and almost as gullible; some few were wholly innocent. Many raved of vengeance by law or by weapon. There was much suspicion of Verpool, who however went about unmoved, albeit with a bruised face, which was reported to be the result of a railway accident; and he did not boast, as he might have done, that he had "busted" the whole scheme. Public wrath had to content itself without a victim, for nearly all who appeared to have been Jocelyn's intimates or allies were already ruined, and Jocelyn himself was gone.

The news of the New York calamities and giant frauds reached Europe, and even created a sensation there, although old Europe in general takes rather more interest in the affairs of Dahomey than in those of America. The news reached the ears of Lady Judith, who had taken her bitter spirit and her wounded heart to Rome, and was enduring there the society of her parents. She heard that Atheling was ruined, and in her cold way she was sorry for it, and she tried to pity the girl to whom the ruin of her adopted father would be another blow; but she could not pity her, and she told herself that Heaven had ordained the visitation on the children of the parents' sin. The news, be sure, travelled fast to the ears of Atheling, then living quietly and hidden away in a Styrian village with his wife and Isolind. He could not tell how much of truth was in the report of his ruin; he did not yet clearly know how far Jocelyn might have pledged his name, his means, and his credit. But he resolved to go back to New York at once and face the storm, do his best to clear himself of the moral iniquity of the transaction, and to the full extent of his means make good any losses he had been made the instrument of inflicting on others. He would not take his wife and Isolind with him; he positively insisted on going alone. So he left the two sad women and went his way, and the letters of Angelo Volney never reached them. As Isolind wandered through Styrian roads and hills in the long, dreary, monotonous summer evenings, with good, querulous Mrs. Atheling clinging to her arm and chattering at her ear, it seemed to her, even as it had lately seemed to Angelo, that some earthquake had swallowed up all her old life and her hopes and those she most dearly loved, and left her purposeless in the world and alone.

So the weeks and months went on, and the sun shone and the rain rained upon the just and the unjust, and new adventures came to Angelo Volney, and fresh fears and pangs and fever fits to poor Alexia, wife of Eric Walraven, and the old monotony of suffering clung to Lady Judith and to Isolind, but could no more break the pure and gentle spirit of the girl than it could yet bend the proud nature of the woman. Against woman's unselfish devotion and woman's egotistic pride the stars in their courses sometimes seem to war in vain.

CHAPTER XXII.

ANGELO'S NEW LIFE INTRODUCES A NEW ACQUAINTANCE.

On the shore of a vast and land-locked harbor, with islands of which some are rugged, bold, and rocky, stands one of the young giant cities of the world. It is a city whose houses seem indeed to have been literally built on sand; a city climbing up the sides of sand-hills, overlooked and girt and crowned by sand-hills; a city the color of dust and ashes; a summerless, winterless city, where men and even women have no seasons of change in the substance of garments; where you may wear furs if you like them in July or in December. Nature has given a monotony of climate to the region, and the young city has added its dusty monotony of color. Three days out of four a dull mist hangs over the city and over so much of the bay as seems to come within its shadow. Half an hour of steam or sail will bring you indeed to shores and valleys and villages which seem to be steeped in an unfading sunlight, and to glow in all the gorgeousness of unwithering flowers. Only a few miles to drive, and you reach one of the most wonderful and delightful stretches of soft, sandy beach to be found in the world, with a sunny silvery ocean rolling in, gentle in the very majesty of its strength; and you see close to the shore the huge rocks rising from the waters, whereon a countless army of restless, romping seals is perpetually clambering and barking.

But if this city be monotonous in its color, and seem as though it were built in sport by some Brobdingnagian Boffin along the sides of some of his vastest and aridest mounds of dust, it is anything but monotonous in the life that foams along its streets. One or two of its broad and busy thoroughfares remind you of New York by day; but when you pass through the same streets at night there is something in the aspect and condition of things, in the noisy, unrestrained gayety, in the glittering singing-saloons, and supper-rooms, and drinking-cellars, which sends a thrill through the wandering Briton's manly heart, for he almost fancies that he is once more in the Strand, London. But day or night there are figures and groups to be seen here which are not often discernible in London or New York. Here in this busy commercial street, with its great banks and bullion-dealers, its dainty bonnets and shimmering silks, its long-visaged eager business men in their stove-pipe hats, observe what strange companions are brought together. Look at that reckless rider in the broad sombrero and Mexican stirrups; he seems as if he ought to be only found in Captain Mayne Reid's novels, and yet he is quite at home here gallopping among hackney-coaches and omnibuses and the inevitable street-car of American civilization. That miserable, shivering, beggarly group of copper-colored women and children, with black ropy hair and clad in robes that look like filthy old matting—that group lounging outside the windows of a bank or a newspaper office or a telegraph office—

these are Digger Indians, lowest, meanest, most stupid, shiftless, helpless, of all the Indian race. Lo, every other man you meet is a blue-gowned and pig-tailed Chinese. Turn right out of one of the greatest commercial thoroughfares, and you step into Pekin—at least, you come into a quarter as entirely Chinese as any part of Pekin itself well can be. Leave the Chinese and the Indians and the Mexican and the negro (and bear in mind, pray, that the city is ruled by none of these, nor even by the keen New Englanders and other lordly Americans who came there and made it; but by pushing and versatile Pat from Ireland, whose appearance it is not necessary to describe)—leave all these, and if you want a little more variety, just follow this great leading thoroughfare a little up the hill. Only a little way, not far at all; and lo! the banks and the bullion-stores and the mantua-makers and theatres and newspaper offices are gone, and you have gaudy-looking houses of a sort of villa pattern on either side, and the doorsteps and windows of these houses swarm with painted women who flaunt their tawdry finery and their startlingly naked bosoms in the face of busy day. These are the Christian daughters of folly, please to understand. Turn to the right, down one of those lanes, so narrow that a cart could hardly get in, and you pass through a double row of little houses over-populated by their Chinese sisters, equally coarse, equally brazen, equally painted and repulsive, but by no means equally naked. In the one street and in a walk of five minutes you can see the solid wealth of London, the eager rushing commerce of New York, the Chinese tailor of "Aladdin and the Wonderful Lamp," the Mexican cavalier, the Indian of the plains, the rowdy whom Seven Dials or the old Five Points might be proud to own, and the half-naked harlots whom even Hamburg and Antwerp keep in a back slum, but who here enjoy all the privileges of free exhibition in the open street and in the glare of day. Convert the hills of Rome into dust-heaps and plant them around the harbor of Queenstown; crowd on their sides a city made up indiscriminately of the Strand, Broadway, Wapping, Donnybrook, Hong Kong, Denver, Vera Cruz, and Hamburg, and you may create in your mind's eye something like an adequate picture of San Francisco.

It was in San Francisco that Angelo Volney made what may be called his new start in life. Mr. Verpool had at present several mining speculations in his mind, of which San Francisco would be the appropriate headquarters and starting-point. He proposed to employ Angelo as a sort of peripatetic private secretary—if one can be a secretary who travels without his principal. He expected to make Angelo useful as much by virtue of what he did not know as of what he did know. The young man's ignorance of the principles of American speculation would, as Verpool believed, render him a pliant and willing agent in the forwarding of enterprises to which, if he fully understood their meaning, he might have been scrupulous enough to object. On the other hand, Angelo's positive knowledge of geology, of chemistry, and especially of the assaying of metals, was very considerable and remarkable; he spoke three or four European languages quite fluently, and could have learned to talk almost any language in a few weeks; he was very quick, intelligent, and energetic; and having long acted as secretary to one of the most methodical women in the world, he was precise, punctual, and business like in his ways.

Mr. Verpool possessed, as Jocelyn once told him, a wonderful insight into human capacities and characters. The uncultured old Vermont peddler read men off at a glance. Thus he had seen in a moment that Jocelyn was proposing to convert their oint enterprise into one of a composite order, having separate and special advantages for Chesterfield Jocelyn, and he therefore, to use his own phrase, "busted the whole thing." He saw at once the firmness, the faithful loyalty of Angelo's nature, as well as his remarkable capacity, and he resolved to serve the young man so as to make him really grateful, and thus to have the full benefit of his devotion and fidelity. Verpool had the one grand and indispensable qualification of a ruler of men—he appreciated men's good qualities and knew that through them are human creatures best governed. He was just as selfish and as unmoral (not immoral) as any Napoleon of them all; but like the great Napoleon he understood the reality and the value of other men's virtues, and strove to have them on his side. Your merely suspicious creature, who looks at the bad side of everything and assumes that the way to understand and govern men and women is by appealing to their selfish and mean qualities, is a charlatan predestined to failure. Never yet did such a being govern men.

Verpool saw where Angelo's value lay. He saw that by a seemingly generous helping hand in the beginning he could buy and secure the unswerving fidelity of the young man, and he knew that that was worth having. He set to work therefore to attach Angelo to him, and he proposed to appreciate distant persons as well as metals and ores by Angelo's eyes and judgment. He counted complacently also on the fact that it would do no little to enhance his own value (especially with those who did not know him personally) to be represented in far-off cities by a secretary who was vaguely reported to be a scion of British aristocracy, who had undoubtedly lived among earls and countesses, and who looked a distinguished gentleman and talked several languages.

The newspapers began to fill with paragraphs about Angelo, according to the agreeable practice of all save a very few honorable exceptions among American journals. Verpool, who picked up a handful of papers every day wherever he went, read these paragraphs with great satisfaction, regarding them as so much cheap advertising of himself.

Sometimes the allusions were florid and complimentary. Thus:

"Our illustrious fellow countryman, the millionaire philanthropist, the Hon. Ezekiel Verpool, has engaged as one of his secretaries a distinguished young English gentleman, the Hon. Angelo Volney, M. P., stepson of the Hon. Lady Judith Scarlett, daughter of Earl Coryden. The Hon. Mr. Volney was travelling through the United States for pleasure, when he chanced to make the acquaintance of the Hon. Mr. Verpool, who was so struck with his abilities that he made him the magnificent offer which has induced the young English nobleman to become secretary to the American millionaire. Mr. Volney is a remarkably handsome man, and speaks all the European languages."

Sometimes it would be more curt and familiar:

"Old Verpool is running a swell Englishman, stepson of a countess. The girls are all in love with the Henglishman."

Or:

"The new sensation in San Francisco is Verpool's splendid secretary. Only think! The nephew of an English duchess, a youth with a lovely dark moustache, who can jabber French and Italian in the European fashion, and not only talks German but dances the German like sixty."

Or:

"Mr. Verpool's new secretary is a brilliant young English aristocrat, who is said to have quarrelled with his mother, a countess, because he wished to marry an American girl. Bully for him!"

Or perhaps it came down to brief, casual notice like this:

"Mr. Verpool, the great capitalist, pays his new secretary, Lord Volney, the young English nobleman, $10,000 a year."

Or it might even be a patriotic remonstrance:

"Verpool is again toadying to England. He has just been engaging the poor relation of some great London countess as his secretary, and giving him a fabulous sum per year. The new secretary is a raw cub from the English universities, a mere Lord Dundreary, whom Verpool has engaged to please some of his English patrons."

All this amused and delighted Verpool, and at first intensely annoyed poor Angelo. The latter even thought at one time, in his greenness, of writing to disclaim any aristocratic rank whatever. But Verpool persuaded him to "let the thing slide;" and indeed after a while so many paragraphs had broken out here and there, and so many people had spoken to Volney of paragraphs which they had seen and he had not seen, that any idea of setting to the work of correction became obviously hopeless and absurd.

Verpool liked it all. It told for him and redounded to his credit. He had all the glory of employing a young British aristocrat and of paying him a huge salary, while he really did neither the one thing nor the other. Angelo had told him exactly what his position was, and Verpool's conviction of the young man's sterling value was greatly strengthened by his unhesitating candor. But Verpool was quite willing and anxious that the world should suppose he had a young English nobleman in his employment and paid him ten or twenty thousand dollars a year. Even when in private Angelo assured people he was not an English nobleman, the assurance went for nothing. Or rather the net result was a paragraph like this:

"The Hon. Angelo Volney, now secretary to Mr. Verpool, is said to have been so much impressed by republican institutions that he insists on renouncing all his aristocratic titles. But as the report is that Mr. Volney quarrelled with his mamma, the Countess Volney, because he wanted to marry an American girl, it may be that love has more to do with his conversion than the principles of true democracy."

One advantage, however, about this sort of thing is that it seldom lasts long in any individual case. Angelo was not an author, artist, or politician, whose new efforts would be constantly attracting fresh attention from the journals and the public. Other curious people and things soon came up and sent him out of notice. A great European singer finished him up in one city; a four-legged girl stamped him into oblivion in another. He was soon forgotten and at rest.

Angelo flung himself with intense energy into his new life, and in several instances showed remarkable judgment. This kind of existence had much charm in it, and it had the special advantage that it banished thought and melancholy. Many expeditions had to be made into the rude, wild mining regions of California and neighboring territories—a kind of journeying which leaves little room for sentimental reflection. Angelo soon learned that people in such places must now and then depend on their own hands to keep their heads. The mere physical inconveniences, dangers, and toils of such an existence, with their never-ending vexations and absurdities, render morbid mental brooding impossible. There is no place in the active life of the Far West for a self-torturing sophist or a bewailing lover. Angelo became more healthy of mind and soul every day, and the love that, had it been merely sentimental, might have faded with his growing physical and mental energies, only waxed stronger and deeper with his strength. Isolind was always with him. Her love and her memory were in his breast and filled it, to adopt the words of Richter, "as warmly as a living heart." As the truly religious soul makes every poor humble piece of work a religious duty, until "the ploughing becomes as holy as the praying," thus did Angelo's deep and passionate love consecrate and glorify the vulgarest toils and meanest vexations of his new life, and cause them to seem noble and lofty. For he always knew that he worked to win his love. He fought to win his true love as literally as though she were in a Saracen castle and he were battling with the paynim for her rescue. It is one of the most exquisite properties of love that thus in its trial-time it makes mean things sacred. I have said "in its trial-time," because the glorious glamour then prevails with all, but only with the few lasts on and on beyond the trial-time and for ever, so that the love of Rachel glorifies Jacob in his fields and his ploughing, even when the hairs of both are whitening and their period of probation has become a fading memory. It is not love's fault, but ours—the fault of heedlessness and selfishness, of the world, the flesh, and the devil—that the glorifying power ever loses its command over any life.

Angelo had not yet been long enough absent from Europe to feel greatly surprised at not having heard from the Athelings. Nor was he much concerned about the reports of Mr. Atheling having been involved in Jocelyn's smash. There were so many extravagant reports in circulation for some time that had one believed them all, or half of them, he must have come to the conclusion that every prominent man in the United States was ruined. The idea of Atheling's being mixed up in the plot itself Angelo never for a moment entertained, and he was probably in too exalted a condition of mind, what between his love and his resolve, to attach much consequence to a mere pecuniary loss on the part of even his best friends. Say that Atheling had lost money in Wall street. What then? Isolind was not lost with the dollars.

It was in San Francisco, during his preparations for a lengthened expedition to a rather distant region where new mining promise had suddenly broken out, that Angelo met with an adventure which seemed at first to amount to nothing, but in reality proved of great moment to him and to others.

Early, very early, one morning he was walking toward the outskirts of the city to hunt up a sturdy follower of other journeys who was to be his companion on the new expedition. He was mounting the hilly part of one of the principal streets, a busy, populous thoroughfare at its best, but which gradually changes its character as it climbs the hill, and at last threatens to become like the road Longfellow speaks of, which if you follow it out dwindles to a squirrel track and runs up a tree, only that here in the region of San Francisco was no tree for the street to run up. The neighborhood became low in character as it grew higher in physical range. Just now few people were stirring, but as Angelo passed a narrow cross-street he saw a little group two or three yards down, and he heard one or two shrill squeaks which, as he was yet in the Quixotic age, drew him quickly to the spot.

Two rowdies, going homeward apparently after a carouse that had lasted all night, were worrying a poor placid-looking Chinaman. The latter apparently had been carrying a bundle of clothes which he had washed, and it had pleased the passing revellers to upset the basket and scatter the shirts, chemises, and "pantalettes" in the dust. Doubtless the Chinaman had resented this treatment, and the lordly Caucasians were now punishing him for his impertinence. One was dragging him backward by his pigtail, the other was kicking him in the stomach. The Chinaman thought not of resistance; he only closed his eyes, poor fellow, and squealed. Lately, one is glad to know, the Chinamen in San Francisco, em ploying that teachable and imitative faculty which belongs to them, have learned the use of the knife, and there are even gratifying instances of a tortured Mongolian having thus successfully "gone for" a Caucasian antagonist's flesh. But this day now spoken of was before John Chinaman had ventured to do more than squeal.

Angelo had lived in England through all the fervor of the epoch of muscular Christianity. He wasted no words, but applied an argument just between the eyes of the kicker, which sent him staggering back until he finally lay prostrate. The other ruffian instantly let go the Chinaman's pigtail and began fumbling for his pistol. Had he got it promptly to hand Angelo's days were probably done, for Angelo had not yet turned round from his falling foe. But at that moment a fifth figure joined the group, and called in a clear, calm voice to the fellow who was fumbling for his revolver:

"Too late, my good friend, too late! Look here!"

In fact the new-comer had the rowdy "covered" with a neat revolver which he held in his hand. Your Western ruffian, if he is not mad with drink or passion, will not attempt to produce a weapon against one who already has him thus covered. What would be the use? The very faintest movement of his hand for such an object would be the signal for his adversary to fire.

So this particular rowdy only grumbled out, "All right!" and ceased to grope for his weapon.

Angelo, meanwhile, had his own revolver out, ready for the worst.

"Get that chum of yours on his feet and take him away," said the stranger. "He isn't much hurt, I dare say, and I suppose neither of you means any particular harm. Neither do we, if you let us alone. Now, then, just you git."

The one rowdy helped up the other, and looked, meanwhile, at the stranger with an air of semi-bewildered recognition and respect.

"You've seen me before?" the stranger said.

"Reckon I have," was the answer.

"Very well; get your chum away and let these poor Chinese alone. Where is that Chinaman? Ah, he has gone. He was prudent enough not to wait to thank his protector; he naturally expected that the protector would begin to exercise the right of kicking and tormenting on his own account. That is how we prove the superiority of our race and our religion here. Sir, I see you are a stranger. You were going this way? So am I, for a little. Let us go. No, we are quite safe; these fellows won't molest us."

This last remark was in answer to a doubtful glance of Angelo's at his late antagonist, who had now risen to his feet. The stranger put up his revolver, took the arm of Angelo and led him away, without even a glance at the two rowdies, who might now if they pleased have shot our hero and his guide in the back with perfect ease and impunity. Angelo, ashamed of showing fear or suspicion, put up his revolver too.

"I know these fellows and their like," said the stranger. "They are better than civilized men for the most part; they are not mean, or treacherous, or bitterly resentful. They think none the worse of you for what you have done, except that they may consider you a fool for caring about a kick given to a Chinaman. What would you have? They are overgrown children; a Chinaman is to them no more than a cat or a butterfly to a child, or a fox or a hare to *you*. I see in men but little real difference. All men feel pleasure in inflicting suffering on something. The Californian rough claims the right to kick his Chinaman; the English rough the right to kick his wife; but a Californian who pretends to be a gentleman does not kick the Chinese, while an Englishman of the highest class demands the sacred, heaven-sent privilege of torturing his wife. You, sir, are from England. I saw that by your manner of hitting out; but I take it that you are not an Englishman, by your features and complexion."

"I come from England indeed," said Volney, "and have lived there all my life; but I am at most only half an Englishman."

Angelo now seized a chance of quietly studying his companion's appearance. The stranger was a slender man, firmly and gracefully made, but hardly up to middle height. He was of fair complexion, much, however, embrowned by sun and air. His forehead was growing bald and was deeply lined and seamed by wrinkles; his hair was turning gray, though his full beard and moustache still retained their bright fair color. He had a handsome striking face, with a quick, flashing blue or gray eye. He spoke like a cultivated gentleman, although when he admonished the roughs he had adopted now and then a phraseology and manner approaching to their own. He was dressed in plain, dark clothes. There was in his whole manner something that told of one in the habit of asking questions, and who conceived that he had some kind of privilege or duty to interrogate people. Angelo was struck with the idea, he could not tell why, that his new acquaintance might be a Roman Catholic missionary, although the prompt production of the revolver might perhaps even in California have been enough to negative any such conjecture.

But the face perplexed Angelo especially. He was tortured by the impression that it was like some face he knew well. He glanced again and again; he could not distinctly confirm the impression, yet he could not shake it off.

"You," said Angelo, hazarding a guess, "are an Englishman?"

"I have no country. I was born in England, if you care to know."

"Pray excuse me, I hardly meant any inquiry. I spoke quite at random."

"Why should you not inquire? I asked of you. I live here, sir, and this is as much my country as any other. But I don't live—thank Heaven—in San Francisco, or any other city."

"Thank Heaven that you were in San Francisco to-day," said Volney cordially, "else I don't know where I should be now. You have rendered me a service which I can never forget—and I suppose shall never have a chance of repaying."

"Have I really served you?" the other said, turning his deep eyes full on Angelo and sending a wild, bewildering thrill through the young man—a thrill of tortured conjecture and memory—"have I really served you? I am glad of it—I am glad to have it anywhere recorded that I served anybody."

Then he came to a stand, as if their ways were parting.

"Will you give me your name?" Angelo asked. "I owe you too much not to wish to see you again."

"No, thanks, my name would be of no interest to you. Men can know each other without names. If there is any purpose in our meeting again, we are sure to meet. I hardly ever come to this city—have not been here for years. I live in many places—I fly from towns and cities and newspapers. Cities are men's curse and scourge. Are you travelling for pleasure?"

"No; I am poor, and am only trying to make a living."

"Your father and mother?"

"Both died when I was a child."

"You loved them both?"

"I loved my mother dearly; I hardly remember my father."

"Your mother was kind and good?"

"All kindness and goodness."

"Ah, it was *he* then who was otherwise! Who brought you up then?"

"A generous and kind-hearted London lady."

"Had *she* a husband?"

"She had."

"Was *he* bad?"

Angelo could hardly help smiling at the evident persistence with which the other clung to the theory, that in matrimony one party or the other must be bad. But he answered gravely:

"She certainly was not happy in her married life." Then as if to put a stop to all further questions, he said: "If you know London at all, the story can hardly be new to you. Every one there has heard of Lady Judith Scarlett's unhappy marriage."

The stranger looked at Angelo with a surprise which he made no attempt to conceal.

"Lady Judith Scarlett? Was it she who brought you up? Was it she who was so kind? Yes. I have heard of her, and of her wrongs." This he said with a kind of sneer. "I have heard of her as very proper and pious, but."

"She is one of the noblest women in the world."

"And *she* adopted you?—as she had no child of her own?"

"No son of her own. She has a daughter."

The other looked with a glance of suspicion and disappointment on Angelo, and said in a tone of contempt:

"Your information is rather inaccurate, sir. Lady Judith Scarlett had no child."

Angelo smiled.

"I lived all my life in Lady Judith's house. She had and has a daughter, born soon after her husband's desertion of her."

The stranger looked unspeakably surprised and perplexed.

"I am sure you tell me what is true, sir; but this seems quite extraordinary to me. Yet I never could have known of it; I don't ever meet English people or hear English news. She has a daughter—living?"

"Living and married." Then Angelo hesitated, dreading that his new companion's mournful marriage theory would be pressed into a question in this case. But the other seemed absorbed in thought.

Meanwhile Angelo gazed at him. When the stranger first appeared to show emotion at the mention of Lady Judith's name, a wild conjecture had flashed across Angelo's mind—one which had invaded it before in the case of Edwin Dare Jocelyn. Could this man before him possibly be Charles Scarlett? But he had to dismiss the conjecture in a moment. He knew from many descriptions that Scarlett was a tall, robust, and stately man, well fitted at least in form and bearing to be the husband of the imperial Lady Judith. This man was slender and rather short.

Suddenly the stranger looked up and said:

"I hope we may meet again; will you give me your name, though I haven't given you mine?"

Angelo handed him a card, at which he looked eagerly, and then seemed somewhat disappointed.

"I don't know the name," he murmured, and was going away.

"One word," Angelo interposed; "do you know anything of Charles Scarlett's present life?"

"Why do you ask?"

"Because you seem to know something of his past history."

"Which you have just said is known to every one who knows London!"

"But, excuse me, *you* evidently feel more interest in it than is felt by everybody in London. Sir, I earnestly entreat of you, if you know anything of Mr. Scarlett's present existence, or if he is alive, not to refuse to tell me. Help me to find him, and it will be a far greater obligation than the one you have already conferred!"

The stranger seemed for a moment wavering. But he turned away and said in a tone that was almost harsh:

"Sir, I can tell you nothing about Charles Scarlett. I presume that whenever he feels inclined to open up a correspondence with his wife, he knows how to do so. *I* never was his confidant and am not likely to be in his secrets; I can tell you nothing."

"But you know him—you know that he is alive; you know where he is."

"If I do know all this, I could hardly have known it on condition of telling it to everybody I chanced to meet in the streets of San Francisco. Good-morning."

"Stay," said Angelo, laying his hand firmly on the other's arm. "You positively shan't go until you have heard from me a message to Mr. Scarlett. When next you see him, tell him that his daughter wasted all her brightest years in vain longing and praying for *him*, and that at last, in utter recklessness, she has flung herself away on a man quite unworthy of her, and doomed herself, I fear to a life of misery! Tell him his absence has done this, and tell him it has brought shame and scandal and cruel suffering on some others—on one other—of the noblest creatures in the world, whom his presence or a word from him might have saved; and tell him too that I who send this message am no messenger or agent of his wife; that I honor and love Lady Judith, but that I have left her house and lost her friendship for ever."

"You are very earnest, sir," said the stranger; and he now spoke in tones which were respectful and sympathetic; "but your message as delivered by me would be only a thing of enigmas, I fancy. Suppose a chance should ever arise how far would you go out of your way to deliver the message yourself?"

"To the other end of the earth," Angelo exclaimed.

"Well, no further talk now would do us any particular good. If any chance should arise I shall contrive to find you. If any time, say within the next three months, you should come near *this* place"— he drew out a scrap of paper and laying it on the palm of his left hand wrote a few words on it with a pencil—"if you come near this place you are pretty certain to find *me*."

He gave Angelo the piece of paper, bade him, somewhat peremptorily a good-morning, and went his way with the resolute manner of one who has said quite as much as he meant to say, and whom it would be useless to press or question any further.

Angelo stood for awhile and gazed after him. Excited and bewildered as he was by the sudden, utterly unexpected appearance of what promised to be a clue to the solution of a mystery that so long had seemed hopeless, yet the question now uppermost in Angelo's mind was, "Where have I seen a look like that, and eyes like those?"

CHAPTER XXIII.

ALEXIA KNOWS HER HUSBAND.

It was fortunate for Isolind that she had such a companion as poor Mrs. Atheling. For it became impossible that the girl could brood over her own sources of sorrow. Mrs. Atheling was in such a perpetual flutter of alarm, anxiety, and distress, and was seized in consequence by such a variety of complicated ailments, exhausting even her own power of description and baffling all medical skill, that Isolind's faculties were taxed to the uttermost to become consoler, guide, and nurse. When the good old lady turned from her own distresses to Isolind's, the change was yet more disturbing to the luxury of grief's indulgence; for Mrs. Atheling's sympathy was so restless, excitable, nervous, and withal sincere and loving, that out of sheer selfishness a sufferer would have feigned joy to escape it. So Isolind preferred to hide her own troubles quite away and be the strengthener and consoler, the more especially as Mrs. Atheling had real need of consolation in the absence of her husband and its cause, and was one of the most kind and single-minded creatures living.

The old lady had many little troubles too. The Styrian serving-maidens did not know and could not learn how to make milk-toast. Pumpkin pie was unknown to them. There was no green corn to be "eaten off the cob" with butter. Mrs. Atheling vilipended the fruits, as all true Americans vilipend the fruits of all other countries. The promised land itself could not have satisfied her for the absence of the delicious little peaches of New Jersey, which are sold by the quart in the streets of New York. Mrs. Atheling had travelled a great deal in her time, but she belonged to that class, much more common in Europe than in America, from whom no extent or variety of travelling ever rubs off the early wonder and irritation at finding that there are places where the dainties they love are not relished and the habits which are their life are unknown.

All this was good for Isolind. She had to be always making herself useful (*par exemple*, she made the milk-toast), and she could not brood and mourn over her own trials. But even as it was, the light went sadly out of her eyes and the color from her cheeks. Indeed, she had a great many troubles heaped suddenly on her young head. The terrible scandal on her mother and her birth, the existence of such a father as Dysart or Jocelyn, the calamity which seemed to have been brought by him on her best friends, and finally the sacrifice of her love and of her lover—all these surely made up a heavy weight of suffering. There was an added pain, too, in Angelo's silence. She was firm in her resolve—indeed, she could not think how any pure soul could resolve otherwise; she was thankful in one sense to him for not resisting it and inflicting on her useless torture. But yet—but yet, he might have written! He might have written once! Just a few lines from him to her of tender farewell and love—a few lines to be carried in her bosom always, to be preserved there like an amulet, so that some vague sense of the enfolding presence of his love might shed itself from his written words to her heart—something to be always borne by her when living and to lie in her coffin when she lay there dead.

Letters came regularly from Atheling; but they gave little account of his business affairs, and even Isolind had now no knowledge of how deeply he might have been involved.

At last he wrote something distinct, and, on the whole, it was cheering. Things were not so bad as they might have been. He had lost the bulk of his property, he was no longer a rich man, and as he did not propose ever again to try to be, he might be called, in the Wall street sense, a ruined man. But out of the wreck was saved enough for the old lady and Issy and himself to live comfortably, though frugally, and their habits had always been modest. He hoped Issy wouldn't cry when she heard that they couldn't hire a house in Fifth avenue for the winter any more, and that he didn't see his way to making much of a figure at Saratoga this season. This, be it understood, was the good Judge's fun—this allusion to Isolind—for he knew that she cared nothing for Fifth avenue and detested Saratoga. He wanted to put things in as easy and jocular a light as he could; and he said the whole affair had been a good lesson to him against speculation and trying to amass useless heaps of money, and that he would be content with modest means for the future. This artful and disingenuous Judge wanted thus to make it appear as if he had gone into the financial speculation of his own accord and out of a desire for the mere possession of superfluous gain. Such was the policy of this crafty man in order that poor Issy might not have the pain of knowing that he had been ruined by her father, and for her sake.

Then he went on to say that he thought for a little time they had better remain in Europe, where things were cheaper, and he would join them as soon as he could. But as he could not bear the idea of having to wander in search of them away into Styria (perhaps he wrote—he certainly would have said—"way into Styria") and longed to think of their welcoming him when he landed, he recommended that they should remove to a quiet pretty bathing place which he named on the French coast, where he hoped soon to find them.

Finally, he added: "I have heard of Angelo Volney. He is gone to California, and is likely to do well, I am told. Old Verpool has taken him up. To be sure, Verpool ain't over-honest, but Volney is; and if he can't convert Verpool, which I take to be a moral impossibility, I am sure old Verpool can't pervert him."

Some things in this letter were consoling and gratifying to Isolind. She was glad to hear that Judge Atheling's affairs were not looking so bad as they might have been, although she suspected he was doing all he could to make the calamity seem less than it really was. Then she was glad to be up and doing; to have to leave Styria and go anywhere. Then a new rush of life seemed to come with a shock like a pang into her heart at the mention of Angelo's name. He was alive; he was well; people heard of him and from him. Though he was many, many thousands of miles away from her, yet she had read his name. Only the heart that has been sick and faint with love's privation can know the nourishment and stimulus which may thus be found in the few seemingly barren words which enclose the beloved one's name.

So the two women left the Styrian village and settled themselves—dropped anchor for the hour—in the French watering-place. This was a newly-discovered spot; a poet had found it out and built there a villa, hoping to be lonely or at least to have the place all to himself and a few of his friends. But the friends had told other friends, and the rocks and the strand began to obtain a sort of celebrity. As yet, however, it was only in its transition stage and not wholly given over, body and soul, to fashion. Isolind and Mrs. Atheling found pleasant lodgings there; and they walked by the sea of evenings, along secluded parts of the strand, and were perhaps not unhappy.

There was a new hotel in the place already—a somewhat pretentious establishment with a great ball-room where there were dances of evenings; and Isolind and her elderly charge usually avoided the hotel in their rambles. One evening, however, they chanced to pass its door, and a pale sad little lady seated at one of the upper windows saw them and called to them, and as they did not hear her came quickly down stairs and followed them, and then Isolind hearing the rapid step turned round and saw Alexia Walraven.

Alexia came up with all her old impetuosity.

"Don't you know me, Isolind, and didn't you hear me call you? Am I so changed as all that? I am Alexia Scarlett—at least I was so once."

Isolind embraced the girl again and again. She could hardly speak at first, for the sight of Alexia brought back memories that sent the tears rushing into her eyes. But the very silence of her welcome was so eloquent, that it thrilled poor Alexia's heart with a strange and softening pang.

"You are changed, Isolind," she said; "you have grown pale and thin. You too are miserable?"

"My dear Mrs. Walraven——"

"Oh don't, Isolind, please, please don't! Don't call me Mrs.—anything! Call me Alexia."

"Dear Alexia, I have had some troubles, but it is a joy to see *you*. Have you been long here?"

"We only came the day before yesterday, and I was sick of the place already and hated it; but now that you are here I think I shall like it, if I can like anything."

Isolind was observing in her own mind the change that had come over Alexia, who, always pale and fragile, had now a nervous eccentricity of glance and gesture, and a changing glitter in her eyes, which sadly marred the beauty that once was hers. But she had little more time for observation or reflection just then; for Eric Walraven broke from a group of smoking loungers near the hotel door, and came up hat in hand to greet the Athelings. He, too, did not seem to have improved in appearance of late. There was a tone of flashiness and a sort of social defiance in his bearing which were new to him. He was less careful and elegant in his dress than of old, his complexion looked yellower than it used to do, and there were deeper lines in his face.

He paid Isolind so many extravagant compliments that she was longing to get away, even though Alexia seemed almost to cling to her. Suddenly Alexia said:

"You are going out this evening, Eric?"

He merely nodded assent.

"Then I'll walk up with Mrs. Atheling and Isolind—if they will allow me—and sit with them in their rooms, and you can come for me. I may, Isolind, may I not? I *so* want to talk to you, and I am so lonely."

"Alexia dislikes society in general," Eric interposed, "and she dislikes French society in especial. She *will* keep herself secluded. Only you, Miss

Atheling, have the charm that can call her from her self-imposed solitude. For her—and for others—your presence sheds a new light over sea and shore."

After one or two other compliments and with a grand bow he rejoined his friends, and the three women walked to the cottage. Alexia leaned on Isolind's arm, and indeed clung to it, and they talked little on the way. When they reached the cottage Isolind brought Alexia into her bedroom, and they were alone.

Alexia plucked off her hat and flung it on a chair, and gathered herself up, half reclining, half crouching, on a little sofa. Isolind was coming over to sit by her and caress her when she said:

"Stand there, Isolind; do, please, stand just there as you are and let me look at you."

Isolind smiled, blushed perhaps a little, but stood.

"How long, dear, shall I remain?"

"Just a moment. Yes, you are changed since the day when I first saw you; that day in Paris, don't you remember? I hated you then, Isolind, because I thought your very looks insulted me with your happiness. I don't hate you now."

"Dear Alexia, I hope not. May I sit down yet?"

"In a moment. You look so picturesque now I like to see you. No, there is nothing in your face now to insult me with happiness, and I am sorry for it, very, very sorry! I wish I could see that bright light in your eyes again. I suppose you are hardly enough of a true Christian, Isolind, to be consoled by the knowledge that there are others more unhappy than yourself, but there are such. I wish I could give back to you your happiness of that day in Paris, and bring back my own unhappiness with it."

"Indeed, I wouldn't accept such a sacrifice——"

"Wouldn't you? Thanks. You mean it well, Isolind. There, I tire you by keeping you in that one attitude; but I like to look at you, and you are so good a girl that I know you are willing to give people pleasure. Strange that *I* should like you, and yet that you should be good. Will *your* days be long in the land, I wonder? Mine won't, for I never honored my mother; but if the Powers above think it will be anything of a punishment to me to cut short my thread of life, they are rather mistaken."

Isolind looked with pain on Alexia's worn face, and listened with pain to her wild talk. She tried to bring her into some more cheerful mood by telling her of the beauty of the scenery all around and of the pleasant rambles they should have together. But Alexia said:

"I shall be glad to be with *you*, Isolind, but I hate nature and natural beauty, and sea and sky, and all the rest of it. I detest this place and every place. We are in banishment here, and shall have to stay here, I dare say. I only thank the fates that have sent you here into exile as well."

"It is really a kind of exile to me," said Isolind smiling, "and yet I like the place, and I mean to try to make you like it too."

"Oh, I don't dislike it more than any other spot on earth. London is detestable. Paris is odious. There is only one little scrap of the whole world to which I look forward with any interest or liking or longing—and I don't even know where that little scrap is to be found. I only mean my grave, Isolind—don't look shocked. This place, I believe, is unluckily very healthy, although you don't seem evidence that way. Ah, yes, I see more and more how much you have changed. You are worn and thin, but you look all the handsomer for it, I think. Isolind, you will look beautiful when you are dead—I mean if the kind gods send you death soon, now that you are young. Don't you ever pray for death?"

"Dear Alexia, what funereal thoughts! No, I don't pray for death; there are some people who don't want me to die, and would miss me if I were not with them, and so I am content to live—although indeed I have little to hope for that makes life worth having. But you, Alexia, you surely can't have—— "

"Any reason to long for death, you were going to say? Oh, no, of course not. I am very happy—don't I look so?"

"You don't look so," said Isolind, coming over to the girl and kneeling beside her sofa, and taking one of Alexia's thin white hands in hers. "You have been sick, I am afraid."

"We seem a remarkably happy pair of women, don't we? No, I haven't been sick; at least I don't remember if I have. But I have been sick of life, and I am so, and that's worse than other sickness, Isolind."

"Yet you have much, dear, to be happy and thankful for. If you only knew how my life is darkened and saddened, and how very hopeless it is in some ways. Alexia, your mother will send for you some day and be reconciled to you, and you have your husband——"

"No, Isolind, no," cried Alexia, so suddenly and sharply that Isolind started back. "I have not my husband any more. I have lost him. I never loved any one in all the world but him, and he cares nothing about me—nothing, nothing, nothing!"

And the poor young woman buried her face among the cushions of the sofa and sobbed like a heartbroken child.

Isolind put her arms round Alexia and raised her, and drew her toward her own bosom, and tried to console her. Alexia was so small and slight that Isolind could have carried her like a child in her arms, and she now felt to her almost as she might feel to a child. Alexia sobbed and sobbed until utter exhaustion came on, and then she told Isolind in broken and hardly coherent sentences her miserable story, of which the whole purport and burden simply was that Eric did not love her any more. Isolind made some efforts to reassure her, to persuade her that she was mistaken, that she was only too sensitive and wrongly interpreted her husband's manner perhaps. The attempt was quite in vain. Alexia only repeated the dismal refrain of her wail.

"He cares nothing for me any more; he doesn't even pretend or try to keep up an appearance. I am only a bore and an annoyance to him; he would be glad if I were dead. I don't blame him so much. Nobody ever liked me, except perhaps Angelo Volney; for Charles Escombe didn't know anything about me, so he counts for nothing. Everybody always detested me, from my mother down. But I didn't care; I detested everybody else. Only him, only him I loved, and now he hates me too!"

That was a sad and weary evening. Alexia rallied a little after a while, and occasionally showed some flashes of her old spirit in conversation when Mrs. Atheling was present. But the sadness was always overhanging, and when Eric Walraven came his presence did little to brighten the atmosphere. It was painful and pitiful to see how Alexia hung upon his words and looks, and fawned upon him, and almost crouched at his feet. All the old fierceness of her nature seemed to have died out of her, to have been extinguished in the glare of her unhappy love as a fire is extinguished by the sunlight. For him, he seemed to take a positive pleasure in humiliating or ignoring her, and his attentions to Isolind were such as to make the latter feel always uncomfortable and sometimes resentful.

During the next few days Mrs. Walraven was a constant visitor to the cottage of the Athelings, and Isolind and she had many rambles together. Alexia was a depressing and sad companion, but Isolind gladly sacrificed all feeling of personal comfort to the task of endeavoring to console and encourage her. Mr. Eric did not present himself often. Isolind's manner had been too decidedly repelling, and he had a cluster of friends in and about the hotel with whom he smoked and played billiards a good deal. In truth, Eric was at present literally an exile. London could no longer contain him. Creditors were importunate and unrelenting, and he had fled to France in order to gain time to think over his situation and find out what was next to be done.

Things had come to an almost desperate pass with him. His poem, "The Mystery of the Universe," had attracted no attention. He owed so much money to his publisher that he did not care to attempt any further literary enterprise, inasmuch as his labor could only go in liquidation of the debt. He had exhausted all his friends and their purses; the Hon. Oscar McAlpine had lately thrown him over altogether. He had begged of Gostick in vain. Lady Judith proved to be calmly implacable as destiny itself. In Alexia he had found not a treasure and source of income, but a mere incumbrance and nuisance.

One evening he came in from the billiard-room to his wife's apartment looking specially dispirited and sullen. Alexia's eyes brightened—they always did—when she saw the manly form of her noble master.

Eric flung himself on the sofa. "Alexia," he said, "I wish to Heaven you could do anything to help us. It's too bad that you can do nothing. Look here, can't you write to old Gostick?"

"Write to Mr. Gostick, Eric—for what?"

"For money of course. Do you think we can live on air? If we don't get some money somewhere, we can't even stay here. You really might try to do something since you have been the cause of all this. I think if you wrote to old Gostick and begged of him, it might soften him a bit; I'll tell you what to say. Though I don't know, perhaps you could do it better in your own kind of way."

"Eric, I can't turn beggar, indeed I can't, and beg of poor Mr. Gostick, whom we always laughed at. Are we really so poor as all that?"

He laughed a bitter laugh.

"So poor that we shall soon have nothing at all. If I hadn't won a few napoleons at cards the other night, I don't know where we should be. Will you write to old Gostick—yes or no?"

"I will not write to him," she said, some of her old temper reasserting itself. "I won't write a begging letter to him or to anybody. Let us starve or poison ourselves if we can do nothing in life; but I am no beggar, and never will stoop to crave for alms!"

"Very spirited indeed," Eric calmly said. "Nothing can be finer. Well, then, you must only accept your mother's conditions and go back to her. I can't support you any longer, Alexia, and that's the sum of the situation."

"Eric, what do you mean by accepting my mother's conditions? I don't understand you."

"Lady Judith offers," he answered very composedly, "to receive you back under her roof rather than allow you to starve. I think you had better go to her."

"But, Eric, dear love, you terrify me! Good God! you don't mean to say you have humbled yourself and me so far as to write to Lady Judith?"

"I have written several letters to Lady Judith," he coldly replied. "I can't afford to stand on dignity."

Alexia stood up, all trembling with wonder, shame, and anger.

"You wrote to Lady Judith! You stooped to her—asked her for money?"

"Certainly. I wrote to her many very eloquent and powerful letters, beseeching her to consider the destitute condition of her daughter and to open her purse-strings on our behalf."

"Oh, my God! And she; what did she reply?"

"She did not condescend to take the slightest notice of my supplications until at last I told her, with what I consider highly honorable frankness, that I should soon be positively unable to support her dear daughter any more, and that the granddaughter of the Earl of Coryden—to whom, by the way, I also wrote, praying for his intercession and coöperation—that the granddaughter o. the Earl would have to go into the workhouse. Then her ladyship wrote offering to receive *you* under her roof—you can see her letter, it is remarkably cool and curt—and I think, dear, you had better go."

"Oh Eric, for shame, for shame; oh, you coward—you mean, unmanly coward! Oh, why did I ever marry you. I hate you—I hate you!"

Alexia flung herself down on the floor and hid her face from the light.

Eric looked down at her with perfect indifference. Her attitude was quite unpicturesque, so there was positively nothing to interest him.

Presently she rose and confronted him.

"First of all," she asked—and there was a strange glitter in her eyes—"is this true?"

"Is what true?"

"This story you tell me about your having written to my mother?"

"True as gospel. I will show you the noble lady's autograph reply."

"I will never go near my mother—never! Find where my father is—you know something of him—and I will go to *him*."

Eric laughed.

"I think that little comedy ought to be now regarded as played out. My dear Alexia, I know no more about your father than the child unborn."

"But you did—you did——"

"Not I, child—nothing at all. I never knew anything but what I heard from you and guessed."

"But all that you told me—and the messages—and the letters in the 'Times'?"

"All pious frauds, child, and very cleverly done, I think. In love, Alexia, all is held to be fair. I wrote those mysterious missives with mine own hand."

"My God, can this be true? All that was a fraud and a lie?"

"At lovers' perjuries, Alexia, Jove laughs. I swear to you—and I am now no longer a lover perjuring myself—I swear to you that I never knew anything about your father, and that I invented the whole thing to captivate your filial little heart."

"Oh, was there ever in all the world such a wretched, ruined, miserable girl! Was there ever known such base and wicked treachery! Oh, how I loved you, Eric, and trusted in you! Why did you marry me—why? You have been cruelly candid with me at last—let me have that question candidly answered too! Why did you marry me?"

"Partly," he answered with unmoved composure, "because I had great, and as it seems now quite absurd, expectations from your family. I thought your father might possibly have assigned you a fortune. I thought your mother would certainly forgive us in the regular 'Bless you, my children' fashion, and give us plenty of money."

"One question more. Did you ever—in all this time—really love me?" There was a terrible choking and gasping in the throat of the poor girl as she put this sad question.

Eric threw back his curls and looked at his white hands.

"Do you press for an answer, Alexia?"

"I do."

"Well, then, I don't fancy I ever did love you in your sense—in the romantic kind of way. I don't think I have much of that sort of thing in me, and besides women have generally fallen in love with me and spared me all that trouble. I liked you well enough—you were a new sensation; but you know very well that you are rather a provoking sort of woman, and you tire me immensely. I am not made perhaps for the joys of domestic life, and at all events I haven't now the means of paying for them. So I really don't see that you can do anything better, Alexia, than to eat humble pie for once and go back to your mother."

And with these words he rose from the sofa, took out his cigar-case, lighted a cigar, and left the room. As he went he hummed some bars of "Dites lui" from "La Grande Duchesse," then in the zenith of its popularity. He was feeling better already, some of the burthen of his care having been lifted off his shoulders. The revelation had been made which must have come soon in any case, and Alexia had really raised less of a row about it than he expected. She would go back to her mother now. She would never stay with him after what he had told her, and he should be rid of her. She really was a dreadful little bore and nuisance, and it was horrible when one was so poor to have to drag a wife about with one, and he couldn't support Alexia and didn't know what to do with her. Then, if her mother should relent and leave Alexia any money, he could take his wife back again. He would have no difficulty in any case in geting hold of the money. But his own impression now was that Lady Judith would never give Alexia a sixpence, and therefore it was much better she should go back.

So his heart felt considerably relieved. As he went down the stairs one of the chambermaids of the hotel passed up. He observed that she was a pretty and *piquante* looking *fille*, and as he gazed after her he quite admired her neat ankles. Then he noted mentally the fact that for days back he had not been in spirit enough to observe whether any woman was pretty or ugly, and he became complacent and encouraged by this evidence of improving condition, and he thought there was still balm in Gilead and that he might yet have a bright future. There was quite a charming elasticity and buoyancy in this poet's nature, and things began to wear a rosy aspect in his eyes again. Even marriage, Eric thought, is not always irreparable.

CHAPTER XXIV.

"HOW IS IT WITH ME WHEN EVERY NOISE APPALS ME?"

LADY JUDITH had returned to London, and again occupied the house where she had passed so many weary years. She scorned to yield so much even to her own weakness as to seek out a place less haunted by the ghosts of old memories. She went back to the sadly familiar rooms, and never shrank for one moment from crossing any threshold, whatever the shadows which hovered around it. She was glad to get back from Rome, which oppressed her with a sense of hopeless idleness and ignoble ruin. She was still more glad to escape from the society of her own family, who had urged on her marriage in the first instance, and who, having always disapproved of her adoption of Angelo, were now inclined to congratulate her and themselves on his disappearance. Nc society could be more uncongenial to her than that of her father and mother; no atmosphere so oppressive to her active, energetic mind as that of the Papal city. She could not breathe freely in a place where there were so many beggars, where idle men lay all day in the sun on the steps of a church, waiting for other men hardly less idle, but calling themselves artists, to employ them as models and paint them into pictures.

She threw herself at once into her old life of beneficent activity. There was no useful institution which had not her helping hand; and she strove to found new institutions and to diffuse new thoughts. There was no great foreign cause to which she did not give her full sympathies and her ready aid. She understood politics, home and foreign, as few women did. When nine out of every ten of her class were making dolts of themselves on the subject of the American war; when members of the House of Lords, in the confidence and plenitude of their grotesque ignorance, were incessantly wondering why the Mississippi could not be accepted as the boundary between North and South, Lady Judith could have talked over every branch of the subject with Charles Sumner or Wendell Phillips, and never shown herself lacking in knowledge. Gradually she had become a sort of celebrity, a person of authority and influence, and men of mark and power, men whose brains were big with schemes which promised to revolutionize material worlds and worlds of thought, came to talk with her and to consult her. To her fresh and vigorous intellect nothing was too new to receive consideration. She had not one single taint of the "old fogy" disposition in her. Her mind was as clear as her complexion. More than forty years of age, Lady Judith was only in her prime of womanhood; and yet the charm, the one charm which with all her queenly beauty and superbly feminine outlines of form she specially wanted, was the simple charm of womanhood.

Her life was, for all its activity and its beneficence, a sad and weary existence. One terrible dread had lately haunted her, one fearful doubt, almost as appalling to a woman of her nature as a doubt of heaven and God. She began to doubt of her own capacity to see and act aright. Her whole life had hitherto been moulded and guided by a profound egotistic faith in her own judgment, her own moral principles, and even her own impulses. She had lived in that faith, and now it was breaking down. Only profound stupidity can always, despite every shock, keep up a belief in its own infallibility; and Lady Judith had no stupidity about her, and had received many severe shocks of late. Everything which she had taken in hand, and into the elements of which human love and human passion entered, had gone wrong with her and failed; and her mind was too active, her principles were too just, to allow her to be content always with throwing the blame on destiny or the perverse wickedness of others. She began to doubt seriously whether she had dealt wisely or even justly with Alexia's younger days. She even found herself going over mentally her own early married life, and wondering why it was that all people used to regard her husband as noble, high-minded, and pure, a man made to guide and to rule; and why she had never understood him in that sense, seen him in that light. Thus painfully studying herself, thus growing so far into doubt of her past that all the good she could do in the present began to seem an expiation rather than a spontaneous work of benevolence, she came gradually into a faint understanding of the utter feebleness and untrustworthiness of human codes of justice, and that love, after all, is the law and the light.

In the true sense, Lady Judith with all her religious devotion had never hitherto been a Christian. Love and mercy and pity, not the mere practical doing of good, distinguish the new dispensation from the old. Lady Judith would have been greatly amazed to hear that she was now for the first time, having passed her fortieth year, being converted to Christianity by events and the discipline of sorrow. Yet this and none other was the process going on within her.

But she could not yet bring herself to forgive Eric Walraven. He had deceived her; he had taught Alexia to deceive her; and she hated deceit. Then she despised him for his cowardice and meanness. He began to persecute her with letters which she contemptuously flung into the fire. Had he held a firm and manly front and stood aloof from her, perhaps in the change which was growing in her nature she might have relented towards him. But his craven supplications utterly disgusted her; and she did not even believe that he was as needy as he pretended to be. As he had told Alexia, he wrote to the Earl of Coryden, beseeching the Earl's intercession with his daughter, Lady Judith; and Coryden, a stingy and selfish old peer, who always hated Alexia because she never showed him the least respect, and who was horribly alarmed at the idea of any appeal for money being made to him, told Lady Judith in affright that she was really bound to do something for her child's husband; and this sort of interference only rendered Lady Judith less placable than before.

A little discovery that she made by chance somewhat altered Lady Judith's resolve, and urged her to endeavor at least to succor and rescue Alexia. Among her many charitable undertakings was one for the reclamation of the class of persons whom we upright individuals who never have sinned complacently term "fallen women." Lady Judith became interested in one poor girl of this class, who seemed to have some education and a good disposition. She became a special benefactress to this girl; and although she never made any prying inquiry, yet she won the girl's confidence and heard, unasking, her melancholy story. She learned that this girl owed her degradation to Eric Walraven, and had been abandoned by him. This was in fact a young woman already passingly alluded to, whom Eric always remembered with pleasure and satisfaction because of the picturesque attitude into which she had fallen in the wild agony and passion of her grief when she learned that he was leaving her forever. One discovery leads to others, and Lady Judith came gradually to know that her poet son-in-law was one of the meanest and most pitiful of sensualists and profligates—a man without the fierce passions and stupendous guilt of a Don Juan or a Lovelace; but a sensuous heartless thing, who delighted to play with any and every woman who could be fooled without trouble or danger. Lady Judith rightly judged that for a paltry sinner of this class reclamation is far more difficult than for an offender of graver and grander mould. There is some stuff to work in the one; there is nothing in the other. She thought the best thing that could be done was to get Alexia out of such a man's clutches altogether; and therefore she wrote the letter of which Walraven had spoken, and offered to take back her daughter, but refused to receive her daughter's husband. Lady Judith knew that such an offer made directly by her to Alexia would be rejected with disdain. But she rightly guessed that Walraven, seeing no prospect of personal advantage, would now be tired of Alexia and anxious to get rid of her; and she counted much upon the indignation Alexia would feel towards him when his willingness to send her home should be made apparent. She did not count upon or understand the strength of Alexia's unreasonable love for the husband who had beguiled and was willing to abandon her. Lady Judith had not yet come to understand fully what love should reckon for in human calculations.

One day, when she returned from some of her charitable expeditions, she found a visitor awaiting her whom she had hardly expected to see, but whom she welcomed with real cordiality. This was Charles Escombe, just come back from his long tour in America and round the world. The proud forlorn lady's heart warmed and softened toward Alexia's old lover and suitor. He looked healthy and hardy, deeply embrowned by sun and sea, and he wore a huge fair beard.

When they had interchanged friendly greetings, and talked for some time over Escombe's travels and his plans for a career in English politics, he suddenly plunged into another subject, and said, with the manner of one who is determined to have a thing out somehow:

"Oh, by the way, Lady Judith, you know I came home through France—landed at Marseilles, you know."

"Yes, Charles."

"Well, I just ran on to Paris, and coming home I stayed a day or two to see a fellow at the new place they have found out near Trouville, you know—nice little place, too."

"So I am told." Lady Judith now began to guess what was coming, and why Escombe's brown complexion was growing red and he kept his eyes fixed on the carpet.

"Yes, very nice. Well, you know, I heard that Alexia—I mean Mrs. Walraven—was there."

"She is there, I believe. Did you see her?"

"No, I didn't see her. I thought perhaps she mightn't care to; and indeed, Lady Judith, I don't think I felt quite up to the mark; but I saw that fellow—I mean I saw her husband."

"You knew him before?"

"I knew him in a kind of way, as one knows all sorts of fellows. But I'm afraid, Lady Judith, he will prove a downright cad. He's up to his eyes in debt, and he only gambles and hangs around there with a very queer lot; and, by Jove, it's a pity if something can't be done."

"What could be done, Charles? I can't reform the man."

"No; but perhaps, for her sake, you know, if something could be done to set him up in some way, he is the sort of fellow that might get on well enough if he only had anything to live on. You see, Lady Judith, there are plenty of us who only get on decently because we haven't to work hard for our living. I dare say half of us would be no better than he only just for our good luck and having money enough. Now if some place could be found for him, or—or—something done of that kind, and some of his debts paid off, I dare say he would turn out a very good husband, and make her happy. I know you'll excuse me, Lady Judith; I want to see Alexia happy, and I couldn't help just saying this."

Escombe had heard a great deal more than he cared to tell, and Lady Judith guessed as much. He had heard that Walraven was sinking into more and more doubtful companionship, and that poor Alexia's ways were growing more and more eccentric and alarming. He had been approached by Walraven, and had refrained, for her sake, from rebuffing him; and he had freely lent him money, and had come away with sad misgivings for Alexia's future.

"You have a good heart, Charles Escombe; and I have reason to grieve, and you have cause to be glad, that that unhappy and lost girl did not appreciate you as you deserved. But I, at least, don't feel inclined to pay tribute to a swindling adventurer—to reward him because he robbed me of my daughter."

"But, Lady Judith—pray excuse me—something will have to be done. It will indeed. Not for his sake, of course, but for hers. You don't know—you haven't been over there, and don't know what people say; but I do assure you he won't do anything for himself or for her, and you can't leave things to go on much longer as they are going."

Lady Judith thought her cup of shame and misery was pretty nearly full. Her daughter was the wife of an outcast English adventurer, whose poverty, shifts, and swindlings were the scandal even of the very unfastidious society of a French bathing-place!

"Nothing shall be done for him—at least nothing by me or with my consent, Charles," she said decisively; "but I must try to do something to save her, before it is too late!"

The very next day she had occasion to attend a meeting of some charitable society in Exeter Hall; and when the proceedings were over and the crowd was breaking up, Lady Judith, who was accompanied by Charles Escombe (when in town the young man delighted to be her faithful henchman), saw a stout, gray person, who was very shabbily dressed, bustling over toward her. This person carried a thick stick, and wore cotton gloves.

"Beg pardon, Lady Judith," he began to say; "you don't remember me, I suppose. How d'ye do, Mr. Escombe? Glad to see you back again in England."

Charles Escombe, who made it part of the business of his life to know everybody, hastened to anticipate Lady Judith's struggling memory, into which some painful association was beginning to force itself, by presenting Mr. Gostick. Lady Judith bowed coldly.

"No pleasant association with me, ma'am, I dare say," the Lancashire man went on; "don't wonder that you should wish to forget me and mine; but I'd take it as a favor if you would allow me to say six words to you just now."

Lady Judith was somewhat softened by Mr. Gostick's blunt honesty.

"I owe you thanks, Mr. Gostick. You once did your best to serve and help me; you, at least, have nothing with which to reproach yourself. Pray say anything you please; I am wholly at your service."

Charles Escombe fell back a little and talked with two or three of the orators of the evening. The great hall was now studded with little chatting groups of people, waiting for the crowd to get out of the doors.

"Well, Lady Judith," Mr. Gostick began, "it's about this poor little girl and that nephew of mine. I wish I hadn't to talk about such a subject, for of course I know how painful it is; but you see this fellow is always writing to me, and, I dare say, to you——"

"He has written to me several times, but I have not replied to most of his appeals, Mr. Gostick."

"Nor I, Lady Judith—nor I, ma'am. I don't care one straw what becomes of him, now that his poor father and mother are both dead; but then the poor girl, you see! Lady Judith, that fellow is capable of anything—I mean anything shabby and sneaking. I don't think he would have the spirit to commit a burglary or a murder. He left his mother to die—the mother who loved the scamp like the apple of her eye—he left her to die, and never went near her. He'll desert that young woman, ma'am, take my word for it, the moment he finds he can't squeeze anything out of us."

"Us!" Lady Judith was growing to respect the man, but still this conjunction was very trying. "Us!" Lady Judith Scarlett and the Lancashire weaver with the cotton gloves! Gostick said "us" quite fearlessly. Lady Judith and he were the only persons with money in the business, and he knew perfectly well that he had as much money as any aristocratic lady in the land.

"I have no doubt, Mr. Gostick, that your nephew is capable of any baseness [for the life of her she could not help dealing the little stab contained in the words "your nephew"], and I would rescue my daughter if I could——"

"Rescue, ma'am, is rather late, I fear, where we are talking of man and wife" (that was Mr. Gostick's touch in return; the proud lady's daughter was, after all, the wife of Gostick's nephew); "but I was thinking that the first loss is the best, you know, and that it would be better even to support an idle, worthless fellow than to run the risk of bringing misery on an innocent girl. I think of my own daughters, Lady Judith, and I am very uneasy about that poor young woman, though I never set eyes upon her in all my life. Now you know I was thinking that your ladyship—excuse my blunt way of coming to the point—has plenty of money, and I am pretty well to do. Can't we combine to pay this fellow into good behavior? Can't we make him an allowance, conditional entirely upon his living a decent life and taking care of his wife? I worked hard to make my own money, but still I am ready to go pound for pound with your ladyship in some arrangement like that. Fix the allowance at anything you like, I don't care what; I'll pay the half of it, and I'll make all the arrangements—you shan't have a bit of trouble."

The red blood mounted into Lady Judith's face. Good God! had it come to this, that her only daughter was to be supported by subscription from the pocket of a vulgar plebeian! True, that even at the moment her better nature saw how much there was of sterling benevolence and honest manhood about Gostick's proposal. None the less she felt it like an insult and an outrage. Her lips quivered, her limbs trembled, her eyebrows contracted.

"Mr. Gostick," she said coldly, "I don't need any combination or partnership in the support of my daughter. I am obliged to you for your concern on her behalf. It does you credit, and you are naturally grieved for the wrong done by your nephew; but you need not trouble yourself about my daughter. I can take care of her. Good evening."

And she made a stately bow, and, taking Charles Escombe's arm, she turned away and left poor Gostick "*planté là.*"

"What an ass I am!" grumbled that senator. "Serves me quite right! What business was it of mine if the Earl of Coryden's granddaughter hadn't a rag to her back or went into the union workhouse? If ever I interfere again! Well, I've done my part, and my mind is clear, and I'm sorry for the poor young woman; but her mother has let me see plainly enough that it's no business of mine. 'Proffered service stinks,' says the proverb."

"Now, Gostick, what about that committee?" said a great railway contractor, a baronet and member of Parliament, to whom Gostick was of more importance than all the aristocratic dames who ever wore a petticoat; and he hooked his arm in Gostick's and bore him away, talking into his ear as they traversed the hall and descended the stairs. The Lancashire member soon forgot all about Lady Judith's *hauteur*, and even had no pressing recollection for the moment of poor Alexia's possible misery.

As Escombe was handing Lady Judith to her carriage she stopped for a moment and asked him abruptly:

"Do you know, have you heard anything of *her*, of Alexia, Charles, which you have not told me?"

"How do you mean, Lady Judith? I don't quite understand."

"Did you hear anything which made you believe that she herself is unhappy, that her mind seems disturbed?"

"Well, you know of course I didn't take everything I heard for granted. People talk so much in those little places—and then French people think we are all so odd—and Alexia always rather piqued herself on not being like everybody else——"

"But what did you hear? Do pray tell me. Remember I am the girl's mother."

Charles Escombe was too kind-hearted and had too profound a regard for Lady Judith to feel inclined to ask whether she had always remembered the fact herself. Still the question did for the moment embarrass him and make him hesitate, and Lady Judith saw this and hastened to say:

"No one can know how faithfully I tried to do my duty to my daughter, and how utterly ungovernable she proved to be. But she still is my daughter, and if the man to whom she has given herself up is unable to protect her, I must of course try to do so. Tell me, then, what it was that people said of Alexia?"

"Well, they seemed to think that her health was giving way, and that perhaps—but one can't mind such rumors——"

"That perhaps what?"

"That her mind was becoming a little affected. He, that fellow Walraven," Escombe said with a great burst, "he told me as much himself. He made a sort of whining appeal and declared he didn't know what to do; but indeed, Lady Judith, I have discovered the fellow to be such a confounded liar that one can hardly attach any importance to a word coming out of his mouth."

Not a syllable more said Lady Judith on the subject. But a chord had been struck to which all her secret fears, and suspicions, and conscience-prompted doubts gave ready and terrible echo. With her growing emancipation from the imprisonment of mere egotism had been rising the doubt whether in dealing with Alexia lately as a sane and sound and wilfully erring daughter she had not been making a sad mistake. Lady Judith had of late set down her daughter's eccentricity of manner and temper as sheer affectation, and had resented any other suggestion as impertinent and absurd. As a person blessed with powerful vision finds it hard to realize the fact that another person can be short-sighted, as a lover of money can hardly understand that there are other beings indifferent to gain, so Lady Judith's clear, firm, egotistic intellect was skeptical on the subject of lurking insanity in others. One of the many sources of torment to her in her bringing up of Alexia was the conviction that ill-judging lookers-on were constantly pitying the girl and making allowances for her on the score of personal eccentricities and extravagances which she, Lady Judith, secretly believed to be wilful and malignant affectations. But the doubt now began to intrude upon her, ghastly and appalling as a phantom, that perhaps she had utterly misunderstood her daughter and failed in her duty all the time; that while she rashly believed herself to be dealing justly and following Heaven's guidance and approval, she was playing false to nature and perverting the ordinance of Providence itself. Great Heavens! how otherwise could she explain the terrible reality of the fact that everything had gone wrong with her, that the elements themselves seemed to war against her?

Indeed, the poor lady was heavily punished for her pride. She went to her lonely home feeling that she could have welcomed better the more utter solitude of a cavern. Perhaps now for the first time did she begin to feel really deserted. Her pride and her sense of personal righteousness had fled from her at last, even as her husband, her daughter, and her adopted son had done.

Lady Judith had now a companion or reader, a superior sort of young woman from Scotland, who could write most of her letters for her and who had not lived with her in the days of Alexia and Angelo. Lady Judith could not endure anybody in the house who had seen her in one of her former epochs. Therefore, as she had done when her husband disappeared, so she did after the flight of Alexia and the secession of Angelo—made a clean sweep of the household and introduced wholly new faces.

"Shall I read you something, Lady Judith?" said Miss Bruce, when the great lady, looking weary and haggard, entered her study or boudoir—more of study or even oratory than boudoir.

"Do, please, Miss Bruce. That review of Darwin, perhaps, from the 'Quarterly.'"

Lady Judith leaned forward in her chair, her elbow resting on her knee, her hand supporting her chin. Her lips were compressed, her eyebrows contracted. She must have been deeply absorbed in Darwinian theories, for she never stirred or looked up, her dress never rustled, her brow never relaxed as Miss Bruce read on and on. Miss Bruce, however, was not without her own share of keenness and observation, and while immensely admiring Lady Judith's beauty and dignity, and greatly envying her wealth, she had begun to think that there was something heavy at the lady's heart, more difficult perhaps than even poverty to bear. Miss Bruce suspected that Lady Judith was not listening to a word of the article on Darwin. She ventured upon an audacious experiment. She read one sentence twice over, then thrice over; it was all the same to Lady Judith.

At last a deep sigh broke from the heart and the lips of the lady, and seemed to recall her to herself. She started, looked up, faintly smiled, and said:

"I think, Miss Bruce, I shall not trouble you to read any more to-night. Or stay, perhaps you will kindly read me a few verses from the Bible."

"The Old Testament, madam?"

"The Old Testament, yes. Anywhere will do. Just where you chance to open it."

Was Lady Judith trying for a word of supernatural guidance and oracle? Or did she hope to hear some lesson of stern strength from the voice of the Old Dispensation bidding her not to be ashamed and tremble even though she had hated those who sinned against her?

Miss Bruce opened and read:

"And Jephthah came to Mizpeh unto his house: and, behold, his daughter came out to meet him with timbrels and with dances, and she was his only child; beside her he had neither son nor daughter."

"No, not that, Miss Bruce, not that. Some other passage if you please."

Miss Bruce turned some pages on, and quietly glancing under her eyes at her listener began again:

"And it was told Joab, Behold, the king weepeth and mourneth for Absalom. And the victory that day was turned into mourning unto all the people; for the people heard say that day how the king was grieved for his son. And the people gat them by stealth that day into the city, as people being ashamed steal away when they flee in battle. But the king covered his face, and the king cried with a loud voice, O my son Absalom, O Absalom, my son, my son!"

Lady Judith rose from her seat with a flush upon her ordinarily pale face. There was a little round table near her elbow, and her sudden movement caused it to fall with a crash.

"Shall I read on?" Miss Bruce asked timidly.

"Thank you; no more now. I will not detain you longer, Miss Bruce. Perhaps, as you are going toward your room, you may see my maid Elise."

"Yes, Lady Judith. Shall I send her to you?"

"Tell her, please, that I don't want her to-night. Let her be sure not to come. Good night, Miss Bruce."

Miss Bruce returned a gentle good-night and left Lady Judith alone.

How long Lady Judith remained that night seated in her chair with her chin resting on her hand, she herself could never have told. Hours and hours after Miss Bruce, who had been writing letters in her own room, stole quietly down stairs and saw that the light was still streaming from under the door of Lady Judith's chamber. Miss Bruce went to bed, but Judith Scarlett still remained sitting and thinking. Doubtless it was owing to the excited condition of her mind, the painful tension of her nerves, the lateness and loneliness of the hour, that she found her senses serve her less faithfully this once than was their wont. For as she sat alone she seemed to hear a wild shrill scream ring through the silent house, and it was as the voice of her daughter, and Lady Judith started from her chair and called aloud "Alexia, Alexia!" and sprang to the door. All was dark and silent without. Lady Judith stood and listened with beating heart. At last she quietly closed the door and returned to her place. She flung herself on her knees and pressed her forehead against her hands.

"It was only the voice of my own heart, of my grief, of my conscience!" murmured the unhappy woman. "I will go to my daughter and save her if I can."

And for the first time in this story Lady Judith burst into a passion of unrestrained tears.

CHAPTER XXV

"HABET!"

ALEXIA, it has already been remarked, was a rather weary companion for Isolind. The unhappy daughter of Lady Judith had always in life had her horizon limited to just the extent of her own personal experiences and vexations. Now that her vexations had expanded into genuine sufferings, they absorbed her wholly, and Isolind heard nothing from her but the sad tale of her mother's coldness and her husband's lack of love. Every day seemed to make Alexia wilder and more morbid, and Isolind began to grow gravely alarmed for her mental condition. She spoke to Mrs. Atheling on the subject, but Mrs. Atheling had never much liked Alexia. The good old lady was always a little afraid of the petulant, sharp tongue of the little English aristocrat. She could never understand Alexia, and always while the latter was present lived in doubt and dread, not knowing what the girl might say next—what piece of impertinence or impiety might escape from her ungoverned lips. Besides, Mrs. Atheling shrank from young women who didn't honor and obey their mothers. Therefore she gave no sympathetic response to Isolind's alarms, and only guessed that Mrs. Walraven could be sane enough if she wanted to, and that if she had any insane tendencies it was only the lunacy of pride and insolence.

Isolind was not satisfied, and only racked her brain to find out whether there was anything she could do. To write to Lady Judith or any of her family would have been for her simply impossible. Was there then no one to whom she could urge her growing conviction that Alexia's mind was giving way under the pressure of her loneliness and her disappointment, and that those who loved the poor girl—if there were yet any such—had better look to her in time lest worse befall?

Thus thinking, Isolind set out alone, on the evening when Walraven made his revelation to his wife, to visit Alexia. Our Anglo-American girl was in the habit of rambling alone, accoutred in high boots and with kilted skirts, through the French village, to the wonder and dismay of all respectable French matrons and maids, in whose minds such solitary promenading by an unmarried woman bespoke a worse than heathenish license. The sun was setting over the sea as Isolind drew near the hotel, and with her ever-present delight in sky and waves and sunset, she paused to enjoy the beauty of the scene and the hour, and to her, as to most of us, something of her own life and love and suffering seemed shining sadly out of the waters and steeped in the fading sunlight. So she became for the moment almost unconscious of where she was, and a gentleman approached and nearly jostled against her, and made a lowly bow and an apology. It was Eric Walraven, who had just left his wife, and in a moment it flashed into Isolind's mind that at whatever risk of misconstruction or of seeming officiousness she must tell him her fears for Alexia.

"I am going to call on Mrs. Walraven," said Isolind.

"She will be delighted; she adores you, but that is not strange. Allow me to return with you."

"Pray no, thank you. I can go alone. I am not at all afraid of walking without escort. But—but—Mr. Walraven."

"My dear Miss Atheling?"

"May I say a word to you without seeming officious or bold?"

"How can you ask? As if any word from *you* could be anything but a favor. Pray honor me by taking my arm and let me walk with you."

"No, Mr. Walraven, there is no need. What I wish to say will be soon said, and perhaps I am wrong in saying it, but I feel as if I could not help it. Mr. Walraven, Alexia is very unhappy, and I sometimes think that if great care be not taken, and in time, her mind will give way. Do, pray, forgive me for obtruding my opinions—perhaps I am wrong altogether—but her manner alarms me sometimes."

"Alexia then has been complaining of me?" said Eric with darkling brow. "She has been pouring out to you some story of imaginary wrongs and sufferings?"

"Not imaginary sufferings at least, Mr. Walraven. Oh, no! The sufferings are all real! I only fear for the constant strain upon her mind. Perhaps those who are nearest to her—and who—who love her best," said Isolind with a great effort, "are naturally the last to observe the changes which the eye of a stranger sees. But, Mr. Walraven, oh do take care of her, and be kind to her! Remember that she has lost her mother, and that she has no one but you."

"Alexia is rather fond of exhibiting herself *en victime*," Walraven coolly replied. "She comes of an eccentric family; you have heard the strange mysterious story of her father? But she is shrewd and sensible when she pleases; and, my dear Miss Isolind, I should be sorry indeed for my own sake, that you took all her capricious utterances as literal and sound. I beg you will do me justice. I am no monster of cruelty, but the very kind, indulgent husband of a pretty little freakish child-wife, who does not know her own mind for an hour together."

"You mistake my purpose," Isolind said coldly. "I was not implying anything against you, Mr. Walraven—I was not even thinking of you—I was thinking only of *her*."

"And I am deeply indebted to you for the kindness. But there is no danger. Strangers often, indeed always, are alarmed by dear Alexia's capricious ways and exaggerated words. *I* understand them; it is my duty to bear with them. I hope—I trust—I am not a bad husband. If there are moments when one looks into other faces and other intellects and thinks of what might have been, and remembers what *is* and sighs at the contrast, *you*, Miss Atheling, will surely not regard an involuntary and uncontrollable emotion as a crime?"

"I know nothing of all that; I have no opinion to give. Once more, Mr. Walraven, I am concerned solely for Alexia."

"You are cruel," the poet replied, and he gently touched her hand, which she quickly drew away. "You are cruel, Isolind! You know that to me the combination of intellect and beauty in woman is the one exquisite, divine ideal I have always sighed for; you have seen how I master and keep down my feelings; and yet you treat me like a criminal! Have I not always borne myself to you with the profoundest respect?"

"You would hardly venture to bear yourself otherwise, Mr. Walraven," Isolind quietly said. "I suppose an English gentleman of education would not knowingly hurt or insult an unprotected girl. I expect of course that much from you, and therefore pray let us not say any more about our own miserable little personalities. I knew I ran some risk of misconstruction when I ventured to obtrude my advice; but I couldn't help it. I felt as if I must speak, and perhaps I have no right to complain of a freedom of speech which I myself provoked. I was brought up, Mr. Walraven, in a country where even unmarried women claim the right to speak and act like free human creatures, and where men acknowledge the right and respect it. No American gentleman would have mistaken my purpose or taken unfair advantage of my impulsive interference."

"You are angry, Isolind," he said, and he gently interposed to prevent her from passing on; "you are angry, and you are consequently unjust. Am I to blame if I admire youth and beauty and genius—if I, a poet, cannot be blind to the gifts and the graces of a Corinna?"

"Pray, Mr. Walraven, forbear compliments that only offend me, and make you seem ridiculous. Life is very serious and sad to me just now" (there were tears which she could not restrain shining in her eyes), "and I have no heart or ear for folly. Mr. Walraven, I trust that you too may not find life serious and sad."

Then she went firmly on; and Walraven, after a moment's hesitation, pursued his way. The poet felt a little vexed with himself and a great deal vexed with Alexia, for he was convinced that the latter had been complaining of him to Isolind and telling tales out of school. So he quietly resolved that Alexia must be made to shed some tears by way of punishment. He was quite proud of being able to make Alexia cry, and he proposed that this very night perhaps he should enjoy his power. Isolind had humbled him; but he did not much mind that. It was rather interesting to hint love to the girl. He always enjoyed hinting at love to women when no better pastime could be had; and he reflected with a certain almost sensuous complacency that words had passed between Isolind and himself which are not commonly interchanged in the beaten way of friendship and society between man and woman. He was both piqued and interested by Isolind; but he felt toward her no emotion deep or strong enough to have prevented him from making love to half a dozen other women on the same evening had they come in his way.

He went on then, annoyed with Alexia, but on the whole in hopeful and brightening mood. He began to see once more that the crescent promise of his spirit had not set; that life and woman had yet charms for him; and he hoped soon to be free. He was incapable of any deep emotion, good or bad, and even the ruin of all his schemes and hopes failed to sink him down. He had just the levity and the buoyancy of a cork.

Meanwhile, Isolind went on to the hotel and had her walk for nothing. To her utter surprise, Alexia, who had haunted her unceasingly for days, refused now to see her. Mrs. Walraven had a bad headache, Isolind was told, and could not see any one. So Isolind returned home, not offended or even vexed, but very much surprised.

Alexia had no headache, but she would not see Isolind. She had made a resolve which she would not expose to the risk of a moment's contact with any healthy and vigorous mind and heart. She feared that if she spoke with Isolind the resolve might give way, and it was a resolve now dear beyond words to her sick sad soul.

The moment Eric revealed his whole real nature to her, Alexia felt that life's purpose and meaning were over for her, and she resolved to die. She sentenced herself to death. She could not think coherently over the past; she could only remember in her wild way that Eric had been her only hope and her only love, that she had given up all for him, staked all on him, and that now she was nothing more to him, that she had lost everything. In her fretful and freakish hours the thought of suicide had been familiar to her. For years she had only reconciled herself to the endurance of life by complacently remembering that she could finish it whenever she pleased. The circumstances of her birth and early training, as well as her physical and mental condition, had rendered her utterly impervious to any sense of religious obligation. Religion had always seemed to her only as a weapon of oppression and torment wielded by cold, hard mothers to punish and subdue children. Alexia's own will, her fears and her angers, had always been a law unto her. Love might have been a better law, if Heaven had but allowed it. Love, however, now seemed her bitterest foe and her worst betrayer.

She therefore doomed herself to death. She thought with a fierce delight that when she lay dead on her bed, killed by her own hand, even her mother's heart would feel a pang of agony. She smiled bitterly at the thought of the scandal and shock it would spread among the precise and stately Corydens; and she exulted in anticipation over the trick she was about to play them. Perhaps when *he*—when Eric—came and looked upon her cold, dead body, he might be sorry for her, and might wish he had loved her—might perhaps then love her once more.

She went to her dressing-case and found her little dagger, the treasured relic of the Paris Exposition, and she gloated over its glittering blade and felt its sharp point. She delighted to touch it to her flesh and feel how sharp it was, and she loosed her dress and found out where her heart was beating and put the dagger's point there; and revelled in the thought that one strong thrust would finish all. Ah, what a goodly vengeance upon her enemies! how thrilling a rebuke to Eric, whom she so loved! Yes, that would bring back his love! He would come and look upon her corpse, and he would take it in his arms, and he would be sorry and reproach himself and shed tears because he had not loved her always. Would not death be sweet to purchase that atonement? Love and revenge won by one thrust of an inch of steel—love and revenge and sleep! Her poor, passionate, disordered heart revelled in the prospect of speedy death, as a voluptuary revels in the anticipation of a festival.

There she sat with the dagger pressed against the side beneath which beat her heart—that wild, sad heart which had throbbed with so many fierce emotions, and into which love had only come at last, not to redeem, but to destroy. Ah, what sudden spites, and hates, and fitful fierce desires had kept that poor little heart in fever-throbs, and now was all going to be still at last? Hardly more than a child in years, and already more than an orphan, and worse than a widow! Where is the father who should have guarded her, the mother who should have loved her? Oh, if they two, whose ill-assorted union and whose selfish quarrels and rancors had left her thus desolate, left her thus a prey to fate and her own disordered passion—if they could but have seen and known, would they not have recognized that Heaven had punished their wrong-doing with unrelenting hand? Is not the time soon to come when they shall know it—too late?

The evening shadows deepened, and the murmur of the sea seemed to grow louder as the twilight grew more gray. Slowly over the water rose at last a mild moon. Hardly, it might be thought, could Passion or even Despair have looked upon the calm, pure beauty of that scene, and not felt something of its soothing spirit, and turned toward some memory of innocence and some hope in God. But the murmur of the sea, the unspeakable beauty of the scene and the hour, pleaded vainly, pleaded unheard to the ears, the eyes, the soul of Eric Walraven's wretched wife. Alexia said truly when she declared that the face of Nature had never had any charm for her. She never learned its lesson. It never won her for one moment from herself. Now, in her hour of supreme despair, there was no sea or sky or star for her. She was blinded and maddened; all around was but blood and fire.

Yet there was a certain fierce and practical composure about her. When the evening grew dark she lighted her lamp and began to write letters to Eric and to her mother, which she tore up as fast as they were written. At last she renounced the idea of writing to either of them, but determined to leave a letter for Isolind. Having less emotion in this piece of work, she succeeded easily enough. She wrote, sealed, and addressed a letter to "Miss Isolind Atheling," and placed it on her dressing-table, hidden away under various articles so that it could hardly be found unless when actual search was made. For some reason—she could hardly tell what—she would not have her death discovered before the morning. When night had come and partly gone, when all were hushed in sleep, then she would do the deed; and when Eric awoke in the morning he would see a dead wife lying by his side. She would undress soon now, and would be in bed and apparently asleep when Eric came in, and then when he fell asleep she would kiss him for the last time—and then! Ah God, it may be that in the mind of the wretched girl there yet lingered some faint sad ghost of a hope that when Eric came back he might be kind and loving to her, and unsay some of his hard, cruel words, and the sky might fall and the old love and life return. It may be that one word of love could yet have saved and redeemed that heart and brain, and left the world richer by the prevention of one deed of blood.

Night had come, and no sounds were heard but the occasional cry of a fisher in his boat, the rare tramp of a horse or tread of a human foot. The moon grew brighter and brighter. Alexia undressed; she now had no maid to help her. She folded and arranged her clothes with a very unusual care, thinking that the trouble was not much, and that she should never have to do it again, and that she should like to have things look neat in the morning. She started, hearing a voice in the room; and then she found it was her own voice, and that she had been talking aloud. She started once again, seeing the room, as she thought, filled with flame; but there was no flame. The fire had flashed from her own bewildered brain and throbbing eyeballs.

Being undressed, she crept into bed, and kept her dagger, her last treasure and anodyne, in her hand, pressed to her bare bosom, as Cleopatra might have held her asp. A sound on the stairs, on the threshold, and she started so that the dagger grazed sharply against her skin, and Eric entered the room. She turned toward him with eager, sparkling eyes. He never looked at her or near her, and she turned away, closed her eyes, and feigned to sleep.

Eric took up a book and began to read. He was rather displeased that his wife was not awake and up to receive him; for although he always told her not to wait for him but to go to bed, he wanted this particular night to have scolded her for her complaining of him to Isolind. Otherwise he was in a rather good humor with everything, except Alexia. He had won a few napoleons at play; and he was in good hope to be soon again a free man.

He read and read on into the night, and Alexia watched his shadow as it fell upon the wall near her bed. She watched with straining eyes that seemed to burn in their sockets, and she listened with ears wherein the crash of a thousand cataracts seemed to be thundering. Strange wild forms and faces appeared every now and then to crowd around her and gesticulate and gibber at her. She longed to scream aloud, and often was on the point of relieving her tortured heart by a wild cry; but the mastering pride of her fierce resolution restrained her and upheld her, and the minutes or hours, she little knew which they were, went inexorably on.

At last Eric put away his book and looked at his watch and wound it, and yawned. Then he undressed himself slowly and lazily, and extinguished the lamp and went into bed. He did not even glance at his wife, and he stretched himself as far away from her as he conveniently could. People who are not good never get any sound sleep in romances and dramas, but in common real life they habitually sleep rather more soundly than the virtuous, who are apt to torment themselves about their own supposed defects and their neighbors' trials and sufferings. Neither subject ever gave Eric Walraven any concern, and he soon sank into a sleep as peaceful and sweet as that of infancy.

Then Alexia raised herself on her elbow. Now her time had come. Farewell to the troubled dream, the fever, the delirium which had been life to her. Farewell to Eric, her one love. She could not but gaze at him as he lay sleeping and the silver moonlight fell upon his face. Ah, how handsome he looked! Like a sleeping god, Alexia thought. How beautiful his dark curls as they lay upon his pillow. How beautiful the mouth, which had something of the helpless appealing look of childhood about it, with its parted lips and the lower jaw slightly dropped. How noble and glorious he had always seemed to her, and how kind and loving and chivalrous he used to be. Into the gloomy, phantom-haunted atmosphere of her life he had flashed all beauty, brightness, and strength, like another Perseus, to deliver a poor little Andromeda from bondage and pain. She bent over him thinking of all this. What a picture it was, the pale, wild, dark-eyed girl, with her long black hair floating over her white garment, and the dagger glittering in her hand, and the man sleeping unconsciously under her eyes, and the pure moonlight flooding the silent room.

"Oh Eric, my Eric!" the girl at last exclaimed with a plaintive cry, "good-by, good-by!"

She bent over him and pressed on his lips one last passionate kiss, and she raised the dagger that she might die upon the kiss.

But the sleeper, half disturbed by the cry and the kiss, turned angrily away, and consciously or unconsciously thrust her from him with the arm which had been lying outside the clothes—thrust her from him with such vehemence and such suddenness that it seemed like a blow on the girl's unprotected breast. Then a shrill scream of passion, of something more than passion, burst from Alexia's lips, and her cherished purpose was gone, had vanished, was swallowed up and drowned in a flood of new, resistless fury; and she remembered no more who she was or what arm had thrust her aside, and her dagger descended sharp and fierce into the white throat of the sleeper. Once he opened his eyes and gazed into hers, and gave a cry of terror and horror and tried to rise, and once more the dagger came down; and with a sob and a gurgle Walraven succumbed to his fate, and the poet who sang the "Mystery of the Universe" had solved its greatest mystery at last.

All of Alexia's purpose was gone. The stroke which had extinguished her husband's life seemed to have extinguished the last gleams of her flickering reason. Only a dead man and a mad woman were in that ghastly chamber.

Alexia appeared to have caught up some kind of notion of flight and escape from danger. She opened the window, which was quite a low one within a few inches of the ground, and, half clad as she was, sprang into the moonlight, and ran across the grass plot surrounding the hotel and out through the gate, and sped along the road that wound by the verge of the cliffs. Not a cry or sound of any kind escaped her.

That night Isolind Atheling lay long awake. There was a kind of fighting in her heart, as in Hamlet's, which would not let her sleep. She thought of her own sad life, of the shame which had fallen so heavily on her, of the love she had renounced, of Angelo, and in all her own sorrows she thought too of Alexia's unhappy fate and the danger which seemed to threaten her. The brightness of the moon, the murmur of the waves, were tempting to the heart of the young poetess, and she arose and wrapped a shawl around her and stood at the window and fed her soul for a while on the old, the immemorial thought of all lovers, that the eyes of the loved one are now perhaps fixed like mine on that moon. With that thought arose the proud, consoling reflection that at least she was loved; that were she never to see Angelo more, yet she held his love in her heart and had the privilege of always loving him. Thinking of this, she thought of poor Alexia, whose fate was so much harder, and her heart was pierced with a pang of pity.

Was it her thought which had so filled her as to call up a mind-created phantom before her? Surely that was the figure of a girl all in white and with streaming black hair—a figure like the ghost of Alexia, which appeared on the road in front of the cottage! For a moment a shudder ran through Isolind's frame; the imaginative nature never can purge itself wholly of the sudden recognition of the supernatural. But the form had disappeared. No, behold it comes again, emerges from behind the shrubs that grow in front of the cottage. It comes wandering, or flickering, vaguely, like a very ghost, on the scrap of lawn or turf under the cottage windows. It *is* a girl in a night-dress; some somnambulist perhaps. And then it looks up, with such eyes! at the windows, and Isolind sees that it is indeed Alexia, and all her old misgivings and fears rush in upon her with terrible confirmation. Not a moment to be lost; the white wanderer is already turning away. Isolind waits to give no alarm, but hurries down stairs, gently opens the door, with swift steps pursues the fugitive, and throws her arms round Alexia.

"Alexia, dear Alexia, don't you know me? I am Isolind. Come with me."

For the first glance has told her that it is no case of somnambulism, that such sense as is left to the wretched girl is not locked in sleep.

Alexia looks at her with purposeless, affrighted, unanswering gaze; and struggles a little and tries to escape, but utters no word or sound.

Isolind was strong, active, and resolute. She lifts Alexia in her arms as if she had been a child, and carries her into the cottage. Alexia struggles no more, but allows her head to rest on the shoulder of her bearer as a tired infant might do. Isolind carries her into her own room, and lays her in her own bed, and covers her carefully and closely; so closely that the covering forms a kind of bondage to check any sudden attempt at escape. But Alexia makes no attempt; she lies motionless and stares at Isolind and round the room with wide-open, vacant, wild eyes, and with a little quiver and tremble round her mouth as if cries or tears were coming, which, however, came not. Then Isolind, having made fast the window and pulled down the blinds, lights her lamp, and partly shading it with her hand draws near the girl in the bed; and it requires all her self-control to repress a shriek when she sees for the first time that Alexia's night-dress and her own are spattered and stained with blood.

CHAPTER XXVI.

ALEXIA RECOGNIZES HER MOTHER.

WAS there ever a night that seemed so long to human watcher as the night when she sheltered Alexia seemed to Isolind? It was late, very late, when Isolind brought in her arms her unhappy friend and laid her in her bed; the dawn came soon, and yet how terrible a time it seemed! Isolind did not see any use in giving a wild alarm, in awakening Mrs. Atheling or the woman who owned the cottage, or either of the two servants. It seemed to her that the best thing to do for Alexia would probably be to give her a few hours of perfect quiet, if possible to induce her to sleep. So she dressed herself and then sat like a nurse by Alexia's side, and endeavored gently to soothe and compose her, as one deals with a convulsive child. She had no suspicion whatever of all the terrible truth. She assumed that that had happened which she had been lately dreading, that Alexia's reason had suddenly broken down, and that in Eric Walraven's absence the girl had escaped from her home. On Alexia's arms and hands she found some scratches and wounds, evidently caused by her having fallen somewhere among the cliffs as she came along; and this fact seemed enough to account for the blood-stains on the night-dress. So she made no alarm, but quietly sat by her patient, bathed her temples, hands, and wrists in water, gave her some water to drink, which Alexia swallowed mechanically—oh, how Isolind longed for some of the plenteous, ever-abundant ice-water of New York!—and tried to induce her to sleep.

Alexia spoke no word. In her eyes gleamed no sign of recognition. The black orbs now dilated, now shrank, the form sometimes cowered and contracted, the lips sometimes quivered as if a scream were about to come, but no sound came forth. Sometimes a fit of violent shuddering and shivering came over the girl, and then her face and form were cold as marble, and when Isolind held her in her arms she seemed to cling to the warmth thus given. Again a sudden heat came over her, and perspiration stood upon her white forehead and neck; and Isolind drew the bed-clothes partly down, and fanned and cooled the poor creature; and Alexia seemed to feel the soothing and refreshing influence. But there was no sensation indicated other than one of the lower animals might have felt. No ray of responding intelligence shone in the gleaming, glaring eyes; and the tremulous lips trembled all in vain.

Meanwhile the dawn came, and Isolind extinguished her lamp. The first beams of the sun—Isolind once used to call them "the sun-dogs," a phrase familiar to American children—glittered over the sea, and the orange and purple splendor of the sunrise shone on the eastern waves. The household would soon begin to be astir. Already there were tramplings and clatterings of wooden shoes heard on the road and among the stones of the beach; and the bathing-carts would soon begin to be in demand, and the horses to be harnessed which were to drag the modern Tritons and Nereids out to meet the welcome of the advancing waves. People rose very early in this little place, and the shrill voice of Madame the owner of the house was usually heard with first cock-crow, as the lady scolded and urged her two serving-women. Isolind did not venture to leave Alexia for a moment, and yet she was very reluctant to summon either of the servants and prematurely, perhaps needlessly, expose to common gossip a calamity which might yet possibly be healed, or at least kept from public observation. She took it for granted that before morning had far advanced Eric Walraven would come to seek his wife—Eric Walraven, who was now lying a hideous spectacle in the purple rays of the rising sun, with the blood clotted all over his neck and shoulders, and glueing to the pillows the beautiful black curls of which the child he married used to be so fond and so proud.

Sometimes Alexia made a sudden effort to rise from the bed as if to escape. Once when Isolind, hearing a step on the lobby outside, went to the door hoping to see Mrs. Atheling, poor Alexia sprang out of bed and crossed the floor, and Isolind only caught her when she had reached the window. But these attempts seemed only vague impulses springing feebly from some passing memory or association, and in no way belonging to the fixed and cunning purpose which is so common an accompaniment of madness. For when Isolind gently laid her in bed again she made no resistance, but rather seemed each time to welcome the recovered warmth and shelter. Yet even these feeble attempts at escape made Isolind less and less willing to leave her for a moment.

At last, after a delay which seemed to Isolind long and fearful enough to have turned her hair gray, she heard Mrs. Atheling's footstep outside and she gently called to her. Then she seated herself on the bed so as completely to hide poor Alexia, in order that she might gain time to prepare Mrs. Atheling and prevent any outburst of alarm. Mrs. Atheling bustled into the room, and came over with a dash of uneasiness in her face to kiss Isolind.

"Why, Isolind, my love, I'm afraid you're sick; kiss me good-morning. What is the matter with you?"

"Dear mamma, will you please be very calm, and don't be alarmed in the least, and above all don't make any noise. Poor Alexia is here, in my bed, and I'm afraid—I'm afraid her senses are quite gone."

Then she gently withdrew, and allowed Mrs. Atheling to see the poor girl in the bed. She was afraid of the effect upon Alexia of a new figure at her bedside. But it was a lost fear. There might have been two or twenty. No new expression came into Alexia's eyes; her lips quivered as idly and vainly as before.

Then Mrs. Atheling, thus prepared, and being really a capital nurse and charged with all manner of healing devices and expedients, proved herself a wonderfully humane, tender, and useful auxiliary to Isolind. The two women agreed that the thing must, if possible, be kept quiet until Mr. Walraven should come to look for his wife, which he was certain to do whenever he missed her.

Leaving Mrs. Atheling in charge of the patient, Isolind presently went down stairs to get at and prepare some soothing medicines which the old lady regarded as of ineffable value. She heard the voices of Madame, of the two servants, and of some man, all in a chorus of wonder, pity, and horror, over some news apparently brought by the man who stood at the open door.

"O mon Dieu!" "O Grand Dieu." "Quelle tragédie!" "Comment, le mari de cette petite dame Anglaise?" "Mais, c'est affreux!" "Comme il était grand et beau avec ses cheveux noirs!" "Assassiné—dans son lit—la nuit passée?" "Par des assassins, des voleurs, dit-on?" "Eh mon Dieu, je n'en sais rien." "Et sa femme, est-ce qu'elle aussi est tuée?"

And so on, through exclamations, inquiries, and replies which made Isolind's blood run cold, and her knees tremble beneath her. Good heavens, what new calamity was this? Was it indeed of Eric Walraven that she heard them talk? Could it be that he had really been murdered by some enemy in the night, and that the sight had driven Alexia mad?

Isolind constrained herself into composure of manner, and joining the group she asked what the terrible story might be. Her fears were only too soon confirmed. The tall and handsome English gentleman with the pretty little dark-haired English wife had been found murdered in his bed at the Hôtel Impérial—murdered with several wounds and with a dagger left in his heart! No one could conjecture how it had been done. No one knew what had become of the lady his wife. Perhaps she had been murdered and her body hidden somewhere, perhaps the assassins had carried her off; who knows?

"But assassins, brigands, ravishers in Villefleurs, and in the Hôtel Impérial, and this the nineteenth century!" said the hostess, shrugging her shoulders.

"Eh! but was there not the affair Dumollard the other day—more strange by far?" urged the man who had brought the news, "and then those English quarrel among themselves, and have such strange, droll ways of revenge."

"The little English lady was very beautiful; perhaps there was some discarded lover who cherished vengeance against the husband," suggested one of the two women."

"Perhaps a lover not discarded, the man began; but madame frowned him down, and said in an undertone, "*Taisez vous donc!* The lady is of the friends most intimate of mademoiselle."

"That which is certain then," the man replied with the air of one who consents to close an unwelcome discussion, "is that monsieur lies dead yonder, murdered in his bed with a poniard in his heart, and that the little madame has not been found anywhere."

Isolind had heard quite enough. Her limbs shivered, her head throbbed, she could scarcely stand or walk. Wild and frightful conjectures now at last began to force themselves upon her. Even without time to consider the terrible business coolly, it yet seemed impossible to believe that either mercenary assassins or personal enemies could have slain Walraven during the night in a crowded hotel, and no one have seen or known anything of their purpose or existence. Walraven had always seemed to her a creature too mean and miserable to have any relentless melodramatic enemies. But Alexia in utter madness, Alexia's night-dress stained with blood—did not all this point to a solution of the mystery far more awful to conceive than any that the curiosity or morbid conjecture of the gossiping talkers at the door had yet suggested?

Isolind made up her mind that, leaving Alexia to Mrs. Atheling's care, she would fly in the face of all French decorum by going over alone to the Hôtel Impérial, and finding out for herself all that could yet be known. She resolved that she would not hint any of her dreadful suspicions to Mrs. Atheling unless something should come to make them more than suspicions. She hurried up stairs, and merely told the old lady that she thought she must go over to the hotel and ask for Mr. Walraven.. Alexia lay still and open-eyed as before, and Isolind knew that Mrs. Atheling could take good care of her.

So she put on a hat and shawl and went on her dismal walk. As she was in the habit of going out before breakfast most mornings, no one in the house felt any surprise now.

But she had not gone a dozen paces from the door when she saw a little chambermaid from the Hôtel Impérial, whom she well knew as the usual attendant at Alexia's apartment, come hurriedly and out of breath toward her. The girl hardly waited to answer Isolind's question as to the truth of the story about Walraven's death, but pulled hastily from her bosom a letter which she thrust into Isolind's hand. She was the first who entered the room, the girl said, and she found a letter there addressed to Isolind which—which she thought mademoiselle would like to have, would think it well to have, before justice should proceed to inform itself of why monsieur had slain himself. The girl eyed Isolind with intense curiosity and interest. Isolind took the letter—she knew Alexia's hand—with eager and trembling fingers. She thanked the girl cordially, gave her a few francs out of her very slender purse, and hurried back toward the cottage. Isolind will never to her dying day have the faintest suspicion of the conjecture formed by that French girl as to the reason of monsieur's "suicide," and the purport of the letter found on his dressing-table and addressed to the belle Américaine, the friend of the little dark-haired dame Anglaise, his wife.

Isolind did not wait to get home before opening and reading the letter. She turned down a little rocky path, or rather cleft in the cliffs and rocks leading to the strand, and there, where no eye could see her emotion, she read poor Alexia's words of farewell.

WEDNESDAY EVENING.

MY DEAR ISOLIND: I suppose I ought to begin this in the regular style of a heroine of romance, and say: Before these lines touch your hand the writer will be no more. Seriously—and indeed, my dear, things look very serious with me now—I have made up my mind to die. *You know why!* I am of no value to any one; I have no motive in living. I always hated life until lately, for a short happy time, and now I hate it more than ever. Please don't be too much shocked and horrified. I am going to kill myself to-night, late, when I have seen Eric for the last time. Of course he shall know nothing about it until he wakes in the morning and finds that his unhappy distracted wife is dead. Perhaps he can make a poem out of it; I shouldn't wonder! O God, how I loved him!

Tell Lady Judith, if ever you should see her again, that she needn't distress herself too much about my eternal salvation. I dare say I shall come out all right; I don't feel at all afraid. I don't believe God is half as bad as some people make him out.

Some time, Isolind, you will be happy and will marry Angelo Volney. Tell him I always loved him dearly, and that I think him a youth favored of the gods—first because he marries you, and next because he escaped me.

Is it not strange, I feel in quite a wild, excited, half-delighted condition at such a time, not at all like one sentenced to death? I feel as if I had been taking opium or hasheesh, or the greenish stuff they drink in Paris. Because I have been so sick of life and I long for rest. Didn't some philosopher or poet or somebody say life was only a disease of the soul? Ah, God, how some of us have felt the truth of that!

Perhaps I shall meet my father! Good-by, Isolind. Think sometimes of the friend you have lost!

Don't blame *him* too much. It is not his fault! ALEXIA.

Isolind's tears fell thick and fast as she read and re-read these lines, seemingly the last farewell of the writer's extinguishing reason. She could sometimes scarcely read the pages for the tears that blotted them, could hardly hold the letter in her trembling fingers. The characteristic style, full to the last of petulance and audacity, covering still a heart that might have been full of love and rich in the power of giving happiness—the style, so reckless, bold, and cynical—added new and unspeakable pathos to the sadness of the whole tragedy. But the letter, with all its audacious frankness, threw hardly any light on the subsequent events. One passage only, that in which Alexia spoke of waiting to see Eric once more, served in any way to help Isolind to guess at the reality. Alexia had waited to see him once more, had perhaps wholly lost her reason in the mean time, or had perhaps been driven wild by some slight or harshness on his part. This seemed the only possible explanation, as we now know it was in substance the true one. But, however it had come to pass, Isolind now felt not the slightest doubt that from the hand of Alexia Walraven came the death-blow to her husband.

Even at that moment Isolind could hardly spare one gleam of pity for the dead man. That he, that any creature, had been so suddenly slain and by such a hand, was a thing appalling to contemplate; but Isolind's pity went wholly to Alexia. In this case the victim seemed indeed the evil-doer, the slayer the object of compassion and sympathy. From the first hour when she saw him, Iso lind had felt an unaccountable dislike and contempt for Eric Walraven. She had read the man's shallow nature like a book. Pure and womanly as was her own noble heart, yet she had enough of dramatic perception to see into the feeble viciousness of his character, combining as it did the meanest cunning of a low woman with the most selfish passions of the basest man. Her thoughts were now therefore all for Alexia; how to save her, if it might be, from exposure; how, perhaps, even to save her from the knowledge of what she had done, should reason one day return to her distracted and tempest-tossed mind.

It seemed to Isolind that the two things now to be hoped for and aimed at were, that Eric Walraven should be supposed to have died by suicide, and that Alexia's madness should be regarded as the result of the shock produced upon her by the sight of his dead body. Oh, how she longed for Judge Atheling to be near! The counsel and the active assistance of a tyrant man like him, to whom everything could be trusted, would have been of inestimable value. Isolind came mournfully to the conclusion that she had better not make a *confidante* of good Mrs. Atheling, whose discretion and skill were to be implicitly trusted in ministering to an ordinary patient, in preparing a soothing draught, smoothing a pillow, or changing a garment; but whose courage and discretion might perhaps give way before the utterly unexpected difficulty of having to care for an insane woman who had killed her husband.

Meanwhile, it was certain that the fact of Alexia's being in Isolind's room could not much longer be concealed. Isolind therefore at once made a virtue of necessity, and returning home took the madame into her confidence and told her that the young English lady, evidently driven mad by the sight of her husband's dead body, had wandered during the night to her threshold and was now lying in Isolind's bed. Madame was a little shocked at first; if we all kept lodging-houses, we should not like to hear of maniacs in our apartments; but she soon warmed into sympathy, and agreed with Isolind that the little lady must not be removed, at least, until her mother could be sent for. It must be owned that Isolind dwelt strongly on the immense wealth, splendid rank, and august pride of the little lady's mother, leaving madame to form vague and vast expectations of the possible advantages which might accrue to those who helped to render a service to so rich and powerful a personage. So madame promised to do all she could, and to exert herself to the utmost in order to keep the servants quiet and discreet.

Isolind requested madame to send for a physician, who came and saw poor Alexia, but of course could say nothing of her condition which was not already patent to every eye. He opined that he should have to make a report to the authorities, and that justice would presently inform herself; intimated that perhaps she might feel called on to take charge of Alexia pending the development of instructions. Whereupon Isolind declared that she was herself ready to lend every aid and give every information in her power to further the mission of justice; and that if justice desired to come and see Alexia in her bed, justice was welcome to do so. But our heroine peremptorily announced that until Lady Judith Scarlett could be sent for and arrive, neither justice nor anybody else save herself, Isolind, and her mother should take charge of the unhappy girl. The physician began perhaps to have vague ideas of Isolind's spreading the flag of the Stars and Stripes across the threshold of the cottage, and defying the Emperor himself to tread where that emblem lay. He undertook at her suggestion to telegraph at once to Lady Judith Scarlett, whose address in London Isolind gave him, and summon her to the bedside of her child.

Presently justice did make her appearance, in the person of a magistrate and one or two other functionaries. They were admitted to see Alexia, who gazed on them with her open black eyes, but was utterly unconscious of their presence. Isolind told all that she knew of Eric Walraven's circumstances, his poverty, his debts, and his probable despair when he found that Lady Judith would do nothing for him. She described plainly and truthfully Alexia's wandering round the cottage, and how she had seen her and brought her in. She did not feel bound to produce or even allude to the letter written by Alexia to her. In truth Isolind was, like most other persons, women especially, totally indifferent to the maintenance of all the formulas of legal procedure in a foreign country; and she felt neither inclined nor in duty bound to help French justice to a true understanding of all this sad and shocking story.

Meanwhile the whole population of Villefleurs began to learn what had happened and to grow excited about it. In the Etablissement, a new building where in wet weather you could look at the sea from a glass gallery, and where journals were read, billiards and croquet were played, and fashions were exhibited, it formed the grand theme of conversation. In the small cabarets at the port, where groups of bearded men in blouses played dominoes and drank an extraordinary liquid supposed to be beer, the story was told and commented on and criticised. The *bonnes* on the beach chattered of nothing else The bare-legged fisher girls even had the tale distorted out of all reality by grotesque and hideous additions. The English residents held a meeting, presided over by the Vice-Consul, at which they adopted resolutions of sympathy with the poet's bereaved widow, and laid the basis of a subscription for a monument to the poet himself. Those who the previous day sneered at Eric Walraven, or cut him dead on the pier, or denounced him as a humbug, cad, and swindler, were now among the loudest in their appreciation of his high poetic genius and their admiration of his noble character. Eric himself held lordly *levée* all the time in his room in the Hôtel Impérial. He lay in his bed, as supreme an object of interest, as completely master of the hour's attention, as though he had been the Grand Monarch himself. If the poor poet was really at that moment looking down upon his body as it lay there, and if Eric Walraven in the skies retained any flavor of the nature of Eric Walraven on the earth, how proud and delighted he must have been to find himself the object of so intense and general an interest. Why, it was almost like being canonized. Vanity itself could have asked for no richer satisfaction. All his life through the poor wretch now dead had placed himself in attitude to extort human admiration. To be looked at, to be pointed out, to be admired by the eyes of women, to be envied by the hearts of men—this had been the object and motive of his life; and if he could only have seen himself now in death, he must have owned with pride that he had at last achieved a great part of his ambition. Surely it would be worth the while of such a man to die, if he could, a thousand deaths, were it but to enjoy the tears and the ejaculations of admiration which broke from the eyes and lips of the few privileged women who were permitted to enter the room and peep at him as he lay dead. His last public exhibition had been as carefully and picturesquely arranged as he himself could have planned it. The bedclothes were neatly disposed so as to show to the utmost advantage his face, his curls, his arms, and his wounds. He looked so young, so noble, and so beautiful, that no chambermaid saw him without shedding tears of sentiment. Justice came and inspected him; took solemn note of his wounds, and carried off, as a useful and valuable memento, the little poniard wherewith he was done to death. Surgery came and studied him and did him honor; minutely inspected his gashes as if they had been those which let out the life of Julius Cæsar, and prepared reports of his corporeal condition solemn and specific enough to have registered the fate of the first of murdered men. Every official personage, French, English, and American, in the place was allowed to enter and pass through the room where the dead body lay in state. Several photographers, native, English, and American, were permitted to reproduce the fine face and rich black curls of the dead man in cheap and ready portraiture. The poet who had discovered or invented the locality, and who has been already mentioned, was prompt to pay his respects to his dead brother; and although he had never read one line of the writings of Eric Walraven or of any English versemaker whatever, yet he was stricken by such an inspiration of fraternity and admiration that he threw off some powerful and thrilling lines that very evening, about the minstrel from the foreign soil, tossed on the shore of beauteous France, "*expirant*" there "*sur sa lyre*," and having chaplets of myrtle and laurel flung upon his immature *cercueil* by the hands of those who, rivals once, were only votaries and admirers now.

This little place had as yet no direct communication with any foreign country. The English and American visitors who began to pour in there came from Paris by railway to a station some seven miles away, and made the rest of the journey on wheels, or they came from England to one of the established and famous bathing places on the coast, and journeyed thence by diligence or carriage. This particular day, when the evening was beginning to descend, a carriage with postillions drove into the town, coming from one of the places lately mentioned, and drew up in front of the Hôtel Impérial. Monsieur the landlord came out, and a stately, beautiful English lady (he knew by her accent that she was English, although she spoke French admirably) alighted, followed by another lady and a maid, and inquired for Madame Walraven. The startled landlord told the lady the appalling story which such a question naturally invited, and Judith Scarlett heard that her daughter's husband lay dead within a few paces of where she stood. Her errand of mercy came all too late. She had tamed her proud heart and relented in vain.

Lady Judith had left London, as we know, on her own impulse. She had, of course, not received the telegraphic message of that morning. She had left town the previous night. She was on her way to save her daughter even while the daughter's hand was descending madly to seek that heart which in life Eric Walraven had never showed that he possessed. Too late by one day, by one night—too late by a thousand years, by all time!

"May God forgive him—and me!" was Lady Judith's murmured ejaculations. Then she asked more loudly:

"Where is my daughter?"

Monsieur the landlord hardly knew; he was not clear; he knew she was somewhere; he had heard that an American lady had taken her in charge.

Half a dozen loungers round the door were better informed. They could direct the coachman to the very place.

Lady Judith got into her carriage again. She spoke not one word to Miss Bruce, who was her companion. The carriage drove on for a little way along the cliffs, and then stopped at a pretty cottage, the wrong one; then at another, the right one. Madame of the house came out, and was surprised to find that she stood already in the presence of the grand English lady, the mother of the poor mad creature within. Madame began in her kindly way to prepare Lady Judith for what she was to see, telling her that the shock had been too much for the nerves of *la pauvre petite dame*, but that without doubt the good God would soon restore her, and that meantime the American ladies had been all kindness and devotion. But Lady Judith hardly heard a word of this, and did not heed what she heard. She only asked in weary tones to be allowed to see her daughter.

Then Madame led her up stairs, tapped at a door, said a word or two to Isolind which caused her to start and grow red, and presently the good woman led in the visitor, and Lady Judith stood by the bedside of her daughter.

The Venetian blinds of the room were partly closed to shut out the slanting, pitiless rays of the evening sun. Lady Judith did not stay to observe who was the other figure in the room. She hastened to the bed and bent over Alexia. At the other side of the bed, withdrawing herself as well as she might from observation, stood Isolind. Mrs. Atheling was not then in the room.

Judith Scarlett bent her proud and beautiful form over her pallid child, whose black bright eyes looked vacantly up.

"Alexia—O my child, my daughter—don't you know me?"

And it was then that Alexia gave her first sign of the possession of any ray of consciousness. The voice seemed to rouse her into a vague, dim sort of recognition; and the girl's form shrank together, and she drew herself away as far as she could, drew herself to the other side of the bed, and there, becoming in some way conscious of Isolind's presence, feebly made a movement as if she would extend her arms toward her. Isolind did not at first respond to this sign of unexpected recognition, this pathetic appeal. In the presence of Alexia's mother it seemed like a cruelty, almost a profanity, for any other arms to enfold the child.

Lady Judith was stricken to the heart. She had seen her daughter's first impulse of recognition, and it was shown in an involuntary, a convulsive effort to escape from her. But the bitterness of the pang was still to come. For when Alexia turned toward the other figure in the room the English lady assumed that it was that of the person who, as she now vaguely remembered having heard the landlady say, had taken Alexia in charge—some kindly and generous woman utterly unknown to her, but whom she was now in her humbled and agonized condition prepared to acknowledge as a benefactress. Following then with a quick glance the movement of her daughter, Lady Judith looked for the first time closely at the figure which on the other side of the bed seemed retiring into the dim light, and she saw that Alexia, from the touch of her mother, was feebly trying to stretch her arms to embrace Isolind Atheling.

A cry broke from the afflicted mother—a wail which no agony of her previous life had ever wrung from her—the death-shriek of her haughty self-reliance and long-enduring pride. She pressed her hands to her forehead and covered her eyes for a moment—only a moment—during which her whole heart and nature were torn by one of those terrible struggles which now and then convulse strong souls, and which in a mere flash can destroy or reorganize a whole character. Then Lady Judith said in a low, calm tone, not speaking that any one might hear, but as if she were uttering an acknowledgment which she felt to be a solemn and righteous expiation:

"This is indeed the judgment of God! Thy will be done!"

Then she looked firmly and bravely to where Isolind still seemed shrinking back, and said in a voice that hardly trembled:

"She appeals to you, Miss Atheling. Don't refuse the appeal. Take my poor child in your arms; you have the right, for you have been kind and loving to her. I thank you from my heart for trying to spare my feelings—I did not try once to spare yours."

"Oh, Lady Judith," murmured Isolind with eyes full of tears, "I never blamed you, and I loved you so much."

A light of sudden and genuine surprise came, even at that moment, into Lady Judith's eyes. There was then some one who loved her, and that was the daughter of the woman she had hated most on earth.

Now she knelt by the bedside of her own daughter and prayed in silence. For more than an hour no word was spoken as the sinking sun still faintly lighted that melancholy room.

CHAPTER XXVII.

"JOHN."

A SMALL blue lake lies glowing under a sky of burning blue. The lake itself is but the ornament of a great grassy plain, through which a river now trickles and now flows. Sometimes the river becomes a broad stream, sometimes and suddenly it is seen only as a thin thread of water; sometimes its progress or even its existence can hardly be traced at all, except through the fact that the grass shows wet and marshy where the water still oozes along. The lake is very deep and marvellously clear and blue. The eye can see down, down to its lowest depths, so transparent is the water. The shoal of little fish you see below, and which you think you could touch with your hand, are twenty feet beneath the surface. This pool which we call a lake is not known by such a name or by any name, there on that broad plain which it adorns. In England or Ireland, in Switzerland, or Northern Italy, it would be a lake with a name and a fame. Here, where the name of lake suggests a great sea furrowed by perpetual lines of steamers, and having populous commercial cities rising everywhere on its shores, this pretty little pond is not worth classifying or naming. Even when this plain grows peopled that water will still be a nameless little pond.

The plain is completely girt around by mountains. They are bare and stony, but of exquisite and noble outline, like the mountains of Greece. They are of lofty height—higher far than any of the hills of Attica—but they are only the spurs, the stragglers of a grand and celebrated chain of mountains, and have themselves no fame and hardly any name. There are few trees anywhere over the plain—none indeed except a little clump which stands near the lake—and there is hardly any verdure on the mountains. The grass on the plain is still green; it keeps its color along the river-track even through the heats of summer, when the ground elsewhere changes its hue to a kind of arid, ashy white. The weather just now is beautiful, fit to lull the soul of a poet or a dreamer into a heaven of sensuous delight. But the changes of climate are sudden, fierce, and, to a stranger, seem sometimes almost supernatural. The traveller has perhaps toiled across the plain some burning September day, when the sky was dazzlingly bright and the torrid rays of the sun were almost insupportable. He has camped on the ground at night, and even in sleep has revelled in a growing and unexpected coolness, and he opens his eyes in the morning to find the ground covered everywhere with a thick white mantle of snow.

This plain and that cincture of hills form a scene common enough in the region where we see them. The traveller may journey for days, nay, for weeks, through a succession of such landscapes. This is in the western region of the

United States; the reader may locate the precise place either in the neighborhood of the Rocky Mountains or the Sierra Nevada, according to his pleasure. Some years ago this plain was bare of all inhabitants. It lay out of the track of the regular emigrant trains, which would have had to turn aside and cross ranges of mountain barriers to reach it; and it was not a good hunting ground, and therefore was avoided by the Indians. Long ago, it is believed, there was a small offshoot of an Indian tribe settled there, having gone there to escape some powerful enemies. But the enemies discovered their retreat, hunted them down, and slaughtered them all—every one to the last man, the last woman, the youngest baby. Then the victors took the scalps of the vanquished, left the corpses to bleach and rot, and returned to their own hunting-ground. It lay in the track of civilization represented by emigrant trains and military forts, and therefore they in their turn were gradually extirpated. Since the raid of the conquerors this valley with the blue lake had known little or nothing of the Indians.

More lately a few refugees from civilization had found out this place and settled there. They planted the trees which grow by the lake and pleasantly shade the spot, and they built a few log houses, and lived secluded, peaceful, sometimes very laborious lives there. They were men brought together by no other bond or affinity than a common desire and determination to live away from civilization, and perhaps, too, a common vague faith, or at least hope, that a better life, a stronger inspiring principle, a purer element of religious intuition, might grow up among them in the work and the ways of this lonely companionship, this hermitage fraternity. They were not the founders of any new sect; there was no name by which to define or classify them, even if they had been numerous enough to invite any attempt at classification; they sought no adherents, not to speak of converts, and asked of the world and civilization nothing but to be let alone. Which the world and civilization readily did, nobody caring or knowing anything of this small group of self-made exiles.

In the United States here and there are many such little groups, not nearly large enough to be called settlements, or to be heard of in books of travel or in newspapers. There is no form of human eccentricity so absurd or extravagant that it cannot find some one man of force and ability ready to become its glorifier and apostle, and some few other men willing to come out of the world and associate in a sort of exile for its sake. In one of the States which used to be called the Far West, but which are recently beginning to be regarded as Middle States, and will be classed as Eastern the day after to-morrow or thereabouts, there lately stood, and probably still stands, a solitary house on a hillside, containing a whole sect or community thus associated as voluntary outcasts from society. This was a community of Free-Lovers. It had never numbered more than ten; the other day it had dwindled down to five. Yet the Free-Lovers insisted on regarding themselves as a community of exiles, and were proud of their withdrawal from civilization in the neighboring town, where their very existence had been long forgotten.

But such associations are by no means generally, or even often, made up of persons who hold any extraordinary views, or come together for the indulgence of any freaks of sensualism or fantastic humor. The facility for isolation in such a country as America naturally suggests and tempts to voluntary isolation. Many of the fraternities least known to society at large are perfectly harmless, inoffensive, honorable communities, made up of men who, out of a fellowship of disappointment or aspiration, rather than of creed, are drawn together into a settlement isolated from civilization and progress all around. These for the most part attract no attention—are wholly unknown, indeed, to the public outside. The curiosity and observation which follow such eccentric, positive, and comparatively influential associations as that of the Mormons or that of the Shakers never touch these small and purposeless unions. The *vates sacer* who made the Brook Farm enterprise immortal is wanting to them, as well perhaps as the high poetic purpose and the adornment of varied intellect and culture which would have rendered the Brook Farm scheme interesting even though Hawthorne had never enshrined it in romance. You may find a dozen or twenty such little settlements in the United States as this of which we are now speaking, too small and insignificant even for Hepworth Dixon to think them worth study or description.

Such a little cluster of ten or a dozen men had settled some years ago in this valley by the lake. They had come there from some place further eastward, because there the land around them was becoming too thickly populated, and they fled before the coming of their kind. Wandering hither and thither, far and wide, they had come at length upon this lonely plain within its rampart of mountains, quite out of the way, off the line of the steady westward march of civilization. There they had set up their staff, and for some few years had had undisturbed quiet. But of late the mountain girdle had been discovered to be as rich in precious minerals as the zone of a sultana; and in all the passes and gullies of the mountains, and along the beds of the mountain rivers, rough, reckless explorers were soon swarming, and on the edges of the plain canvas towns were rising. A canvas town, it may be well to explain, to some European readers at least, is a cluster of tents to cover and shelter the miners and squatters who have been attracted by some new-found riches in the earth. One tent has a bar, with perhaps a couple of flashy colored lithographs over it, and a few bottles and glasses, and this institution has a sign hung up outside proclaiming it to be hotel or restaurant or sample-room, as the case may be. The owner of another tent goes in for financial dealings, and announces his canvas house as the Bank or the Exchange. Another sets up a "grocery" store, wherein he sells everything he can get together, from candies and canned oysters to bowie-knives and huge thigh boots. In a canvas town of considerable standing, large population, and bold social pretensions, may be seen a tent which displays half a dozen crinolines swinging in the breeze, and has bright shawls and ribbons and women's boots inside. But the canvas settlement at the feet of the mountains we are now describing was very far as yet from this stage of civilization. Not one solitary crinoline could have found a purchaser there. The ungracious Saints Senanus and Kevin, of the Irish legends, might have been happy there. No voice of woman would ever have disturbed the sacred stillness of their prayerful thoughts.

Unwelcome indeed was the intrusion of this form of active civilization to the hermits by the lake. It became wearily apparent that they must endure a constantly increasing pressure of rough companionship, or pull up stakes and seek elsewhere a new home. Some of the hermits were now getting old, and shrank from further wandering; were perhaps losing faith in the possibility of anywhere escaping from their busy brother man. Some perhaps were losing faith in the dream of isolation altogether. There was therefore much hesitancy and delay, and meanwhile they began inevitably to get known among the new-comers, the mining folk. They were not misanthropists, and they were able to render many good turns to the invading barbarians. They could always give medicine to any one who was sickly; they could act as surgeons to a wounded or injured man; they had plenty of gunpowder; they were not afraid of anything; they acted sometimes as advisers and arbiters in disputes; they had joined energetically in the expulsion or other punishment of robbers, murderers, and such like evil-doers. They came to be respected among the barbarians, and it was understood that they were to be treated with some consideration, and that their settlement was to be held sacred against all disturbance or molestation.

Now in this little community of hermits, apparently about to be driven on to seek a new home, were two or three natives of Great Britain, two or three native Americans, a German, two Swedes, and a Wallachian Jew. No one knew or cared to know the real name of the other, or any of his antecedents and history. It was understood that no allusion to the past or the outer world was to be made. If by chance any one of the fraternity should come to hear of anything going on in New York, or San Francisco, or Europe, he kept it to himself and said nothing of it. Sometimes it became necessary that one of the body should journey to the nearest large city to make purchases. When he did so, he avoided as far as he could hearing anything of what might be going on in the active world. If he did nevertheless hear anything, he bore with it and said nothing about it. They lived on game, on fish, on maize, and fruits which they had with infinite labor compelled the desert to grow abundantly. They lived in separate huts quite independently of each other, not even praying together. Sometimes one of the body never for days interchanged a word with any of his fellows; sometimes two or three would work or read together for a long succession of days. Each respected as far as possible the peculiarities and idiosyncrasies of the others. The bond of union was the understanding that each considered himself absolutely cut off from the living world, and was striving to purify himself from earthly passion and selfishness, and to prepare his soul for the better life.

The oldest man in this little brotherhood was a tall, lean, dry Scotchman, a man apparently of great scientific attainments, and who seemed to have travelled far over the earth's surface. He was growing gray and shrivelled; had a hard, thin face, lighted by gray eyes, which sometimes gleamed with a sparkle of humor. He was a mystic and a humorist at once; Swedenborg and Captain Lismahago in one. He believed that through a pure life of labor and unselfish devotion man would at last become perfect, absolutely impervious to temptation and to sin upon this earth; and when the mood was on him and he could find listeners he loved to expatiate upon this faith of his, and to explain and illumine it by all manner of illustrations drawn from history and science, from the Scriptures and the open book of Nature. There was something wonderful now and then in the rich roll of his eloquence when the talking fit was on him, and in accents like those of a Chalmers, with gesticulation like that of a Guthrie, he poured out his argument for the new creed which ordered man to seek not merely perfection, but even immortality, on this earth by the culture of the soil, by habitual seclusion, by absolute purity of body, by the conquest of the passions and bitternesses of the heart.

This man, though the eldest, was not the founder or pioneer of the little body of companions. The leader was younger in years and far less fixed in habits. Lately this founder of the society had taken to long wanderings away from the place. He would disappear for weeks or months, so that his companions sometimes thought he would reappear among them no more. He always, however, did come back; and a certain quick energy and forcefulness of character en abled him to retain tacitly the kind of virtual leadership which he had held from the beginning. He never expounded any faith, or cared to listen to an exposition from the lips of others. He frankly told his fellows that there were times when he could not endure any companionship, and when he could not rest tranquilly in any place. He therefore commonly made any expeditions which were requisite for the benefit of the whole company. Expiation, rather than aspiration, seemed to be the impulse of his self-banishment from the world.

One of the Swedes was a man of high culture, who had evidently at one time been in the military service. The death of his young wife in child-bed long ago had so deeply affected him that his friends believed his reason was touched. He wandered out to America, crossed the plains, fell in with the leader of this party on one of the latter's expeditions, and joined the settlement. The other Swede was a mere peasant who had been enticed out to the Mormon community, became disgusted with it, and came at last to the scene and the people with whom we find him. The German had been a professor in a college in Baden. He got mixed up with the Baden revolution, was severely wounded in the head, and escaped to the United States, where he was seized with a passion or craze for a new religion and new kind of life. The Wallachian was little better than a religious lunatic—at best, an extravagant and hyperbolical enthusiast. The Americans, two of whom had been ministers of churches, belonged to that class more common in America than in any other country—the class of able, well-educated, and restless devotees of new "isms" and crotchets, men who thirst always for a new theory to put into practice, with whom nothing is settled, and who, the moment they are stricken by any notion or conceit, however wild, clamor for a new school, a new religion, to give it expression. There is in America a constant collision or at least contrast of two forces, which in great measure explains the fact, so odd-looking to a stranger, that every little crotchet or craze gathers a little school or sect around it. Nowhere is there less reverence for authority, more audacity of freakish thought, than among certain classes in the United States; nowhere is there a more slow and solid conviction and conservatism than among others. There are small American towns, there are sects and churches in American towns, small or large, which are as rigorous as the infallible Pope himself could be in refusing to their members any personal independence, any conceivable laxity from set and orthodox opinion. If you will start a new theory in one of these communities, you must in self-defence endeavor to cincture yourself by a seceding sect; and probably in the end you will find it more convenient to betake yourself and your fellow rebels into the seclusion and freedom of a voluntary exile. Thus had the American members of this little community been led to adhere to it for the present. They had all the sense of dignity and complacent martyrdom which self-exile naturally gives; and although their fellow-exiles were not upholders of their special crotchet or of any other, yet they were free to nurse and indulge their craze to the full, pending the longed-for time when they could induce a whole school to rally round it and force it on the world. None of the Americans had been very long residents of this little camp, and none was likely to cling to it even for its brief day.

Three of the brotherhood have been described as natives of Great Britain. These were the founder, an Englishman; the elderly Scotchman; and an Englishman who had joined the group when they were on their search for this very valley, and had remained with them ever since. It should be said that some changes had taken place since then. The number had always been about the same; but now a companion died, now one wandered away and did not return, making his way probably to the track of the regular emigrant trains, and so getting back to civilization somewhere. Chance brought accessions to the group to supply the vacant places. The oldest members now in the body were the two Englishmen, the Scotchman, and the mystic Swede. Of these, the second Englishman was the latest accession. Each man was called but by one name—Alexander, Paul, John, and so on.

The evening was beginning to set in on this beautiful scene, when the Scotchman, who was known among his fellows simply as Brother Alexander, came out of his little hut, around which he had with wondrous labor and patience managed to cultivate a rich and glowing garden of flowers. He wore a long gray coat of some rough material, buttoned up to his chin despite the heat of the season, and a broad-brimmed felt hat. He walked slowly along by the lake. On his way his eyes rested upon the second Englishman, who was lying on the ground under a tree reading a book. The two men interchanged a friendly greeting. Alexander stopped in his walk and the Englishman rose to his feet. These two men had perhaps more of social companionship between them than any other two in the eccentric family.

The Englishman was dressed in a plain blue shirt or blouse, and wore high boots drawn up over his trousers, and a broad-leaved hat. He was dressed indeed like three out of four of the figures to be seen in a Western settlement. He was a tall man, finely made, with a certain quiet dignity about him. His face was handsome and noble, although worn and deeply lined. Exposure to sun and breeze had not affected in the least the remarkable whiteness of his broad forehead and his small hands. He wore a full beard, and except on his temples, which were growing bald, his hair curled thickly. His eyes had that oddly-combined expression of dreaminess and restlessness in them which seems to be peculiar to the mystic or the hermit, and which to the ordinary or hasty observer is almost sure at first to suggest the idea of insanity. In all men who lead a life remarkably diverging from the commonplace, the eye soon comes to have something of this peculiar expression.

There was a singular and winning sweetness in the smile with which the Englishman, who was known in the community simply as John, welcomed the other.

"Always reading, John? Not got over your book-reading days yet, at your time of life!" Alexander spoke with a good-humored glance of affected anger. The Englishman's time of life was apparently under fifty. "What are ye poring over the day, man?"

"I've been reading Sophocles, Alexander. Isn't it good reading?"

"Well, it's not just that bad reading; it's very good in fact. But I think a man ought to have done all his reading of books at thirty years of age. You don't learn anything out of books after that time. I dare say you'll have read the 'Electra' and 'Antigone' and all the rest of it many times over already."

"Several times. I think I know some of the plays almost by heart."

"Then what do you read them any more for?"

"How often have you sat for hours looking at that water and that sunset? Why do you look at them now?"

"Ah, lad, I have you there, though. The sun and the sky and the water never look the same twice over, nor the same for two mortal minutes. They always tell you something new, but your bonny Greek Antigone is always just the same."

"Not at all. I get new ideas from her every time.'

Alexander shook his head. "Books at best only bind one to the old world and the old flesh. They don't set us free and make us strong and self-reliant, as Nature and Thought do. But you are all the same, you young fellows."

"Why, you were talking of my advanced years just now."

"Advanced for book-studying like a schoolboy, lad—young and frivolous when compared with me or with Christian" (the Swede). "The last time Paul was here" (Paul was the founder of the community), "what d'ye think I found him reading? Rousseau, man, Rousseau! All the sentimentalities about Julie —was that her name? To think that mountains and lakes like yon" (Alexander jerked his head to indicate more clearly the precise location of Switzerland) "should turn out a Rousseau for their prophet! When's Paul coming back?"

"I don't know," John replied, with something of the curt coldness of the British national manner now for the first time perceptible in him. The truth was that Paul and he had but little association or intercourse.

"But he *is* coming back?"

"I presume so, Alexander."

"The place doesn't seem quite itself without him, although there's no arguing him into anything or keeping him still for any time. Perhaps, with his clever head and his journeyings, he can find out where we are to go next, for I don't see how we can remain here much longer, and I'm sore grieved for it. I've gotten to love this place, and that itself is a weakness and a reason why I should leave it; for no place is more dumb than another, and all can help in teaching the grand lesson."

"I am sorry for the place," said the other. "I can't help regretting it. I have grown to love it. I have had calm and happy years here. I begin to despond and to doubt the use of trying new scenes any more."

"Hush, man; ye mustn't despond ever. The Lord is everywhere except only where the crowds are. Only the money-changers pollute the temple—and a pretty lot of money-changers we are having about us down yonder;" and he glanced toward the canvas town on the edge of the plain.

"Well, Alexander, I wish they wouldn't come and drive us out of this place; I don't feel the spirit for new wanderings. I seem to have grown to be a part of this place. There was until lately such a splendid sense of seclusion and safety about it. I spent years, Alexander, in a monastery on Mount Athos; I wandered through Asia in the dress of a Mussulman pilgrim; and I never felt the same sense of freedom from the intrusion of the world that I have felt here. I begin to be afraid and to doubt; it almost seems as if the world would never relax its hold upon us."

Alexander shaded his eyes and gazed steadily toward the west. Out of the radiance of the sinking sun, as it seemed, two figures came riding rapidly, dark against the lustrous and golden glow.

"Here's the lad Paul coming home," he said. It was one of the ways of Alexander to treat John and Paul, and all others whose age did not much exceed fifty, as lads. He himself looked hardly more than fifty, but he had in reality passed his seventieth year.

John looked in the same direction.

"Yes, it is Paul," he said, and he turned as if to go to his hut.

"Who can this be that comes riding with him, I wonder?" the old man asked.

"I don't know, Alexander; but whoever it is, you will welcome him more agreeably than I could, and I shall go in."

This little community, fleeing from human society, yet never refused temporary shelter, welcome, and hospitality to any wayfarer, even though he came utterly without recommendation. Paul had been the means of introducing to the brotherhood some of its best members, John included; and anybody coming with him was therefore sure to be received with honor and affection.

But John turned away and presently disappeared within his log-cabin.

Alexander looked after him curiously and rather sadly. He never could understand why John and Paul seemed always anxious to avoid each other. He loved them both, and they seemed to respect each other; yet they did not willingly associate or even meet.

Presently Paul and his companion came galloping up, and Paul, seeing Alexander, checked his stout little Mexican horse and leaped to the ground. His companion, a dark-haired and handsome young man, also alighted, looking rather puzzled and anxious, as one who is not quite certain what he is to do next. If it were not rather a frivolous sort of comparison, one might say that a guest brought by a friend to the dinner-table of a host whom he has never seen before, and in a country whose language he only imperfectly understands, might have worn on his face such an expression as that which was now seen on the countenance of Paul's companion.

"Brother Alexander," said Paul (whom we have seen before in San Francisco), "I have brought a friend with me for whom I ask your welcome."

Alexander made a bow which had in it a dignified and grand association of the finest days of society in Edinburgh, Auld Reekie, "mine auld romantic town," and pressed the hand of the new-comer.

"Shall I introduce you," Paul asked, turning to the latter, "by your worldly, I mean your usual name? Here we only care for realities, not names. Every one calls himself what he will."

"My own name, by all means," the other replied with a bright smile. "It isn't worth concealing, and I can't readily invent any other. My name is Angelo Volney."

"Let us say Angelo for shortness," said Alexander cheerily. "Well, Angelo, I give you a welcome, and we here haven't much more to give. Paul has doubtless told you something about us. Stay as long as ye like; go when ye will. We will do all we can to make your stay tolerable, and to help and speed your going if ye must go."

"Is John anywhere near?" asked Paul.

"John was here two moments ago; he is now in his home."

"Then I'll leave Angelo in your charge for a short time. He has come to see John, and I had better go in first and ask John to receive him."

Paul walked toward John's hut, leaving Angelo with Alexander. The latter sounded a whistle, and one of the fraternity came and looked after the horses: each denizen of the place took his regular turn of such service. Then Alexander pointed out to Angelo the beauties and wonders of the scene, described the changes that had taken place there and the sudden incursion of the mining population, and played in every respect the part of a courteous and genial host. But courtesy at that moment was almost thrown away upon Angelo Volney. The young man's heart and mind were wholly engrossed by the wonderful nature of the situation in which he found himself placed, and the possible results which might arise from it. The mystery of a life, nay, of many lives—at least involving directly the fate of many lives—had blind chance then thrown this into his power to solve? Since his childhood he had been haunted by the overhanging presence of one mystery, oppressing, torturing, and bewildering the lives of those then most near and dear to him. Lately this one same mystery had come to involve and enwrap another life—another fame dearer to him than any, than all. Could it be possible that Heaven, working apparently through the agency of a wild, sightless chance, had singled him out to bring back the lost, to restore to life the living dead, to explain the enigma which so deeply concerned the happiness of his benefactress, his heart-sister, and his love?

Meanwhile Paul knocked at the door of John's hut, and a deep, sweet voice called out "Come in," and Paul entered.

The occupant of the cottage was seated in the sunlight by the window, still reading his Sophocles. The furniture of the hut consisted of a table, two chairs, a bed in a camp bedstead, and some neatly carved wooden shelves, on which books were lying.

John looked a little surprised at the appearance of his visitor, but at once arose, laid his book aside, and courteously offered him a chair.

"Thanks—I don't need to sit down," the other replied rather coldly. "I have come on an unpleasant errand; at least one that will hardly earn me any thanks. I have brought you a visitor."

The occupant of the hut looked surprised.

"A visitor to me—to me in particular?"

"To you, and you alone. One who knows you only by your worldly name, and desires to see you."

A flush came over John's face, and his eyes flashed with momentary anger. But he controlled himself and said calmly:

"*You* know that I will see no such visitor. You know, too, that no such person could have found me out unaided by you. Have you then betrayed me? If so, it was to no purpose. Tell the emissary, whoever he may be, that his journey is for nothing. I'll not see him; and I don't even ask who he is."

"I have not betrayed you. He doesn't even yet know where you are to be found; and he is not an emissary from any one. Only the strangest chance brought him and me together, and he told me strange news which I think you ought to hear."

"What news can affect me any more?" John asked with an impatient gesture. "Why do you torment me in this useless way? Do you think I can be dragged back to the world again? Do you—*you*, of all men—want to help in urging me back? Am I never, to the end of my life, to have the security of peace?"

He sprang to his feet and walked impatiently up and down.

"I knew that you would blame me for bringing this on you," Paul calmly said; "but I felt that I must do it. Do, pray, do me justice. I am not likely to interfere needlessly in what does not concern me. We have not been friends; we *can't* be friends. There are memories which rise up between us and keep us apart. I look on you as the principal cause of the misery that fell on my sister's whole existence. But if we can't be friends, neither can we be enemies; and you must know that I am incapable of doing anything to give you needless pain. But I have thought this thing over, and I tell you again this man outside has some news for you which you ought to know."

"Then tell it to me at once yourself, and be done with it. Perhaps I can guess it. If it be as I conjecture, God knows I am sorry for it. I lament for a life ruined like my own, but I envy the early stroke of fate."

"You can't guess it; you are wholly wrong."

"Tell me then, in heaven's name——"

"Not I. Let it come with its full effect from one who knows all that I don't know. You *must* see this man!"

"What is his name?"

"You don't know it. He is called Angelo Volney."

"Is he sent by——"

"He is sent by no one, except, as I firmly believe, by God!"

The other stopped in his walk and laid his hand on Paul's shoulder.

"If you are distracting and torturing me uselessly," he said, in a deep stern voice, "then may God forgive you for inflicting wanton pain on one whose only prayer in life is to be allowed to repent the past in peace. You know me well; you know how I have been tormented between my hatred of the world, my dread of it, and yet all the old impulses and temptations of ambition. Deal fairly with me, Paul. We are not friends, I suppose. I am indeed the destroyer—the murderer if you choose to have it so—of your sister; but you know that I would have given my life to save her, and that I flung away every worldly prospect and hope for her. Don't tempt and torture me for nothing. I have been expecting this or something like it. Some presentiment I can't explain told me that this temptation was coming. Tell me, on your word, on your soul, is this meeting inevitable?"

"On my word, on my soul, I believe you must meet this man, and that when you have heard what he has to tell you, you would curse any obstacle which could have held you back from hearing it. You *must* see him."

"Strange that there can be anything to be told which could affect me and my ways in life!" John said, irresolutely. "In one word, is it news of death?"

"In one word, no."

John turned away and again walked impatiently to and fro across the narrow floor—the bare earth that formed the floor—of the hut, hardly a broader surface than the lion's cage gives to the restless, impatient lion. At last he stopped, looked fixedly at Paul, and said:

"You would not torment me idly. I can't believe such a thing possible of you. I have never known any levity in you which could allow me to think it. Bring in your new acquaintance—I *will* see him!"

While the man called John was speaking these words, the strange look in his eyes which has been already mentioned became so remarkable that any ordinary spectator might well have been excused for supposing that he saw before him a madman. When the words were finished, the speaker turned away and flung himself into his chair and leaned his chin upon his hand.

Paul left the hut without speaking. In a few moments its inmate heard footsteps at the door, and he rose to receive his scarcely welcome visitors. He stood in a calm and dignified attitude, hardly evincing now any emotion, even of curiosity, as the stranger entered, introduced by Paul. The latter said to Angelo Volney:

"All that you want to say or to ask is to be said now and here! You remember the conditions and the pledge on which I have consented to bring you here. I leave you."

And he left the hut, closing the door behind him.

Angelo Volney saw before him a tall, dignified, and handsome man, whose rough garb and rugged surroundings could hardly keep any intelligent eye from recognizing in him a cultivated and high-bred gentleman. The occupant of the hut bowed, handed a chair to his visitor, and looked at the latter with a penetrating glance. But he did not open the conversation, and Angelo had to begin.

"I am afraid I must appear a very unwelcome and intrusive visitor," he said. "But I know I can justify my intrusion. I believe I have the honor of speaking to a gentleman who can at least help me to communicate with—with Mr. Charles Grey Scarlett?"

"Your business will have to be urgent and important indeed," the other said, coldly and firmly, "to justify a visit to one who desires, above all things on earth, to be left to the life of seclusion he has chosen for himself. Pray let us not waste time or words. My name is Charles Grey Scarlett."

CHAPTER XXVIII.

"I MIGHT HAVE SAVED HER; NOW SHE'S GONE FOREVER!"

"CALL it not vain," sings the Minstrel of the North; "they do not err who say that, when a poet dies, mute Nature mourns her worshipper and celebrates his obsequies." Accepting this declaration as a scientific fact, we take it for granted that mute Nature went into mourning when Eric Walraven died. Mute Nature had the mourning all to herself. No one else wept. The poet had no funeral cortége, no funeral oration, chaplet, or other gratifying mark of public sorrow. The general conviction that he had killed himself—which was all that Justice could make of the matter when she came to inquire into it—chilled and scared away any desire to do honor to the dead. So Walraven was laid in earth with funeral rites very much maimed. The absence of any positive proof that he had killed himself allowed him a corner in the little Protestant cemetery then recently opened, and where, since then, many consumptive English and many pale-cheeked daughters of American dyspepsia have been laid to rest. Mr. Gostick came to Villefleurs and had a cheap and decent monument erected over the grave, simply announcing that there lay the mortal remains of Eric G. Walraven, of London, son of the late Rev. Edward Walraven and Jane his wife. A few lines of obituary appeared in the leading daily and weekly papers of London, wherein Walraven was gently spoken of as a poet whose first efforts had had some promise in them, and who perhaps, if he had lived, might have achieved something worthy of preservation. That was his funeral dirge. That moan was soon made. Next day he was utterly forgotten. The only monument to his fame that seems likely to be abiding in London is a solitary dusty copy of "The Mystery of the Universe," sticking up in a bookstall in Southampton Row, Holborn, and vainly offered to the public for eightpence.

Meanwhile Walraven's young, unhappy wife was fading away. She remained for days and days in the same condition of almost utter unconsciousness that has already been described. Lady Judith took up her residence altogether in the cottage with the Athelings. They offered to give up the place wholly to her, but the poor stricken lady, with a sudden revulsion of feeling, seemed to cling to the companionship of Isolind, and to dread being left alone. Lady Judith's maid was left with Miss Bruce at the hotel, to be ready when needed; but Lady Judith had seldom need of them. She watched by her daughter night and day, except in the intervals when sheer physical exhaustion compelled her to lie down and sleep. A great London doctor and a great Paris doctor were sent for and kept in constant attendance. Madame who owned the house was literally bewildered by the prodigality of expense which seemed to be going on, and felt herself immensely elevated in personal dignity by the whole series of events. Mrs. Atheling kept habitually in the background. She never could quite warm to Lady Judith, even in the latter's hour of deep affliction.

After a while Alexia seemed to rally a little, both in physical and mental condition. She swallowed certain foods and drinks with apparent relish. She smiled on Isolind when Isolind entered the room, and looked wistfully after her when she left it. By degrees, under the influence of Lady Judith's devoted attention, the girl's heart appeared to thaw toward her mother, and she would smile sometimes upon her and take food from her hand. Lady Judith felt a thrill of joy and gratitude pass through her when first she saw this change. An infant of six months would have shown much clearer and more cordial signs of recognition than Alexia did; and yet Lady Judith welcomed the faint dawn of that first smile as if it were the proudest triumph a mother's heart could win. Ah, heaven! what a miserable anomaly sometimes is human happiness! Lady Judith felt almost happy that first day of kindly recognition, and turned to Isolind with a proud, triumphant smile, as if to say, "You see my daughter pardons and loves her mother, after all!"

What strange days those were for the two watching women—those days when Alexia was still weak as a new-born infant, and almost as unconscious. What strange days and still more strange nights! How often Isolind and Lady Judith together saw the dawn flush over the sea, together heard the bells chime the midnight. Isolind's helpful, loving, pitying, womanly nature took all weariness from her task; and the whole vitality and energy of Lady Judith's frame was engrossed in it, and allowed her to feel no fatigue. Sometimes, when the two sat together by the bedside of the patient, the thought would arise in the mind of each, "How strange that she and I should be fellow-watchers!" Lady Judith now and then sent a sudden glance of her dark eyes to where Isolind sat, and wondered within herself that anything could have so wrought a charm upon her bitter vindictiveness as to make her cling to the companionship of Agnes Revington's daughter. But she did cling to it; she could hardly endure the girl's absence. "Am I the same—am I really Judith Scarlett?" she would ask of her own heart. "Is it the Spirit of God that has poured grace into my soul; or is it only that my misfortune has enfeebled my mind and broken my spirit?" More than once did Lady Judith start suddenly from her chair and walk up and down the room, and Isolind looked at her with kindly sympathizing eyes, believing that she was thinking only of her sinking daughter; but the mother was asking of her distracted soul whether the love growing up within her for the fair-haired watching girl was a heaven-sent inspiration or a sinful and shameful weakness. More than once did Lady Judith suddenly pause in her walk and stoop over Isolind and kiss her forehead; and Isolind never knew what a victory of sweetness and love over rancor and bitterness was symbolized by that kiss of affection and peace.

A change began to take place in Alexia's condition. She grew physically stronger, and the state of torpid unconsciousness seemed to have almost wholly vanished. It was succeeded by fitful, frequent outbursts of genuine madness—wild, delirious raving—and then intervals which might be called comparatively lucid; intervals, that is, when the patient knew those around her and called them by their names, and talked an irregular and incoherent talk indeed, having seldom much meaning in it, but yet not frenzied or extravagant. In such times it did not appear that Alexia had any recollection of anything that had passed, nor did her manner now show any of the old bitternes towards her mother,

She would ask Lady Judith questions and not wait for an answer; she would begin long and rambling accounts of imaginary walks and rides and adventures; she would ask Isolind to sing for her, and burst into talk again in the middle of the singing. Once or twice she asked when Angelo was coming home, and she went off into some talk in which Charles Escombe's name occurred; and the two watchers turned pale and exchanged glances of significant alarm, believing that she would next come to speak of Eric Walraven. But she did not now appear to have any recollection whatever of him.

The physicians had still some hope that when the merely physical prostration of the shock should have passed away, and the shattered nerve-system should have begun to reorganize itself, Alexia's reason might return. But they were therefore the more anxious that her memory should if possible be guarded against any intrusion from the terrible associations of the tragedy which had broken her down. They, like Lady Judith and everybody else save Isolind alone, assumed that Walraven had committed suicide, and that the sight of the deed had overthrown Alexia's reason. Isolind of course had never breathed a hint of her terrible suspicions; and she had kept Alexia's farewell letter a secret.

One night Lady Judith received a new and fearful shock. During Alexia's wilder moods it was often necessary to have the attendance of a hired nurse. But this particular night the patient seemed very tranquil, and Lady Judith not only insisted that Isolind must go to bed early, but sent away the nurse as well, and chose to spend the night alone with her daughter. It was a warm night, and Lady Judith was dressed in a light muslin wrapper wherein she looked wonderfully picturesque and stately. The whole scene was a picture ready to the hand of any artist could he have seen it. The simply-furnished French room with its little white bed; the pale, thin, beautiful face of the girl, whose arms wandered vaguely outside the coverlet, whose short-cropped black hair (how long and luxuriant it was the other day!) looked so black against the white pillow, and whose ever-open glittering eyes beamed restlessly everywhere; and then the statuesque and noble figure of the pale, sad, dark-haired woman, in the loose light-colored dress who sat by the bedside, her chin resting on her arm—a very embodiment of sleepless sorrow. The murmur of the waves could be faintly heard in the room; save for that sound and the occasional cry of a seabird across the waters, all was silent.

Lady Judith held a book in one hand, but she had not been reading. In the silence of the hour the sad past had once again been unrolling itself before her newly-opening eyes. She saw her own proud, egotistic, and loveless youth; her ill-assorted marriage; her cold and stern refusal to practise any of the genial arts by which a woman seeks to conquer the love of a man; the lonely, disdainful independence wherein she had wrapped herself as in a mantle of pride. She saw the husband of her youth, so noble, so gifted, so much admired by all the world else, but to whose heart she never could approach—alas! never tried to approach from the fatal hour when she learned that he had once loved another woman in vain. She saw herself deserted by him—and then by all; she saw that all had gone wrong with her; and at last, at last she was learning to the full the lesson which pride and egotism find it so hard to learn—the lesson that the world goes wrong only with those who have not themselves gone right. Now at last she saw with clear sad eyes where her own fault had been. Calamity had beaten down the rampart of pride, and there came from out the very heart of the solitary woman the vain immemorial cry, "Oh, give me back the years I flung away; give me back the opportunities I wasted or scorned;

let it not be too late, let it not be all too late!" Unknown to her, thousands of miles away the same hopeless appeal against Time and Destiny was going up from another heart, once erring like hers, now penitent like hers, and which in the hour of her present trial ought to have been pressed against her own.

Lady Judith had become thus buried so completely in her memories of self-reproach, that she had almost lost any consciousness of the present. Suddenly, however, she was recalled to quick keen life and attention by a shriek which rang out through the tortured air. Alexia was sitting upright in the bed, her thin arms flung over her head, the hands clasped together, and her white breast gleaming through her disarranged night-dress. Pouring out shriek after shriek, she tried to rise and to escape from the bed. Lady Judith put her strong white arms around the child and tenderly held her down—it was an easy task—and tried to soothe and quiet her. After a few struggles and shivers Alexia resisted no more, but she broke into a passion of tears and sobs, through which there came again and again in disjointed words one fearful accusation of herself, one revelation which made her mother start and tremble, and then put her hand over the girl's mouth and try to hush her wailing voice. Again Alexia's mood changed, and her face became rigid, and she spoke in a low, calm tone, more terrible than her most ear-piercing scream; but in the altered tone there still came with thrilling distinctness the same tale of horror. Sometimes with frantic gestures she reënacted the scene of tragedy; sometimes she moaned and crooned and murmured to herself; but while the fit lasted every gesticulation she used, every word she uttered bore distinct and ghastly evidence of the truth of the one story.

Lady Judith's blood was running cold while she listened to this awful revelation. In the first moment, so great was the shock and so profound the horror, that she actually drew away her arms from her daughter's support and let the girl fall back upon the bed. There was a terrible preciseness, a cruel coherency in the words she heard, which seemed to distinguish them from the meaningless outbursts of mere raving in which Alexia's disorder sometimes displayed itself. What the feelings of that mother were during the watches of that heavy night, no man could attempt to describe.

"Oh, my unhappy child!" murmured the wretched lady, "if this be true, I must pray no more for the restoration of that reason which would be only a torture to you! And yet not you—not you, poor child, are guilty of any crime! The guilt is mine—all mine! May Heaven visit it on me alone, and grant me life long enough to expiate and atone for it!"

More tenderly than before did she press her daughter to her bosom. Never when Alexia was an infant had she felt so much of the unfathomable love and pity which belong to motherhood as now, when she held to her heart the frenzied girl whose innocently-guilty hands were stained with the blood of a husband.

With the early morning came a soft, low tapping at the door, and Lady Judith, well knowing who was there, called "Come in!" and Isolind entered. After a night of wild and sobbing delirium Alexia had relapsed into her old condition of almost utter unconsciousness.

"You look very pale and worn, dear Lady Judith," Isolind said. "You have not slept all the night? Where is the nurse? Did she not come?"

"She came, dear, but I sent her away. Come here, Isolind; I want to ask you something."

Lady Judith was seated by the bedside. Isolind approached her, and Lady

Judith took the girl's hand in hers and looked earnestly into her gray sympathetic eyes.

"Isolind, answer me frankly; don't think of my feelings or of anything but the reality! Do you know or suspect anything about—about—the death—of that wretched man—that man Walraven, which others don't know or don't guess at?"

"Oh, Lady Judith," Isolind answered, turning pale, as though she were herself accused of the guilt of blood, "why ask me such a question? Why even think of it? Should we not try to shut out from our minds such terrible conjectures? Nothing about it can ever be known as a certainty except to God. What is the use of trying to know?"

"There is some use, dear; for we can at least endeavor to prevent others from hearing what I heard last night."

"Then she spoke—she told you?"

"She spoke in delirium; but there was a terrible clearness in her words! Isolind, I want you to tell me all you know—all you suspect or conjecture about this—all, every word! The only kindness is to tell me all; the worst of cruelty is to keep anything back from me!"

Thus pressed, Isolind told her in low whispering tones all that she had conjectured; and she could not withhold Alexia's last letter. Cruel as it was to allow the eyes of the mother to fall upon Alexia's bitter allusion to her, Isolind saw no choice for herself but to produce the letter.

Lady Judith read it with lips compressed. Once she started as if she had been smitten. It was when she came to the words which spoke of herself. But she bowed her head, as if she meant to signify her acceptance of one other cruel rebuke from Heaven, and she made no allusion to that passage in the letter. She sighed deeply.

"This, then," she said, "is all that is left to throw any light on the poor child's fate?"

"This is all, Lady Judith, thank God! We may be quite wrong in our wild ideas, and her delirious words are as nothing."

Lady Judith made no reply. To her, too, the whole truth now seemed clear. She knew that Eric Walraven had not killed himself. From that hour she never allowed any nurse to attend Alexia, and she ceased to supplicate Heaven that her daughter might live and be restored to reason.

The days passed languidly and heavily away for Isolind and Lady Judith. Perhaps it may seem strange at first to say that Isolind, with all her anxiety, her nursing, and her watching, was looking better in health, and even brighter in face, than when her pale cheeks attracted the attention of poor, lost Alexia. In truth, Isolind's was a nature which can bear anything better than inactivity, which must work for somebody, help somebody, or perish. Eating her own heart, in her first loneliness of grief, she was pining and withering away. Now, the knowledge that she could be useful, that there was some one she could help, some load of sorrow she could at least try to lighten, consoled and even animated her. Her step grew firmer, and her eyes lost the expression of vacant and brooding sadness which was becoming habitual to them. Her time was very busily engaged; she had hardly a moment to spare for thoughts of herself. She had to take care of Mrs. Atheling; to walk with her, read to her, and be as much as possible a companion to her. For, although the dear old lady insisted that there must be no thought of her in the matter, and that the poor sick girl and her mother must have all the attention, yet "our Isolind" was not likely, from any consideration of sympathy or pity toward others, to neglect one who had ever been more than a mother to her, motherless. So, in that, the brave girl had no time to give to brooding and personal sorrow. She delighted to go into the little market-place of the town every morning, and bring fresh flowers and fruits, in the hope that they might please Alexia; and she brought the London papers to Lady Judith, who felt, of course, a close interest in all the stirrings of Parliament and politics. Isolind even contrived to pay several visits to poor Miss Bruce, who moped piteously at the Hôtel Impérial, and she took Miss Bruce out for a little walk now and then, and showed her most of the points of interest around the village. Once she nearly induced Miss Bruce to join her in a bath in the sea, one of Isolind's most cherished delights. But Miss Bruce was fresh from Scotland, and though she got so far as to put on the bathing tunic and the picturesque *caleçons*, she utterly refused to emerge from the cover of the bathing-hut and allow even the sea to behold her in such unmaidenly attire. So Isolind gave up for the rest of the time any attempt at lightening the load of Miss Bruce's monotony by persuading her to shake it off in the salt waves.

Ah, but one day, one memorable day, there came to Villefleurs something which caused Isolind's cheek to flush with a long unaccustomed glow, and her eyes to sparkle, and then to stream with tears, born of the blended passions of gladness and grief. It was Angelo's letter, written ever so many months—or was it not years and ages?—ago, pledging himself to unchangeable, eternal love, and vowing that he would never, never consent to renounce her, let her resolve be what it might. This was the letter which, enclosed in one addressed to Judge Atheling, Angelo had sent off before he left for America, and which, wandering about from place to place ever since, or lying sometimes for weeks amid heaps of dusty documents in some post-office, had at last reached its destination, having twice crossed the Atlantic, in the effort to get from London to Isolind on the north coast of France. How proud and glad it made the girl! What cruel grief, what bitter shame it brought to her! She could not be otherwise than proud and glad to know that she was so passionately and truly loved. She had always felt, despite of her resolve and of herself, a gnawing pang of pain and doubt, because Angelo seemed to have accepted her farewell without even a protest. But the letter brought her grief, because she still was as resolute as ever that she would not marry Angelo; and she wept, not for her own sorrow alone, but also for the cruel wound she must deal to that loving, gallant, tender heart. And it brought shame, for it renewed the memory of the stigma which rested on her, and which doomed her to a blank and lonely life.

Yet the sum of her emotions was gladness. "He loves me! He loves me!" Nothing, no shame, no agony, can countervail the pride and joy of that conviction, when it is brought home to the hearts of the loving and the absent. When Isolind went to Lady Judith's room, with the precious letter—the crumpled, faded, yellowing, travel-soiled letter—lying hidden in her bosom, there was a brightness in her eyes, tear-stained though they were, which even the sad watcher by the bedside could not fail to observe. Lady Judith looked up at the strong, shapely form of the girl, with her clustering fair hair falling upon her neck and shoulders, her cheeks once more colored with the roseate and purple lights and hues of youth and health; her eyes, like those of one of Chaucer's lovely heroines, "gray as glass"; her elastic step, her graceful movements; and then she looked down at the pale, wasted, fading little face in the bed, and she could not suppress a sigh. Isolind saw the glance and knew the meaning of the sigh, and sighed herself and felt her heart bleed for the mother.

Yes, that day was remarkable. Isolind will never forget it. She did not leave Lady Judith's side for many hours. They two kept watch, seldom speaking, by Alexia's bedside. A change had set in; the fierce feverishness had gone, the girl's pulse was low and feeble, her eyes had lost much of their unmeaning restlessness. She seemed composed and tranquil, and more like a rational creature than at any time since the night when Isolind brought her into the cottage. The doctors had seen her and shaken their heads, and did not appear to think there was anything in particular which they could do. They did not speak of any immediate danger, but they had ceased to talk of hope. They agreed in declining to regard it as a favorable symptom that Alexia had once or twice that day put a question which was quite calm and rational, and had waited for an answer, and understood the answer when it was given.

What a lovely day it was! The sky was pure and cloudless, and yet with no intense heat; the sea was of brightest emerald; all objects, the hills, the houses, the trees, the boats, were outlined with a radiant clearness that reminded Isolind of the atmosphere of her own much-loved bay of New York. The shore in front of the little town made a great curve, thus embracing in its arms the expanse of water where the bathers enjoyed themselves; and beyond the chord of that arc stretched the sea, whose further waves lapped against the shingly beaches of the English coast. All over the shore and the sands of Villefleurs there was color, life, movement, animation. Children scrambled and shouted, dug holes in the sand, gathered shells, or tried in vain to catch the swift-darting, infinitesimal, bloodless, boneless things in the shape of fish, which shot like tiny shadows beneath the surface of the small salt pools left by the receding sea in the little rock-beds among the sands. Up a steep path that climbed the cliffs went a merry procession of fisher-girls bearing baskets of shining, scaly fish on their heads, and singing as they went, their short red petticoats, scarcely reaching to the knee, displaying bare, bronze-colored legs, firm and shapely enough to have excited the futile envy of a whole ballet chorus in the Opéra Comique. Along the sand lounged a little, idling group of soldiers from the neighboring *caserne*—soldiers in blue coats and scarlet trousers—adding with their bright-colored uniforms gleaming in the sunlight another element of life and brilliancy to the many-tinted scene. All along the edge of the shore the green waves were studded with laughing, joyous bathers—girls in costumes of pink and white and crimson and purple. A blind man seated on the sand had before him a tray covered with glittering, variously-colored shells, which he was hoping to sell; and as the light fell upon the contents of his tray it made the spot where he sat to gleam and flash like a sun, so that the eyes of gazers from far-off windows were suddenly dazzled into darkness by the beams that seemed to shoot directly from his poor little unpurchased collection. A short distance further out than the line of bathers the boat belonging to the local society for the rescue of drowning persons was lazily rowing up and down—a good Samaritan keeping a keen eye out for any possible object of rescue. On the horizon were seen the white wings of a whole flotilla of fishing boats sailing in, twenty abreast, and the smoke of a passing steamer now and then revealed itself faint against the sky. Blue sky, green sea, white sails, golden sunlight, yellow strand, and on that strand all manner of colors, purple, crimson, gray, orange, black, fantastically contrasting, blending, and constantly changing—here was a display of Nature at her brightest, humanity in its mood the gayest, the most careless, gleesome, and happy.

The room became too hot where Alexia lay, watched by Lady Judith and Iso-

find, this glorious day. Isolind threw the windows open, and the pure soft air came in, too late to bear healing on its wings. The young poetess looked out upon the scene which these pages have attempted so vainly to describe.

Lady Judith noticed the kind of silent rapture with which Isolind gazed out upon the scene, and said in a low tone:

"It seems a beautiful day, Isolind, and you ought not to be pent up here. Go out, my dear, and breathe the fresh air."

"Dear Lady Judith, I can breathe it here, and I don't care to go out. But the whole scene is so bright and delightful that I could not keep from admiring it. Do come here and look out; it will do you ever so much good. I will sit by Alexia, and you hardly ever now enjoy the pure air and see the sunlight on the water."

Isolind left the window and came quietly over and took Lady Judith's seat. Lady Judith went to the window, leaned upon the sill, and surveyed the scene. Perhaps she was endeavoring to find out whether she too could not open her eyes and soul to the sacred influence of that charm with which sea and sky and sunlight can touch the wounds of certain suffering natures and bid them to be healed. But the flashing colors, the joyous sounds fell sadly on the ears and eyes of the unhappy woman. She had never cared, in her days of pride, for the charm and the glory of Nature, and Nature now refused to accept the offer of a homage that came so late. In certain stern creeds it is held that when a sinner has been too long impenitent, Heaven itself hardens his heart so that if he afterward would fain repent his utmost effort shall be unavailing, and he shall not know the sacred sweetness of expiating sorrow. Would it be too fanciful to suggest that perhaps Nature sometimes exercises such a remorseless power—that when one has refused to open the heart and the mind to her in good time, she deliberately and sternly closes both, so that they may be barred against her consoling, sweetening influence forever?

Some such feeling may perhaps have vaguely suggested itself to Lady Judith's breast. She turned away from the window, and approaching Isolind touched her gently on the shoulder and quietly whispered:

"Go back, my dear, and enjoy the scene and the sunlight while you can. Leave me to sit here, Isolind. All that brightness outside is lost on me. I don't believe my eyes were ever opened to the loveliness of Nature and the world when I was young, and it is too late to hope to cure their blindness now. I wish it hadn't been so; but how few things there are in me and my life of which I could not say the same with all my heart!"

An hour or two passed away, and the sun was beginning to sink and the sound of the waves to be heard more clearly as the noisy life of the day grew quieter. Alexia now and then looked up and asked a question calmly and rationally enough, and having received an answer seemed each time to fade away into unconsciousness again. Since her outburst of grief and passion on the night when she so appalled her mother, she had never made the faintest allusion to the tragedy of her life. Even when she was most clear and rational she seemed now to have no recollection of her recent days and sufferings. When she was not frenzied she was merely infantile.

The sounds of sprightly music were heard somewhere on the road outside. Alexia's ear caught the strains, and she smiled a weak, sweet smile, and asked, as a little child might do:

"What is that?"

"What, my child?"

"That sound."

"It is music, dear."

"Yes; but what music?"

Isolind, hearing the question addressed by Alexia to her mother, looked out of the window in the hope of being able to give an answer. She saw a procession of young men and women, some bearing garlands and some with musical instruments, winding along the road.

She drew near the bed, and Alexia smiled and held a hand toward her. "It is the music of some procession, dear Alexia; some young men and women."

There was a moment's pause, and the watchers thought Alexia had fallen away into forgetfulness again, as she commonly did after the exertion of the shortest conversation. But she presently said, in her child-like tones:

"Please tell me what the procession is—I should like to know."

"I'll find out, dear."

Isolind stepped to the door and asked one of the maids to learn what the procession was and let her know. She and Lady Judith exchanged glances of satisfaction. There seemed something hopeful to them in this awakened and sustained curiosity.

Presently the *fille* returned, tapped at the door, and being allowed to come in said in a tone intended to be soft and low:

"But, milady, it is a marriage procession—a youth and girl who have just been married."

A wild, agonized cry broke from Alexia. The unlucky serving-woman hastily disappeared. Lady Judith gently put her arm round her daughter. Alexia sobbed and sobbed, and fell from convulsion into convulsion; it seemed as though she could hardly struggle through her agony with life. Isolind sent at once for one of the physicians, who came and remained for some time, and gave all the aid and advice he could—which indeed availed but little. As he was leaving the room—Lady Judith did not care that he should remain—he invited Isolind by a glance to follow him. She did so; and when they had crossed the threshold of the room and the door was closed behind them, he told her quietly that the utmost care must be taken to keep the patient undisturbed; that the least shock caused by the revival of any painful memory might be fatal. At the same time he acknowledged the almost total impossibility of securing perfect mental quietude for a patient whose own mind might at any moment, without any external impulse or reminder, bring back all the bitterest associations of the past, and in any case he feared there was little hope or chance.

"And is there nothing to be done—nothing?"

"Absolutely nothing. You can but wait. The end is not far off. Perhaps to-night even—perhaps to-morrow, or later; but unless a miracle should come, the end is near."

So Isolind returned to the already darkening room. Lady Judith, wholly engrossed with the care of her daughter, had not noticed Isolind's absence.

Isolind again drew near the window. A certain sense of the sanctity of the mother's place and right generally urged her to keep at some little distance from the bed, unless when there was some help to be rendered, or when Alexia called to her, or Lady Judith signed to her to draw near. She leaned upon the window her noble head and neck and bust outlined darkly, like a statue, against the violet evening sky.

Alexia murmured:

"Is Isolind there?

Isolind came over and kneeled by the bed. Alexia's little hand wandered feebly out. Isolind took it in her own. Lady Judith held her daughter's other hand.

"Mamma!"

"My child?"

"I want you to love Isolind very much. She was very kind to me."

Then she remained silent for a few moments, and though she still held their hands, and her eyes were open, she appeared to have no consciousness of their presence. Suddenly she withdrew both her hands and stretched them out as if to reach toward some distant object, and there came a light of ineffable sweetness and gladness into her face; an expression quite new to it during all her time of prostration. She endeavored to raise herself up, and with her eyes still looking brightly out, she cried:

"Oh, mamma, I see him, I see him!"

Lady Judith started and laid her finger on her lips as a sign to Isolind to ask no question. She feared that Alexia was speaking of Eric Walraven, and that to her present flush of joy would succeed a terrible reaction into memory and grief. The same thought was uppermost in Isolind's mind, and both women listened with bated breath and beating hearts, hoping that Alexia's fancy might fade away. But Alexia still looked bright and joyous, and she said:

"Oh, yes, I saw him—I can see him still! Mamma, don't you see him too? Look there! Don't you see him?"

Her voice grew so thrilling, her manner became so excited, that Lady Judith could not choose but answer.

"See whom, my child? There is no one here but Isolind."

"Oh yes; my father, my father! I see him now again, oh so clearly—and he beckons to me—see, he takes my hand in his. Mamma, give me your hand too—quick, quick!"

Lady Judith, all trembling, laid her cold hand in the thin, burning fingers of the girl, who pressed it almost fiercely, and smiled delightedly now at her mother, now at the form which her delirium made her believe that she saw. Then with a tranquil, satisfied air, Alexia said:

"I knew we should find him at last."

She closed her eyes, and the hand she had held outstretched gradually sank by her side. Lady Judith found the hand that lay in hers growing weaker in its pressure, then lax and languid, then colder and colder. Alexia gave forth a sigh which seemed rather one of relief and gratification than of sorrow, and she breathed heavily once or twice, and then more softly, and then the room was hushed in silence.

Isolind stooped over the bed, drew gently back, and whispered:

"She is asleep."

Lady Judith pressed to her lips the cold hand she still held clasped in her own, and said:

"She is awake—in heaven!"

The moon which had been rising over the sea now looked into the room. Its first entering light fell upon the face of the dead girl, and, leaving all else in shadow, seemed to glorify with a pure and silvery halo the pallid cheeks and the lips whereon yet lingered the smile with which Alexia had welcomed the dawn of her new life.

CHAPTER XXIX.

"HAST THOU FOUND ME, O MINE ENEMY?"

MORE than two hours passed away before the conversation between Angelc and Charles Scarlett came to an end. Perhaps it could hardly have been called a conversation, for Scarlett uttered scarcely a word other than an occasional question necessary to direct the course of Angelo's narrative. This narrative was itself rather a broken stream; for although Angelo had much of the fluency of the great story-telling southern race, the race of Boccaccio and Ariosto, and although his whole heart was filled with his subject, yet he often found it difficult to get words and to tell his tale. The situation, the experience were so wholly new. A keen double sense of embarrassment and even of awe possessed him. To speak to Lady Judith's long-lost husband seemed like speaking to a ghost. Then what could be more novel and trying than to have to tell to such a man the strange, sad story which the man's own deeds, unknown to him, had woven to be his fate?

The sinking sunlight streamed in for a while through the open door of the cabin. Then it became faint and purple, and disappeared; and the floor was dark. Scarlett sat in the deepest shade. He held his hand over his chin and listened, and hardly ever changed his attitude, never showed any sign of emotion. When he put any question, it was uttered in a deep, sweet, clear tone, that thrilled through Angelo with a power as of eloquence. Angelo could not have told the reason why, but it was certain that as he sat and spoke and pleaded, he became more and more impressed with a vague admiration and even reverence for his listener. The man before him had spoken but a few words, and yet he had already inspired Angelo with a sense of dignity and nobleness of character.

At last the whole tale was told, and there was for a moment a profound silence. Scarlett had heard of the noble charity, the splendid generosity, the almost unconquerable pride, the deep suffering of the wife who ever seemed to him made only of passionless and soulless marble. He had heard of the daughter whose existence was before unknown to him; he had heard of Isolind and of the cruel stigma which rested upon her. He knew too for certain, and now for the first time, that Agnes Dysart was dead. Was ever such story of his own life so told before to mortal man? Had Scarlett been dead and come back to earth from the grave, he could not have known less of all this history than he did when Angelo Volney began his revelation.

The silence was broken by something like a faint sigh from Scarlett, the only evidence of emotion he had hitherto given. Then Scarlett rose to his feet, and Angelo rose too.

"Mr. Volney," Scarlett said in his deep, calm voice, "you at least have deserved well of all my family—since I have a family—and of me. The chance that brought you here is so strange that it ought, I suppose, in itself to be received by me as a command. But I must think over all this to-night. For nearly twenty years I have deliberately and with good purpose withdrawn myself utterly from human life. I cannot in a moment recall all that resolve and order myself back to the life I fled from. But I always believed that my life was wholly my own, and that no human creature could suffer by my having consigned myself to a living grave. Now I learn that this is not so. I must think of what you have told me."

He made a movement as if to accompany Angelo to the door of the cabin. Then he paused again, and after a moment's silence he said :

"The story of my own past life *is* my own. I have not to account to any human being for *that;* and so far as I am concerned, I care nothing how any one may choose to read it. But I tell you at once, for I can guess how deep and natural is your interest in it, that the daughter of Agnes Revington is the daughter of as pure and good a woman as ever lived and suffered—and—and died. I tell you that now, because I don't think you ought to be a night, or even an hour, without knowing it; but I can do more than say this—I can prove it."

Angelo's heart leaped up. For the moment he forgot everything in the delight of this revelation. He could hardly keep from crying aloud the name of Isolind. For this meant that Isolind would be his wife.

"You remain here to-night?" Scarlett asked.

"I suppose so."

"Oh, yes ; you will be provided for ; we try to be hospitable here in our desert. Let me walk with you to where we shall find some of our friends. Men have friends here, Mr. Volney, and no enemies. To-morrow I will tell you what I mean to do. The night will bring counsel."

He smiled a faint smile as he spoke these words, and he motioned Angelo to precede him.

They walked out of the hut, and silently trod the silent prairie. The stars were already beginning to light the sky. Far on the edge of the scene some glowworm-like sparkles were glimmering from torches and kerosene lamps in the canvas town. Myriads of insects twittered and rustled in the grass. The faint odor of flowers came from some of the little garden-plots of the quiet brotherhood. A heron now and then swooped across the plain with throbbing wings. The mountains, now black against the purple star-studded heaven, girdled the whole scene with their awful cincture.

Scarlett glanced toward the mountain wall, and a perceptible tremor passed over him.

"Beyond those mountains!" he murmured. "Mr. Volney, you cannot know what it means to my mind, to speak or think of the world that lies beyond those mountains! I have lived many years here of a quiet which was, at least, a sort of ghost of happiness. I loved to regard myself as free of all earthly bonds and duties and hopes. There is a delicious kind of madness in such isolation; there is the madman's joy of utter abandonment to self."

"You have not lived here always—I mean since you left?" and Angelo broke down, embarrassed to find that he had been drawn into putting a question that might seem intrusive.

Scarlett looked keenly at him, and then calmly answered, as if Angelo's face satisfied and inspired him with confidence.

"When I left England—alone," he said, with some emphasis on the latter word, "I went into Greece, and found refuge in a Greek monastery. I remained there for a long time—how long I hardly know, for I was not myself part of the time. Then I went on to Asia, and adopted the dress and tried to reconcile myself to the life of the East. I thought to bury myself and drown my own individuality by accepting the life of Damascus or Bagdad. I could not endure it. I required a deeper solitude and a fresher nature. I crossed Asia, and sailed from China to San Francisco. Thence I penetrated the American desert, going eastward. Chance—no, I'll not call it chance ; there's no such thing—led me to meet the brother who has now brought you here, and whom we call Paul. Do you know who *he* is? Have you not guessed?"

"No, I have guessed nothing; but I have been tortured by the likeness of his face to some face I know."

"He is the brother of Agnes Revington."

Angelo started. Full light flashed upon him. The brother of Isolind's mother! These, then, were the eyes which seemed sometimes dimly to look into his when Paul turned a gaze upon him.

"This place is full of wonders. It is enchanted!" Angelo exclaimed.

"His story is not mine to tell," said Scarlett; "we are friends, and yet an eternal wall, higher and stronger than those mountains, divides us. Until I found him, he knew nothing of his sister's unhappiness. We could find no clue to and knowledge of her fate—no, none whatever. Now I know why! There are no gravestones or burial registers in this American desert; and she must have found rest for her suffering and noble heart years before I had left Asia. I shall never even look upon her grave; and it is right and just. My presence, my very sorrow would only profane it. One thing you have not told me: does her wretched husband live?"

"He does."

"In England?"

"No; in America!"

Scarlett seemed much surprised at this news, and was apparently about to ask some other and eager questions, but he checked himself, and said:

"No; I don't ask you anything more about him. I had rather not know. I have no further quarrel with him, or enmity against him. There was a time, Mr. Volney, when one of my strongest temptations was a thirst for revenge upon that man. It was one of the temptations which I specially sought to conquer in the purer life of this loneliness; and I thank God that I have conquered it. I have no enmity to Dysart any more, and I don't ask you anything else about him. Let him live, and prosper if he will. If Heaven can endure him, why not earth?"

Scarlett's manner, although it grew gradually somewhat warmer and more confidential with Angelo, under the cover of deepening night, yet had a certain exaltation and solemnity about it, such as solitude almost always gives to a brooding, thoughtful man. Angelo seemed to be walking with one of the prophetic hermits of olden days, and could hardly understand or realize to himself that this dignified recluse, this melancholy, stately visionary, was once the brilliant rising star of London fashion and politics.

They passed a little cabin, near the door of which stood two or three of the brotherhood. One of these advanced and greeted Scarlett by the name of "John." Scarlett stopped. Angelo stopped. The man who spoke was Christian, the Swede, the mystic.

"And so you leave us, John," he said, in clear, pure English, although with a marked foreign accent. "So you *will* go back to the world and all its temptations—away from the Better Life?" There was a blending of anger and sadness in his voice as he spoke.

"Who said so, Christian? Which of us knows anything yet, that leads him to say so?"

"No one said so; but I have seen it. I have seen you leaving us. I have had a vision, and saw you preparing to leave this valley, and to cross the mountains. This dark-complexioned youth"—and he turned on Angelo so suddenly that the latter involuntarily drew back a little—"I also saw in my vision, just as plainly as I see him now. So when he came galloping up from the west, from the evening glow, to-day, I knew he was the messenger who had come for you! Yes, you will yield to the temptation, and you will go. I am sorry for you, John, my brother. But you want the true strength and the spiritual insight, and I always felt that you could never be one of us."

The old Swede turned away half angrily, half sadly, and left them.

"Is he mad?" asked Angelo rather precipitately.

"Perhaps he would be called so in England—in the world," replied Scarlett coldly. "We don't call distinct, self-reliant individuality madness, here. The fact that a man *is* here proves that he is unlike most other men. That fact alone would be enough with most other men to warrant them in setting him down as mad."

"But does he see visions? Is it possible that he can really have seen, in anticipation, what he told us?"

"I don't know. He believes that he did; and if you had lived ten years of a lonely life among these mountains, Mr. Volney, you would perhaps begin to find the horizon of your physical and spiritual vision somewhat enlarged. At least, you would become slow to limit the possibilities of other men's vision. May I now leave you for the night? There is Paul. Having brought you here, he claims the right of giving you a shelter. To-morrow we shall speak together again. I am deeply grateful to you, and if my friendship were in any sense worth having, I would offer it to you. Good night."

Then Scarlett turned away, and his tall form soon disappeared in the growing darkness. Paul and Alexander came up, and courteously took Angelo in charge. He was assigned a little cabin, all to himself, and shared in Alexander's domicile a very modest and temperate banquet of potatoes, apples, and "biscuit," as exceedingly soft, half-baked, doughy cakes are called in America. Paul ate no supper, but remained with his guest until the time came for all to sleep, or try to sleep. Paul talked but little, and did not ask Angelo a single question touching his long interview with Scarlett.

Alexander, on the contrary, talked a great deal, and very shrewdly and pleasantly. Angelo was much impressed by his varied knowledge of countries and people, of literature and of science. One thing struck him as strange and almost inexplicable. The old Scotchman's acquaintance with the literature, politics, and public figures of Europe and America seemed absolutely to have ceased twenty years before, but he was perfectly acquainted with the very latest developments of science. He knew nothing of what followed Kossuth in Hungary, and had never even heard of Count Cavour or Bismarck. But he was familiar with Darwin and Huxley. He had followed Vambery's wanderings, and been amused by Du Chaillu. Angelo failed to understand how a man could thus have contrived to fill his mind so freely with the one class of knowledge, and hermetically seal it against the other. What messenger, living or printed, bore the news of the great Darwinian controversy, but dropped no hint of reform in the English Constitution, of the reconstitution of Italy, and the breaking up of the old Germanic Confederation? Angelo began to find that human eccentricity is marvellously fertile in resources, and ingenious in expedients to indulge its special whims. Alexander refused to taste of political or social "news," as the Brahmin refuses to taste of flesh; and his cultivated keenness of scent placed him on his guard against pollution even by the touch of the grease in a cartridge.

Angelo slept little that night. The strange things he had seen, the strange possibilities and prospects they opened up, the new and confident hope they brought to his own life and love, and the torturing doubt which all new hope brings blended in it for the absent lover—the doubt whether some terrible frustration may not yet intervene—all this was enough to secure for him a sleepless night. Let us do him the justice to say that his own personal hopes and fears and love did not engross him wholly. His mind was deeply filled with hopes and doubts as to the effect which his appeal to Charles Scarlett might have on the lives of Lady Judith and Alexia. It is almost needless to say that Angelo knew nothing of the calamities that had lately fallen on his friend; he did not even know that Eric Walraven had been showing his real nature to his wife; he only knew that he, Angelo, suspected the man, and feared that he would, sooner or later, make Alexia miserable. Would Charles Scarlett return to London? If he did, could he do much to brighten the life of his daughter? How would Lady Judith receive him? Could these two ever become reconciled? Could they ever be a happy husband and wife? Was it not all too late?

Sadly did Angelo own to himself that he could hardly realize in his own mind the possibility of the past being annulled for these two, and their living in one happy home of love together. He could not picture to himself that woman folded in the arms of that man.

At least, Scarlett might protect Alexia, and save her from poverty. That would be something.

And then—and then—Scarlett could vindicate the fame of Isolind's mother, and make Isolind happy. No wonder that Angelo found little sleep that night.

How passed the hours with Charles Scarlett himself? When he left Angelo he walked slowly back with bowed head toward his cabin. The memories of twenty years ago poured in upon him, and oppressed his consciousness and his very frame. As he slowly walked along, there came back to his mind that other night, when he crossed St. James's Park, and looked back for the last time upon the Houses of Parliament. Again he entered his own stately, lonely house, and wrote his parting letter to his wife; again he repaired to the rendezvous appointed, and he learned that Agnes Dysart had sacrificed herself rather than yield to the impulses of a misguiding love. Again he devoted himself, as then, to a life of utter exile and of solitude. Again the fire of ambition burned within him, and again he flung on it the extinguishing coldness of his self-condemning resolve, and quenched and crushed it.

And now he learned that all had been but a wild and fatal mistake. He had ruined the fame of the woman he loved; he had brought calamity upon her child; he had devoted his own wife to a life of misery—that wife whom he had believed incapable of any emotion whatever, but who now seemed to have a nature so rich in splendid possibilities; and he who regarded himself as a childless man had a daughter who loved his very name, and whom the want of his protecting hand had consigned perhaps to life-long sorrow. How bitterly now he repented his rash and wild resolve! How clearly he saw the whole ghastly extent of the sin against himself and his which he had committed when he fled from his post in society! How selfish, sensuous, ignoble, cowardly, seemed the life of quietude and seclusion in which he had vainly hoped to find expiation and purification!

He reached his hut, and he flung himself down, with his face to the earth, and thought of all this in agony and shame.

Was it too late to repair his wrong-doing? At any cost of terrible humiliation—and here, even here in the desert and the night, he winced at the bare thought of a return to life in London, and the wonder and scandal which his appearance there would revive—at any penalty of humiliation, he would go back; he would reclaim his position as a husband and a father; he would bend himself contritely before his wife, if by doing this he could earn the love and secure the happiness of his child. Sometimes, too, a gleam of the old ambition flamed up in his heart. He heard once again the ringing cheers of the crowded House of Commons; he saw the brightening faces of his admiring friends and partisans; he thought of the brilliant, manly career, the noble game of politics, which he had abandoned; and he asked himself, "Is it yet, after all, too late?" Then he thrust the thought, the wild dream, away from him, and he scorned and cursed himself for having given it even a moment's endurance.

Above all other thoughts rose and remained the torturing agony of the reflection that all which he now deplored need not have been, but for his fatal, foolish error—the error of regarding that as heroic self-sacrifice which now showed but as selfish and dastardly desertion. "I have wrecked my own life and the lives of others, only to prove to myself in the end that I am a selfish coward!"

Thus thought Scarlett, as he lay prostrate on the floor of his hut, or paced silently the turf of the prairie, under the unpitying stars. His sensitive and self-torturing soul exaggerated error into crime, and racked him with the agony of late and futile remorse. The errors or the wrong-doings of others now counted as nothing; the Aaron's serpent of his own sin had swallowed up all the rest, and all memory of the rest, for him.

At last he said to himself firmly and calmly, "I will go back, even though it *be* too late."

So he felt somewhat relieved. The resolve stepped between him and his fighting soul; and when the day began to dawn he even slept a little.

Throughout the day the news gradually became diffused through the little community that "John" was going back to the life of the world. All were sorry; one or two felt angry; but there was no thought of remonstrance or even argument. The basis of the association was full individual liberty. Each lived his own life, and could go whither he would unchallenged.

Angelo was surprised and touched at the evident earnestness and depth of the affection with which the brothers nearly all took leave of Scarlett.

"Ye'll be for making a stir in the world, I doubt not," said Alexander sadly. "Eh, man, I fear your heart will turn back sometimes with sadness to the memory of your quiet life with us here among the mountains. If ye ever should come out again, I doubt ye'll not find us here. We can't abide yon roaring companionship much longer," and he pointed toward the distant canvas tents.

Scarlett could hardly speak to any one. He could only press the hand of each.

Paul came up somewhat abruptly, and took Scarlett's hand. Scarlett seemed a little agitated, but he grasped the hand.

"Good-by," Paul said; "I always thought you had no place here. You *have* work to do. Go and do it. The best thing I can hope for you is that you may never think of us again. There is peace between *us?*"

"Peace," Scarlett replied in a low tone—"peace, if you can but forgive me."

"From my soul I forgive you and pray for you. You are doing right now Go in peace!"

Scarlett pressed his hand again, and lingered a little.

"And you" he asked; "*you*—is there no chance of your return?"

"I have no duties in life, and my only task is expiation."

Paul walked quickly away.

Suddenly up came Christian, very much excited, and calling for "John!

"John" approached him.

"Have you any arrangements to make, any injunctions to bequeath, any papers?" the mystic began in an alarmed tone.

"My arrangements are soon and easily made. Christian, I am leaving in a few hours."

"Never!" replied Christian solemnly. "You will never leave this place! I have dreamed of it, and I know it. Take courage, the hour of your release is near! But waste no time; put your house in order! The hour is nearly come!"

Charles Scarlett turned pale and a slight shudder passed over him. But in an instant he regained his self-command and his usual quiet dignity.

"Why have you sentenced me to death so soon, Christian?" he asked with a calm smile.

"Not I, but Heaven."

"I don't want to die just now, Christian; I specially want to live; and so if you can show me where my present danger is, I'll endeavor to avoid it, and so cheat the fates."

"I can't show you where the danger is," said Christian quite seriously and gravely.

"That's the worst of most of Christian's visions," good-humoredly interposed Alexander. "They only tell us something which it in no wise imports us to know, or they warn us of some danger which we can't avert or avoid. What did ye see this time, man?"

"I saw John's grave dug here on this prairie," Christian calmly replied. "He will never leave this place. Farewell."

Perhaps the old man's prophet-dignity was a little hurt by the want of respect for his prediction. At all events he turned away and left the group.

Angelo and Charles Scarlett were to leave the place that evening. Civilization had of late so far encroached upon the hermits, that a mountain ride of some forty miles would bring them to a mining settlement so considerable that a "stage" made regular journeys from it to another and much larger town. Thus they could gradually and easily reach the great highways, and so the self-exiled man could at last return to life.

"I defy augury," Scarlett said with a faint smile; "but I will make some preparations for this doom with which Christian threatens me. There are some things, Mr. Volney, which I must put it in your power to say for me, if I cannot say them for myself. I will go and arrange some papers, and write a few pages which shall be intrusted to you; and then, unless the doom of prophecy is to involve you as well as myself, we may perhaps bid Destiny do her worst."

This Scarlett said in an easy and cheerful tone, almost like that of an ordinary man of the world. Perhaps it was the prospect of a return to England, perhaps the meeting with one who had lately come thence, which led Scarlett, in his occasional words of conversation with Angelo (after their one long conference of the previous night), to lay aside the somewhat *exalté* manner which in his exile had grown familiar to him. But though he treated thus lightly Christian's prediction, it had not wholly failed to impress him. As he returned to his cottage he kept murmuring to himself:

"If it were to be so, if Providence so willed it, what better way out of the difficulty could there be? I dread to go back—I dare not stay! The past looks dreadful and shameful now; but does the future look any better? Are there not things which, once done, can never be atoned for? Am I not too late—too late?"

But he quickened his pace and soon disappeared within his cottage, where for two hours he remained arranging papers and writing. No one intruded on him during those hours. We can only guess what his mental emotions were, what his bitter and useless pangs, as some of the written memorials of the past came once again under his eyes, and reminded him of ruined lives and broken hearts, of love more strong than death, of hate that strove to war with love.

The time went on, and evening drew nigh. Angelo sat under the shade of one of the trees and talked with Alexander and one or two others. The preparations of Scarlett and himself for departure were very easily made, and their horses only waited until Scarlett should appear and give the word for their going. Angelo talked and listened, but he only talked and listened as one might seem to do in a dream. The events of the past day were so strange, the whole scene seemed so unreal, that had all he saw around him suddenly vanished from his eyes, such a phenomenon would have appeared simple and natural. The one most wonderful thing was that the scene endured and did not vanish; that Angelo did not suddenly awake and find himself lying in his room in San Francisco, or perhaps in his long familiar bedroom in Lady Judith's house in far-off London.

Suddenly the sound of several shots fired in rapid succession broke the sacred stillness of the evening. The sound came from the direction of the miners' settlement. Alexander leaped to his feet and surveyed the plain. Angelo after a moment rose too. A man mounted on a horse was seen galloping furiously toward the trees which sheltered the peaceful exiles. He was hotly pursued by some five or six others, who fired shot after shot at him. He now and then flung himself, Indian fashion, flat on his horse, to escape the bullets; and while in this position he twice fired back on his pursuers, in one case at least not without some effect, for the horse of the pursuer fell and flung his rider. The fugitive still dashed madly along, and the thunder of the panting horses' hoofs was now full in the ears of Alexander and his fellows.

"Half a dozen against one will never do," Alexander said coolly. "We must shelter yon poor fellow."

He and another mounted the horses that were already saddled, and galloped out across the plain. When the pursuers saw them come, they slackened their pace and seemed inclined to abandon the hunt. The little community of the brethren had come to be regarded as a kind of sanctuary. More than one poor scoundrel, outcast even from the social laws and life of the rough squatters in the tents, owed the safety of his neck to the intercession and protection of Alexander and his friends.

The fugitive dashed past the two brothers, apparently leaving them to settle matters with the pursuers as best they could. He galloped close up to the clump of trees, under which was gathered a little group of observers. From a further distance Angelo, again lying on the ground, watched the scene with keen and astonished interest. The flying outcast pulled up his horse, and two or three of the brothers came kindly around him and assured him that there he would be in perfect safety, if only he had committed no deed of blood.

The man leaped from his horse with an agility which would hardly have been expected of him by an observer, for he was not young, and he was very heavily built. He was a dark-bearded man with an aquiline nose and keen black eyes. His disordered and torn clothes and dusty face and beard gave him an uncouth and even savage appearance, which contrasted oddly with his voice and manner the moment he began to speak.

"Thanks, a thousand times thanks, gentlemen, for your shelter," he said: and at the same time he removed his felt hat, displaying a head nearly bald, and he made a grand and florid bow. "I have been a good deal over the world in my time, and had many escapes, but never, I think, so close a run as that. I pledge you my honor as a gentleman—which I still claim to be—that I aroused the wrath of yonder savages by no deed of blood, and by no crime worse than that of endeavoring to introduce the truest principles of modern finance to the business and the bosoms of ignorant cads. May I ask whom I have the honor of addressing?"

The brother to whom he appeared to direct his inquiry answered civilly by mentioning the simple Christian names assumed by himself and one or two others, and explaining that they did not, in that little community, care to retain the names which belonged to them in the world.

"A very wise and sensible practice indeed," the stranger remarked, as he thrust his revolver into his pocket, "and one which at the present moment suits me admirably. I heard something about your ways among those brutes over there; lucky for me that I did so, for it gave me some notion of where to turn for shelter when attacked by half a dozen blackguards at once. So I see our friends seem to have at last succeeded in talking the ruffians into a retreat. Truly I breathe again. I am indebted to you, gentlemen, especially for a new lease of life! Allow me to express my deepest sense of obligation; and what so poor a man as Hamlet can—I mean, what a man at present under the very blackest possible cloud of financial ruin can do to prove his sense of obligation, God willing, shall not lack."

This last speech was addressed with several bows and flourishes to Alexander and his companion, who had returned and dismounted.

"Ye owe us no manner of personal obligation, sir," Alexander replied, after he had taken a cool, keen survey of the new-comer, and seemed not quite delighted with the subject of his inspection. "We save life whenever we can, without regard to person or character, except when a man has done a murder. We save life as much for the sake of the blood-shedders as of the intended victim—sometimes more for their sakes, may be. They're a rough lot yonder, but not dishonest, nor without certain rude notions of justice."

"Very rude notions of justice indeed," the stranger coolly said, as he lighted a fresh cigar from the stump of that which he had been smoking, and which in all his flight he had not permitted to go out. "To murder a man because he is clever enough to win the money of some coarse blackguards, is a rather rude and quite primeval exhibition of justice! But I don't know that it is any worse than Wall street."

While most of this talk was going on, Angelo Volney had remained lying on the grass as before. But he was suddenly so much struck by something in the appearance, the figure, the swagger of the rescued man, that he leaped to his feet, amazed, incredulous, yet already half convinced. He rapidly approached the group. The voice of the man then plainly reached his ear, and his conviction deepened. He drew nearer. Yes, it *was* he! It could be none other! There was no possibility of mistaking that form, that head, that voice, with its strangely-blended tones of pompousness and ferocity, that insolent and swaggering affectation of politeness. The fugitive with the torn clothes and the dusty beard was undoubtedly none other than Chesterfield Jocelyn—Thomas Thynne Dysart!

Angelo would now have given much not to be seen and recognized by this man. He was about to draw back, but he saw that retreat was already too late. Jocelyn's hawk-like glance had caught him, and a fierce flash of surprise, anger, and hatred blazed in the dark eyes. But in a moment the face resumed its habitual expression, and Jocelyn, with his familiar *fanfaronnade* of florid courtesy, advanced toward Angelo.

"My dear Volney! this is indeed a surprise and a delight! Do I then really find a friend where I thought the foot of civilized man had never trodden before my own? Is our dear friend Verpool anywhere around? How pleased I should be to meet him; and how glad, I doubt not, he would be to meet *me!* How did *you* come here? Are you, like me, a temporary exile from civilization? Are you alone? Or is there any other little surprise in store for me? Is there any other dear friend near at hand?"

CHAPTER XXX.

"RED HAND."

ANGELO's capacity for surprise had not been so utterly exhausted but that the sudden appearance of Jocelyn on such a scene and at such a moment started fresh emotions of amazement. Nor did the apparition so completely scatter his presence of mind but that he remembered how undesirable it was to have Jocelyn made aware of the existence of Charles Scarlett. He felt much inclined to wish that the enemies who were hunting Jocelyn had been lucky enough to run him to earth before he succeeded in obtaining the protection of Alexander and his friends. He had no alternative now, however, but to acknowledge the acquaintanceship so unexpectedly thrust upon him, and he therefore answered Jocelyn's greeting with cold civility.

"I've been singularly unfortunate since I saw you last, Volney," Jocelyn again broke out. "Every damned thing has gone wrong with me. I had to go into a sort of retreat until that confounded explosion, caused by your amiable friend Verpool's treason, should have done its worst; for, by Jove, San Francisco would have been just as hot for me as New York. Some cursed misfortune sent me out to the mining regions, where I fancied I might have struck a streak of good luck, as they say. I made a fortune that way in '49 and '50, doing smart financial business for the lucky diggers. God! what a chance that was; and what a career I had before me then if I had only played my cards better. It wasn't my luck this time—and those damned fellows yonder said I tried to cheat them—and you know the rest. Is old Verpool here?"

"No; I haven't seen Mr. Verpool for months."

"But you are prospecting and speculating out here for him? Look here, Volney, the life I've been lately leading makes a man as savage as a wolf. I hate all this sort of thing, and it fell on me just when I thought I was on the eve of getting back to civilization, by God! I blame old Verpool for much of it, and if he were here it would give me some comfort to finish up the work with him which you interrupted in New York. *You* can't have any idea of the infernal sense of degradation a gentleman feels in this kind of life. You know I am a gentleman, don't you—or that I was?"

"I know what you were, Mr. Jocelyn; and there are reasons which make *me* at least anxious to forget if possible what you are."

"Stop!" cried Jocelyn in a savage tone and with a face that grew livid with anger, and he seized Volney's arm; "tell me who *that* is. God in heaven! I can't be mistaken—that is *he!* That is Charles Scarlett!"

"Keep these two from meeting," cried Angelo to Alexander, "at any cost."

It was too late. Alexander, who had not been near enough to hear any part of the previous dialogue, looked merely bewildered. Charles Scarlett was seen slowly approaching. Angelo interposed between Dysart and him, and endeavored to prevent Dysart from passing.

"I see it all now," the latter cried. "I see it all! You, Volney fellow, were sent out on an expedition by Judith Scarlett to bring her precious husband home. That's the game; but I'll spoil it. God, this repays me for all! Let me go, you lying lackey!" and he broke from Angelo and stood right before Charles Scarlett.

For the moment the latter did not recognize him. Years and obesity, and now dust and disorder, had done heavy work with Dysart. The latter touched his hat with ferocious affectation of politeness, and said:

"So we *do* meet again, Mr. Charles Grey Scarlett, after all, and it is here then that you have been skulking all these years. Don't you know *me?*"

Scarlett started at first out of mere surprise, to hear his name mentioned, a name by which he had not once been addressed for more than seventeen long years. Then he looked keenly and quite composedly at the man confronting him, and said:

"I can hardly say that I should have recognized you, but I presume you can only be——"

"Yes, I am he. I knew *you* at the first glance. You have had all your usual good luck. Years have not done you much harm. Yes, I am Thomas Thynne Dysart. I am the man whom you contrived to hunt out of Parliament and whose wife you seduced. Gentlemen all, this man has been my worst enemy; he is the seducer of my wife."

"Gentlemen all," said Scarlett calmly, "this man's wife lived and died a pure and innocent woman. I can prove it even to him."

"You lie!" screamed Jocelyn. "You were always a liar with your sham sobriety and sanctity. Your existence was a living lie."

Scarlett's face was terrible to see, while Dysart, standing close up to him and with fists clenched, yelled this language into his ears. All the natural passions of manhood and of a peculiarly sensitive and emotional nature were struggling within Scarlett against the pleadings and the pressure of a self-discipline which for years he had taught himself to regard as man's highest duty. He was a strong man. His life of rugged labor and open air had added every year new power to his limbs and sinews. He could with perfect ease have crushed between his arms the life from out Jocelyn's bloated body.

"Never heed him," Alexander interposed. Look here, my fine man, whoever ye are——"

"I don't heed him, Alexander," said Scarlett at last, recovering completely his self-control. "I never harmed the man; for a long time I tried in vain to serve him."

"You think to sneak back to London and be a successful man there again, and be welcomed to your wife's bosom. By God, you sha'n't! Heaven or the devil—I don't care which—has brought me here to stop you on your way. You shall die here, Scarlett, by my hand; or you shall finish up all the evil you have done me by taking my life. Come, will you fight me here like a man, shot for shot, until one of us falls dead?"

"Dysart, I'll not fight with you. I don't fight; and of all men in the world you are the last——"

"Ha, coward, coward—O coward!"

"My friends here," Scarlett said, "know perfectly well whether I have ever hesitated to risk my life where I thought I was doing right. They know whether I am a coward. Even if they didn't, I had rather bear their unjust contempt than stand justly contemptible in my own eyes. I don't mean to fight you, Dysart."

A new figure suddenly thrust itself in upon the scene. Paul, the brother of Agnes Revington, had kept aloof from his fellows for some little time, anxious perhaps to avoid the parting scene with Scarlett. But some straggling member of the community, meeting him as he wandered idly over the prairie, had told him that something remarkable was going on, and he hastened back and arrived just in time to hear Scarlett call the fugitive by the name of Dysart and refuse to fight him. In an instant Paul thrust aside every one who stood between, and planted himself face to face with Dysart. Paul was slender and sinewy; in mere weight Dysart might almost have crushed him. But as he stood there with his gray eyes flashing, his teeth set, and his fair hair flung back from his forehead, there was an overmastering energy about him which gave him for the moment the foremost place in the scene, and made all others seem as though they had been cast into the background. Angelo drew his breath with difficulty, so intense was his anxiety for what was next to come; and even at that moment, and in features that burned with all the white heat of half-suppressed passion, he could see a wonderful resemblance to the fair, firm beauty of Isolind's face.

"Are you Thomas Dysart?" Paul said, in a voice made low by the very depth of its passion. "Has Heaven really sent you here?"

Dysart looked at him with a kind of contemptuous wonder.

"Are you Thomas Dysart, the husband of Agnes Revington?" Paul asked again.

"I am. What the devil's that to you?" was the ferocious answer.

"I am Agnes Revington's brother, and blessed be God who has brought you here! I have the first claim on your life! I'll fight you, Dysart, scoundrel, swindler, profligate though you are—outcast from all society where honor or truth is cared for—I'll fight you and kill you!"

And Paul struck Dysart a fierce blow in the breast, which made the heavy adventurer recoil and stagger.

For the first time since we have had the privilege of seeing him, Dysart-Jocelyn seemed to lose the brazen self-possession of his effrontery. Some faint ghost of a feeling of conscience may perhaps have even yet lingered within him, and made him for a moment to quail. He did indeed strike mechanically back at his assailant, but there was in his face and manner a momentary gleam of something like abasement and trepidation. Meantime Angelo and two or three of the spectators interposed and kept Paul and Dysart apart.

"No, no," said Alexander, throwing round Paul's shoulders a friendly arm, with a strength in it which no one would have expected from his years, "we'll have no fighting here. What's gone wrong with ye, Paul, my brother, that ye set such an example?"

"If you are really my wife's brother," Dysart exclaimed, "I want no quarrel with you! Go and be damned your own way! But I have an old quarrel to settle with him, and by God he shall fight me!"

He rushed toward Scarlett, who stood with perfect composure. Before Angelo, Alexander, or any other could interpose, Dysart was close upon his adversary. But Scarlett put out one hand and grasped his savage enemy by the chest, and kept him thus at a distance, purple and foaming with rage. Dysart could neither advance further nor break away.

"Will you fight?" he roared.

"I will not! Now listen to me for the last time, Dysart. You know well that, even according to the false code of honor which used to prevail in England, you have long since forfeited all claim to be allowed to fight or to feast with men of character. Out here, men only fight those whom they want to kill, and I don't want to kill you. I don't fight! I have sins to atone for and wrongs to repair if I can! Go away, and mend your life if you can! Do what you will, I'll not fight with you!"

He pushed Jocelyn from him, apparently with the lightest possible exertion of force; and yet such was the muscle of that arm, long inured to severe labor, that the outcast staggered several paces back. Jocelyn set his teeth, and for a moment hell-fire flashed in his dark, cruel eyes, and his teeth glittered like those of a hunted wolf.

"Then die like a coward!" he yelled, "and carry your hypocrisy down to hell!"

Scarlett had already turned away. Jocelyn was standing nearly alone. Alexander and Angelo still kept their friendly pressure on Paul, who now seemed the fiercest and most dangerous of the company. All looked after Scarlett, but his resolute determination not to fight, and the manly strength which secured him from insolent outrage, seemed to banish all thought of danger in his direction. No one dreamed for a moment of what was coming. The scene was still lighted by the sun about to sink, and the trees behind Jocelyn cast their black fantastic shadows on the grass. He stood there, dark against the sunset, a hideous, ominous blot upon the fading, glorious light. Alexander, Angelo, Paul, and four or five others were together in a group. Suddenly two loud reports, following each other in quick succession, rang out from where Jocelyn stood, and the adventurer was for a moment lost to the eyes of the spectators in a little cloud of smoke. Angelo distinctly saw Scarlett stop and turn quickly round, as if gazing with the same surprise as all the rest at the place whence the sound had come, and was for an instant in doubt whether it was Jocelyn who had fired, or whether he had fired at any of the party or attempted to kill himself. But before Angelo could rush forward, he saw Scarlett sway and reel and fall prostrate on the grass, and Jocelyn, with a fierce hurrah of gratified vengeance, flung his now empty revolver high in air, and, thrusting his hands deep into his pockets, swaggered toward the spot whither now all were rushing.

Angelo first reached the fallen man, and raised his head. A packet of papers which Scarlett had held in his left hand had dropped from his relaxing grasp, and lay on the grass near him. Scarlett made two or three gasping efforts to speak, but could not articulate a word. Then he motioned eagerly and convulsively toward the papers on the ground, and his struggle for utterance grew fearful to look at; and then a shiver passed through him, his arms sank, his head dropped back on Angelo's knee, his lower jaw fell with a sigh or groan, and Lady Judith is a widow and knows it not. The career so suddenly checked at its splendid rising is never to be resumed; all old grievances vanish, all old enmities are avenged, all hopes are finished, and Charles Scarlett is dead. His enemy had found him out and killed him.

Three or four seized Jocelyn. He made no effort at resistance. The first words he spoke were:

"Is the fellow dead?"

Paul drew a revolver, and exclaiming, "He is dead, assassin, and you shall follow him!" was about to fire point-blank at Dysart, who still betrayed no sign whatever of any emotion but that of exulting and gratified revenge. Alexander seized Paul's arm and forced it down.

"Nay, nay," he said; "assassin he is, and shall have assassin's punishment; but he shall have the formality of a trial anyhow. It will all come to the same thing in the end, Paul; but the fellow shan't go into the other world to boast that we sent him off without giving him a chance of saying a word in his own behalf. Here, lads, lend a hand and tie this red-handed murderer's wrists."

"You needn't trouble yourselves to tie me," Jocelyn coolly said. "I have emptied my revolver, I have no way of defending myself, and I'm not exactly the build for running away. I suppose I am at the mercy of you fellows, and I don't care a curse what you do with me. I would have given ten years of my life when it was worth having for the pleasure of killing *him;* and if you'll oblige me so far of your great courtesy as to let me have just one final look at him, to satisfy me that I have really done the thing completely, I shall be entirely at your honorable service. Just one look, if you please."

With his usual insolent swagger he was approaching the dead body of his victim, but Alexander cried out:

"Drag him away, and tie him up in yon cabin, until we have time to come to him! Deeds of blood find no countenance with us; a short shrift and a long rope will be his reward!"

Two or three of the brethren bound Jocelyn tightly, and he was dragged with little ceremony into one of the log houses.

The body of Scarlett was carried tenderly and lovingly into the hut which had been his, and where he had passed so many years of quietude and of penitence. It was laid there decently upon the bed. Angelo could not but admire the noble contour of the massive head and the serene handsome face; the powerful, graceful, statuesque frame, the very perfection of that robust manhood which belongs to the finest type of what we call the English gentleman. Other emotions Angelo could hardly be said to have. His mind was not calm enough to allow him to feel sorrow for the wasted career, for the great heart of the man who lay dead. The events of the day had become only like those of some terrible sensation drama, or the weird incidents of a ghastly dream. Angelo could not yet recognize them and feel them as sober, inexorable realities.

Jocelyn had wasted a shot. Either of his bullets would have done the work. One had lodged in the neck, one in the chest. The whole college of surgeons could have done nothing in the case but look on and see the victim die.

Angelo was left alone for a while in the hut with the dead man. A kerosene lamp was burning there, and by that light the young man half-unconsciously examined the packet of papers, which at Scarlett's latest motion he had lifted from the grass. The package contained two envelopes, one sealed and addressed to "Lady Judith Scarlett," the other unsealed and having Angelo's own name written on it. This envelope contained two or three separate papers. Angelo did not then stop to read them, but made them up carefully in the envelope and put the whole package in an inner and well-protected pocket in the breast of his coat.

A step was heard on the threshold, and Paul entered.

"Come with me," the latter gravely said. "You are about to see a strange sight, if anything can seem strange to you after what has already passed under your eyes."

Angelo rose to follow him; but Revington (we may call him by his real name) stopped for a moment and bent over the bed where the dead body lay, and gazed sadly and at first silently at it.

"There's a great spirit gone!" he said at last. "A noble career was marred in *him*. I never knew of a finer nature, Mr. Volney, and yet misfortune seemed to pursue him and all who were bound up with him! How many victims! Three, at least—victims, Mr. Volney of our English society and our social marriages! One purer than he was a victim before him. May they never meet in the other world to be tortured by the struggle between Love and Law again! He was too strong to be Society's faithful bond slave, not strong enough to be her master; and so he wasted his life away, and lies murdered by the meanest of his enemies! Come, now, and see how justice is dealt out to murderers among us."

Paul strode out of the hut, and Angelo mechanically followed him. They walked in silence across the prairie toward Alexander's dwelling. The homes of the brothers stood each apart and isolated; not arranged in any manner so as to form streets, but every one planted according to the taste or the whim of its owner, and adorned after his fancy. Paul's cabin was a square naked structure of logs. Alexander's had quite an extensive garden of flowers and vegetables round it. The visitor entered through a pretty wooden gate, in a paling which encircled the whole, and he passed along a walk between beds of fragrant flowers to reach the door. The purple evening light yet glowed among masses of dark clouds—"black Vesper's pageants." In a moment night will have come. In this region there is hardly any twilight known. The sun falls down rather than sinks, and then comes darkness.

Angelo followed Paul into Alexander's dwelling, and there he saw indeed a strange spectacle. The one room which the hut contained was crowded up by the presence of the whole community. Two or three kerosene lamps, some brought from other cottages, gave their dull smoky light to the place, and added their stifling vapors to the density of the atmosphere, which even the open windows and the night air could not wholly purify. Alexander sat at one end of the room, evidently having assumed the functions of judge. Six of the brethren, among whom were all the American members, seated some on logs and some on stools, acted as a jury. Two or three others stood beside and behind Chesterfield Jocelyn, who, at the nearer end of the room, as Paul and Angelo entered was put up to take his trial. The first words that fell upon Angelo's ears were in the harsh and strident tones of the prisoner.

"I decline to plead before this sort of tribunal. Play out any buffoonery you like, but don't expect an English gentleman to take any part in it."

"Man," said Alexander solemnly, "your life depends as much upon the issue of this trial here as if you were before the most pompous assize court in England. Think of that, and if ye can defend yourself, do so. If yon jury finds ye guilty, no power on earth can prolong your life for four-and-twenty hours!"

Jocelyn only shrugged his shoulders, and said, "Go on!"

"Who accuses this man?" Alexander asked.

"I accuse him." The words came out in Revington's deep stern accents, and he pushed his way forward and confronted the prisoner. The eyes of the two men met, and Jocelyn's sank for a moment. Then Jocelyn looked up and said:

"I can save this honorable and learned court some time and trouble. It is hardly worth the while of the eminent judge and the highly intelligent jury whom I have the honor to see before me—it's hardly worth their while to try the question whether a man has a nose on his face! We needn't have witnesses called to prove what we have all seen."

"Then you plead guilty?"

"Pardon, most righteous judge, I don't do anything of the kind. I assume that I am charged with murder, and I utterly deny having committed any murder. But I killed Charles Scarlett—I don't know what idiotic name you choose to call him here—I killed him; and if it were to do again, I would do it again if all the rowdies in California were ready to murder me by Lynch Law for doing it. I am proud of having killed him! I gave the fellow a chance he didn't deserve when I offered to fight him—as you all saw and heard—and he wouldn't fight, and then I killed him. He seduced my wife; and I was resolved that whenever or wherever we met I would kill him, or he should kill me."

A sort of murmur denoting something like sympathy or approval ran round the jury. Jocelyn's fierce assumption of the character and rights of an injured husband appealed sharply to the sympathies of the stern men who listened to him. Jocelyn saw his chance and his advantage, and a sudden hope flashed up within him.

"Is there any one of you," he demanded vehemently, "who wouldn't have done the same? Is there anywhere a creature with the heart of a man who wouldn't have done it? If the man I killed was your friend, I am sorry for you, but he was my enemy! He had done me the worst possible wrong, and I would have killed him if he were clinging to the horns of the altar! My life is in your hands, of course, and you can murder me if you will; but I did only what every man has a right to do, and I am not afraid to die!"

Alexander looked doubtfully first at the jury and then at Paul. He grieved deeply for Scarlett; but he had always assumed that Scarlett sought exile for the sake of expiation, and it was not impossible that he might have thus wronged Jocelyn, years ago. Certainly Jocelyn appeared to be passionately in earnest, and he had offered his victim the chances of open fight; and Alexander did not see his way to a capital conviction, by such a jury, of a man who even after many years should thus enforce the wild justice of revenge.

Jocelyn's eyes were sparkling with hope and triumph. In another moment the rude, extemporized court of justice would probably have been dissolved, and the prisoner would have been free; but Paul, who had been watching Jocelyn with an expression of blended curiosity and contempt, coolly interposed with the words:

"There is no truth in what this man says. His wife was my sister, whom he brutally ill-treated; and she was as good and pure as she was unhappy."

"Can you prove that?" Alexander asked.

"He can't prove it," Jocelyn exclaimed. "I pity his feelings, as he was her brother; but she ran away with Scarlett, the man I killed!"

"She never did!" Paul answered fiercely. "She fled from *his* house because he was a scoundrel, and she tried to put herself under the protection of her worthless brother—myself—and she died on the way! That's her whole history. The man whom *he* killed told me over and over again that he left England alone, that he never saw her after leaving England, and that she was only too pure and virtuous for the life and the people who surrounded her!"

"Is this supposed to be evidence? Is this quite regular?" Jocelyn asked.

"We don't profess to be governed by the rules of the Old Bailey," Alexander coldly answered; "we only want to get at the truth."

"And is the truth supposed to be found in Scarlett's own excuse for himself, told at second hand?"

"We here knew the man you call Scarlett, and we know he couldn't say anything but the truth. Anything *he* said we accept as evidence."

"Well, suppose it were true—as true as gospel—what's that to me? I didn't know it! I only knew that my wife left my house, that Scarlett disappeared at the same time, and that everybody believed they had gone together. Scarlett's own wife believed it. Didn't she, Mr. Volney—that man there? If I was made the victim of a conspiracy and a puzzle, and left to believe that my wife had deserted me for him, and if I was driven half mad by the thought, am I to be held accountable? Am I to blame? Grant that this extraordinary tale, this pretty bit of Arcadian romance is true—that she left her husband, and he left his wife, out of sheer innocence and virtue, and that my wife died in the very odor of sanctity—grant all this if you like, but remember that *I* didn't know anything of it. The whole thing is as new to me as it is to you!"

Some of the jury murmured again. There was another chance for Jocelyn, and he saw it.

"How say *you?*" the judge asked, addressing the accuser.

"I say that this is not new to him. I say that he knew all about it, and that he no more believed his wife had gone away with Scarlett than I did! I say more than that; I say that my sister left his house and took her baby with her, because he—that man there—her husband, endeavored to traffic in her beauty and her misery, and to induce her to sell herself to Scarlett—to buy her husband's advancement at the price of her own dishonor!"

A groan or growl of astonishment and horror went round the room at this unexpected and terrible declaration. Every eye was turned upon Jocelyn. Even in the dim and flickering light, all could see the change that had come over his face and expression. His lips quivered; the muscles of his forehead worked like the strings of a piano; a hot perspiration shone upon his bald temples, and for a moment he seemed unable to meet the steady gaze of Paul's gray eyes. There were a few seconds of anxious oppressive silence, and then the prisoner plucked up his courage again and exclaimed:

"It's a lie—all a base, damnable lie! Let him prove it! Make him prove it, or leave it to me to make him retract it!"

"Do you want much more proof," Paul asked contemptuously, "than was seen in his face when I made the charge against him? But I can bring some proof too, if you only give me a few moments' time to search for some papers which belonged to Scarlett. Perhaps you know something of them?" he asked, suddenly addressing Angelo, who now for the first time found himself required to lay aside the part of mere listener.

"I have some papers which were meant to be given into my charge. One packet is addressed to myself and unsealed; the other is sealed and addressed to a lady in London. I can't give that up."

"Will you let us see the other?"

"Give me a few minutes—I have not yet looked at any of the papers—and I will see whether I am at liberty to make any of their contents public."

"Quite right," Alexander approvingly remarked. "Let us suspend the proceedings for half an hour, till our friend gets time to look over his papers."

"The prisoner has something to say," one of the jury interposed, observing that Jocelyn was making gestures as if about to speak.

"Only, most honored judge, to beseech that I may not be supposed guilty of contempt of court if I proceed to beguile the time by smoking a cigar."

Without waiting for a reply, he took out a cigar, lighted it, and smoked away. His short hope was nearly gone, and he was beginning to assume the desperado again. But he glanced every now and then to where Angelo stood in a corner of the hut, reading some papers by the light of a smoking, sputtering, foul-smelling kerosene lamp. Some of the members of the court had left the hut, and were enjoying the sweet, pure air of night and the sublime starlight outside. Within there was a profound silence, except for the impatient puffing of Jocelyn's cigar.

Angelo had glanced over the papers in the envelope addressed to himself, and satisfied himself quickly that justice to the dead man and to others excused and even demanded their production. He quietly left his corner, said a word or two to Paul, and put the papers into his hands. Paul looked at one of them—it was in a woman's hand, and was all faded and yellow—with a gaze of profound sadness, and his hands trembled as they touched it.

"Out of the grave," he murmured to himself, "out of the grave, almost, comes her testimony to convict him! Little did she think when she wrote these lines that some day they would come to be his sentence of death! If she could have thought that, poor girl, she never would have written them! No matter; my duty is quite clear to me."

He spoke a few words to Alexander, and the odd little court of justice was soon reconstituted. Jocelyn still smoked his cigar, but his eyes watched Angelo and Paul, and he drew little comfort from what he saw.

Paul said: "I accuse this man of the murder of Charles Scarlett! I accuse him of murder because I can prove that he knew his wife had not gone away with Scarlett, and that he knew she left him because he was urging her to dishonor herself that he might benefit by her shame! I have here a letter from his wife, which shows that this was the only reason why she left him, and that he knew it. He may see the letter if he will."

Jocelyn held out his hand. Paul made his way toward him, and held a paper as if for him to read, while one of the spectators brought a lamp.

"Pray permit me," Jocelyn said, and he took the lamp in his own hand. "This is a serious affair, you see, for me; it is a charge against my honor as a gentleman! Let me see if that really is my wife's writing."

With a sudden dash he seized the paper, and, affecting to bring the light of the lamp more closely, that he might read it, he set the paper aflame. It shrivelled and blazed in an instant, and he let drop the burning, useless fragments.

"Pardon my awkwardness," he said, with a sneer. "My sight is not good. I hope the document was not very valuable; it certainly was not in my wife's handwriting."

A terribly suspicious murmur ran round the room, and some of the jurymen moved rather impatiently. They clearly were beginning to think the trial had lasted long enough. Jocelyn's latest movement had been a complete mistake.

That "court" could have made any allowance for man's passion, but it was utterly intolerant of knavery or trick.

Paul quietly said :

"I expected something of the kind ! I knew it ! Therefore I didn't endanger the letter which is of importance. He is quite right ; the paper he burned was not in his wife's handwriting. It was Scarlett's own memorandum of facts and dates—valuable, perhaps, for other purposes, but to us now absolutely worthless. My sister's letter I now hand up for the inspection of the court. It can be read to the prisoner if he cares to hear it ; but we need not risk the placing of it in the hands which would have destroyed it."

"Stop !" cried Jocelyn savagely, "and let this mummery end ! I made a false move, and my game is up—confound my stupid rashness. It was always my way—some cursed burst of impatience destroyed my prettiest plans ! I don't know what's in that letter, and I don't care now one cent ! I knew perfectly well that my wife never went off with that fellow or anybody else. She hadn't blood and marrow enough to commit sin ! But I knew that he admired her, and that she loved him, and I hated them both for that ; and I did tell her that I cared nothing for her damned anatomical chastity, and that as she loved the fellow for herself, she had better turn him to some account for me ! She wouldn't, and I suppose he wouldn't ; and everybody always praised and admired them and denounced me. He might have had her, and welcome, if he would have paid me my price. As he had her heart, he might have had her body too, for me ! But he set himself up as a pure and lofty sort of person, and he affected to look on me with horror ; and yet he did try to win her away all the same ! I always hated him, and then more than ever. I thank God, or the devil, who gave me the chance of killing him, and I want no more of your damned buffoonery ! Murder me as soon as you like ! I have killed him ! Most wise and honored judge" (here Jocelyn suddenly resumed his familiar tone of affected and extravagant politeness), "you may at once proceed to charge the jury, if such a formality prevails among you, and I shall be happy to hear you pass sentence !"

He put his cigar in his mouth and puffed at it again. He glared round the cottage, answering every eye that looked into his with a reckless and defiant stare.

Angelo could not endure the scene any longer. He pushed his way out of the cottage and stood under the patient stars. His heart was throbbing fearfully, and he was growing sick at the thought of the other ghastly and hideous tragedy which he felt must be soon approaching. There was to his unaccustomed senses something awful and even loathsome in the stern, fierce composure and self-reliance with which the men inside had taken on themselves the right of ordaining life or death. Chesterfield Jocelyn was clearly a doomed man, and detestable as were his crimes, Angelo could not endure to hear his sentence pronounced by such a tribunal. He flung himself down on the grass and turned away from the lights which gleamed lurid, red, and fateful out of the windows of the cottage where the life of a man was about to be coolly voted away. His mind went back to the calm and happy evening—that evening which was the dawn and gateway of so much sweet, sad experience to him—when first he saw Edwin Dare Jocelyn. He saw again the bright skies and lustrous waters of New York bay, and clear against the evening sky, the noble, supple form, the golden hair of Isolind. He remembered her sudden, instinctive dread of Jocelyn—of the man who proved to be her own father—the man whose well-merited, shameful, awful doom he, Angelo Volney, her lover, had unconsciously helped to bring about. His heart beat as feverishly, his whole being and nature sickened as utterly as though he were himself under sentence of death, or rather as if he himself were compelled by some hideous, inexorable fate to act the part of executioner.

A hand was laid upon his shoulder; he started and sprang to his feet. Paul Revington stood there pale in the rising moonlight, but very calm.

"*Consummatum est*," said Revington. "They have found him guilty, and he dies at sunrise."

"But, God in heaven! is this right? have these men the right——?"

"They have the power, and they have the right. Murderers are not to rule here. We are stern in our punishment of such crimes always. Our systems of trial are rough and ready, but they are entirely honest and impartial. No money can bribe us, and no personal influence or feeling warps us. Well would it be for New York if she could boast of such justice! You saw how near that wretch inside, soaked in the stains of a thousand crimes—how near he was to escaping, just because he claimed to have been wronged?"

"Yes, I saw all that, and I have nothing to say for the man, but it seems fearful——"

"To you, no doubt, it seems fearful that criminals should be condemned to death by judges who don't wear wigs and gowns. To us simple and manly justice, based on human feeling and sympathy, seems the purest of all law. That man dies, not because he yielded to one temptation and committed one crime, but because in the history of the crime he proves himself an intolerable pest and nuisance to all human society. However, it is useless talking of all this. The man is to die at sunrise, and in the mean while he has asked to see you. Of course you won't refuse to see him? Then come with me."

They walked toward a hut near to that where the rude trial had taken place. Outside the little paling Revington seemed to be struck suddenly by some idea. He stopped and asked:

"Have you any weapons—a revolver or anything?"

"Only a revolver."

"Nothing else?"

"Nothing else."

"Would you object to lending it to me for a few moments?"

"Surely not."

Angelo produced his revolver, much wondering why Revington wanted it then. But he handed it over and asked no question.

In another moment Angelo stood in the room which was now Jocelyn-Dysart's prison-cell. Jocelyn was watched by two of the brothers. One little lamp gave dull light to the room. Jocelyn was not manacled or bound in any way, and he was walking up and down, crossing the little floor in two strides each time, and still smoking a cigar. When Angelo came in the prisoner scowled at his guards, and said:

"Perhaps these affectionate gentlemen would be kind enough to relieve us of their company for a few moments. They may perhaps be aware that a gentleman doesn't usually discuss his private affairs *coram populo;* and I needn't give my word that I won't try to escape, seeing that there isn't the remotest possibility of my accomplishing such a feat."

The watchers quietly went out of the cottage. Nothing could be more sober, decent, even dignified, than their behavior. Even in an execution by Lynch law among the rude, fierce population of an ordinary mining settlement in California, there is usually a good deal of a kind of grim and rugged decorum. The doomed man, when once his sentence has been pronounced, is safe from levity or insult. In the little community by which Dysart was condemned, a certain air of religious exaltation dignified all their proceedings, and lent to this business in which they were now engaged, and which they regarded as a sad and stern duty, all the grave and rigorous decorum of a sacrifice.

Jocelyn strode over to Angelo and seized him by the hand. Jocelyn's own hand was hot and damp.

"Volney!" he said in a hoarse, thick voice, and he had to moisten his lips with his tongue before he could get any further—"Volney, these blackguards are quite in earnest. They are, by Heaven! They really mean to murder me. Now look here—you know some of them—you must have some influence—can't you say something or do something to save me? You can, I know you can!"

Volney shook his head.

"Mr. Jocelyn, I can do nothing, even if you were innocent of murder and I were anxious to save you. I never saw the people or the place until yesterday. I can do nothing."

"You can, man, you can! Damn it, you can try at all events. Think of a man like me—a gentleman, an English gentleman—hanged like an Old Bailey felon, or a dog—or a dog, by Jove!—and by a gang of nameless blackguards on a prairie. You won't see me die in such a way without making an effort to save me? Why, don't I know well that you are in love with my daughter? Do you mean to tell me that you can have the face to go back and ask Isa—Isola—what the devil is her name?—to marry you when you have allowed her father to die like a dog?"

"Mr. Jocelyn, I beg of you, in the name of Heaven, to put such thoughts out of your head and prepare for death. Nothing could save you. Don't waste the few hours you have. Think of repentance—turn to God."

"Stuff, man; it hasn't come to that yet—it can't have. They'll never dare—yes, confound it all, they will though. There's no law here. Talking of repentance is all rot. I never in my life felt any of the thing people talk about—stings of conscience and all that. I don't believe there's any such thing. Look here, Volney, I don't feel sorry for anything I ever did in my life, unless, of course, where it injured me. I'm sorry I made so many confounded mistakes. I'm sorry I didn't strangle old Verpool that day. But as to being penitent for sins, and all that, I'm not penitent, and I don't believe anybody ever is. So we needn't waste any time over that sort of thing. But you must go to these fellows and try to talk them over—you must indeed. You shan't leave me to die, Volney, without making an effort to save me. Think of *her*—I always forget the ridiculous name they gave her—and remember that I am her father."

Angelo yielded at last to the terrible urgency of the wretch, and he did seek out Paul and Alexander and try to plead for Jocelyn's life. They listened to him patiently for a few moments, but they assured him that he pleaded in vain.

He came back to the condemned man, who rushed at him with glowing eyes. When Angelo told him the result he broke into an outburst of savage execrations which seemed to the excited fancy of the young man to be like outrages flung into the very face of Heaven. Angelo would have left the place in horror and disgust but that Jocelyn clung to him. Suddenly another idea flashed across the mind of the latter, and he began to ask whether there was no chance of escape. He demanded in a frantic way whether there was no possibility of getting out of the cottage unseen and reaching his horse, and so on. Angelo quietly and earnestly showed him the vanity of all such ideas, the utter impossibility of escape.

"Well, then, if I must die, if you can't do anything to save me you can at least help me to die like a gentleman. Volney, my father spent his money and ruined himself, and then blew his brains out. Like father like son! What was good enough for him is good enough for me. Lend me your revolver and see if I don't cheat these scoundrels yet."

He squeezed Angelo's hand fiercely. Angelo drew back. He now for the first time knew why Revington had borrowed his revolver. He owned to himself that if he still had the weapon there would have been a terrible temptation to give it to Jocelyn, and save Isolind's father from a base and ignominious death.

"I have no revolver," he answered, "and no weapon of any kind. I gave up my revolver before I came in here. I know now—I didn't know then—why I was asked for it."

"So you can neither help me to live nor to die?"

"Neither. I can only implore of you, for your own sake, to think no more of anything but preparation for death."

"Thank you, you are very kind. Quite an estimable and model young man in every way. You can leave me now. I don't trouble you with any messages for my daughter. I am not by any means sentimental. I can die, Volney, as I have lived. I never was afraid of anything in life, and I will show these ruffians that a gentleman can die without trembling."

Yet, though he was bracing up all his energies, and though he strove to assume his old swagger, he was actually trembling. His nerves had failed him. He was cowed—quite cowed.

"You see, Volney, I'm not afraid—the fellows must acknowledge that at all events. Don't go yet—must you go? Stay a little—I don't like to be alone. What's the hour now? Good God, is it so late? How the time passes. These wretches will soon be here. Oh, damn them! I don't care, I won't die! They shan't kill me! Volney, Volney, save me—save me for *her* sake. Don't let them kill me. God, my nerve is all gone! You coward, you could have saved me if you would, but you want to have me out of the way that you may marry my daughter! You are all in one damned conspiracy against me. Don't go, Volney; stand by me. Save me, save me!"

When Angelo at last made his escape from the hut and breathed the pure air, he felt as if he had come out of the foul and lurid vapors of blasphemous, despairing hell, into the sacred atmosphere of a starlighted court of heaven. He saw at length the dawn flame up all yellow and crimson over the plain, and he fled to the furthest hut on the verge of the little shallow stream, and he buried himself there and closed his ears as well as he could against all sounds from without. The morning had far advanced when he came out and mingled with the living again. Then he learned briefly that the hideous tragedy was all over, and he heard that Thomas Thynne Dysart, Chesterfield Jocelyn, the outcast of English aristocracy, the forger and swindler, the fearless, audacious adventurer, the bloodthirsty and desperate murderer, had utterly broken down at the last, and died not like a bravo, not like a felon, not even as he had himself said, like a dog, but like a coward.

CHAPTER XXXI.

A GLANCE BACKWARD.

ANGELO did not remain long among the brethren of the little community. He saw the last of Charles Grey Scarlett; saw the earth of the prairie close over that career of promise so suddenly self-arrested. He took a cordial, friendly farewell of Paul Revington, whom he never expected to meet again in life; said good-by to Alexander and others of the friends, and went his way back to San Francisco.

Angelo resolved at once that he would return to England. The tidings he had to convey, the documents he had to carry, were such as he did not feel inclined to trust to any other care than his own. He felt that at whatever inconvenience to himself he was bound by every obligation of gratitude and duty to hasten back to Lady Judith and lay fully before her, as no letters could do, all that he had known. Therefore he made the best arrangements he could in San Francisco, that his place might be filled in his absence, and he sailed for New York by the Panama route. The great railway that now binds together New York and San Francisco, that marries Atlantic to Pacific, was not yet finished. On many a soft, sunny day, as he lay upon the deck while the steamer made her way through the bland and amber mists of the Pacific, or in the glittering brightness of the Caribbean Sea, he read and read again the papers given into his charge and left unsealed by Scarlett. From these he endeavored to reconstruct the sad story which had run parallel with that of his own life thus far, and on which he had seen the green curtain of the prairie turf so lately fall.

The papers which he had were two letters from Isolind's mother, both addressed to Scarlett, and both written in the early part of 1851. When Angelo first received them they were accompanied by a paper containing a few explanatory words and dates, written by Scarlett himself. That paper, as we have seen, was seized and burned by Jocelyn. But Angelo had read it carefully through beforehand, had quite mastered its contents in fact, and having an excellent memory, was able still to avail himself of all the data it furnished for the elucidation of the mystery so long hidden.

We need not read the melancholy letters, offspring of so much trial and agony. Let us be content with a short survey of the history which revealed itself gradually to Angelo from the study of them.

In the early part of the year 1851 Agnes Dysart found that she could no longer live with her husband. His profligacy and his cruelty would never have driven her from him. His ferocious and frequent taunts about her former engagement with Scartlett she patiently bore. But at last, when debt and difficulties began to make Dysart desperate, the latter again and again savagely urged upon his wife that she must turn to account her supposed influence over Scarlett, and it was then that Agnes Dysart resolved upon leaving her husband forever, and taking her infant daughter with her out of the reach of contamination. She resolved at all hazards to endeavor to find her brother in America, and put herself under his protection, glad to endure any life of drudgery and poverty, if needs were, where shame and sin were not to be. But she could not bear the idea that the one man whom alone on earth she had ever loved and trusted should misunderstand her flight, and she therefore wrote a long, pathetic, heartbroken letter to Charles Scarlett, telling him that she was at last compelled to leave her husband, and why. Never, perhaps, even from the often-tortured heart of woman, was there wrung a confession so full of pain and shame as this. This was the paper which passed sentence of death on Thomas Thynne Dysart.

At this time it would seem (for we supplement Angelo's conjectures here by the testimony which Robert May and afterward Lady Judith herself could have offered) that the estrangement between Scarlett and his wife had grown so profound and apparently so hopeless, that it cast a gloom over Scarlett's whole existence. He believed he had made a fatal mistake in life, and he could not recncile himself yet to patient endurance. With his over-sensitive heart and a certain tendency toward morbid nerve excitement, like that which shattered poor Alexia, it became terrible to him to have to live under the same roof with the cold and apparently unfeeling woman who, as he believed, detested him. He had even more than once poured out his soul to his old friend May so far as to tell him that he thought of separating from his wife; and May always earnestly advised him not to take such a step. Then came Agnes Dysart's letter, and Scarlett, driven almost wild by pity, irrepressible love, and bitter disappointment, resolved to throw everything away that lent honor to life and hope to ambition, and tear her from her misery even at the expense of her self-respect. So fiercely, recklessly did he urge this sudden, half-insane resolve, that Agnes Dysart began to tremble for him and for herself, and at last she determined, as May once said, to fly at once from the man she hated and the man she loved.

Her second letter, in a few brief, piteous, agonized sentences, explained this. She had allowed Scarlett to believe that she was yielding to the urgencies of his despair, only that she might gain time to escape, and save him and herself. In her second and last letter she told him of this, told him she had gone forever, besought and prayed of him not ever to think of following or finding her, and with all love and pity and agony commended him to his duty, his honor, his home, and his God. One sentence in the letter besought him never to quarrel with Dysart, and also revealed the fact that she had left a letter for her husband announcing that she had gone to seek her brother's protection, and imploring of him, as the only reparation he could make for his sins and crimes toward her, not to allow slander to fall on her fair fame. Thus then it became clear that Dysart had never really believed his wife to have gone away with Charles Scarlett. But Dysart hated his old rival none the less—nay, all the more, because he felt sure all his own baseness had been revealed to Scarlett. He had tried to traffic in the beauty of his wife and had failed; he had all the shame and none of the profits. So far as he could, he revenged himself on his wife and his enemy by publicly denouncing and stigmatizing them both as accomplices in guilt.

But Agnes Dysart's resolve had unfortunately a result of which she never had dreamed. Scarlett's soul revolted against the thought of resuming his old life, taking up the broken threads of his career. He had gone too far to go back. His awakened conscience branded him as a criminal. The sin he would have committed seemed to him as heavy and black a stain as though it had been done. He had already pronounced on himself the doom of exile, and he carried out the sentence—alone. He wandered into Greece and Turkey, and in a Greek monastery his reason for a time deserted him. But in whatever mood or phase of temporary insanity, he always remained true to his purpose, and never betrayed his identity, never revealed his name.

Restored to intellect, he crossed Asia, entered America, met with Paul Revington—and the rest is known. How far some original taint of the mental excitability and weakness which afterward showed itself may have been responsible for his one profound error, his one fatal resolve, no moralizing critic can venture to say. The man had genius, courage, great ambition, great depth and capacity of love. Something was wanting, the lack of which doomed all these to disappointment and frustration. Charles Scarlett lived, loved, thought, spoke, dared, and suffered in vain. A rude wooden cross was set up to mark where he lay, and it was faithfully preserved in safety while the little community among whom he had passed so many years still remained on the scene. But they soon migrated thence, some in search of a new place wherein to pitch their tents unvexed of encroaching civilization, some to return once more to the active world.

Then the storms and snows of winter soon swept away the simple monument that marked the spot, and nothing remained to guide any friendly eye to Charles Scarlett's grave. When the great railway to the Pacific was made, there came out to that region certain who sought for the place—a stately, grave lady in black, a fair-haired, noble-looking younger woman, and a dark-complexioned young man. They sought for the place where the grave was made, and one of the party had been there on that prairie when the grave was dug and the body laid therein. But Angelo could not find the spot. He endeavored patiently to recall the position of the log huts and the canvas town, and thus to guess at the grave of Charles Scarlett. But the tents were gone, the huts were gone; a quite pretentious town stood near, which had negro minstrel performers and a newspaper; the very river had oozed into a new course, and the search was vain. The earth had swallowed its prey, and Scarlett's widow never knew where the body of her husband returned to the dust.

From this glimpse of the future our story returns to its course, now not long.

Angelo reached New York, found out old Verpool, and obtained from him a leave of absence long enough to cover his visit to Europe. It may as well be said at once that the absence *en congé* was changed into one in perpetuity, and that Angelo never again entered the service of the tough old Vermonter. The very day he reached New York he wrote to Lady Judith a few lines to announce his coming, and to prepare her in some degree for the news he was to bear.

He remained but a few days in New York—only long enough to make the arrangements needful for his journey. But short as his stay was, he found time for one little expedition. One bright evening he took the train from the city and went to the little railway station close to the place where the Athelings had lived and where he first saw Isolind. The house was let to other tenants now; but Angelo crossed the paling which divided the woods from the road and made his way among the trees until he found the spot where Isolind and he were seated side by side on the day when he first broke into a confession of his love. The tree still lay there, and Angelo hewed and hacked a precious fragment, a sacred relic, from it. Then seated on the tree he abandoned himself to all the sweet and bitter memories of the scene. The sun went down in gorgeous, heaven-suffusing effulgence of purple and flame, its latest rays gleaming through the trees with an almost intolerable brightness, and then the short twilight passed like a breath or like youth, and soon the fireflies sparkled and glittered on the grass and among the trees. Angelo rose, not without reluctance, and turned to leave the spot. One last glance he gave, and then obeying an involuntary, irrepressible influence, he flung himself down beside the sacred tree, pressed his forehead and his lips to it in token of farewell, and hastened away, looking back no more.

He was pacing up and down the platform of the little station waiting for the train, when he heard a heavy step behind him, a heavy arm was flung over his shoulders, and turning round he saw Judge Atheling standing there. The warmth of that mutual greeting seemed to welcome Angelo back to the old life and hopes and love from which he had lately been exiled. Atheling, too, had been down to see the old place. They returned to town together, and sat up until late in the night exchanging confidences and explanations. Each had much to tell which astonished and thrilled the other. Not even the delight with which Angelo listened to every word that told of Isolind could wholly overcome the pain and sorrow with which he learned of Alexia's untimely death.

CHAPTER THE LAST.

"FOR LOVE IS CROWNED WITH THE PRIME."

LADY JUDITH SCARLETT has returned to London and resumed sadly and resolutely the duties of her life as they seemed to her. She labors in every good cause, or cause that appears to her good, in social and moral reform; she feeds the hungry and clothes the naked as of old. Alexia her daughter sleeps in the family graveyard of the Corydens, and is closer to the heart of her mother in death than ever she was in life. To the outer world the character of Lady Judith shows the same as ever; but those who come nearer to her, whether poor or rich, can notice a wonderful softness and sweetness in her which were not so before. One mark the trial she has passed through has set upon her brow to be seen of all eyes. Her hair is now as white as snow. The contrast between the face and form, still superb in the prime and pride of womanhood, and this coronal of white hair, has only added something like a new dignity and grandeur to her. She looks like some majestic woman of the Scriptures, enduring life that she might be helpful to her people.

Mrs. Atheling and Isolind have left Villefleurs, and are living in another little watering-place on the same coast. The associations which clung around Villefleurs rendered the place intolerable to them.

The parting between Lady Judith and Isolind was surcharged with strange emotions for both. Now that the two women were awakened out of the kind of feverish dream in which they had lived together during Alexia's sickness, each looked at the other with a certain timidity and shame. As in a night alarm of fire or wreck people almost strangers to each other rush half-dressed and huddle and cling together, and then when the terror is over and the gray light of morning begins to shine on them they are ashamed and shrink back, so there was a certain shamefaced shrinking back, or at least an impulse that way, on the part of Lady Judith and of Isolind alike. Perhaps each felt that it was needful they should separate. But each now felt toward the other only the truest regard, compassion, and love.

"Shall we not meet any more—ever again?" Lady Judith asked, and conquering a certain emotion she took Isolind's hand in hers.

"I suppose not," Isolind answered with moistened eyes, "unless Heaven wills us to be useful to each other. I suppose I shall soon go back to my own country—I mean to America, which was my own country so long that I can't think of it otherwise."

"Wherever you go, dear, I shall always follow you in my thoughts with gratefulness and love and prayer. I wish I could serve you—I wish I could make you happy."

Isolind shook her head.

"Could I not make you happy, Isolind—could I not do something toward making you happy, if you would only allow me?"

Lady Judith spoke with infinite tenderness and softness; and Isolind understood her meaning. Isolind knew it was this: "Let me bring you and Angelo together, that you may be married." But even Isolind did not know what a magnamimity of self-chastening and noble penitence was expressed in these few quiet words.

"Ah, no, Lady Judith! Nothing can be done for me—nothing!"

"Your resolution then is so fixed—unchangeable?"

This was the nearest approach to any direct allusion to the past on which

Lady Judith ventured. She did not look at Isolind while she spoke; nor did Isolind raise her eyes while she replied in the one sad firm word:

"Unchangeable."

"Then, good-by, my dear. I appreciate and honor your purposes and your motives. You have taught me some lessons, Isolind, which will last me for my life! I hope Heaven will give you happiness in some form. But you carry with you always the grand talisman against unhappiness, in your pure conscience and your noble heart. Good-by!"

Then she kissed Isolind, and soon after began her sad journey homeward with the coffin of her dead daughter.

Soon after Mrs. Atheling and Isolind too left Villefleurs for their new residence. There the days and weeks dragged heavily along. Judge Atheling had not yet returned to Europe. The present was dreary to Isolind, and she thought of the future with a blank dismay. What was to be her life? If it should please Heaven to take away while she yet remained young her kind and loving friends and protectors, into what sad and loveless path was she destined to wander with heavy feet and heavier heart? Would a time ever come when she and Angelo might meet even as friends? Must she never see Angelo again? Could it be that a time ever would come when Angelo and she, living in the same world, should be nothing to each other? This was the most torturing thought of all.

After the excitement and strain of the events which had lately passed, and which had for the time torn her away from her own sorrows, the reaction that plunged her back again into lonely meditation was terrible and desolating. There were times when Nature and Passion raged within Isolind, and she longed to break away from the regular monotony of her life and plunge into utter solitude, or into some existence of active work. There came days when she said to herself, "This kind of life will kill me! I must do something or die!"

But she always strove to discipline her nature, and to remember what she owed to others. She could not affect to doubt that her companionship was dear and needful to Mrs. Atheling, and therefore she resisted all impulses which would have driven her into any more active sphere of woman's work. Poetry no longer came to her relief. Thackeray has laid it down as a law that when a man or woman can begin making rhymes about a grief, the sense of grief can no longer be very strong. But this is only true of those who are not great inspired poets. Such do indeed sometimes find relief from utmost sorrow in pouring forth poetic plaint and passion. Isolind knew now only too well that she did not belong to this great inspired order; and she felt her own sorrow too acutely to put it, being uninspired, into rhyme and verse.

The best thing she could do in one of these often-recurring paroxysms of agony was to take a long, quick walk somewhere by the sea. If the day was not fine, all the better. If the sun was overcast by storm-clouds, and the wind blew and the waves tossed and roared, all the better. There are moods of the human mind when nothing soothes like the tempest.

Autumn was beginning, and beginning rather early. There came one day when the heaven was wholly overhung with thick brooding cloud, and the gray heavy sea murmured in low, dull, ominous tone, and everything seemed to forebode a stormy evening and night, and Mrs. Atheling would not venture out, and Isolind could not stay at home. She wrapped herself in a shawl and went for a quick walk along the edge of the cliffs. Glancing down at the little pier, she saw the steamer come in which brought people from Dieppe or one of the other great and fashionable places; and she was conscious of a sense of gladness that the boat had got in before the threatening storm began. Otherwise he heeded it not; she felt no curiosity about the passengers it might have brought; she never went down to the pier as so many others did, making such expedition the grand event of their idle day, to see the new arrivals. The boats came and went, but not for Isolind. As she walked along she met two merry, bright English girls, who had seen the smoke of the steamer and were hastening to the pier. Their hair was blowing in the breeze, their complexions were rosy, their figures were well wrapped in gray waterproof cloaks in expectation of the coming rain; their short petticoats fluttered around their stout Balmoral boots; their white teeth gleamed healthily as they chattered and laughed; they were a very "living picture" of youth and health and good spirits. Isolind looked at them and after them with admiration, and a certain irrepressible feeling of envy, and a certain wonder—wonder that there could be gleeful and happy girls. Perhaps some father, or brother, or lover is coming in that boat? There are then still happy women who expect fathers, brothers, lovers to come to them? And I!—but Isolind walked only the more rapidly along the road on the cliffs, and strove to banish by movement and by battling with the rising wind the fierce pangs which were tormenting her.

She walked on and on, and the wind grew wilder and the sea tossed more passionately, and at length the rain began to fall. Isolind never at any time was afraid of a shower of rain, or even was much concerned about a very drenching therein; and at the present moment the wildness of the storm and the loneliness it created were welcome to her. So she still went on, observing with interest how the cloud and mist began gradually to obliterate the sea. The gloom and utter dreariness of the scene were congenial with the girl's sad mood. There crept up to her memory as something that ought to be part of the scene and the hour the sorrowful sweet wail of Thekla, the prayer to the Holy One to call home his child who had enjoyed all the earthly happiness that could be hers, having lived and loved. "Oh," exclaimed poor Isolind, "if I might only die to-day! I have lived and loved; and my love is all in vain; and I have nothing now to live for, and I shall never see Angelo any more!" And she stood still on the open road, pressed her hands to her eyes, and burst at last into passionate tears.

Terror! She had fancied that no one could be near, that the wind and mists had made an utter solitude of the place; and now she heard a quick step behind her—the tread of a man hastening on. He must have seen her—seen that she was weeping; and shamefaced she hurried away. But in a moment the tread was close behind her, the man was beside her, his arm was flung round her waist, and Isolind, startled, bewildered, indignant, looked up—and saw Angelo! Oh, the divine ecstasy of that moment, when every thought was lost in the one delight of meeting! Stream mist, blow wind, toss and moan gray and mournful sea; not the most glorious scene and heaven of a fabled summer-land could have for Isolind one tithe of the glory and delight of that enraptured moment! True, it would have been but a moment of rapture, for the sad existence of a resolve needful and inexorable apparently as fate itself would soon have reasserted its right, and told the girl she and her lover must part. But the moment of rapture was destined to remain forever a memory of unbroken joy, for Angelo exclaimed:

"I have you, Isolind, and I will never leave you again! You are mine forever. I give you the pure fame of your mother, made clear as light; and I claim you in return!"

Let the gathering mist and the deepening dusk of evening enfold these two, as in the veil of a sanctuary, while they walk slowly home and pour out in such broken words as spring from supreme emotion their hearts to each other. We have no right to listen to their talk, or to try to reduce to the dull literature of printed report the all-imperfect expressions of their joy and confidence and hope and love. While they live, it will always be that an autumn evening of wind and rain and gloom, which fills other hearts with drear and melancholy feeling, shall come to them full of the brightest and gladdest association, for it will remind them of that first meeting after a separation that seemed hopeless—of that hour which gave them back to each other, and made them one for life or death.

The rest is not long to tell. Angelo had been in London, had seen Lady Judith and told her the sad and shocking story of her husband's death, and given her the papers which he bore. What words of self-condemnation or vindication—what appeal for generous judgment, or for pardon, may have been contained in Charles Scarlett's letter to his wife, no one but his wife ever knew. Events had lately broken down so completely the intrenchments of egotism which once ramparted Lady Judith against the influence of her better nature, that she was prepared to judge more sympathetically, and therefore more justly, of her husband and of herself, than she ever could have done before. Alone in that familiar room where we have so often seen her, she read the letter again and again. "If we had but known each other!" she said with a deep sigh—"if we had but known each other!" The words and the sigh were the fitting epitaph and dirge of her married life—the history and confession of the error of two noble lives.

Then she set herself resolutely to carry out to practical purpose the wishes expressed in Scarlett's writing, so far as these could any longer be realized. There was one earnest wish of his which could no more find fulfilment on earth. His knowledge of his daughter's existence came, as so much other knowledge had come to him, too late.

When Charles Scarlett was preparing for his flight from London, he had no thought of a luxurious exile. He meant to enter upon a life of obscurity and labor of some kind, perhaps literary, probably in some Western city of the American States. He had therefore taken with him but a comparatively inconsiderable sum of money. It seemed to him that the step he was about to take would have brought with it utter degradation and the forfeiture of all self-respect, if it did not bring with it some personal sacrifice. He left behind him a will, in which he bequeathed the whole of his property to his wife, "provided she will consent to accept it, and will believe my solemn assurance that this disposition of my property is not meant to add by insult further wrong to that I have already done her, but because I believe it to be right, and do her the justice to believe that she will make the wealth which was useless to me serviceable in some way for good." If, however, Lady Judith should refuse to accept it, then it was to be disposed of in the founding of certain institutions for popular education, which he described. In any case, there was a legacy of a few thousand pounds to Robert May.

When Scarlett was nearing the other great crisis of his life—preparing, as he believed, for a return to England—he was apparently impressed more profoundly than might have been expected by the stern prediction of Christian, the Swede. Perhaps his coming fate had cast its shadow before. Certainly he wrote his letter to Lady Judith as if it were the last message of a man about to die. In it he referred to his will, and begged of her to act upon its disposition, only with a distinct expression of a desire that a proper provision should be made for the daughter "of whose existence I did not know until yesterday." Also the letter contained a request that five hundred pounds a year should be made over upon Angelo; "enough to allow him to choose his path in life, but not enough to deprive him of the healthy stimulus of a need to labor"—this gift being described as "a poor recompense for a life of devotion to duties which I deserted, for the earnestness which conquered my reluctance to return to active life, and for the honest and truthful eloquence with which he taught me to understand for the first time the real character of my wife." The letter contained no allusion to Isolind. Evidently Scarlett felt that she would not care to accept any benefit at his hand, and that even her name would hardly find a fitting place in this his first and last long and confidential letter to his wife.

That part of the letter which referred to the will was the only portion made known to any one by Lady Judith. It is due to her to say that she was deeply and sincerely rejoiced to find that the memory of Isolind's mother was free from stain. "I might have known it," she said; "no sinful mother ever yet had such a daughter." For the stern old theology had still its hold over Lady Judith's heart and mind. She could not let the sin of a mother be blotted out, but she rejoiced over the daughter now proved to have sprung from the womb of a mother who had not committed the sin.

"Go to her, Angelo," said Lady Judith, "and tell her I shall not believe you have both forgiven me until you have made each other happy."

So Angelo went and found Isolind, and when Judge Atheling comes to Europe the pair will be married. Atheling has, out of the wreck of his fortune, enough left for himself and his wife to live quietly and happily; and these two can always be happy together. Angelo does not think of leading an idle life. He will keep to his practical study of mines and mining both in Europe and in America, and means to make a business out of it, and to be a citizen in this sense of both continents. Thus the Athelings, when they return to America, will still have a chance of sometimes seeing the daughter of their heart and the husband of her love.

One last pang awaited Lady Judith, in the revived gossip and gabble which were the result of the steps necessary to be taken in order to prove the death of her husband, that his property might be administered according to his wishes. She bore it bravely and patiently; and the traditional nine days passed away. She did not habitually take in any American papers, and she therefore did not see the four closely-printed columns which appeared in the "Sunday Sociable" of New York, wherein the London correspondent of that journal gave a *verbatim* report of an interview he professed to have had with herself, in which she told him the whole story of her life, drew a terrible picture of her husband's crimes and violences toward her, and assured him in language of lurid efflorescence and dazzling grandeur that such was the common domestic life of the British aristocracy, and such the sufferings woman has to endure in the select circles of Belgravian fashion. Judge Atheling heard of this; not that he ever read the "Sunday Sociable," but he did read the "Tribune," the "Times," the "Evening Post," the "Nation," and the other respectable papers of New York—journals unsurpassed by the press of any city on earth, alike for ability and for character—and he observed therein certain expressions of disgust and contempt for the coarse and slanderous invention.

Lady Judith resolved to dedicate the whole of her husband's property—and it was large—with the exception, of course, of the specified legacies—to the educational projects indicated in his will. She will have in this work the constant aid, counsel, and coöperation of Robert May, of Charles Escombe, of Angelo, and less directly of Judge Atheling, who helps with suggestion and information drawn from some of the splendid school systems of the United States. Thus she proposes to battle with her own sorrow, and to coöperate for the first time in her life with the husband of whom she had known so little. "Thus at least," she said to herself, "it may come about that we shall not both have lived and died in vain! In this way I may raise his monument and help to make my own expiation."

One secret, and one only, Angelo has kept as yet from Isolind. He has told her of the death of Thomas Thynne Dysart and of Scarlett, but she does not know how either died. In time even this will be gradually unfolded to her, for Angelo loves no life-long secrets; but for the present he will not scare away her happiness by that tale of horror. He will not have her earliest days of married life clouded by the knowledge that her wretched father crowned his life of sin and wickedness by one supreme crime, and was punished for it by the death of a felon.

And so, for these two we may hope for a life of happiness and of usefulness. Neither the one nor the other ever could be happy in a life which lacked purpose and the desire to do good. The character of each will strengthen and elevate that of the other; their souls will grow together and develop in the noblest sympathy and harmony. They are not rich thus far, and probably never may be; but each has learned from the same experience how much of a superstition, of a mere vulgar unreality, is the idea that riches have anything to do either in the making or the marring of happiness. They have alike the courage to be themselves, to live their own lives. Nothing but inexorable misfortune—which we trust will be kept from them—can make these two unhappy; not even misfortune can make either of them ignoble. Richer promise no two lives ever had when starting together in the partnership of love.

In the story which closes here the author has endeavored to illustrate principally one great truth, as certain as any physical or scientific law, but which among grave people would probably be regarded rather as a pretty piece of sentimentalism, or one of the exaggerations of poetical enthusiasm—the truth that Love is the great human strength, the one grand, eternal principle and guiding power of life. Woe to those who have false gods before it, or who take its name in vain, or who have eyes and see it not! They who enthrone Egotism, or Pride, or Ambition, or Money, or Lust in its sacred place, shall fall down and be abased, and shall perish; or shall only save themselves on condition that they acknowledge its divinity at last, and purely, unselfishly pay it their tribute of homage and devotion. Never yet did pure, unselfish love betray any heart, or lead any one astray, who honestly listened to its voice of counsel. Never yet did it fail to avenge itself of neglect or outrage. Never was there uttered by philosopher a profounder truth than that contained in the words of the American poet—words already quoted in this story, and which may most fittingly be adopted as its *envoi* and moral—the words which tell the ruler of Olympus that "Thou and all strength shall crumble, except Love!"

THE END.

www.ingramcontent.com/pod-product-compliance
Lightning Source LLC
LaVergne TN
LVHW020225110826
845151LV00003B/825

* 9 7 8 1 4 2 5 5 3 1 6 6 9 *